THREE EARLY NOVELS

• THE BARNES & NOBLE LIBRARY OF ESSENTIAL READING •

THREE EARLY NOVELS

Liza of Lambeth, Mrs Craddock, The Magician

W. Somerset Maugham

Introduction by Philip Holden

BARNES & NOBLE BOOKS
NEW YORK

THE BARNES & NOBLE
LIBRARY OF ESSENTIAL READING

Liza of Lambeth (1897). *Mrs Craddock* (1902). *The Magician* (1908).

This edition published by Barnes & Noble Publishing, Inc.

Cover Design by Stacey May

2005 Barnes & Noble Publishing, Inc.

ISBN 0-7607-6862-5

Printed and bound in the United States of America

1 3 5 7 9 10 8 6 4 2

CONTENTS

INTRODUCTION

"I have never quite got out of my astonishment at being a writer," wrote Somerset Maugham when looking back at his long and successful career. Maugham's apparently effortless, economical, and elegant style influenced major modern novelists as disparate as George Orwell and V. S. Naipaul. Yet if the author's mature fiction was popular throughout the twentieth century and is still widely read today, his earlier novels have perhaps been unjustly neglected. The three novels in this collection, *Liza of Lambeth* (1897), *Mrs Craddock* (1902), and *The Magician* (1908), were all written before their author achieved celebrity status. Their settings are various, ranging from the South London slums through the Kentish countryside to the British expatriate community in early twentieth-century Paris, and yet they have common qualities. Each is marked by a compelling plot, and by the detached narrational irony that would become a central feature of Maugham's work. In each, the protagonist is isolated from or ostracized by a traditional community and yet unable to create the new bonds of reciprocity through personal relationships that might enable survival in a changing society. The three novels thus dramatize a dilemma Maugham faced in his own life that is also the central theme of much literature in the modern world.

Although he is best known as a playwright and writer of short stories, W. Somerset Maugham (1874-1965) enjoyed one of the longest and most varied literary careers of any author in the

English language. He was born in Paris, orphaned at ten, and abruptly transported first to the house of a provincial English clergyman uncle and then the harsh environment of a British boarding school. After studying in Germany Maugham trained as a doctor in London, and the social deprivation he witnessed in the outpatient's department at Saint Thomas' Hospital, South London, provided background material for the gritty realism of his first novel, *Liza of Lambeth.* A closeted homosexual moving with increasing comfort in bohemian circles in London and Paris, Maugham took his revenge on his past suffering and present insecurities through fiction. His second important novel, *Mrs Craddock,* is a caustic portrayal of the sterility of middle-class provincial English life. The third novel collected here, *The Magician,* is a thinly-veiled account of his encounter in Paris in the early 1900s with the "wickedest man alive," occultist Aleister Crowley. After the success of the play *Lady Frederick* in 1907, Maugham's popularity and financial security were assured, and yet he continued to exhibit creative versatility. Returning to prose fiction with the autobiographical novel *Of Human Bondage* (1915), Maugham continued to write popular short stories and novels until well after the Second World War. In doing so, he drew on an intense and varied life. His work for British Intelligence in Switzerland provided material for the Ashenden stories, and later extensive travels in the South Pacific and Asia with his lover Gerald Haxton resulted in novels such as *The Moon and Sixpence* and *The Narrow Corner.* His short stories of the foibles of British colonialists in colonial Malaya were influential enough that Malaya in the twilight of British rule is often thought of as "Maugham Country." In 1926, Maugham bought a villa at Cap Ferrat, France, where he would live, apart from a hiatus in the United States during the Second World War which provided material for the frame narrative of his most popular novel, *The Razor's Edge* (1944), until his death in 1965. Maugham's last book, *Purely for My Pleasure,* was published in 1962, when its author was eighty-eight years old.

In his autobiographical *The Summing Up* Maugham recalled his experience working in the outpatient department in St Thomas'. At one time he served as an obstetrics clerk. "I had," the author noted, "to attend a certain number of confinements to get a certificate, and this meant going into the slums of Lambeth, often into foul courts that the police hesitated to enter, but in which my black bag amply protected me." One of these confinements would give rise to the final scene of his first novel in which the unmarried Liza Kemp, pregnant by a married man, dies of an unspecified condition related to her pregnancy. Published in 1897, *Liza of Lambeth* made a strong impact on critics and the reading public. In a reader's report for Unwin, who would later publish the book, Edward Garnett praised it as a "very clever and realistic study" but warned that critics might object to the strong language and unflinchingly realistic description of working class life. He was proved right. A review in the *Academy* condemned the work as "a sordid story of vulgar seduction," while *The National Review* characterized it as "gratuitously brutal." The novel was even the subject of a Sunday sermon at Westminster Abbey. As Maugham discovered later in his career, controversy sells books, and *Liza of Lambeth* soon went into its second printing.

Whether wittingly or not, Maugham displayed impeccable timing in his publication of a novel of working class life. Novels showing the squalor of the conditions in city slums had become popular in England with the publication of George Gissing's *The Nether World* (1889). More immediate models for Maugham were Arthur Morrison's *Tales of Mean Streets* (1894) and *A Child of the Jago* (1896), the latter published in the year in which the author of *Liza* wrote the bulk of his novel. Morrison's novels were set in working-class London, and attempted to represent Cockney slang phonetically in their dialogue. Yet Maugham's bilingual background allowed him to draw on other influences. The author himself acknowledged the decisive impact of French fiction writer Guy de Maupassant on his first novel. His wide knowledge of French Literature would have suggested a further antecedent: Emile Zola's *L'Assomoir*, with its naturalistic representation of Parisian working-class life, and Zola's pioneering use of Parisian slang. Philosophically, Maugham was clearly also influenced by naturalistic conventions embodied in Zola's writings. He would later claim that in *Liza of Lambeth* he "described without addition or exaggeration the people I met. . ., the incidents that had struck me when I went from house to house as the work called, or, when I had nothing to do, on my idle saunterings," and note with considerable self-deprecation that the success of the book was due to the vividness of the material presented, not to his own skill or artistic imagination.

Despite Maugham's modesty, *Liza* is clearly a novel of promise, which succeeds as much through technical virtuosity as it does through its subject matter. Its author did not have the direct experience of working-class life possessed by Gissing and Morrison, and attempted to overcome this through copious research, making careful notes to himself on Lambeth court and hospital cases as well as Cockney pronunciation for later use in the book. Yet Maugham's need to work hard to enter into the world of working-class life does not damage the book, but rather proves its strength, developing it in a different direction from its predecessors. Gissing's and Morrison's novels of slum life, for all their illumination of the horror of inner-city squalor, were largely read by a firmly middle-class reading public. In *Liza of Lambeth* Maugham cultivates a close relationship with this middle-class readership. At one point Maugham's narrator playfully describes Liza and her youthful suitor, Tom, as "Corydon and Phyllis," the shepherd and shepherdess lovers of Classical mythology in a scene which culminates in a very unpastoral spitting competition. This, and the painterly narrational distance of several descriptive passages, foreshadows the detached and ironic narrator of Maugham's later fiction. The doctor who appears at the end of the novel is clearly a self-portrait of Maugham himself, yet he appears distant from the scene, delivering harsh pronouncements with little emotional content in crisp Received Pronunciation. He might usefully be thought of as a precursor of a number of Maugham's detached characters, observers, and narrators who have a close resemblance to the author, blurring the boundary between fiction and autobiography, a process culminating in the appearance of a character called "Somerset Maugham" in the novel *The Razor's Edge.*

Mrs Craddock, written in 1899 but not published until 1902, extends Maugham's encounter with naturalism. After an exuberant but unsuccessful foray into historical fiction with his second novel, *The Making of a Saint,* Maugham perhaps felt the need to return to material with which he was more familiar. Searching for experiences on which to draw, its author looked back beyond his time at Saint Thomas' hospital to his teenage years in Kent. Place names in the novel are thus transparent adaptations of real ones, much in the style of Thomas Hardy's use of "Casterbridge" for Dorchester. Whitstable, where Maugham lived with his clergyman uncle and his wife after he was orphaned, becomes, with rather wicked irony, "Blackstable," while the first two syllables of Canterbury are transposed in the name of Maugham's town "Tercanbury." The parsimonious curate Mr. Glover in *Mrs Craddock* is a direct if rather jaundiced portrait of Maugham's uncle, Henry MacDonald Maugham. Yet the protagonist of *Mrs Craddock,* Bertha Leys, loving life but married to the stolid and uninspiring Edward Craddock, is drawn not from Maugham's life but from fiction. In temperament and situation, if not in eventual fate, she resembles the protagonist of one of Maugham's favorite novels, Gustave Flaubert's *Madame Bovary.* Indeed, the closeness of the titles is not incidental: in both Maugham's and Flaubert's novels, the protagonists find themselves constricted by the roles that they must play as wives in conservative provincial settings.

Maugham's novel was largely well received. Novelist Arthur St John Aldcock noted in the *Bookman* that the narrative marked "a distinct advance on what Mr Maugham had previously accomplished," and praised Maugham's capacity to "reflect the truth" of unhappy marriages rather than writing "improbable romances of ideal men and women." If anything, Maugham was perhaps too liberal with the truth. Publishers initially objected to the explicitness of his descriptions of Bertha's passion for her husband and lover, and Heinemann only consented to publish the novel if a key passage was deleted. Maugham had been unhappy about the paucity of royalties received from Fisher Unwin for *Liza of Lambeth*, and the book's publication marked the beginning of his long and lucrative publishing relationship with Heinemann, which would last for his lifetime. The cut passage was quietly restored in a later edition.

Re-reading the novel half a century after its composition, Maugham confessed that the late Victorian milieu it described was now unfamiliar to him, and he felt impelled to discuss its author in the third, rather than the first person. The "author of *Mrs Craddock*," he remarked in a 1955 preface to the book, "was not only a foolish young man; he was supercilious, cocksure and often wrongheaded," although he did note elsewhere that the novel was "not unsuccessful" in giving a picture of a now vanished world. The novel is certainly very much of its time, describing with acerbic penetration the torpor of upper- and middle-class late Victorian provincial life. Bertha's frustration in a marriage to a man who is not her social, intellectual, and emotional equal allows Maugham to respond to the "Woman question" that vexed late Victorian and Edwardian England. Bertha does not make the same choices as "New Women" such as Herminia Barton in Grant Allen's *The Woman Who Did* (1895), who would support themselves through newly open professions such as teaching, and live a life independent of men. However, her restlessness in her role reflects societal changes at the end of the nineteenth century in which women were gradually gaining visibility in the public sphere. Maugham's sympathetic portrayal of Bertha, like his portrait of Liza in his first novel, complicates a commonplace but mistaken view of him as an unrepentant misogynist.

Maugham's ability to observe with precision and wry humor the antics of the provincial upper and upper-middle classes was no doubt honed by his own experiences. His seven years as a child and teenager at Whitstable had produced both an intimate knowledge of and yet a continued sense of distance from Kentish landscape and society. After the excitement of an early childhood in Paris, Whitstable seemed dull and stifling, and Maugham exorcised some demons of the past through his portrayal of Mr. Glover's narrow-mindedness and Edward Craddock's boorish love of hunting, farming, King, and Country. Yet in describing the setting of *Mrs Craddock*, Maugham encountered a problem which he was later to note with reference to Flaubert: How might a writer "describe a boring time without boring the reader"? The author achieves this through a variety of strategies, allowing Bertha trips to London and abroad where she encounters the seductions of Bohemia, while at the same time making her a fully-realized character with a strongly drawn inner life. We thus follow Bertha through her initial infatuation with Edward to her growing realization of his shallowness. In doing so, we encounter what is perhaps the central theme in Maugham's fiction. Musing on Edward's unresponsiveness, Bertha's confidante Miss Ley quotes a maxim from the French moralist François La Rochefoucauld, "*entre deux amants il y a toujours in qui aime et un qui se laisse aimer*" (of any two lovers there is always one who loves and the other who allows him or herself to be loved). Bertha's passion causes her "to abase herself before the strong man, to be low and humble before him," and yet such self-denial eventually leads to her resentment at her loss of personal autonomy, her love slowly being transformed into hatred.

Most significant in terms of Maugham's future career, however, is not characterization but his use of dialogue. Many of the early exchanges between Bertha, Miss Ley, and other characters are extremely witty in their trenchant irony and *double entendre,* and read more like a play script than a novel. Such dialogue would not be out of place in the Shropshire country house of Oscar Wilde's

The Importance of Being Earnest (1895), and indicates that Maugham was already honing skills that he would put to use as a popular playwright in the next phase of his literary career.

The Magician, the last of the novels collected here, was published in 1908, having been written during Maugham's residence in Paris from 1904 onwards. The novel represents a new departure for its author, constituting an early attempt to synthesize the sharp social observation of *Liza of Lambeth* and *Mrs Craddock* with an interest in the spiritual and the fantastic which marked less successful novels such as *The Making of a Saint*. Like Maugham's earlier fiction, *The Magician* proved controversial. Its publication was delayed because its original publishers read it while in proof, and were shocked enough by the content to promptly return the manuscript to its author. "I have always thought that publishers should never learn to read," Maugham commented dryly on the incident. "It is enough if they can sign their names."

If the events of the plot are fictional, many of the early scenes of the novel are again drawn from life: In this case they are replete with thinly disguised portraits of the Parisian expatriate community in which Maugham moved. The two lovers in the novel, solid Englishman Arthur Burdon and his fiancée Margaret Dauncy, rendezvous at the Chien Noir (Black Dog) restaurant; in actuality, the restaurant was a meeting place for artists and intellectuals in the rue d'Odessa known as the Chat Blanc (White Cat). Many of the regulars at the café in the novel are identifiable as members of Maugham's circle, and the villain of the novel, Oliver Haddo, is clearly the occultist Aleister Crowley, with whom Maugham was acquainted in Paris. Haddo, indeed, is pivotal in bringing together the two halves of the book. He enslaves Margaret mentally, marries her, and then takes her to England where she dies in diabolic experiments to create new forms of life on Haddo's country estate. Arthur's pursuit of Margaret transforms the book from a nuanced observation of expatriate life into a reprise of the late Victorian gothic quest. Haddo's magnetic personality, country house, and spiritual possession of a woman are reminiscent of Bram Stoker's *Dracula* (1897), while the relationship between Haddo and Margaret, and the Parisian expatriate setting suggest the influence of George du Maurier's *Trilby* (1894). The novel's central theme of the struggle between rationality and what lies beyond the rational, as well as some of the descriptive passages towards the end of the narrative, are perhaps influenced by Robert Louis Stevenson's *Dr Jekyll and Mr Hyde* (1886).

Since Maugham was already a successful playwright by the time of its publication, critical attention was elsewhere, and this might explain why *The Magician* attracted only a smattering of contemporary interest. The most vehement response was from Crowley himself, who reviewed the book in *Vanity Fair* under the pseudonym "Oliver Haddo," and noted that the "photographically-accurate portrait" of the Chat Blanc set was Maugham's attempted revenge for the "cutting contempt" in which members of the group held the writer. Crowley argued that the novel was both extremely derivative, rewriting scenes from popular novelist Mabel Collins' *The Blossom and the Fruit* and H. G. Wells' *The Island of Doctor Moreau.* He also, more devastatingly, located and documented passages that were plagiarized from contemporary books about the occult. Accusations of lack of originality and of wafer-thin fictionalization of reality would dog Maugham for the rest of his career. In 1925, for instance, his publishers had to physically cut out pages from the first edition of *The Painted Veil* and replace them with new ones in order to head off a threatened libel suit.

Retrospectively, Maugham would also belittle *The Magician* as the last of a series of "exercises by which I sought to learn my business." Re-reading his novel when it was re-published half a century after he wrote it, the author did find that the narrative "held my interest," although he now felt the style to be overly "lush and turgid." Since the novel was published at a time when its author had made his breakthrough on the London stage, it closes the early, formative phase of his literary career. He would move away from fiction in the next few years, and only return to writing fiction in the next decade.

Despite these criticisms, however, *The Magician* foreshadows important themes in Maugham's later, and more substantial fiction. Like Maugham's earlier novels, and in particular *Mrs Craddock*, it explores the tyranny of unreciprocated love. Margaret is infatuated with Haddo despite recognizing his innate evil; Arthur is almost destroyed by Margaret's rejection of him on the day of their marriage; and Susie Boyd, Margaret's companion in Paris, is motivated by a deeply sublimated infatuation with her friend's fiancé. This, as we have seen, is perhaps the most persistent of Maugham's themes: In an 1894 entry in *A Writer's Notebook* he would note that "the love that lasts longest is the love that is never returned." Such concerns would become central in Maugham's partially autobiographical novel, *Of Human Bondage*, and remain prominent in his later novels and short stories, and indeed be exemplified in his long and frequently tortured relationship with Gerald.

The freedom accorded by the Parisian setting and the structure of the horror tale used in *The Magician* enabled its author to introduce new motifs. Maugham's novel is Orientalist in the sense used by Edward Said, in that it draws a binary opposition between Western rationality and Eastern spirituality. Haddo ensnares Margaret by telling her of "strange Eastern places" and, of "many-colored webs and of silken carpets" that promise "a life of vivacity" in contrast to the "narrow round" of humdrum marriage to the stolid Arthur. Yet Maugham's use of this binarism is not simple. Arthur is in fact born in Egypt and only defeats Haddo by recognizing the irrational, "oriental" side of his personality long suppressed by a British education. Here Maugham is creating an imaginary, textual Orient in order to provide a place of refuge from, and critique of, the West. The Egypt of *The Magician* is thus the first in a long line of exotic locations that would be thematically central in his later writing: The Tahiti that enables English painter Charles Strickland to discover a primordial selfhood in *The Moon and Sixpence*, for example, or the India which causes Larry Darrel to reject his affluent American background in *The Razor's Edge*.

Bohemian Paris also gives Maugham greater scope to represent homosexual desire, albeit in a coded manner. Wandering in the Louvre, Arthur finds that a statue of a Greek athlete attracts his "prolonged attention." Later, Maugham devotes an elaborate and sensuous descriptive passage to a painting which is easily identifiable as Bronzino's *Portrait of a Man Holding a Statuette*, a work of art used by Marcel Proust to indicate the homosexual desire of Charlus for Morel in *The Captive*. Extended quotation from Oscar Wilde's *Salome* is matched by further passages from Walter Pater's *The Renaissance*. While Maugham would later affect to despise Pater, both Pater and Wilde would have been associated with the representation of male homosexual desire in the community in which Maugham moved. In a note written before the composition of *The Magician* Maugham writes of "the hothouse beauties of Pater's style," of being overwhelmed by its oppressive sensuality. The displacement of homosexual desire into prolonged sensual descriptive passages would become a staple of short stories such as "Red," and indeed it is significant that Maugham's only published discussions of homosexuality are in reference to artistic and literary texts, in essays concerning the painter El Greco and the American novelist Herman Melville.

Collectively, the three novels show the development of Maugham's writing talent. Each is written following the conventions of a different genre, and each succeeds on its own terms as more than simply a curiosity of literary history. *Liza of Lambeth* extends the genre of the slum novel through its detached narrational strategies, while *Mrs Craddock*, in its depiction of provincial ennui, displays the other side of women's experiences to fiction regarding the New Woman. *The Magician* mixes the genres of the expatriate novel and the gothic tale, and, in its representation of exoticism, aestheticism, and homosexual desire, is an important precursor for Maugham's subsequent fiction.

Maugham's long career provided him many opportunities to look back at his earlier work, and in doing so he was acutely conscious of his strengths and limitations as a writer. His best work, he was aware, was of limited but detailed scope, skillfully written yet without the breadth of theme or imagination possessed by the great novelists of the nineteenth century whom he read and admired. "I have painted easel pictures, not frescoes," he noted aiming for detailed observations rather than grand thematic gestures, and cultivating an ironic detachment from the subjects of his fiction. Yet Maugham's pictures of late Victorian and Edwardian life reproduced here would have a lasting influence on his own writing practice and on that of his literary successors. And, as Maugham would repeatedly stress, there are virtues in limited scope, and in distance. "There is no need for the writer to eat a whole sheep to be able to tell you what mutton tastes like," he wrote in *A Writer's Notebook.* "It is enough if he eats a cutlet. But he should do that."

Philip Holden is Associate Professor in the Department of English Language and Literature at the National University of Singapore. He is the author of three books and many articles about literary production under colonialism.

LIZA OF LAMBETH

CHAPTER I

IT was the first Saturday afternoon in August; it had been broiling hot all day, with a cloudless sky, and the sun had been beating down on the houses, so that the top rooms were like ovens; but now with the approach of evening it was cooler, and everyone in Vere Street was out of doors.

Vere Street, Lambeth, is a short, straight street leading out of the Westminster Bridge Road; it has forty houses on one side and forty houses on the other, and these eighty houses are very much more like one another than ever peas are like peas, or young ladies like young ladies. They are newish, three-storied buildings of dingy grey brick with slate roofs, and they are perfectly flat, without a bow-window or even a projecting cornice or window-sill to break the straightness of the line from one end of the street to the other.

This Saturday afternoon the street was full of life; no traffic came down Vere Street, and the cemented space between the pavements was given up to children. Several games of cricket were being played by wildly excited boys, using coats for wickets, an old tennis-ball or a bundle of rags tied together for a ball, and, generally, an old broomstick for bat. The wicket was so large and the bat so small that the man in was always getting bowled, when heated quarrels would arise, the batter absolutely refusing to go out and the bowler absolutely insisting on going in. The girls were more peaceable; they were chiefly employed in skipping, and only abused one another mildly when the rope was not properly turned or the skipper did not jump sufficiently high. Worst off of all were the very young children, for there had been no rain for weeks, and the street was as dry and clean as a covered court, and, in the lack of mud to wallow in, they sat about the road, disconsolate as poets. The number of babies was prodigious; they sprawled about everywhere, on the pavement, round the doors, and about their mothers' skirts. The grown-ups were gathered round the open doors; there were usually two women squatting on the doorstep, and two or three more seated on either side on chairs; they were invariably nursing babies, and most of them showed clear signs that the present object of the maternal care would be soon ousted by a new arrival. Men were less numerous but such as there were leant against the walls, smoking, or sat on the sills of the ground-floor windows. It was the dead season in Vere Street as much as in Belgravia, and really if it had not been for babies just come or just about to come, and an opportune murder in a neighbouring doss-house, there would have been nothing whatever to talk about. As it was, the little groups talked quietly, discussing the atrocity or the merits of the local midwives, comparing the circumstances of their various confinements.

'You'll be 'avin' your little trouble soon, eh, Polly?' asked one good lady of another.

'Oh, I reckon I've got another two months ter go yet,' answered Polly.

'Well,' said a third, 'I wouldn't 'ave thought you'd go so long by the look of yer!'

'I 'ope you'll have it easier this time, my dear,' said a very stout old person, a woman of great importance.

'She said she wasn't goin' to 'ave no more, when the last one come.' This remark came from Polly's husband.

'Ah,' said the stout old lady, who was in the business, and boasted vast experience, 'That's wot they all says; but, Lor' bless yer, they don't mean it.'

'Well, I've got three, and I'm not goin' to 'ave no more bli'me if I will; 'tain't good enough—that's wot I says.'

'You're abaht right there, ole gal,' said Polly, 'My word, 'Arry, if you 'ave any more I'll git a divorce, that I will.'

At that moment an organ-grinder turned the corner and came down the street.

'Good biz; 'ere's an organ!' cried half a dozen people at once.

The organ-man was an Italian, with a shock of black hair and a ferocious moustache. Drawing his organ to a favourable spot, he stopped, released his shoulder from the leather straps by which he dragged it, and cocking his large soft hat on the side of his head, began turning the handle. It was a lively tune, and in less than no time a little crowd had gathered round to listen, chiefly the young men and the maidens, for the married ladies were never in a fit state to dance, and therefore disinclined to trouble themselves to stand round the organ. There was a moment's hesitation at opening the ball; then one girl said to another:

'Come on, Florrie, you and me ain't shy; we'll begin, and bust it!'

The two girls took hold of one another, one acting gentleman, the other lady; three or four more pairs of girls immediately joined them, and they began a waltz. They held themselves very upright; and with an air of grave dignity which was quite impressive, glided slowly about, making their steps with the utmost precision, bearing themselves with sufficient decorum for a court ball. After a while the men began to itch for a turn, and two of them, taking hold of one another in the most approved fashion, waltzed round the circle with the gravity of judges.

All at once there was a cry: 'There's Liza!' And several members of the group turned and called out: 'Oo, look at Liza!'

The dancers stopped to see the sight, and the organ-grinder, having come to the end of his tune, ceased turning the handle and looked to see what was the excitement.

'Oo, Liza!' they called out. 'Look at Liza; oo, I sy!'

It was a young girl of about eighteen, with dark eyes, and an enormous fringe, puffed-out and curled and frizzed, covering her whole forehead from side to side, and coming down to meet her eyebrows. She was dressed in brilliant violet, with great lappets of velvet, and she had on her head an enormous black hat covered with feathers.

'I sy, ain't she got up dossy?' called out the groups at the doors, as she passed.

'Dressed ter death, and kill the fashion; that's wot I calls it.'

Liza saw what a sensation she was creating; she arched her back and lifted her head, and walked down the street, swaying her body from side to side, and swaggering along as though the whole place belonged to her.

''Ave yer bought the street, Bill?' shouted one youth; and then half a dozen burst forth at once, as if by inspiration:

'Knocked 'em in the Old Kent Road!'

It was immediately taken up by a dozen more, and they all yelled it out:

'Knocked 'em in the Old Kent Road. Yah, ah, knocked 'em in the Old Kent Road!'

'Oo, Liza!' they shouted; the whole street joined in, and they gave long, shrill, ear-piercing shrieks and strange calls, that rung down the street and echoed back again.

'Hextra special!' called out a wag.

'Oh, Liza! Oo! Ooo!' yells and whistles, and then it thundered forth again:

'Knocked 'em in the Old Kent Road!'

Liza put on the air of a conquering hero, and sauntered on, enchanted at the uproar. She stuck out her elbows and jerked her head on one side, and said to herself as she passed through the bellowing crowd:

'This is jam!'

'Knocked 'em in the Old Kent Road!'

When she came to the group round the barrel-organ, one of the girls cried out to her:

'Is that yer new dress, Liza?'

'Well, it don't look like my old one, do it?' said Liza.

'Where did yer git it?' asked another friend, rather enviously.

'Picked it up in the street, of course,' scornfully answered Liza.

'I believe it's the same one as I saw in the pawnbroker's dahn the road,' said one of the men, to tease her.

'Thet's it; but wot was you doin' in there? Pledgin' yer shirt, or was it yer trousers?'

'Yah, I wouldn't git a second-'and dress at a pawnbroker's!'

'Garn!' said Liza indignantly. 'I'll swipe yer over the snitch if yer talk ter me. I got the mayterials in the West Hend, didn't I? And I 'ad it mide up by my Court Dressmiker, so you jolly well dry up, old jelly-belly.'

'Garn!' was the reply.

Liza had been so intent on her new dress and the comment it was exciting that she had not noticed the organ.

'Oo, I say, let's 'ave some dancin',' she said as soon as she saw it. 'Come on, Sally,' she added, to one of the girls, 'you an' me'll dance togither. Grind away, old cock!'

The man turned on a new tune, and the organ began to play the Intermezzo from the 'Cavalleria'; other couples quickly followed Liza's example, and they began to waltz round with the same solemnity as before; but Liza outdid them all; if the others were as stately as queens, she was as stately as an empress; the gravity and dignity with which she waltzed were something appalling, you felt that the minuet was a frolic in comparison; it would have been a fitting measure to tread round the grave of a *première danseuse,* or at the funeral of a professional humorist And the graces she put on, the languor of the eyes, the contemptuous curl of the lips, the exquisite turn of the hand, the dainty arching of the foot! You felt there could be no questioning her right to the tyranny of Vere Street.

Suddenly she stopped short, and disengaged herself from her companion.

'Oh, I sy,' she said, 'this is too bloomin' slow; it gives me the sick.'

That is not precisely what she said, but it is impossible always to give the exact unexpurgated words of Liza and the other personages of the story; the reader is therefore entreated with his thoughts to piece out the necessary imperfections of the dialogue.

'It's too bloomin' slow,' she said again; 'it gives me the sick. Let's 'ave somethin' a bit more lively than this 'ere waltz. You stand over there, Sally, an' we'll show 'em 'ow ter skirt dance.'

They all stopped waltzing.

'Talk of the ballet at the Canterbury and South London. You just wite till you see the ballet at Vere Street, Lambeth—we'll knock 'em!'

She went up to the organ-grinder.

'Na then, Italiano,' she said to him, 'you buck up; give us a tune that's got some guts in it! See?'

She caught hold of his big hat and squashed it down over his eyes. The man grinned from ear to ear, and, touching the little catch at the side, began to play a lively tune such as Liza had asked for.

The men had fallen out, but several girls had put themselves in position, in couples, standing face to face; and immediately the music struck up, they began. They held up their skirts on each side, so as to show their feet, and proceeded to go through the difficult steps and motions of the dance. Liza was right; they could not have done it better in a trained ballet. But the best dancer of them all was Liza; she threw her whole soul into it; forgetting the stiff bearing which she had thought proper to the waltz, and casting off its elaborate graces, she gave herself up entirely to the present pleasure. Gradually the other couples stood aside, so that Liza and Sally were left alone. They paced it carefully, watching each other's steps, and as if by instinct performing corresponding movements, so as to make the whole a thing of symmetry.

'I'm abaht done,' said Sally, blowing and puffing. 'I've 'ad enough of it.'

'Go on, Liza!' cried out a dozen voices when Sally stopped.

She gave no sign of having heard them other than calmly to continue her dance. She glided through the steps, and swayed about, and manipulated her skirt, all with the most charming grace imaginable, then, the music altering, she changed the style of her dancing, her feet moved more quickly, and did not keep so strictly to the ground. She was getting excited at the admiration of the onlookers, and her dance grew wilder and more daring. She lifted her skirts higher, brought in new and more difficult movements into her improvisation, kicking up her legs she did the wonderful twist, backwards and forwards, of which the dancer is proud.

'Look at er' legs!' cried one of the men.

'Look at 'er stockin's!' shouted another; and indeed they were remarkable, for Liza had chosen them of the same brilliant hue as her dress, and was herself most proud of the harmony.

Her dance became gayer: her feet scarcely touched the ground, she whirled round madly.

'Tike care yer don't split!' cried out one of the wags, at a very audacious kick.

The words were hardly out of his mouth when Liza, with a gigantic effort, raised her foot and kicked off his hat. The feat was greeted with applause, and she went on, making turns and twists, flourishing her skirts, kicking higher and higher, and finally, among a volley of shouts, fell on her hands and turned head over heels in a magnificent catharine-wheel; then scrambling to her feet again, she tumbled into the arms of a young man standing in the front of the ring.

'That's right, Liza,' he said. 'Give us a kiss, now,' and promptly tried to take one.

'Git aht!' said Liza, pushing him away, not too gently.

'Yus, give us a kiss,' cried another, running up to her.

'I'll smack yer in the fice!' said Liza, elegantly, as she dodged him.

'Ketch 'old on 'er, Bill,' cried out a third, 'an' we'll all kiss her.'

'Na, you won't!' shrieked Liza, beginning to run.

'Come on,' they cried, 'we'll ketch 'er.'

She dodged in and out, between their legs, under their arms, and then, getting clear of the little crowd, caught up her skirts so that they might not hinder her, and took to her heels along the street. A score of men set in chase, whistling, shouting, yelling; the people at the doors looked up to see the fun, and cried out to her as she dashed past; she ran like the wind. Suddenly a man from the side darted into the middle of the road, stood straight in her way, and before she knew where she was, she had jumped shrieking into his arms, and he, lifting her up to him, had imprinted two sounding kisses on her cheeks.

'Oh, you—!' she said. Her expression was quite unprintable; nor can it be euphemized.

There was a shout of laughter from the bystanders, and the young men in chase of her, and Liza, looking up, saw a big, bearded man whom she had never seen before. She blushed to the very roots of her hair, quickly extricated herself from his arms, and, amid the jeers and laughter of everyone, slid into the door of the nearest house and was lost to view.

CHAPTER II

LIZA and her mother were having supper. Mrs Kemp was an elderly woman, short, and rather stout, with a red face, and grey hair brushed tight back over her forehead. She had been a widow for many years, and since her husband's death had lived with Liza in the ground-floor front room in which they were now sitting. Her husband had been a soldier, and from a grateful country she received a pension large enough to keep her from starvation, and by charring and doing such odd jobs as she could get she earned a little extra to supply herself with liquor. Liza was able to make her own living by working at a factory.

Mrs Kemp was rather sulky this evening.

'Wot was yer doin' this afternoon, Liza?' she asked.

'I was in the street.'

'You're always in the street when I want yer.'

'I didn't know as 'ow yer wanted me, mother,' answered Liza.

'Well, yer might 'ave come ter see! I might 'ave been dead, for all you knew.'

Liza said nothing.

'My rheumatics was thet bad to-dy, thet I didn't know wot ter do with myself. The doctor said I was to be rubbed with that stuff 'e give me, but yer won't never do nothin' for me.'

'Well, mother,' said Liza, 'your rheumatics was all right yesterday.'

'I know wot you was doin'; you was showin' off thet new dress of yours. Pretty waste of money thet is, instead of givin' it me ter sive up. An' for the matter of thet, I wanted a new dress far worse than you did. But, of course, I don't matter.'

Liza did not answer, and Mrs Kemp, having nothing more to say, continued her supper in silence.

It was Liza who spoke next.

'There's some new people moved in the street. 'Ave you seen 'em?' she asked.

'No, wot are they?'

'I dunno; I've seen a chap, a big chap with a beard. I think 'e lives up at the other end.'

She felt herself blushing a little.

'No one any good you be sure,' said Mrs Kemp. 'I can't swaller these new people as are comin' in; the street ain't wot it was when I fust come.'

When they had done, Mrs Kemp got up, and having finished her half-pint of beer, said to her daughter:

'Put the things awy, Liza. I'm just goin' round to see Mrs Clayton; she's just 'ad twins, and she 'ad nine before these come. It's a pity the Lord don't see fit ter tike some on 'em—thet's wot I say.'

After which pious remark Mrs Kemp went out of the house and turned into another a few doors up.

Liza did not clear the supper things away as she was told, but opened the window and drew her chair to it. She leant on the sill, looking out into the street. The sun had set, and it was twilight, the sky was growing dark, bringing to view the twinkling stars; there was no breeze, but it was pleasantly and restfully cool. The good folk still sat at their doorsteps, talking as before on the same inexhaustible subjects, but a little subdued with the approach of night. The boys were still playing cricket, but they were mostly at the other end of the street, and their shouts were muffled before they reached Liza's ears.

She sat, leaning her head on her hands, breathing in the fresh air and feeling a certain exquisite sense of peacefulness which she was not used to. It was Saturday evening, and she thankfully remembered that there would be no factory on the morrow; she was glad to rest. Somehow she felt a little tired, perhaps it was through the excitement of the afternoon, and she enjoyed the quietness of the evening. It seemed so tranquil and still; the silence filled her with a strange delight, she felt as if she could sit there all through the night looking out into the cool, dark street, and up heavenwards at the stars. She was very happy, but yet at the same time experienced a strange new sensation of melancholy, and she almost wished to cry.

Suddenly a dark form stepped in front of the open window. She gave a little shriek.

''Oo's thet?' she asked, for it was quite dark, and she did not recognize the man standing in front of her.

'Me, Liza,' was the answer.

'Tom?'

'Yus!'

It was a young man with light yellow hair and a little fair moustache, which made him appear almost boyish; he was light-complexioned and blue-eyed, and had a frank and pleasant look mingled with a curious bashfulness that made him blush when people spoke to him.

'Wot's up?' asked Liza.

'Come aht for a walk, Liza, will yer?'

'No!' she answered decisively.

'You promised ter yesterday, Liza.'

'Yesterday an' ter-day's two different things,' was her wise reply.

'Yus, come on, Liza.'

'Na, I tell yer, I won't.'

'I want ter talk ter yer, Liza.' Her hand was resting on the window-sill, and he put his upon it. She quickly drew it back.

'Well, I don't want yer ter talk ter me.'

But she did, for it was she who broke the silence.

'Say, Tom, 'oo are them new folk as 'as come into the street? It's a big chap with a brown beard.'

'D'you mean the bloke as kissed yer this afternoon?'

Liza blushed again.

'Well, why shouldn't 'e kiss me?' she said, with some inconsequence.

'I never said as 'ow 'e shouldn't; I only arst yer if it was the sime.'

'Yes, thet's 'oo I mean.'

''Is nime is Blakeston—Jim Blakeston. I've only spoke to 'im once; he's took the two top rooms at No. 19 'ouse.'

'Wot's 'e want two top rooms for?'

''Im? Oh, 'e's got a big family—five kids. Ain't yer seen 'is wife abaht the street? She's a big, fat woman, as does 'er 'air funny.'

'I didn't know 'e 'ad a wife.'

There was another silence; Liza sat thinking, and Tom stood at the window, looking at her.

'Won't yer come aht with me, Liza?' he asked, at last.

'Na, Tom,' she said, a little more gently, 'it's too lite.'

'Liza,' he said, blushing to the roots of his hair.

'Well?'

'Liza'—he couldn't go on, and stuttered in his shyness—'Liza, I—I—I loves yer, Liza.'

'Garn awy!'

He was quite brave now, and took hold of her hand.

'Yer know, Liza, I'm earnin' twenty-three shillin's at the works now, an' I've got some furniture as mother left me when she was took.'

The girl said nothing.

'Liza, will you 'ave me? I'll make yer a good 'usband, Liza, swop me bob, I will; an' yer know I'm not a drinkin' sort. Liza, will yer marry me?'

'Na, Tom,' she answered quietly.

'Oh, Liza, won't you 'ave me?'

'Na, Tom, I can't.'

'Why not? You've come aht walkin' with me ever since Whitsun.'

'Ah, things is different now.'

'You're not walkin' aht with anybody else, are you, Liza?' he asked quickly.

'Na, not that.'

'Well, why won't yer, Liza? Oh Liza, I do love yer, I've never loved anybody as I love you!'

'Oh, I can't, Tom!'

'There ain't no one else?'

'Na.'

'Then why not?'

'I'm very sorry, Tom, but I don't love yer so as ter marry yer.'

'Oh, Liza!'

She could not see the look upon his face, but she heard the agony in his voice; and, moved with sudden pity, she bent out, threw her arms round his neck, and kissed him on both cheeks.

'Never mind old chap!' she said. 'I'm not worth troublin' abaht.'

And quickly drawing back, she slammed the window to, and moved into the further part of the room.

CHAPTER III

THE following day was Sunday. Liza when she was dressing herself in the morning, felt the hardness of fate in the impossibility of eating one's cake and having it; she wished she had reserved her new dress, and had still before her the sensation of a first appearance in it. With a sigh she put on her ordinary everyday working dress, and proceeded to get the breakfast ready, for her mother had been out late the previous night, celebrating the new arrivals in the street, and had the 'rheumatics' this morning.

'Oo, my 'ead!' she was saying, as she pressed her hands on each side of her forehead. 'I've got the neuralgy again, wot shall I do? I dunno 'ow it is, but it always comes on Sunday mornings. Oo, an' my rheumatics, they give me sich a doin' in the night!'

'You'd better go to the 'orspital, mother.'

'Not I!' answered the worthy lady, with great decision. 'You 'as a dozen young chaps messin' you abaht, and lookin' at yer; and then they tells yer ter leave off beer and spirrits. Well, wot I says, I says I can't do withaht my glass of beer.' She thumped her pillow to emphasize the statement.

'Wot with the work I 'ave ter do, lookin' after you and the cookin' and gettin' everythin' ready and doin' all the 'ousework, and goin' aht charring besides—well, I says, if I don't 'ave a drop of beer, I says, ter pull me together, I should be under the turf in no time.'

She munched her bread-and-butter and drank her tea.

'When you've done breakfast, Liza,' she said, 'you can give the grate a cleanin', an' my boots'd do with a bit of polishin'. Mrs Tike, in the next 'ouse, 'll give yer some blackin'.'

She remained silent for a bit, then said:

'I don't think I shall get up ter-day, Liza. My rheumatics is bad. You can put the room straight and cook the dinner.'

'Arright, mother; you stay where you are, an' I'll do everythin' for yer.'

'Well, it's only wot yer ought to do, considerin' all the trouble you've been ter me when you was young, and considerin' thet when you was born the doctor thought I never should get through it. Wot 'ave you done with your week's money, Liza?'

'Oh, I've put it awy,' answered Liza quietly.

'Where?' asked her mother.

'Where it'll be safe.'

'Where's that?'

Liza was driven into a corner.

'Why d'you want ter know?' she asked.

'Why shouldn't I know; d'you think I want ter steal it from yer?'

'Na, not thet.'

'Well, why won't you tell me?'

'Oh, a thing's sifer when only one person knows where it is.'

This was a very discreet remark, but it set Mrs Kemp in a whirlwind of passion. She raised herself and sat up in the bed, flourishing her clenched fist at her daughter.

'I know wot yer mean, you—you!' Her language was emphatic, her epithets picturesque, but too forcible for reproduction. 'You think I'd steal it,' she went on. 'I know yer! D'yer think I'd go an' tike yer dirty money?'

'Well mother,' said Liza, 'when I've told yer before, the money's perspired like.'

'Wot d'yer mean?'

'It got less.'

'Well, I can't 'elp thet, can I? Anyone can come in 'ere and tike the money.'

'If it's 'idden awy, they can't, can they, mother?' said Liza.

Mrs Kemp shook her fist.

'You dirty slut, you,' she said, 'yer think I tike yer money! Why, you ought ter give it me every week instead of savin' it up and spendin' it on all sorts of muck, while I 'ave ter grind my very bones down to keep yer.'

'Yer know, mother, if I didn't 'ave a little bit saved up, we should be rather short when you're dahn in yer luck.'

Mrs Kemp's money always ran out on Tuesday, and Liza had to keep things going till the following Saturday.

'Oh, don't talk ter me!' proceeded Mrs Kemp. 'When I was a girl I give all my money ter my mother. She never 'ad ter ask me for nothin'. On Saturday when I come 'ome with my wiges, I give it 'er every farthin'. That's wot a daughter ought ter do. I can say this for myself, I be'aved by my mother like a gal should. None of your prodigal sons for me! She didn't 'ave ter ask me for three 'apence ter get a drop of beer.'

Liza was wise in her generation; she held her tongue, and put on her hat.

'Now, you're goin' aht, and leavin' me; I dunno wot you get up to in the street with all those men. No good, I'll be bound. An' 'ere am I left alone, an' I might die for all you care.'

In her sorrow at herself the old lady began to cry, and Liza slipped out of the room and into the street.

Leaning against the wall of the opposite house was Tom; he came towards her.

''Ulloa!' she said, as she saw him. 'Wot are you doin' 'ere?'

'I was waitin' for you ter come aht, Liza,' he answered.

She looked at him quickly.

'I ain't comin' aht with yer ter-day, if thet's wot yer mean,' she said.

'I never thought of arskin' yer, Liza—after wot you said ter me last night.'

His voice was a little sad, and she felt so sorry for him.

'But yer did want ter speak ter me, didn't yer, Tom?' she said, more gently.

'You've got a day off ter-morrow, ain't yer?'

'Bank 'Oliday. Yus! Why?'

'Why, 'cause they've got a drag startin' from the "Red Lion" that's goin' down ter Chingford for the day—an' I'm goin'.'

'Yus!' she said.

He looked at her doubtfully.

'Will yer come too, Liza? It'll be a regular beeno; there's only goin' ter be people in the street. Eh, Liza?'

'Na, I can't.'

'Why not?'

'I ain't got—I ain't got the ooftish.'

'I mean, won't yer come with me?'

'Na, Tom, thank yer; I can't do thet neither.'

'Yer might as well, Liza; it wouldn't 'urt yer.'

'Na, it wouldn't be right like; I can't come aht with yer, and then mean nothin'! It would be doin' yer aht of an outing.'

'I don't see why,' he said, very crestfallen.

'I can't go on keepin' company with you—after what I said last night.'

'I shan't enjoy it a bit without you, Liza.'

'You git somebody else, Tom. You'll do withaht me all right.'

She nodded to him, and walked up the street to the house of her friend Sally. Having arrived in front of it, she put her hands to her mouth in trumpet form, and shouted:

''I! 'I! 'I! Sally!'

A couple of fellows standing by copied her.

''I! 'I! 'I! Sally!'

'Garn!' said Liza, looking round at them.

Sally did not appear and she repeated her call. The men imitated her, and half a dozen took it up, so that there was enough noise to wake the seven sleepers.

''I! 'I! 'I! Sally!'

A head was put out of a top window, and Liza, taking off her hat, waved it, crying:

'Come on dahn, Sally!'

'Arright, old gal!' shouted the other. 'I'm comin'!'

'So's Christmas!' was Liza's repartee.

There was a clatter down the stairs, and Sally, rushing through the passage, threw herself on to her friend. They began fooling, in reminiscence of a melodrama they had lately seen together.

'Oh, my darlin' duck!' said Liza, kissing her and pressing her, with affected rapture, to her bosom.

'My sweetest sweet!' replied Sally, copying her.

'An' 'ow does your lidyship ter-day?'

'Oh!'—with immense languor—'fust class; and is your royal 'ighness quite well?'

'I deeply regret,' answered Liza, 'but my royal 'ighness 'as got the collywobbles.'

Sally was a small, thin girl, with sandy hair and blue eyes, and a very freckled complexion. She had an enormous mouth, with terrible, square teeth set wide apart, which looked as if they could masticate an iron bar. She was dressed like Liza, in a shortish black skirt and an old-fashioned bodice, green and grey and yellow with age; her sleeves were tucked up to the elbow, and she wore a singularly dirty apron, that had once been white.

'Wot 'ave you got yer 'air in them things for?' asked Liza, pointing to the curl-papers. 'Goin' aht with yer young man ter-day?'

'No, I'm going ter stay 'ere all day.'

'Wot for, then?'

'Why, 'Arry's going ter tike me ter Chingford ter-morrer.'

'Oh? In the "Red Lion" brake?'

'Yus. Are you goin'?'

'Na!'

'Not! Well, why don't you get round Tom? 'E'll tike yer, and jolly glad 'e'll be, too.'

''E arst me ter go with 'im, but I wouldn't.'

'Swop me bob—why not?'

'I ain't keeping company with 'im.'

'Yer might 'ave gone with 'im all the sime.'

'Na. You're goin' with 'Arry, ain't yer?'

'Yus!'

'An' you're goin' to 'ave 'im?'

'Right again!'

'Well, I couldn't go with Tom, and then throw him over.'

'Well, you are a mug!'

The two girls had strolled down towards the Westminster Bridge Road, and Sally, meeting her young man, had gone to him. Liza walked back, wishing to get home in time to cook the dinner. But she went slowly, for she knew every dweller in the street, and as she passed the groups sitting at their doors, as on the previous evening, but this time mostly engaged in peeling potatoes or shelling peas, she stopped and had a little chat. Everyone liked her, and was glad to have her company. 'Good old Liza,' they would say, as she left them, 'she's a rare good sort, ain't she?'

She asked after the aches and pains of all the old people, and delicately inquired after the babies, past and future; the children hung on to her skirts and asked her to play with them, and she would hold one end of the rope while tiny little ragged girls skipped, invariably entangling themselves after two jumps.

She had nearly reached home, when she heard a voice cry:

'Mornin'!'

She looked round and recognized the man whom Tom had told her was called Jim Blakeston. He was sitting on a stool at the door of one of the houses, playing with two young children, to whom he was giving rides on his knee. She remembered his heavy brown beard from the day before, and she had also an impression of great size; she noticed this morning that he was, in fact, a big man, tall and broad, and she saw besides that he had large, masculine features and pleasant brown eyes. She supposed him to be about forty.

'Mornin'!' he said again, as she stopped and looked at him.

'Well, yer needn't look as if I was goin' ter eat yer up, 'cause I ain't,' he said.

''Oo are you? I'm not afeard of yer.'

'Wot are yer so bloomin' red abaht?' he asked pointedly.

'Well, I'm 'ot.'

'You ain't shirty 'cause I kissed yer last night?'

'I'm not shirty; but it was pretty cool, considerin' like as I didn't know yer.'

'Well, you run into my arms.'

'Thet I didn't; you run aht and caught me.'

'An' kissed yer before you could say "Jack Robinson".' He laughed at the thought. 'Well, Liza,' he went on, 'seein' as 'ow I kissed yer against yer will, the best thing you can do ter make it up is to kiss me not against yer will.'

'Me?' said Liza, looking at him, open-mouthed. 'Well you are a pill!'

The children began to clamour for the riding, which had been discontinued on Liza's approach.

'Are them your kids?' she asked.

'Yus; them's two on 'em.'

''Ow many 'ave yer got?'

'Five; the eldest gal's fifteen, and the next one 'oo's a boy's twelve, and then there are these two and baby.'

'Well, you've got enough for your money.'

'Too many for me—and more comin'.'

'Ah well,' said Liza, laughing, 'thet's your fault, ain't it?'

Then she bade him good morning, and strolled off.

He watched her as she went, and saw half a dozen little boys surround her and beg her to join them in their game of cricket. They caught hold of her arms and skirts, and pulled her to their pitch.

'No, I can't,' she said trying to disengage herself. 'I've got the dinner ter cook.'

'Dinner ter cook?' shouted one small boy. 'Why, they always cooks the cats' meat at the shop.'

'You little so-and-so!' said Liza, somewhat inelegantly, making a dash at him.

He dodged her and gave a whoop; then turning he caught her round the legs, and another boy catching hold of her round the neck they dragged her down, and all three struggled on the ground, rolling over and over; the other boys threw themselves on the top, so that there was a great heap of legs and arms and heads waving and bobbing up and down.

Liza extricated herself with some difficulty, and taking off her hat she began cuffing the boys with it, using all the time the most lively expressions. Then, having cleared the field, she retired victorious into her own house and began cooking the dinner.

CHAPTER IV

BANK Holiday was a beautiful day: the cloudless sky threatened a stifling heat for noontide, but early in the morning, when Liza got out of bed and threw open the window, it was fresh and cool. She dressed herself, wondering how she should spend her day; she thought of Sally going off to Chingford with her lover, and of herself remaining alone in the dull street with half the people away. She almost wished it were an ordinary work-day, and that there were no such things as bank holidays. And it seemed to be a little like two Sundays running, but with the second rather worse than the first. Her mother was still sleeping, and she was in no great hurry about getting the breakfast, but stood quietly looking out of the window at the house opposite.

In a little while she saw Sally coming along. She was arrayed in purple and fine linen—a very smart red dress, trimmed with velveteen, and a tremendous hat covered with feathers. She had reaped the benefit of keeping her hair in curl-papers since Saturday, and her sandy fringe stretched from ear to ear. She was in enormous spirits.

''Ulloa, Liza!' she called as soon as she saw her at the window.

Liza looked at her a little enviously.

''Ulloa!' she answered quietly.

'I'm just goin' to the "Red Lion" to meet 'Arry.'

'At what time d'yer start?'

'The brake leaves at 'alf-past eight sharp.'

'Why, it's only eight; it's only just struck at the church. 'Arry won't be there yet, will he?'

'Oh, 'e's sure ter be early. I couldn't wite. I've been witin' abaht since 'alf-past six. I've been up since five this morning.'

'Since five! What 'ave you been doin'?'

'Dressin' myself and doin' my 'air. I woke up so early. I've been dreamin' all the night abaht it. I simply couldn't sleep.'

'Well, you are a caution!' said Liza.

'Bust it, I don't go on the spree every day! Oh, I do 'ope I shall enjoy myself.'

'Why, you simply dunno where you are!' said Liza, a little crossly.

'Don't you wish you was comin', Liza?' asked Sally.

'Na! I could if I liked, but I don't want ter.'

'You are a coughdrop—thet's all I can say. Ketch me refusin' when I 'ave the chanst.'

'Well, it's done now. I ain't got the chanst any more.' Liza said this with just a little regret in her voice.

'Come on dahn to the "Red Lion", Liza, and see us off,' said Sally.

'No, I'm damned if I do!' answered Liza, with some warmth.

'You might as well. P'raps 'Arry won't be there, an' you can keep me company till 'e comes. An' you can see the 'orses.'

Liza was really very anxious to see the brake and the horses and the people going; but she hesitated a little longer. Sally asked her once again. Then she said:

'Arright; I'll come with yer, and wite till the bloomin' old thing starts.'

She did not trouble to put on a hat, but just walked out as she was, and accompanied Sally to the public-house which was getting up the expedition.

Although there was still nearly half an hour to wait, the brake was drawn up before the main entrance; it was large and long, with seats arranged crosswise, so that four people could sit on each; and it was drawn by two powerful horses, whose harness the coachman was now examining. Sally was not the first on the scene, for already half a dozen people had taken their places, but Harry had not yet arrived. The two girls stood by the public-door, looking at the preparations. Huge baskets full of food were brought out and stowed away; cases of beer were hoisted up and put in every possible place—under the seats, under the driver's legs, and even beneath the brake. As more people came up, Sally began to get excited about Harry's non-appearance.

'I say, I wish 'e'd come!' she said.' 'E is lite.'

Then she looked up and down the Westminster Bridge Road to see if he was in view.

'Suppose 'e don't turn up! I will give it 'im when 'e comes for keepin' me witin' like this.'

'Why, there's a quarter of an hour yet,' said Liza, who saw nothing at all to get excited about.

At last Sally saw her lover, and rushed off to meet him. Liza was left alone, rather disconsolate at all this bustle and preparation. She was not sorry that she had refused Tom's invitation, but she did wish that she had conscientiously been able to accept it. Sally and her friend came up; attired in his Sunday best, he was a fit match for his lady-love—he wore a shirt and collar, unusual luxuries—and he carried under his arm a concertina to make things merry on the way.

'Ain't you goin', Liza?' he asked in surprise at seeing her without a hat and with her apron on.

'Na,' said Sally, 'ain't she a soft? Tom said 'e'd tike 'er, an' she wouldn't.'

'Well, I'm dashed!'

Then they climbed the ladder and took their seats, so that Liza was left alone again. More people had come along, and the brake was nearly full. Liza knew them all, but they were too busy taking their places to talk to her. At last Tom came. He saw her standing there and went up to her.

'Won't yer change yer mind, Liza, an' come along with us?'

'Na, Tom, I told yer I wouldn't—it's not right like.' She felt she must repeat that to herself often.

'I shan't enjoy it a bit without you,' he said.

'Well, I can't 'elp it!' she answered, somewhat sullenly.

At that moment a man came out of the public-house with a horn in his hand; her heart gave a great jump, for if there was anything she adored it was to drive along to the tootling of a horn. She really felt it was very hard lines that she must stay at home when all these people were going to have such a fine time; and they were all so merry, and she could picture to herself so well the delights of the drive and the picnic. She felt very much inclined to cry. But she mustn't go, and she wouldn't go: she repeated that to herself twice as the trumpeter gave a preliminary tootle.

Two more people hurried along, and when they came near Liza saw that they were Jim Blakeston and a woman whom she supposed to be his wife.

'Are you comin', Liza?' Jim said to her.

'No,' she answered. 'I didn't know you was goin'.'

'I wish you was comin',' he replied, 'we shall 'ave a game.'

She could only just keep back the sobs; she so wished she were going. It did seem hard that she must remain behind; and all because she wasn't going to marry Tom. After all, she didn't see why that should prevent her; there really was no need to refuse for that. She began to think she had acted foolishly: it didn't do anyone any good that she refused to go out with Tom, and no one thought it anything specially fine that she should renounce her pleasure. Sally merely thought her a fool.

Tom was standing by her side, silent, and looking disappointed and rather unhappy. Jim said to her, in a low voice:

'I am sorry you're not comin'!'

It was too much. She did want to go so badly, and she really couldn't resist any longer. If Tom would only ask her once more, and if she could only change her mind reasonably and decently, she would accept; but he stood silent, and she had to speak herself. It was very undignified.

'Yer know, Tom,' she said, 'I don't want ter spoil your day.'

'Well, I don't think I shall go alone; it 'ud be so precious slow.'

Supposing he didn't ask her again! What should she do? She looked up at the clock on the front of the pub, and noticed that it only wanted five minutes to the half-hour. How terrible it would be if the brake started and he didn't ask her! Her heart beat violently against her chest, and in her agitation she fumbled with the corner of her apron.

'Well, what can I do, Tom dear?'

'Why, come with me, of course. Oh, Liza, do say yes.'

She had got the offer again, and it only wanted a little seemly hesitation, and the thing was done.

'I should like ter, Tom,' she said. 'But d'you think it 'ud be arright?'

'Yus, of course it would. Come on, Liza!' In his eagerness he clasped her hand.

'Well,' she remarked, looking down, 'if it'd spoil your 'oliday—'

'I won't go if you don't—swop me bob, I won't!' he answered.

'Well, if I come, it won't mean that I'm keepin' company with you.'

'Na, it won't mean anythin' you don't like.'

'Arright!' she said.

'You'll come?' he could hardly believe her.

'Yus!' she answered, smiling all over her face.

'You're a good sort, Liza! I say, 'Arry, Liza's comin'!' he shouted.

'Liza? 'Oorray!' shouted Harry.

''S'at right. Liza?' called Sally.

And Liza feeling quite joyful and light of heart called back:

'Yus!'

''Oorray!' shouted Sally in answer.

'Thet's right, Liza,' called Jim; and he smiled pleasantly as she looked at him.

'There's just room for you two 'ere,' said Harry, pointing to the vacant places by his side.

'Arright!' said Tom.

'I must jest go an' get a 'at an' tell mother,' said Liza.

'There's just three minutes. Be quick!' answered Tom, and as she scampered off as hard as she could go, he shouted to the coachman: ''Old 'ard; there' another passenger comin' in a minute.'

'Arright, old cock,' answered the coachman: 'no 'urry!'

Liza rushed into the room, and called to her mother, who was still asleep:

'Mother! mother! I'm going to Chingford!'

Then tearing off her old dress she slipped into her gorgeous violet one; she kicked off her old ragged shoes and put on her new boots. She brushed her hair down and rapidly gave her fringe a twirl and a twist—it was luckily still moderately in curl from the previous Saturday—and putting on her black hat with all the feathers, she rushed along the street, and scrambling up the brake steps fell panting on Tom's lap.

The coachman cracked his whip, the trumpeter tootled his horn, and with a cry and a cheer from the occupants, the brake clattered down the road.

CHAPTER V

As soon as Liza had recovered herself she started examining the people on the brake; and first of all she took stock of the woman whom Jim Blakeston had with him.

'This is my missus!' said Jim, pointing to her with his thumb.

'You ain't been dahn in the street much, 'ave yer?' said Liza, by way of making the acquaintance.

'Na,' answered Mrs Blakeston, 'my youngster's been dahn with the measles, an' I've 'ad my work cut out lookin' after 'im.'

'Oh, an' is 'e all right now?'

'Yus, 'e's gettin' on fine, an' Jim wanted ter go ter Chingford ter-day, an' 'e says ter me, well, 'e says, "You come along ter Chingford, too; it'll do you good." An' 'e says, "You can leave Polly"—she's my eldest, yer know—"you can leave Polly,' says 'e, "ter look after the kids." So I says, "Well, I don't mind if I do," says I.'

Meanwhile Liza was looking at her. First she noticed her dress: she wore a black cloak and a funny, old-fashioned black bonnet; then examining the woman herself, she saw a middle-sized, stout person anywhere between thirty and forty years old. She had a large, fat face with a big mouth, and her hair was curiously done, parted in the middle and plastered down on each side of the head in little plaits. One could see that she was a woman of great strength, notwithstanding evident traces of hard work and much child-bearing.

Liza knew all the other passengers, and now that everyone was settled down and had got over the excitement of departure, they had time to greet one another. They were delighted to have Liza among them, for where she was there was no dullness. Her attention was first of all taken up by a young coster who had arrayed himself in the traditional costume—grey suit, tight trousers, and shiny buttons in profusion.

'Wot cheer, Bill!' she cried to him.

'Wot cheer, Liza!' he answered.

'You are got up dossy; you'll knock 'em.'

'Na then, Liza Kemp,' said his companion, turning round with mock indignation, 'you let my Johnny alone. If you come gettin' round 'im I'll give you wot for.'

'Arright, Clary Sharp, I don't want 'im,' answered Liza. 'I've got one of my own, an' thet's a good 'andful—ain't it, Tom?'

Tom was delighted, and, unable to find a repartee, in his pleasure gave Liza a great nudge with his elbow.

''Oo, I say,' said Liza, putting her hand to her side. 'Tike care of my ribs; you'll brike 'em.'

'Them's not yer ribs,' shouted a candid friend—'them's yer whale-bones yer afraid of breakin'.'

'Garn!'

''Ave yer got whale-bones?' said Tom, with affected simplicity, putting his arm round her waist to feel.

'Na, then,' she said, 'keep off the grass!'

'Well, I only wanted ter know if you'd got any.'

'Garn; yer don't git round me like thet.'

He still kept as he was.

'Na then,' she repeated, 'tike yer 'and away. If yer touch me there you'll 'ave ter marry me.'

'Thet's just wot I wants ter do, Liza!'

'Shut it!' she answered cruelly, and drew his arm away from her waist.

The horses scampered on, and the man behind blew his horn with vigour.

'Don't bust yerself, guv'nor!' said one of the passengers to him when he made a particularly discordant sound. They drove along eastwards, and as the hour grew later the streets became more filled and the traffic greater. At last they got on the road to Chingford, and caught up numbers of other vehicles going in the same direction—donkey-shays, pony-carts, tradesmen's carts, dog-carts, drags, brakes, every conceivable kind of wheel thing, all filled with people, the wretched donkey dragging along four solid rate-payers to the pair of stout horses easily managing a couple of score. They exchanged cheers and greetings as they passed, the 'Red Lion' brake being noticeable above all for its uproariousness. As the day wore on the sun became hotter, and the road seemed more dusty and threw up a greater heat.

'I am getting 'ot!' was the common cry, and everyone began to puff and sweat.

The ladies removed their cloaks and capes, and the men, following their example, took off their coats and sat in their shirt-sleeves. Whereupon ensued much banter of a not particularly edifying kind respecting the garments which each person would like to remove—which showed that the innuendo of French farce is not so unknown to the upright, honest Englishman as might be supposed.

At last came in sight the half-way house, where the horses were to have a rest and a sponge down. They had been talking of it for the last quarter of a mile, and when at length it was observed on the top of a hill a cheer broke out, and some thirsty wag began to sing 'Rule Britannia', whilst others burst forth with a different national ditty, 'Beer, Glorious Beer!' They drew up before the pub entrance, and all climbed down as quickly as they could. The bar was besieged, and potmen and barmaids were quickly busy drawing beer and handing it over to the eager folk outside.

THE IDYLL OF CORYDON AND PHYLLIS.

Gallantry ordered that the faithful swain and the amorous shepherdess should drink out of one and the same pot.

''Urry up an' 'ave your whack,' said Corydon, politely handing the foaming bowl for his fair one to drink from.

Phyllis, without replying, raised it to her lips and drank deep. The swain watched anxiously.

''Ere, give us a chanst!' he said, as the pot was raised higher and higher and its contents appeared to be getting less and less.

At this the amorous shepherdess stopped and handed the pot to her lover.

'Well, I'm dashed!' said Corydon, looking into it; and added: 'I guess you know a thing or two.' Then with courtly grace putting his own lips to the place where had been those of his beloved, finished the pint.

'Go' lumme!' remarked the shepherdess, smacking her lips, 'that was somethin' like!' And she put out her tongue and licked her lips, and then breathed deeply.

The faithful swain having finished, gave a long sigh, and said:

'Well, I could do with some more!'

'For the matter of thet, I could do with a gargle!'

Thus encouraged, the gallant returned to the bar, and soon brought out a second pint.

'You 'ave fust pop,' amorously remarked Phyllis, and he took a long drink and handed the pot to her.

She, with maiden modesty, turned it so as to have a different part to drink from; but he remarked as he saw her:

'You are bloomin' particular.'

Then, unwilling to grieve him, she turned it back again and applied her ruby lips to the place where his had been.

'Now we shan't be long!' she remarked, as she handed him back the pot.

The faithful swain took out of his pocket a short clay pipe, blew through it, filled it, and began to smoke, while Phyllis sighed at the thought of the cool liquid gliding down her throat, and with the pleasing recollection gently stroked her stomach. Then Corydon spat, and immediately his love said:

'I can spit farther than thet.'

'I bet yer yer can't.'

She tried, and did. He collected himself and spat again, further than before, she followed him, and in this idyllic contest they remained till the tootling horn warned them to take their places.

At last they reached Chingford, and here the horses were taken out and the drag, on which they were to lunch, drawn up in a sheltered spot. They were all rather hungry, but as it was not yet feeding-time, they scattered to have drinks meanwhile. Liza and Tom, with Sally and her young man, went off together to the nearest public-house, and as they drank beer, Harry, who was a great sportsman, gave them a graphic account of a prize-fight he had seen on the previous Saturday evening, which had been rendered specially memorable by one man being so hurt that he had died from the effects. It had evidently been a very fine affair, and Harry said that several swells from the West End had been present, and he related their ludicrous efforts to get in without being seen by anyone, and their terror when someone to frighten them called out 'Copper!' Then Tom and he entered into a discussion on the subject of boxing, in which Tom, being a shy and undogmatic sort of person, was entirely worsted. After this they strolled back to the brake, and found things being prepared for luncheon; the hampers were brought out and emptied, and the bottles of beer in great profusion made many a thirsty mouth thirstier.

'Come along, lidies an' gentlemen—if you are gentlemen,' shouted the coachman; 'the animals is now goin' ter be fed!'

'Garn awy,' answered somebody, 'we're not hanimals; we don't drink water.'

'You're too clever,' remarked the coachman; 'I can see you've just come from the board school.'

As the former speaker was a lady of quite mature appearance, the remark was not without its little irony. The other man blew his horn by way of grace, at which Liza called out to him:

'Don't do thet, you'll bust, I know you will, an' if you bust you'll quite spoil my dinner!'

Then they all set to. Pork-pies, saveloys, sausages, cold potatoes, hard-boiled eggs, cold, bacon, veal, ham, crabs and shrimps, cheese, butter, cold suet-puddings and treacle, gooseberry-tarts, cherry-tarts, butter, bread, more sausages, and yet again pork-pies! They devoured the provisions like ravening beasts, stolidly, silently, earnestly, in large mouthfuls which they shoved down their throats unmasticated. The intelligent foreigner seeing them thus dispose of their food would have understood why England is a great nation. He would have understood why Britons never, never will be slaves. They never stopped except to drink, and then at each gulp they emptied their glass; no heel-taps! And still they ate, and still they drank—but as all things must cease, they stopped at last, and a long sigh of content broke from their two-and-thirty throats.

Then the gathering broke up, and the good folk paired themselves and separated. Harry and his lady strolled off to secluded byways in the forest, so that they might discourse of their loves and digest their dinner. Tom had all the morning been waiting for this happy moment; he had counted on the expansive effect of a full stomach to thaw his Liza's coldness, and he had pictured himself sitting on the grass with his back against the trunk of a spreading chestnut-tree, with his arm round his Liza's waist, and her head resting affectionately on his manly bosom. Liza, too, had foreseen the separation into couples after dinner, and had been racking her brains to find a means of getting out of it.

'I don't want 'im slobberin' abaht me,' she said; 'it gives me the sick, all this kissin' an' cuddlin'!'

She scarcely knew why she objected to his caresses; but they bored her and made her cross. But luckily the blessed institution of marriage came to her rescue, for Jim and his wife naturally had no particular desire to spend the afternoon together, and Liza, seeing a little embarrassment on their part, proposed that they should go for a walk together in the forest.

Jim agreed at once, and with pleasure, but Tom was dreadfully disappointed. He hadn't the courage to say anything, but he glared at Blakeston. Jim smiled benignly at him, and Tom began to sulk. Then they began a funny walk through the woods. Jim tried to go on with Liza, and Liza was not at all disinclined to this, for she had come to the conclusion that Jim, notwithstanding his 'cheek', was not ''alf a bad sort'. But Tom kept walking alongside of them, and as Jim slightly quickened his pace so as to get Liza on in front, Tom quickened his, and Mrs Blakeston, who didn't want to be left behind, had to break into a little trot to keep up with them. Jim tried also to get Liza all to himself in the conversation, and let Tom see that he was out in the cold, but Tom would break in with cross, sulky remarks, just to make the others uncomfortable. Liza at last got rather vexed with him.

'Strikes me you got aht of bed the wrong way this mornin',' she said to him.

'Yer didn't think thet when yer said you'd come aht with me.' He emphasized the 'me'.

Liza shrugged her shoulders.

'You give me the 'ump,' she said. 'If yer wants ter mike a fool of yerself, you can go elsewhere an' do it.'

'I suppose yer want me ter go awy now,' he said angrily.

'I didn't say I did.'

'Arright, Liza, I won't stay where I'm not wanted.' And turning on his heel he marched off, striking through the underwood into the midst of the forest.

He felt extremely unhappy as he wandered on, and there was a choky feeling in his throat as he thought of Liza: she was very unkind and ungrateful, and he wished he had never come to Chingford. She might so easily have come for a walk with him instead of going with that beast of a Blakeston; she wouldn't ever do anything for him, and he hated her—but all the same, he was a poor foolish thing in love, and he began to feel that perhaps he had been a little exacting and a little forward to take offence. And then he wished he had never said anything, and he wanted so much to see her and make it up. He made his way back to Chingford, hoping she would not make him wait too long.

Liza was a little surprised when Tom turned and left them.

'Wot 'as 'e got the needle abaht?' she said.

'Why, 'e's jealous,' answered Jim, with a laugh.

'Tom jealous?'

'Yus; 'e's jealous of me.'

'Well, 'e ain't got no cause ter be jealous of anyone—that 'e ain't!' said Liza, and continued by telling him all about Tom: how he had wanted to marry her and she wouldn't have him, and how she had only agreed to come to Chingford with him on the understanding that she should preserve her entire freedom. Jim listened sympathetically, but his wife paid no attention; she was doubtless engaged in thought respecting her household or her family.

When they got back to Chingford they saw Tom standing in solitude looking at them. Liza was struck by the woebegone expression on his face; she felt she had been cruel to him, and leaving the Blakestons went up to him.

'I say, Tom,' she said, 'don't tike on so; I didn't mean it.'

He was bursting to apologize for his behaviour.

'Yer know, Tom,' she went on, 'I'm rather 'asty, an' I'm sorry I said wot I did.'

'Oh, Liza, you are good! You ain't cross with me?'

'Me? Na; it's you thet oughter be cross.'

'You are a good sort, Liza!'

'You ain't vexed with me?'

'Give me Liza every time; that's wot I say,' he answered, as his face lit up. 'Come along an' 'ave tea, an' then we'll go for a donkey-ride.'

The donkey-ride was a great success. Liza was a little afraid at first, so Tom walked by her side to take care of her, she screamed the moment the beast began to trot, and clutched hold of Tom to save herself from falling, and as he felt her hand on his shoulder, and heard her appealing cry: 'Oh, do 'old me! I'm fallin'!' he felt that he had never in his life been so deliciously happy. The whole party joined in, and it was proposed that they should have races; but in the first heat, when the donkeys broke into a canter, Liza fell off into Tom's arms and the donkeys scampered on without her.

'I know wot I'll do,' she said, when the runaway had been recovered, 'I'll ride 'im straddlewyse.'

'Garn!' said Sally, 'yer can't with petticoats.'

'Yus, I can, an' I will too!'

So another donkey was procured, this time with a man's saddle, and putting her foot in the stirrup, she cocked her leg over and took her seat triumphantly. Neither modesty nor bashfulness was to be reckoned among Liza's faults, and in this position she felt quite at ease.

'I'll git along arright now, Tom,' she said; 'you garn and git yerself a moke, and come an' jine in.'

The next race was perfectly uproarious. Liza kicked and beat her donkey with all her might, shrieking and laughing the while, and finally came in winner by a length. After that they felt rather warm and dry, and repaired to the public-house to restore themselves and talk over the excitements of the racecourse.

When they had drunk several pints of beer Liza and Sally, with their respective adorers and the Blakestons, walked round to find other means of amusing themselves; they were arrested by a coconut-shy.

'Oh, let's 'ave a shy!' said Liza, excitedly, at which the unlucky men had to pull out their coppers, while Sally and Liza made ludicrously bad shots at the coconuts.

'It looks so bloomin' easy,' said Liza, brushing up her hair, 'but I can't 'it the blasted thing. You 'ave a shot, Tom.'

He and Harry were equally unskilful, but Jim got three coconuts running, and the proprietors of the show began to look on him with some concern.

'You are a dab at it,' said Liza, in admiration.

They tried to induce Mrs Blakeston to try her luck, but she stoutly refused.

'I don't old with such foolishness. It's wiste of money ter me,' she said.

'Na then, don't crack on, old tart,' remarked her husband, 'let's go an' eat the coconuts.'

There was one for each couple, and after the ladies had sucked the juice they divided them and added their respective shares to their dinners and teas. Supper came next. Again they fell to sausage-rolls, boiled eggs, and saveloys, and countless bottles of beer were added to those already drunk.

'I dunno 'ow many bottles of beer I've drunk—I've lost count,' said Liza; whereat there was a general laugh.

They still had an hour before the brake was to start back, and it was then the concertinas came in useful. They sat down on the grass, and the concert was begun by Harry, who played a solo; then there was a call for a song, and Jim stood up and sang that ancient ditty, 'O dem Golden Kippers, O'. There was no shyness in the company, and Liza, almost without being asked, gave another popular comic song. Then there was more concertina playing, and another demand for a song. Liza turned to Tom, who was sitting quietly by her side.

'Give us a song, old cock,' she said.

'I can't,' he answered. 'I'm not a singin' sort.' At which Blakeston got up and offered to sing again.

'Tom is rather a soft,' said Liza to herself, 'not like that cove Blakeston.'

They repaired to the public-house to have a few last drinks before the brake started, and when the horn blew to warn them, rather unsteadily, they proceeded to take their places.

Liza, as she scrambled up the steps, said: 'Well, I believe I'm boozed.'

The coachman had arrived at the melancholy stage of intoxication, and was sitting on his box holding his reins, with his head bent on his chest. He was thinking sadly of the long-lost days of his youth, and wishing he had been a better man.

Liza had no respect for such holy emotions, and she brought down her fist on the crown of his hat, and bashed it over his eyes.

'Na then, old jellybelly,' she said, 'wot's the good of 'avin' a fice as long as a kite?'

He turned round and smote her.

'Jellybelly yerself!' said he.

'Puddin' fice!' she cried.

'Kite fice!'

'Boss eye!'

She was tremendously excited, laughing and singing, keeping the whole company in an uproar. In her jollity she had changed hats with Tom, and he in her big feathers made her shriek with laughter. When they started they began to sing 'For 'e's a jolly good feller', making the night resound with their noisy voices.

Liza and Tom and the Blakestons had got a seat together, Liza being between the two men. Tom was perfectly happy, and only wished that they might go on so for ever. Gradually as they drove along they became quieter, their singing ceased, and they talked in undertones. Some of them slept; Sally and her young man were leaning up against one another, slumbering quite peacefully. The night was beautiful, the sky still blue, very dark, scattered over with countless brilliant stars, and Liza, as she looked up at the heavens, felt a certain emotion, as if she wished to be taken in someone's arms, or feel some strong man's caress; and there was in her heart a strange sensation as though it were growing big. She stopped speaking, and all four were silent. Then slowly she felt Tom's arm steal round her waist, cautiously, as though it were afraid of being there; this time both she and Tom were happy. But suddenly there was a movement on the other side of her, a hand was advanced along her leg, and her hand was grasped and gently pressed. It was Jim Blakeston. She started a little and began trembling so that Tom noticed it, and whispered:

'You're cold, Liza.'

'Na, I'm not, Tom; it's only a sort of shiver thet went through me.'

His arm gave her waist a squeeze, and at the same time the big rough hand pressed her little one. And so she sat between them till they reached the 'Red Lion' in the Westminster Bridge Road, and Tom said to himself: 'I believe she does care for me after all.'

When they got down they all said good night, and Sally and Liza, with their respective slaves and the Blakestons, marched off homewards. At the corner of Vere Street Harry said to Tom and Blakeston:

'I say, you blokes, let's go an' 'ave another drink before closin' time.'

'I don't mind,' said Tom, 'after we've took the gals 'ome.'

'Then we shan't 'ave time, it's just on closin' time now,' answered Harry.

'Well, we can't leave 'em 'ere.'

'Yus, you can,' said Sally. 'No one'll run awy with us.'

Tom did not want to part from Liza, but she broke in with:

'Yus, go on, Tom. Sally an' me'll git along arright, an' you ain't got too much time.'

'Yus, good night, 'Arry,' said Sally to settle the matter.

'Good night, old gal,' he answered, 'give us another slobber.'

And she, not at all unwilling, surrendered herself to him, while he imprinted two sounding kisses on her cheeks.

'Good night, Tom,' said Liza, holding out her hand.

'Good night, Liza,' he answered, taking it, but looking very wistfully at her.

She understood, and with a kindly smile lifted up her face to him. He bent down and, taking her in his arms, kissed her passionately.

'You do kiss nice, Liza,' he said, making the others laugh.

'Thanks for tikin' me aht, old man,' she said as they parted.

'Arright, Liza,' he answered, and added, almost to himself: 'God bless yer!'

''Ulloa, Blakeston, ain't you comin'?' said Harry, seeing that Jim was walking off with his wife instead of joining him and Tom.

'Na,' he answered, 'I'm goin' 'ome. I've got ter be up at five ter-morrer.'

'You are a chap!' said Harry, disgustedly, strolling off with Tom to the pub, while the others made their way down the sleeping street.

The house where Sally lived came first, and she left them; then, walking a few yards more, they came to the Blakestons', and after a little talk at the door Liza bade the couple good night, and was left to walk the rest of the way home. The street was perfectly silent, and the lamp-posts, far apart, threw a dim light which only served to make Liza realize her solitude. There was such a difference between the street at midday, with its swarms of people, and now, when there was neither sound nor soul besides herself, that even she was struck by it. The regular line of houses on either side, with the even pavements and straight, cemented road, seemed to her like some desert place, as if everyone were dead, or a fire had raged and left it all desolate. Suddenly she heard a footstep, she started and looked back. It was a man hurrying behind her, and in a moment she had recognized Jim. He beckoned to her, and in a low voice called:

'Liza!'

She stopped till he had come up to her.

'Wot 'ave yer come aht again for?' she said.

'I've come aht ter say good night to you, Liza,' he answered.

'But yer said good night a moment ago.'

'I wanted to say it again—properly.'

'Where's yer missus?'

'Oh, she's gone in. I said I was dry and was goin' ter 'ave a drink after all.'

'But she'll know yer didn't go ter the pub.'

'Na, she won't, she's gone straight upstairs to see after the kid. I wanted ter see yer alone, Liza.'

'Why?'

He didn't answer, but tried to take hold of her hand. She drew it away quickly. They walked in silence till they came to Liza's house.

'Good night,' said Liza.

'Won't you come for a little walk, Liza?'

'Tike care no one 'ears you,' she added, in a whisper, though why she whispered she did not know.

'Will yer?' he asked again.

'Na—you've got to get up at five.'

'Oh, I only said thet not ter go inter the pub with them.'

'So as yer might come 'ere with me?' asked Liza.

'Yus!'

'No, I'm not comin'. Good night.'

'Well, say good night nicely.'

'Wot d'yer mean?'

'Tom said you did kiss nice.'

She looked at him without speaking, and in a moment he had clasped his arms round her, almost lifting her off her feet, and kissed her. She turned her face away.

'Give us yer lips, Liza,' he whispered—'give us yer lips.'

He turned her face without resistance and kissed her on the mouth.

At last she tore herself from him, and opening the door slid away into the house.

CHAPTER VI

NEXT morning on her way to the factory Liza came up with Sally. They were both of them rather stale and bedraggled after the day's outing; their fringes were ragged and untidily straying over their foreheads, their back hair, carelessly tied in a loose knot, fell over their necks and threatened completely to come down. Liza had not had time to put her hat on, and was holding it in her hand. Sally's was pinned on sideways, and she had to bash it down on her head every now and then to prevent its coming off. Cinderella herself was not more transformed than they were; but Cinderella even in her rags was virtuously tidy and patched up, while Sally had a great tear in her shabby dress, and Liza's stockings were falling over her boots.

'Wot cheer, Sal!' said Liza, when she caught her up.

'Oh, I 'ave got sich a 'ead on me this mornin'!' she remarked, turning round a pale face: heavily lined under the eyes.

'I don't feel too chirpy neither,' said Liza, sympathetically.

'I wish I 'adn't drunk so much beer,' added Sally, as a pang shot through her head.

'Oh, you'll be arright in a bit,' said Liza. Just then they heard the clock strike eight, and they began to run so that they might not miss getting their tokens and thereby their day's pay; they turned into the street at the end of which was the factory, and saw half a hundred women running like themselves to get in before it was too late.

All the morning Liza worked in a dead-and-alive sort of fashion, her head like a piece of lead with electric shocks going through it when she moved, and her tongue and mouth hot and dry. At last lunch-time came.

'Come on, Sal,' said Liza, 'I'm goin' to 'ave a glass o' bitter. I can't stand this no longer.'

So they entered the public-house opposite, and in one draught finished their pots. Liza gave a long sigh of relief.

'That bucks you up, don't it?'

'I was dry! I ain't told yer yet, Liza, 'ave I? 'E got it aht last night.'

'Who d'yer mean?'

'Why, 'Arry. 'E spit it aht at last.'

'Arst yer ter nime the day?' said Liza, smiling.

'Thet's it.'

'And did yer?'

'Didn't I jest!' answered Sally, with some emphasis. 'I always told yer I'd git off before you.'

'Yus!' said Liza, thinking.

'Yer know, Liza, you'd better tike Tom; 'e ain't a bad sort.' She was quite patronizing.

'I'm goin' ter tike 'oo I like; an' it ain't nobody's business but mine.'

'Arright, Liza, don't get shirty over it; I don't mean no offence.'

'What d'yer say it for then?'

'Well, I thought as seeing as yer'd gone aht with 'im yesterday thet yer meant ter after all.'

''E wanted ter tike me; I didn't arsk 'im.'

'Well, I didn't arsk my 'Arry, either.'

'I never said yer did,' replied Liza.

'Oh, you've got the 'ump, you 'ave!' finished Sally, rather angrily.

The beer had restored Liza; she went back to work without a headache, and, except for a slight languor, feeling no worse for the previous day's debauch. As she worked on she began going over in her mind the events of the preceding day, and she found entwined in all her thoughts the burly person of Jim Blakeston. She saw him walking by her side in the Forest, presiding over the meals, playing the concertina, singing, joking, and finally, on the drive back, she felt the heavy form by her side, and the big, rough hand holding hers, while Tom's arm was round her waist. Tom! That was the first time he had entered her mind, and he sank into a shadow beside the other. Last of all she remembered the walk home from the pub, the good nights, and the rapid footsteps as Jim caught her up, and the kiss. She blushed and looked up quickly to see whether any of the girls were looking at her; she could not help thinking of that moment when he took her in his arms; she still felt the roughness of his beard pressing on her mouth. Her heart seemed to grow larger in her breast, and she caught for breath as she threw back her head as if to receive his lips again. A shudder ran through her from the vividness of the thought.

'Wot are you shiverin' for, Liza?' asked one of the girls. 'You ain't cold.'

'Not much,' answered Liza, blushing awkwardly on her meditations being broken into. 'Why, I'm sweatin' so—I'm drippin' wet.'

'I expect yer caught cold in the Faurest yesterday.'

'I see your mash as I was comin' along this mornin'.'

Liza stared a little.

'I ain't got one, 'oo d'yer mean, ay?'

'Yer only Tom, of course. 'E did look washed aht. Wot was yer doin' with 'im yesterday?'

''E ain't got nothin' ter do with me, 'e ain't.'

'Garn, don't you tell me!'

The bell rang, and, throwing over their work, the girls trooped off, and after chattering in groups outside the factory gates for a while, made their way in different directions to their respective homes. Liza and Sally went along together.

'I sy, we are comin' aht!' cried Sally, seeing the advertisement of a play being acted at the neighbouring theatre.

'I should like ter see thet!' said Liza, as they stood arm-in-arm in front of the flaring poster. It represented two rooms and a passage in between; in one room a dead man was lying on the floor, while two others were standing horror-stricken, listening to a youth who was in the passage, knocking at the door.

'You see, they've 'killed im,' said Sally, excitedly.

'Yus, any fool can see thet! an' the one ahtside, wot's 'e doin' of?'

'Ain't 'e beautiful? I'll git my 'Arry ter tike me, I will. I should like ter see it. 'E said 'e'd tike me to the ply.'

They strolled on again, and Liza, leaving Sally, made her way to her mother's. She knew she must pass Jim's house, and wondered whether she would see him. But as she walked along the street she saw Tom coming the opposite way; with a sudden impulse she turned back so as not to meet him, and began walking the way she had come. Then thinking herself a fool for what she had done, she turned again and walked towards him. She wondered if he had seen her or noticed her movement, but when she looked down the street he was nowhere to be seen; he had not caught sight of her, and had evidently gone in to see a mate in one or other of the houses. She quickened her step, and passing the house where lived Jim, could not help looking up; he was standing at the door watching her, with a smile on his lips.

'I didn't see yer, Mr Blakeston,' she said, as he came up to her.

'Didn't yer? Well, I knew yer would; an' I was witin' for yer ter look up. I see yer before ter-day.'

'Na, when?'

'I passed be'ind yer as you an' thet other girl was lookin' at the advertisement of thet ply.'

'I never see yer.'

'Na, I know yer didn't. I 'ear yer say, you says: "I should like to see thet."'

'Yus, an' I should too.'

'Well, I'll tike yen.'

'You?'

'Yus: why not?'

'I like thet; wot would yer missus sy?'

'She wouldn't know.'

'But the neighbours would!'

'No they wouldn't, no one 'd see us.'

He was speaking in a low voice so that people could not hear.

'You could meet me ahtside the theatre,' he went on.

'Na, I couldn't go with you; you're a married man.'

'Garn! wot's the matter—jest ter go ter the ply? An' besides, my missus can't come if she wanted, she's got the kids ter look after.'

'I should like ter see it,' said Liza meditatively.

They had reached her house, and Jim said:

'Well, come aht this evenin' and tell me if yer will—eh, Liza?'

'Na, I'm not comin' aht this evening.'

'Thet won't 'urt yer. I shall wite for yer.'

''Tain't a bit of good your witing', 'cause I shan't come.'

'Well, then, look 'ere, Liza; next Saturday night's the last night, an' I shall go to the theatre, any'ow. An' if you'll come, you just come to the door at 'alf-past six, an' you'll find me there. See?'

'Na, I don't,' said Liza, firmly.

'Well, I shall expect yer.'

'I shan't come, so you needn't expect.' And with that she walked into the house and slammed the door behind her.

Her mother had not come in from her day's charing, and Liza set about getting her tea. She thought it would be rather lonely eating it alone, so pouring out a cup of tea and putting a little condensed milk into it, she cut a huge piece of bread-and-butter, and sat herself down outside on the doorstep. Another woman came downstairs, and seeing Liza, sat down by her side and began to talk.

'Why, Mrs Stanley, wot 'ave yer done to your 'ead?' asked Liza, noticing a bandage round her forehead.

'I 'ad an accident last night,' answered the woman, blushing uneasily.

'Oh, I am sorry! Wot did yer do to yerself?'

'I fell against the coal-scuttle and cut my 'ead open.'

'Well, I never!'

'To tell yer the truth, I 'ad a few words with my old man. But one doesn't like them things to get abaht; yer won't tell anyone, will yer?'

'Not me!' answered Liza. 'I didn't know yer husband was like thet.'

'Oh, 'e's as gentle as a lamb when 'e's sober,' said Mrs Stanley, apologetically. 'But, Lor' bless yer, when 'e's 'ad a drop too much 'e's a demond, an' there's no two ways abaht it.'

'An' you ain't been married long, neither?' said Liza.

'Na, not above eighteen months; ain't it disgriceful? Thet's wot the doctor at the 'orspital says ter me. I 'ad ter go ter the 'orspital. You should have seen 'ow it bled!—it bled all dahn' my fice, and went streamin' like a bust water-pipe. Well, it fair frightened my old man, an' I says ter 'im, "I'll charge yer," an' although I was bleedin' like a bloomin' pig I shook my fist at 'im, an' I says, "I'll charge ye—see if I don't!" An' 'e says, "Na," says 'e, "don't do thet, for God's sike, Kitie, I'll git three months." "An' serve yer damn well right!" says I, an' I went aht an' left 'im. But, Lor' bless yer, I wouldn't charge 'im! I know 'e don't mean it; 'e's as gentle as a lamb when 'e's sober.' She smiled quite affectionately as she said this.

'Wot did yer do, then?' asked Liza.

'Well, as I wos tellin' yer, I went to the 'orspital, an' the doctor 'e says to me, "My good woman," says 'e, "you might have been very seriously injured." An' me not been married eighteen months! An' as I was tellin' the doctor all about it, "Missus," 'e says ter me, lookin' at me straight in the eyeball, "Missus," says 'e, "'ave you been drinkin'?" "Drinkin'?" says I; "no! I've 'ad a little drop, but as for drinkin'! Mind," says I, "I don't say I'm a teetotaller—I'm not, I 'ave my glass of beer, and I like it. I couldn't do withaht it, wot with the work I 'ave, I must 'ave somethin' ter keep me tergether. But as for drinkin' 'eavily! Well! I can say this, there ain't a soberer woman than myself in all London. Why, my first 'usband never touched a drop. Ah, my first 'usband, 'e was a beauty, 'e was."'

She stopped the repetition of her conversation and addressed herself to Liza.

''E was thet different ter this one. 'E was a man as' ad seen better days. 'E was a gentleman!' She mouthed the word and emphasized it with an expressive nod.

''E was a gentleman and a Christian. 'E'd been in good circumstances in 'is time; an' 'e was a man of education and a teetotaller, for twenty-two years.'

At that moment Liza's mother appeared on the scene.

'Good evenin', Mrs Stanley,' she said, politely.

'The sime ter you, Mrs Kemp,' replied that lady, with equal courtesy.

'An' 'ow is your poor 'ead?' asked Liza's mother, with sympathy.

'Oh, it's been achin' cruel. I've hardly known wot ter do with myself.'

'I'm sure 'e ought ter be ashimed of 'imself for treatin' yer like thet.'

'Oh, it wasn't 'is blows I minded so much, Mrs Kemp,' replied Mrs Stanley, 'an' don't you think it. It was wot 'e said ter me. I can stand a blow as well as any woman. I don't mind thet, an' when 'e don't tike a mean advantage of me I can stand up for myself an' give as good as I tike; an' many's the time I give my fust husband a black eye. But the language 'e used, an' the things 'e called me! It made me blush to the roots of my 'air; I'm not used ter bein' spoken ter like thet. I was in good circumstances when my fust 'usband was alive, 'e earned between two an' three pound a week, 'e did. As I said to 'im this mornin', "'Ow a gentleman can use sich language, I dunno."'

''Usbands is cautions, 'owever good they are,' said Mrs Kemp, aphoristically. 'But I mustn't stay ant 'ere in the night air.'

''As yer rheumatism been troublin' yer litely?' asked Mrs Stanley.

'Oh, cruel. Liza rubs me with embrocation every night, but it torments me cruel.'

Mrs Kemp then went into the house, and Liza remained talking to Mrs Stanley, she, too, had to go in, and Liza was left alone. Some while she spent thinking of nothing, staring vacantly in front of her, enjoying the cool and quiet of the evening. But Liza could not be left alone long, several boys came along with a bat and a ball, and fixed upon the road just in front of her for their pitch. Taking off their coats they piled them up at the two ends, and were ready to begin.

'I say, old gal,' said one of them to Liza, 'come an' have a gime of cricket, will yer?'

'Na, Bob, I'm tired.'

'Come on!'

'Na, I tell you I won't.'

'She was on the booze yesterday, an' she ain't got over it,' cried another boy.

'I'll swipe yer over the snitch!' replied Liza to him, and then on being asked again, said:

'Leave me alone, won't yer?'

'Liza's got the needle ter-night, thet's flat,' commented a third member of the team.

'I wouldn't drink if I was you, Liza,' added another, with mock gravity. 'It's a bad 'abit ter git into,' and he began rolling and swaying about like a drunken man.

If Liza had been 'in form' she would have gone straight away and given the whole lot of them a sample of her strength; but she was only rather bored and vexed that they should disturb her quietness, so she let them talk. They saw she was not to be drawn, and leaving her, set to their game. She watched them for some time, but her thoughts gradually lost themselves, and insensibly her mind was filled with a burly form, and she was again thinking of Jim.

''E is a good sort ter want ter tike me ter the ply,' she said to herself. 'Tom never arst me!'

Jim had said he would come out in the evening; he ought to be here soon, she thought. Of course she wasn't going to the theatre with him, but she didn't mind talking to him; she rather enjoyed being asked to do a thing and refusing, and she would have liked another opportunity of doing so. But he didn't come and he had said he would!

'I say, Bill,' she said at last to one of the boys who was fielding close beside her, 'that there Blakeston—d'you know 'im?'

'Yes, rather; why, he works at the sime plice as me.'

'Wot's 'e do with 'isself in the evening; I never see 'im abaht?'

'I dunno. I see 'im this evenin' go into the "Red Lion". I suppose 'e's there, but I dunno.'

Then he wasn't coming. Of course she had told him she was going to stay indoors, but he might have come all the same—just to see.

'I know Tom 'ud 'ave come,' she said to herself, rather sulkily.

'Liza! Liza!' she heard her mother's voice calling her.

'Arright, I'm comin',' said Liza.

'I've been witin' for you this last 'alf-hour ter rub me.'

'Why didn't yer call?' asked Liza.

'I did call. I've been callin' this last I dunno 'ow long; it's give me quite a sore throat.'

'I never 'eard yer.'

'Na, yer didn't want ter 'ear me, did yer? Yer don't mind if I dies with rheumatics, do yer? I know.'

Liza did not answer, but took the bottle, and, pouring some of the liniment on her hand, began to rub it into Mrs Kemp's rheumatic joints, while the invalid kept complaining and grumbling at everything Liza did.

'Don't rub so 'ard, Liza, you'll rub all the skin off.'

Then when Liza did it as gently as she could, she grumbled again.

'If yer do it like thet, it won't do no good at all. You want ter sive yerself trouble—I know yer. When I was young girls didn't mind a little bit of 'ard work—but, law bless yer, you don't care abaht my rheumatics, do yer?'

At last she finished, and Liza went to bed by her mother's side.

CHAPTER VII

Two days passed, and it was Friday morning. Liza had got up early and strolled off to her work in good time, but she did not meet her faithful Sally on the way, nor find her at the factory when she herself arrived. The bell rang and all the girls trooped in, but still Sally did not come. Liza could not make it out, and was thinking she would be shut out, when just as the man who gave out the tokens for the day's work was pulling down the shutter in front of his window, Sally arrived, breathless and perspiring.

'Whew! Go' lumme, I am 'ot!' she said, wiping her face with her apron.

'I thought you wasn't comin',' said Liza.

'Well, I only just did it; I overslep' myself. I was aht lite last night.'

'Were yer?'

'Me an' 'Arry went ter see the ply. Oh, Liza, it's simply spiffin'! I've never see sich a good ply in my life. Lor'! Why, it mikes yer blood run cold: they 'ang a man on the stige; oh, it mide me creep all over!'

And then she began telling Liza all about it—the blood and thunder, the shooting, the railway train, the murder, the bomb, the hero, the funny man—jumbling everything up in her excitement, repeating little scraps of dialogue—all wrong—gesticulating, getting excited and red in the face at the recollection. Liza listened rather crossly, feeling bored at the detail into which Sally was going; the piece really didn't much interest her.

'One 'ud think yer'd never been to a theatre in your life before,' she said.

'I never seen anything so good, I can tell yer. You tike my tip, and git Tom ter tike yer.'

'I don't want ter go; an' if I did I'd py for myself an' go alone.'

'Cheese it! That ain't 'alf so good. Me an' 'Arry, we set together, 'im with 'is arm round my wiste and me oldin' 'is 'and. It was jam, I can tell yer!'

'Well, I don't want anyone sprawlin' me abaht, thet ain't my mark!'

'But I do like 'Arry; you dunno the little ways 'e 'as; an' we're goin' ter be married in three weeks now. 'Arry said, well, 'e says, "I'll git a licence." "Na," says I, "'ave the banns read aht in church; it seems more reg'lar like to 'ave banns; so they're goin' ter be read aht next Sunday. You'll come with me 'an 'ear them, won't yer, Liza?'

'Yus, I don't mind.'

On the way home Sally insisted on stopping in front of the poster and explaining to Liza all about the scene represented.

'Oh, you give me the sick with your "Fital Card", you do! I'm goin' 'ome.' And she left Sally in the midst of her explanation.

'I dunno wot's up with Liza,' remarked Sally to a mutual friend. 'She's always got the needle, some 'ow.'

'Oh, she's barmy,' answered the friend.

'Well, I do think she's a bit dotty sometimes—I do really,' rejoined Sally.

Liza walked homewards, thinking of the play; at length she tossed her head impatiently.

'I don't want ter see the blasted thing; an' if I see that there Jim I'll tell 'im so; swop me bob, I will.'

She did see him; he was leaning with his back against the wall of his house, smoking. Liza knew he had seen her, and as she walked by pretended not to have noticed him. To her disgust, he let her pass, and she was thinking he hadn't seen her after all, when she heard him call her name.

'Liza!'

She turned round and started with surprise very well imitated. 'I didn't see you was there!' she said.

'Why did yer pretend not ter notice me, as yer went past—eh, Liza?'

'Why, I didn't see yer.'

'Garn! But you ain't shirty with me?'

'Wot 'ave I got to be shirty abaht?'

He tried to take her hand, but she drew it away quickly. She was getting used to the movement. They went on talking, but Jim did not mention the theatre; Liza was surprised, and wondered whether he had forgotten.

'Er—Sally went to the ply last night,' she said, at last.

'Oh!' he said, and that was all.

She got impatient.

'Well, I'm off!' she said.

'Na, don't go yet; I want ter talk ter yer,' he replied.

'Wot abaht? anythin' in partickler?' She would drag it out of him if she possibly could.

'Not thet I knows on,' he said, smiling.

'Good night!' she said, abruptly, turning away from him.

'Well, I'm damned if 'e ain't forgotten!' she said to herself, sulkily, as she marched home.

The following evening about six o'clock, it suddenly struck her that it was the last night of the 'New and Sensational Drama".

'I do like thet Jim Blakeston,' she said to herself; 'fancy treatin' me like thet! You wouldn't catch Tom doin' sich a thing. Bli'me if I speak to 'im again, the—Now I shan't see it at all. I've a good mind ter go on my own 'ook. Fancy 'is forgettin' all abaht it, like thet!'

She was really quite indignant; though, as she had distinctly refused Jim's offer, it was rather hard to see why.

''E said 'e'd wite for me ahtside the doors; I wonder if 'e's there. I'll go an' see if 'e is, see if I don't—an' then if e's there, I'll go in on my own 'ook, jist ter spite 'im!'

She dressed herself in her best, and, so that the neighbours shouldn't see her, went up a passage between some model lodging-house buildings, and in this roundabout way got into the Westminster Bridge Road, and soon found herself in front of the theatre.

'I've been witin' for yer this 'alf-hour.'

She turned round and saw Jim standing just behind her.

''Oo are you talkin' to? I'm not goin' to the ply with you. Wot d'yer tike me for, eh?'

''Oo are yer goin' with, then?'

'I'm goin' alone.'

'Garn! don't be a bloomin' jackass!'

Liza was feeling very injured.

'Thet's 'ow you treat me! I shall go 'ome. Why didn't you come aht the other night?'

'Yer told me not ter.'

She snorted at the ridiculous ineptitude of the reply.

'Why didn't you say nothin' abaht it yesterday?'

'Why, I thought you'd come if I didn't talk on it.'

'Well, I think you're a—brute!' She felt very much inclined to cry.

'Come on, Liza, don't tike on; I didn't mean no offence.' And he put his arm round her waist and led her to take their places at the gallery door. Two tears escaped from the corners of her eyes and ran down her nose, but she felt very relieved and happy, and let him lead her where he would.

There was a long string of people waiting at the door, and Liza was delighted to see a couple of niggers who were helping them to while away the time of waiting. The niggers sang and danced, and made faces, while the people looked on with appreciative gravity, like royalty listening to de Reské, and they were very generous of applause and halfpence at the end of the performance. Then, when the niggers moved to the pit doors, paper boys came along offering *Tit-Bits* and 'extra specials'; after that three little girls came round and sang sentimental songs and collected more half-pence. At last a movement ran through the serpent-like string of people, sounds were heard behind the door, everyone closed up, the men told the women to keep close and hold tight; there was a great unbarring and unbolting, the doors were thrown open, and, like a bursting river, the people surged in.

Half an hour more and the curtain went up. The play was indeed thrilling. Liza quite forgot her companion, and was intent on the scene; she watched the incidents breathlessly, trembling with excitement, almost beside herself at the celebrated hanging incident. When the curtain fell on the first act she sighed and mopped her face.

'See 'ow 'ot I am,' she said to Jim, giving him her hand.

'Yus, you are!' he remarked, taking it.

'Leave go!' she said, trying to withdraw it from him.

'Not much,' he answered, quite boldly.

'Garn! Leave go!' But he didn't, and she really did not struggle very violently.

The second act came, and she shrieked over the comic man; and her laughter rang higher than anyone else's, so that people turned to look at her, and said:

'She is enjoyin' 'erself.'

Then when the murder came she bit her nails and the sweat stood on her forehead in great drops; in her excitement she even called out as loud as she could to the victim, 'Look aht!' It caused a laugh and slackened the tension, for the whole house was holding its breath as it looked at the villains listening at the door, creeping silently forward, crawling like tigers to their prey.

Liza trembling all over, and in her terror threw herself against Jim, who put both his arms round her, and said:

'Don't be afride, Liza; it's all right.'

At last the men sprang, there was a scuffle, and the wretch was killed, then came the scene depicted on the posters—the victim's son knocking at the door, on the inside of which were the murderers and the murdered man. At last the curtain came down, and the house in relief burst forth into cheers and cheers; the handsome hero in his top hat was greeted thunderously; the murdered man, with his clothes still all disarranged, was hailed with sympathy; and the villains—the house yelled and hissed and booed, while the poor brutes bowed and tried to look as if they liked it.

'I am enjoyin' myself,' said Liza, pressing herself quite close to Jim; 'you are a good sort ter tike me—Jim.'

He gave her a little hug, and it struck her that she was sitting just as Sally had done, and, like Sally, she found it 'jam'.

The *entr'actes* were short and the curtain was soon up again, and the comic man raised customary laughter by undressing and exposing his nether garments to the public view; then more tragedy, and the final act with its darkened room, its casting lots, and its explosion.

When it was all over and they had got outside Jim smacked his lips and said:

'I could do with a gargle; let's go onto thet pub there.'

'I'm as dry as bone,' said Liza; and so they went.

When they got in they discovered they were hungry, and seeing some appetising sausage-rolls, ate of them, and washed them down with a couple of pots of beer; then Jim lit his pipe and they strolled off. They had got quite near the Westminster Bridge Road when Jim suggested that they should go and have one more drink before closing time.

'I shall be tight,' said Liza.

'Thet don't matter,' answered Jim, laughing. 'You ain't got ter go ter work in the mornin' an' you can sleep it aht.'

'Arright, I don't mind if I do then, in for a penny, in for a pound.'

At the pub door she drew back.

'I say, guv'ner,' she said, 'there'll be some of the coves from dahn our street, and they'll see us.'

'Na, there won't be nobody there, don't yer 'ave no fear.'

'I don't like ter go in for fear of it.'

'Well, we ain't doin' no 'arm if they does see us, an' we can go into the private bar, an' you bet your boots there won't be no one there.'

She yielded, and they went in.

'Two pints of bitter, please, miss,' ordered Jim.

'I say, 'old 'ard. I can't drink more than 'alf a pint,' said Liza.

'Cheese it,' answered Jim. 'You can do with all you can get, I know.'

At closing time they left and walked down the broad road which led homewards.

'Let's 'ave a little sit dahn,' said Jim, pointing to an empty bench between two trees.

'Na, it's gettin' lite; I want ter be 'ome.'

'It's such a fine night, it's a pity ter go in already;' and he drew her unresisting towards the seat. He put his arm round her waist.

'Un'and me, villin!' she said, in apt misquotation of the melodrama, but Jim only laughed, and she made no effort to disengage herself.

They sat there for a long while in silence; the beer had got to Liza's head, and the warm night air filled her with a double intoxication. She felt the arm round her waist, and the big, heavy form pressing against her side; she experienced again the curious sensation as if her heart were about to burst, and it choked her—a feeling so oppressive and painful it almost made her feel sick. Her hands began to tremble, and her breathing grew rapid, as though she were suffocating. Almost fainting, she swayed over towards the man, and a cold shiver ran through her from top to toe. Jim bent over her, and, taking her in both arms, he pressed his lips to hers in a long, passionate kiss. At last, panting for breath, she turned her head away and groaned.

Then they again sat for a long while in silence, Liza full of a strange happiness, feeling as if she could laugh aloud hysterically, but restrained by the calm and silence of the night. Close behind struck a church clock—one.

'Bless my soul!' said Liza, starting, 'there's one o'clock. I must get 'ome.'

'It's so nice out 'ere; do sty, Liza.' He pressed her closer to him. 'Yer know, Liza, I love yer—fit ter kill.'

'Na, I can't stay; come on.' She got up from the seat, and pulled him up too. 'Come on,' she said.

Without speaking they went along, and there was no one to be seen either in front or behind them. He had not got his arm round her now, and they were walking side by side, slightly separated. It was Liza who spoke first.

'You'd better go dahn the Road and by the church an' git into Vere Street the other end, an' I'll go through the passage, so thet no one shouldn't see us comin' together,' she spoke almost in a whisper.

'Arright, Liza,' he answered, 'I'll do just as you tell me.'

They came to the passage of which Liza spoke; it was a narrow way between blank walls, the backs of factories, and it led into the upper end of Vere Street. The entrance to it was guarded by two iron posts in the middle so that horses or barrows should not be taken through.

They had just got to it when a man came out into the open road. Liza quickly turned her head away.

'I wonder if 'e see us,' she said, when he had passed out of earshot. ''E's lookin' back,' she added.

'Why, 'oo is it?' asked Jim.

'It's a man aht of our street,' she answered. 'I dunno 'im, but I know where 'e lodges. D'yer think 'e sees us?'

'Na, 'e wouldn't know 'oo it was in the dark.'

'But he looked round; all the street'll know it if he see us.'

'Well, we ain't doin' no 'arm.'

She stretched out her hand to say good night.

'I'll come a little wy with yer along the passage,' said Jim.

'Na, you mustn't; you go straight round.'

'But it's so dark; p'raps summat'll 'appen to yer.'

'Not it! You go on 'ome an' leave me,' she replied, and entering the passage, stood facing him with one of the iron pillars between them.

'Good night, old cock,' she said, stretching out her hand. He took it, and said:

'I wish yer wasn't goin' ter leave me, Liza.'

'Garn! I must!' She tried to get her hand away from his, but he held it firm, resting it on the top of the pillar.

'Leave go my 'and,' she said. He made no movement, but looked into her eyes steadily, so that it made her uneasy. She repented having come out with him. 'Leave go my 'and.' And she beat down on his with her closed fist.

'Liza!' he said, at last.

'Well, wot is it?' she answered, still thumping down on his hand with her fist.

'Liza,' he said a whisper, 'will yer?'

'Will I wot?' she said, looking down.

'You know, Liza. Sy, will yer?'

'Na,' she said.

He bent over her and repeated—

'Will yer?'

She did not speak, but kept beating down on his hand.

'Liza,' he said again, his voice growing hoarse and thick—'Liza, will yer?'

She still kept silence, looking away and continually bringing down her fist. He looked at her a moment, and she, ceasing to thump his hand, looked up at him with half-opened mouth. Suddenly he shook himself, and closing his fist gave her a violent, swinging blow in the belly.

'Come on,' he said.

And together they slid down into the darkness of the passage.

CHAPTER VIII

Mrs Kemp was in the habit of slumbering somewhat heavily on Sunday mornings, or Liza would not have been allowed to go on sleeping as she did. When she woke, she rubbed her eyes to gather her senses together and gradually she remembered having gone to the theatre on the previous evening; then suddenly everything came back to her. She stretched out her legs and gave a long sigh of delight. Her heart was full; she thought of Jim, and the delicious sensation of love came over her. Closing her eyes, she imagined his warm kisses, and she lifted up her arms as if to put them round his neck and draw him down to her; she almost felt the rough beard on her face, and the strong heavy arms round her body. She smiled to herself and took a long breath; then, slipping back the sleeves of her nightdress, she looked at her own thin arms, just two pieces of bone with not a muscle on them, but very white and showing distinctly the interlacement of blue veins; she did not notice that her hands were rough, and red and dirty with the nails broken, and bitten to the quick. She got out of bed and looked at herself in the glass over the mantelpiece; with one hand she brushed back her hair and smiled at herself; her face was very small and thin, but the complexion was nice, clear and white, with a delicate tint of red on the cheeks, and her eyes were big and dark like her hair. She felt very happy.

She did not want to dress yet, but rather to sit down and think, so she twisted up her hair into a little knot, slipped a skirt over her nightdress, and sat on a chair near the window and began looking around. The decorations of the room had been centred on the mantelpiece; the chief ornament consisted of a pear and an apple, a pineapple, a bunch of grapes, and several fat plums, all very beautifully done in wax, as was the fashion about the middle of this most glorious reign. They were appropriately coloured—the apple blushing red, the grapes an inky black, emerald green leaves were scattered here and there to lend finish, and the whole was mounted on an ebonised stand covered with black velvet, and protected from dust and dirt by a beautiful glass cover bordered with red plush. Liza's eyes rested on this with approbation, and the pineapple quite made her mouth water. At either end of the mantelpiece were pink jars with blue flowers on the front; round the top in Gothic letters of gold was inscribed: 'A Present from a Friend'—these were products of a later, but not less artistic age. The intervening spaces were taken up with little jars and cups and saucers—gold inside, with a view of a town outside, and surrounding them, 'A Present from Clacton-on-Sea,' or, alliteratively, 'A Memento of Margate.' Of these many were broken, but they had been mended with glue, and it is well known that pottery in the eyes of the connoisseur loses none of its value by a crack or two. Then there were portraits innumerable—little yellow cartes-de-visite in velvet frames, some of which were decorated with shells; they showed strange people with old-fashioned clothes, the women with bodices and sleeves fitting close to the figure, stern-featured females with hair carefully parted in the middle and plastered down on each side, firm chins and mouths, with small, pig-like eyes and wrinkled faces, and the men were uncomfortably clad in Sunday garments, very stiff and uneasy in their awkward postures, with large whiskers and shaved chins and upper lips and a general air of horny-handed toil. Then there were one or two daguerreotypes, little full-length figures framed in gold paper. There was one of Mrs Kemp's father and one of her mother, and there were several photographs of betrothed or newly-married couples, the lady sitting down and the man standing behind her with his hand on the chair, or the man sitting and the woman with her hand on his shoulder. And from all sides of the room, standing on the mantelpiece, hanging above it, on the wall and over the bed, they stared full-face into the room, self-consciously fixed for ever in their stiff discomfort.

The walls were covered with dingy, antiquated paper, and ornamented with coloured supplements from Christmas Numbers—there was a very patriotic picture of a soldier shaking the hand of a fallen comrade and waving his arm in defiance of a band of advancing Arabs; there was a 'Cherry Ripe,' almost black with age and dirt; there were two almanacks several years old, one with a coloured portrait of the Marquess of Lorne, very handsome and elegantly dressed, the object of Mrs Kemp's adoration since her husband's demise; the other a Jubilee portrait of the Queen, somewhat losing in dignity by a moustache which Liza in an irreverent moment had smeared on with charcoal.

The furniture consisted of a wash-hand stand and a little deal chest of drawers, which acted as sideboard to such pots and pans and crockery as could not find room in the grate; and besides the bed there was nothing but two kitchen chairs and a lamp. Liza looked at it all and felt perfectly satisfied; she put a pin into one corner of the noble Marquess to prevent him from falling, fiddled about with the ornaments a little, and then started washing herself. After putting on her clothes she ate some bread-and-butter, swallowed a dishful of cold tea, and went out into the street.

She saw some boys playing cricket and went up to them.

'Let me ply,' she said.

'Arright, Liza,' cried half a dozen of them in delight; and the captain added: 'You go an' scout over by the lamppost.'

'Go an' scout my eye!' said Liza, indignantly. 'When I ply cricket I does the battin'.'

'Na, you're not goin' ter bat all the time. 'Oo are you gettin' at?' replied the captain, who had taken advantage of his position to put himself in first, and was still at the wicket.

'Well, then I shan't ply,' answered Liza.

'Garn, Ernie, let 'er go in!' shouted two or three members of the team.

'Well, I'm busted!' remarked the captain, as she took his bat. 'You won't sty in long, I lay,' he said, as he sent the old bowler fielding and took the ball himself. He was a young gentleman who did not suffer from excessive backwardness.

'Aht!' shouted a dozen voices as the ball went past Liza's bat and landed in the pile of coats which formed the wicket. The captain came forward to resume his innings, but Liza held the bat away from him.

'Garn!' she said; 'thet was only a trial.'

'You never said trial,' answered the captain indignantly.

'Yus, I did,' said Liza; 'I said it just as the ball was comin'— under my breath.'

'Well, I am busted!' repeated the captain.

Just then Liza saw Tom among the lookers-on, and as she felt very kindly disposed to the world in general that morning, she called out to him:

''Ulloa, Tom!' she said. 'Come an' give us a ball; this chap can't bowl.'

'Well, I got yer aht, any'ow,' said that person.

'Ah, yer wouldn't 'ave got me aht plyin' square. But a trial ball—well, one don't ever know wot a trial ball's goin' ter do.'

Tom began bowling very slowly and easily, so that Liza could swing her bat round and hit mightily; she ran well, too, and pantingly brought up her score to twenty. Then the fielders interposed.

'I sy, look 'ere, 'e's only givin' 'er lobs; 'e's not tryin' ter git 'er aht.'

'You're spoilin' our gime.'

'I don't care; I've got twenty runs—thet's more than you could do. I'll go aht now of my own accord, so there! Come on, Tom.'

Tom joined her, and as the captain at last resumed his bat and the game went on, they commenced talking, Liza leaning against the wall of a house, while Tom stood in front of her, smiling with pleasure.

'Where 'ave you been idin' yerself, Tom? I ain't seen yer for I dunno 'ow long.'

'I've been abaht as usual; an' I've seen you when you didn't see me.'

'Well, yer might 'ave come up and said good mornin' when you see me.'

'I didn't want ter force myself on yer, Liza.'

'Garn! You are a bloomin' cuckoo, I'm blowed!'

'I thought yer didn't like me 'angin' round yer; so I kep' awy.'

'Why, yer talks as if I didn't like yer. Yer don't think I'd 'ave come aht beanfeastin' with yer if I 'adn't liked yer?'

Liza was really very dishonest, but she felt so happy this morning that she loved the whole world, and of course Tom came in with the others. She looked very kindly at him, and he was so affected that a great lump came in his throat and he could not speak.

Liza's eyes turned to Jim's house, and she saw coming out of the door a girl of about her own age; she fancied she saw in her some likeness to Jim.

'Say, Tom,' he asked, 'thet ain't Blakeston's daughter, is it?'

'Yus, thet's it.'

'I'll go an' speak to 'er,' said Liza, leaving Tom and going over the road.

'You're Polly Blakeston, ain't yer?' she said.

'Thet's me!' said the girl.

'I thought you was. Your dad, 'e says ter me, "You dunno my daughter, Polly, do yer?" says 'e. "Na," says I, "I don't." "Well," says 'e, "You can't miss 'er when you see 'er." An' right enough I didn't.'

'Mother says I'm all father, an' there ain't nothin' of 'er in me. Dad says it's lucky it ain't the other wy abaht, or e'd 'ave got a divorce.'

They both laughed.

'Where are you goin' now?' asked Liza, looking at the slop-basin she was carrying.

'I was just goin' dahn into the road ter get some ice-cream for dinner. Father 'ad a bit of luck last night, 'e says, and 'e'd stand the lot of us ice-cream for dinner ter-day.'

'I'll come with yer if yer like.'

'Come on!' And, already friends, they walked arm-in-arm to the Westminster Bridge Road. Then they went along till they came to a stall where an Italian was selling the required commodity, and having had a taste apiece to see if they liked it, Polly planked down sixpence and had her basin filled with a poisonous-looking mixture of red and white ice-cream.

On the way back, looking up the street, Polly cried:

'There's father!'

Liza's heart beat rapidly and she turned red; but suddenly a sense of shame came over her, and casting down her head so that she might not see him, she said:

'I think I'll be off 'ome an' see 'ow mother's gettin' on.' And before Polly could say anything she had slipped away and entered her own house.

Mother was not getting on at all well.

'You've come in at last, you—, you!' snarled Mrs Kemp, as Liza entered the room.

'Wot's the matter, mother?'

'Matter! I like thet—matter indeed! Go an' matter yerself an' be mattered! Nice way ter treat an old woman like me—an' yer own mother, too!'

'Wot's up now?'

'Don't talk ter me; I don't want ter listen ter you. Leavin' me all alone, me with my rheumatics, an' the neuralgy! I've 'ad the neuralgy all the mornin', and my 'ead's been simply splittin', so thet I thought the bones 'ud come apart and all my brains go streamin' on the floor. An' when I wake up there's no one ter git my tea for me, an' I lay there witin' an' witin', an' at last I 'ad ter git up and mike it myself. And, my 'ead simply cruel! Why, I might 'ave been burnt ter death with the fire alight an' me asleep.'

'Well, I am sorry, mother; but I went aht just for a bit, an' didn't think you'd wike. An' besides, the fire wasn't alight.'

'Garn with yer! I didn't treat my mother like thet. Oh, you've been a bad daughter ter me—an' I 'ad more illness carryin' you than with all the other children put togither. You was a cross at yer birth, an' you've been a cross ever since. An' now in my old age, when I've worked myself ter the bone, yer leaves me to starve and burn to death.' Here she began to cry, and the rest of her utterances was lost in sobs.

The dusk had darkened into night, and Mrs Kemp had retired to rest with the dicky-birds. Liza was thinking of many things; she wondered why she had been unwilling to meet Jim in the morning.

'I was a bally fool,' she said to herself.

It really seemed an age since the previous night, and all that had happened seemed very long ago. She had not spoken to Jim all day, and she had so much to say to him. Then, wondering whether he was about, she went to the window and looked out; but there was nobody there. She closed the window again and sat just beside it; the time went on, and she wondered whether he would come, asking herself whether he had been thinking of her as she of him; gradually her thoughts grew vague, and a kind of mist came over them. She nodded. Suddenly she roused herself with a start, fancying she had heard something; she listened again, and in a moment the sound was repeated, three or four gentle taps on the window. She opened it quickly and whispered:

'Jim.'

'Thet's me,' he answered, 'come aht.'

Closing the window, she went into the passage and opened the street door; it was hardly unlocked before Jim had pushed his way in; partly shutting it behind him, he took her in his arms and hugged her to his breast. She kissed him passionately.

'I thought yer'd come ter-night, Jim; summat in my 'eart told me so. But you 'ave been long.'

'I wouldn't come before, 'cause I thought there'd be people abaht. Kiss us!' And again he pressed his lips to hers, and Liza nearly fainted with the delight of it.

'Let's go for a walk, shall we?' he said.

'Arright!' They were speaking in whispers. 'You go into the road through the passage, an' I'll go by the street.'

'Yus, thet's right,' and kissing her once more, he slid out, and she closed the door behind him.

Then going back to get her hat, she came again into the passage, waiting behind the door till it might be safe for her to venture. She had not made up her mind to risk it, when she heard a key put in the lock, and she hardly had time to spring back to prevent herself from being hit by the opening door. It was a man, one of the upstairs lodgers.

''Ulloa!' he said, ''oo's there?'

'Mr 'Odges! Strikes me, you did give me a turn; I was just goin' aht.' She blushed to her hair, but in the darkness he could see nothing.

'Good night,' she said, and went out.

She walked close along the sides of the houses like a thief, and the policeman as she passed him turned round and looked at her, wondering whether she was meditating some illegal deed. She breathed freely on coming into the open road, and seeing Jim skulking behind a tree, ran up to him, and in the shadows they kissed again.

CHAPTER IX

THUS began a time of love and joy. As soon as her work was over and she had finished tea, Liza would slip out and at some appointed spot meet Jim. Usually it would be at the church, where the Westminster Bridge Road bends down to get to the river, and they would go off, arm-in-arm, till they came to some place where they could sit down and rest. Sometimes they would walk along the Albert Embankment to Battersea Park, and here sit on the benches, watching the children play. The female cyclist had almost abandoned Battersea for the parks on the other side of the river, but often enough one went by, and Liza, with the old-fashioned prejudice of her class, would look after the rider and make some remark about her, not seldom more forcible than ladylike. Both Jim and she liked children, and tiny, ragged urchins would gather round to have rides on the man's knees or mock fights with Liza.

They thought themselves far away from anyone in Vere Street, but twice, as they were walking along, they were met by people they knew. Once it was two workmen coming home from a job at Vauxhall: Liza did not see them till they were quite near; she immediately dropped Jim's arm, and they both cast their eyes to the ground as the men passed, like ostriches, expecting that if they did not look they would not be seen.

'D'you see 'em, Jim?' asked Liza, in a whisper, when they had gone by. 'I wonder if they see us.' Almost instinctively she turned round, and at the same moment one of the men turned too; then there was no doubt about it.

'Thet did give me a turn,' she said.

'So it did me,' answered Jim; 'I simply went 'ot all over.'

'We was bally fools,' said Liza; 'we oughter 'ave spoken to 'em! D'you think they'll let aht?'

They heard nothing of it, when Jim afterwards met one of the men in a public-house he did not mention a meeting, and they thought that perhaps they had not been recognized. But the second time was worse.

It was on the Albert Embankment again. They were met by a party of four, all of whom lived in the street. Liza's heart sank within her, for there was no chance of escape; she thought of turning quickly and walking in the opposite direction, but there was not time, for the men had already seen them. She whispered to Jim:

'Back us up,' and as they met she said to one of the men: ''Ulloa there! Where are you off to?'

The men stopped, and one of them asked the question back.

'Where are you off to?'

'Me? Oh, I've just been to the 'orspital. One of the gals at our place is queer, an' so I says ter myself, "I'll go an' see 'er."' She faltered a little as she began, but quickly gathered herself together, lying fluently and without hesitation.

'An' when I come aht,' she went on, ''oo should I see just passin' the 'orspital but this 'ere cove, an' 'e says to me, "Wot cheer," says 'e, "I'm goin' ter Vaux'all, come an' walk a bit of the wy with us." "Arright," says I, "I don't mind if I do."'

One man winked, and another said: 'Go it, Liza!'

She fired up with the dignity of outraged innocence.

'Wot d'yer mean by thet?' she said; 'd'yer think I'm kiddin'?'

'Kiddin'? No! You've only just come up from the country, ain't yer?'

'Think I'm kidding? What d'yer think I want ter kid for? Liars never believe anyone, thet's fact.'

'Na then, Liza, don't be saucy.'

'Saucy! I'll smack yer in the eye if yer sy much ter me. Come on,' she said to Jim, who had been standing sheepishly by; and they walked away.

The men shouted: 'Now we shan't be long!' and went off laughing.

After that they decided to go where there was no chance at all of their being seen. They did not meet till they got over Westminster Bridge, and thence they made their way into the park; they would lie down on the grass in one another's arms, and thus spend the long summer evenings. After the heat of the day there would be a gentle breeze in the park, and they would take in long breaths of the air; it seemed far away from London, it was so quiet and cool; and Liza, as she lay by Jim's side, felt her love for him overflowing to the rest of the world and enveloping mankind itself in a kind of grateful happiness. If it could only have lasted! They would stay and see the stars shine out dimly, one by one, from the blue sky, till it grew late and the blue darkened into black, and the stars glittered in thousands all above them. But as the nights grew cooler, they found it cold on the grass, and the time they had there seemed too short for the long journey they had to make; so, crossing the bridge as before, they strolled along the Embankment till they came to a vacant bench, and there they would sit, with Liza nestling close up to her lover and his great arms around her. The rain of September made no difference to them; they went as usual to their seat beneath the trees, and Jim would take Liza on his knee, and, opening his coat, shelter her with it, while she, with her arms round his neck, pressed very close to him, and occasionally gave a little laugh of pleasure and delight. They hardly spoke at all through these evenings, for what had they to say to one another? Often without exchanging a word they would sit for an hour with their faces touching, the one feeling on his cheek the hot breath from the other's mouth; while at the end of the time the only motion was an upraising of Liza's lips, a bending down of Jim's, so that they might meet and kiss. Sometimes Liza fell into a light doze, and Jim would sit very still for fear of waking her, and when she roused herself she would smile, while he bent down again and kissed her. They were very happy. But the hours passed by so quickly, that Big Ben striking twelve came upon them as a surprise, and unwillingly they got up and made their way homewards; their partings were never ending—each evening Jim refused to let her go from his arms, and tears stood in his eyes at the thought of the separation.

'I'd give somethin',' he would say, 'if we could be together always.'

'Never mind, old chap!' Liza would answer, herself half crying, 'it can't be 'elped, so we must jolly well lump it.'

But notwithstanding all their precautions people in Vere Street appeared to know. First of all Liza noticed that the women did not seem quite so cordial as before, and she often fancied they were talking of her; when she passed by they appeared to look at her, then say something or other, and perhaps burst out laughing; but when she approached they would immediately stop speaking, and keep silence in a rather awkward, constrained manner. For a long time she was unwilling to believe that there was any change in them, and Jim who had observed nothing, persuaded her that it was all fancy. But gradually it became clearer, and Jim had to agree with her that somehow or other people had found out. Once when Liza had been talking to Polly, Jim's daughter, Mrs Blakeston had called her, and when the girl had come to her mother Liza saw that she spoke angrily, and they both looked across at her. When Liza caught Mrs Blakeston's eye she saw in her face a surly scowl, which almost frightened her; she wanted to brave it out, and stepped forward a little to go and speak with the woman, but Mrs Blakeston, standing still, looked so angrily at her that she was afraid to. When she told Jim his face grew dark, and he said: 'Blast the woman! I'll give 'er wot for if she says anythin' ter you.'

'Don't strike 'er, wotever 'appens, will yer, Jim?' said Liza.

'She'd better tike care then!' he answered, and he told her that lately his wife had been sulking, and not speaking to him. The previous night, on coming home after the day's work and bidding her 'Good evenin',' she had turned her back on him without answering.

'Can't you answer when you're spoke to?' he had said.

'Good evenin',' she had replied sulkily, with her back still turned.

After that Liza noticed that Polly avoided her.

'Wot's up, Polly?' she said to her one day. 'You never speaks now; 'ave you 'ad yer tongue cut aht?'

'Me? I ain't got nothin' ter speak abaht, thet I knows of,' answered Polly, abruptly walking off. Liza grew very red and quickly looked to see if anyone had noticed the incident. A couple of youths, sitting on the pavement, had seen it, and she saw them nudge one another and wink.

Then the fellows about the street began to chaff her.

'You look pale,' said one of a group to her one day.

'You're overworkin' yerself, you are,' said another.

'Married life don't agree with Liza, thet's wot it is,' added a third.

''Oo d'yer think yer gettin' at? I ain't married, an' never like ter be,' she answered.

'Liza 'as all the pleasures of a 'usband an' none of the trouble.'

'Bli'me if I know wot yer mean!' said Liza.

'Na, of course not; you don't know nothin', do yer?'

'Innocent as a bibe. Our Father which art in 'eaven!'

''Aven't been in London long, 'ave yer?'

They spoke in chorus, and Liza stood in front of them, bewildered, not knowing what to answer.

'Don't you mike no mistake abaht it, Liza knows a thing or two.'

'O me darlin', I love yer fit to kill, but tike care your missus ain't round the corner.' This was particularly bold, and they all laughed.

Liza felt very uncomfortable, and fiddled about with her apron, wondering how she should get away.

'Tike care yer don't git into trouble, thet's all,' said one of the men, with burlesque gravity.

'Yer might give us a chanst, Liza, you come aht with me one evenin'. You oughter give us all a turn, just ter show there's no ill-feelin'.'

'Bli'me if I know wot yer all talkin' abaht. You're all barmy on the crumpet,' said Liza indignantly, and, turning her back on them, made for home.

Among other things that had happened was Sally's marriage. One Saturday a little procession had started from Vere Street, consisting of Sally, in a state of giggling excitement, her fringe magnificent after a whole week of curling-papers, clad in a perfectly new velveteen dress of the colour known as electric blue; and Harry, rather nervous and ill at ease in the unaccustomed restraint of a collar; these two walked arm-in-arm, and were followed by Sally's mother and uncle, also arm-in-arm, and the procession was brought up by Harry's brother and a friend. They started with a flourish of trumpets and an old boot, and walked down the middle of Vere Street, accompanied by the neighbours' good wishes; but as they got into the Westminster Bridge Road and nearer to the church, the happy couple grew silent, and Harry began to perspire freely, so that his collar gave him perfect torture. There was a public-house just opposite the church, and it was suggested that they should have a drink before going in. As it was a solemn occasion they went into the private bar, and there Sally's uncle, who was a man of means, ordered six pots of beer.

'Feel a bit nervous, 'Arry?' asked his friend.

'Na,' said Harry, as if he had been used to getting married every day of his life; 'bit warm, thet's all.'

'Your very good 'ealth, Sally,' said her mother, lifting her mug; 'this is the last time as I shall ever address you as miss.'

'An' may she be as good a wife as you was,' added Sally's uncle.

'Well, I don't think my old man ever 'ad no complaint ter mike abaht me. I did my duty by 'im, although it's me as says it,' answered the good lady.

'Well, mates,' said Harry's brother, 'I reckon it's abaht time to go in. So 'ere's to the 'ealth of Mr 'Enry Atkins an' 'is future missus.'

'An' God bless 'em!' said Sally's mother.

Then they went into the church, and as they solemnly walked up the aisle a pale-faced young curate came out of the vestry and down to the bottom of the chancel. The beer had had a calming effect on their troubled minds, and both Harry and

Sally began to think it rather a good joke. They smiled on each other, and at those parts of the service which they thought suggestive violently nudged one another in the ribs. When the ring had to be produced, Harry fumbled about in different pockets, and his brother whispered:

'Swop me bob, 'e's gone and lorst it!'

However, all went right, and Sally having carefully pocketed the certificate, they went out and had another drink to celebrate the happy event.

In the evening Liza and several friends came into the couple's room, which they had taken in the same house as Sally had lived in before, and drank the health of the bride and bridegroom till they thought fit to retire.

CHAPTER X

IT was November. The fine weather had quite gone now, and with it much of the sweet pleasure of Jim and Liza's love. When they came out at night on the Embankment they found it cold and dreary; sometimes a light fog covered the river-banks, and made the lamps glow out dim and large; a light rain would be falling, which sent a chill into their very souls; foot passengers came along at rare intervals, holding up umbrellas, and staring straight in front of them as they hurried along in the damp and cold; a cab would pass rapidly by, splashing up the mud on each side. The benches were deserted, except, perhaps, for some poor homeless wretch who could afford no shelter, and, huddled up in a corner, with his head buried in his breast, was sleeping heavily, like a dead man. The wet mud made Liza's skirts cling about her feet, and the damp would come in and chill her legs and creep up her body, till she shivered, and for warmth pressed herself close against Jim. Sometimes they would go into the third-class waiting-rooms at Waterloo or Charing Cross and sit there, but it was not like the park or the Embankment on summer nights; they had warmth, but the heat made their wet clothes steam and smell, and the gas flared in their eyes, and they hated the people perpetually coming in and out, opening the doors and letting in a blast of cold air; they hated the noise of the guards and porters shouting out the departure of the trains, the shrill whistling of the steam-engine, the hurry and bustle and confusion. About eleven o'clock, when the trains grew less frequent, they got some quietness; but then their minds were troubled, and they felt heavy, sad and miserable.

One evening they had been sitting at Waterloo Station; it was foggy outside—a thick, yellow November fog, which filled the waiting-room, entering the lungs, and making the mouth taste nasty and the eyes smart. It was about half-past eleven, and the station was unusually quiet; a few passengers, in wraps and overcoats, were walking to and fro, waiting for the last train, and one or two porters were standing about yawning. Liza and Jim had remained for an hour in perfect silence, filled with a gloomy unhappiness, as of a great weight on their brains. Liza was sitting forward, with her elbows on her knees, resting her face on her hands.

'I wish I was straight,' she said at last, not looking up.

'Well, why won't yer come along of me altogether, an' you'll be arright then?' he answered.

'Na, that's no go; I can't do thet.' He had often asked her to live with him entirely, but she had always refused.

'You can come along of me, an' I'll tike a room in a lodgin' 'ouse in 'Olloway, an' we can live there as if we was married.'

'Wot abaht yer work?'

'I can get work over the other side as well as I can 'ere. I'm abaht sick of the wy things is goin' on.'

'So am I; but I can't leave mother.'

'She can come, too.'

'Not when I'm not married. I shouldn't like 'er ter know as I'd—as I'd gone wrong.'

'Well, I'll marry yer. Swop me bob, I wants ter badly enough.'

'Yer can't; yer married already.'

'Thet don't matter! If I give the missus so much a week aht of my screw, she'll sign a piper ter give up all clime ter me, an' then we can get spliced. One of the men as I works with done thet, an' it was arright.'

Liza shook her head.

'Na, yer can't do thet now; it's bigamy, an' the cop tikes yer, an' yer gits twelve months' 'ard for it.'

'But swop me bob, Liza, I can't go on like this. Yer knows the missus—well, there ain't no bloomin' doubt abaht it, she knows as you an' me are carryin' on, an' she mikes no bones abaht lettin' me see it.'

'She don't do thet?'

'Well, she don't exactly sy it, but she sulks an' won't speak, an' then when I says anythin' she rounds on me an' calls me all the nimes she can think of. I'd give 'er a good 'idin', but some'ow I don't like ter! She mikes the plice a 'ell ter me, an' I'm not goin' ter stand it no longer!'

'You'll ave ter sit it, then; yer can't chuck it.'

'Yus I can, an' I would if you'd come along of me. I don't believe you like me at all, Liza, or you'd come.'

She turned towards him and put her arms round his neck.

'Yer know I do, old cock,' she said. 'I like yer better than anyone else in the world; but I can't go awy an' leave mother.'

'Bli'me me if I see why; she's never been much ter you. She mikes yer slave awy ter pay the rent, an' all the money she earns she boozes.'

'Thet's true, she ain't been wot yer might call a good mother ter me—but some'ow she's my mother, an' I don't like ter leave 'er on 'er own, now she's so old—an' she can't do much with the rheumatics. An' besides, Jim dear, it ain't only mother, but there's yer own kids, yer can't leave them.'

He thought for a while, and then said:

'You're abaht right there, Liza; I dunno if I could get on without the kids. If I could only tike them an' you too, swop me bob, I should be 'appy.'

Liza smiled sadly.

'So yer see, Jim, we're in a bloomin' 'ole, an' there ain't no way aht of it thet I can see.'

He took her on his knees, and pressing her to him, kissed her very long and very lovingly.

'Well, we must trust ter luck,' she said again, 'p'raps somethin' 'll 'appen soon, an' everythin' 'll come right in the end—when we gets four balls of worsted for a penny.'

It was past twelve, and separating, they went by different ways along the dreary, wet, deserted roads till they came to Vere Street.

The street seemed quite different to Liza from what it had been three months before. Tom, the humble adorer, had quite disappeared from her life. One day, three or four weeks after the August Bank Holiday, she saw him dawdling along the pavement, and it suddenly struck her that she had not seen him for a long time; but she had been so full of her happiness that she had been unable to think of anyone but Jim. She wondered at his absence, since before wherever she had been there was he certain to be also. She passed him, but to her astonishment he did not speak to her. She thought by some wonder he had not seen her, but she felt his gaze resting upon her. She turned back, and suddenly he dropped his eyes and looked down, walking on as if he had not seen her, but blushing furiously.

'Tom,' she said, 'why don't yer speak ter me.'

He started and blushed more than ever.

'I didn't know yer was there,' he stuttered.

'Don't tell me,' she said, 'wot's up?'

'Nothin' as I knows of,' he answered uneasily.

'I ain't offended yer, 'ave I, Tom?'

'Na, not as I knows of,' he replied, looking very unhappy.

'You don't ever come my way now,' she said.

'I didn't know as yer wanted ter see me.'

'Garn! Yer knows I likes you as well as anybody.'

'Yer likes so many people, Liza,' he said, flushing.

'What d'yer mean?' said Liza indignantly, but very red; she was afraid he knew now, and it was from him especially she would have been so glad to hide it.

'Nothin',' he answered.

'One doesn't say things like thet without any meanin', unless one's a blimed fool.'

'You're right there, Liza,' he answered. 'I am a blimed fool.' He looked at her a little reproachfully, she thought, and then he said 'Good-bye,' and turned away.

At first she was horrified that he should know of her love for Jim, but then she did not care. After all, it was nobody's business, and what did anything matter as long as she loved Jim and Jim loved her? Then she grew angry that Tom should suspect her; he could know nothing but that some of the men had seen her with Jim near Vauxhall, and it seemed mean that he should condemn her for that. Thenceforward, when she ran against Tom, she cut him; he never tried to speak to her, but as she passed him, pretending to look in front of her, she could see that he always blushed, and she fancied his eyes were very sorrowful. Then several weeks went by, and as she began to feel more and more lonely in the street she regretted the quarrel; she cried a little as she thought that she had lost his faithful gentle love and she would have much liked to be friends with him again. If he had only made some advance she would have welcomed him so cordially, but she was too proud to go to him herself and beg him to forgive her—and then how could he forgive her?

She had lost Sally too, for on her marriage Harry had made her give up the factory; he was a young man with principles worthy of a Member of Parliament, and he had said:

'A woman's plice is 'er 'ome, an' if 'er old man can't afford ter keep 'er without 'er workin' in a factory—well, all I can say is thet 'e'd better go an' git single.'

'Quite right, too,' agreed his mother-in-law; 'an' wot's more, she'll 'ave a baby ter look after soon, an' thet'll tike 'er all 'er time, an' there's no one as knows thet better than me, for I've 'ad twelve, ter sy nothin' of two stills an' one miss.'

Liza quite envied Sally her happiness, for the bride was brimming over with song and laughter; her happiness overwhelmed her.

'I am 'appy,' she said to Liza one day a few weeks after her marriage. 'You dunno wot a good sort 'Arry is. 'E's just a darlin', an' there's no mistikin' it. I don't care wot other people sy, but wot

I says is, there's nothin' like marriage. Never a cross word passes his lips, an' mother 'as all 'er meals with us an' 'e says all the better. Well I'm thet 'appy I simply dunno if I'm standin' on my 'ead or on my 'eels.'

But alas! it did not last too long. Sally was not so full of joy when next Liza met her, and one day her eyes looked very much as if she had been crying.

'Wot's the matter?' asked Liza, looking at her. 'Wot 'ave yer been blubberin' abaht?'

'Me?' said Sally, getting very red. 'Oh, I've got a bit of a toothache, an'—well, I'm rather a fool like, an' it 'urt so much that I couldn't 'elp cryin'.'

Liza was not satisfied, but could get nothing further out of her. Then one day it came out. It was a Saturday night, the time when women in Vere Street weep. Liza went up into Sally's room for a few minutes on her way to the Westminster Bridge Road, where she was to meet Jim. Harry had taken the top back room, and Liza, climbing up the second flight of stairs, called out as usual,

'Wot ho, Sally!'

The door remained shut, although Liza could see that there was a light in the room; but on getting to the door she stood still, for she heard the sound of sobbing. She listened for a minute and then knocked: there was a little flurry inside, and someone called out:

''Oo's there?'

'Only me,' said Liza, opening the door. As she did so she saw Sally rapidly wipe her eyes and put her handkerchief away. Her mother was sitting by her side, evidently comforting her.

'Wot's up, Sal?' asked Liza.

'Nothin',' answered Sally, with a brave little gasp to stop the crying, turning her face downwards so that Liza should not see the tears in her eyes; but they were too strong for her, and, quickly taking out her handkerchief, she hid her face in it and began to sob broken-heartedly. Liza looked at the mother in interrogation.

'Oh, it's thet man again!' said the lady, snorting and tossing her head.

'Not 'Arry?' asked Liza, in surprise.

'Not 'Arry—'oo is it if it ain't 'Arry? The villin!'

'Wot's 'e been doin,' then?' asked Liza again.

'Beatin' 'er, that's wot 'e's been doin'! Oh, the villin, 'e oughter be ashimed of 'isself 'e ought!'

'I didn't know 'e was like that!' said Liza.

'Didn't yer? I thought the 'ole street knew it by now,' said Mrs Cooper indignantly. 'Oh, 'e's a wrong 'un, 'e is.'

'It wasn't 'is fault,' put in Sally, amidst her sobs; 'it's only because 'e's 'ad a little drop too much. 'E's arright when 'e's sober.'

'A little drop too much! I should just think 'e'd 'ad, the beast! I'd give it 'im if I was a man. They're all like thet—'usbinds is all alike; they're arright when they're sober—sometimes—but when they've got the liquor in 'em, they're beasts, an' no mistike. I 'ad a 'usbind myself for five-an'-twenty years, an' I know 'em.'

'Well, mother,' sobbed Sally, 'it was all my fault. I should 'ave come 'ome earlier.'

'Na, it wasn't your fault at all. Just you look 'ere, Liza: this is wot 'e done an' call 'isself a man. Just because Sally'd gone aht to 'ave a chat with Mrs. McLeod in the next 'ouse, when she come in 'e start bangin' 'er abaht. An' me, too, wot d'yer think of that!' Mrs Cooper was quite purple with indignation.

'Yus,' she went on, 'thet's a man for yer. Of course, I wasn't goin' ter stand there an' see my daughter bein' knocked abaht; it wasn't likely—was it? An' 'e rounds on me, an' 'e 'its me with 'is fist. Look 'ere.' She pulled up her sleeves and showed two red and brawny arms.' ''E's bruised my arms; I thought 'e'd broken it at fust. If I 'adn't put my arm up, 'e'd 'ave got me on the 'ead, an' 'e might 'ave killed me. An' I says to 'im, "If you touch me again, I'll go ter the police-station, thet I will!" Well, that frightened 'im a bit, an' then didn't I let 'im 'ave it! "You call yerself a man," says I, "an' you ain't fit ter clean the drains aht." You should 'ave 'eard the language 'e used. "You dirty old woman," says 'e, "you go away; you're always interferin' with me." Well, I don't like ter repeat wot 'e said, and thet's the truth. An' I says ter 'im, "I wish yer'd never married my daughter, an' if I'd known you was like this I'd 'ave died sooner than let yer."'

'Well, I didn't know 'e was like thet!' said Liza.

''E was arright at fust,' said Sally.

'Yus, they're always arright at fust! But ter think it should 'ave come to this now, when they ain't been married three months, an' the first child not born yet! I think it's disgraceful.'

Liza stayed a little while longer, helping to comfort Sally, who kept pathetically taking to herself all the blame of the dispute; and then, bidding her good night and better luck, she slid off to meet Jim.

When she reached the appointed spot he was not to be found. She waited for some time, and at last saw him come out of the neighbouring pub.

'Good night, Jim,' she said as she came up to him.

'So you've turned up, 'ave yer?' he answered roughly, turning round.

'Wot's the matter, Jim?' she asked in a frightened way, for he had never spoken to her in that manner.

'Nice thing ter keep me witin' all night for yer to come aht.'

She saw that he had been drinking, and answered humbly.

'I'm very sorry, Jim, but I went in to Sally, an' 'er bloke 'ad been knockin' 'er abaht, an' so I sat with 'er a bit.'

'Knockin' 'er abaht, 'ad 'e? and serve 'er damn well right too; an' there's many more as could do with a good 'idin'!'

Liza did not answer. He looked at her, and then suddenly said:

'Come in an' 'ave a drink.'

'Na, I'm not thirsty; I don't want a drink,' she answered.

'Come on,' he said angrily.

'Na, Jim, you've had quite enough already.'

''Oo are you talkin' ter?' he said. 'Don't come if yer don't want ter; I'll go an' 'ave one by myself.'

'Na, Jim, don't.' She caught hold of his arm.

'Yus, I shall,' he said, going towards the pub, while she held him back. 'Let me go, can't yer! Let me go!' He roughly pulled his arm away from her. As she tried to catch hold of it again, he pushed her back, and in the little scuffle caught her a blow over the face.

'Oh!' she cried, 'you did 'urt!'

He was sobered at once.

'Liza,' he said. 'I ain't 'urt yer?' She didn't answer, and he took her in his arms. 'Liza, I ain't 'urt you, 'ave I? Say I ain't 'urt yer. I'm so sorry, I beg your pardon, Liza.'

'Arright, old chap,' she said, smiling charmingly on him. 'It wasn't the blow that 'urt me much; it was the wy you was talkin'.'

'I didn't mean it, Liza.' He was so contrite, he could not humble himself enough. 'I 'ad another bloomin' row with the missus ter-night, an' then when I didn't find you 'ere, an' I kept witin' an' witin'—well, I fair downright lost my 'air. An' I 'ad two or three pints of four 'alf, an'—well, I dunno—'

'Never mind, old cock, I can stand more than thet as long as yer loves me.'

He kissed her and they were quite friends again. But the little quarrel had another effect which was worse for Liza. When she woke up next morning she noticed a slight soreness over the ridge of bone under the left eye, and on looking in the glass saw that it was black and blue and green. She bathed it, but it remained, and seemed to get more marked. She was terrified lest people should see it, and kept indoors all day; but next morning it was blacker than ever. She went to the factory with her hat over her eyes and her head bent down; she escaped observation, but on the way home she was not so lucky. The sharp eyes of some girls noticed it first.

'Wot's the matter with yer eye?' asked one of them.

'Me?' answered Liza, putting her hand up as if in ignorance. 'Nothin' thet I knows of.'

Two or three young men were standing by, and hearing the girl, looked up.

'Why, yer've got a black eye, Liza!'

'Me? I ain't got no black eye!'

'Yus you 'ave; 'ow d'yer get it?'

'I dunno,' said Liza. 'I didn't know I 'ad one.'

'Garn! tell us another!' was the answer. 'One doesn't git a black eye without knowin' 'ow they got it.'

'Well, I did fall against the chest of drawers yesterday; I suppose I must 'ave got it then.'

'Oh yes, we believe thet, don't we?'

'I didn't know 'e was so 'andy with 'is dukes, did you, Ted?' asked one man of another.

Liza felt herself grow red to the tips of her toes.

'Who?' she asked.

'Never you mind; nobody you know.'

At that moment Jim's wife passed and looked at her with a scowl. Liza wished herself a hundred miles away, and blushed more violently than ever.

'Wot are yer blushin' abaht?' ingenuously asked one of the girls.

And they all looked from her to Mrs Blakeston and back again. Someone said: ''Ow abaht our Sunday boots on now?' And a titter went through them. Liza's nerve deserted her; she could think of nothing to say, and a sob burst from her. To hide the tears which were coming from her eyes she turned away and walked homewards. Immediately a great shout of laughter broke from the group, and she heard them positively screaming till she got into her own house.

CHAPTER XI

A few days afterwards Liza was talking with Sally, who did not seem very much happier than when Liza had last seen her.

''E ain't wot I thought 'e wos,' she said. 'I don't mind sayin' thet; but 'e 'as a lot ter put up with; I expect I'm rather tryin' sometimes, an' 'e means well. P'raps 'e'll be kinder like when the biby's born.'

'Cheer up, old gal,' answered Liza, who had seen something of the lives of many married couples; 'it won't seem so bad after yer gets used to it; it's a bit disappointin' at fust, but yer gits not ter mind it.'

After a little Sally said she must go and see about her husband's tea. She said good-bye, and then rather awkwardly:

'Say, Liza, tike care of yerself!'

'Tike care of meself—why?' asked Liza, in surprise.

'Yer know wot I mean.'

'Na, I'm darned if I do.'

'Thet there Mrs Blakeston, she's lookin' aht for you.'

'Mrs Blakeston!' Liza was startled.

'Yus; she says she's goin' ter give you somethin' if she can git 'old on yer. I should advise yer ter tike care.'

'Me?' said Liza.

Sally looked away, so as not to see the other's face.

'She says as 'ow yer've been messin' abaht with 'er old man.'

Liza didn't say anything, and Sally, repeating her good-bye, slid off.

Liza felt a chill run through her. She had several times noticed a scowl and a look of anger on Mrs Blakeston's face, and she had avoided her as much as possible; but she had no idea that the woman meant to do anything to her. She was very frightened, a cold sweat broke out over her face. If Mrs Blakeston got hold of her she would be helpless, she was so small and weak, while the other was strong and muscular. Liza wondered what she would do if she did catch her.

That night she told Jim, and tried to make a joke of it.

'I say, Jim, your missus—she says she's goin' ter give me socks if she catches me.'

'My missus! 'Ow d'yer know?'

'She's been tellin' people in the street.'

'Go' lumme,' said Jim, furious, 'if she dares ter touch a 'air of your 'ead, swop me dicky I'll give 'er sich a 'idin' as she never 'ad before! By God, give me the chanst, an' I would let 'er 'ave it; I'm bloomin' well sick of 'er sulks!' He clenched his fist as he spoke.

Liza was a coward. She could not help thinking of her enemy's threat; it got on her nerves, and she hardly dared go out for fear of meeting her; she would look nervously in front of her, quickly turning round if she saw in the distance anyone resembling Mrs Blakeston. She dreamed of her at night; she saw the big, powerful form, the heavy, frowning face, and the curiously braided brown hair; and she would wake up with a cry and find herself bathed in sweat.

It was the Saturday afternoon following this, a chill November day, with the roads sloshy, and a grey, comfortless sky that made one's spirits sink. It was about three o'clock, and Liza was coming home from work; she got into Vere Street, and was walking quickly towards her house when she saw Mrs Blakeston coming towards her. Her heart gave a great jump. Turning, she walked rapidly in the direction she had come; with a screw round of her eyes she saw that she was being followed, and therefore went straight out of Vere Street. She went right round, meaning to get into the street from the other end and, unobserved, slip into her house, which was then quite close; but she dared not risk it immediately for fear Mrs Blakeston should still be there; so she waited about for half an hour. It seemed an age. Finally, taking her courage in both hands, she turned the corner and entered Vere Street. She nearly ran into the arms of Mrs Blakeston, who was standing close to the public-house door.

Liza gave a little cry, and the woman said, with a sneer:

'Yer didn't expect ter see me, did yer?'

Liza did not answer, but tried to walk past her. Mrs Blakeston stepped forward and blocked her way.

'Yer seem ter be in a mighty fine 'urry,' she said.

'Yus, I've got ter git 'ome,' said Liza, again trying to pass.

'But supposin' I don't let yer?' remarked Mrs Blakeston, preventing her from moving.

'Why don't yer leave me alone?' Liza said. 'I ain't interferin' with you!'

'Not interferin' with me, aren't yer? I like thet!'

'Let me go by,' said Liza. 'I don't want ter talk ter you.'

'Na, I know thet,' said the other; 'but I want ter talk ter you, an' I shan't let yer go until I've said wot I wants ter sy.'

Liza looked round for help. At the beginning of the altercation the loafers about the public-house had looked up with interest, and gradually gathered round in a little circle. Passers-by had joined in, and a number of other people in the street, seeing the crowd, added themselves to it to see what was going on. Liza saw that all eyes were fixed on her, the men amused and excited, the women unsympathetic, rather virtuously indignant. Liza wanted to ask for help, but there were so many people, and they all seemed so much against her, that she had not the courage to. So, having surveyed the crowd, she turned her eyes to Mrs Blakeston, and stood in front of her, trembling a little, and very white.

'Na, 'e ain't there,' said Mrs Blakeston, sneeringly, 'so yer needn't look for 'im.'

'I dunno wot yer mean,' answered Liza, 'an' I want ter go awy. I ain't done nothin' ter you.'

'Not done nothin' ter me?' furiously repeated the woman. 'I'll tell yer wot yer've done ter me—you've robbed me of my 'usbind, you 'ave. I never 'ad a word with my 'usbind until you took 'im from me. An' now it's all you with 'im. 'E's got no time for 'is wife an' family—it's all you. An' 'is money, too. I never git a penny of it; if it weren't for the little bit I 'ad saved up in the siving-bank, me an' my children 'ud be starvin' now! An' all through you!' She shook her fist at her.

'I never 'ad any money from anyone.'

'Don' talk ter me; I know yer did. Yer dirty bitch! You oughter be ishimed of yourself tikin' a married man from 'is family, an' 'im old enough ter be yer father.'

'She's right there!' said one or two of the onlooking women. 'There can't be no good in 'er if she tikes somebody else's 'usbind.'

'I'll give it yer!' proceeded Mrs Blakeston, getting more hot and excited, brandishing her fist, and speaking in a loud voice, hoarse with rage. 'Oh, I've been tryin' ter git 'old on yer this four weeks. Why, you're a prostitute—that's wot you are!'

'I'm not!' answered Liza indignantly.

'Yus, you are,' repeated Mrs Blakeston, advancing menacingly, so that Liza shrank back. 'An' wot's more, 'e treats yer like one. I know 'oo give yer thet black eye; thet shows what 'e thinks of yer! An' serve yer bloomin' well right if 'e'd give yer one in both eyes!'

Mrs Blakeston stood close in front of her, her heavy jaw protruded and the frown of her eyebrows dark and stern. For a moment she stood silent, contemplating Liza, while the surrounders looked on in breathless interest.

'Yer dirty little bitch, you!' she said at last. 'Tike that!' and with her open hand she gave her a sharp smack on the cheek.

Liza started back with a cry and put her hand up to her face.

'An' tike thet!' added Mrs Blakeston, repeating the blow. Then, gathering up the spittle in her mouth, she spat in Liza's face.

Liza sprang on her, and with her hands spread out like claws buried her nails in the woman's face and drew them down her cheeks. Mrs Blakeston caught hold of her hair with both hands and tugged at it as hard as she could. But they were immediately separated.

‘'Ere, 'old 'ard!' said some of the men. 'Fight it aht fair and square. Don't go scratchin' and maulin' like thet.'

'I'll fight 'er, I don't mind!' shouted Mrs Blakeston, tucking up her sleeves and savagely glaring at her opponent.

Liza stood in front of her, pale and trembling; as she looked at her enemy, and saw the long red marks of her nails, with blood coming from one or two of them, she shrank back.

'I don't want ter fight,' she said hoarsely.

'Na, I don't suppose yer do,' hissed the other, 'but yer'll damn well 'ave ter!'

'She's ever so much bigger than me; I've got no chanst,' added Liza tearfully.

'You should 'ave thought of thet before. Come on!' and with these words Mrs Blakeston rushed upon her. She hit her with both fists one after the other. Liza did not try to guard herself, but imitating the woman's motion, hit out with her own fists; and for a minute or two they continued thus, raining blows on one another with the same windmill motion of the arms. But Liza could not stand against the other woman's weight; the blows came down heavy and rapid all over her face and head. She put up her hands to cover her face and turned her head away, while Mrs Blakeston kept on hitting mercilessly.

'Time!' shouted some of the men—'Time!' and Mrs Blakeston stopped to rest herself.

'It don't seem 'ardly fair to set them two on tergether. Liza's got no chanst against a big woman like thet,' said a man among the crowd.

'Well, it's er' own fault,' answered a woman; 'she didn't oughter mess about with 'er 'usbind.'

'Well, I don't think it's right,' added another man. 'She's gettin' it too much.'

'An' serve 'er right too!' said one of the women. 'She deserves all she gets an' a damn sight more inter the bargain.'

'Quite right,' put in a third; 'a woman's got no right ter tike someone's 'usbind from 'er. An' if she does she's bloomin' lucky if she gits off with a 'idin'—thet's wot I think.'

'So do I. But I wouldn't 'ave thought it of Liza. I never thought she was a wrong 'un.'

'Pretty specimen she is!' said a little dark woman, who looked like a Jewess. 'If she messed abaht with my old man, I'd stick 'er—I swear I would!'

'Now she's been carryin' on with one, she'll try an' git others—you see if she don't.'

'She'd better not come round my 'ouse; I'll soon give 'er wot for.'

Meanwhile Liza was standing at one corner of the ring, trembling all over and crying bitterly. One of her eyes was bunged up, and her hair, all dishevelled, was hanging down over her face. Two young fellows, who had constituted themselves her seconds, were standing in front of her, offering rather ironical comfort. One of them had taken the bottom corners of her apron and was fanning her with it, while the other was showing her how to stand and hold her arms.

'You stand up to 'er, Liza,' he was saying; 'there ain't no good funkin' it, you'll simply get it all the worse. You 'it 'er back. Give 'er one on the boko, like this—see; yer must show a bit of pluck, yer know.'

Liza tried to check her sobs.

'Yus, 'it 'er 'ard, that's wot yer've got ter do,' said the other. 'An' if yer find she's gettin' the better on yer, you close on 'er and catch 'old of 'er 'air and scratch 'er.'

'You've marked 'er with yer nails, Liza. By gosh, you did fly on her when she spat at yer! thet's the way ter do the job!'

Then turning to his fellow, he said:

'D'yer remember thet fight as old Mother Cregg 'ad with another woman in the street last year?'

'Na,' he answered, 'I never saw thet.'

'It was a cawker; an' the cops come in and took 'em both off ter quod.'

Liza wished the policemen would come and take her off; she would willingly have gone to prison to escape the fiend in front of her; but no help came.

'Time's up!' shouted the referee. 'Fire away!'

'Tike care of the cops!' shouted a man.

'There's no fear abaht them,' answered somebody else. 'They always keeps out of the way when there's anythin' goin' on.'

'Fire away!'

Mrs Blakeston attacked Liza madly; but the girl stood up bravely, and as well as she could gave back the blows she received. The spectators grew tremendously excited.

'Got 'im again!' they shouted. 'Give it 'er, Liza, thet's a good 'un!—'it 'er 'ard!'

'Two ter one on the old 'un!' shouted a sporting gentleman; but Liza found no backers.

'Ain't she standin' up well now she's roused?' cried someone.

'Oh, she's got some pluck in 'er, she 'as!'

'Thet's a knock-aht!' they shouted as Mrs Blakeston brought her fist down on to Liza's nose; the girl staggered back, and blood began to flow. Then, losing all fear, mad with rage, she made a rush on her enemy, and rained down blows all over her nose and eyes and mouth. The woman recoiled at the sudden violence of the onslaught, and the men cried:

'By God, the little 'un's gettin' the best of it!'

But quickly recovering herself the woman closed with Liza, and dug her nails into her flesh. Liza caught hold of her hair and pulled with all her might, and turning her teeth on Mrs Blakeston tried to bite her. And thus for a minute they swayed about, scratching, tearing, biting, sweat and blood pouring down their faces, and their eyes fixed on one another, bloodshot and full of rage. The audience shouted and cheered and clapped their hands.

'Wot the 'ell's up 'ere?'

'I sy, look there,' said some of the women in a whisper. 'It's the 'usbind!'

He stood on tiptoe and looked over the crowd.

'My Gawd,' he said, 'it's Liza!'

Then roughly pushing the people aside, he made his way through the crowd into the centre, and thrusting himself between the two women, tore them apart. He turned furiously on his wife.

'By Gawd, I'll give yer somethin' for this!'

And for a moment they all three stood silently looking at one another.

Another man had been attracted by the crowd, and he, too, pushed his way through.

'Come 'ome, Liza,' he said.

'Tom!'

He took hold of her arm, and led her through the people, who gave way to let her pass. They walked silently through the street, Tom very grave, Liza weeping bitterly.

'Oh, Tom,' she sobbed after a while, 'I couldn't 'elp it!' Then, when her tears permitted, 'I did love 'im so!'

When they got to the door she plaintively said: 'Come in,' and he followed her to her room. Here she sank on to a chair, and gave herself up to her tears.

Tom wetted the end of a towel and began wiping her face, grimy with blood and tears. She let him do it, just moaning amid her sobs:

'You are good ter me, Tom.'

'Cheer up, old gal,' he said kindly, 'it's all over now.'

After a while the excess of crying brought its cessation. She drank some water, and then taking up a broken handglass she looked at herself, saying:

'I am a sight!' and proceeded to wind up her hair. 'You 'ave been good ter me, Tom,' she repeated, her voice still broken with sobs; and as he sat down beside her she took his hand.

'Na, I ain't,' he answered; 'it's only wot anybody 'ud 'ave done.'

'Yer know, Tom,' she said, after a little silence, 'I'm so sorry I spoke cross like when I met yer in the street; you ain't spoke ter me since.'

'Oh, thet's all over now, old lidy, we needn't think of thet.'

'Oh, but I 'ave treated yer bad. I'm a regular wrong 'un, I am.'

He pressed her hand without speaking.

'I say, Tom,' she began, after another pause. 'Did yer know thet—well, you know—before ter-day?'

He blushed as he answered:

'Yus.'

She spoke very sadly and slowly.

'I thought yer did; yer seemed so cut up like when I used to meet yer. Yer did love me then, Tom, didn't yer?'

'I do now, dearie,' he answered.

'Ah, it's too lite now,' she sighed.

'D'yer know, Liza,' he said, I just abaht kicked the life aht of a feller 'cause 'e said you was messin' abaht with—with 'im.'

'An' yer knew I was?'

'Yus—but I wasn't goin' ter 'ave anyone say it before me.'

'They've all rounded on me except you, Tom. I'd 'ave done better if I'd tiken you when you arst me; I shouldn't be where I am now, if I 'ad.'

'Well, won't yer now? Won't yer 'ave me now?'

'Me? After wot's 'appened?'

'Oh, I don't mind abaht thet. Thet don't matter ter me if you'll marry me. I fair can't live without yer, Liza—won't yer?'

She groaned.

'Na, I can't, Tom, it wouldn't be right.'

'Why, not, if I don't mind?'

'Tom,' she said, looking down, almost whispering, 'I'm like that—you know!'

'Wot d'yer mean?'

She could scarcely utter the words—

'I think I'm in the family wy.'

He paused a moment; then spoke again.

'Well—I don't mind, if yer'll only marry me.'

'Na, I can't, Tom,' she said, bursting into tears; 'I can't but you are so good ter me; I'd do anythin' ter mike it up ter you.'

She put her arms round his neck and slid on to his knees.

'Yer know, Tom, I couldn't marry yer now; but anythin' else—if yer wants me ter do anythin' else, I'll do it if it'll mike you 'appy.'

He did not understand, but only said:

'You're a good gal, Liza,' and bending down he kissed her gravely on the forehead.

Then with a sigh he lifted her down, and getting up left her alone. For a while she sat where he left her, but as she thought of all she had gone through her loneliness and misery overcame her, the tears welled forth, and throwing herself on the bed she buried her face in the pillows.

Jim stood looking at Liza as she went off with Tom, and his wife watched him jealously.

'It's 'er you're thinkin' abaht. Of course you'd 'ave liked ter tike 'er 'ome yerself, I know, an' leave me to shift for myself.'

'Shut up!' said Jim, angrily turning upon her.

'I shan't shut up,' she answered, raising her voice. 'Nice 'usbind you are. Go' lumme, as good as they mike 'em! Nice thing ter go an' leave yer wife and children for a thing like thet! At your age, too! You oughter be ashimed of yerself. Why. it's like messin' abaht with your own daughter!'

'By God!'—he ground his teeth with rage—'if yer don't leave me alone, I'll kick the life aht of yer!'

'There!' she said, turning to the crowd—'there, see 'ow 'e treats me! Listen ter that! I've been 'is wife for twenty years, an' yer couldn't 'ave 'ad a better wife, an' I've bore 'im nine children, yet say nothin' of a miscarriage, an' I've got another comin', an' thet's 'ow 'e treats me! Nice 'usbind, ain't it?' She looked at him scornfully, then again at the surrounders as if for their opinion.

'Well, I ain't goin' ter stay 'ere all night; get aht of the light!' He pushed aside the people who barred his way, and the one or two who growled a little at his roughness, looking at his angry face, were afraid to complain.

'Look at 'im!' said his wife. ''E's afraid, 'e is. See 'im slinkin' awy like a bloomin' mongrel with 'is tail between 'is legs. Ugh!' She walked just behind him, shouting and brandishing her arms.

'Yer dirty beast, you,' she yelled, 'ter go foolin' abaht with a little girl! Ugh! I wish yer wasn't my 'usbind; I wouldn't be seen drowned with yer, if I could 'elp it. Yer mike me sick ter look at yer.'

The crowd followed them on both sides of the road, keeping at a discreet distance, but still eagerly listening.

Jim turned on her once or twice and said:

'Shut up!'

But it only made her more angry. 'I tell yer I shan't shut up. I don't care 'oo knows it, you're a—, you are! I'm ashimed the children should 'ave such a father as you. D'yer think I didn't know wot you was up ter them nights you was awy—courtin', yus, courtin'? You're a nice man, you are!'

Jim did not answer her, but walked on. At last he turned round to the people who were following and said:

'Na then, wot d'you want 'ere? You jolly well clear, or I'll give some of you somethin'!'

They were mostly boys and women, and at his words they shrank back.

''E's afraid ter sy anythin' ter me,' jeered Mrs Blakeston. ''E's a beauty!'

Jim entered his house, and she followed him till they came up into their room. Polly was giving the children their tea. They all started up as they saw their mother with her hair and clothes in disorder, blotches of dried blood on her face, and the long scratch-marks.

'Oh. mother.' said Polly, 'wot is the matter?'

''E's the matter,' she answered, pointing to her husband. 'It's through 'im I've got all this. Look at yer father, children; e's a father to be proud of, leavin' yer ter starve an' spendin' 'is week's money on a dirty little strumper.'

Jim felt easier now he had not got so many strange eyes on him.

'Now, look 'ere,' he said, 'I'm not goin' ter stand this much longer, so just you tike care.'

'I ain't frightened of yer. I know yer'd like ter kill me, but yer'll get strung up if you do.'

'Na, I won't kill yer, but if I 'ave any more of your sauce I'll do the next thing to it.'

'Touch me if yer dare,' she said, 'I'll 'ave the law on you. An' I shouldn't mind 'ow many month's 'ard you got.'

'Be quiet!' he said, and, closing his hand, gave her a heavy blow in the chest that made her stagger.

'Oh, you—!" she screamed.

She seized the poker, and in a fury of rage rushed at him.

'Would yer?' he said, catching hold of it and wrenching it from her grasp. He threw it to the end of the room and grappled with her. For a moment they swayed about from side to side, then with an effort he lifted her off her feet and threw her to the ground; but she caught hold of him and he came down on the top of her. She screamed as her head thumped down on the floor, and the children, who were standing huddled up in a corner, terrified, screamed too.

Jim caught hold of his wife's head and began beating it against the floor.

She cried out: 'You're killing me! Help! help!'

Polly in terror ran up to her father and tried to pull him off.

'Father, don't 'it 'er! Anythin' but thet—for God's sike!'

'Leave me alone,' he said, 'or I'll give you somethin' too.'

She caught hold of his arm, but Jim, still kneeling on his wife, gave Polly a backhanded blow which sent her staggering back.

'Tike that!'

Polly ran out of the room, downstairs to the first-floor front, where two men and two women were sitting at tea.

'Oh, come an' stop father!' she cried. ''E's killin' mother!'

'Why, wot's 'e doin'?'

'Oh, 'e's got 'er on the floor, an' 'e's bangin' 'er 'ead. 'E's payin' 'er ant for givin' Liza Kemp a 'idin'.'

One of the women started up and said to her husband:

'Come on, John, you go an' stop it.'

'Don't you, John,' said the other man. 'When a man's givin' 'is wife socks it's best not ter interfere.'

'But 'e's killin' 'er,' repeated Polly, trembling with fright.

'Garn!' rejoined the man, 'she'll git over it; an' p'raps she deserves it, for all you know.'

John sat undecided, looking now at Polly, now at his wife, and now at the other man.

'Oh, do be quick—for God's sike!' said Polly.

At that moment a sound as of something smashing was heard upstairs, and a woman's shriek. Mrs Blakeston, in an effort to tear herself away from her husband, had knocked up against the wash-hand stand, and the whole thing had crashed down.

'Go on, John,' said the wife.

'No, I ain't goin'; I shan't do no good, an' 'e'll only round on me.'

'Well, you are a bloomin' lot of cowards, thet's all I can say,' indignantly answered the wife. 'But I ain't goin' ter see a woman murdered; I'll go an' stop 'im.'

With that she ran upstairs and threw open the door. Jim was still kneeling on his wife, hitting her furiously, while she was trying to protect her head and face with her hands.

'Leave off!' shouted the woman.

Jim looked up.' 'Oo the devil are you?' he said.

'Leave off, I tell yer. Aren't yer ashimed of yerself, knockin' a woman abaht like that?' And she sprang at him, seizing his fist.

'Let go,' he said, 'or I'll give you a bit.'

'Yer'd better not touch me,' she said. 'Yer dirty coward! Why, look at 'er, she's almost senseless.'

Jim stopped and gazed at his wife. He got up and gave her a kick.

'Git up!' he said; but she remained huddled up on the floor, moaning feebly. The woman from downstairs went on her knees and took her head in her arms.

'Never mind, Mrs Blakeston. 'E's not goin' ter touch yer. 'Ere, drink this little drop of water.' Then turning to Jim, with infinite disdain: 'Yer dirty blackguard, you! If I was a man I'd give you something for this.'

Jim put on his hat and went out, slamming the door, while the woman shouted after him: 'Good riddance!'

'Lord love yer,' said Mrs Kemp, 'wot is the matter?'

She had just come in, and opening the door had started back in surprise at seeing Liza on the bed, all tears. Liza made no answer, but cried as if her heart were breaking. Mrs Kemp went up to her and tried to look at her face.

'Don't cry, dearie; tell us wot it is.'

Liza sat up and dried her eyes.

'I am so un'appy!'

'Wot 'ave yer been doin' ter yer fice? My!'

'Nothin'.'

'Garn! Yer can't 'ave got a fice like thet all by itself.'

'I 'ad a bit of a scrimmage with a woman dahn the street,' sobbed out Liza.

'She 'as give yer a doin'; an' yer all upset—an' look at yer eye! I brought in a little bit of stike for ter-morrer's dinner; you just cut a bit off an' put it over yer optic, that'll soon put it right. I always used ter do thet myself when me an' your poor father 'ad words.'

'Oh, I'm all over in a tremble, an' my 'ead, oo, my 'ead does feel bad!'

'I know wot yer want,' remarked Mrs Kemp, nodding her head, 'an' it so 'appens as I've got the very thing with me.' She pulled a medicine bottle out of her pocket, and taking out the cork smelt it. Thet's good stuff, none of your firewater or your methylated spirit. I don't often indulge in sich things, but when I do I likes to 'ave the best.'

She handed the bottle to Liza, who took a mouthful and gave it her back; she had a drink herself, and smacked her lips.

'Thet's good stuff. 'ave a drop more.'

'Na,' said Liza, 'I ain't used ter drinkin' spirits.'

She felt dull and miserable, and a heavy pain throbbed through her head. If she could only forget!

'Na, I know you're not, but, bless your soul, thet won' 'urt yer. It'll do you no end of good. Why, often when I've been feelin' thet done up thet I didn't know wot ter do with myself, I've just 'ad a little drop of whisky or gin—I'm not partic'ler wot spirit it is—an' it's pulled me up wonderful.'

Liza took another sip. a slightly longer one; it burnt as it went down her throat, and sent through her a feeling of comfortable warmth.

'I really do think it's doin' me good.' she said, wiping her eyes and giving a sigh of relief as the crying ceased.

'I knew it would. Tike my word for it, if people took a little drop of spirits in time, there'd be much less sickness abaht.'

They sat for a while in silence, then Mrs Kemp remarked:

'Yer know, Liza, it strikes me as 'ow we could do with a drop more. You not bein' in the 'abit of tikin' anythin' I only brought just this little drop for me; an' it ain't took us long ter finish thet up. But as you're an invalid like we'll git a little more this time; it's sure ter turn aht useful.'

'But you ain't got nothin' ter put it in.'

'Yus, I 'ave,' answered Mrs Kemp; 'there's thet bottle as they gives me at the 'orspital. Just empty the medicine aht into the pile, an' wash it aht, an' I'll tike it round to the pub myself.'

Liza, when she was left alone, began to turn things over in her mind. She did not feel so utterly unhappy as before, for the things she had gone through seemed further away.

'After all,' she said, 'it don't so much matter.'

Mrs Kemp came in.

''Ave a little drop more, Liza,' she said.

'Well, I don't mind if I do. I'll get some tumblers, shall I? There's no mistike abaht it,' she added, when she had taken a little, 'it do buck yer up.'

'You're right, Liza—you're right. An' you wanted it badly. Fancy you 'avin' a fight with a woman! Oh, I've 'ad some in my day, but then I wasn't a little bit of a thing like you is. I wish I'd been there, I wouldn't 'ave stood by an' looked on while my daughter was gettin' the worst of it; although I'm turned sixty-five, an' gettin' on for sixty-six, I'd 'ave said to 'er: "If you touch my daughter you'll 'ave me ter deal with, so just look aht!"'

She brandished her glass, and that reminding her, she refilled it and Liza's.

'Ah, Liza,' she remarked, 'you're a chip of the old block. Ter see you settin' there an' 'avin' your little drop, it mikes me feel as if I was livin' a better life. Yer used ter be rather 'ard on me, Liza, 'cause I took a little drop on Saturday nights. An', mind, I don't sy I didn't tike a little drop too much sometimes—accidents will occur even in the best regulated of families, but wot I say is this—it's good stuff, I say, an' it don't 'urt yer.'

'Buck up, old gal!' said Liza, filling the glasses, 'no 'eel-taps. I feel like a new woman now. I was thet dahn in the dumps—well, I shouldn't 'ave cared if I'd been at the bottom of the river, an' thet's the truth.'

'You don't sy so,' replied her affectionate mother.

'Yus, I do, an' I mean it too, but I don't feel like thet now. You're right, mother, when you're in trouble there's nothin' like a bit of spirits.'

'Well, if I don't know, I dunno 'oo does, for the trouble I've 'ad, it 'ud be enough to kill many women. Well, I've 'ad thirteen children, an' you can think wot thet was; everyone I 'ad I used ter sy I wouldn't 'ave no more—but one does, yer know. You'll 'ave a family some day, Liza, an' I shouldn't wonder if you didn't 'ave as many as me. We come from a very prodigal family, we do, we've all gone in ter double figures, except your Aunt Mary, who only 'ad three—but then she wasn't married, so it didn't count, like.'

They drank each other's health. Everything was getting blurred to Liza, she was losing her head.

'Yus,' went on Mrs Kemp, 'I've 'ad thirteen children an' I'm proud of it. As your poor dear father used ter sy, it shows as 'ow one's got the blood of a Briton in one. Your poor dear father, 'e was a great 'and at speakin' 'e was: 'e used ter speak at parliamentary meetin's—I really believe 'e'd 'ave been a Member of Parliament if 'e'd been alive now. Well, as I was sayin', your father 'e used ter sy, "None of your small families for me, I don't approve of them," says 'e. 'E was a man of very 'igh principles, an' by politics 'e was a Radical. "No," says 'e, when 'e got talkin', "when a man can 'ave a family risin' into double figures, it shows 'e's got the backbone of a Briton in 'im. That's the stuff as 'as built up England's nime and glory! When one thinks of the mighty British Hempire," says 'e, "on which the sun never sets from mornin' till night, one 'as ter be proud of 'isself, an' one 'as ter do one's duty in thet walk of life in which it 'as pleased Providence ter set one—an' every man's fust duty is ter get as many children as 'e bloomin' well can." Lord love yer—'e could talk, I can tell yer.'

'Drink up, mother,' said Liza. 'You're not 'alf drinkin'.' She flourished the bottle. 'I don't care a twopanny 'ang for all them blokes; I'm quite 'appy, an' I don't want anythin' else.'

'I can see you're my daughter now,' said Mrs Kemp. 'When yer used ter round on me I used ter think as 'ow if I 'adn't carried yer for nine months, it must 'ave been some mistike, an' yer wasn't my daughter at all. When you come ter think of it, a man 'e don't know if it's 'is child or somebody else's, but yer can't deceive a woman like thet Yer couldn't palm off somebody else's kid on 'er.'

'I am beginnin' ter feel quite lively,' said Liza. 'I dunno wot it is, but I feel as if I wanted to laugh till I fairly split my sides.'

And she began to sing: Tor 'e's a jolly good feller—for 'e's a jolly good feller!'

Her dress was all disarranged; her face covered with the scars of scratches, and clots of blood had fixed under her nose; her eye had swollen up so that it was nearly closed, and red; her hair was hanging over her face and shoulders, and she laughed stupidly and leered with heavy, sodden ugliness.

'Disy, Disy! I can't afford a kerridge.
But you'll look neat, on the seat
Of a bicycle mide for two."

She shouted out the tunes, beating time on the table, and her mother, grinning, with her thin, grey hair hanging dishevelled over her head, joined in with her weak, cracked voice—

'Oh, dem golden kippers, oh!'

Then Liza grew more melancholy and broke into 'Auld Lang Syne'.

'Should old acquaintance be forgot
And never brought to mind?

. . . .

For old lang syne'.

Finally they both grew silent, and in a little while there came a snore from Mrs Kemp; her head fell forward to her chest; Liza tumbled from her chair on to the bed, and sprawling across it fell asleep.

'Although I am drunk and bad, be you kind,
Cast a glance at this heart which is bewildered and distressed.
O God, take away from my mind my cry and my complaint.
Offer wine, and take sorrow from my remembrance.
Offer wine.'

CHAPTER XII

ABOUT the middle of the night Liza woke; her mouth was hot and dry, and a sharp, cutting pain passed through her head as she moved. Her mother had evidently roused herself, for she was lying in bed by her side, partially undressed, with all the bedclothes rolled round her. Liza shivered in the cold night, and taking off some of her things—her boots, her skirt, and jacket—got right into bed; she tried to get some of the blanket from her mother, but as she pulled Mrs Kemp gave a growl in her sleep and drew the clothes more tightly round her. So Liza put over herself her skirt and a shawl, which was lying over the end of the bed, and tried to go to sleep.

But she could not; her head and hands were broiling hot, and she was terribly thirsty; when she lifted herself up to get a drink of water such a pang went through her head that she fell back on the bed groaning, and lay there with beating heart. And strange pains that she did not know went through her. Then a cold shiver seemed to rise in the very marrow of her bones and run down every artery and vein, freezing the blood; her skin puckered up, and drawing up her legs she lay huddled together in a heap, the shawl wrapped tightly round her, and her teeth chattering. Shivering, she whispered:

'Oh, I'm so cold, so cold. Mother, give me some clothes; I shall die of the cold. Oh, I'm freezing!'

But after awhile the cold seemed to give way, and a sudden heat seized her, flushing her face, making her break out into perspiration, so that she threw everything off and loosened the things about her neck.

'Give us a drink,' she said. 'Oh, I'd give anythin' for a little drop of water!'

There was no one to hear; Mrs Kemp continued to sleep heavily, occasionally breaking out into a little snore.

Liza remained there, now shivering with cold, now panting for breath, listening to the regular, heavy breathing by her side, and in her pain she sobbed. She pulled at her pillow and said:

'Why can't I go to sleep? Why can't I sleep like 'er?'

And the darkness was awful; it was a heavy, ghastly blackness, that seemed palpable, so that it frightened her and she looked for relief at the faint light glimmering through the window from a distant street-lamp. She thought the night would never end—the minutes seemed like hours, and she wondered how she should live through till morning. And strange pains that she did not know went through her.

Still the night went on, the darkness continued, cold and horrible, and her mother breathed loudly and steadily by her side.

At last with the morning sleep came; but the sleep was almost worse than the wakefulness, for it was accompanied by ugly, disturbing dreams. Liza thought she was going through the fight with her enemy, and Mrs Blakeston grew enormous in size, and multiplied, so that every way she turned the figure confronted her. And she began running away, and she ran and ran till she found herself reckoning up an account she had puzzled over in the morning, and she did it backwards and forwards, upwards and downwards, starting here, starting there, and the figures got mixed up with other things, and she had to begin over again, and everything jumbled up, and her head whirled, till finally, with a start, she woke.

The darkness had given way to a cold, grey dawn, her uncovered legs were chilled to the bone, and by her side she heard again the regular, nasal breathing of the drunkard.

For a long while she lay where she was, feeling very sick and ill, but better than in the night. At last her mother woke.

'Liza!' she called.

'Yus, mother,' she answered feebly.

'Git us a cup of tea, will yer?'

'I can't, mother, I'm ill.'

'Garn!' said Mrs Kemp, in surprise. Then looking at her: 'Swop me bob, wot's up with yer? Why, yer cheeks is flushed, an' yer forehead—it is 'ot! Wot's the matter with yer, gal?'

'I dunno,' said Liza. 'I've been thet bad all night, I thought I was goin' ter die."

'I know wot it is,' said Mrs Kemp, shaking her head; 'the fact is, you ain't used ter drinkin', an' of course it's upset yer. Now me, why I'm as fresh as a disy. Tike my word, there ain't no good in teetotalism; it finds yer aht in the end, an' it's found you aht.'

Mrs Kemp considered it a judgment of Providence. She got up and mixed some whisky and water.

''Ere, drink this,' she said. 'When one's 'ad a drop too much at night, there's nothin' like havin' a drop more in the mornin' ter put one right. It just acts like magic.'

'Tike it awy,' said Liza, turning from it in disgust; 'the smell of it gives me the sick. I'll never touch spirits again.'

'Ah, thet's wot we all says sometime in our lives, but we does, an' wot's more we can't do withaht it. Why, me, the 'ard life I've 'ad—' It is unnecessary to repeat Mrs Kemp's repetitions.

Liza did not get up all day. Tom came to inquire after her, and was told she was very ill. Liza plaintively asked whether anyone else had been, and sighed a little when her mother answered no. But she felt too ill to think much or trouble much about anything. The fever came again as the day wore on, and the pains in her head grew worse. Her mother came to bed, and quickly went off to sleep, leaving Liza to bear her agony alone. She began to have frightful pains all over her, and she held her breath to prevent herself from crying out and waking her mother. She clutched the sheets in her agony, and at last, about six o'clock in the morning, she could bear it no longer, and in the anguish of labour screamed out, and woke her mother.

Mrs Kemp was frightened out of her wits. Going upstairs she woke the woman who lived on the floor above her. Without hesitating, the good lady put on a skirt and came down.

'She's 'ad a miss,' she said, after looking at Liza. 'Is there anyone you could send to the 'orspital?'

'Na, I dunno 'oo I could get at this hour?'

'Well, I'll git my old man ter go.'

She called her husband, and sent him off. She was a stout, middle-aged woman, rough-visaged and strong-armed. Her name was Mrs Hodges.

'It's lucky you came ter me,' she said, when she had settled down. 'I go aht nursin', yer know, so I know all abaht it.'

'Well, you surprise me,' said Mrs Kemp. 'I didn't know as Liza was thet way. She never told me nothin' abaht it.'

'D'yer know 'oo it is 'as done it?'

'Now you ask me somethin' I don't know,' replied Mrs Kemp. 'But now I come ter think of it, it must be thet there Tom. 'E's been keepin' company with Liza. 'E's a single man, so they'll be able ter get married—thet's somethin'.'

'It ain't Tom,' feebly said Liza.

'Not 'im; 'oo is it then?'

Liza did not answer.

'Eh?' repeated the mother,' 'oo is it?'

Liza lay still without speaking.

'Never mind, Mrs Kemp,' said Mrs Hodges, 'don't worry 'er now; you'll be able ter find aht all abaht it when she gits better.'

For a while the two women sat still, waiting the doctor's coming, and Liza lay gazing vacantly at the wall, panting for breath. Sometimes Jim crossed her mind, and she opened her mouth to call for him, but in her despair she restrained herself.

The doctor came.

'D'you think she's bad, doctor?' asked Mrs Hodges.

'I'm afraid she is rather,' he answered. 'I'll come in again this evening.'

'Oh, doctor,' said Mrs Kemp, as he was going, 'could yer give me somethin' for my rheumatics? I'm a martyr to rheumatism, an' these cold days I 'ardly knows wot ter do with myself. An', doctor, could you let me 'ave some beef-tea? My 'usbind's dead, an' of course I can't do no work with my daughter ill like this, an' we're very short—"

The day passed, and in the evening Mrs Hodges, who had been attending to her own domestic duties, came downstairs again. Mrs Kemp was on the bed sleeping.

'I was just 'avin' a little nap,' she said to Mrs Hodges, on waking.

''Ow is the girl?' asked that lady.

'Oh,' answered Mrs Kemp, 'my rheumatics 'as been thet bad I really 'aven't known wot ter do with myself, an' now Liza can't rub me I'm worse than ever. It is unfortunate thet she should get ill just now when I want so much attendin' ter myself, but there, it's just my luck!'

Mrs Hodges went over and looked at Liza; she was lying just as when she left in the morning, her cheeks flushed, her mouth open for breath, and tiny beads of sweat stood on her forehead.

''Ow are yer, ducky?' asked Mrs Hodges; but Liza did not answer.

'It's my belief she's unconscious,' said Mrs Kemp. 'I've been askin' 'er 'oo it was as done it, but she don't seem to 'ear wot I say. It's been a great shock ter me, Mrs 'Odges.'

'I believe you,' replied that lady, sympathetically.

'Well, when you come in and said wot it was, yer might 'ave knocked me dahn with a feather. I knew no more than the dead wot 'ad 'appened.'

'I saw at once wot it was,' said Mrs Hodges, nodding her head.

'Yus, of course, you knew. I expect you've 'ad a great deal of practice one way an' another.'

'You're right, Mrs Kemp, you're right. I've been on the job now for nearly twenty years, an' if I don't know somethin' abaht it I ought.'

'D'yer finds it pays well?'

'Well, Mrs Kemp, tike it all in all, I ain't got no grounds for complaint. I'm in the 'abit of askin' five shillings, an' I will say this, I don't think it's too much for wot I do.'

The news of Liza's illness had quickly spread, and more than once in the course of the day a neighbour had come to ask after her. There was a knock at the door now, and Mrs Hodges opened it. Tom stood on the threshold asking to come in.

'Yus, you can come,' said Mrs Kemp.

He advanced on tiptoe, so as to make no noise, and for a while stood silently looking at Liza. Mrs Hodges was by his side.

'Can I speak to 'er?' he whispered.

'She can't 'ear you.'

He groaned.

'D'yer think she'll get arright?' he asked.

Mrs Hodges shrugged her shoulders.

'I shouldn't like ter give an opinion,' she said, cautiously.

Tom bent over Liza, and, blushing, kissed her; then, without speaking further, went out of the room.

'Thet's the young man as was courtin' 'er,' said Mrs Kemp, pointing over her shoulder with her thumb.

Soon after the Doctor came.

'Wot do yer think of 'er, doctor?' said Mrs Hodges, bustling forwards authoritatively in her position of midwife and sick-nurse.

'I'm afraid she's very bad.'

'D'yer think she's goin' ter die?' she asked, dropping her voice to a whisper.

'I'm afraid so!'

As the doctor sat down by Liza's side Mrs Hodges turned round and significantly nodded to Mrs Kemp, who put her handkerchief to her eyes. Then she went outside to the little group waiting at the door.

'Wot does the doctor sy?' they asked, among them Tom.

''E says just wot I've been sayin' all along; I knew she wouldn't live.'

And Tom burst out: 'Oh, Liza!'

As she retired a woman remarked:

'Mrs 'Odges is very clever, I think.'

'Yus,' remarked another, 'she got me through my last confinement simply wonderful. If it come to choosin' between 'em I'd back Mrs 'Odges against forty doctors.'

'Ter tell yer the truth, so would I. I've never known 'er wrong yet.'

Mrs Hodges sat down beside Mrs Kemp and proceeded to comfort her.

'Why don't yer tike a little drop of brandy ter calm yer nerves, Mrs Kemp?' she said, 'you want it.'

'I was just feelin' rather faint, an' I couldn't 'elp thinkin' as 'ow twopenneth of whisky 'ud do me good.'

'Na, Mrs Kemp,' said Mrs Hodges, earnestly, putting her hand on the other's arm. 'You tike my tip—when you're queer there's nothin' like brandy for pullin' yer togither. I don't object to whisky myself, but as a medicine yer can't beat brandy.'

'Well, I won't set up myself as knowin' better than you Mrs 'Odges; I'll do wot you think right.'

Quite accidentally there was some in the room, and Mrs Kemp poured it out for herself and her friend.

'I'm not in the 'abit of tikin' anythin' when I'm aht on business,' she apologized, 'but just ter keep you company I don't mind if I do.'

'Your 'ealth, Mrs 'Odges.'

'Sime ter you, an' thank yer, Mrs Kemp.'

Liza lay still, breathing very quietly, her eyes closed. The doctor kept his fingers on her pulse.

'I've been very unfortunate of lite,' remarked Mrs Hodges, as she licked her lips, 'this mikes the second death I've 'ad in the last ten days—women, I mean, of course I don't count bibies.'

'Yer don't sy so.'

'Of course the other one—well, she was only a prostitute, so it didn't so much matter. It ain't like another woman is it?'

'Na, you're right.'

'Still, one don't like 'em ter die, even if they are thet. One mustn't be too 'ard on 'em.'

'Strikes me you've got a very kind 'eart, Mrs 'Odges,' said Mrs Kemp.

'I 'ave thet; an' I often says it 'ud be better for my peace of mind an' my business if I 'adn't. I 'ave ter go through a lot, I do; but I can say this for myself, I always gives satisfaction, an' thet's somethin' as all lidies in my line can't say.'

They sipped their brandy for a while.

'It's a great trial ter me that this should 'ave 'appened,' said Mrs Kemp, coming to the subject that had been disturbing her for some time. 'Mine's always been a very respectable family, an' such a thing as this 'as never 'appened before. No, Mrs 'Odges, I was lawfully married in church, an' I've got my marriage lines now ter show I was, an' thet one of my daughters should 'ave gone wrong in this way—well, I can't understand it. I give 'er a good education, an' she 'ad all the comforts of a 'ome. She never wanted for nothin'; I worked myself to the bone ter keep 'er in luxury, an' then thet she should go an' disgrace me like this!'

'I understand wot yer mean, Mrs Kemp.'

'I can tell you my family was very respectable; an' my 'usband, 'e earned twenty-five shillings a week, an' was in the sime plice seventeen years; an' 'is employers sent a beautiful wreath ter put on 'is coffin; an' they tell me they never 'ad such a good workman an' sich an 'onest man before. An' me! Well, I can sy this—I've done my duty by the girl, an' she's never learnt anythin' but good from me. Of course I ain't always been in wot yer might call flourishing circumstances, but I've always set her a good example, as she could tell yer so 'erself if she wasn't speechless.'

Mrs Kemp paused for a moment's reflection.

'As they sy in the Bible,' she finished, 'it's enough ter mike one's grey 'airs go dahn into the ground in sorrer. I can show yer my marriage certificate. Of course one doesn't like ter say much, because of course she's very bad; but if she got well I should 'ave given 'er a talkin' ter.'

There was another knock.

'Do go an' see 'oo thet is; I can't, on account of my rheumatics.'

Mrs Hodges opened the door. It was Jim.

He was very white, and the blackness of his hair and beard, contrasting with the deathly pallor of his face, made him look ghastly. Mrs Hodges stepped back.

''Oo's 'e?' she said, turning to Mrs Kemp.

Jim pushed her aside and went up to the bed.

'Doctor, is she very bad?' he asked.

The doctor looked at him questioningly.

Jim whispered: 'It was me as done it. She ain't goin' ter die, is she?'

The doctor nodded.

'O God! wot shall I do? It was my fault! I wish I was dead!'

Jim took the girl's head in his hands, and the tears burst from his eyes.

'She ain't dead yet, is she?'

'She's just living,' said the doctor.

Jim bent down.

'Liza, Liza, speak ter me! Liza, say you forgive me! Oh, speak ter me!'

His voice was full of agony. The doctor spoke.

'She can't hear you.'

'Oh, she must hear me! Liza! Liza!'

He sank on his knees by the bedside.

They all remained silent: Liza lying stiller than ever, her breast unmoved by the feeble respiration, Jim looking at her very mournfully; the doctor grave, with his fingers on the pulse. The two women looked at Jim.

'Fancy it bein' 'im!' said Mrs Kemp. 'Strike me lucky, ain't 'e a sight!'

'You 'ave got 'er insured, Mrs Kemp?' asked the midwife. She could bear the silence no longer.

'Trust me fur thet!' replied the good lady. 'I've 'ad 'er insured ever since she was born. Why, only the other dy I was sayin' ter myself thet all thet money 'ad been wisted, but you see it wasn't; yer never know yer luck, you see!'

'Quite right, Mrs Kemp; I'm a rare one for insurin'. It's a great thing. I've always insured all my children.'

'The way I look on it is this,' said Mrs Kemp—'wotever yer do when they're alive, an' we all know as children is very tryin' sometimes, you should give them a good funeral when they dies. Thet's my motto, an' I've always acted up to it.'

'Do you deal with Mr Stearman?' asked Mrs Hodges.

'No, Mrs 'Odges, for undertikin' give me Mr Footley every time. In the black line 'e's fust an' the rest nowhere!'

'Well, thet's very strange now—thet's just wot I think. Mr Footley does 'is work well, an' 'e's very reasonable. I'm a very old customer of 'is, an' 'e lets me 'ave things as cheap as anybody.'

'Does 'e indeed! Well Mrs 'Odges if it ain't askin' too much of yer, I should look upon it as very kind if you'd go an' mike the arrangements for Liza.'

'Why, certainly, Mrs Kemp. I'm always willin' ter do a good turn to anybody, if I can.'

'I want it done very respectable,' said Mrs Kemp: 'I'm not goin' ter stint for nothin' for my daughter's funeral. I like plumes, you know, although they is a bit extra.'

'Never you fear, Mrs Kemp, it shall be done as well as if it was for my own 'usbind, an' I can't say more than thet. Mr Footley thinks a deal of me, 'e does! Why, only the other dy as I was goin' inter 'is shop 'e says "Good mornin', Mrs 'Odges," "Good mornin', Mr Footley," says I. "You've jest come in the nick of time," says 'e. "This gentleman an' myself," pointin' to another gentleman as was standin' there, "we was 'avin' a bit of an argument. Now you're a very intelligent woman, Mrs 'Odges, and a good customer too." "I can say thet for myself," say I, "I gives yer all the work I can." "I believe you," says 'e. "Well," 'e says, "now which do you think? Does hoak look better than helm, or does helm look better than hoak? Hoak *versus* helm, thet's the question." "Well, Mr Footley," says I, "for my own private opinion, when you've got a nice brass plite in the middle, an' nice brass 'andles each end, there's nothin' like hoak." "Quite right," says 'e, "thet's wot I think; for coffins give me hoak any day, an' I 'ope," says 'e, "when the Lord sees fit ter call me to 'Imself, I shall be put in a hoak coffin myself." "Amen," says I.'

'I like hoak,' said Mrs Kemp. 'My poor 'usband 'e 'ad a hoak coffin. We did 'ave a job with 'im, I can tell yer. You know 'e 'ad dropsy, an' 'e swell up—oh, 'e did swell; 'is own mother wouldn't 'ave known 'im. Why, 'is leg swell up till it was as big round as 'is body, swop me bob, it did.'

'Did it indeed!' ejaculated Mrs Hodges.

'Yus, an' when 'e died they sent the coffin up. I didn't 'ave Mr Footley at thet time; we didn't live 'ere then, we lived in Battersea, an' all our undertikin' was done by Mr Brownin'; well, 'e sent the coffin up, an' we got my old man in, but we couldn't get the lid down, he was so swell up. Well, Mr Brownin', 'e was a great big man, thirteen stone if 'e was a ounce. Well, 'e stood on the coffin, an' a young man 'e 'ad with 'im stood on it too, an' the lid simply wouldn't go dahn; so Mr Browning', 'e said, "Jump on, missus," so I was in my widow's weeds, yer know, but we 'ad ter git it dahn, so I stood on it, an' we all jumped, an' at last we got it to, an' screwed it; but, lor', we did 'ave a job; I shall never forget it.'

Then all was silence. And a heaviness seemed to fill the air like a grey blight, cold and suffocating; and the heaviness was Death. They felt the presence in the room, and they dared not move, they dared not draw their breath. The silence was terrifying.

Suddenly a sound was heard—a loud rattle. It was from the bed and rang through the room, piercing the stillness.

The doctor opened one of Liza's eyes and touched it, then he laid on her breast the hand he had been holding, and drew the sheet over her head.

Jim turned away with a look of intense weariness on his face, and the two women began weeping silently. The darkness was sinking before the day, and a dim, grey light came through the window. The lamp spluttered out.

MRS CRADDOCK

CHAPTER I

THIS book might be called also *The Triumph of Love.*

Bertha was looking out of the window at the bleakness of the day. The sky was grey and the clouds were heavy and low; the neglected drive leading to the gates was swept by the bitter wind, and the elm trees that bordered it were bare of leaf; their naked branches seemed to shiver with horror of the cold. It was the end of November and the day was cheerless. The dying year seemed to have cast over all nature the terror of death; the imagination would not bring to the wearied mind thoughts of the merciful sunshine, thoughts of the spring coming as a maiden to scatter from her baskets the flowers and the green leaves.

Bertha turned round and looked at her aunt cutting the leaves of a new *Spectator.* Wondering what book to get down from Mudie's, Miss Ley read the autumn lists and the laudatory expressions that the adroitness of publishers extracts from unfavourable reviews.

'You're very restless this afternoon, Bertha,' she remarked, in answer to her niece's steady gaze.

'I think I shall walk down to the gate.'

'You've already done that twice in the last hour. Do you find in it something alarmingly novel?'

Bertha did not reply, but turned again to the window; the scene in the last two hours had fixed itself upon her mind with monotonous accuracy.

'What are you thinking about, Aunt Polly?' she asked, suddenly turning back to her aunt and catching the eyes fixed upon her.

'I was thinking that one must be very penetrative to discover a woman's emotions from the view of her back hair.'

Bertha laughed: 'I don't think I have any emotions to discover. I feel—' she sought for some way of expressing the sensation. 'I feel as if I should like to take my hair down.'

Miss Ley made no rejoinder, but looked down at her paper. She hardly wondered what her niece meant, having long ceased to be astonished at Bertha's ways and doings; indeed, her only surprise was that they never sufficiently corroborated the common opinion that Bertha was an independent young woman from whom anything might be expected. In the three years they had spent together since the death of Bertha's father, the two women had learned to tolerate one another extremely well. Their mutual affection was mild and perfectly respectable, in every way suitable to ladylike persons bound together by ties of convenience and decorum. Miss Ley, called to the death-bed of her brother in Italy, made Bertha's acquaintance over the dead man's grave, and she was then too old and of too independent character to accept a stranger's authority; nor had Miss Ley the smallest desire to exert authority over anybody. She was a very indolent woman, who wished nothing more than to leave people alone and be left alone by them. But if it was obviously her duty to take charge of an orphan niece, it was also an advantage that Bertha was eighteen and but for conventions of decent society could very well take charge of herself. Miss Ley was not unthankful to a merciful providence on the discovery that her ward had every intention of going her own way and none whatever of hanging about the skirts of a maiden aunt who was passionately devoted to her liberty.

They travelled on the Continent, seeing many churches, pictures and cities, in the examination of which their chief desire appeared to be to conceal from one another the emotions they felt. Like the Red Indian, who will suffer the most horrid tortures without wincing, Miss Ley would have thought it highly disgraceful to display feeling at some touching scene. She used polite cynicism as a cloak for sentimentality, laughing that she might not cry—and her want of originality herein, the old repetition of Grimaldi's doubleness, made her snigger at herself; she felt that tears were unbecoming and foolish.

'Weeping makes a fright even of a good-looking woman,' she said, 'but if she is ugly they make her simply repulsive.'

Finally, letting her own flat in London, Miss Ley settled down with Bertha to cultivate rural delights at Court Leys near Blackstable, in the county of Kent. The two ladies lived together with much harmony, although the demonstrations of their affection did not exceed a single kiss morning and night, given and received with almost equal indifference. Each had considerable respect for the other's abilities, and particularly for the wit that occasionally exhibited itself in little friendly sarcasms. But they were too clever to get on badly, and since they neither hated nor loved one another excessively, there was really no reason why they should not continue to live together on the best of terms. The general result of their relations was that Bertha's restlessness on this particular day aroused in Miss Ley no more question than was easily explained by the warmth of her young blood; and her eccentric curiosity in respect of the gate on a very cold and unpleasant winter afternoon did not even elicit from her a shrug of disapproval or an upraising of the eyebrows in wonder.

Bertha put on a hat and walked out. The avenue of elm trees reaching from the façade of Court Leys in a straight line to the gates had once been rather an imposing sight, but now announced clearly the ruin of an ancient house. Here and there a tree had died and fallen, leaving an unsightly gap, and one huge trunk still lay upon the ground after a terrific storm of the preceding year, left there to rot in the indifference of bailiffs and tenants. On either side of the elm trees was a broad strip of meadow that once had been a well-kept lawn, but now was foul with docks and rank weeds; a few sheep nibbled the grass where upon a time fine ladies in hoops and gentlemen with tie-wigs had sauntered, discussing the wars and the last volumes of Mr Richardson. Beyond was an ill-trimmed hedge and then the broad fields of the Ley estate. Bertha walked down, looking at the highway beyond the gate; it was a relief no longer to feel Miss Ley's cold eyes fixed upon her. She had emotions enough in her breast, they beat against one another like birds in a net struggling to get free; but not for worlds would she have bidden anyone look into her heart, full of expectation, of longing and of a hundred strange desires. She went out on the high-road that led from Blackstable to Tercanbury; she looked up and down with a tremor and a quick beating of the heart. But the road was empty, swept by the winter wind, and she almost sobbed with disappointment.

She could not return to the house; a roof just then would stifle her, and the walls seemed like a prison; there was a certain pleasure in the biting wind that blew through her clothes and chilled her to the bone. The waiting was terrible. She entered the grounds and looked up the carriage-drive to the big white house that was hers. The very roadway was in need of repair, and the dead leaves that none troubled about rustled hither and thither in the gusts of wind. The house stood out in its squareness without relation to its environment. Built in the reign of George II, it seemed to have acquired no hold upon the land that bore it; with its plain front and many windows, the Doric portico exactly in the middle, it looked as if it were merely placed upon the ground as a house of cards is built upon the floor, with no foundations. The passing years had given it no beauty, and it stood now, as for more than a century it had stood, a blot upon the landscape, vulgar and new. Surrounded by the fields, it had no garden but for a few beds planted about its feet, and in them the flowers, uncared for, had grown wild or withered away.

The day was declining and the lowering clouds seemed to shut out the light. Bertha gave up hope. But she looked once more down the hill, and her heart gave a great thud against her chest. She felt herself blushing furiously. Her blood seemed to be rushing through the vessels with sudden rapidity, and in dismay at her want of composure she had an impulse to turn quickly and go back to the house. She forgot the sickening expectation and the hours that she had spent in looking for the figure that tramped up the hill.

He came nearer, a tall fellow of twenty-seven, massively set together, big-boned, with long arms and legs and a magnificent breadth of chest. One could well believe him as strong as an ox. Bertha recognized the costume that always pleased her, the knickerbockers and gaiters, the Norfolk jacket of rough tweed, the white stock and the cap—all redolent of the country which for his sake she was beginning to love, and all intensely masculine. Even the huge boots that covered his feet gave her by their very size a thrill of pleasure; their dimensions suggested a firmness of character and a masterfulness that were intensely reassuring. The style of dress fitted perfectly the background of brown road and ploughed field. Bertha wondered if he knew that he was exceedingly picturesque as he climbed the hill.

'Afternoon, Miss Bertha,' the man said as he passed.

He showed no sign of stopping, and the girl's heart sank at the thought that he might go on with only a commonplace word of greeting.

'I thought it was you I saw coming up the hill,' she said, stretching out her hand.

He stopped and shook it. The touch of his big, firm fingers made her tremble. His hand was as massive and hard as if it were hewn of stone. She looked up at him and smiled.

'Isn't it cold?' she said.

It is terrible to be desirous of saying all sorts of passionate things while convention prevents you from any but the most commonplace.

'You haven't been walking at the rate of five miles an hour,' he said cheerily. 'I've been into Blackstable to see about buying a nag.'

He was the very picture of health. The winds of November were like summer breezes to him, and his face glowed with the pleasant cold. His cheeks were flushed and his eyes glistened; his vitality was intense, shining out upon others with almost a material warmth.

'Were you going out?' he asked.

'Oh, no,' Bertha replied without strict regard to truth. 'I just walked down to the gate and I happened to catch sight of you.'

'I'm very glad. I see you so seldom now, Miss Bertha.'

'I wish you wouldn't call me Miss Bertha,' she cried. 'It sounds horrid.'

It was worse than that, it sounded almost menial.

'When we were boy and girl we used to call each other by our Christian names.'

He blushed a little, and his modesty filled Bertha with pleasure.

'Yes, but when you came back six months ago you had changed so much—I didn't dare; and besides, you called me Mr Craddock.'

'Well, I won't any more,' she said, smiling. 'I'd much sooner call you Edward.'

She did not add that the word seemed to her the most beautiful in the whole list of Christian names, nor that in the past few weeks she had already repeated it to herself a thousand times.

'It'll be like the old days,' he said. 'D'you remember what fun we used to have when you were a little girl, before you went abroad with Mr Ley?'

'I remember that you used to look upon me with great contempt because I *was* a little girl,' she replied, laughing.

'Well, I was awfully frightened the first time I saw you again, with your hair up and long dresses.'

'I'm not really very terrible,' she answered.

For five minutes they had been looking into one another's eyes, and suddenly, without obvious reason, Edward Craddock blushed. Bertha noticed it, and a strange little thrill went through her. She blushed too, and her dark eyes flashed even more brightly than before.

'I wish I didn't see you so seldom, Miss Bertha,' he said.

'You have only yourself to blame, fair sir,' she replied. 'You perceive the road that leads to my palace, and at the end of it you will certainly find a door.'

'I'm rather afraid of your aunt,' he said.

It was on the tip of Bertha's tongue to say that faint heart never won fair lady, but, for modesty's sake, she refrained. Her spirits had suddenly gone up and she felt extraordinarily happy.

'Do you want to see me very badly?' she asked, her heart beating at quite an absurd rate.

Craddock blushed again and seemed to have some difficulty in finding a reply; his confusion and his ingenuous air were new delights to Bertha.

'If he only knew how I adore him!' she thought; but naturally could not tell him in so many words.

'You've changed so much in these years,' he said. 'I don't understand you.'

'You haven't answered my question.'

'Of course I want to see you, Bertha,' he said quickly, seeming to take his courage in both hands. 'I want to see you always.'

'Well,' he said, with a charming smile, 'I sometimes take a walk after dinner to the gate and observe the shadows of night.'

'By Jove, I wish I'd known that before.'

'Foolish creature!' said Bertha to herself with amusement. 'He doesn't gather that this is the first night upon which I shall have done anything of the kind.'

Then aloud, she bade him a laughing good-bye and they separated.

CHAPTER II

WITH swinging step Bertha returned to the house, and, like a swarm of birds, a hundred amorets flew about her head; Cupid leapt from tree to tree and shot his arrows into her willing heart; her imagination clothed the naked branches with tender green and in her happiness the grey sky turned to azure. It was the first time that Edward Craddock had shown his love in a manner that was unmistakable; if, before, much had suggested that he was not indifferent, nothing had been absolutely convincing, and the doubt had caused her every imaginable woe. As for her, she made no effort to conceal it from herself; she was not ashamed, she loved him passionately, she worshipped the ground he trod on; she confessed boldly that he of all men was the one to make her happy, her life she would give into his strong and manly hands; she had made up her mind firmly that Craddock should lead her to the altar.

'I want to be his wife,' she gasped, in the extremity of her passion.

Times without number already had she thought of herself resting in his arms—in his strong arms, the very thought of which was a protection against all the ills of the world. Oh, yes, she wanted him to take her in his arms and kiss her; in imagination she felt his lips upon hers, and the warmth of his breath made her faint with the anguish of love.

She asked herself how she could wait till the evening, how on earth she was to endure the slow passing of the hours. And she must sit opposite her aunt and pretend to read, or talk on this subject or that. It was insufferable. Then inconsequently she asked herself if Edward knew that she loved him; he could not dream how intense was her desire.

'I'm sorry I'm late for tea,' she said, on entering the drawing-room.

'My dear,' said Miss Ley, 'the buttered toast is probably horrid, but I don't see why you should not eat cake.'

'I don't want anything to eat,' cried Bertha, flinging herself on a chair.

'But you're dying with thirst,' added Miss Ley, looking at her niece with sharp eye. 'Wouldn't you like your tea out of a breakfast cup?'

Miss Ley had come to the conclusion that the restlessness and the long absence could only be due to some masculine cause. Mentally she shrugged her shoulders, hardly wondering who the creature was.

'Of course,' she thought, 'it's certain to be someone quite ineligible. I hope they won't have a long engagement.'

Miss Ley could not have supported for several months the presence of a bashful and love-sick swain. She found lovers invariably ridiculous and felt that they should be hidden—just as the sons of Noah covered their father's nakedness. She watched Bertha gulp down six cups of tea. Of course those shining eyes, the flushed cheeks and the breathlessness indicated some amorous excitement; it amused her, but she thought it charitable and wise to pretend that she noticed nothing.

'After all, it's no business of mine,' she thought, 'and if Bertha is going to get married at all, it would be much more convenient for her to do it before next quarter day, when the Brownes give up my flat.'

Miss Ley sat on the sofa by the fireside. She was a woman neither short nor tall, very slight, with a thin and much-wrinkled face. Of her features the mouth was the most noticeable, not large, with lips that were a trifle too thin; it was always so tightly compressed as to give her an air of great determination, but there was about the corners an expressive mobility, contradicting in rather an unusual manner the inferences that might be drawn from the rest of her person. She had a habit of fixing her cold eyes on people with a steadiness that was not a little embarrassing. They said Miss Ley looked as if she thought them great fools, and as a matter of fact that usually was precisely what she did think. Her thin grey hair was very plainly done, and the extreme simplicity of her costume gave her a certain primness, so that her favourite method of saying rather absurd things in the gravest and most decorous manner often disconcerted the casual stranger. She was a woman who, one felt, had never been handsome, but now, in middle age, was of distinctly prepossessing appearance. Young men thought her somewhat terrifying till they discovered that they were to her a constant source of amusement, while elderly ladies asserted that, though of course a perfect gentlewoman, she was a little queer.

'You know, Aunt Polly,' said Bertha, finishing her tea and getting up, 'I think you ought to have been called Martha or Matilda. I don't think Polly suits you.'

'My dear, you need not remind me so pointedly that I'm forty-five—and you need not smile in that fashion because you know that I'm really forty-seven. I say forty-five merely as a round number; in another year I shall call myself fifty. A woman never acknowledges such a nondescript age as forty-eight unless she is going to marry a widower with seventeen children.'

'I wonder why you never married, Aunt Polly?' said Bertha looking away.

Miss Ley smiled almost imperceptibly; she found Bertha's remark highly significant.

'My dear,' she said, 'why should I? I had five hundred a year of my own. Ah, yes, I know it's not what might have been expected; I'm sorry for your sake that I had no hopeless amour. The only excuse for an old maid is that she has pined thirty years for a lover who is buried under the snowdrops or has married another.'

Bertha made no answer; she was feeling that the world had turned good, and wanted to hear nothing that could suggest imperfections in human nature. Going upstairs she sat at the window, gazing towards the farm where lived her heart's desire. She wondered what Edward was doing. Was he awaiting the night as anxiously as she? It gave her quite a pang that a sizable hill should intervene between herself and him. During dinner she hardly spoke, and Miss Ley was mercifully silent. Bertha could not eat. She crumpled her bread and toyed with the various meats put before her. She looked at the clock a dozen times and started absurdly when it struck the hour.

She did not trouble to make any excuse to Miss Ley, whom she left to think as she chose. The night was dark and cold. Bertha slipped out of the side-door with a delightful feeling of doing something venturesome. But her legs would scarcely carry her she had a sensation that was entirely novel: never before had she experienced that utter weakness of the knees so that she feared to fall; her breathing was strangely oppressive, her heart beat painfully. She walked down the carriage-drive hardly knowing what she did. And supposing he was not there, supposing he never came? She had forced herself to wait in-doors till the desire to go out became uncontrollable, she dared not imagine her dismay if there was no one to meet her when she reached the gate. It would mean he did not love her. She stopped with a sob. Ought she not to wait longer? It was still early. But her impatience forced her on.

She gave a little cry. Craddock had suddenly stepped out of the darkness.

'Oh, I'm sorry,' he said, 'I frightened you. I thought you wouldn't mind my coming this evening. You're not angry?'

She could not answer, it was an immense load off her heart. She was extremely happy. Then he did love her; and he feared she was angry with him.

'I expected you,' she whispered.

What was the good of pretending to be modest and bashful? She loved him and he loved her. Why should she not tell him all she felt?

'It's so dark,' he said. 'I can't see you.'

She was too deliriously happy to speak, and the only words she could have said were, '*I love you, I love you!*' She moved a step nearer so as to touch him. Why did he not open his arms and take her in them and kiss her as she had dreamt that he would kiss her?

But he took her hand, and the contact thrilled her; her senses were giving way, and she almost tottered.

'What's the matter?' he said. 'Are you trembling?'

'I'm only a little cold.'

She was trying with all her might to speak naturally. Nothing came into her head to say.

'You've got nothing on,' he said. 'You must wear my coat.'

He began to take it off.

'No,' she said, 'then you'll be cold.'

'Oh, no, I shan't.'

What he was doing seemed to her a marvel of unselfish kindness. She was beside herself with gratitude.

'It's awfully good of you, Edward,' she whispered, almost tearfully.

When he put it round her shoulders the touch of his hands made her lose the little self-control she had left. A curious spasm passed through her and she pressed herself closer to him; at the same time his hands sank down, dropping the cloak and encircled her waist Then she surrendered herself entirely to his embrace and lifted up her face to his. He bent down and kissed her. The kiss was such utter rapture that she almost groaned. She could not tell if it was pain or pleasure. She flung her arms round his neck and drew him to her.

'What a fool I am,' she said at last, with something between a sob and a laugh.

She drew herself a little away, though not so violently as to make him withdraw the arm that so comfortably encircled her. But why did he say nothing? Why did he not swear he loved her? Why did he not ask what she was so willing to grant? She rested her head on his shoulder.

'Do you like me at all, Bertha?' he asked. 'I've been wanting to ask you ever since you came home.'

'Can't you see?' She was reassured; she understood that it was only timidity that clogged his tongue. 'You're so absurdly bashful.'

'You know who I am, Bertha; and—' he hesitated.

'And what?'

'And you're Miss Ley of Court Leys, while I'm just one of your tenants with nothing whatever to my back.'

'I've got very little,' she said. 'And if I had ten thousand a year my only wish would be to lay it at your feet.'

'Bertha, what d'you mean? Don't be cruel to me. You know what I want—but—'

'Well, as far as I can make out,' she said, smiling, 'you want me to propose to you.'

'Oh, Bertha, don't laugh at me. I love you. I want to ask you to marry me. But I haven't got anything to offer you, and I know I oughtn't. Don't be angry with me, Bertha.'

'But I love you with all my heart,' she cried. 'I want no better husband. You can give me happiness, and I want nothing else in the world.'

Then he caught her again in his arms quite passionately and kissed her.

'Didn't you see that I loved you?' she whispered.

'I thought perhaps you did; but I wasn't sure, and I was afraid that you wouldn't think me good enough.'

'I love you with all my heart. I never imagined it possible to love anyone as I love you. Oh, Eddie, you don't know how happy you've made me.'

He kissed her again, and again she flung her arms around his neck.

'Oughtn't you to be going in?' he said at last. 'What will Miss Ley think?'

'Oh, no—not yet,' she cried.

'How will you tell her? D'you think she'll like me? She'll try and make you give me up.'

'Oh, I'm sure she'll love you. Besides, what does it matter if she doesn't? She isn't going to marry you.'

'She can take you abroad again, and then you may see someone you like better."

'But I'm twenty-one tomorrow, Edward—didn't you know? And I shall be my own mistress. I shan't leave Blackstable till I'm your wife.'

They were walking slowly towards the house, whither he, in his anxiety lest she should stay out too long, had guided her steps. They went arm in arm, and Bertha enjoyed her happiness.

'Dr Ramsay is coming to luncheon tomorrow,' she said. 'I shall tell them both that I'm going to be married to you.'

'He won't like it,' said Craddock rather nervously.

'I'm sure I don't care. If you like it and I like it the rest can think what they like.'

'I leave everything in your hands,' he said.

They had arrived at the portico, and Bertha looked at it doubtfully.

'I suppose I ought to go in,' she said, wishing Edward to persuade her to take one more turn in the garden.

'Yes, do,' he said. 'I'm so afraid you'll catch cold.'

It was charming of him to be so solicitous about her health, and of course he was right. Everything he did and said was right; for the moment Bertha forgot her wayward nature and wished suddenly to subject herself to his strong guidance. His very strength made her feel strangely weak.

'Good night, my beloved,' she whispered passionately.

She could not tear herself away from him; it was utter madness. Their kisses never ended.

'Goodnight!'

She watched him at last disappear into the darkness and finally shut the door behind her.

CHAPTER III

WITH old and young great sorrow is followed by a sleepless night, and with the old great joy is as disturbing; but youth, I suppose, finds happiness more natural and its rest is not disturbed by it. Bertha slept without dreams, and awaking, for the moment did not remember the occurrence of the previous day; but suddenly it came back to her, and she stretched herself with a sigh of great content. She lay in bed to contemplate her well-being. She could hardly realize that she had attained her dearest wish. God was very good and gave His creatures what they asked; without words, from the fullness of her heart she offered up thanks. It was quite extraordinary, after the maddening expectation, after the hopes and fears, the lover's pains that are nearly pleasures, at last to be satisfied. She had now nothing more to desire, her happiness was complete. Ah, yes, indeed, God was very good!

Bertha thought of the two months she had spent at Blackstable. After the first excitement of getting into the house of her fathers she had settled down to the humdrum of country life. She spent the day wandering about the lanes or on the sea-shore watching the desolate sea. She read a great deal and looked forward to the ample time at her disposal to satisfy an immoderate desire for knowledge. She spent many hours looking at the books in the library, gathered mostly by her father, for it was only with falling fortunes that the family of Ley had taken to reading books; it had only applied itself to literature when it was too poor for any other pursuit. Bertha looked at the titles, receiving a certain thrill as she read over the great names of the past, and imagined the future delights that they would give her. Beside the vicar and his sister, Dr Ramsay, who was Bertha's guardian, and his wife, she saw no one.

One day she was calling at the vicarage, and Edward Craddock, just returned from a short holiday, happened to be there. She had known him in days gone by; his father had been her father's tenant, and he still fanned the same land, but for eight years they had not seen one another, and now Bertha hardly recognized him. She thought him, however, a good-looking fellow in his knickerbockers and thick stockings, and was not displeased when he came up to speak to her, asking if she remembered him. He sat down, and a certain pleasant odour of the farmyard was wafted over to Bertha, a mingled perfume of strong tobacco, of cattle and horses. She did not understand why it made her heart beat; but she inhaled it voluptuously, and her eyes glittered. He began to talk, and his voice sounded like music in her ears; he looked at her, and his eyes were rather large and grey; she found them highly sympathetic. He was clean-shaven, and his mouth was very attractive. She blushed and felt herself a fool. She took pains to be as charming as possible. She knew her own dark eyes were beautiful, and kept them fixed upon his. When at last he bade her good-bye and shook hands with her, she blushed again; she was extraordinarily troubled, and as, with his rising, the strong, masculine odour of the countryside again reached her nostrils, her head whirled. She was very glad Miss Ley was not there to see her.

She walked home in the darkness, trying to compose herself. She could think of nothing but Edward Craddock. She recalled the past, trying to bring back to her memory incidents of their old acquaintance. At night she dreamt of him, and she dreamt he kissed her.

She awoke thinking of Craddock, and felt it impossible to go through the day without seeing him. She thought of sending him an invitation to luncheon or tea, but hardly dared to; and she did not want Miss Ley to see him yet. Suddenly she thought of the farm; she would walk there, was it not hers? The god of Love was propitious, and in a field she saw him, directing some operation. She trembled at the sight, her heart beat very quickly; and when, seeing her, he came forward with a greeting, she turned red and then white in the most compromising fashion. But he was very handsome as with easy gait he sauntered up to the hedge; above all he was manly; the thought passed through Bertha that his strength must be quite herculean. She scarcely concealed her admiration.

'Oh, I didn't know this was your farm,' she said, shaking hands. 'I was just walking at random.'

'I should like to show you round, Miss Bertha.'

He opened the gate and took her to the sheds where he kept his carts, pointing out a couple of sturdy horses ploughing an adjacent field; he showed her his cattle and poked the pigs to let her admire their excellent condition; he gave her sugar for his hunter, and took her to the sheep, explaining everything while she listened spellbound. When with great pride Craddock showed her his machines and explained the use of the horse-tosser and the expense of the reaper, she thought that never in her life had she heard anything so enthralling. But above all Bertha wanted to see the house in which he lived.

'D'you mind giving me a glass of water?' she said. 'I'm so thirsty.'

'Do come in,' he answered, opening the door.

He led her into a little parlour with an oilcloth on the floor. On the table, which took up the middle of the room, was a stamped red doth; the chairs and the sofa, covered with worn old leather, were arranged with the greatest possible stiffness. On the chimney-piece, along with pipes and tobacco-jars, were bright china vases with rushes in them, and in the middle a marble clock.

'Oh, how pretty!' cried Bertha with enthusiasm. 'You must feel very lonely here by yourself.'

'Oh, no. I'm always out. Shall I get you some milk? It'll be better for you than water.'

But Bertha saw a napkin laid out on the table, a jug of beer and some bread and cheese.

'Have I been keeping you from your lunch?' she asked. 'I'm so sorry.'

'It doesn't matter at all; I just have a little snack at eleven.'

'Oh, may I have some too?' she cried. 'I love bread and cheese, and I'm perfectly ravenous.'

They sat down opposite one another, seeing a great joke in the impromptu meal. The bread, which he cut in a great chunk, was delicious, and the beer, of course, was nectar. But afterwards, Bertha feared that Craddock must be thinking her rather queer.

'D'you think it's very eccentric of me to come and lunch with you in this way?'

'I think it's awfully good of you. Mr Ley often used to come and have a snack with my father.'

'Oh, did he?' said Bertha. Of course that made her proceeding quite natural. 'But I really must go now,' she said. 'I shall get in awful trouble with Aunt Polly.'

He begged her to take some flowers, and hastily cut a bunch of dahlias. She accepted them with embarrassing gratitude; and when they shook hands at parting her heart went pit-a-pat again in the most ridiculous fashion.

Miss Ley inquired from whom she had got her flowers.

'Oh,' said Bertha coolly. 'I happened to meet one of the tenants and he gave them to me.'

'H'm,' murmured Miss Ley. 'It would be more to the purpose if they paid their rent.'

Miss Ley presently left the room, and Bertha looked at the prim dahlias with a heart full of emotion. She gave a laugh.

'It's no good trying to hide it from myself,' she thought, 'I suppose I'm in love.'

She kissed the flowers and felt very glad. She evidently was in that condition, since by the night Bertha had made up her mind to marry Edward Craddock or die. She lost no time, for less than a month had passed, and their wedding-day was certainly in sight.

Miss Ley loathed all manifestations of feeling; Christmas, when everybody is supposed to take his neighbour to his bosom and harbour towards him a number of sentimental emotions, caused her such discomfort that she habitually buried herself for the time in some continental city where she knew no one and could escape the overbrimming of other people's hearts, their compliments of the season, and their state of mind generally. Even in summer Miss Ley could not see a holly tree without a little shiver of disgust; her mind went immediately to the decorations of middle-class houses, the mistletoe hanging from a gas chandelier and the foolish old gentlemen who found amusement in kissing stray females. She was glad that Bertha had thought fit to refuse the display of enthusiasm from servants and impoverished tenants that, on the attainment of her majority, Dr Ramsay had wished to arrange; Miss Ley could imagine that the festivities possible on such an occasion, the hand-shaking, the making of good cheer and the obtrusive joviality of the country Englishman, might surpass even the tawdry celebrations of Yuletide. But Bertha fortunately detested such festivities as sincerely as did Miss Ley herself, and suggested to the persons concerned that they could not oblige her more than by taking no notice of an event that really did not seem to her very significant.

But her guardian's heartiness could not be entirely restrained; he had a fine old English sense of fitness of things. He insisted on solemnly meeting Bertha to offer congratulations, a blessing, and some statement of his stewardship. Bertha came downstairs when Miss Ley was already eating breakfast, a very feminine breakfast consisting of nothing more substantial than a square inch of bacon and some dry toast. Miss Ley was really somewhat nervous, she was bothered by the necessity of referring to her niece's birthday.

'That is one advantage of women,' she told herself, 'after twenty-five they gloss over their birthdays like improprieties. A man is so impressed with his cleverness in having entered the world at all that the anniversary always interests him; and the foolish creature thinks it interests other people as well.'

But Bertha came into the room and kissed her.

'Good morning, dear,' said Miss Ley, and then, pouring out her niece's coffee: 'Our estimable cook has burnt the milk in honour of your majority; I trust she will not celebrate the occasion by getting drunk—at all events, till after dinner.'

'I hope Dr Ramsay won't enthuse too vigorously,' replied Bertha, understanding Miss Ley's feeling.

'Oh, my dear, I tremble at the prospect of his jollity. He's a good man, I should think his principles were excellent, and I don't suppose he's more ignorant than most general practitioners, but his friendliness is sometimes painfully aggressive.'

But Bertha's calm was merely external, her brain was in a whirl and her heart beat madly. She was full of impatience to declare her news. Bertha had some sense of dramatic effect, and looked forward a little to the scene when, the keys of her kingdom being handed over to her, she made the announcement that she had already chosen a king to rule by her side. She felt also that between herself and Miss Ley alone the necessary explanations would be awkward. Dr Ramsay's outspoken bluffness made him easier to deal with; there is always a certain difficulty in conducting oneself with a person who ostentatiously believes that everyone should mind her own business, and who, whatever her thoughts, takes more pleasure in the concealment than in the expression of them. Bertha sent a note to Craddock, telling him to come at three o'clock to be introduced as the future lord and master of the Ley estate.

Dr Ramsay arrived and burst at once into a prodigious stream of congratulation, partly jocose, partly grave and sentimental, but entirely distasteful to the fastidiousness of Miss Ley. Bertha's guardian was a big, broad-shouldered man, with a mane of fair hair, now turning white, and Miss Ley vowed he was the last person upon this earth to wear mutton-chop whiskers; he was very red-cheeked, and by his size, joviality and florid complexion gave one an idea of unalterable health. With his shaven chin and his loud-voiced burliness he looked like a yeoman of the old school, before bad times and the spread of education had made the farmer a sort of cross between the city clerk and the Newmarket trainer. Dr Ramsay's frock-coat and top-hat, notwithstanding the habit of many years, sat uneasily upon him with the air of Sunday clothes upon an agricultural labourer. Miss Ley, who liked to find absurd descriptions of people or hit upon an apt comparison, had never been able exactly to suit him. and that somewhat irritated her. In her eyes the only link that connected him with humanity was a certain love of antiquities, which had filled his house with old snuff-boxes, china and other precious things. Humanity, Miss Ley took to be a small circle of persons, mostly feminine, middle-aged, unattached and of independent means, who travelled on the Continent, read good literature and abhorred the vast majority of their fellow-creatures, especially when these shrieked philanthropically, thrust their religion in your face, or cultivated their muscle with aggressive ardour.

Dr Ramsay ate his luncheon with a voracity that Miss Ley thought must be a source of satisfaction to his butcher. She asked politely after his wife, to whom she secretly objected for her meek submission to the doctor. Miss Ley made a practice of avoiding those women who had turned themselves into mere shadows of their husbands, more especially when their conversation was of household affairs; and Mrs Ramsay, except on Sundays, when her mind was turned to the clothes of the congregation, thought of nothing beyond her husband's enormous appetite and the methods of subduing it.

They returned to the drawing-room, and Dr Ramsay began telling Bertha about the property; who this tenant was and the condition of that farm; winding up with the pitiful state of the times and the impossibility of getting any rents.

'And now, Bertha, what are you thinking of doing?' he asked.

This was the opportunity for which Bertha had been looking.

'I? Oh, I intend to get married.'

Dr Ramsay, opening his mouth, threw back his head and laughed immoderately.

'Very good indeed,' he cried.

Miss Ley looked at him with uplifted eyebrows.

'Girls are coming on nowadays,' he said, with much amusement. 'Why, in my time, a young woman would have been all blushes and downcast glances. If anyone had talked of marriage she would have prayed Heaven to send an earthquake to swallow her up.'

'Fiddlesticks!' said Miss Ley.

Bertha was looking at Dr Ramsay with a smile that she difficultly repressed, and Miss Ley caught the expression.

'So you intend to be married, Bertha?' said the doctor, again laughing.

'Yes,' she replied.

'When?' asked Miss Ley, who did not take Bertha's remarks as merely playful and fantastic.

Bertha was looking out of the window, wondering when Edward would arrive.

'When?' she repeated, turning round. 'This day four weeks.'

'What!' cried Dr Ramsay, jumping up. 'You don't mean to say you've found someone! Are you engaged? Oh, I see, I see! You've been having a little joke with me. Why didn't you tell me that Bertha was engaged all the time, Miss Ley?'

'My good doctor,' answered Miss Ley, with great calmness, 'until this moment I knew nothing whatever about it. I suppose we ought to offer our congratulations; it's a blessing to get them all over on one day.'

Dr Ramsay looked from one to the other with perplexity.

'Well, upon my word,' he said, 'I don't understand.'

'Neither do I,' said Miss Ley, 'but I keep calm.'

'It's very simple,' said Bertha. 'I got engaged last night, and I mean to be married exactly four weeks from today—to Mr Craddock.'

This time Dr Ramsay was more surprised than ever.

'What!' he cried, jumping up in his astonishment and causing the floor to quake in the most dangerous way. 'Craddock! What d'you mean? Which Craddock?'

'Edward Craddock,' replied Bertha with perfect calm, 'of Bewlie's Farm.'

'Brrh!' Dr Ramsay's exclamation cannot be transcribed, but it sounded horrid. 'It's absurd. You'll do nothing of the sort.'

Bertha looked at him with a gentle smile, she did not trouble to answer.

'You're very emphatic, dear doctor,' said Miss Ley. 'Who is this gentleman?'

'He isn't a gentleman,' said Dr Ramsay, becoming purple with vexation.

'He's going to be my husband, Dr Ramsay,' said Bertha compressing her lips in the manner which with Miss Ley had become habitual, and turned to that lady: 'I've known him all my life. Father was a great friend of his father's. He's a gentleman-farmer.'

'The definition of which,' said Dr Ramsay, 'is a man who's neither a farmer nor a gentleman.'

'I forget what your father was,' said Bertha, who remembered perfectly well.

'My father was a farmer,' replied Dr Ramsay with some heat, 'and, thank God! he made no pretence of being a gentleman. He worked with his own hands, and I've seen him often enough with a pitchfork turning over a heap of manure, when no one else was handy.'

'I see,' said Bertha.

'But my father can have nothing to do with it; you can't marry him because he's been dead these thirty years, and you can't marry me because I've got a wife already.'

Miss Ley concealed a smile; Bertha was too clever for it not to give the elder lady some slight pleasure to see her snubbed. Bertha was getting angry, she thought the doctor rude.

'And what have you against him?' she asked.

'If you want to make a fool of yourself, he's got no right to encourage you. He knows he's not a fit match for you.'

'Why not, if I love him?'

'Why not?' shouted Dr Ramsay. 'Because he's the son of a farmer—like I am—and you're Miss Ley of Court Leys. Because a man in that position, without fifty pounds to his back, doesn't make love on the sly to a girl with a fortune.'

'Five thousand acres that pay no rent,' murmured Miss Ley, who was always in opposition.

'You have nothing whatever against him,' retorted Bertha. 'You told me yourself that he had the very best reputation.'

'I didn't know you were asking me with a view to matrimony,' said the doctor.

'I wasn't. I care nothing for his reputation. If he were drunken and idle and dissolute, I'd marry him—because I love him.'

'My dear Bertha,' said Miss Ley, 'the doctor will have an apoplectic fit if you say such things.'

'You told me he was one of the best fellows you knew, Dr Ramsay,' said Bertha.

'I don't deny it,' shouted the doctor, and his red cheeks really had in them a purple tinge that was quite alarming. 'He knows his business and he works hard and he's straight and steady.'

'Good heavens, doctor,' cried Miss Ley, 'he must be a miracle of rural excellence. Bertha would surely never have fallen in love with him if he were faultless.'

'If Bertha wanted an agent,' Dr Ramsay proceeded, 'I could recommend no one better—but as for marrying him—'

'Does he pay his rent?' asked Miss Ley.

'He's one of the best tenants we've got,' growled the doctor. Miss Ley's frivolous interruptions annoyed him.

'Of course in these bad times,' added Miss Ley, who was determined not to allow the doctor to play the heavy father with too much seriousness, 'I suppose about the only resource of the respectable farmer is to marry his landlady.'

'Here he is!' interrupted Bertha.

'Good God, is he coming here?' cried her guardian.

'I sent for him. Remember he is going to be my husband.'

'I'm damned if he is!' said Dr Ramsay.

Miss Ley laughed gently; she rather liked an occasional oath, it relieved the commonplace of masculine conversation in the presence of ladies.

CHAPTER IV

BERTHA threw off her troubled looks and the vexation that the argument had caused her. She blushed charmingly as the door opened, and with the entrance of the fairy prince her face was wreathed in smiles. She went towards him and took his hands.

'Aunt Polly,' she said, 'this is Mr Edward Craddock. Dr Ramsay you know.'

He shook hands with Miss Ley and looked at the doctor, who promptly turned his back on him. Craddock flushed a little and sat down by Miss Ley's side.

'We were talking about you, dearest,' said Bertha. The pause at his arrival had been disconcerting, and while Craddock was nervously thinking of something to say, Miss Ley made no effort to help him. 'I have told Aunt Polly and Dr Ramsay that we intend to be married four weeks from today.'

This was the first that Craddock had heard of the date, but he showed no astonishment. He was in fact trying to recall the speech that he had composed for the occasion.

'I will try to be a good husband to your niece, Miss Ley,' he began.

But that lady interrupted him; she had already come to the conclusion that he was a man likely to say on a given occasion the sort of thing that might be expected; and that in her eyes was a hideous crime.

'Oh, yes, I have no doubt,' she replied. 'Bertha, as you know, is her own mistress and responsible for her acts to no one.'

Craddock was a little embarrassed; he had meant to express his sense of unworthiness and his desire to do his duty, also to explain his own position; but Miss Ley's remark seemed to prohibit further explanation.

'Which is really very convenient,' said Bertha, coming to his rescue. 'Because I have a mind to manage my life in my own way without interference from anybody.'

Miss Ley wondered whether the young man looked upon Bertha's statement as auguring complete tranquillity in the future; but Craddock seemed to see in it nothing ominous, he looked at Bertha with a grateful smile, and the glance that she returned to him was full of the most passionate devotion. Since his arrival Miss Ley had been observing Craddock with great minuteness, and being a woman she could not help finding some pleasure in the knowledge that Bertha was trying with anxiety to discover her judgement. Craddock's appearance was pleasing. Miss Ley liked young men generally, and this was a very good-looking member of the species. His eyes were good, but otherwise there was nothing remarkable in his physiognomy; he looked healthy and good-tempered. Miss Ley noticed even that he did not bite his nails and that his hands were strong and firm. There was really nothing to distinguish him from the common run of healthy young Englishmen with good morals and fine physique; but the class is pleasant. Miss Ley's only wonder was that Bertha had chosen him rather than ten thousand others of the same variety; for that Bertha had chosen him rather actively there was in Miss Ley's mind not the shadow of a doubt.

Miss Ley turned to him.

'Has Bertha shown you our chickens?' she asked calmly.

'No,' he said, rather surprised at the question. 'I hope she will.'

'Oh, no doubt. You know I am quite ignorant of agriculture. Have you ever been abroad?'

'No, I stick to my own country,' he replied, 'it's good enough for me.'

'I daresay it is,' said Miss Ley, looking to the ground. 'Bertha must certainly show you our chickens. They interest me because they're very like human beings; they're so stupid.'

'I can't get mine to lay at all at this time of year,' said Craddock.

'Of course I'm not an agriculturist,' repeated Miss Ley. 'But chickens amuse me.'

Dr Ramsay began to smile, and Bertha flushed angrily.

'You have never shown any interest in the chickens before, Aunt Polly.'

'Haven't I, my dear? Don't you remember last night I remarked how tough was that one we had for dinner? How long have you known Bertha, Mr Craddock?'

'It seems all my life,' he replied. 'And I want to know her more.'

This time Bertha smiled, and Miss Ley, though she felt certain it was unintentional, was not displeased with the manner in which he had parried her question. Dr Ramsay sat in a peevish silence.

'I have never seen you sit so still before, Dr Ramsay,' said Bertha, not too pleased with him.

'I think what I have to say would scarcely please you, Miss Bertha,' he answered bluntly.

Miss Ley was anxious that no altercation should disturb the polite discomfort of the meeting.

'You're thinking about those rents again, doctor,' she said, and turning to Craddock: "The poor doctor is unhappy because half our tenants say they cannot pay.'

The poor doctor grunted and sniffed, and Miss Ley thought it high time for the young man to take his leave. She looked at Bertha, who quickly understood, and getting up, said:

'Let us leave them alone, Eddie; I want to show you the house.'

He rose with great alacrity, evidently much relieved at the end of the ordeal. He shook Miss Ley's hand, and this time could not be restrained from making a little speech.

'I hope you're not angry with me for taking Bertha away from you. I hope I shall soon get to know you better and that we shall become great friends.'

Miss Ley was taken aback, but really she thought his effort not bad. It might have been much worse, and at all events he had kept out of it references to the Almighty and his Duty. Then Craddock turned to Dr Ramsay and went up to him with an outstretched hand that could not be refused.

'I should like to see you some time, Dr Ramsay,' he said, looking at him steadily. 'I fancy you want to have a talk with me, and I should like it too. When can you give me an appointment?'

Bertha flushed with pleasure at his frank words, and Miss Ley was pleased at the courage with which be had attacked the old curmudgeon.

'I think it would be a very good idea,' said the doctor. 'I can see you tonight at eight.'

'Good! Good-bye, Miss Ley.'

He went out with Bertha.

Miss Ley was not one of those persons who consider it indiscreet to form an opinion upon small evidence. Before knowing a person five minutes she made up her mind about him, and liked nothing better than to impart her impression to anyone who asked her.

'Upon my word, doctor,' she said as soon as the door was shut upon the young couple, 'he's not so terrible as I expected.'

'I never said he was not good-looking,' pointedly answered Dr Ramsay, who was convinced that any and every woman was willing to make herself a fool with a handsome man.

Miss Ley smiled. 'Good looks, my dear doctor, are three parts of the necessary equipment in the battle of life. You can't imagine the miserable existence of a really plain girl.'

'Do you approve of Bertha's ridiculous idea?'

'To tell you the truth, I think it makes very little difference if you and I approve or not; therefore we'd much better take the matter quietly.'

'You can do what you like, Miss Ley,' replied the doctor very bluntly, 'but I mean to stop this business.'

'You won't, my dear doctor,' said Miss Ley, smiling again. 'I know Bertha so much better than you. I've lived with her three years, and I've found constant entertainment in the study of her character. Let me tell you how I first knew her. Of course you know that her father and I hadn't been on speaking terms for years: having played ducks and drakes with his own money, he wanted to play the same silly game with mine; and as I strongly objected he flew into a violent passion, called me an ungrateful wretch, and nourished the grievance to the end of his days. Well, his health broke down after his wife's death, and he spent several years with Bertha wandering about the Continent. She was educated as best could be in half a dozen countries, and it's a marvel to me that she is not entirely ignorant or entirely vicious. She's a brilliant example in favour of the opinion that the human race is inclined to good rather than to evil.'

Miss Ley smiled, for she was herself none too certain of it.

'Well, one day,' she proceeded, 'I got a telegram, sent through my solicitors. "Father dead, please come if convenient, Bertha Ley." It was addressed from Naples, and I was in Florence. Of course I rushed down, taking nothing but a bag, a few yards of crape and some smelling-salts. I was met at the station by Bertha, whom I hadn't seen for ten years. I saw a tall and handsome young woman, self-possessed and admirably gowned in the very latest fashion. I kissed her in a subdued way, proper to the occasion, and as we drove back inquired when the funeral was to be, holding the smelling-salts in readiness for an outburst of weeping. "Oh, it's all over," she said. "I didn't send my wire till everything was settled. I thought it would only upset you. I've given notice to the landlord of the villa and to the servants. There was really no need for you to come at all, only the doctor and the English parson seemed to think it rather queer of me to be here alone." I used the smelling-salts myself! Imagine my emotion! I expected to find a hobbledehoy of a girl in hysterics, everything topsy-turvy and all sorts of horrid things to do; instead of which I found everything arranged perfectly well and the hobbledehoy rather disposed to manage me, if I let her. At luncheon she looked at my travelling-dress. "I suppose you left Florence in rather a hurry," she remarked. "If you want to get anything black you'd better go to my dressmaker. She's not bad. I must go there this afternoon myself to try some things on."'

Miss Ley stopped and looked at the doctor to see the effect of her words. He said nothing.

'And the impression I gained then,' she added, 'has only been strengthened since. You'll be a very clever man if you prevent Bertha from doing a thing upon which she has set her mind.'

'D'you mean to tell me that you're going to sanction this marriage?' asked the doctor.

Miss Ley shrugged her shoulders: 'My dear Dr Ramsay, I tell you it won't make the least difference whether we either of us bless or curse. And he seems an average sort of young man. Let us be thankful that she's done no worse; he's not uneducated.'

'No, he's not that. He spent ten years at Regis School, Tercanbury; so he ought to know something.'

'What exactly was his father?'

'His father was the same as himself—a gentleman-farmer. He'd been educated at Regis School as his son was. He knew most of the gentry, but he wasn't quite one of them; he knew all the farmers and he wasn't quite one of them either. And that's what they've been for generations, neither flesh, fowl, nor good red-herring.'

'It's those people that the newspapers tell us are the backbone of the country, Dr Ramsay.'

'Let 'em remain in their proper place then, in the back,' said the doctor. 'You can do as you please, Miss Ley; I'm going to put a stop to this nonsense. After all, Mr Ley made me the girl's guardian, and though she is twenty-one I think it's my duty to see that she doesn't fall into the hands of the first penniless scamp who asks her to marry him.'

'You can do as you please,' retorted Miss Ley, who was somewhat bored with the good man. 'You'll do no good with Bertha.'

'I'm not going to Bertha, I'm going to Craddock direct, and I mean to give him a piece of my mind.'

Miss Ley shrugged her shoulders. Dr Ramsay evidently did not see who was the active party in the matter, and she did not feel it her duty to inform him. The doctor took his leave, and in a few minutes Bertha joined Miss Ley. The latter obviously intended to make no efforts to disturb the course of true love.

'You'll have to be thinking of ordering your trousseau, my dear,' she said with a dry smile.

'We're going to be married quite privately,' answered Bertha. 'We neither of us want to make a fuss.'

'I think you're very wise. Most people when they get married fancy they're doing a very original thing. It never occurs to them that quite a number of persons have committed matrimony since Adam and Eve.'

'I've asked Edward to come to luncheon tomorrow,' said Bertha.

CHAPTER V

NEXT day, after luncheon, Miss Ley retired to the drawing-room and unpacked the books that had just arrived from Mudie. She looked through them and read a page here and there to see what they were like, thinking meanwhile of the meal they had just finished. Edward Craddock had been rather nervous, sitting uncomfortably on his chair, and too officious perhaps in handing things to Miss Ley, salt and pepper and such like, as he saw she wanted them; he evidently wished to make himself amiable. At the same time he was subdued, and not gaily enthusiastic, as might be expected from a happy lover. Miss Ley could not help asking herself if he really loved her niece. Bertha was obviously without a doubt on the subject; she had been radiant, keeping her eyes all the while fixed upon the young man as if he were the most delightful and wonderful thing she had ever seen. Miss Ley was surprised at the girl's expansiveness, contrasting with her old reserve; she seemed now not to care a straw if all the world saw her emotions. She was not only happy to be in love, she was proud. Miss Ley laughed aloud at the doctor's idea that he could disturb the course of such passion. But if Miss Ley, well aware that the watering-pots of reason could not put out those raging fires, had no intention of hindering the match, neither had she a desire to witness the preliminaries thereof; and after luncheon, remarking that she felt tired and meant to lie down, she had gone into the drawing-room alone. It pleased her to think that she could at the same time suit the lovers' pleasure and her own convenience.

She chose the book from the bundle that seemed most promising and began to read. Presently the door was opened by a servant and Miss Glover was announced. A look of annoyance passed over Miss Ley's face, but it was immediately succeeded by one of mellifluous amiability.

'Oh, don't get up, dear Miss Ley,' said the visitor as her hostess slowly rose from the sofa upon which she had been so comfortably lying.

Miss Ley shook hands and began to talk. She said she was delighted to see Miss Glover, thinking meanwhile that this estimable person's sense of etiquette was very tiresome. The Glovers had dined at Court Leys during the previous week, and punctually seven days afterwards Miss Glover was paying a ceremonious call.

Miss Glover was a worthy person, but tedious; and that Miss Ley could not forgive. Better ten thousand times, in her opinion, was it to be Becky Sharp and a monster of wickedness than Amelia and a monster of stupidity.

Miss Glover was one of the best-natured and most charitable creatures upon the face of the earth, a miracle of abnegation and unselfishness; but a person to be amused by her could have been only an absolute lunatic.

'She's a dear kind thing,' said Miss Ley of her, 'and she does endless good in the parish; but she's really too dull, she's only fit for heaven.'

And the image passed through Miss Ley's mind, unsobered by advancing years, of Miss Glover, with her colourless hair hanging down her back, wings and a golden harp, singing hymns in a squeaky voice, morning, noon and night. Indeed, the general conception of paradisaical costume suited Miss Glover very ill. She was a woman of about eight and twenty, but might have been any age between one score and two; you felt that she had always been the same and that years would have no power over her strength of mind. She had no figure, and her clothes were so stiff and unyielding as to give an impression of armour. She was always dressed in a tight black jacket of ribbed cloth that was evidently most durable, the plainest of skirts, and strong, really strong, boots. Her hat was suited to wear in all weathers, and she had made it herself. She never wore a veil, and her skin was dry and hard, drawn so tightly over the bones as to give her face extraordinary angularity; over her prominent cheek-bones was a red flush, the colour of which was not uniformly suffused, but with the capillaries standing out distinctly forming a network. Her nose and mouth were what is politely termed of a determined character, her pale blue eyes slightly protruded; ten years of East Anglian winds had blown all the softness out of her face, and their bitter fury seemed to have bleached even her hair. One could not tell if this was brown and had lost its richness, or gold from which the shimmer had vanished; the roots sprang from the cranium with a curious apartness, so that Miss Ley always thought how easy in her case it would be to number the hairs. But notwithstanding the hard, uncompromising exterior which suggested extreme determination, she was so bashful, so absurdly self-conscious as to blush at every opportunity, and in the presence of a stranger to go through utter misery from inability to think of a single word to say. At the same time she had the tenderest of hearts, sympathetic, compassionate; she overflowed with love and pity for her fellow-creatures. She was excessively sentimental.

'And how is your brother?' asked Miss Ley.

Mr Glover was the Vicar of Leanham, which was about a mile from Court Leys on the Tercanbury Road, and Miss Glover had kept house for him since his appointment to the living.

'Oh, he's very well. Of course he's rather worried about the dissenters. You know they're putting up a new chapel in Leanham? It's perfectly dreadful.'

'Mr Craddock mentioned the fact at luncheon.'

'Oh, was he lunching with you? I didn't know you knew him well enough for that.'

'I suppose he's here now,' said Miss Ley, 'he's not been in to say good-bye.'

Miss Glover looked at her with some want of intelligence. But it was not to be expected that Miss Ley would explain before making the affair a good deal more complicated.

'And how is Bertha?' asked Miss Glover, whose conversation was chiefly concerned with inquiries about common acquaintances.

'Oh, of course, she's in the seventh heaven of delight.'

'Oh!' said Miss Glover, not understanding at all what Miss Ley meant. She was somewhat afraid of the elder lady: even though her brother Charles said he feared she was worldly, Miss Glover could not fail to respect a woman who had lived in London and on the Continent, who had met Dean Farrer and seen Miss Marie Corelli. 'Of course,' she said, 'Bertha is young, and naturally high-spirited,'

'Well, I'm sure I hope she'll be happy.'

'You must be very anxious about her future, Miss Ley.'

Miss Glover found her hostess's observations cryptic, and feeling foolish blushed a fiery red.

'Not at all,' said Miss Ley. 'She's her own mistress and as able-bodied and reasonable-minded as most young women. But, of course, it's a great risk.'

'I'm very sorry, Miss Ley,' said the vicar's sister, in such distress as to give Miss Ley certain qualms of conscience, 'but I really don't understand. What is a great risk?'

'Matrimony, my dear.'

'Is Bertha—going—to get married? Oh, dear Miss Ley, let me congratulate you. How happy and proud you must be!'

'My dear Miss Glover, please keep calm. And if you want to congratulate anybody congratulate Bertha—not me.'

'But I'm so glad, Miss Ley. To think of dear Bertha getting married! Charles will be so pleased.'

'It's to Mr Edward Craddock,' drily said Miss Ley, interrupting these transports.

'Oh!' Miss Glover's jaw dropped and she changed colour; then recovering herself: 'You don't say so!'

'You seem surprised, dear Miss Glover,' said the elder lady with a thin smile.

'I am surprised. I thought they scarcely knew one another; and besides—' Miss Glover stopped with embarrassment.

'And besides what?' inquired Miss Ley sharply.

'Well, Miss Ley, of course Mr Craddock is a very good young man, and I like him; but I shouldn't have thought him a suitable match for Bertha.'

'It depends on what you mean by a suitable match,' answered Miss Ley.

'I was always hoping Bertha would marry young Mr Branderton of the Towers.'

'H'm!' said Miss Ley, who did not like the neighbouring squire's mother. 'I don't know what Mr Branderton has to recommend him beyond the possession of four or five generations of particularly stupid ancestors and two or three thousand acres that he can neither let nor sell.'

'Of course Mr Craddock is a very worthy young man,' added Miss Glover, who was afraid she had said too much. 'If you approve of the match no one else can complain.'

'I don't approve of the match, Miss Glover, but I'm not such a fool as to oppose it. Marriage is always a hopeless idiocy for a woman who has enough of her own to live upon.'

'It's an institution of the Church, Miss Ley,' replied Miss Glover.

'Is it?' retorted Miss Ley. 'I always thought it was an institution to provide work for the judges in the Divorce Court.'

To this Miss Glover very properly made no answer.

'Do you think they'll be happy together?' she asked finally.

'I think it very improbable,' said Miss Ley.

'Well, don't you think it's your duty—excuse my mentioning it, Miss Ley—to do something?'

'My dear Miss Glover, I don't think they'll be more unhappy than most married couples; and one's greatest duty in this world is to leave people alone.'

'There I cannot agree with you,' said Miss Glover, bridling. 'If duty was not more difficult than that, there would be no credit in doing it.'

'Ah, my dear, your idea of a happy life is always to do the disagreeable thing; mine is to gather the roses—with gloves on, so that the thorns should not prick me.'

'That's not the way to win the battle, Miss Ley. We must all fight.'

Miss Ley raised her eyebrows. She fancied it somewhat impertinent for a woman twenty years younger than herself to exhort her to lead a better life. But the picture of that poor, scraggy, ill-dressed creature fighting with a devil, cloven-footed, betailed and behorned, was as pitiful as it was comic; and with difficulty Miss Ley repressed an impulse to argue and startle a little her estimable friend. But at that moment Dr Ramsay came in. He shook hands with the two ladies.

'I thought I'd look in to see how Bertha was,' he said.

'Poor Mr Craddock has another adversary,' remarked Miss Ley. 'Miss Glover thinks I ought to take the affair—seriously.'

'I do indeed,' said Miss Glover.

'Ever since I was a young girl,' said Miss Ley, 'I've been trying not to take things seriously; and I'm afraid now I'm hopelessly frivolous.'

The contrast between this assertion and Miss Ley's prim manner was really funny; but Miss Glover saw only something quite incomprehensible.

'After all,' added Miss Ley, 'nine marriages out often are more or less unsatisfactory. You say young Branderton would have been more suitable; but really a string of ancestors is no particular assistance to matrimonial felicity, and otherwise I see no marked difference between him and Edward Craddock. Mr Branderton has been to Eton and Oxford, but he conceals the fact with very great success. Practically he's just as much a gentleman-farmer as Mr Craddock; but one family is working itself up and the other is working itself down. The Brandertons represent the past and the Craddocks the future; and though I detest reform and progress, so far as matrimony is concerned I myself prefer the man who founds a family to the man who ends it. But, good Heavens, you're making me sententious!'

Opposition was making Miss Ley almost a champion of Edward Craddock.

'Well,' said the doctor in his heavy way, 'I'm in favour of everyone sticking to his own class. Nowadays, whoever a man is he wants to be the next thing better; the labourer apes the tradesman, the tradesman apes the professional man.'

'And the professional man is worst of all, dear doctor,' said Miss Ley, 'for he apes the noble lord, who seldom affords a very admirable example. And the amusing thing is that each set thinks itself quite as good as the set above it and has a profound contempt for the set below it. In fact the only members of society who hold themselves in proper estimation are the servants. I always think that the domestics of gentlemen's houses in South Kensington are several degrees less odious than their masters.'

This was not a subject that Miss Glover and Dr Ramsay could discuss, and there was a momentary pause. 'What single point can you bring in favour of this marriage?' asked the doctor suddenly.

Miss Ley looked at him as if she were thinking, then with a dry smile: 'My dear doctor, Mr Craddock is so matter of fact—the moon will never arouse him to poetic ecstasies.'

'Miss Ley!' said the parson's sister in a tone of entreaty.

Miss Ley glanced from one to the other. 'Do you want my serious opinion?' she asked, rather more gravely than usual. 'The girl loves him, my dear doctor. Marriage, after all, is such a risk that only passion makes it worth while.'

Miss Glover looked up rather uneasily at the word.

'Yes, I know what you all think in England,' said Miss Ley, catching the glance and its meaning. 'You expect people to marry from every reason except the proper one—and that is the instinct of reproduction.'

'Miss Ley!' exclaimed Miss Glover, blushing.

'Oh, you're old enough to take a sensible view of the matter,' answered Miss Ley brutally. 'Bertha is merely the female attracted to the male, and that is the only decent foundation of marriage; the other way seems to me merely pornographic. And what does it matter if the man is not of the same station? The instinct has nothing to do with the walk in life. If I'd ever been in love I shouldn't have cared if it was a pot-boy, I'd have married him—if he asked me.'

'Well, upon my word!' said the doctor.

But Miss Ley was roused now, and interrupted him: 'The particular function of a woman is to propagate her species, and if she's wise she'll choose a strong and healthy man to be the father of her children. I have no patience with those women who marry a man because he's got brains. What is the good of a husband who can make abstruse mathematical calculations? A woman wants a man with strong arms and the digestion of an ox.'

'Miss Ley,' broke in Miss Glover, 'I'm not clever enough to argue with you, but I know you're wrong. I don't think I ought to listen to you; I'm sure Charles wouldn't like it.'

'My dear, you've been brought up like the majority of English girls, that is, like a fool.'

Poor Miss Glover blushed. 'At all events I've been brought up to regard marriage as a holy institution. We're here upon earth to mortify the flesh, not to indulge it. I hope I shall never be tempted to think of such matters in the way you've suggested. If ever I marry, I know that nothing will be further from me than carnal thoughts. I look upon marriage as a spiritual union in which it's my duty to love, honour and obey my husband, to assist and sustain him, to live with him such a life that when the end comes we may be prepared for it.'

'Fiddlesticks!' said Miss Ley.

'I should have thought you of all people,' said Dr Ramsay, 'would object to Bertha's marrying beneath her.'

'They can't be happy,' said Miss Glover.

'Why not? I used to know in Italy Lady Justitia Shawe, who married her footman. She made him take her name, and they drank like fishes. They lived for forty years in complete happiness, and when he drank himself to death, poor Lady Justitia was so grieved that her next attack of *delirium tremens* carried her off. It was most pathetic.'

'I can't think you look forward with pleasure to such a fate for your only niece, Miss Ley,' said Miss Glover, who took everything seriously.

'I have another niece, you know,' answered Miss Ley. 'My sister, who married Sir James Courte, has three children.'

But the doctor broke in: 'Well, I don't think you need trouble yourselves about the matter, for I have authority to announce to you that the marriage of Bertha and young Craddock is broken off.'

'What!' cried Miss Ley. 'I don't believe it.'

'You don't say so,' ejaculated Miss Glover at the same moment. 'Oh, I *am* relieved!'

Dr Ramsay rubbed his hands, beaming with delight. 'I knew I should stop it,' he said. 'What do you think now, Miss Ley?'

He was evidently rejoicing over her discomfiture. It made her cross.

'How can I think anything till you explain yourself?' she asked.

'He came to see me last night—you remember he asked for an interview of his own accord—and I put the case before him. I talked to him, I told him that the marriage was impossible, and I said the Leanham and Blackstable people would call him a fortune-hunter. I appealed to him for Bertha's sake. He's an honest, straightforward fellow. I always said he was. I made him see he wasn't doing the straight thing, and at last he promised to break it off.'

'He won't keep a promise of that sort,' said Miss Ley.

'Oh, won't he!' cried the doctor. 'I've known him all his life, and he'd rather die than break his word.'

'Poor fellow,' said Miss Glover, 'it must have pained him terribly.'

'He bore it like a man.'

Miss Ley pursed her lips till they practically disappeared. 'And when is he supposed to carry out your ridiculous suggestion, Dr Ramsay?' she asked.

'He told me he was lunching here today, and would take the opportunity to ask Bertha for his release.'

'The man's a fool!' muttered Miss Ley to herself, but quite audibly.

'I think it's very noble of him,' said Miss Glover, 'and I shall make a point of telling him so.'

'I wasn't thinking of Mr Craddock,' snapped Miss Ley, 'but of Dr Ramsay.'

Miss Glover looked at the worthy man to see how he took the rudeness; but at that moment the door opened and Bertha walked in. Miss Ley caught her mood at a glance. Bertha was evidently not at all distressed, there was no sign of tears, but her cheeks showed more colour than usual and her lips were firmly compressed; Miss Ley concluded that her niece was in a very pretty passion. She drove away the appearance of anger, and her face was full of smiles, however, as she greeted her visitors.

'Miss Glover, how kind of you to come! How d'you do, Dr Ramsay? By the way, I think I must ask you not to interfere in future with my private concerns.'

'Dearest,' broke in Miss Glover, 'it's an for the best.'

Bertha turned to her, and the flush on her face deepened. 'Ah, I see you've been discussing the matter. How good of you! Edward has been asking me to release him.'

Dr Ramsay nodded with satisfaction.

'But I refused!'

Dr Ramsay sprang up, and Mitt Glover, lifting her hands, cried: 'Oh, dear! Oh, dear!'

This was one of the rare occasions in her life upon which Miss Ley was known to laugh outright. Bertha now was simply beaming with happiness. 'He pretended that he wanted to break the engagement, but I utterly declined.'

'You mean to say you wouldn't let him go when he asked you?' said the doctor.

'Did you think I was going to let my happiness be destroyed by you?' she asked contemptuously. 'I found out that you had been meddling, Dr Ramsay. Poor boy, he thought his honour required him not to take advantage of my inexperience. I told him, what I've told him a thousand times, that I love him and that I can't live without him. Oh, I think you ought to be ashamed of yourself, Dr Ramsay. What d'you mean by coming between me and Edward?'

Bertha said the last words passionately. She was breathing hard. Dr Ramsay was taken aback, and Miss Glover, thinking such a manner of speech unladylike, looked down. Miss Ley's sharp eyes played from one to the other.

'Do you think he really loves you?' said Miss Glover at last. 'It seems to me that if he had, he would not have been so ready to give you up.'

Miss Ley smiled; it was certainly curious that a creature of quite angelic goodness should make so machiavellian a suggestion.

'He offered to give me up because he loved me,' said Bertha proudly. 'I adore him ten thousand times more for the suggestion.'

'I have no patience with you,' cried the doctor, unable to contain himself. 'He's marrying you for your money.'

Bertha gave a little laugh. She was standing by the fire, and turned to the glass. She looked at her hands, resting on the edge of the chimney-piece, small and exquisitely modelled, the fingers tapering, the nails of the softest pink; they were the gentlest hands in the world, made for caresses; and, conscious of their beauty, she wore no rings. With them Bertha was well satisfied. Then, raising her glance, she saw herself in the mirror. For a while she gazed into her dark eyes, flashing sometimes and at others conveying the burning messages of love. She looked at her ears, small and pink like a shell; they made one feel that no materials were so grateful to the artist's hands as the materials that make up the body of man. Her hair was dark too, so abundant that she scarcely knew how to wear it, curling, and one wanted to pass one's hands through it, imagining that its touch must be delightful. She put her fingers to one side, to arrange a stray lock; they might say what they liked, she thought, but her hair was good. Bertha wondered why she was so dark; her olive skin suggested, indeed, the South with its burning passion; she had the complexion of the women of Umbria, clear and soft beyond description: a painter once had said that her skin had in it all the colours of the setting sun, of the setting sun at its borders, where the splendour mingles with the sky; it had a hundred mellow tints—cream and ivory, the palest yellow of the heart of roses and the faintest, the very faintest green, all flushed with radiant light. She looked at her full red lips, almost passionately sensual; it made the heart beat to imagine the kisses of that mouth. Bertha smiled at herself, and saw the even, glistening teeth. The scrutiny had made her blush, and the colour rendered still more exquisite the pallid, marvellous complexion. She turned slowly and faced the three persons looking at her.

'Do you think it impossible for a man to love me for myself? You are not flattering, dear doctor.'

Miss Ley thought Bertha certainly very bold thus to challenge the criticism of two women, both unmarried; but she silenced it. Miss Ley's eyes went from the statuesque neck to the arms as finely formed, and to the shapely body.

'You're looking your best, my dear,' she said with a smile.

The doctor uttered an expression of annoyance: 'Can you do nothing to hinder this madness, Miss Ley?'

'My dear Dr Ramsay, I have trouble enough in arranging my own life; do not ask me to interfere with other people's.'

CHAPTER VI

BERTHA gave herself over completely to the enjoyment of her love. Her sanguine temperament never allowed her to do anything half-heartedly, and she took no care now to conceal her feelings; love was a great sea into which she boldly plunged, uncaring whether she would swim or sink.

'I am such a fool,' she told Craddock. 'I can't realize that anyone has loved before. I feel that the world is only now beginning.'

She hated any separation from him. In the morning she existed for nothing but her lover's visit at luncheon time and the walk back with him to his farm; then the afternoon seemed endless, and she counted the hours that must pass before she saw him again. But what bliss it was when, after his work was over, he arrived and they sat side by side near the fire, talking! Bertha would have no other light than the fitful flaming of the coals: but for the little space where they sat the room was dark, and the redness of the fire threw on Edward's face a glow and weird shadows. She loved to look at him, at his clean-cut features and his curly hair, into his grey eyes. Then her passion knew no restraint.

'Shut your eyes,' she whispered, and kissed the closed lids; she passed her lips slowly over his lips, and the soft contact made her shudder and laugh. She buried her face in his clothes inhaling those masterful scents of the countryside that had always fascinated her. 'What have you been doing today, my dearest?'

'Oh, there's nothing much doing on the farm just now. We've just been ploughing and root-carting.'

It enchanted her to receive information on agricultural subjects, and she could have listened to him for hours. Every word that Edward spoke was charming and original. Bertha never took her eyes off him, she loved to hear him speak but often scarcely listened to what he said, merely watching the play of his expression. It puzzled him sometimes to catch her smile of intense happiness when he was discussing the bush-drainage of a field. However, she really took a deep interest in all his stock, and never failed to inquire after a bullock that was indisposed; it pleased her to think of the strong man among his beasts, and the thought gave a tautness to her own muscles. She determined to learn riding and tennis and golf, so that she might accompany him in all his amusements. Her own accomplishments seemed unnecessary and even humiliating. Looking at Edward Craddock she realized that Man was indeed the lord of creation. She saw him striding over his fields with long steps, ordering his labourers here and there, able to direct their operations, fearless, brave and free. It was astonishing how many excellent traits she derived from the examination of his profile.

He talked of the men he employed, and she could Imagine no felicity greater than to have such a master.

'I should like to be a milkmaid on your farm,' she said.

'I don't keep milkmaids,' he replied. 'I have a milkman, it's more useful.'

'You dear old thing,' she cried. 'How matter-of-fact you are!'

She caught hold of his hands and looked at them.

'I'm rather frightened of you sometimes,' she said, laughing. 'You're so strong. I feel so utterly weak and helpless beside you.'

'Are you afraid I shall beat you?' he asked, with a smile.

She looked up at him and then down at the strong hands she was still holding.

'I don't think I should mind if you did,' she said. 'I think I should only love you more.'

He burst out laughing and kissed her.

'I'm not joking,' she said. 'I understand now those women who love beasts of men. It's a commonplace that some wives will stand anything from their husbands; it seems they love them all the more because they're brutal. I think I'm like that. But I've never seen you in a passion, Eddie. What are you like when you're angry?'

'I never am angry,' he answered.

'Miss Glover told me that you had the best temper in the world. I'm terrified of all these perfections.'

'Don't expect too much from me, Bertha. I'm not a model man, you know.'

'I'm pleased,' she answered. 'I don't want perfection. Of course you've got faults, though I can't see them yet. But when I do, I know I shall only love you better. When a woman loves an ugly man, they say his ugliness only makes him more attractive, and I shall love your faults as I love everything that is yours.'

They sat for a while without speaking, and the silence was even more entrancing than the speech. Bertha wished she could remain thus for ever, resting in his arms; she forgot that soon Craddock would develop a healthy appetite and demolish a substantial dinner.

'Let me look at your hands,' she said.

She loved them too. They were large and roughly made, hard with work and exposure, ten times nicer, she thought, than the soft hands of the townsman. She felt them firm and intensely masculine; they reminded her of a hand in an Italian museum, sculptured in porphyry, but for some reason left unfinished; the lack of detail gave the same impression of massive strength. His hands too might have been those of a demi-god or of a hero. She stretched out the long, strong fingers. Craddock looked at her with some wonder, mingled with amusement; he knew her really very little. She caught his glance, and with a smile bent down to kiss the upturned palms. She wanted to abase herself before the strong man, to be low and humble before him. She would have been his handmaiden, and nothing could have satisfied her so much as to perform for him menial services. She knew not how to show the immensity of her passion.

It pleased Bertha to walk into Blackstable with her lover and catch the people's glances, knowing how intensely the marriage interested them. What did she care if they were surprised at her choosing Edward Craddock, whom they had known all his life? She was proud of him, proud to be his wife.

One day, when it was very warm for the time of the year, she was resting on a stile, while Craddock stood by her side. They did not speak, but looked at one another in ecstatic happiness.

'Look,' said Craddock suddenly, 'there's Arthur Branderton.' He glanced up at Bertha, then from side to side uneasily, as if he wished to avoid a meeting.

'He's been away, hasn't he?' asked Bertha. 'I wanted to meet him.' She was quite willing that all the world should see them. 'Good afternoon, Arthur,' she called out as the youth approached.

'Oh, is it you, Bertha? Hulloa, Craddock.'

He looked at Edward, wondering what he did there with Miss Ley.

'We've just been walking into Leanham and I was tired.'

'Oh!'

Young Branderton thought it queer that Bertha should take walks with Craddock.

Bertha burst out laughing. 'Oh, he doesn't know, Edward. He's the only person in the county who hasn't heard the news.'

'What news?' asked Branderton. 'I've been in Yorkshire for the last week at my brother-in-law's.'

'Edward and I are going to be married.'

'Are you, by Jove?'

He looked at Craddock, and then awkwardly offered his congratulations. They could not help seeing his astonishment, and Craddock flushed, knowing it was due to the fact that Bertha had consented to marry a penniless beggar like himself and a man of no family.

'I hope you'll invite me to the wedding,' said the young man to cover his confusion.

'Oh, it's going to be very quiet. There will only be ourselves, Dr Ramsay, my aunt and Edward's best man.'

'Then mayn't I come?' asked Branderton.

Bertha looked quickly at Edward. It had caused her some uneasiness to think that he might be supported by a person of no great consequence in the place. After all she was Miss Ley; and she had already discovered that some of her lover's friends were not too desirable. Chance offered her means of surmounting the difficulty.

'I'm afraid it's impossible,' she said, 'unless you can get Edward to offer you the important post of best man.'

She succeeded in making the two men very uncomfortable. Branderton had no great wish to perform that office for Edward. 'Of course, Craddock was a very good fellow and a fine sportsman, but not the sort of chap you'd expect a girl like Bertha Ley to marry.' And Edward, understanding the young man's feelings, was silent. But Branderton had some knowledge of polite society, and broke the momentary silence.

'Who is going to be your best man, Craddock?' he asked. He could do nothing else.

'I don't know; I haven't thought of it.'

But Branderton, catching Bertha's eye, suddenly realized her desire and the reason of it.

'Won't you have me?' he said quickly. 'I daresay you'll find me intelligent enough to learn the duties.'

'I should like it very much,' answered Craddock. 'It's very good of you.'

Branderton looked at Bertha, and she smiled her thanks; he saw she was pleased.

'Where are you going for your honeymoon?' he asked now, to make conversation.

'I don't know,' answered Craddock. 'We've hardly had time to think of it yet.'

'You certainly are very vague in all your plans.'

He shook hands with them, receiving from Bertha a grateful pressure, and went off.

'Have you really not thought of our honeymoon, foolish boy?' asked Bertha.

'No.'

'Well, I have. I've made up my mind and settled it all. We're going to Italy, and I mean to show you Florence and Pisa and Sienna. It'll be simply heavenly. We won't go to Venice, because it's too sentimental; self-respecting people can't make love in gondolas at the end of the nineteenth century. Oh, I long to be with you in the South, beneath the blue sky and the countless stars of night.'

'I've never been abroad before,' he said, without much enthusiasm.

But her fire was quite enough for two: 'I know. I shall have the pleasure of unfolding it all to you. I shall enjoy it more than I ever have before; it'll all be so new to you. And we can stay six months if we like.'

'Oh, I couldn't possibly,' he cried. 'Think of the farm.'

'Oh, bother the farm. It's our honeymoon, *sposo mio.*'

'I don't think I could possibly stay away more than a fortnight.'

'What nonsense! We can't go to Italy for a fortnight. The farm can get on without you.'

'And in January and February, too, when all the lambing is coming on.'

He did not want to distress Bertha, but really half his lambs would die if he were not there to superintend their entrance into the world.

'But you must go,' said Bertha. 'I've set my heart upon it.'

He looked down for a while, looking rather unhappy.

'Wouldn't a month do?' he asked. 'I'll do anything you really want, Bertha.'

But his obvious dislike to the suggestion cut Bertha's heart. She was only inclined to be stubborn when she saw he might resist her; and his first word of surrender made her veer round penitently.

'What a selfish beast I am!' she said. 'I don't want to make you miserable, Eddie. I thought it would please you to go abroad, and I'd planned it all so well. But we won't go; I hate Italy. Let's just go up to town for a fortnight like two country bumpkins.'

'Oh, but you won't like that,' he said.

'Of course I shall. I like everything you like. D'you think I care where we go as long as I'm with you? You're not angry with me, darling, are you?'

Mr Craddock was good enough to intimate that he was not.

Miss Ley, much against her will, had been driven by Miss Glover into working for some charitable institution, and was knitting babies' socks (as the smallest garments she could make) when Bertha told her of the altered plans. She dropped a stitch. She was too wise to say anything, but she wondered if the world was coming to an end; Bertha's schemes were shattered like brittle glass and she really seemed delighted; a month ago opposition would have made Bertha traverse seas and scale precipices rather than abandon a notion that she had got into her head. Verily love is a prestidigitator who can change the lion into the lamb as easily as a handkerchief into a flower-pot! Miss Ley began to admire Edward Craddock.

He, on his way home after leaving Bertha, was met by the Vicar of Leanham. Mr Glover was a tall man, angular, fair, thin and red-cheeked, a somewhat feminine edition of his sister, but smelling in the most remarkable fashion of antiseptics; Miss Ley vowed he peppered his clothes with iodoform and bathed daily in carbolic acid. He was strenuous and charitable, he hated a dissenter and was over forty.

'Ah, Craddock, I wanted to see you.'

'Not about the banns, vicar, is it? We're going to be married by special licence.'

Like many countrymen, Edward saw something funny in the clergy—one should not grudge it them, for it is the only jest in their lives—and he was given to treating the parson with more humour than he used in the other affairs of this world. The vicar laughed; it is one of the best traits of the country clergy that they are willing to be amused with their parishioners' jocosity.

'The marriage is all settled then? You're a very lucky young man.'

Craddock put his arm through Mr Glover's with the unconscious friendliness that had gained him a hundred friends.

'Yes, I am lucky,' he said. 'I know you people think it rather queer that Bertha and I should get married, but—we're very much attached to one another, and I mean to do my best by her. You know I've never racketted about, vicar, don't you?'

'Yes, my boy,' said the vicar, touched by Edward's confidence. 'Everyone knows you're steady enough.'

'Of course, she could have found men of much better social position than mine, but I'll try and make her happy. And I've got nothing to hide from her as some men have; I go to her almost as straight as she comes to me.'

'That is a very fortunate thing to be able to say,' replied the vicar.

'I have never loved another woman in my life, and as for the rest—well, of course, I'm young and I've been up to town sometimes; but I always hated and loathed it. And the country and the hard work keep one pretty clear of anything nasty.'

'I'm very glad to hear you say that,' answered Mr Glover, 'I hope you'll be happy, and I think you will.'

The vicar felt a slight pricking of conscience, for at first his sister and himself had called the match a *mésalliance* (they pronounced the word vilely), and not till they learned it was inevitable did they begin to see that their attitude was a little wanting in charity. The two men shook hands when they parted.

'I hope you don't mind me spitting out these things to you, vicar. I suppose it's your business in a sort of way. I wanted to tell Miss Ley something of the kind; but somehow or other I can never get an opportunity.'

CHAPTER VII

EXACTLY one month after the attainment of her majority, as Bertha had announced, the marriage took place and the young couple started off to spend their honeymoon in London. Bertha, knowing she would not read, took with her notwithstanding a book, to wit the *Meditations of Marcus Aurelius,* and Edward, thinking that railway journeys were always tedious, bought for the occasion *The Mystery of the Six-fingered Woman,* the title of which attracted him. He was determined not to be bored, for not content with his novel he purchased at the station a *Sporting Times.*

'Oh,' said Bertha when the train had started, heaving a great sigh of relief, 'I'm so glad to be alone with you at last. Now we shan't have anybody to worry us and no one can separate us, and we shall be together for the rest of our lives.'

Craddock put down the newspaper which, from force of habit, he had opened after settling himself down in his seat.

'I'm glad to have the ceremony over, too.'

'D'you know,' she said, 'I was terrified on the way to church; it occurred to me that you might not be there—that you might have changed your mind and fled.'

He laughed. 'Why on earth should I change my mind?'

'Oh, I can't sit solemnly opposite you as if we'd been married a century. Make room for me, boy.'

She came over to his side and nestled close to him.

'Tell me you love me,' she whispered.

'I love you very much.'

He bent down and kissed her, then putting his arm round her waist drew her closer to him. He was a little nervous, he would not really have been very sorry if some officious person had disregarded the *engaged* on the carriage and entered. He felt scarcely at home with his wife, and was still a little bewildered by his change of fortune; there was, indeed, a vast difference between Court Leys and Bewlie's Farm.

'I'm so happy,' said Bertha. 'Sometimes I'm afraid. D'you think it can last, d'you think we shall always be as happy? I've got everything I want in the world, I'm absolutely and completely content.' She was silent for a minute, caressing his hands. 'You will always love me, Eddie, won't you—even when I'm old and horrible?'

'I'm not the sort of chap to alter,' he said.

'Oh, you don't know how I adore you,' she cried, passionately. '*My* love will never alter, it is too strong. To the end of my days I shall always love you with all my heart. I wish I could tell you what I feel.'

Of late the English language had seemed quite incompetent for the expression of her manifold emotions.

They went to a far more expensive hotel than they could afford; Craddock had prudently suggested something less extravagant, but Bertha would not hear of it; as Miss Ley she had been unused to the second-rate, and she was too proud of her new name to take it to any but the best hotel in London.

The more Bertha saw of her husband's mind the more it delighted her. She loved the simplicity and the naturalness of the man; she cast off like a tattered silken cloak the sentiments with which for years she had lived, and robed herself in the sturdy homespun that so well suited her lord and master. It was charming to see his naïve enjoyment of everything; to him all was fresh and novel; he would explode with laughter at the comic papers and in the dailies continually find observations that struck him as extremely original. He was the unspoiled child of nature, his mind free from the million perversities of civilization. To know him was, in Bertha's opinion, an education in all the goodness and purity, the strength and virtue of the Englishman. They went often to the theatre, and it pleased Bertha to watch her husband's simple enjoyment; the pathetic passages of melodrama that made Bertha's lips curl with amused contempt moved him to facile tears, and in the darkness he held her hand to comfort her, imagining that she experienced the same emotions as himself. Ah, she wished she could; she hated the education in foreign countries that in the study of pictures and palaces and strange peoples had released her mind from its prison of darkness, yet had destroyed half her illusions; now she would far rather have retained the plain and unadorned illiteracy, the ingenuous ignorance of the typical and creamy English girl. What is the use of knowledge? Blessed are the poor in spirit; all that a woman really wants is purity and goodness and perhaps a certain acquaintance with plain cooking.

'Isn't it splendid?' he said, turning to his wife.

'You dear thing!' she whispered.

It touched her to see how deeply he felt it all. She loved him ten times more because his emotions were easily aroused; ah, yes, she abhorred the cold cynicism of the worldly-wise who sneer at the burning tears of the simple-minded.

But the lovers, the injured heroine and the wrongly suspected hero, had bidden one another a heart-rending good-bye, and the curtain descended to rapturous applause. Edward cleared his throat and blew his nose. The curtain rose on the next act, and in his eagerness to see what was going to happen Edward immediately ceased to listen to what Bertha was in the middle of saying, and gave himself over to the play. The feelings of the audience having been sufficiently harrowed, the comic relief was turned on; the funny man made jokes about various articles of clothing, tumbled over tables and chairs, and it charmed Bertha again to hear her husband's peals of unrestrained laughter; he put his head back and with his hands to his sides simply roared.

'He has a charming character,' she thought.

Craddock had the strictest notions of morality, and absolutely refused to take his wife to a music-hall; Bertha had seen abroad many sights the like of which Edward did not dream, but she respected his innocence. It pleased her to see the firmness with which he upheld his principles and it amused her to be treated like a little girl. They went to all the theatres; Edward on his rare visits to London had done his sight-seeing economically, and the purchase of stalls, the getting into evening clothes, were new sensations that caused him great pleasure. Bertha liked to see her husband in evening dress; the black suited his florid style, and the white shirt with a high collar threw up his sunburned, weather-beaten face. He looked strong above all things, and manly; and he was her husband, never to be parted from her except by death. She adored him.

Craddock's interest in the stage was unflagging, he always wanted to know what was going to happen and he was able to follow with the closest attention, even the incomprehensible plot of a musical comedy. Nothing bored him. Even the most ingenuous find a little cloying the humours and the harmonies of a Gaiety burlesque; they are like toffee and butterscotch, delicacies for which we cannot understand our youthful craving. Bertha had learnt something of music in lands where it is cultivated as a pleasure rather than as a duty' and the popular melodies with obvious refrains sent cold shivers down her back. But they stirred Craddock to the depths of his soul; he beat time to the swinging, vulgar tunes, and his face was transfigured when the band played a patriotic march with a great braying of brass and beating of drums. He whistled and hummed it for days afterwards.

'I love music,' he told Bertha in the interval. 'Don't you?'

With a tender smile she confessed she did, and for fear of hurting his feelings did not suggest that the music in question made her almost vomit. What did it matter if his taste in that respect were not beyond reproach? After all there was something to be said for the honest, homely melodies that touched the people's heart.

'When we get home,' said Craddock, 'I want you to play to me, 'I'm so fond of it.'

'I shall love to,' she murmured.

She thought of the long winter evenings which they would spend at the piano, her husband by her side to turn the leaves, while to his astonished ears she unfolded the manifold riches of the great composers. She was convinced that his taste was really excellent.

'I have lots of music that my mother used to play,' he said. 'By Jove, I shall like to hear it again—some of those old tunes I can never hear often enough—"The Last Rose of Summer" and "Home, Sweet Home" and a lot more like that.'

'By Jove, that show was good,' said Craddock when they were having supper. 'I should like to see it again before we go back.'

'We'll do whatever you like, my dear.'

'I think an evening like that does you good. It bucks me up; doesn't it you?'

'It does me good to see you amused,' replied Bertha diplomatically.

The performance had appeared to her vulgar, but in the face of her husband's enthusiasm she could only accuse herself of a ridiculous squeamishness. Why should she set herself up as a judge of these things? Was it not rather vulgar of her to find vulgarity in what gave such pleasure to the unsophisticated? She was like the *nouveau riche* who is distressed at the universal lack of gentility. But she was tired of analysis and subtlety and all the accessories of a decadent civilization.

'For goodness' sake,' she thought, 'let us be simple and easily amused.'

She remembered the four young ladies who had appeared in skin tights and nothing else worth mentioning and danced a singularly ungraceful jig, which the audience in its delight had insisted on having twice repeated.

There is some difficulty in knowing how to spend one's time in London when one has no business to do and no friends to visit. Bertha would have been content to sit all day with Edward in their private sitting-room, contemplating him and her felicity. But Craddock had all the fine energy of the Anglo-Saxon race, that desire to be always doing something or other which has made the English athletes and missionaries and members of Parliament. After his first mouthful of breakfast, he invariably asked: 'What shall we do today?' And Bertha ransacked her brain and a Baedeker to find sights to visit, for to treat London as a foreign town and systematically explore it was their only resource. They went to the Tower of London and gaped at the crowns and sceptres, at the insignia of the various orders; to Westminster Abbey and, joining the party of Americans and country-folk who were being driven hither and thither by a black-robed verger, they visited the tombs of the kings and saw everything that it was their duty to see. Bertha developed a fine enthusiasm for the antiquities of London; she quite enjoyed the sensation of bovine ignorance with which the Cook's tourist surrenders himself into the hands of a custodian, looking as he is told and swallowing with open mouth the most unreliable information. Feeling herself more stupid, Bertha was conscious of a closer connexion with her fellow-men. Edward did not like all things in an equal degree; pictures bored him (they were the only things that really did), and their visit to the National Gallery was not a success. Neither did the British Museum meet with his approval; for one thing, he had great difficulty in directing Bertha's attention so that her eyes should not wander to various naked statues that are exhibited there with no regard at all for the susceptibilities of modest persons. Once she stopped in front of a group that some shields and swords quite inadequately clothed, and remarked on their beauty. Edward looked about uneasily to see whether anyone noticed them, and agreeing with her briefly that they were fine figures, moved her rapidly away to some less questionable object.

'I can't stand all this rot,' he said when they stood opposite the three goddesses of the Parthenon. 'I wouldn't give twopence to come to this place again.'

Bertha felt a little ashamed that she had a sneaking admiration for the statues in question.

'Now tell me,' he said, 'where is the beauty of those creatures without any heads?'

Bertha could not tell him, and he was triumphant. He was a dear, and she loved him with all her heart.

The Natural History Museum, on the other hand, aroused Craddock to enthusiasm. Here he was quite at home, no improprieties were there from which he must keep his wife, and animals were the sort of things that any man could understand. But they brought back to him strongly the country of East Kent and the life which it pleased him most to lead. London was all very well, but he did not feel at home, and it was beginning to pall upon him. Bertha also began talking of home and Court Leys; she had always lived more in the future than in the present, and even in this, the time of her greatest happiness, looked forward to the days to come at Leanham when complete bliss would indeed be hers.

She was contented enough now; it was only the eighth day of her married life, but she ardently wished to settle down and satisfy all her anticipations. They talked of the alterations they must make in the house. Craddock had already plans for putting the park in order, for taking over the Home Farm and working it himself.

'I wish we were home,' said Bertha. 'I'm sick of London.'

'I don't think I should mind much if we'd got to the end of our fortnight,' he replied.

Craddock had arranged with himself to stay in town fourteen days, and he could not change his mind. It made him uncomfortable to alter his plans and think out something new; he prided himself on always doing the thing he had determined.

But a letter came from Miss Ley announcing that she had packed her trunks and was starting for the Continent.

'Oughtn't we to ask her to stay on?' said Craddock. 'It seems rather rough on her to turn her out so quickly.'

'You don't want to have her to live with us, do you?' asked Bertha in dismay.

'No, rather not; but I don't see why you should pack her off like a servant with a month's notice.'

'Oh, I'll ask her to stay,' said Bertha anxious to obey her husband's smallest wish; and obedience was easy, for she knew that Miss Ley would never dream of accepting the offer.

Bertha wished to see no one just now, least of all her aunt, feeling confusedly that her happiness would be diminished by the intrusion of an actor in her old life; her emotions also were too intense for concealment, and she would have been ashamed to display them to Miss Ley's critical sense. Bertha saw only discomfort in meeting the elder lady, with her calm irony and polite contempt for the things which on her husband's account Bertha now sincerely cherished.

But Miss Ley's reply showed perhaps that she guessed her niece's thoughts better than Bertha had given her credit for.

My Dearest Bertha,

I am much obliged to your husband for his politeness in asking me to stay at Court Leys; but I flatter myself that you have too high an opinion of me to think me capable of accepting. Newly married people offer much matter for ridicule (which they say, is the noblest characteristic of man, being the only one that distinguishes him from the brutes), but since I am a peculiarly self-denying creature, I do not propose to avail myself of the opportunity you offer. Perhaps in a year you will have begun to see one another's imperfections, and then, though less amusing, you will be more interesting. No, I am going to Italy—to hurl myself once more into that sea of pensions and second-rate hotels wherein it is the fate of single women with moderate incomes to spend their lives; and I am taking with me a Baedeker so that if ever I am inclined to think myself less foolish than the average man I may look upon its red cover and remember that I am but human. By the way, I hope you do not show your correspondence to your husband, least of all mine; a man can never understand a woman's epistolary communications, for he reads them with his own simple alphabet of twenty-six letters, whereas he requires one of at least fifty-two; and even that is little. It is a bad system to allow a husband to read one's letters, and my observation of married couples has led me to the belief that there is no surer way to the divorce court; in fact it is madness for a happy pair to pretend to have no secrets from one another; it leads them into so much deception. If, however, as I suspect, you think it is your duty to show Edward this note of mine, he will perhaps find it not unuseful for the explanation of my character—on the study of which I myself have spent many entertaining years.

I give you no address, so that you may not be in want of an excuse to leave this missive unanswered.

Your affectionate aunt,
Mary Ley.

Bertha, a trifle impatiently, tossed the letter to Edward.

'What does she mean?' he asked when he had read it.

Bertha shrugged her shoulders: 'She believes in nothing but the stupidity of other people. Poor woman, she has never been in love. But we won't have any secrets from one another, Eddie. I know that you will never hide anything from me, and I—What can I do that is not at your telling?'

'It's a funny letter,' he replied, looking at it again.

'But we're free now, darling,' she said. 'The house is ready for us. Shall we go at once?'

'But we haven't been here a fortnight yet,' he objected.

'What does it matter? We're both sick of London; let us go home and start our life. We're going to lead it for the rest of our lives, so we'd better begin it quickly. Honeymoons are stupid things.'

'Well, I don't mind. By Jove, fancy if we'd gone to Italy for six weeks.'

'Oh, I didn't know what a honeymoon was like. I think I imagined something quite different.'

'You see I was right, wasn't I?'

'Of course you were right,' she answered, flinging her arms round his neck. 'You're always right, my darling. Ah, you can't think how I love you.'

CHAPTER VIII

THE Kentish coast is bleak and grey between Leanham and Blackstable; through the long winter months the winds of the North Sea sweep down upon it, bowing the trees before them, and from the murky waters perpetually arise the clouds, and roll up in heavy banks. It is a country that offers those who live there what they give: sometimes the sombre colours and the silent sea express only restfulness and peace, sometimes the chill breezes send the blood racing through the veins, and red cheeks and swinging stride tell the joy of life; but also the solitude can answer the deepest melancholy, or the cheerless sky a misery that is more terrible than death. One's mood seems always reproduced in the surrounding scenes, and in them may be found, as it were, a synthesis of one's emotions. Bertha stood upon the high road that ran past Court Leys, and from the height looked down upon the lands that were hers. Close at hand the only habitations were a pair of humble cottages, from which time and rough weather had almost effaced the obtrusiveness of human handiwork. They stood away from the road, among fruit trees, a part of nature, and not a blot upon it, as Court Leys had never ceased to be. All around were fields, great stretches of ploughed earth and meadows of coarse herbage. The trees were few, and stood out here and there in the distance, bent before the wind. Beyond was Blackstable, straggling grey houses with a border of new villas built for the Londoners who came in summer; it was a fishing town, and the sea was dotted with smacks.

Bertha looked at the scene with sensations that she had never known. The heavy clouds hung above her, shutting out the whole world, and she felt an invisible barrier between herself and all other things. This was the land of her birth, out of which she, and her fathers before her, had arisen. They had had their day, and one by one returned whence they came and become again united with the earth. She had withdrawn from the pomps and vanities of life to live as her ancestors had lived, ploughing the land, sowing and reaping; but her children, the sons of the future, would belong to a new stock, stronger and fairer than the old. The Leys had gone down into the darkness of death, and her children would bear another name. All these things she gathered out of the brown fields and the grey sea mist. She was a little tired, and the physical sensation caused a mental fatigue, so that she felt in herself suddenly the weariness of a family that had lived too long; she knew she was right to choose new blood to mix with the old blood of the Leys. It needed the freshness and youth, the massive strength of her husband, to bring life to the decayed race. Her thoughts wandered to her father, the dilettante who wandered in Italy in search of beautiful things and emotions that his native country could not give him; to Miss Ley, whose attitude towards life was a shrug of the shoulders and a well-bred smile of contempt. Was not she, the last of them, wise? Feeling herself too weak to stand alone, she had taken a mate whose will and vitality would be a pillar of strength to her frailty; her husband had still in his sinews the might of his mother, the Earth, a barbaric power that knew not the subtleties of weakness; he was the conqueror and she was his handmaiden.

But an umbrella was being waved at Mrs Craddock from the bottom of the hill, and she smiled, recognizing the masculine walk of Miss Glover. Even from a distance the maiden's determination was apparent; she approached, her face redder even than usual after the climb, encased in a braided jacket that fitted her as severely as sardines are fitted in their tin.

'I was coming to see you, Bertha,' she cried. 'I heard you were back.'

'We've been home several days, getting to rights.'

Miss Glover shook Bertha's hand with vigour, and together they walked back to the house, along the avenue bordered with leafless trees.

'Now, do tell me all about your honeymoon; I'm so anxious to hear everything.'

But Bertha was not communicative, she had an instinctive dislike to telling her private affairs, and never had any overpowering desire for sympathy.

'Oh, I don't think there's much to tell,' she answered, when they were in the drawing-room and she was pouring out tea for her guest. 'I suppose all honeymoons are more or less alike.'

'You funny girl,' said Miss Glover. 'Didn't you enjoy it?'

'Yes,' said Bertha, with a smile that was almost ecstatic; then after a little pause: 'We had a very good time; we went to all the theatres.'

Miss Glover felt that marriage had caused a difference in Bertha, and it made her nervous to realize the change. She looked uneasily at the married woman and occasionally blushed.

'And are you really happy?' she blurted out suddenly.

Bertha smiled, and, reddening, looked more charming than ever.

'Yes, I think I'm perfectly happy.'

'Aren't you sure?' asked Miss Glover, who cultivated precision and strongly disapproved of persons who did not know their own minds.

Bertha looked at her for a moment, as if considering the question.

'You know,' she answered at last, 'happiness is never quite what one expected it to be. I hardly hoped for so much; but I didn't imagine it quite as it is.'

'Ah, well, I think it's better not to go into these things,' replied Miss Glover, a little severely, thinking the suggestion of self-analysis scarcely suitable in a young married woman. 'We ought to take things as they are and be thankful.'

'Ought we?' said Bertha lightly. 'I never do. I'm never satisfied with what I have.'

They heard the opening of the front door, and Bertha jumped up.

'There's Edward! I must go and see him. You don't mind, do you?'

She almost skipped out of the room; marriage, curiously enough, had dissipated the gravity of manner that had made people find so little girlishness in her. She seemed younger, lighter of heart.

'What a funny creature she is!' thought Miss Glover. 'When she was a girl she had all the ways of a married woman, and now that she's married she might be a schoolgirl.'

The parson's sister was not certain whether the irresponsibility of Bertha was fit to her responsible position, whether her unusual bursts of laughter were proper to a mystic state demanding gravity.

'I hope she'll turn out all right,' she sighed.

But Bertha impulsively rushed up to her husband and kissed him. She helped him off with his coat.

'I'm so glad to see you again,' she cried, laughing a little at her own eagerness, for it was only after luncheon that he had left her.

'Is anyone here?' he asked, noticing Miss Glover's umbrella.

He returned his wife's embrace somewhat mechanically.

'Come and see,' said his wife, taking his arm and dragging him along. 'You must be dying for tea, you poor thing.'

'Miss Glover!' he said, shaking the lady's hand as energetically as she shook his. 'How good of you to come and see us. I *am* glad to see you! You see, we came home sooner than we expected; there's no place like the country, is there?'

'You're right there, Mr Craddock; I can't bear London.'

'On, you don't know it,' said Bertha. 'For you it's Aerated Bread Shops, Exeter Hall and Church Congresses.'

'Bertha!' cried Edward in a tone of surprise; he could not understand frivolity with Miss Glover.

That good creature was far too kind-hearted to take offence at any remark of Bertha's, and smiled grimly; she could smile in no other way.

'Tell me what you did in London; I can't get anything out of Bertha.'

Craddock, on the other hand, was communicative; nothing pleased him more than to give people information, and he was always ready to share his knowledge with the world at large. He never picked up a fact without rushing to tell it to somebody else. Some persons when they know a thing immediately lose interest in it and it bores them to discuss it. Craddock was not of these. Nor could repetition exhaust his eagerness to enlighten his fellows; he would tell a hundred people the news of the day, and be as fresh as ever when it came to the hundred and first. Such a characteristic is undoubtedly a gift, useful in the highest degree to schoolmasters and politicians, but slightly tedious to their hearers. Craddock favoured his guest with a detailed account of all their adventures in London, the plays they had seen, their plots and the actors who played in them. He gave the complete list of the museums and churches and public buildings they had visited. Bertha looked at him the while, smiling happily at his enthusiasm; she cared little what he spoke of, the mere sound of his voice was music to her ears, and she would have listened delightedly while he read aloud from end to end *Whitaker's Almanack*; that was a thing, by the way, that he was quite capable of doing. Edward corresponded far more with Miss Glover's conception of the newly-married man than did Bertha with that of the newly-married woman.

'He is a nice fellow,' she said to her brother afterwards when they were eating their supper of cold mutton, solemnly seated at either end of a long table.

'Yes,' answered the vicar, in his tired, patient voice. 'I think he'll turn out a good husband.'

Mr Glover was patience itself, which a little irritated Miss Ley, who liked a man of spirit, and of that Mr Glover had never had a grain. He was resigned to everything: he was resigned to his food being badly cooked, to the perversity of human nature, to the existence of dissenters (almost), to his infinitesimal salary; he was resignation driven to death. Miss Ley said he was like those Spanish donkeys whom one sees plodding along in a long string, listlessly bearing over-heavy loads, patient, patient, patient. But not so patient as Mr Glover, the donkey sometimes kicked: the Vicar of Leanham never!

'I do hope it will turn out well, Charles,' said Miss Glover.

'I hope it will,' he answered; then, after a pause: 'Did you ask them if they were coming to church tomorrow?'

Helping himself to mashed potatoes, he noticed long-sufferingly that they were burnt again; the potatoes were always burnt; but he made no comment.

'Oh, I quite forgot to, but I think they're sure to. Edward Craddock was always a regular attendant.'

Mr Glover made no reply, and they kept silence for the rest of the meal. Immediately afterwards the parson went into his study to finish his sermon, and Miss Glover took out of her basket her brother's woollen socks and began to darn them. She worked for more than an hour, thinking meanwhile of the Craddocks; she liked Edward better and better each time she saw him, and she felt he was a man who could be trusted. She upbraided herself a little for her disapproval of the marriage; her action was unchristian, and she asked herself whether it was not her duty to apologize to Bertha or Craddock; the thought of doing something humiliating to her own self-respect attracted her wonderfully. But Bertha was different from other girls; Miss Glover, thinking of her, grew confused.

But a tick of the clock to announce an hour to strike made her look up. She saw it wanted but five minutes to ten.

'I had no idea it was so late.'

She got up and tidily put away her work, then taking from the top of the harmonium the Bible and the big prayer-book that were upon it, placed them at the end of the table. She drew a chair for her brother and sat patiently to await his coming. As the clock struck she heard the study door open. The vicar walked in. Without a word he went to the books and, sitting down, found his place in the Bible.

'Are you ready,' she asked.

He looked up one moment: 'Yes.'

Miss Glover leant forward and rang the bell. The servant appeared with a basket of eggs, which she placed on the table. Mr Glover looked at her till she was settled on her chair and began the lesson. Afterwards the servant lit two candles and bade them good night. Miss Glover counted the eggs.

'How many are there today?' asked the parson.

'Seven,' she answered, dating them one by one, and entering the number in a book kept for the purpose.

'Are you ready?' asked Mr Glover.

'Yes, Charles,' she said, taking up one of the candles.

He put out the lamp and with the other candle followed her upstairs. She stopped outside her door and bade him good night, he kissed her coldly on the forehead and they went into their respective rooms.

There is always a certain flurry in a country-house on Sunday morning. There is in the air a feeling peculiar to the day, a state of alertness and expectation; even when they are repeated for years, week by week, the preparations for church cannot be taken coolly. The odour of clean linen is unmistakable, everyone is highly starched and somewhat ill at ease; there is a hunt for prayer-books and hymn-books; the ladies of the party are never ready in time and sally out at last buttoning their gloves; the men stamp and fume and take out their watches. Edward, of course, wore a tail-coat and a top-hat, which is quite the proper costume for the squire to go to church in, and no one gave more thought to the proprieties than Edward; he held himself very upright, cultivating the slightly self-conscious gravity thought fit for the occasion.

'We shall be late, Bertha,' he said. 'It will look so bad—the first time we come to church since our marriage, too.'

'My dear,' said Bertha, 'you may be quite certain that even if Mr Glover is so indiscreet as to start, for the congregation the ceremony will not really begin till we appear.'

They drove up in an old-fashioned brougham used only for going to church and to dinner-parties and the word was immediately passed by the loungers at the porch to the devout within; there was a rustle of attention as Mr and Mrs Craddock walked up the aisle to the front pew that was theirs by right.

'He looks at home, don't he?' murmured the natives, for the behaviour of Edward interested them more than that of his wife, who was sufficiently above them to be almost a stranger.

Bertha sailed up with a royal unconsciousness of the eyes upon her; she was pleased with her personal appearance and intensely proud of her good-looking husband. Mrs Branderton, the mother of Craddock's best man, fixed her eye-glass upon her and stared as is the custom of great ladies. Mrs Branderton was a woman who cultivated the mode in the depths of the country, a little, giggling, grey-haired creature, who talked stupidly in a high, cracked voice and had her too juvenile bonnets straight from Paris. She was a gentlewoman, and this, of course, is a very fine thing to be; she was proud of it (in a quite gentlewomanly way), and in the habit of saying that gentlefolk were gentlefolk, which, if you come to think of it, is a profound remark.

'I mean to go and speak to the Craddocks afterwards,' she whispered to her son. 'It will have a good effect on the Leanham people; I wonder if poor Bertha feels it yet.'

Mrs Branderton had a self-importance that was almost sublime; it never occurred to her that there might be persons sufficiently ill-conditioned as to resent her patronage. She showered advice upon all and sundry, besides soups and jellies upon the poor, to whom when they were ill she even sent her cook to read the Bible. She would have gone herself, only she strongly disapproved of familiarity with the lower classes; it made them independent and often rude. Mrs Branderton knew without possibility of question that she and her equals were made of different clay from common people; but, being a gentlewoman did not throw this fact in their faces, unless, of course, they gave themselves airs, when she thought a straight talking to did them good. Without any striking advantages of birth, money or intelligence, Mrs Branderton never doubted her right to direct the affairs and fashions, even the modes of thought of her neighbours, and by sheer force of self-esteem had caused them to submit for thirty years to her tyranny, hating her and yet looking upon her invitations to a bad dinner as something quite desirable.

Mrs Branderton had debated with herself how she should treat the Craddocks.

'I wonder if it's my duty to cut them,' she said. 'Edward Craddock is not the sort of man a Miss Ley ought to marry. But there are so few gentlefolk in the neighbourhood, and of course people do make marriages which they wouldn't have dreamt of twenty years ago. Even the very best society is mixed nowadays. Perhaps I'd better err on the side of mercy.'

Mrs Branderton was a little pleased to think that the Leys required her support, as was proved by the request of her son's services at the wedding.

'The fact is, gentlefolk are gentlefolk, and they must stand by one another in these days of pork-butchers and furniture people.'

After the service, when the parishioners were standing about the churchyard, Mrs Branderton sailed up to the Craddocks, followed by Arthur, and in her high, cracked voice began to talk to Edward. She kept an eye on the Leanham people to see that her action was being duly noticed, and spoke to Craddock in the manner a gentlewoman should adopt with a man who, though possibly a gentleman, was not county. He was pleased and flattered.

CHAPTER IX

SOME days later, after the due preliminaries which Mrs Branderton would on no account have neglected, the Craddocks received an invitation to dinner. Bertha read and silently passed it to her husband.

'I wonder who she'll ask to meet us,' he said.

'D'you want to go?' asked Bertha.

'Why, don't you? We've got no engagement, have we?'

'Have you ever dined there before?'

'No. I've been to tennis-parties and that sort of thing, but I've hardly set foot inside their house.'

'Well, I think it's an impertinence of her to ask you now.'

Edward opened his mouth wide: 'What on earth d'you mean?'

'Oh, don't you see?' cried his wife. 'They're merely asking you because you're my husband. It's humiliating.'

'Nonsense!' replied Edward, laughing. 'And if they are, what do I care? I'm not so thin-skinned as that. Mrs Branderton was very nice to me on Sunday; it would be funny if we didn't accept.'

'Did you think she was nice? Didn't you see that she was patronizing you as if you were a groom. It made me boil with rage. I could hardly hold my tongue.'

Edward laughed again. 'I never noticed anything. It's just your fancy, Bertha.'

'I'm not going to the horrid dinner-party.'

'Then I shall go by myself.'

Bertha started and turned white; it was as if she had received a sudden blow; but he was laughing. Of course he did not mean what he said. She hurriedly agreed to all he asked.

'Of course if you want to go, Eddie, I'll come too. It was only for your sake that I didn't wish to.'

'We must be neighbourly. I want to be friends with everybody.'

She sat on the arm of his chair, and put her arm round his neck. Edward patted her hand, and she looked at him with eyes full of eager love. She bent down and kissed his hair. How foolish had been her sudden thought that he did not love her!

But Bertha had another reason for not wishing to go to Mrs Branderton's. She knew Edward would be bitterly criticized, and the thought made her wretched; they would talk of his appearance and manner, and wonder how they got on together. Bertha understood well enough the position Edward had occupied in Leanham: the Branderton's and their like, knowing him all his life, had treated him as a mere acquaintance, for then he had been a person to whom you are civil and that is all. This was the first occasion upon which he had been dealt with as an equal; it was his introduction into what Mrs Branderton was pleased to call the upper ten of Leanham. It did indeed make Bertha's blood boil; and it cut her to the heart to think that for years he had been used in so infamous a fashion. He did not seem to mind.

'If I were he,' she said, 'I'd rather die than go. They've ignored him always, and now they take him up as a favour to me.'

But Edward appeared to have no pride. He neither resented the former neglect of the Brandertons nor their present impertinence.

Bertha was in a tremor of anxiety. She guessed who the other guests would be. Would they laugh at him? Of course, not openly; Mrs Branderton, the least charitable of them all, prided herself on her breeding; but Edward was shy and among strangers rather awkward. To Bertha this was a charm rather than a defect; his bashful candour touched her, and she compared it favourably with the foolish worldliness of the imaginary man about town whose dissipation she always opposed to her husband's virtues. But she knew that a spiteful tongue would find another name for what she called a delightful *naïveté.*

When at last the great day arrived and they trundled off in the old-fashioned brougham, Bertha was thoroughly prepared to take mortal offence at the merest shadow of a slight offered to her husband. The Lord Chief Justice himself could not have been more careful of a company promoter's fair name than was Mrs Craddock of her husband's susceptibilities; Edward, like the financier, treated the affair with indifference.

Mrs Branderton had routed out the whole countryside for her show of gentlefolk. They had come from Blackstable and Tercanbury and Faversley, and from the seats and mansions that surrounded those places. Mrs Mayston Ryle was there in a wonderful black wig and a voluminous dress of violet silk; Lady Waggett was there.

'Merely the widow of a city knight, my dear,' said the hostess to Bertha; 'but if she isn't distinguished, she's good, so one mustn't be too hard upon her.'

General Hancock arrived with two frizzle-haired daughters, who were dreadfully plain, but pretended not to know it. They had walked, and while the old soldier toddled in, blowing like a grampus, the girls (whose united ages made the respectable total of sixty-five years) stayed behind to remove their boots and put on the shoes that they had brought in a bag. Then in a little while came the Dean, meek and rather talkative; Mr Glover had been invited for his sake, and of course Charles's sister could not be omitted. She was looking almost festive in very shiny black satin.

'Poor dear,' said Mrs Branderton to another guest, 'it's her only dinner dress; I've seen it for years. I'd willingly give her one of my old ones, only I'm afraid I should offend her by offering it. People in that class are so ridiculously sensitive.'

Mr Atthill Bacot was announced. He had once contested the seat, and ever after been regarded as an authority upon the nation's affairs. Mr James Lycett and Mr Molson came next, both red-faced squires with dogmatic opinions. They were as alike as two peas, and it had been the local joke for thirty years that no one but their wives could tell them apart. Mrs Lycett was thin and quiet and staid, wearing two little strips of lace on her hair to represent a cap; Mrs Molson was so insignificant that no one had ever noticed what she was like. It was one of Mrs Branderton's representative gatherings; moral excellence was joined to perfect gentility, and the result could not fail to edify. She was herself in high spirits, and her cracked voice rang high and shrill. She was conscious of a successful frock; it was quite pretty, and would have looked charming on a woman half her age.

The dinner just missed being eatable. Mrs Branderton, a woman of fashion, disdained the solid fare of a country dinner-party—thick soup, fried soles, mutton cutlets, roast mutton, pheasant, charlotte russe and jellies—and saying she must be a little more 'distangay' than that, provided her guests with clear soup, *entreés* from the Stores, chicken *en casserole* and a fluffy sweet that looked pretty and tasted horrid. The feast was elegant, but it was not filling, which is unpleasant to elderly squires with large appetites.

'I never get enough to eat at the Brandertons',' said Mr Atthill Bacot indignantly.

'Well, I know the old woman,' replied Mr Molson. (Mrs Branderton was the same age as himself, but he was rather a dog, and thought himself quite young enough to flirt with the least plain of the two Miss Hancocks.) 'I know her well, and I make a point of drinking a glass of sherry with a couple of eggs beaten up in it before I come.'

'The wines are positively immoral,' said Mrs Mayston Ryle, who prided herself on her palate. 'I'm always inclined to bring with me a flask with a little good whisky in it.'

But if the food was not heavy, the conversation was. It is an axiom of narration that truth should coincide with probability, and the realist is perpetually hampered by the wild exaggeration of actual facts. A verbatim report of the conversation at Mrs Branderton's dinner-party would read like shrieking caricature. The anecdote reigned supreme. Mrs Mayston Ryle was a specialist in the clerical anecdote; she successively related the story of Bishop Thorold and his white hands and the story of Bishop Wilberforce and the bloody shovel. (This somewhat shocked the ladies, but Mrs Mayston Ryle could not spoil her point by the omission of a swear word.) The Dean gave an anecdote about himself, to which Mrs Mayston Ryle retorted with one about the Archbishop of Canterbury and the tedious curate. Mr Atthill Bacot gave political anecdotes—Mr Gladstone and the table of the House of Commons, Dizzy and the agricultural labourer. The climax came when General Hancock gave his celebrated stories about the Duke of Wellington. Edward laughed heartily at them all.

Bertha's eyes were constantly upon her husband. She was horribly anxious. She felt it mean to think the thoughts that ran through her head; that they should ever come to her was disparaging to him and made her despise herself. Was he not perfect and handsome and adorable? Why should she tremble before the opinion of a dozen stupid people? She could not help it. However much she despised her neighbours, she could not prevent herself from being miserably affected by their judgement. And what did Edward feel? Was he as nervous as she? She could not bear the thought of him suffering pain. It was an immense relief when Mrs Branderton rose from the table. Bertha looked at Arthur holding open the door; she would have given anything to ask him to took after Edward, but dared not. She was terrified lest those horrid old men should leave him in the cold and he be humiliated. On reaching the drawing-room, Miss Glover found herself by Bertha's side, a little apart from the others, and the accident seemed to be designed by higher powers to give her an opportunity for the amends which she felt it her duty to make Mrs Craddock for her former disparagement of Edward. She had been thinking the matter over, and she thought an apology distinctly needful. But Miss Glover suffered terribly from nervousness, and the notion of broaching so delicate a subject caused her indescribable tortures. The very unpleasantness of it reassured her: if speech was so disagreeable it must obviously be her duty. But the words stuck in her throat, and she began talking of the weather; she reproached herself for cowardice, she set her teeth and grew scarlet.

'Bertha, I want to beg your pardon,' she blurted out suddenly.

'What on earth for?' Bertha opened her eyes wide and looked at the poor woman with astonishment.

'I feel I've been unjust to your husband. I thought he wasn't a proper match for you, and I said things about him which I shouldn't even have thought. I'm very sorry. He's one of the best and kindest men I've ever seen, and I'm very glad you married him, and I'm sure you'll be very happy.'

Tears came to Bertha's eyes as she laughed; she felt inclined to throw her arms round the grim Miss Glover's neck, for such a speech at that moment was very comforting.

'Of course, I know you didn't mean what you said.'

'Oh, yes, I did, I'm sorry to say,' replied Miss Glover, who could allow no extenuation of her crime.

'I'd quite forgotten all about it, and I believe you'll soon be as madly in love with Edward as I am.'

'My dear Bertha,' replied Miss Glover, who never jested. 'With your husband? You must be joking.'

But Mrs Branderton interrupted them with her high voice.

'Bertha, dear, I want to talk to you.'

Bertha, smiling, sat down beside her, and Mrs Branderton proceeded in undertones:

'I must tell you. Everyone has been saying you're the handsomest couple in the county, and we all think your husband is so nice.'

'He laughed at all your jokes,' replied Bertha.

'Yes,' said Mrs Branderton, looking upwards and sideways like a canary, 'he has such a merry disposition. But I've always liked him, dear. I was telling Mrs Mayston Ryle that I've known him intimately ever since he was born. I thought it would please you to know that we all think your husband is nice.'

'I'm very much pleased. I hope Edward will be equally satisfied with all of you.'

The Craddocks' carriage came early, and Bertha offered to drive the Glovers home.

'I wonder if that lady has swallowed a poker,' said Mr Molson, as soon as the drawing-room door was closed upon them.

The two Miss Hancocks went into shrieks of laughter at this sally, and even the Dean smiled gently.

'Where did she get her diamonds from?' asked the elder Miss Hancock. 'I thought they were as poor as church mice.'

'The diamonds and the pictures are the only things they have left,' said Mrs Branderton. 'Her family always refused to sell them; though of course it's absurd for people in that position to have such jewels.'

'He's a remarkably nice fellow,' said Mrs Mayston Ryle in her deep, authoritative voice. 'But I agree with Mr Molson, she's distinctly inclined to give herself airs.'

'The Leys for generations have been as proud as turkey-cocks,' added Mrs Branderton.

'I shouldn't have thought Mrs Craddock had much to be proud of now, at all events,' said the elder Miss Hancock, who had no ancestors and thought people who had were snobs.

'Perhaps she was a little nervous,' said Lady Waggett, who, though not distinguished, was good. 'I know when I was a bride I used to be all of a tremble when I went to dinner-parties.'

'Nonsense,' said Mrs Mayston Ryle. 'She was extremely self-possessed. I don't think it looks well for a young woman to have so much assurance.'

'Well, what do you think she said to me?' said Mrs Branderton, waving her thin arms. 'I was telling her that we were all so pleased with her husband; I thought it would comfort her a little, poor thing; and she said she hoped he would be equally satisfied with us.'

Mrs Mayston Ryle for a moment was stupefied. 'How very amusing!' she cried, rising from her chair. 'Ha! Ha! She hopes Mr Edward Craddock will be satisfied with Mrs Mayston Ryle.'

The two Miss Hancocks said 'Ha! Ha!' in chorus. Then, the great lady's carriage being announced, she bade the assembly good night and swept out with a great rustling of her violet silk. The party might now really be looked upon as concluded, and the others obediently flocked off.

When they had put the Glovers down, Bertha nestled close to her husband.

'I'm so glad it's all over,' she whispered; 'I'm only happy when I'm alone with you.'

'It was a jolly evening, wasn't it?' he said. 'I thought they were all ripping.'

'I'm so glad you enjoyed it, dear; I was afraid you'd be bored.'

'Good Heavens, that's the last thing I should be. It does one good to hear conversation like that now and then; it brightens one up.'

Bertha started a little.

'Old Bacot is a very well-informed man, isn't he? I shouldn't wonder if he was right in thinking that the Government would go out at the end of their six years.'

'He always leads one to believe that he's in the Prime Minister's confidence,' said Bertha.

'And the General is a funny old chap,' added Edward. 'That was a good story he told about the Duke of Wellington.'

This remark had a curious effect upon Bertha; she could not restrain herself, but burst suddenly into shrieks of hysterical laughter. Her husband, thinking she was laughing at the anecdote, burst also into peal upon peal.

'And the story about the Bishop's gaiter!' cried Edward, shouting with merriment.

The more he laughed, the more hysterical became Bertha, and as they drove through the silent night they both screamed and yelled and shook with uncontrollable mirth.

CHAPTER X

AND so the Craddocks began their journey along the great road that is called the road of Holy Matrimony. The spring came and with it a hundred new delights. Bertha watched the lengthening days, the coloured crocus spring from the ground, the snowdrops; the warm damp days of February brought the primroses and then the violets. February is a month of languors; the world's heart is heavy, listless of the unrest of April and the vigorous life of May; throughout nature the seed is germinating and the pulse of all things throbs, like a woman when first she is with child. The sea mists arose from the North Sea and covered the Kentish land with a veil of moisture, white and almost transparent, so that through it the leafless trees were seen strangely distorted, their branches like long arms writhing to free themselves from the shackles of winter; the grass was very green in the marshes and the young lambs frisked and gambolled, bleating to their mothers. Already the thrushes and the blackbirds were singing in the hedgerows. March roared in boisterously, and the clouds, higher than usual, swept across the sky before the tearing winds, sometimes heaped up in heavy masses and then blown asunder, flying westwards, tripping over one another's heels in their hurry. Nature was resting, holding her breath, as it were, before the great effort of birth.

Gradually Bertha came to know her husband better. At her marriage she had really known nothing but that she loved him; the senses only had spoken, she and he were merely puppets that nature had thrown together and made attractive in one another's eyes that the race might be continued. Bertha, desire burning within her like a fire, had flung herself into her husband's arms, loving as the beasts love—and as the gods. He was the man and she was the woman, and the world was a garden of Eden conjured up by the power of passion. But greater knowledge brought only greater love. Little by little, reading in Edward's mind, Bertha discovered to her delight an unexpected purity; it was with a feeling of curious happiness that she recognized his extreme innocence. She saw that he had never loved before, that woman to him was a strange thing, a thing he had scarcely known. She was proud that her husband had come to her unsoiled by foreign embraces, the lips that kissed hers were dean: no speech on the subject had passed between them, and yet she felt certain of his extreme chastity. His soul was truly virginal.

And this being so how could she fail to adore him? Bertha was only happy in her husband's company, and it was an exquisite pleasure for her to think that their bonds could not be sundered, that as long as they lived they would always be together, always inseparable. She followed him like a dog, with a subjection that was really touching; her pride had vanished, and she desired to exist only in Edward, to fuse her character with his and be entirely one with him. She wanted him to be her only individuality, likening herself to ivy clinging to the oak tree, for he was an oak tree, a pillar of strength, and she was very weak. In the morning after breakfast she accompanied him on his walk round the farms, and only when her presence was impossible did she stay at home to look after her house. The attempt to read was hopeless, and she had thrown aside her books. Why should she read? Not for entertainment, since her husband was a perpetual occupation, and if she knew how to love what other knowledge was useful? Often, left alone, for a while, she would take up some volume, but her mind quickly wandered and she thought of Edward again, wishing to be with him.

Bertha's life was an exquisite dream, a dream that need never end, for her happiness was not of that boisterous sort that breeds excursions and alarums, but equable and smooth; she dwelt in a paradise of rosy tints, in which were neither violent shadows nor glaring lights. She was in heaven, and the only link attaching her to earth was the weekly service at Leanham. There was a delightful humanity about the bare church with its pitchpine, highly varnished pews, and the odours of hair-pomade and Reckitt's Blue. Edward was in his sabbath garments, the organist made horrid sounds and the village choir sang out of tune; Mr Glover's mechanical delivery of the prayers cleverly extracted all beauty from them and his sermon was matter-of-fact. Those two hours of church gave Bertha just the touch of earthliness that was necessary to make her realize that life was not entirely spiritual.

Now came April; the elm trees before Court Leys were beginning to burst into leaf, the green buds covered the branches like a delicate rain, like a verdant haze that was visible from a little distance and vanished when one came near. The brown fields clothed themselves with a summer garment, the clover sprang up green and luscious, and the crops showed good promise for the future. There were days when the air was almost balmy, when the sun was warm and the heart leapt, certain at last that spring was at hand. The warm and comfortable rain soaked into the ground, and from the branches continually hung the countless drops, glistening in the succeeding sun. The self-conscious tulip unfolded her petals and carpeted the ground with gaudy colour. The clouds above Leanham were lifted up and the world was stretched out in a greater circle. The birds now sang with no uncertain notes as in March, but from a full throat, filling the air; and in the hawthorn behind Court Leys the first nightingale poured out his richness. And the full scents of the earth arose, the fragrance of the mould and of the rain, the perfumes of the sun and of the soft breezes.

But sometimes, without ceasing, it rained from morning till night, and then Edward rubbed his hands.

'I wish this would keep on for a week: it's just what the country wants.'

One such day Bertha was lounging on a sofa while Edward stood at the window, looking at the pattering rain. She thought of the November afternoon when she had stood at the same window considering the dreariness of the winter, but her heart full of hope and love.

'Come and sit down beside me, Eddie dear,' she said. 'I've hardly seen you all day.'

'I've got to go out,' he said, without turning round.

'Oh, no, you haven't; come here and sit down.'

'I'll come for two minutes,' he said, 'while they're putting the trap in.'

He sat down and she put her arm round his neck.

'Kiss me.'

He kissed her, and she laughed.

'You funny boy, I don't believe you care about kissing me a bit.'

He could not answer this, for at that moment the trap came to the door and he sprang up.

'Where are you going?'

'I'm driving over to see old Potts at Herne about some sheep.'

'Is that all? Don't you think you might stay in for an afternoon when I ask you?'

'Why?' he replied. 'There's nothing to do in here. Nobody is coming, I suppose.'

'I want to be with you, Eddie,' she said, rather plaintively.

He laughed. 'I'm afraid I can't break an appointment just for that.'

'Shall I come with you then?'

'What on earth for?' he asked, with surprise.

'I want to be with you, I hate being always separated from you.'

'But we're not always separated,' said Edward. 'Hang it all, it seems to me that we're always together.'

'You don't notice my absence as I notice yours,' said Bertha in a low voice, looking down.

'But it's raining cats and dogs, and you'll get wet through if you come.'

'What do I care about that if I'm with you?'

'Then come by all means if you like.'

'You don't care if I come or not; it's nothing to you.'

'Well, I think it would be very silly of you to come in the rain. You bet I shouldn't go if I could help it.'

'Then go,' she said.

She kept back with difficulty the bitter words that were on the tip of her tongue.

'You're much better at home,' said her husband cheerfully. 'I shall be in for tea at five. Ta-ta!'

He might have said a thousand things. He might have said that nothing would please him more than that she should accompany him, that the appointment could go to the devil and he would stay with her. But he went off cheerfully, whistling. He didn't care. Bertha's cheeks grew red with the humiliation of his refusal.

'He doesn't love me,' she said, and suddenly burst into tears, the first tears of her married life, the first she had wept since her father's death; and they made her ashamed. She tried to control them, but could not, and wept on ungovernably. Edward's words seemed terribly cruel, she wondered how he could have said them.

'I might have expected it,' she said. 'He doesn't love me.'

She grew angry with him, remembering the little coldnesses that had often pained her. Often he almost pushed her away when she came to caress him, because he had at the moment something else to occupy him; often he had left unanswered her protestations of undying affection. Did he not know that he cut her to the quick? When she said she loved him with all her heart, he wondered if the clock was wound up! Bertha brooded for two hours over her unhappiness, and, ignorant of the time, was surprised to hear the trap again at the door; her first impulse was to run and let Edward in, but she restrained herself. She was very angry with him. He entered, and, shouting to her that he was wet and must change, pounded upstairs. Of course he had not noticed that for the first time since their marriage his wife had not met him in the hall when he came in: he never noticed anything.

Edward entered the room, his face glowing with the fresh air.

'By Jove, I'm glad you didn't come. The rain simply poured down. How about tea? I'm starving.'

He thought of his tea when Bertha wanted apologies, humble excuses, and a plea for pardon. He was as cheerful as usual, and quite unconscious that his wife had been crying herself into a towering passion.

'Did you buy your sheep?' she said in an indignant tone.

She was anxious for Edward to notice her discomposure, so that she might reproach him for his sins; but he noticed nothing.

'Not much,' he cried. 'I wouldn't have given a fiver for the lot.'

'You might as well have stayed with me, as I asked you,' said Bertha bitterly.

'As far as business goes, I really might. But I daresay the drive across country did me good.'

He was a man who always made the best of things. Bertha took up a book and began reading.

'Where's the paper?' asked Edward. 'I haven't read the leading articles yet.'

'I'm sure I don't know,' replied Bertha.

They sat till dinner, Edward methodically going through the *Standard,* column after column, Bertha turning over the pages of her book, trying to understand, but occupied the whole time only with her injuries. They ate dinner almost in silence, for Edward was not talkative and the conversation rested usually with Bertha. He merely remarked that soon they would be having new potatoes and that he had met Dr Ramsay. Bertha answered in monosyllables.

'You're very quiet, Bertha,' he remarked later in the evening. 'What's the matter?'

'Nothing.'

'Got a headache?'

'No.'

He made no more inquiries, satisfied that her quietness was due to natural causes. He did not seem to notice that she was in any way different from usual. She held herself in as long as she could, but finally burst out, referring to his remark of an hour before.

'Do you care if I have a headache or not?' she cried. It was hardly a question so much as a taunt.

He looked up with surprise: 'What's the matter?'

She looked at him, and then, with a gesture of impatience, turned away. But coming to her, he put his arm round her waist.

'Aren't you well, dear?' he asked with concern.

She looked at him again, but now her eyes were full of tears and she could not repress a sob.

'Oh, Eddie, be nice to me,' she said, suddenly weakening.

'Do tell me what's wrong.'

He put his arms round her and kissed her lips. The contact revived the passion that for an hour had been a-dying, and she burst into tears.

'Don't be angry with me, Eddie,' she sobbed; it was she who apologized and made excuses. 'I've been horrid to you. I couldn't help it. You're not angry, are you?'

'What on earth for?' he asked, completely mystified.

'I was so hurt this afternoon because you didn't seem to care about me two straws. You must love me, Eddie. I can't live without it.'

'You are silly,' he said, laughing.

She dried her tears, smiling. His forgiveness greatly comforted her, and she felt now trebly happy.

CHAPTER XI

BUT Edward was certainly not an ardent lover. Bertha could not tell when first she had noticed his unresponsiveness to her passionate outbursts; at the beginning she had known nothing but that she loved her husband with all her heart, and her ardour had lit up his slightly pallid attachment till it seemed to glow as fiercely as her own. Yet, little by little, she seemed to see very small return for the wealth of affection that she lavished upon him. The causes of her dissatisfaction were scarcely explicable, a slight motion of withdrawal, an indifference to her feelings—little nothings that had seemed almost comic. Bertha at first likened Edward to the Hippolytus of Phaedra; he was untamed and wild, the kisses of women frightened him, his phlegm, disguised as rustic savagery, pleased her, and she said her passion should thaw the icicles in his heart. But soon she ceased to consider his passiveness amusing, sometimes she upbraided him, and often, when alone, she wept.

'I wonder if you realize what pain you cause me at times,' said Bertha.

'Oh, I don't think I do anything of the kind.'

'You don't see it. When I come up and kiss you it's the most natural thing in the world for you to push me away, as if—almost as if you couldn't bear me.'

'Nonsense,' he replied.

To himself Edward was the same now as when they were first married.

'Of course after four months of married life you can't expect a man to be the same as on his honeymoon. One can't always be making love and canoodling. Everything in its proper time and season.'

After the day's work he liked to read his *Standard* in peace, so when Bertha came up to him he put her gently aside.

'Leave me alone for a bit, there's a good girl,' he said.

'Oh, you don't love me,' she cried then, feeling as if her heart would break.

He did not look up from his paper or make reply: he was in the middle of a leading article.

'Why don't you answer?' she cried.

'Because you're talking nonsense.'

He was the best-humoured of men, and Bertha's bad temper never disturbed his equilibrium. He knew that women felt a little irritable at times, but if a man gave 'em plenty of rope they'd calm down after a bit.

'Women are like chickens,' he told a friend. 'Give 'em a good run, properly closed in with stout wire-netting so that they can't get into mischief, and when they cluck and cackle just sit tight and take no notice.'

Marriage had made no great difference in Edward's life. He had always been a man of regular habits, and these he continued to cultivate. Of course he was more comfortable.

'There's no denying it, a fellow wants a woman to look after him,' he told Dr Ramsay, whom he sometimes met on the latter's rounds. 'Before I was married I used to find my shirts worn out in no time, but now when I see a cuff getting a bit groggy I just give it to the missus, and she makes it as good as new.'

'There's a good deal of extra work, isn't there, now you've taken on the Home Farm?'

'Oh, bless you, I enjoy it. Fact is, I can't get enough work to do. And it seems to me that if you want to make farming pay nowadays you must do it on a big scale.'

All day Edward was occupied, if not on the farms, then with business at Blackstable, Tercanbury or Faversley.

'I don't approve of idleness,' he said. 'They always say the devil finds work for idle hands to do, and upon my word I think there's a lot of truth in it.'

Miss Glover, to whom this sentiment was addressed, naturally approved, and when Edward immediately afterwards went out, leaving her with Bertha, she said: 'What a good fellow your husband is! You don't mind my saying so, do you?'

'Not if it pleases you,' said Bertha, drily.

'I hear praise of him from every side. Of course Charles has the highest opinion of him.'

Bertha did not answer, and Miss Glover added: 'You can't think how glad I am that you're so happy.'

Bertha smiled: 'You've got such a kind heart, Fanny.'

The conversation dragged, and after five minutes of heavy silence Miss Glover rose to go. When the door was closed upon her Bertha sank back in her chair, thinking. This was one of her unhappy days: Eddie had walked into Blackstable, and she had wished to accompany him.

'I don't think you'd better come with me,' he said. 'I'm in rather a hurry and I shall walk fast.'

'I can walk fast too,' she said, her face clouding over.

'No, you can't. I know what you call walking fast. If you like you can come and meet me on the way back.'

'Oh, you do everything you can to hurt me. It looks as if you welcomed an opportunity of being cruel.'

'How unreasonable you are, Bertha! Can't you see that I'm in a hurry, and I haven't got time to saunter along and chatter about the buttercups?'

'Well, let's drive in.'

'That's impossible. The mare isn't well and the pony had a hard day yesterday; he must rest today.'

'It's simply because you don't want me to come. It's always the same, day after day. You invent anything to get rid of me, you push me away even when I want to kiss you.'

She burst into tears, knowing that what she said was unjust, but feeling notwithstanding extremely ill-used. Edward smiled with irritating good-temper.

'You'll be sorry for what you've said when you've calmed down, and then you'll want me to forgive you.'

She looked up, flushing: 'You think I'm a child and a fool.'

'No I just think you're out of sorts today.'

Then he went out whistling, and she heard him give an order to the gardener in his usual manner, as cheerful as if nothing had happened. Bertha knew that he had already forgotten the little scene; nothing affected his good humour—she might weep, she might tear her heart out (metaphorically) and bang it on the floor. Edward would not be perturbed; he would still be placid, good-tempered and forbearing. Hard words, he said, broke nobody's bones. 'Women are like chickens, when they cluck and cackle sit tight and take no notice.'

On his return Edward appeared not to see that his wife was out of temper. His spirits were always equable, and he was an observant person; she answered him in monosyllables, but he chattered away, delighted at having driven a good bargain with a man in Blackstable. Bertha longed for him to remark upon her condition, so that she might burst into reproaches, but Edward was hopelessly dense—or else he saw and was unwilling to give her an opportunity to speak. Bertha, almost for the first time, was seriously angry with her husband, and it frightened her: suddenly Edward seemed an enemy, and she wished to inflict some hurt upon him. She did not understand herself. What was going to happen next? Why wouldn't he say something so that she might pour forth her woes and then be reconciled? The day wore on and she preserved a sullen silence; her heart was beginning to ache terribly. The night came, and still Edward made no sign; she looked about for a chance of beginning the quarrel, but nothing offered. They went to bed, and, turning her back on him, Bertha pretended to go to sleep; she did not give him the kiss, the never-ending kiss of lovers, that they always exchanged at night. Surely he would notice it, surely he would ask what troubled her, and then she could at last bring him to his knees. But he said nothing, he was dog-tired after a hard day's work, and without a word went to sleep. In five minutes Bertha heard his heavy, regular breathing.

Then she broke down; she could never sleep without saying good night to him, without the kiss of his lips.

'He's stronger than I,' she said, 'because he doesn't love me.'

Bertha sobbed silently; she couldn't bear to be angry with her husband. She would submit to anything rather than pass the night in wrath and the next day as unhappily as this. She was entirely humbled. At last, unable any longer to bear the agony, she awoke him.

'Eddie, you've not said good night to me.'

'By Jove, I forgot all about it,' he answered sleepily.

Bertha stifled a sob.

'Hulloa, what's the matter? You're not crying just because I forgot to kiss you? I was awfully fagged, you know.'

He really had noticed nothing. While she was passing through utter distress he had been as happily self-satisfied as usual. But the momentary recurrence of Bertha's anger was quickly stifled. She could not afford now to be proud.

'You're not angry with me?' she said. 'I can't sleep unless you kiss me.'

'Silly girl!' he whispered.

'You do love me, don't you?'

'Yes.'

He kissed her as she loved to be kissed, and in the delight of it her anger was entirely forgotten.

'I can't live unless you love me.' She nestled against his bosom, sobbing. 'Oh, I wish I could make you understand how I love you. We're friends again now, aren't we?'

'We haven't been ever otherwise.'

Bertha gave a sigh of relief, and lay in his arms completely happy. A minute more and Edward's breathing told her that he had already fallen asleep; she dared not move for fear of waking him.

The summer brought Bertha new pleasures, and she set herself to enjoy the pastoral life that she had looked forward to. The elms of Court Leys now were dark with leaves, and the heavy, close-fitting verdure gave quite a stately look to the house. The elm is the most respectable of trees, over-pompous if anything, but perfectly well-bred, and the shade it casts is no ordinary shade, but solid and self-assured as befits the estate of a county family. The fallen trunk had been removed, and in the autumn young trees were to be placed in the vacant spaces. Edward had set himself with a will to put the place to rights. The spring had seen a new coat of paint on Court Leys, so that it looked as spick and span as the suburban mansion of a stockbroker; the beds, which for years had been neglected, now were trim with the abominations of carpet bedding; squares of red geraniums contrasted with circles of yellow calceolarias; the overgrown boxwood was cut down to a just height; the hawthorn hedge was doomed, and Edward had arranged to enclose the grounds with a wooden palisade and laurel bushes. The drive was decorated with several loads of gravel, so that it became a thing of pride to the successor of an ancient and lackadaisical race. Craddock had not reigned in their stead a fortnight before the grimy sheep were expelled from the lawns on either side of the avenue, and since then the grass had been industriously mown and rolled. Now a tennis-court had been marked out, which, as Edward said, made things look homely. Finally, the iron gates were gorgeous in black and gold, as suited the entrance to a gentleman's mansion, and the renovated lodge proved to all and sundry that Court Leys was in the hands of a man who knew what was what and delighted in the proprieties.

Though Bertha abhorred all innovations, she had meekly accepted Edward's improvements; they formed an inexhaustible topic of conversation, and his enthusiasm delighted her.

'By Jove,' he said, rubbing his hands, 'the changes will make your aunt simply jump, won't they?'

'They will indeed,' said Bertha, smiling, but with a shudder at the prospect of Miss Ley's sarcastic praise.

'She'll hardly recognize the place; the house looks as good as new, and the grounds might have been laid out only half a dozen years ago. Give me five years more, and even you won't know your old home.'

Miss Ley had at last accepted one of the invitations that Edward had insisted should be showered upon her, and wrote to say she was coming down for a week. Edward was, of course, much pleased; as he said, he wanted to be friends with everybody, and it didn't seem natural that Bertha's only relative should make a point of avoiding them.

'It looks as if she didn't approve of our marriage, and it makes people talk.'

He met the good lady at the station, and, somewhat to her dismay, greeted her with effusion.

'Ah, here you are at last!' he bellowed in his jovial way. 'We thought you were never coming. Here, porter!'

He raised his voice so that the platform shook and rumbled. He seized both Miss Ley's hands, and the terrifying thought flashed through her head that he would kiss her before the assembled multitude. Six people.

'He's cultivating the airs of the country squire,' she thought. 'I wish he wouldn't.'

He took the innumerable bags with which she travelled and scattered them among the attendants. He even tried to induce her to take his arm to the dog-cart, but this honour she stoutly refused.

'Now, will you come round to this side, and I'll help you up. Your luggage will come on afterwards with the pony.'

He was managing everything in a self-confident and masterful fashion. Miss Ley noticed that marriage had dispelled the shyness that had been in him father an attractive feature. He was becoming bluff and hearty. Also he was filling out; prosperity and a consciousness of his greater importance had broadened his back and straightened his shoulders; he was quite three inches more round the chest than when she had first known him, and his waist had proportionately increased.

'If he goes on developing in this way,' she thought, 'the good man will be colossal by the time he's forty.'

'Of course, Aunt Polly,' he said, boldly dropping the respectful *Miss Ley* that hitherto he had invariably used, though his new relative was not a woman whom most men would have ventured to treat familiarly, 'of course, it's all rot about your leaving us in a week; you must stay a couple of months at least.'

'It's very good of you, dear Edward,' replied Miss Ley drily. 'But I have other engagements.'

'Then you must break them. I can't have people leave my house immediately they come.'

Miss Ley raised her eyebrows and smiled. Was it *his* house already? Dear me!

'My dear Edward,' she answered, 'I never stay anywhere longer than two days—the first day I talk to people, the second I let them talk to me and the third I go. I stay a week at hotels so as to go *en pension* and get my washing properly aired.'

'You're treating us like a hotel,' said Edward, laughing.

'It's a great compliment; in private houses one gets so abominably waited on.'

'Ah, well, we'll say no more about it. But I shall have your boxes taken to the box-room, and I keep the key of it.'

Miss Ley gave the short dry laugh that denoted that the remark of the person she was with had not amused her, but something in her own mind. They arrived at Court Leys.

'D'you see all the differences since you were last here?' asked Edward jovially.

Miss Ley looked round and pursed her lips.

'It's charming,' she said.

'I knew it would make you sit up,' he cried, laughing.

Bertha received her aunt in the hall, and embraced her with the grave decorum that had always characterized their relations.

'How clever you are, Bertha,' said Miss Ley. 'You manage to preserve your beautiful figure.'

Then she set herself solemnly to investigate the connubial bliss of the youthful couple.

CHAPTER XII

THE passion to analyse the casual fellow-creature was the most absorbing vice that Miss Ley possessed, and no ties of relationship or affection prevented her from exercising her talents in this direction. She observed Bertha and Edward during luncheon. Bertha was talkative, chattering with a vivacity that seemed suspicious about the neighbours—Mrs Branderton's new bonnets and new hair, Miss Glover's good works and Mr Glover's visit to London. Edward was silent, except when he pressed Miss Ley to take a second helping. He ate largely, and the maiden lady noticed the enormous mouthfuls he took and the heartiness with which he drank his beer. Of course she drew conclusions; and she drew further conclusions when, having devoured half a pound of cheese and taken a last drink of all, he pushed back his chair with a sort of low roar reminding one of a beast of prey gorged with food, and said:

'Ah, well, I suppose I must set about my work. There's no rest for the weary.'

He pulled a new briarwood pipe out of his pocket, filled and lit it.

'I feel better now. Well, good-bye, I shall be in to tea.'

Conclusions buzzed about Miss Ley like midges on a summer's day. She drew them all the afternoon and again at dinner. Bertha was effusive too, unusually so; and Miss Ley asked herself a dozen times if this stream of chatter, these peals of laughter, proceeded from a light heart or from a base desire to deceive a middle-aged and inquiring aunt. After dinner, Edward, telling her that of course she was one of the family, so he hoped she did not wish him to stand on ceremony, began reading the paper. When Bertha at Miss Ley's request played the piano, good manners made him put it aside, and he yawned a dozen times in a quarter of an hour.

'I mustn't play any more,' said Bertha, 'or Eddie will go to sleep. Won't you, darling?'

'I shouldn't wonder,' he replied, laughing. 'The fact is that the things Bertha plays when we've got company give me the fair hump.'

'Edward only consents to listen when I play "The Blue Bells of Scotland" or "Yankee Doodle".'

Bertha made the remark, smiling good-naturedly at her husband, but Miss Ley drew conclusions.

'I don't mind confessing that I can't stand all this foreign music. What I say to Bertha is, Why can't you play English stuff?'

'If you must play at all,' interposed his wife.

'After all's said and done, "The Blue Bells of Scotland" has got a tune about it that a fellow can get his teeth into.'

'You see, there's the difference,' said Bertha, strumming a few bars of 'Rule, Britannia,' 'it sets mine on edge.'

'Well, I'm patriotic,' retorted Edward. 'I like the good, honest, homely English airs. I like 'em because they're English. I'm not ashamed to say that for me the best piece of music that's ever been written is "God Save the Queen".'

'Which was written by a German, dear Edward,' said Miss Ley, smiling.

'That's as it may be,' said Edward, unabashed, 'but the sentiment's English, and that's all I care about.'

'Hear! Hear!' cried Bertha. 'I believe Edward has aspirations towards a political career. I know I shall finish up as the wife of the local M.P.'

'I'm patriotic,' said Edward, 'and I'm not ashamed to confess it.'

'Rule, Britannia,' sang Bertha, 'Britannia rules the waves, Britons never, never shall be slaves. Ta-ra-ra-boom-de-ay! Ta-ra-ra-boom-de-ay!'

'It's the same everywhere now,' proceeded the orator. 'We're chock full of foreigners and their goods. I think it's scandalous. English music isn't good enough for you; you get it from France and Germany. Where do you get your butter from? Brittany! Where d'you get your meat from? New Zealand!' This he said with great scorn, and Bertha punctuated it with a resounding chord. 'And as far as the butter goes, it isn't butter—it's margarine. Where does your bread come from? America. Your vegetables from Jersey.'

'Your fish from the sea,' interposed Bertha.

'And so it is all along the line; the British farmer hasn't got a chance.'

To this speech Bertha played a burlesque accompaniment that would have irritated a more sensitive man than Craddock; but he merely laughed good-naturedly.

'Bertha won't take these things seriously,' he said, passing his hand affectionately over her hair.

She suddenly stopped playing, and his good humour, joined with the loving gesture, filled her with remorse. Her eyes filled with tears.

'You are a dear good thing,' she faltered, 'and I'm utterly horrid.'

'Now don't talk stuff before Aunt Polly. You know shell laugh at us.'

'Oh, I don't care,' said Bertha, smiling happily. She stood up and linked her arm with his. 'Eddie's the best-tempered person in the world; he's perfectly wonderful.'

'He must be indeed,' said Miss Ley, 'if you have preserved your faith in him after six months of marriage.'

But the maiden lady had stored so many observations, her impressions were so multitudinous, that she felt an urgent need to retire to the privacy of her bed-chamber and sort them. She kissed Bertha and held out her hand to Edward.

'Oh, if you kiss Bertha, you must kiss me too,' said he, bending forward with a laugh.

'Upon my word!' said Miss Ley, somewhat taken aback, then, as he was evidently insisting, she embraced him on the cheek. She positively blushed.

The upshot of Miss Ley's investigation was that once again the hymeneal path had not been found strewn with roses; and the notion crossed her head, as she laid it on the pillow, that Dr Ramsay would certainly come and crow over her; it was not in masculine human nature, she thought, to miss an opportunity of exulting over a vanquished foe.

'He'll vow that I was the direct cause of the marriage. The dear man, he'll be so pleased with my discomfiture that I shall never hear the last of it. He's sure to call tomorrow.'

Indeed the news of Miss Ley's arrival had been by Edward industriously spread abroad, and promptly Mrs Ramsay put on her blue velvet calling dress and in the doctor's brougham drove with him to Court Leys. The Ramsays found Miss Glover and the Vicar of Leanham already in possession of the field. Mr Glover looked thinner and older than when Miss Ley had last seen him; he was more weary, meek and brow-beaten. Miss Glover never altered.

'The parish?' said the parson, in answer to Miss Ley's polite inquiry, 'I'm afraid it's in a bad way. The dissenters have got a new chapel, you know; and they say the Salvation Army is going to set up "barracks", as they call them. It's a great pity the Government doesn't step in; after all, we are established by law, and the law ought to protect us from encroachment.'

'You don't believe in liberty of conscience?' asked Miss Ley.

'My dear Miss Ley,' said the vicar in his tired voice, 'everything has its limits. I should have thought there was in the Established Church enough liberty of conscience for anyone.'

'Things are becoming dreadful in Leanham,' said Miss Glover. 'Practically all the tradesmen go to chapel now, and it makes it so difficult for us.'

'Yes,' replied the vicar with a weary sigh, 'and as if we hadn't enough to put up with, I hear that Walker has ceased coming to church.'

'Oh, dear! oh, dear!' said Miss Glover.

'Walker, the baker?' asked Edward.

'Yes, and now the only baker in Leanham who goes to church is Andrews.'

'Well, we can't possibly deal with him, Charles,' said Miss Glover. 'His bread is too bad.'

'My dear, we must,' groaned her brother. 'It would be against all my principles to deal with a tradesman who goes to chapel. You must tell Walker to send his book in, unless he will give an assurance that he'll come to church regularly.'

'But Andrews's bread always gives you indigestion, Charles,' cried Miss Glover.

'I must put up with it. If none of our martyrdoms were more serious than that we should have no cause to complain.'

'Well, it's quite easy to get your bread from Tercanbury,' said Mrs Ramsay, who was severely practical.

Both Mr and Miss Glover threw up their hands in dismay.

'Then Andrews would go to chapel too. The only thing that keeps them at church, I'm sorry to say, is the vicarage custom, or the hope of getting it.'

Presently Miss Ley found herself alone with the parson's sister.

'You must be very glad to see Bertha again, Miss Ley.'

'Now she's going to crow,' thought the good lady. 'Of course I am,' she said aloud.

'And it must be such a relief to you to see how well it's all turned out.'

Miss Ley looked sharply at Miss Glover, but saw no trace of irony.

'Oh, I think it's beautiful to see a married couple so thoroughly happy. It really makes me feel a better woman when I come here and see how those two worship one another.'

'Of course the poor thing's a perfect idiot,' thought Miss Ley. 'Yes, it's very satisfactory,' she said, drily.

She glanced round for Dr Ramsay, looking forward, notwithstanding that she was on the losing side, to the tussle she foresaw. She had the instinct of the fighting woman, and even though defeat was inevitable, never avoided an encounter. The doctor approached.

'Well, Miss Ley, so you have come back to us. We're all delighted to see you.'

'How cordial these people are,' thought Miss Ley, rather crossly, thinking Dr Ramsay's remark preliminary to coarse banter or reproach. 'Shall we take a turn in the garden? I'm sure you wish to quarrel with me.'

'There's nothing I should like better. To walk in the garden, I mean; of course no one could quarrel with so charming a lady as yourself.'

'He would never be so polite if he did not mean afterwards to be very rude,' thought Miss Ley. 'I'm glad you like the garden.'

'Craddock has improved it so wonderfully. It's a perfect pleasure to look at all he's done.'

This Miss Ley considered a gibe, and she looked for a repartee, but, finding none, was silent: Miss Ley was a wise woman. They walked a few steps without a word, and then Dr Ramsay suddenly burst out:

'Well, Miss Ley, you were right after all.'

She stopped and looked at the speaker. He seemed quite serious.

'Yes,' he said, 'I don't mind acknowledging it. I was wrong. It's a great triumph for you, isn't it?'

He looked at her and shook with good-tempered laughter.

'Is he making fun of me?' Miss Ley asked herself, with something not very far removed from dismay; this was the first occasion upon which she had been unable to understand, not only the good doctor, but his inmost thoughts as well. 'So you think the estate has been improved?'

'I can't make out how the man's done so much in so short a time. Why, just look at it!'

Miss Ley pursed her lips. 'Even in its most dilapidated days, Court Leys looked gentlemanly; now all this,' she glanced round with upturned nose, 'might be the country mansion of a pork-butcher.'

'My dear Miss Ley, you must pardon my saying so, but the place wasn't even respectable.'

'But it is now; that is my complaint. My dear doctor, in the old days the passer-by could see that the owners of Court Leys were decent people; that they could not make both ends meet was a detail; it was possibly because they burnt one end too rapidly, which is the sign of a rather delicate mind,'—Miss Ley was mixing her metaphors—'And he moralized accordingly. For a gentleman there are only two decorous states, absolute poverty or overpowering wealth; the middle condition is vulgar. Now the passer-by sees thrift and careful management, the ends meet, but they do it aggressively, as if it were something to be proud of. Pennies are looked at before they are spent; and, good Heavens, the Leys serve to point a moral and adorn a tale. The Leys who gambled and squandered their sustenance, who bought diamonds when they hadn't got bread, and pawned the diamonds to give the king a garden-party, now form the heading of a copy-book and the ideal of a market-gardener.'

Miss Ley had the characteristics of the true phrase-maker, for so long as her period was well rounded off she did not mind how much nonsense it contained. Coming to the end of her tirade, she looked at the doctor for the signs of disapproval which she thought her right; but he merely laughed.

'I see you want to rub it in,' he said.

'What on earth does the creature mean?' Miss Ley asked herself.

'I confess I did believe things would turn out badly,' the doctor proceeded. 'And I couldn't help thinking he'd be tempted to play ducks and drakes with the whole property. Well, I don't mind frankly acknowledging that Bertha couldn't have chosen a better husband; he's a thoroughly good fellow, no one realized what he had in him, and there's no knowing how far he'll go.'

A man would have expressed Miss Ley's feeling with a little whistle, but that lady merely raised her eyebrows. Then Dr Ramsay shared the opinion of Miss Glover?

'And what precisely is the opinion of the county?' she asked. 'Of that odious Mrs Branderton, of Mrs Ryle (she has no right to the *Mayston* at all), of the Hancocks and the rest?'

'Edward Craddock has won golden opinions all round. Everyone likes him and thinks well of him. He's not conceited—he never had an ounce of conceit and he's not a bit changed. No, I assure you, although I'm not so fond as all that of confessing I was wrong, he's the right man in the right place. It's extraordinary how people look up to him and respect him already. I give you my word for it, Bertha has reason to congratulate herself; a girl doesn't pick up a husband like that every day of the week.'

Miss Ley smiled; it was a great relief to find that she really was no more foolish than most people (so she modestly put it), for a doubt on the subject had for a short while given her some uneasiness.

'So everyone thinks they're as happy as turtle-doves?'

'Why, so they are,' cried the doctor. 'Surely you don't think otherwise?'

Miss Ley never considered it a duty to dispel the error of her fellow-creatures, and whenever she had a little piece of knowledge, vastly preferred keeping it to herself.

'I?' she answered. 'I make a point of thinking with the majority; it's the only way to get a reputation for wisdom.' But Miss Ley, after all, was only human. 'Which do you think is the predominant partner?' she asked, smiling drily.

'The man, as he should be,' gruffly replied the doctor.

'Do you think he has more brains?'

'Ah, you're a feminist,' said Dr Ramsay, with great scorn.

'My dear doctor, my gloves are sixes, and perceive my shoes.' She put out for the old gentleman's inspection a very pointed, high-heeled shoe, displaying at the same time the elaborate openwork of a silk stocking.

'Do you intend me to take that as an acknowledgement of the superiority of man?'

'Heavens, how argumentative you are!' Miss Ley laughed, for she was getting into her own particular element. 'I knew you wished to quarrel with me. Do you really want my opinion?'

'Yes.'

'Well, it seems to me that if you take the very clever woman and set her beside an ordinary man, you prove nothing. That is how we women mostly argue. We place George Eliot (who, by the way, had nothing of the woman but petticoats, and those not always) beside plain John Smith and ask tragically if such a woman can be considered inferior to such a man. But that's silly. The question I've been asking myself for the last five-and-twenty years is whether the average fool of a woman is a greater fool than the average fool of a man.'

'And the answer?'

'Well, upon my word, I don't think there's much to choose between them.'

'Then you haven't really an opinion on the subject at all?' cried the doctor.

'That is why I give it to you,' said Miss Ley.

'H'm!' grunted Dr Ramsay. 'And how does that apply to the Craddocks?'

'It doesn't apply to them. I don't think Bertha is a fool.'

'She couldn't be, having had the discretion to be born your niece, eh?'

'Why, doctor, you are growing quite pert,' answered Miss Ley, with a smile.

They had finished the tour of the garden, and Mrs Ramsay was seen in the drawing-room bidding Bertha good-bye.

'Now, seriously, Miss Ley,' said the doctor, 'they're quite happy, aren't they? Everyone thinks so.'

'Everyone is always right,' said Miss Ley.

'And what is your opinion?'

'Good Heavens, what an insistent man it is! Well, Dr Ramsay, all I would suggest is that for Bertha, you know, the book of life is written throughout in italics; for Edward it is all in the big round hand of the copy-book heading. Don't you think it will make the reading of the book somewhat difficult?'

CHAPTER XIII

RURAL pastimes had been one of the pleasures to which Bertha had chiefly looked forward, and with the summer Edward began to teach her the noble game of lawn tennis.

In the long evenings, when Craddock had finished his work and changed into the flannels that suited him so well, they played set after set. He prided himself upon his skill in this pursuit, and naturally found it trying to play with a beginner; but on the whole he was very patient, hoping that eventually Bertha would acquire sufficient skill to give him a good game. She did not find the sport so exhilarating as she had expected; it was difficult and she was slow at learning. However, to be doing something with her husband sufficiently amused her; she liked him to correct her mistakes, to show her this stroke and that, she admired his good-nature and inexhaustible spirits; with him she would have found endless entertainment even in such dull games as Beggar-my-Neighbour and Bagatelle. And now she looked for fine days so that their amusement might not be hindered. Those evenings were always pleasant; but the greatest delight for Bertha was to lie on the long chair by the lawn when the game was over and enjoy her fatigue, gossiping of the little nothings that love made absorbingly interesting.

Miss Ley had been persuaded to prolong her stay; she had vowed to go at the end of her week, but Edward, in his highhanded fashion, had ordered the key of the box-room to be given him, and refused to surrender it.

'Oh, no,' he said, 'I can't make people come here, but I can prevent them from going away. In this house everyone has to do as I tell them. Isn't that so, Bertha?'

'If you say it, my dear,' replied his wife.

Miss Ley gracefully acceded to her nephew's desire, which was the more easy since the house was comfortable; she had really no pressing engagements and her mind was set upon making further examination into the married life of her relatives. It would have been weakness, unworthy of her, to maintain her intention for consistence' sake. Why, for days and days, were Edward and Bertha the happiest lovers, and then suddenly why did Bertha behave almost brutally towards her husband, while he remained invariably good-tempered and amiable? The obvious reason was that some little quarrel had arisen, such as, since Adam and Eve, has troubled every married couple in the world; but the obvious reason was that which Miss Ley was least likely to credit. She never saw anything in the way of a disagreement; Bertha acceded to all her husband's proposals; and with such docility on the one hand, such good humour on the other, what on earth could form a bone of contention?

Miss Ley had discovered that when the green leaves of life are turning red and golden with approaching autumn more pleasure can be obtained by a judicious mingling in simplicity of the gifts of nature and the resources of civilization; she was satisfied to come in the evenings to the tennis lawn and sit on a comfortable chair, shaded by trees and protected by a red parasol from the rays of the setting sun. She was not a woman to find distraction in needlework, and brought with her, therefore, a volume of Montaigne, who was her favourite writer. She read a page and then lifted her sharp eyes to the players. Edward was certainly very handsome; he looked very clean; he was one of those men who carry the morning tub stamped on every line of their faces. You felt that Pears' Soap was as essential to him as his belief in the Conservative Party, Derby Day and the Depression of Agriculture.

As Bertha often said, his energy was superabundant; notwithstanding his increasing size he was most agile; he was perpetually doing unnecessary feats of strength, such as jumping and hopping over the net, and holding chairs with outstretched arm.

'If health and a good digestion are all that is necessary in a husband, Bertha certainly ought to be the most contented woman alive.'

Miss Ley never believed so implicitly in her own theories that she was prevented from laughing at them; she had an impartial mind, and saw the two sides of a question clearly enough to find little to choose between them; consequently she was able and willing to argue with equal force from either point of view.

The set was finished, and Bertha threw herself on a chair, panting.

'Find the balls, there's a dear,' she cried.

Edward went off on the search, and Bertha looked at him with a delighted smile.

'He is such a good-tempered person,' she said to Miss Ley. 'Sometimes he makes me feel positively ashamed.'

'He has all the virtues. Dr Ramsay, Miss Glover, even Mrs Branderton have been drumming his praise into my ears.'

'Yes, they all like him. Arthur Branderton is always here, asking his advice about something or other. He's a dear good thing.'

'Who? Arthur Branderton?'

'No, of course not. Eddie.'

Bertha took off her hat and stretched herself more comfortably in the long chair; her hair was somewhat disarranged, and the rich locks wandered about her forehead and the nape of her neck in a way that would have distracted any minor poet under seventy. Miss Ley looked at her niece's fine profile, and wondered again at the complexion made of the softest colours in the setting sun. Her eyes now were liquid with love, languorous with the shade of long lashes, and her full, sensual mouth was half-open with a smile.

'Is my hair very untidy?' asked Bertha, catching Miss Ley's look and its meaning.

'No, I think it suits you when it is not done too severely.'

'Edward hates it; he likes me to be trim. And of course I don't care how I look as long as he's pleased. Don't you think he's very good-looking?'

Then, without waiting for an answer, she asked a second question.

'Do you think me a great fool for being so much in love, Aunt Polly?'

'My dear, it's surely the proper behaviour with one's lord and master.'

Bertha's smile became a little sad as she replied:

'Edward seems to think it unusual.' She followed him with her eyes, picking up the balls one by one, hunting among bushes; she was in the mood for confidences that afternoon. 'You don't know how different everything has been since I fell in love. The world is fuller. It's the only state worth living in.' Edward advanced with the eight balls on his racket. 'Come here and be kissed, Eddie,' she cried.

'Not if I know it,' he replied, laughing. 'Bertha's a perfect terror. She wants me to spend my whole life in kissing her. Don't you think it's unreasonable, Aunt Polly? My motto is: everything in its place and season.'

'One kiss in the morning,' said Bertha, 'one kiss at night will do to keep your wife quiet, and the rest of the time you can attend to your work and read your paper.'

Again Bertha smiled charmingly, but Miss Ley saw no amusement in her eyes.

'Well, one can have too much of a good thing,' said Edward, balancing his racket on the tip of his nose.

'Even of proverbial philosophy,' remarked Bertha.

A few days later, his guest having definitely announced that she must go, Edward proposed a tennis-party as a parting honour. Miss Ley would gladly have escaped an afternoon of small-talk with the notabilities of Leanham, but Edward was determined to pay his aunt every attention, and his inner consciousness assured him that at least a small party was necessary to the occasion. They came, Mr and Miss Glover, the Brandertons, Mr Atthill Bacot, the great politician (of the district), and the Hancocks. But Mr Atthill Bacot was more than political, he was gallant; he devoted himself to the entertainment of Miss Ley. He discussed with her the sins of the Government and the incapacity of the army.

'More men, more guns,' he said. 'An elementary education in common sense for the officers, and the rudiments of grammar if there's time.'

'Good Heavens, Mr Bacot, you mustn't say such things. I thought you were a Conservative.'

'Madam, I stood for the constituency in '85. I may say that if a Conservative member could have got in, I should have. But there are limits. Even the staunch Conservative will turn. Now look at General Hancock.'

'Please don't talk so loud,' said Miss Ley with alarm; for Mr Bacot had instinctively adopted his platform manner, and his voice could be heard through the whole garden.

'Look at General Hancock, I say,' he repeated, taking no notice of the interruption. 'Is that the sort of man whom you would wish to have the handling of ten thousand of your sons?'

'Oh, but be fair,' cried Miss Ley, laughing, 'they're not all such fools as poor General Hancock.'

'I give you my word, madam, I think they are. As far as I can make out, when a man has shown himself incapable of doing anything else they make him a general, just to encourage the others. I understand the reason. It's a great thing, of course, for parents sending their sons into the army to be able to say: "Well, he may be a fool, but there's no reason why he shouldn't become a general".'

'You wouldn't rob us of our generals,' said Miss Ley; 'they're so useful at tea-parties.'

Mr Bacot was about to make a heated retort, when Edward called to him: 'We want you to make up a set at tennis. Will you play with Miss Hancock against my wife and the General? Come on, Bertha.'

'Oh, no, I mean to sit out, Eddie,' said Bertha quickly. She saw that Edward was putting all the bad players into one set, so that they might be got rid of. 'I'm not going to play.'

'You must, or you'll disarrange the next lot,' said her husband. 'It's all settled; Miss Glover and I are going to take on Miss Jane Hancock and Arthur Branderton.'

Bertha looked at him with eyes flashing angrily; of course he did not notice her vexation. He preferred playing with Miss Glover. The parson's sister played well, and for a good game he would never hesitate to sacrifice his wife's feelings. Didn't he know that she cared nothing for the game, but merely for the pleasure of playing with him? Only Miss Glover and young Branderton were within earshot, and in his jovial, pleasant manner, Edward laughingly said:

'Bertha's such a duffer. Of course she's only just beginning. You don't mind playing with the General, do you, dear?'

Arthur Branderton laughed, and Bertha smiled at the sally, but she flushed.

'I'm not going to play at all; I must see to the tea, and I daresay some more people will be coming in presently.'

'Oh, I forgot that,' said Edward. 'No, perhaps you oughtn't to.' And then, putting his wife out of his thoughts and linking his arm with young Branderton's, he sauntered off: 'Come along, old chap, we must find someone else to make up the pat-ball set.'

Edward had such a charming, frank manner, one could not help liking him. Bertha watched the two men go, and turned very white.

'I must just go into the house a moment,' she said to Miss Glover. 'Go and entertain Mrs Branderton, there's a dear.'

And precipitately she fled. She ran to her bedroom and, flinging herself on the bed, burst into a flood of tears. To her the humiliation seemed dreadful. She wondered how Eddie, whom she loved above all else in the world, could treat her so cruelly. What had she done? He knew—ah, yes, he knew well enough the happiness he could cause her—and he went out of his way to be brutal. She wept bitterly, and jealousy of Miss Glover (Miss Glover, of all people!) stabbed her to the heart with sudden pain.

'He doesn't love me,' she moaned, her tears redoubling.

Presently there was a knock at the door.

'Who is it?' she cried.

The handle was turned and Miss Glover came in, red-faced with nervousness.

'Forgive me for coming in, Bertha. But I thought you seemed unwell. Can't I do something for you?'

'Oh, I'm all right,' said Bertha, drying her tears. 'Only the heat upset me, and I've got a headache.'

'Shall I send Edward up to you?' asked Miss Glover, compassionately.

'What do I want with Edward?' replied Bertha, petulantly. 'I shall be all right in five minutes; I often have attacks like this.'

'I'm sure he didn't mean to say anything unkind. He's kindness itself, I know.'

Bertha flushed: 'What on earth d'you mean, Fanny? Who didn't say anything unkind?'

'I thought you were hurt by Edward's saying you were a duffer and a beginner.'

'Oh, my dear, you must think me a fool,' Bertha laughed hysterically. 'It's quite true that I'm a duffer. I tell you it's only the weather. Why, if my feelings were hurt each time Eddie said a thing like that I should lead a miserable life.'

'I wish you'd let me send him up to you,' said Miss Glover, unconvinced.

'Good Heavens, why? See, I'm all right now.' She washed her eyes and passed the powder-puff over her face. 'My dear, it was only the sun.'

With an effort she braced herself, and burst into a laugh joyful enough almost to deceive the vicar's sister.

'Now, we must go down, or Mrs Branderton will complain more than ever of my bad manners.'

She put her arm round Miss Glover's waist and ran her down the stairs, to the mingled terror and amazement of that good lady. For the rest of the afternoon, though her eyes never rested on Edward, she was perfectly charming, in the highest spirits, chattering incessantly, and laughing; everyone noticed her high spirits and commented upon her happiness.

'It does one good to see a couple like that,' said General Hancock. 'Just as happy as the day is long.'

But the little scene had not escaped Miss Ley's sharp eyes, and she noticed with agony that Miss Glover had gone to Bertha; she could not stop her, being at the moment in the toils of Mrs Branderton.

'Oh, these good people are too officious. Why can't she leave the girl alone to have it out with herself?'

But the explanation of everything now flashed across Miss Ley.

'What a fool I am!' she thought, and she was able to cogitate quite clearly while exchanging honeyed impertinences with Mrs Branderton. 'I noticed it the first day I saw them together. How could I ever forget?'

She shrugged her shoulders and murmured the maxim of La Rochefoucauld:

'Entre deux amants il y a toujours un qui aime et un qui se laisse aimer.'

And to this she added another, in the same language, which, knowing no original, she ventured to claim as her own; it seemed to summarize the situation.

'Celui qui aime a toujours tort.'

CHAPTER XIV

BERTHA and Miss Ley passed a troubled night, while Edward, of course, after much exercise and a hearty dinner slept the sleep of the just and of the pure at heart. Bertha was nursing her wrath; she had with difficulty brought herself to kiss her husband before, according to his habit, he turned his back upon her and began to snore. She had never felt so angry; she could hardly bear his touch, and withdrew as far from him as possible. Miss Ley, with her knowledge of the difficulties in store for the couple, asked herself if she could do anything. But what could she do? They were reading the book of life in their separate ways, one in italics, the other in the big round letters of the copy-book; and how could she help them to find a common character? Of course the first year of married life is difficult, and the weariness of the flesh adds to the inevitable disillusionment. Every marriage has its moments of despair. The great danger is in the onlooker, who may pay them too much attention, and by stepping in render the difficulty permanent. Miss Ley's cogitations brought her not unnaturally to the course that most suited her temperament; she concluded that far and away the best plan was to attempt nothing and let things right themselves as best they could. She did not postpone her departure but according to arrangement went on the following day.

'Well, you see,' said Edward, bidding her good-bye, 'I told you that I should make you stay longer than a week.'

'You're a wonderful person, Edward,' said Miss Ley, drily. 'I have never doubted it for an instant.'

He was pleased, seeing no irony in the compliment. Miss Ley took leave of Bertha with a suspicion of awkward tenderness that was quite unusual; she hated to show her feelings, and found it difficult, yet wanted to tell Bertha that if she were ever in difficulties she would always find in her an old friend and a true one. All she said was:

'If you want to do any shopping in London, I can always put you up, you know. And for the matter of that, I don't see why you shouldn't come and stay a month or so with me—if Edward can spare you. It will be a change.'

When Miss Ley drove off with him to the station, Bertha felt suddenly a terrible loneliness. Her aunt had been a barrier between herself and her husband, coming opportunely just when, after the first months of mad passion, she was beginning to see herself linked to a man she did not know. A third person in the house had been a restraint, and the moments alone with her husband had gained a sweetness by their comparative rarity. She looked forward already to the future with something like terror. Her love for Edward was a bitter heart-ache. Oh, yes, she loved him well, she loved him passionately; but he—he was fond of her in his placid, calm way; it made her furious to think of it.

The weather was rainy, and for two days there was no question of tennis. On the third, however, the sun came out, and the lawn was soon dry. Edward had driven over to Tercanbury, but returned towards the evening.

'Hulloa!' he said, 'you haven't got your tennis things on. You'd better hurry up.'

This was the opportunity for which Bertha had been looking. She was tired of always giving way, of humbling herself; she wanted an explanation.

'You're very good,' she said, 'but I don't want to play tennis with you any more.'

'Why on earth not?'

She burst out furiously: 'Because I'm sick and tired of being made a convenience by you. I'm too proud to be treated like that. Oh, don't look as if you didn't understand. You play with me because you've got no one else to play with. Isn't that so? That is how you are always with me. You prefer the company of the veriest fool in the world to mine. You seem to do everything you can to show your contempt for me.'

'Why, what have I done now?'

'Oh, of course, you forget. You never dream that you are making me frightfully unhappy. Do you think I like to be treated before people as a sort of poor idiot that you can laugh and sneer at?'

Edward had never seen his wife so angry, and this time he was forced to pay her attention. She stood before him, at the end of her speech, with her teeth clenched, her cheeks flaming.

'It's about the other day, I suppose. I saw at the time you were in a passion.'

'And didn't care two straws,' she cried. 'You knew I wanted to play with you, but what was that to you so long as you had a good game.'

'You're too silly,' he said, with a laugh. 'We couldn't play together the whole afternoon when we had a lot of people here. They laugh at us as it is for being so devoted to one another.'

'If only they knew how little you cared for me!'

'I might have managed a set with you later on, if you hadn't sulked and refused to play at all.'

'Why didn't you suggest it? I should have been so pleased. I'm satisfied with the smallest crumbs you let fall for me. But it would never have occurred to you; I know you better than that. You're absolutely selfish.'

'Come, come, Bertha,' he cried, good-humouredly. 'That's a thing I've not been accused of before. No one has ever called me selfish.'

'Oh, no. They think you charming. They think because you're cheerful and even-tempered, because you're hail-fellow-well-met with everyone you meet, that you've got such a nice character. If they knew you as well as I do they'd understand it was merely because you're perfectly indifferent to them. You treat people as if they were your bosom friends, and then, five minutes after they've gone, you've forgotten all about them. And the worst of it is that I'm no more to you than anybody else.'

'Oh, come, I don't think you can really find such awful things wrong with me.'

'I've never known you sacrifice your slightest whim to gratify my most earnest desire.'

'You can't expect me to do things that I think unreasonable.'

'If you loved me you'd not always be asking if the things I want are reasonable. I didn't think of reason when I married you.'

Edward made no answer, which naturally added to Bertha's irritation. She was arranging flowers for the table, and broke off the stalks savagely. Edward after a pause went to the door.

'Where are you going?' she asked.

'Since you won't play, I'm just going to do a few serves for practice.'

'Why don't you send for Miss Glover to come and play with you?'

A new idea suddenly came to him (they came at sufficiently rare intervals not to spoil his equanimity), but the absurdity of it made him laugh: 'Surely you're not jealous of her, Bertha?'

'I?' began Bertha with tremendous scorn, and then, changing her mind: 'You prefered to play with her than to play with me.'

He wisely ignored part of the charge: 'Look at her and look at yourself. Do you think I could prefer her to you?'

'I think you're fool enough.'

The words slipped out of Bertha's mouth almost before she knew she had said them, and the bitter, scornful tone added to their violence. They rather frightened her, and going very white, she turned to look at her husband.

'Oh, I didn't mean to say that, Eddie.'

Fearing now that she had really wounded him, Bertha was entirely sorry; she would have given anything for the words to be unsaid. Was he very angry? Edward was turning over the pages of a book, looking at it listlessly. She went up to him gently.

'I haven't offended you, have I, Eddie? I didn't mean to say that.'

She put her arm in his; he didn't answer.

'Don't be angry with me,' she faltered again, and then, breaking down, buried her face in his bosom. 'I didn't mean what I said. I lost command over myself. You don't know how you humiliated me the other day. I haven't been able to sleep at night, thinking of it. Kiss me.'

He turned his face away, but she would not let him go; at last she found his lips.

'Say you're not angry with me.'

'I'm not angry with you,' he said, smiling.

'Oh, I want your love so much, Eddie,' she murmured. 'Now more than ever. I'm going to have a child.' Then, in reply to his astonished exclamation: 'I wasn't certain till today. Oh, Eddie, I'm so glad. I think it's what I wanted to make me happy.'

'I'm glad too,' he said.

'But you will be kind to me, Eddie, and not mind if I'm fretful and bad-tempered? You know I can't help it, and I'm always sorry afterwards.'

He kissed her as passionately as his cold nature allowed, and peace returned to Bertha's tormented heart.

Bertha had intended as long as possible to make a secret of her news; it was a comfort in her distress and a bulwark against her increasing disillusionment. The knowledge that she was at last with child came as a great joy and as an even greater relief. She was unable to reconcile herself to the discovery, seen as yet dimly, that Edward's cold temperament could not satisfy her burning desires. Love to her was a fire, a flame that absorbed the rest of life; love to him was a convenient and necessary institution of Providence, a matter about which there was as little need for excitement as about the ordering of a suit of clothes. Bertha's passion for a while had masked her husband's want of ardour, and she would not see that his temperament was to blame. She accused him of not loving her, and asked herself distractedly how to gain his affection. Her pride found cause for humiliation in the circumstance that her own love was so much greater than his. For six months she had loved him blindly; and now, opening her eyes, she refused to look upon the naked fact, but insisted on seeing only what she wished.

But the truth, elbowing itself through the crowd of her illusions, tormented her. A cold fear seized her that Edward neither loved her nor had ever loved her, and she wavered uncertainly between the old passionate devotion and a new equally passionate hatred. She told herself that she could not do things by halves; she must love or detest, but in either case fiercely. And now the child made up for everything. Now it did not matter if Edward loved her or not; it no longer gave her terrible pain to realize how foolish had been her hopes, how quickly her ideal had been shattered; she felt that the infantine hands of her son were already breaking, one by one, the links that bound her to her husband. When she guessed her pregnancy, she gave a cry, not only of joy and pride, but also of exultation in her approaching freedom.

But when the suspicion was changed into a certainty, and Bertha knew finally that she would bear a child, her feelings veered round. Her emotions were always as unstable as the light winds of April. An extreme weakness made her long for the support and sympathy of her husband; she could not help telling him. In the hateful dispute of that very day she had forced herself to say bitter things, but all the time she wished him to take her in his arms, saying he loved her. It wanted so little to rekindle her dying affection, she wanted his help and she could not live without his love.

The weeks went on, and Bertha was touched to see a change in Edward's behaviour, more noticeable after his past indifference. He looked upon her now as an invalid, and, as such, entitled to consideration. He was really kind-hearted, and during this time did everything for his wife that did not involve a sacrifice of his own convenience. When the doctor suggested some dainty to tempt her appetite, Edward was delighted to ride over to Tercanbury to fetch it, and in her presence he trod more softly and spoke in a gentler voice. After a while he used to insist on carrying her up and downstairs, and though Dr Ramsay assured them it was a quite unnecessary proceeding, Bertha would not allow Edward to give it up. It amused her to feel a little child in his strong arms, and she loved to nestle against his breast. Then with the winter, when it was too cold to drive out, Bertha would lie for long hours on a couch by the window, looking at the line of elm trees, now leafless again and melancholy, and watch the heavy clouds that drove over from the sea; her heart was full of peace.

One day of the new year she was sitting as usual at her window when Edward came prancing up the drive on horseback. He stopped in front of her and waved his whip.

'What d'you think of my new horse?' he cried.

At that moment the animal began to cavort, and backed almost into a flower-bed.

'Quiet, old fellow,' cried Edward. 'Now then, don't make a fuss, quiet!'

The horse stood on its hind legs and laid its ears back viciously. Presently Edward dismounted and led him up to Bertha.

'Isn't he a stunner? Just look at him.'

He passed his hand down the beast's forelegs and stroked its sleek coat.

'I only gave thirty-five guineas for him,' he remarked. 'I must just take him round to the stable, and then I'll come in.'

In a few minutes Edward joined his wife. The riding-clothes suited him well, and in his top-boots he looked more than ever the fox-hunting country squire, which had always been his ideal. He was in high spirits over the new purchase.

'It's the beast that threw Arthur Branderton when we were out last week. Arthur's limping about now with a sprained ankle and a smashed collar-bone. He says the horse is the greatest devil he's ever ridden; he's frightened to try him again.'

Edward laughed scornfully.

'But you haven't bought him?' asked Bertha, with alarm.

'Of course I have,' said Edward; 'I couldn't miss a chance like that. Why, he's a perfect beauty—only he's got a temper, like we all have.'

'But is he dangerous?'

'A bit. That's why I got him cheap. Arthur gave a hundred guineas for him, and he told me I could have him for seventy. "No," I said, "I'll give you thirty-five—and take the risk of breaking my neck." Well, he just had to accept my offer. The horse has got a bad name in the county, and he wouldn't get anyone to buy him in a hurry. A man has to get up early if he wants to do me over a gee.'

By this time Bertha was frightened out of her wits.

'But, Eddie, you're not going to ride him? Supposing something should happen? Oh, I wish you hadn't bought him.'

'He's all right,' said Craddock. 'If anyone can ride him, I can—and, by Jove, I'm going to risk it. Why, if I bought him and then didn't use him, I'd never hear the last of it.'

'To please me, Eddie, don't. What does it matter what people say? I'm so frightened. And now, of all times, you might do something to please me. It isn't often I ask you to do me a favour.'

'Well, when you ask for something reasonable, I always try my best to do it; but really, after I've paid thirty-five guineas for a horse, I can't cut him up for cat's-meat.'

'That means you'll always do anything for me as long as it doesn't interfere with your own likes and dislikes.'

'Ah, well, we're all like that, aren't we? Come, come, don't be nasty about it, Bertha.' He pinched her cheek good-naturedly. Women, we all know, would like the moon if they could get it; and the fact that they can't doesn't prevent them from persistently asking for it Edward sat down beside his wife, holding her hand. 'Now, tell us what you've been up to today. Has anyone been?'

Bertha sighed deeply: she had absolutely no influence over her husband. Neither prayers nor tears would stop him from doing a thing he had set his mind on. However much she argued, he always managed to make her seem in the wrong, and then went his way rejoicing. But she had her child now.

'Thank God for that!' she murmured.

CHAPTER XV

CRADDOCK went out on his new horse, and returned triumphant.

'He was as quiet as a lamb,' he said. 'I could ride him with my arms tied behind my back; and as to jumping—he takes a five-barred gate in his stride.'

Bertha was rather angry with him for having caused her such terror, angry with herself also for troubling so much.

'And it was rather lucky I had him today. Old Lord Philip Dirk was there, and he asked Branderton who I was. "You tell him," says he, "that it isn't often I've seen a man ride as well as he does." You should see Branderton; he isn't half glad at having let me take the beast for thirty-five guineas. And Mr Molson came up to me and said: "I knew that horse would get into your hands before long, you're the only man in this part who can ride it; but if it don't break your neck, you'll be lucky".'

He recounted with satisfaction the compliments paid to him.

'We had a good run today. And how are you, dear? Feeling comfy? Oh, I forgot to tell you: you know Rodgers, the huntsman? Well, he said to me: "That's a mighty fine hack you've got there, governor; but he takes some riding." "I know he does," I said, "but I flatter myself I know a thing or two more than most horses." They all thought I should get rolled over before the day was out, but I just went slick at everything, just to show I wasn't frightened.'

Then he gave details of the affair, and he had as great a passion for the meticulous as a German historian; he was one of those men who take infinite pains over trifles, flattering themselves that they never do things by halves. Bertha had a headache, and her husband bored her; she thought herself a great fool to be so concerned about his safety.

As the months wore on Miss Glover became dreadfully solicitous. The parson's sister looked upon birth as a mysteriously heart-fluttering business which, however, modesty required decent people to ignore. She treated her friend in an absurdly self-conscious manner, and blushed like a peony when Bertha, with the frankness usual in her, referred to the coming event. The greatest torment of Miss Glover's life was that, as lady of the vicarage, she had to manage the Maternity Bag, an institution to provide the infants of the needy with articles of raiment and their mothers with flannel petticoats. Miss Glover could never without much blushing ask the necessary questions of the recipients of her charity: and feeling that the whole thing ought not to be discussed at all, when she did so kept her eyes averted. Her manner caused great indignation among the virtuous poor.

'Well,' said one good lady, 'I'd rather not 'ave her bag at all than be treated like that. Why, she treats you as if—well, as if you wasn't married.'

'Yes,' said another, 'that's just what I complain of. I promise you I 'ad 'alf a mind to take me marriage lines out of me pocket an' show 'er. It ain't nothin' to be ashamed about. Nice thing it would be after 'aving sixteen if I was bashful.'

But of course the more unpleasant a duty was, the more zealously Miss Glover performed it; she felt it right to visit Bertha with frequency, and manfully bore the young wife's persistence in referring to an unpleasant subject. She carried her herosim to the pitch of knitting socks for the forthcoming baby, although to do so made her heart palpitate uncomfortably, and when she was surprised at the work by her brother her cheeks burned like two fires.

'Now, Bertha dear,' she said one day, pulling herself together and straightening her back as she always did when she was mortifying her flesh, 'now, Bertha dear, I want to talk to you seriously.'

Bertha smiled: 'Oh, don't, Fanny, you know how uncomfortable it makes you.'

'I must,' answered the good creature gravely. 'I know you'll think me ridiculous; but it's my duty.'

'I shan't think anything of the kind,' said Bertha, touched by her friend's humility.

'Well, you talk a great deal of—of what's going to happen.' Miss Glover blushed. 'But I'm not sure if you are really prepared for it.'

'Oh, is that all?' cried Bertha. 'The nurse will be here in a fortnight, and Dr Ramsay says she's a most reliable woman.'

'I wasn't thinking of earthly preparations,' said Miss Glover. 'I was thinking of the other. Are you quite sure you're approaching the—the *thing* in the right spirit?'

'What do you want me to do?' asked Bertha.

'It isn't what I want you to do. It's what you ought to do. I'm nobody. But have you thought at all of the spiritual side of it?'

Bertha gave a sigh that was chiefly voluptuous.

'I've thought that I'm going to have a son that's mine and Eddie's, and I'm awfully thankful.'

'Wouldn't you like me to read the Bible to you sometimes?'

'Good Heavens, you talk as if I were going to die.'

'One can never tell, dear Bertha,' replied Miss Glover, gloomily. 'I think you ought to be prepared. In the midst of life we are in death, and one can never tell what may happen.'

Bertha looked at her a trifle anxiously. She had been forcing herself of late to be cheerful, and had found it necessary to stifle a recurring presentiment of evil fortune. The vicar's sister never realized that she was doing everything possible to make Bertha thoroughly unhappy.

'I brought my own Bible with me,' she said. 'Do you mind if I read you a chapter?'

'I should like it,' said Bertha, and a cold shiver went through her.

'Have you got any preference for some particular part?' asked Miss Glover, on extracting the book from a little black bag that she always carried.

On Bertha's answer that she had no preference, she suggested opening the Bible at random and reading on from the first line that crossed her eyes.

'Charles doesn't quite approve of it,' she said. 'He thinks it smacks of superstition. But I can't help doing it, and the early Protestants constantly did the same.'

Miss Glover, having opened the book with closed eyes, began to read: 'The sons of Pharez; Hezron, and Hamul. And the sons of Zerah; Zimri, and Ethan, and Heman, and Calcol, and Dara: five of them in all.' Miss Glover cleared her throat: 'And the sons of Ethan: Azariah. The sons also of Hezron, that were born unto him; Jerahmeel, and Ram, and Chelubai. And Ram begat Amminadab; and Amminadab begat Nahshon, prince of the children of Judah.'

She had fallen upon the genealogical table at the beginning of the Book of Chronicles. The chapter was very long, and consisted entirely of names, uncouth and difficult to pronounce; but Miss Glover shirked not one of them. With grave and rather high-pitched delivery, modelled upon her brother's, she read out the endless list. Bertha looked at her in amazement, but Miss Glover went steadily on.

'That's the end of the chapter,' she said at last. 'Would you like me to read you another one?'

'Yes, I should like it very much; but I don't think the part you've hit on is quite to the point.'

'My dear, I don't want to reprove you—that's not my duty—but all the Bible is to the point.'

And as the time of her delivery approached, Bertha quite lost her courage, and was often seized by a panic fear; suddenly, without obvious cause, her heart sank, and she asked herself frantically how she could possibly get through her confinement. She thought she was going to die, and wondered what would happen if she did. What would Edward do without her? The tears came to her eyes thinking of his bitter grief; but her lips trembled with pity for herself when the suspicion came to her that he would not be heart-broken; he was not a man to feel either grief or joy very poignantly. He would not weep; at the most his gaiety for a couple of days would be obscured, and then he would go about as before. She imagined him relishing the sympathy of his friends. In six months he would almost have forgotten her, and such memory as remained would not be extraordinarily pleasing. He would marry again, she thought bitterly; Edward loathed solitude, and next time doubtless he would choose a different sort of woman, one less remote than she from his ideal. Edward cared nothing for appearance, and Bertha imagined her successor plain as Miss Hancock or dowdy as Miss Glover; and the irony of it lay in the knowledge that either of those two would make a wife more suitable than she to his character, answering better to his conception of a helpmate.

Bertha fancied that Edward would willingly have given her beauty for some solid advantage, such as a knowledge of dressmaking; her taste, her arts and accomplishments were nothing to him, and her impulsive passion was a positive defect. Handsome is as handsome does, said he; he was a plain, simple man, and he wanted a plain, simple wife.

She wondered if her death would really cause him much sorrow. Bertha's will gave him everything of which she was possessed, and he would spend it with a second wife. She was seized with insane jealousy.

'No, I won't die,' she cried between her teeth. 'I won't!'

But one day, while Edward was out hunting, her morbid thoughts took another turn; supposing he should die! The thought was unendurable, but the very horror of it fascinated her; she could not drive away the scenes which, with strange distinctness, her imagination set before her. She was sitting at the piano and heard suddenly a horse stop at the front door—Edward was back. But the bell rang. Why should Edward ring? There was a murmur of voices without, and then Arthur Branderton came in. In her mind's eye she saw every detail most clearly. He was in his hunting things! Something had happened, and, knowing what it was, Bertha was yet able to realize her terrified wonder as one possibility and another rushed through her brain. He was uneasy; he had something to tell, but dared not say it; she looked at him, horror-stricken, and a faintness came over her so that she could hardly stand.

Bertha's heart beat fast; she told herself it was absurd to allow her imagination to run away with her; but while she was arguing with herself the pictures went on developing themselves in her mind: she seemed to be assisting at a ghastly play in which she was the principal actor.

And what would she do when the fact was finally told her that Edward was dead? She would faint or cry out.

'There's been an accident,' said Branderton. 'Your husband is rather hurt.'

Bertha put her hands to her eyes, the agony was dreadful.

'You musn't upset yourself,' he went on, trying to break it to her.

Then, rapidly passing over the intermediate details, she found herself with her husband. He was dead, lying on the floor, and she pictured him to herself; she knew exactly how he would look; sometimes he slept so soundly, so quietly, that she was nervous, and put her ear to his heart to hear if it was beating. Now he was dead. Despair suddenly swept down upon her, overpoweringly. Bertha tried again to shake off her fancies, she even went to the piano and played a few notes; but the morbid attraction was too strong for her, and the scene went on. Now that he was dead he could not repulse her passion; now he was helpless and she kissed him with all her love; she passed her hands through his hair, and stroked his face (he had hated this in life), she kissed his lips and his closed eyes.

The imagined grief was so poignant that Bertha burst into tears. She remained with the body, refusing to be separated from it, and Bertha buried her face in cushions so that nothing might disturb her illusion; she had ceased trying to drive it away. Ah, she loved him passionately, she had always loved him and could not live without him. She knew that she would shortly die—and she had been afraid of death. Ah, now it was welcome! She kissed his hands—he could not prevent her now—and with a little shudder opened one of his eyes; it was glassy, expressionless, immobile. She burst into tears and, clinging to him, sobbed in love and anguish. She would let no one touch him but herself; it was a relief to perform the last offices for him who had been her whole life. She did not know that her love was so great.

She undressed the body and washed it; she washed the limbs one by one and sponged them; then very gently dried them with a towel. The touch of the cold flesh made her shudder voluptuously: she thought of him taking her in his strong arms, kissing her on the mouth. She wrapped him in the white shroud and surrounded him with flowers. They placed him in the coffin, and her heart stood still. She could not leave him, she passed with him all day and all night, looking ever at the quiet, restful face. Dr Ramsay came and Miss Glover came, urging her to go away, but she refused. What was the care of her own health now? She had only wanted to live for him. The coffin was closed, and she saw the faces of the undertakers; she had seen her husband's face for the last time, her beloved; her heart was like a stone, and she clutched at her breast in the pain of the oppression.

Hurriedly now the pictures thronged upon her, the drive to the churchyard, the service, the coffin covered with flowers and finally the graveside. They tried to keep her at home. What cared she for the silly, the abominable convention that sought to prevent her from going to the funeral? Was it not her husband, the only light of her life, whom they were burying? They could not realize the horror of it, the utter despair. And distinctly, by the dimness of the winter day, in the drawing-room of Court Leys, Bertha saw the lowering of the coffin, heard the rattle of earth thrown upon it.

What would her life be afterwards? She would try to live, she would surround herself with Edward's things, so that his memory might be always with her. The loneliness of life was appalling. Court Leys was empty and bare. She saw the endless succession of grey days; the seasons brought no change, and continually the clouds hung heavily above her; the trees were always leafless, and it was desolate. She could not imagine that travel would bring solace; the whole of life was blank, and what to her now were the pictures and churches, the blue skies of Italy? Her only happiness was to weep.

Then distractedly Bertha thought she would kill herself; her life was impossible to endure. No life at all, the blankness of the grave was preferable to the pangs gnawing continually at her heart. It would be so easy to finish, with a little morphia to close the book of trouble; despair would give her courage, and the prick of the needle was the only pain. But her vision became dim, and she had to make an effort to retain it. Her thoughts, growing less coherent, travelled back to previous incidents, to the scene at the grave and to the voluptuous pleasure of washing the body.

It was all so vivid that the entrance of Edward came upon her as a surprise. But the relief was almost too great for words, it was the awakening from a horrible nightmare. When he came forward to kiss her, she flung her arms round his neck and pressed him passionately to her heart.

'Oh, thank God!' she cried.

'Hulloa, what's up now?'

'I don't know what's been the matter with me. I've been so miserable, Eddie. I thought you were dead.'

'You've been crying.'

'It was so awful, I couldn't get the idea out of my head. Oh, I should die also.'

Bertha could hardly realize that her husband was by her side in the flesh, alive and well.

'Would you be sorry if *I* died?' she asked him.

'But you're not going to do anything of the sort,' he said, cheerily.

'Sometimes I'm so frightened, I don't believe I'll get over it.'

He laughed at her, and his joyous tones were peculiarly comforting. She made him sit by her side, and held his strong hands, the hands that to her were the visible signs of his powerful manhood. She stroked them and kissed the palms. She was quite broken with the past emotions; her limbs trembled and her eyes glistened with tears.

CHAPTER XVI

THE nurse arrived, bringing new apprehensions. She was an old woman who for twenty years had brought the neighbouring gentry into the world, and she had a copious store of ghastly anecdotes. In her mouth the terrors of birth were innumerable, and she told her stories with a cumulative art that was appalling. Of course, in her own mind she acted for the best. Bertha was nervous, and the nurse could imagine no better way of reassuring her than to give detailed accounts of patients who for days had been at death's door, given up by all the doctors, and yet had finally recovered and lived happily ever afterwards.

Bertha's quick invention magnified the coming anguish till, for thinking of it, she could hardly sleep at night. The impossibility of even conceiving it rendered it more formidable; she saw before her a long, long agony and then death. She could not bear Eddie to be out of her sight.

'Why, of course you'll get over it,' he said. 'I promise you it's nothing to make a fuss about.'

He had bred animals for years, and was quite used to the process that supplied him with veal, mutton and beef for the local butchers. It was a ridiculous fuss that human beings made over a natural and ordinary phenomenon.

'Why, Dinah, the Irish terrier I used to have, had litters as regular as clockwork, and she was running about ten minutes afterwards.'

Bertha lay with her face to the wall, holding Edward's fingers with a feverish hand.

'Oh, I'm so afraid of the pain. I feel certain that I shan't get over it—it's awful. I wish I hadn't got to go through it.'

Then as the days passed she looked upon Dr Ramsay as her very stay.

'You won't hurt me,' she begged.' I can't bear pain a bit. You'll give me chloroform all the time, won't you?'

'Good Heavens,' cried the doctor, 'one would think no one had ever had a baby before you.'

'Oh, don't laugh at me. Can't you see how frightened I am?'

She asked the nurse how long her agony must last. She lay in bed, white, with terror-filled eyes, her lips set and a little vertical line between the brows.

'I shall never get through it,' she whispered. 'I have a presentiment that I shall die.'

'I never knew a woman yet,' said Dr Ramsay, 'who hadn't a presentiment that she would die, even if she had nothing worse than a finger-ache the matter with her.'

'Oh, you can laugh,' said Bertha. 'I've got to go through it.'

And the thought recurred persistently that she would die.

Another day passed, and the nurse said the doctor must be immediately sent for. Bertha had made Edward promise to remain with her all the time.

'I think I shall have courage if I can hold your hand,' she said.

'Nonsense,' said Dr Ramsay, when Edward told him this. 'I'm not going to have a man meddling about.'

'I thought not,' said Edward, 'but I just promised to keep her quiet.'

'If you'll keep yourself quiet,' answered the doctor, 'that's all I shall expect.'

'Oh, you needn't fear about me. I know all about these things. Why, my dear doctor, I've brought a good sight more living things into the world than you have, I bet.'

Edward was an eminently sensible man, whom any woman might admire. He was neither hysterical nor nervous; calm, self-possessed and unimaginative, he was the ideal person for an emergency.

'There's no good my knocking about the house all the afternoon,' he said. 'I should only mope, and if I'm wanted I can always be sent for.'

He left word that he was going to Bewlie's Farm to see a cow that was sick. He was anxious about her.

'She's the best milker I've ever had. I don't know what I should do if something went wrong with her. She gives her so many pints a day as regular as possible. She's brought in over and over again the money I gave for her.'

He walked along with the free-and-easy stride that Bertha so much admired, glancing now and then at the fields that bordered the highway. He stopped to examine the beans of a rival farmer.

'That soil's no good,' he said, shaking his head. 'It don't pay to grow beans on a patch like that.'

Then, arriving at Bewlie's Farm, he called for the labourer in charge of the sick cow.

'Well, how's she going?'

'She ain't no better, squire.'

'Bad job! Has Thompson been to see her today?'

Thompson was the vet.

''E can't make nothin' of it. 'E thinks it's a habscess she's got, but I don't put much faith in Mister Thompson: 'is father was a labourer same as me, only 'e didn't 'ave to do with farming, bein' a bricklayer; and wot 'is son can know about cattle I don't know.'

'Well, let's go and look at her,' said Edward.

He strode over to the barn, followed by the labourer. The poor beast was standing in one corner, looking even more meditative than is usual with cows, hanging her head and humping her back; she looked profoundly pessimistic.

'I should have thought Thompson could do something,' said Edward.

''E says the butcher's the only thing for 'er,' said the other, with great contempt.

Edward snorted indignantly. 'Butcher indeed! I'd like to butcher him if I got the chance.'

He went into the farmhouse, which for years had been his home, but he was a practical, sensible fellow, and it brought him no memories, no particular emotion.

'Well, Mrs Jones,' he said to the tenant's wife, 'how's yourself?'

'Middlin', sir. And 'ow are you and Mrs Craddock?'

'I'm all right. The missus is having a baby, you know.'

He spoke in the jovial, careless way that endeared him to all and sundry.

'Bless my soul, is she indeed, sir? And I knew you when you was a boy. When d'you expect it?'

'I expect it every minute. Why, for all I know I may be a happy father when I get back to tea.'

'Oh, I didn't know it was so soon as all that.'

'Well, it was about time, Mrs Jones. We've been married sixteen months, and chance it.'

'Ah, well, sir, it's a thing as 'appens to everybody. I 'ope she's takin' it well.'

'As well as can be expected, you know. Of course she's very fanciful. Women are full of ideas; I never saw anything like 'em. Now as I was saying to Dr Ramsay only today, a bitch'll have half a dozen pups and be running about before you can say Jack Robinson. What I want to know is, why aren't women the same? All this fuss and bother; it's enough to turn a man's hair grey.'

'You take it pretty cool, governor,' said Farmer Jones, who had known Edward in the days of his poverty.

'Me?' cried Edward, laughing. 'I know all about this sort of thing, you see. Why, look at all the calves I've had; and, mind you, I've not had an accident with a cow above twice all the time I've gone in for breeding. But I'd better be going to see how the missus is getting on. Good afternoon to you, Mrs Jones.'

'Now what I like about the squire,' said Mrs Jones, 'is that there's no 'aughtiness in 'im. 'E ain't too proud to take a cup of tea with you, although 'e is the squire now.'

''E's the best squire we've 'ad for thirty years,' said Farmer Jones. 'And as you say, my dear, there's not a drop of 'aughtiness in 'im—which is more than you can say for his missus.'

'Oh, well, she's young-like,' replied his wife. 'They do say as 'ow 'e's the master, and I daresay 'e'll teach 'er better.'

'Trust 'im for makin' 'is wife buckle under; 'e's not a man to stand nonsense from anybody.'

Edward swung along the road, whirling his stick round, whistling and talking to the dogs that accompanied him. He was of a hopeful disposition, and did not think it would be necessary to slaughter his best cow. He didn't believe in the vet half so much as in himself, and his private opinion was that she would recover. He walked up the avenue of Court Leys, looking at the young elms he had planted to fill up the gaps; they were pretty healthy on the whole, and he was pleased with his success. He entered, and as he was hanging up his hat a piercing scream reached his ears.

'Hulloa!' he said, 'things are beginning to get a bit lively.'

He went up to the bedroom and knocked at the door. Dr Ramsay opened it, but with his burly frame barred the passage.

'Oh, don't be afraid,' said Edward. 'I don't want to come in. I know when I'm best out of the way. How is she getting on?'

'Well, I'm afraid it won't be such an easy job as I thought,' whispered the doctor. 'But there's no reason to get alarmed. It's only a bit slow.'

'I shall be downstairs if you want me for anything.'

'She was asking for you a good deal just now, but Nurse told her it would upset you if you were there; so then she said: "Don't let him come. I'll bear it alone."'

'Oh, that's all right. In a time like this the husband is much better out of the way, I think.'

Dr Ramsay shut the door upon him. 'Sensible chap that!' he aid. 'I like him better and better. Why, most men would be fussing about and getting hysterical and Lord knows what.'

'Was that Eddie?' asked Bertha, her voice trembling with recent agony.

'Yes, he came to see how you were.'

'Oh, the darling!' she groaned. 'He isn't very much upset, is he? Don't tell him I'm very bad. It'll make him wretched. I'll bear it alone.'

Edward, downstairs, told himself it was no use getting into a state, which was quite true, and taking the most comfortable chair in the room, settled down to read his paper. Before dinner he went upstairs to make more inquiries. Dr Ramsay came out saying he had given Bertha opium and for a while she was quiet.

'It's lucky you did it just at dinner-time,' said Edward, with a laugh.' We'll be able to have a snack together.'

They sat down and began to eat; they rivalled one another in their appetites, and the doctor, liking Edward more and more said it did him good to see a man who could eat well. But before they had reached the pudding a message came from the nurse to say that Bertha was awake, and Dr Ramsay regretfully left the table. Edward went on eating steadily. At last, with the happy sigh of a man conscious of virtue and a distended stomach, he lit his pipe and again settling himself in the armchair in a little while began to nod. The evening was long and he felt bored.

'It ought to be all over by now,' he said.' I wonder if I need stay up.'

Dr Ramsay was looking worried when Edward went up to him a third time.

'I'm afraid it's a difficult case,' he said. 'It's most unfortunate. She's been suffering a good deal, poor thing.'

'Well, is there anything I can do?' asked Edward.

'No, except to keep calm and not make a fuss.'

'Oh, I shan't do that, you needn't fear. I will say that for myself, I have got nerve.'

'You're splendid,' said Dr Ramsay. 'I tell you I like to see a man keep his head so well through a job like this.'

'Well, what I came to ask you was, is there any good in my sitting up? Of course I'll do it if any thing can be done; but if not I may as well go to bed.'

'Yes, I think you'd much better. I'll call you if you're wanted. I think you might come in and say a word or two to Bertha; it will encourage her.'

Edward entered. Bertha was lying with staring, terrified eyes, eyes that seemed to have lately seen entirely new things; they shone glassily. Her face was whiter than ever, the blood had fled from her lips, and the cheeks were sunken: she looked as if she were dying. She greeted Edward with the faintest smile.

'How are you, little woman?' he asked.

His presence seemed to call her back to life, and a faint colour lit up her cheeks.

'I'm all right,' she groaned, making an effort. 'You musn't worry yourself, dear.'

'Been having a bad time?'

'No,' she said, bravely. 'I've not really suffered much. There's nothing for you to upset yourself about.'

He went out, and she called Dr Ramsay.

'You haven't told him what I've gone through, have you? I don't want him to know.'

'No, that's all right. I've told him to go to bed.'

'Oh, I'm glad. He can't bear not to get his proper night's rest. How long d'you think it will last? Already I feel as if I'd been tortured for ever, and it seems endless.'

'Oh, it'll soon be over now, I hope.'

'I'm sure I'm going to die,' she whispered. 'I feel that life is being gradually drawn out of me. I shouldn't mind if it weren't for Eddie. He'll be so cut up.'

'What nonsense!' said the nurse. 'You all say you're going to die. You'll be all right in a couple of hours.'

'D'you think it will last a couple of hours longer? I can't stand it. Oh, doctor, don't let me suffer any more.'

Edward went to bed quietly and soon was fast asleep. But his slumbers were somewhat troubled; generally he enjoyed the heavy, dreamless sleep of the man who has no nerves and takes plenty of exercise; tonight he dreamt. He dreamt not only that one cow was sick, but that all his cattle had fallen ill: the cows stood about with gloomy eyes and hump-backs, surly and dangerous, evidently with their livers totally deranged; the oxen were 'blown' and lay on their backs with legs kicking feebly in the air, and swollen to double their normal size.

'You must send them all to the butcher's,' said the vet. 'There's nothing to be done with them.'

'Good Lord deliver us,' said Edward. 'I shan't get four bob a stone for them.'

But his dream was disturbed by a knock at the door, and Edward awoke to find Dr Ramsay shaking him.

'Wake up, man. Get up and dress quickly.'

'What's the matter?' cried Edward, jumping out of bed and seizing his clothes. 'What's the time?'

'It's half-past four. I want you to go into Tercanbury for Dr Spencer. Bertha is very bad.'

'All right, I'll bring him back with me.'

Edward rapidly dressed.

'I'll go round and wake up the man to put the horse in.'

'No, I'll do that myself; it'll take me half the time.'

He methodically laced his boots.

'Bertha is in no immediate danger. But I must have a consultation. I still hope we shall bring her through it.'

'By Jove,' said Edward, 'I didn't know it was so bad as that.'

'You need not get alarmed yet. The great thing is for you to keep calm and bring Spencer along as quickly as possible. It's not hopeless yet.'

Edward with all his wits about him, was soon ready, and with equal rapidity set to harnessing the horse. He carefully lit the lamps as the proverb 'more haste less speed' passed through his mind. In two minutes he was on the main road, and whipped up the horse. He went with a quick, steady trot through the silent night.

Dr Ramsay, returning to the sick-room, thought what a splendid object a man was who could be relied upon to do anything, who never lost his head or got excited. His admiration for Edward was growing by leaps and bounds.

CHAPTER XVII

EDWARD Craddock was a strong man and unimaginative. Driving through the night to Tercanbury he did not give way to distressing thoughts, but easily kept his anxiety within proper bounds, and gave his whole attention to conducting the horse. He kept his eyes on the road in front of him. The horse stepped out with swift, regular stride, rapidly passing the milestones. Edward rang Dr Spencer up and gave him the note he carried. The doctor presently came down, an undersized man with a squeaky voice and a gesticulative manner. He looked upon Edward with suspicion.

'I suppose you're the husband?' he said, as they clattered down the street. 'Would you tike me to drive? I daresay you're rather upset.'

'No, and don't want to be,' answered Edward with a laugh. He looked down a little upon people who lived in towns, and never trusted a man who was less than six feet high and burly in proportion.

'I'm rather nervous of anxious husbands who drive me at breakneck pace in the middle of the night,' said the doctor. 'The ditches have an almost irresistible attraction for them.'

'Well, I'm not nervous, doctor, so it doesn't matter twopence if you are.'

When they reached the open country, Edward set the horse going at its fastest; he was amused at the doctor's desire to drive. Absurd little man!

'Are you holding on tight?' he asked, with good-natured scorn.

'I can see you can drive,' said the doctor.

'It is not the first time I've had reins in my hands,' replied Edward modestly. 'Here we are.'

He showed the specialist to the bedroom and asked whether Dr Ramsay required him further.

'No, I don't want you just now; but you'd better stay up to be ready, if anything happens. I'm afraid Bertha is very bad indeed. You must be prepared for everything.'

Edward retired to the next room and sat down. He was genuinely disturbed, but even now he could not realize that Bertha was dying; his mind was sluggish and he was unable to imagine the future. A more emotional man would have been white with fear, his heart beating painfully, and his nerves quivering with a hundred anticipated terrors. He would have been quite useless, while Edward was fit for any emergency; he could have been trusted to drive another ten miles in search of some appliance, and with perfect steadiness to help in any necessary operation.

'You know,' he said to Dr Ramsay, 'I don't want to get in your way; but if I should be any use in the room you can trust me not to get flurried.'

'I don't think there's anything you can do; the nurse is very trustworthy and capable.'

'Women,' said Edward, 'get so excited; they always make fools of themselves if they possibly can.'

But the night air had made Craddock sleepy, and after half an hour in the chair, trying to read a book, he dozed off. Presently, however, he awoke, and the first light of day filled the room with a grey coldness. He looked at his watch.

'By Jove, it's a long job,' he said.

There was a knock at the door, and the nurse came in.

'Will you please come?'

Dr Ramsay met him in the passage.

'Thank God, it's over. She's had a terrible time.'

'Is she all right?'

'I think she's in no danger now, but I'm sorry to say we couldn't save the child.'

A pang went through Edward's heart. 'Is it dead?'

'It was still-born. I was afraid it was hopeless. You'd better go to Bertha now, she wants you. She doesn't know about the child.'

Bertha was lying in an attitude of extreme exhaustion: she lay on her back, with arms stretched in utter weakness by her sides. Her face was grey with past anguish, her eyes now were dull and lifeless, half closed, and her jaw hung almost as hangs the jaw of a dead man. She tried to form a smile as she saw Edward, but in her feebleness the lips scarcely moved.

'Don't try to speak, dear,' said the nurse, seeing that Bertha was attempting words.

Edward bent down and kissed her the faintest blush coloured her cheeks, and then she began to cry; the tears stealthily glided down her cheeks.

'Come nearer to me, Eddie,' she whispered.

He knelt down beside her, suddenly touched. He took her hand, and the contact had a vivifying effect; she drew a long breath and her lips formed a weary, weary smile.

'Thank God, it's over,' she groaned. 'Oh, Eddie darling, you can't think what I've gone through. It hurt so awfully.'

'Well, it's all over now,' said Edward.

'And you've been worrying too, Eddie. It encouraged me to think that you shared my trouble. You must go to sleep now. It was good of you to drive to Tercanbury for me.'

'You musn't talk,' said Dr Ramsay, coming back into the room after seeing the specialist sent off.

'I'm better now,' said Bertha, 'since I've seen Eddie.'

'Well, you must go to sleep.'

'You've not told me yet if it's a boy or a girl; tell me, Eddie, you know.'

Edward looked uneasily at the doctor.

'It's a boy,' said Dr Ramsay.

'I knew it would be,' she murmured. An expression of ecstatic pleasure came into her face, chasing away the greyness of death. 'I'm so glad. Have you seen it, Eddie?'

'Not yet.'

'It's our child, isn't it? It's worth going through the pain to have a baby. I'm so happy.'

'You must go to sleep now.'

'I'm not a bit sleepy, and I want to see my son.'

'No, you can't see him now,' said Dr Ramsay, 'he's asleep, and you mustn't disturb him.'

'Oh, I should like to see him—just for one minute. You needn't wake him.'

'You shall see him after you've been asleep,' said the doctor soothingly. 'It'll excite you too much.'

'Well, you go and see him, Eddie, and kiss him; and then I'll go to sleep.'

She seemed so anxious that at least its father should see his child that the nurse led Edward into the next room. On a chest of drawers was lying something covered with a towel. This the nurse lifted, and Edward saw his child; it was naked and very small, hardly human, repulsive, yet very pitiful. The eyes were closed, the eyes that had never opened. Edward looked at it for a minute.

'I promised I'd kiss it,' he whispered.

He bent down and touched with his lips the cold forehead; the nurse drew the towel over the body and they went back to Bertha.

'Is he sleeping?' she asked.

'Yes.'

'Did you kiss him?'

'Yes.'

Bertha smiled: 'Fancy your kissing my baby before me.'

But the soporific that Dr Ramsay had administered was taking its effect, and almost immediately Bertha fell into a happy sleep.

'Let's take a turn in the garden,' said Dr Ramsay, 'I think I ought to be here when she wakes.'

The air was fresh, scented with the spring flowers and the odour of the earth. Both men inspired it with relief after the close atmosphere of the sick-room. Dr Ramsay put his arm in Edward's.

'Cheer up, my boy,' he said. 'You've borne it all magnificently. I've never seen a man go through a night like this better than you; and upon my word you're as fresh as paint this morning.'

'Oh, I'm all right,' said Edward. 'What's to be done about—about the baby?'

'I think she'll be able to bear it better after she's had a sleep. I really didn't dare say it was still-born; I thought the shock would be too much for her.'

They went in and washed and ate, then waited for Bertha to wake. At last the nurse called them.

'You poor things,' cried Bertha as they entered the room. 'Have you had no sleep at all? I feel quite well now, and I want my baby. Nurse says it's sleeping and I can't have it, but I will. I want it to sleep with me, I want to look at my son.'

Edward and the nurse looked at Dr Ramsay, who for once was disconcerted.

'I don't think you'd better have him today, Bertha,' he said. 'It would upset you.'

'Oh, but I must have my baby. Nurse, bring him to me at once.'

Edward knelt down again by the bedside and took her hands. 'Now, Bertha, you musn't be alarmed, but the baby's not well and—'

'What d'you mean?'

Bertha suddenly sprang up in bed.

'Lie down. Lie down,' cried both Dr Ramsay and the nurse, forcing her back on the pillow.

'What's the matter with him, doctor?' she cried, in sudden terror.

'It's as Edward says, he's not well.'

'Oh, he isn't going to die—after all I've gone through.'

She looked from one to the other.

'Oh, tell me, don't keep me in suspense. I can bear it, whatever it is.'

Dr Ramsay touched Edward, encouraging him.

'You must prepare yourself for bad news, darling. You know—'

'He isn't dead?' she shrieked.

'I'm awfully sorry, dear. He was still-born.'

'Oh, God!' groaned Bertha.

It was a cry of despair. And then she burst into passionate weeping. Her sobs were terrible, unbridled, it was her life that she was weeping away, her hope of happiness, all her desires and dreams. Her heart seemed breaking. She put her hands to her eyes in agony.

'Then I went through it all for nothing? Oh, Eddie, you don't know the frightful pain of it. All night I thought I should die. I would have given anything to be put out of my suffering. And it was all useless.'

She sobbed uncontrollably. She was crushed by the recollection of what she had gone through and its futility.

'Oh, I wish I could die.'

The tears were in Edward's eyes, and he kissed her hands.

'Don't give way, darling,' he said, searching in vain for words to console her. His voice faltered and broke.

'Oh, Eddie,' she said, 'you're suffering just as much as I am. I forgot. Let me see him now.'

Dr Ramsay made a sign to the nurse, and she fetched the dead child. She carried it to the bedside, and uncovering its head showed the face to Bertha. She looked a moment, and then asked:

'Let me see the whole body.'

The nurse removed the cloth, and Bertha looked again. She said nothing, but finally turned away, and the nurse withdrew.

Bertha's tears now had ceased, but her mouth was set to a hopeless woe.

'Oh, I loved him already so much,' she murmured.

Edward bent over: 'Don't grieve, darling.'

She put her arms round his neck as she had delighted to do.

'Oh, Eddie, love me with all your heart. I want your love so badly.'

CHAPTER XVIII

FOR days Bertha was overwhelmed with grief. She thought always of the dead child that had never lived, and her heart ached. But above all she was tormented by the idea that all her pain had been futile; she had gone through so much, her sleep still was full of the past agony, and it had been useless, utterly useless. Her body was mutilated so that she wondered it was possible for her to recover, she had lost her old buoyancy, that vitality that had been so enjoyable, and she felt like an old woman. Her weariness was unendurable; she felt so tired that it seemed to her impossible to rest. She lay in bed, day after day, in a posture of hopeless fatigue, on her back, with arms stretched out alongside of her, the pillows supporting her head; and all her limbs were powerless.

Recovery was very slow, and Edward suggested sending for Miss Ley; but Bertha refused.

'I don't want to see anybody,' she said. 'I merely want to lie still and be quiet.'

It bored her to speak with people, and even her affections for the time were dormant; she looked upon Edward as someone apart from her, his presence and absence gave her no particular emotion. She was tired and desired only to be left alone. Sympathy was unnecessary and useless; she knew that no one could enter into the bitterness of her sorrow, and she preferred to bear it alone.

Little by little, however, Bertha regained strength and consented to see the friends who called, some genuinely sorry, others impelled merely by a sense of duty or a ghoul-like curiosity. Miss Glover was a great trial; she felt the sincerest sympathy for Bertha, but her feelings were one thing and her sense of right and wrong was another. She did not think the young wife took her affliction with proper humility. Gradually a rebellious feeling had replaced the extreme prostration of the beginning, and Bertha raged at the injustice of her lot. Miss Glover came every day, bringing flowers and good advice; but Bertha was not docile, and refused to be satisfied with Miss Glover's pious consolations. When the good creature read the Bible, Bertha listened with a firmer closing of her lips, sullenly.

'Do you like me to read the Bible to you, dear?' asked the parson's sister sometimes.

But one day, Bertha, driven beyond her patience, could not as usual command her tongue.

'It amuses you, dear,' she answered bitterly.

'Oh, Bertha, you're not taking it in the proper spirit. You're so rebellious, and it's wrong, it's utterly wrong.'

'I can only think of my baby,' said Bertha, hoarsely.

'Why don't you pray to God, dear? Shall I offer a short prayer now, Bertha?'

'No, I don't want to pray to God. He's either impotent or cruel.'

'Bertha,' cried Miss Glover, 'you don't know what you're saying. Oh, pray to God, to melt your stubbornness, pray to God to forgive you.'

'I don't want to be forgiven. I've done nothing that needs it. It's God who needs my forgiveness—not I His.'

'You don't know what you're saying, Bertha,' said Miss Glover, very gravely and sorrowfully.

Bertha was still so ill that Miss Glover dared not press the subject, but she was grievously troubled. She asked herself whether she should consult her brother, to whom an absurd shyness prevented her from mentioning spiritual matters unless necessity compelled. But she had immense faith in him, and to her he was a type of all that the Christian clergyman should be: although her character was much stronger than his, Mr Glover seemed to his sister a pillar of strength, and often in past times, when the flesh was more stubborn, had she found strength and consolation in his very mediocre sermons. Finally, however, Miss Glover decided to speak with him on the subject that distressed her, with the result that for a week she avoided spiritual topics in her daily conversations with the invalid; then, Bertha having grown a little stronger, without previously mentioning her intention she brought her brother to Court Leys.

Miss Glover went alone to Bertha's room, her ardent sense of propriety fearing that Bertha, in bed, might not be costumed decorously enough for the visit of a clerical gentleman.

'Oh,' she said, 'Charles is downstairs, and would like to see you so much. I thought I'd better come up first to see if you were presentable.'

Bertha was sitting up in bed, with a mass of cushions and pillows behind her; a bright red jacket contrasted with her dark hair and the pallor of her skin. She drew her lips together when she heard that the vicar was below, and a slight frown darkened her forehead. Miss Glover caught sight of it.

'I don't think she likes your coming,' said Miss Glover—to encourage him—when she went to fetch her brother,' but I think it's your duty.'

'Yes, I think it's my duty,' replied Mr Glover, who liked the approaching interview as little as Bertha.

He was an honest man, oppressed by the inroads of dissent, but his ministrations were confined to the services in church, the collecting of subscriptions, and the visiting of the church-going poor. It was something new to be brought before a rebellious gentlewoman, and he did not quite know how to treat her.

Miss Glover opened the bedroom door for her brother, and he entered, a cold wind laden with carbolic acid; she solemnly put a chair for him by the bedside and another for herself at a little distance.

'Ring for the tea before you sit down, Fanny,' said Bertha.

'I think, if you don't mind, Charles would like to speak to you first,' said Miss Glover. 'Am I not right, Charles?'

'Yes, dear.'

'I took the liberty of telling him what you had said to me the other day, Bertha.'

Mrs Craddock pursed her lips, but made no reply.

'I hope you're not angry with me for doing so, but I thought it my duty. Now, Charles.'

The Vicar of Leanham coughed.

'I can quite understand,' he said, 'that you must be most distressed at your affliction. It's a most unfortunate occurrence. I need not say that Fanny and I sympathize with you from the bottom of our hearts.'

'We do indeed,' said his sister.

Still Bertha did not answer, and Miss Glover looked at her uneasily. The vicar coughed again.

'But I always think that we should be thankful for the cross we have to bear. It is, as it were, a measure of the confidence that God places in us.'

Bertha remained silent, and the parson inquiringly looked at his sister. Miss Glover saw that no good would come by beating about the bush.

'The fact is, Bertha,' she said, breaking the awkward silence, 'that Charles and I are very anxious that you should be churched. You don't mind our saying so, but we're both a great deal older than you are, and we think it will do you good. We do hope you'll consent to it; but, more than that, Charles is here as the clergyman of your parish to tell you that it is your duty.'

'I hope it won't be necessary for me to put it in that way, Mrs Craddock.'

Bertha paused a moment longer, and then asked for a prayer-book. Miss Glover gave a smile which for her was radiant.

'I've been wanting for a long time to make you a little present, Bertha,' she said. 'And it occurred to me that you might like a prayer-book with good large print. I've noticed in church that the book you generally use is so small that it must try your eyes and be a temptation to you not to follow the service. So I've brought you one today, which it will give me very much pleasure if you will accept.'

She produced a large volume, bound in gloomy black cloth and redolent of the antiseptic odours that pervaded the Vicarage. The print was indeed large, but since the society that arranged the publication insisted on the combination of cheapness with utility, the paper was abominable.

'Thank you very much,' said Bertha, holding out her hand for the gift. 'It's awfully kind of you.'

'Shall I find you the "Churching of Women"?' asked Miss Glover.

Bertha nodded, and presently the vicar's sister handed her the book open. She read a few lines and dropped the volume.

'I have no wish to "give hearty thanks unto God,"' she said, looking almost fiercely at the worthy couple. 'I'm very sorry to offend your prejudices, but it seems to me absurd that I should prostrate myself in gratitude to God.'

'Oh, Mrs Craddock, I trust you don't mean what you say,' said the vicar.

'This is what I told you, Charles,' said Miss Glover. 'I don't think Bertha is well; but still this seems to me dreadfully wicked.'

Bertha frowned, finding it difficult to repress the sarcasms that rose to her lips; her forbearance was sorely tried. But Mr Glover was a little undecided.

'We must be as thankful to God for the afflictions that He sends us as for the benefits,' he said at last.

'I am not a worm to crawl along the ground and give thanks to the Foot that crushes me.'

'I think that is blasphemous, Bertha,' said Miss Glover.

'Oh, I have no patience with you, Fanny,' said Bertha, a flush lighting up her face. 'Can you realize what I've gone through, the terrible pain of it? Oh, it was too awful. Even now when I think of it I almost scream. Don't you know what it is? It feels as if your flesh were being torn, it's like sharp hooks dragged through your entrails. You try to be brave, you clench your teeth to stop crying out, but the pain is so awful that you're powerless. You shriek in your agony.'

'Bertha, Bertha,' said Miss Glover, horrified that such details should assail the chaste ears of the Vicar of Leanham.

'And the endlessness of it—they stand round you like ghouls, and do nothing. They say you must have patience, that it'll soon be over; and it lasts on. And time after time the awful agony comes, you feel it coming and you think you can't endure it. Oh, I wanted to die, it was too awful.'

'It is by suffering that we rise to our higher selves,' said Miss Glover. 'Suffering is a fire that burns away the grossness of our material natures.'

'What rubbish you talk,' cried Bertha passionately. 'You say that because you've never suffered. People say that suffering ennobles one; it's a lie, it only makes one brutal. But I would have borne it for the sake of my child. It was all useless—utterly useless. Dr Ramsay told me the child had been dead the whole time. Oh, if God made me suffer like that it's infamous. I wonder you're not ashamed to put it down to your God. How can you imagine Him to be so stupid, so cruel? Why, even the vilest, most brutal man on the earth wouldn't cause a woman such frightful and useless agony for the mere pleasure of it. Your God is a ruffian at a cock-fight, drinking in the bloodiness, laughing because the wretched birds, in their faintness, stagger ridiculously.'

Miss Glover sprang to her feet.

'Bertha, your illness is no excuse for this. You must either be mad or utterly depraved and wicked.'

'No, I'm more charitable than you,' cried Bertha. 'I know there is no God.'

'Then I for one can have nothing more to do with you.'

Miss Glover's cheeks were flaming, and a sudden indignation dispelled her habitual shyness.

'Fanny, Fanny,' cried her brother, 'restrain yourself!'

'Oh, this isn't the time to restrain oneself, Charles. It's one's duty to speak out sometimes. No, Bertha, if you're an atheist I can have nothing more to do with you.'

'She spoke in anger,' said the vicar. 'It is not our duty to judge her.'

'It's our duty to protest when the name of God is taken in vain. Charles, if you think Bertha's position excuses her blasphemies, then I think you ought to be ashamed of yourself. But I'm not afraid to speak out. Yes, Bertha, I've known for a long time that you were proud and headstrong, but I thought time would change you. I have always had confidence in you, because I thought at the bottom you were good. But if you deny your Maker, Bertha, there can be no hope for you.'

'Fanny, Fanny,' murmured the vicar.

'Let me speak, Charles. I think you're a bad and wicked woman, and I can no longer feel sorry for you, because everything that you have suffered I think you have thoroughly deserved. Your heart is absolutely hard, and I know nothing so thoroughly wicked as a hard-hearted woman.'

'My dear Fanny,' said Bertha, smiling, 'we've both been absurdly melodramatic.'

'I refuse to laugh at the subject. I see nothing ridiculous in it. Come, Charles, let us go and leave her to her own thoughts.'

But as Miss Glover bounded to the door, the handle was turned from the outside and Mrs Branderton came in. The position was awkward, and her appearance seemed almost providential to the vicar, who could not fling out of the room like his sister, but also could not make up his mind to shake hands with Bertha as if nothing had happened. Mrs Branderton came in, all airs and graces, smirking and ogling, and the gewgaws on her brand-new bonnet quivered with every movement.

'I told the servant I could find my way up alone, Bertha,' she said. 'I wanted so much to see you.'

'Mr and Miss Glover were just going,' said Bertha. 'How kind of you to come!'

Miss Glover bounced out of the room with a smile at Mrs Branderton that was almost ghastly; and Mr Glover, meek, polite and antiseptic as ever, shaking hands with Mrs Branderton, followed his sister.

'What queer people they are!' said Mrs Branderton, standing at the window to see them go out of the front door. 'I really don't think they're quite human. Why, she's walking on in front—she might wait for him—taking such long steps; and he's trying to catch her up. I believe they're having a race. What ridiculous people! Isn't it a pity she will wear short skirts? My dear, her great ankles are positively pornographic. I believe they wear one another's boots indiscriminately. And how are you, dear? I think you're looking much better.'

Mrs Branderton sat in such a position as to have a full view of herself in a mirror.

'What nice looking-glasses you have in your room, my dear. No woman can dress properly without them. Now you've only got to look at poor Fanny Glover to know that she's so modest as never even to look at herself in the glass to put her hat on.'

Mrs Branderton chattered on, thinking that she was doing Bertha good.

'A woman doesn't want to be solemn when she's ill. I know, when I have anything the matter, I like someone to talk to me about the fashions. I remember in my young days when I was ill I used to get old Mr Crowhurst, the former vicar, to come and read the ladies' papers to me. He was such a nice old man, not a bit like a clergyman, and he used to say I was his only parishioner whom he really liked visiting. I'm not tiring you, am I, dear?'

'Oh, dear, no,' said Bertha.

'Now, I suppose the Glovers have been talking all sorts of stuff to you. Of course, one has to put up with it, I suppose, because it sets a good example to the lower classes; but I must say, I think the clergy nowadays sometimes forget their place. I consider it most objectionable when they insist on talking religion with you as if you were a common person. But they're not nearly so nice as they used to be. In my young days the clergy were always gentlemen's sons—but then they weren't expected to trouble about the poor. I can quite understand that now a gentleman shouldn't like to become a clergyman; he has to mix with the lower classes, and they're growing more familiar every day.'

But suddenly, Bertha without warning burst into tears. Mrs Branderton was flabbergasted.

'My dear, what is the matter? Where are your salts? Shall I ring the bell?'

Bertha, sobbing violently, begged Mrs Branderton to take no notice of her. That fashionable creature had a sentimental heart, and would have been delighted to weep with Bertha, but she had several calls to make and therefore could not risk a disarrangement of her person; she was also curious, and would have given much to find out the cause of Bertha's outburst She comforted herself, however, by giving the Hancocks, whose At Home day it was, a detailed account of the affair; and they shortly afterwards recounted it with sundry embellishments to Mrs Mayston Ryle.

Mrs Mayston Ryle, magnificently imposing as ever, snorted like a charger, eager for battle.

'Mrs Branderton sends *me* to sleep, frequently,' she said, 'but I can quite understand that if the poor thing isn't well, Mrs Branderton would make her cry. I never see her myself unless I'm in the most robust health, otherwise I know she'd simply make me howl.'

'But I wonder what was the matter with poor Mrs Craddock,' said Miss Hancock.

'I don't know,' answered Mrs Mayston Ryle, in her majestic manner. 'But I'll find out. I daresay she only wants a little good society, *I* shall go and see her.'

And she did!

CHAPTER XIX

BUT the apathy with which for weeks Bertha had looked upon all terrestrial concerns was passing away before her increasing strength; it had been due only to an utter physical weakness, of the same order as that merciful indifference to all earthly sympathies that gives ease to the final passage into the Unknown. The prospect of death would be unendurable if one did not know that the enfeebled body brought a like enfeeblement of spirit, dissolving the ties of the world: when the traveller must leave the hostel with the double gate, the wine he loved has lost its savour and the bread turned bitter in his mouth. Like useless gauds, Bertha had let fall the interest of life and her soul lay dying. Her spirit was a lighted candle in a lantern, flickering in the wind so that its flame was hardly seen, and the lantern was useless; but presently the wind of Death was stilled, and the light shone out and filled the darkness.

With the increasing strength the old passion returned; Love came back like a conqueror, and Bertha knew that she had not done with life. In her loneliness she yearned for Edward's affection; he now was all she had, and she stretched out her arms to him with a great desire. She blamed herself bitterly for her coldness, she wept at the idea of what he must have suffered. And she was ashamed that the love that she had thought eternal should have been for a while destroyed. But a change had come over her, she did not now love her husband with the old blind passion, but with a new feeling added to it; for to him were transferred the tenderness that she had lavished on her dead child and all the yearning that must now, to her life's end, go unsatisfied. Her heart was like a house with empty chambers, and the fires of love raged through them triumphantly.

Bertha thought a little painfully of Miss Glover, but dismissed her with a shrug of the shoulders. The good creature had kept her resolve never again to come near Court Leys, and for three days nothing had been heard of her.

'What does it matter?' cried Bertha. 'So long as Eddie loves me, the rest of the world is nothing.'

But her bedroom now had the aspect of a prison; she felt it impossible much longer to endure its dreadful monotony. Her bed was a bed of torture, and she fancied that so long as she remained stretched upon it she would never regain her health. She begged Dr Ramsay to allow her to get up, but was always met with the same refusal; and this was backed up by her husband's common sense. All she obtained was the dismissal of the nurse, to whom she had taken a sudden and violent dislike. From no reasonable cause Bertha found the mere presence of the poor woman unendurable; her officious loquacity irritated her beyond measure. If she must remain in bed, Bertha preferred absolute solitude; the turn of her mind was becoming almost misanthropic.

The hours passed endlessly. From her pillow Bertha could see only the sky, now a metallic blue with dazzling clouds swaying heavily across the line of sight, now grey, darkening the room; the furniture and the wallpaper forced themselves distastefully on her mind. Every detail was impressed on her consciousness as indelibly as the potter's mark on the clay.

Finally she made up her mind to get up, come what might. It was the Sunday after the quarrel with Miss Glover; Edward would be indoors, and doubtless intended to spend most of the afternoon in her bedroom, but she knew he disliked sitting there; the closeness, the odours of medicines and perfume, made his head ache. Her appearance in the drawing-room would be a pleasant surprise; she would not tell him that she was getting up, but go downstairs and take him unawares. She got out of bed, but as she put her feet to the ground had to cling to a chair; her legs were so weak that they hardly supported her, and her head reeled. But in a little while she gathered strength and dressed herself, slowly and very painfully; her weakness was almost pain. She had to sit down, and her hair was so wearisome to do that she was afraid she must give up the attempt and return to bed. But the thought of Edward's surprise upheld her; he had said how pleased he would be to have her downstairs with him. At last she was ready, and went to the door, supporting herself on every object at hand. But what a delight it was to be up again, to feel herself once more among the living, away from the grave of her bed!

She came to the top of the stairs and went down, leaning heavily on the banisters; she went one step at a time, as little children do, and she laughed at herself. But the laugh changed into a groan as in exhaustion she sank down and felt it impossible to go further. Then the thought of Edward urged her on. She struggled up and persevered till she reached the bottom. Now she was outside the drawing-room; she heard Edward whistling within. She crept along, eager to make no sound; noiselessly she turned the handle and flung the door open.

'Eddie!'

He turned round with a cry: 'Hulloa, what are you doing here?'

He came towards her, but did not show the great joy that she had expected.

'I wanted to surprise you. Aren't you glad to see me?'

'Yes, of course I am. But you oughtn't to have come without Dr Ramsay's leave. And I didn't expect you today.'

He led her to the sofa and she lay down.

'I thought you'd be so pleased.'

'Of course I am!'

He placed pillows under her and covered her with a rug.

'You don't know how I struggled,' she said. 'I thought I should never get my things on, and then I almost tumbled down the stairs, I was so weak. But I knew you must be lonely here, and you hate sitting in the bedroom.'

'You oughtn't to have risked it. It may throw you back,' he replied, gently. He looked at his watch. 'You must only stay half-an-hour, and then I shall carry you up to bed.'

Bertha gave a laugh, intending to permit nothing of the sort. It was so comfortable to lie on the sofa with Edward by her side. She held his hands.

'I simply couldn't stay in the room any longer. It was so gloomy with the rain pattering all day on the windows.'

It was one of those days of early autumn when the rain seems never ceasing and the air is filled with the melancholy of Nature conscious of the near decay.

'I was meaning to come up to you as soon as I'd finished my pipe.'

Bertha was exhausted, and, keeping silence, pressed Edward's hand in acknowledgement of his kind intention. It was delightful merely to be there with him, her heart was very full. Presently he looked at his watch again.

'Your half-hour's nearly up,' said he. 'In five minutes I'm going to carry you to your room.'

'Oh, no, you're not,' she replied, playfully, treating his remark as humorous. 'I'm going to stay till dinner.'

'No, you can't possibly. It will be very bad for you. To please me, go back to bed now.'

'Well, we'll split the difference and I'll go after tea.'

'No, you must go now.'

'Why, one would think you wanted to get rid of me!'

'I have to go out,' said Edward.

'Oh, no, you haven't; you're merely saying that to induce me to go upstairs. You fibber!'

'Let me carry you up now, there's a good girl.'

'I won't, I won't, I won't.'

'I shall have to leave you alone, Bertha. I didn't know you meant to get up today, and I have an engagement.'

'Oh, but you can't leave me the first time I get up. What is it? You can write a note and break it.'

'I'm awfully sorry,' he replied. 'But I'm afraid I can't do that. The fact is, I saw the Miss Hancocks after church; and they said they had to walk into Tercanbury this afternoon, and as it was so wet I offered to drive them in. I've promised to fetch them at three.'

'You're joking,' said Bertha.

Her eyes had suddenly become hard, and she was breathing fast. Edward looked at her uneasily.

'I didn't know you were going to get up, or I shouldn't have arranged to go out.'

'Oh, well, it doesn't matter,' said Bertha, throwing off the momentary anger. 'You can just write and say you can't come.'

'I'm afraid I can't do that,' he answered, gravely. 'I've given my word, and I can't break it.'

'Oh, but it's infamous!' Her wrath blazed out 'Even you can't be so cruel as to leave me at such a time. I deserve some consideration after all I've suffered. For weeks I lay at death's door, and at last when I'm a little better and come down, thinking to give you pleasure, you're engaged to drive the Miss Hancocks into Tercanbury.'

'Come, Bertha, be reasonable.' Edward condescended to expostulate with his wife, though it was not his habit to humour her extravagances. 'You see it's not my fault. Isn't it enough for you that I'm very sorry? I shall be back in an hour. Stay here, and then we'll spend the evening together.'

'Why did you lie to me?'

'I haven't lied: I'm not given to that,' said Edward, with natural satisfaction.

'You pretended it was for my health's sake that I must go upstairs. Isn't that a lie?'

'It was for your health's sake.'

'You lie again. You wanted to get me out of the way, so that you might go to the Miss Hancocks without telling me.'

'You ought to know me better than that by now.'

'Why did you say nothing about them till you found it impossible to avoid?'

Edward shrugged his shoulders good-humouredly. 'Because I know how touchy you are.'

'And yet you made them the offer.'

'It came out almost unawares. They were grumbling about the weather, and without thinking, I said, "I'll drive you over, if you like." And they jumped at it.'

'You're so good-natured if anyone but your wife is concerned.'

'Well, dear, I can't stay arguing, I shall be late already.'

'You're not really going?'

It had been impossible for Bertha to realize that Edward would carry out his intention.

'I must, my dear, it's my duty.'

'You have more duty to me than to anyone else. Oh, Eddie, don't go. You can't realize all it means to me.'

'I must; I'm not going because I want to. I shall be back in an hour.'

He bent down to kiss her, and she flung her arms round his neck, bursting into tears.

'Oh, please don't go—if you love me at all, if you've ever loved me. Don't you see that you're destroying my love for you?'

'Now, don't be silly, there's a good girl.'

He loosened her arms and moved away; but rising from the sofa, she followed him and took his arm, beseeching him to stay.

'You see how unhappy I am, and you are all I have in the world now. For God's sake stay, Eddie. It means more to me than you know.'

She sank on to the floor, still holding his hand; she was kneeling before him.

'Come, get on to the sofa. All this is very bad for you.'

He carried her to the couch, and then, to finish the scene, hurriedly left the room.

Bertha sprang up to follow him, but sank back as the door slammed, and burying her face in her hands surrendered herself to a passion of sobs. But humiliation and rage almost drove away her grief. She had knelt before her husband for a favour, and he had not granted it.

Suddenly she abhorred him; the love that had been a tower of brass fell like a house of cards. She would not try now to conceal from herself the faults that stared her in the face. He cared only for himself: with him it was only self, self, self. Bertha found a bitter fascination in stripping her idol of the finery with which her madness had bedizened him; she saw him naked now, and he was utterly selfish. But most unbearable of all was her own extreme humiliation.

The rain poured down, unceasing, and the despair of Nature ate into her soul. At last she was exhausted, and, losing thought of time, lay half-unconscious, feeling at least no pain, her brain vacant and weary. When a servant came to ask if Miss Glover might see her, she hardly understood.

'Miss Glover doesn't usually stand on such ceremony,' she said, ill-temperedly, forgetting the incident of the previous week. 'Ask her to come in.'

The parson's sister came to the door and hesitated, growing red; the expression in her eyes was pained and even frightened.

'May I come in, Bertha?'

'Yes.'

She walked straight up to the sofa, and suddenly fell on her knees.

'Oh, Bertha, please forgive me. I was wrong and I've behaved wickedly to you.'

'My dear Fanny,' murmured Bertha, a smile breaking through her misery.

'I withdraw every word I said to you, Bertha; I can't understand how I said it. I humbly beg your forgiveness.'

'There is nothing to forgive.'

'Oh, yes, there is. Good Heavens, I know! My conscience has been reproaching me ever since I was here, but I hardened my heart and would not listen.'

Poor Miss Glover could not have really hardened her heart, however much she tried.

'I knew I ought to come to you and beg your forgiveness, but I wouldn't. I've not slept a wink at night. I was afraid of dying, and if I'd been cut off in the midst of my wickedness I should have been lost.'

She spoke very quickly, finding it a relief to express her trouble.

'I thought Charles would upbraid me, but he's never said a word. Oh, I wish be had; it would have been easier to bear than his sorrowful look. I know he's been worrying dreadfully, and I'm so sorry for him. I kept on saying I'd only done my duty, but in my heart I knew I had done wrong. Oh, Bertha, and this morning I dared not take Communion; I thought God would strike me for blasphemy. And I was afraid Charles would refuse me in front of the whole congregation. It's the first Sunday since I was confirmed that I've missed taking Holy Communion.'

She buried her face in her hands and burst into tears. Bertha heard her almost listlessly; her own trouble was overwhelming her and she could not think of any other. Miss Glover raised her face, tear-stained and red; it was positively hideous; but, notwithstanding, pathetic.

'Then I couldn't bear it any longer. I thought if I begged your pardon I might be able to forgive myself. Oh, Bertha, please forget what I said and forgive me. And I fancied that Edward would be here today, and the thought of exposing myself before him too was almost more than I could bear. But I knew the humiliation would be good for me. Oh, I was so thankful when Jane said he was out. What can I do to earn your forgiveness?'

In her heart of hearts Miss Glover desired some horrible penance that would thoroughly mortify the flesh.

'I have already forgotten all about it,' said Bertha, smiling wearily. 'If my forgiveness is worth anything, I forgive you entirely.'

Miss Glover was pained at Bertha's manifest indifference, yet took it as a just punishment.

'And Bertha, let me say that I love you and admire you more than anyone after Charles. If you really think what you said the other day, I still love you and hope God will turn your heart. Charles and I will pray for you night and day, and soon I hope the Almighty will send you another child to take the place of the one you lost. Believe me, God is very good and merciful, and He will grant you what you wish.'

Bertha gave a low cry of pain. 'I can never have another child. Dr Ramsay told me it was impossible.'

'Oh, Bertha, I didn't know.'

Miss Glover took Bertha protectingly in her arms, crying, and kissed her like a little child.

But Bertha dried her eyes.

'Leave me now, Fanny, please. I'd rather be alone. But come and see me soon, and forgive me if I'm horrid. I'm very unhappy, and I shall never be happy again.'

A few minutes later Edward returned, cheery, jovial, red-faced, and in the best of humours.

'Here we are again!' he shouted. 'You see I've not been gone long, and you haven't missed me a rap. Now well have tea.'

He kissed her and put her cushions right.

'By Jove, it does me good to see you down again. You must pour out the tea for me. Now, confess, weren't you unreasonable to make such a fuss about my going away? And I couldn't help it, could I?'

CHAPTER XX

BUT the love that had taken such despotic possession of Bertha's heart could not be overthrown by any sudden means. When she recovered her health and was able to resume her habits it blazed out again like a fire that has been momentarily subdued, but has gained new strength in its coercion. It dismayed her to think of her extreme loneliness; Edward was now her mainstay and her only hope. She no longer sought to deny that his love was very unlike hers; but his coldness was not always apparent, and she so vehemently wished to find a response to her own ardour that she closed her eyes to all that did not too readily obtrude itself. She had such a consuming desire to find in Edward the lover of her dreams, that for certain periods she was indeed able to live in a fool's paradise, which was none the less grateful because at the bottom of her heart she had an aching suspicion of its true character.

But it seemed that the more passionately Bertha yearned for her husband's love, the more frequent became their differences. As time went on the calm between the storms was shorter, and every quarrel left its mark and made Bertha more susceptible to affront. Realizing finally that Edward could not answer her demonstrations of affection, she became ten times more exacting: even the little tenderness that at the beginning of her married life would have overjoyed her, now too much resembled alms thrown to an importunate beggar to be received with anything but irritation. Their altercations proved conclusively that it does not require two to make a quarrel. Edward was a model of good temper and his equanimity imperturbable. However cross Bertha was, Edward never lost his serenity; he imagined that she was troubled over the loss of her child and that her health was not entirely restored: it had been his experience, especially with cows, that a difficult confinement frequently gave rise to a temporary change in disposition, so that the most docile animal in the world would suddenly develop an unexpected viciousness. He never tried to understand Bertha's varied moods; her passionate desire for love was to him as unreasonable as her outbursts of temper and the succeeding contrition. Now Edward was always the same, contented equally with the world at large and with himself: there was no shadow of doubt about the fact that the world he lived in, the particular spot and period, were the very best possible, and that no existence could be more satisfactory than happily to cultivate one's garden. Not being analytic, he forbore to think about the matter; and, if he had, would not have borrowed the phrases of M. de Voltaire, of whom he had never heard, and whom he would have utterly abhorred as a Frenchman, a philosopher and a wit. But the fact that Edward ate, drank, slept, and ate again as regularly as the oxen on his farm sufficiently proves that he enjoyed a happiness equal to theirs; and what more a decent man can want I certainly have not the faintest notion.

Edward had moreover that magnificent faculty of always doing right and knowing it which is said to be the most inestimable gift of the true Christian; but if his infallibility satisfied himself and edified his neighbours, it did not fail to cause his wife annoyance. She would clench her hands and from her eyes shoot arrows of fire when he stood in front of her smilingly conscious of the justice of his own standpoint and the unreason of hers. And the worst of it was that in her saner moments Bertha had to confess that Edward's view was invariably right and she completely in the wrong. Her injustice appalled her, and she took upon her own shoulders the blame of all their unhappiness. Always, after a quarrel from which Edward had come with his usual triumph, Bertha's rage would be succeeded by a passion of remorse, and she could not find sufficient reproaches with which to castigate herself. She asked frantically how her husband could be expected to love her, and in a transport of agony and fear would take the first opportunity of throwing her arms round his neck and making the most abject apology. Then, having eaten the dust before him, having wept and humiliated herself, she would be for a week absurdly happy, under the impression that henceforward nothing short of an earthquake could disturb their blissful equilibrium. Edward was again the golden idol, clothed in the diaphanous garments of true love; his word was law and his deeds were perfect; Bertha was a humble worshipper offering incense and devoutly grateful to the deity that forbore to crush her. It required very tittle for her to forget the slights and the coldness of her husband's affection; her love was like the tide covering a barren rock; the sea breaks into waves and is dispersed in foam, and the rock remains ever unchanged. This simile, by the way, would not have displeased Edward; when he thought at all he liked to think how firm and steadfast he was.

At night, before going to sleep, it was Bertha's greatest pleasure to kiss her husband on the lips, and it mortified her to see how mechanically he replied to this embrace. It was always she who had to make the advance, and when, to try him, she omitted to do so, he promptly went off to sleep without even bidding her good night. Then she told herself that he must utterly despise her.

'Oh, it drives me mad to think of the devotion I waste on you,' she cried. 'I'm a fool! You are all in the world to me, and I, to you, am a sort of accident: you might have married anyone but me. If I hadn't come across your path you would infallibly have married somebody else.'

'Well, so would you,' he answered, laughing.

'I? Never! If I had not met you, I should have married no one. My love isn't a bauble that I am willing to give to whomever chance throws in my way. My heart is one and indivisible, it would be impossible for me to love anyone but you. When I think that to you, I'm nothing more than any other woman might be, I'm ashamed.'

'You do talk the most awful rot sometimes.'

'Ah, that summarizes your whole opinion. To you I'm merely a fool of a woman. I'm a domestic animal, a little more companionable than a dog, but on the whole not so useful as a cow.'

'I don't know what you want me to do more than I actually do. You can't expect me to be kissing and cuddling all the time; the honeymoon is meant for that, and a man who goes on honeymooning all his life is a fool.'

'Ah, yes, with you love is kept out of sight all day, while you are occupied with the serious affairs of life, such as shearing sheep and hunting foxes; and after dinner it arises in your bosom, especially if you've had good things to eat, and is indistinguishable from the process of digestion. But for me love is everything, the cause and reason of life. Without love I should be non-existent.'

'Well, you may love me,' said Edward, 'but, by Jove, you've got a jolly funny way of showing it. But as far as I'm concerned, if you'll tell me what you want me to do, I'll try to do it.'

'Oh, how can I tell you?' she cried, impatiently. 'I do everything I can to make you love me, and I can't. If you're a stock and a stone, how can I teach you to be the passionate lover? I want you to love me as I love you.'

'Well, if you ask me for my opinion I should say it was rather a good job I don't. Why, the furniture would be smashed up in a week if I were as violent as you.'

'I shouldn't mind if you were violent if you loved me,' replied Bertha, taking his remark with passionate seriousness. 'I shouldn't care if you beat me. I shouldn't mind how much you hurt me, if you did it because you loved me.'

'I think a week of it would about sicken you of that sort of love, my dear.'

'Anything would be preferable to your indifference.'

'But, God bless my soul, I'm not indifferent. Anyone would think I didn't care for you, or was gone on some other woman.'

'I almost wish you were,' answered Bertha. 'If you loved anyone at all, I might have some hope of gaining your affection. But you're incapable of love.'

'I don't know about that. I can say truly that after God and my honour I treasure nothing in the world so much as you.'

'You've forgotten your hunter.'

'No, I haven't,' answered Edward, gravely.

'What do you think I care for a posit ion like that? You acknowledge that I am third; I would as soon be nowhere.'

'"I could not love you half so much, loved I not honour more,"' misquoted Edward.

'The man was a prig who wrote that. I want to be placed above your God and above your honour. The love I want is the love of the man who will lose everything, even his own soul, for the sake of a woman.'

Edward shrugged his shoulders: 'I don't know where you'll get that. My idea of love is that it's a very good thing in its place, but there's a limit to everything. There are other things in life.'

'Oh, yes, I know: there are duty and honour, and the farm and fox-hunting, and the opinion of one's neighbours, and the dogs and the cat, and the new brougham and a million other things. What do you suppose you'd do if I had committed some crime and were likely to be imprisoned?'

'I don't want to suppose anything of the sort. You may be sure I'd do my duty.'

'Oh, I'm sick of your duty. You din it into my ear morning, noon and night. I wish to God you weren't so virtuous, you might be more human.'

Edward found his wife's behaviour so extraordinary that he consulted Dr Ramsay. The general practitioner had been for thirty years the recipient of marital confidences and was sceptical of the value of medicine in the cure of jealousy, talkativeness, incompatibility of temper and the like diseases. He assured Edward that time was the only remedy, by which all differences were reconciled; but after further pressing, consented to send Bertha a bottle of harmless tonic, which it was his habit to give to all and sundry for most of the ills to which the flesh is heir. It would doubtless do Bertha no harm, and that is an important consideration to a medical man. Dr Ramsay advised Edward to keep calm and be confident that Bertha would eventually become the dutiful and submissive spouse whom it is every man's ideal to see by his fireside when he wakes up from his after-dinner snooze.

Bertha's moods were trying. No one could tell one day how she would be the next, and this was peculiarly uncomfortable to a man who was willing to make the best of everything, but on the condition that he had time to get used to it. Sometimes in the twilight of winter afternoons, when the mind was naturally led to a contemplation of the vanity of existence and the futility of all human endeavour, she would be seized with melancholy. Edward, noticing she was pensive, a state which he detested, asked what were her thoughts, and half-dreamily she tried to express them.

'Good Lord deliver us!' he said cheerily. 'What rum things you do get into your little noddle! You must be out of sorts.'

'It isn't that,' she answered, smiling sadly.

'It's not natural for a woman to brood in that way. I think you ought to start taking that tonic again; but I daresay you're only tired and you'll think quite different in the morning.'

Bertha made no answer. She suffered from the nameless pain of existence, and he offered her—iron and quinine: when she required sympathy because her heart ached for the woes of her fellow-men, he poured tincture of nux vomica down her throat. He could not understand, it was no good explaining that she found a savour in the tender contemplation of the evils of mankind. But the worst of it was that Edward was quite right—the brute, he always was! When the morning came, the melancholy had vanished, Bertha was left without a care, and the world did not even need rose-coloured spectacles to seem attractive. It was humiliating to find that her most beautiful thoughts, the ennobling emotions that brought home to her the charming fiction that all men are brothers, were due to mere physical exhaustion.

Some people have extraordinarily literal minds, they never allow for the play of imagination: life for them has no beer and skittles, and, far from being an empty dream, is a matter of the deadly-dullest seriousness. Of such is the man who, when a woman tells him she feels dreadfully old, instead of answering that she looks absurdly young, replies that youth has its drawbacks and age its compensations. And of such was Edward; he could never realize that people did not mean exactly what they said. At first he had always consulted Bertha on the conduct of the estate; but she, pleased to be a nonentity in her own house, had consented to everything he suggested, and even begged him not to ask her. When she informed him that he was absolute lord not only of herself, but of all her worldly goods, it was not surprising that he should at last take her at her word.

'Women know nothing about farming,' he said, 'and it's best that I should have a free hand.'

The result of his stewardship was all that could be desired; the estate was put into apple-pie order and the farms paid rent for the first time for twenty years. The wandering winds, even the sun and rain, seemed to conspire in favour of so clever and hard-working a man; and fortune for once went hand in hand with virtue: Bertha constantly received congratulations from the surrounding squires on the admirable way in which Edward managed the place; and he on his side never failed to tell her his triumphs and the compliments they had occasioned. But not only was Edward looked upon as the master by his farm-hands and labourers; even the servants of Court Leys treated Bertha as a minor personage whose orders were only to be conditionally obeyed. Long generations of servitude have made the countryman peculiarly subtle in hierarchical distinctions, and there was a marked difference between his manner with Edward, on whom his livelihood depended, and his manner with Bertha, who shone only with a reflected light as the squire's missus.

At first it had only amused her, but the most subtle jest may lose its savour after three years. More than once she had to speak sharply to a gardener who hesitated to do as he was bid, because his orders were not from the master. Her pride reviving with the decline of love, Bertha began to find the position intolerable; her mind was now very susceptible to affront, and she was desirous of an opportunity to show that after all she was still the mistress of Court Leys.

It soon came. For it chanced that some ancient lover of trees, unpractical as the Leys had ever been, had planted six beeches in a hedgerow, and these in course of time had grown into stately trees, the admiration of all beholders. But one day as Bertha walked along a hideous gap caught her eyes: one of the six beeches had disappeared. There had been no storm, it could not have fallen of itself. She went up, and found it cut down; the men who had done the deed were already starting on another. A ladder was leaning against it, upon which stood a labourer attaching a line. No sight is more pathetic than an old tree levelled with the ground: the space which it filled suddenly stands out with an unsightly emptiness. But Bertha was more angry than pained.

'What are you doing, Hodgkins?' she angrily asked the foreman. 'Who gave you orders to cut down this tree?'

'The squire, Mum.'

'Oh, it must be a mistake. Mr Craddock never meant anything of the sort.'

''E told us positive to take down this one and them others yonder. You can see his mark, Mum.'

'Nonsense. I'll talk to Mr Craddock about it. Take that rope off and come down from the ladder. I forbid you to touch another tree.'

The man on the ladder looked at her, but made no attempt to do as he was bid.

'The squire said most particular that we was to cut that tree down today.'

'Will you have the goodness to do as I tell you?' said Bertha growing cold with anger. 'Tell that man to unfasten the rope and come down. I forbid you to touch the tree.'

The foreman repeated Bertha's order in a surly voice, and they all looked at her suspiciously, wishing to disobey but not daring to in case the squire should be angry.

'Well, I'll take no responsibility for it,' said Hodgkins.

'Please hold your tongue and do what I tell you as quickly as possible.'

She waited while the men gathered up their various belongings and finally trooped off.

CHAPTER XXI

BERTHA went home fuming, knowing perfectly well that Edward had given the order that she had countermanded, but glad of the chance to have a final settlement of rights. She did not see him for several hours.

'I say, Bertha,' he said, when he came in, 'why on earth did you stop those men cutting down the beeches on Carter's field? You've lost a whole half-day's work. I wanted to set them on something else tomorrow. Now I shall have to leave it over till Thursday.'

'I stopped them because I refuse to have the beeches cut down. They're the only ones in the place. I'm very annoyed that even one should have gone without my knowing about it. You should have asked me before you did a thing like that.'

'My good girl, I can't come and ask you each time I want a thing done.'

'Is the land mine or yours?'

'It's yours,' answered Edward, laughing, 'but I know better than you what ought to be done, and it's silly of you to interfere.'

Bertha flushed: 'In future, I wish to be consulted.'

'You've told me fifty thousands times to do always as I think fit.'

'Well, I've changed my mind.'

'It's too late now,' he laughed. 'You made me take the reins in my own hands, and I'm going to keep them.'

Bertha in her anger hardly restrained herself from telling him she could send him away like a hired servant.

'I want you to understand, Edward, that I'm not going to have those trees cut down. You must tell the men you've made a mistake.'

'I shall tell them nothing of the sort. I'm not going to cut them all down—only three. We don't want them there. For one thing the shade damages the crops, and otherwise Carter's is one of our best fields. And then I want the wood.'

'I care nothing about the crops, and if you want wood you can buy it. These trees were planted nearly a hundred years ago, and I would sooner die than cut them down.'

'The man who planted beeches in a hedgerow was about the silliest jackass I've ever heard of. Any tree's bad enough, but a beech of all things—why, it's drip, drip, drip, all the time, and not a thing will grow under them. That's the sort of thing that has been done all over the estate for years. It'll take me a life-time to repair the blunders of your—of the former owners.'

It is one of the curiosities of sentiment that its most abject slave rarely permits it to interfere with his temporal concerns; it appears as unusual for a man to sentimentalize in his own walk in life as for him to pick his own pocket. Edward, having passed his whole life in contact with the earth, might have been expected to cherish a certain love of Nature: the pathos of transpontine melodrama made him cough and blow his nose, and in literature he affected the titled and consumptive heroine and the soft-hearted, burly hero. But when it came to business, it was another matter: the sort of sentiment that asks a farmer to spare a sylvan glade for aesthetic reasons is absurd. Edward would have willingly allowed advertisement-mongers to put up boards on the most beautiful part of his estate if thereby he could have surreptitiously increased the profits on his farm.

'Whatever you may think of my ancestors,' said Bertha, 'you will kindly pay attention to me. The land is mine, and I refuse to let you spoil it.'

'It isn't spoiling it. It's the proper thing to do. You'll soon get used to not seeing the wretched trees, and I tell you I'm only going to take three down. I've given orders to cut the others tomorrow.'

'D'you mean to say you're going to ignore me absolutely?'

'I'm going to do what's right, and if you don't approve of it, I'm very sorry, but I shall do it all the same.'

'I shall give the men orders to do nothing of the kind.'

Edward laughed: 'Then you'll make an ass of yourself. You try giving them orders contrary to mine and see what they do.'

Bertha gave a cry. In her fury she looked round for something to throw, she would have liked to hit him; but he stood there, calm and self-possessed, very much amused.

'I think you must be mad,' she said. 'You do all you can to destroy my love for you.'

She was in too great a passion for words. This was the measure of his affection, he must indeed utterly despise her; and this was the only result of the love she had humbly laid at his feet. She asked herself what she could do: she could do nothing—but submit. She knew as well as he that her orders would be disobeyed if they did not agree with his; and that he would keep his word she did not for a moment doubt. To do so was his pride. She did not speak for the rest of the day, but next morning, when he was going out, asked what was his intention with regard to the trees.

'Oh, I thought you'd forgotten all about them,' he replied. 'I mean to do as I said.'

'If you have the trees cut down, I shall leave you. I shall go to Aunt Polly's.'

'And tell her that you wanted the moon and I was so unkind as not to give it you?' he replied, smiling. 'She'll laugh at you.'

'You will find me as careful to keep my word as you.'

Before luncheon she went out and walked to Carter's field: the men were still at work, but a second tree had gone; the third would doubtless fall in the afternoon. The men looked at her, and she thought they laughed. She stood looking at them for some while, so that she might thoroughly digest the humiliation. Then she went home and wrote her aunt the following letter.

My dear Aunt Polly,

I have been so seedy these last few weeks that Edward, poor dear, has been quite alarmed, and has been bothering me to come up to town to see a specialist. He's as urgent as if he wanted to get me out of the way, and I'm already half-jealous of my new parlour-maid, who has pink cheeks and golden hair, which is just the type that Edward really admires. I also think that Dr Ramsay hasn't the ghost of an idea what is the matter with me, and not being particularly desirous to depart this life just yet, I think it would be discreet to see somebody who will at least change my medicine. I have taken gallons of iron and quinine, and I'm frightfully afraid that my teeth will go black. My own opinion coinciding so exactly with Edward's, (that horrid Mrs Ryle calls us the humming-birds, meaning the turtle-doves, her knowledge of natural history arouses dear Edward's contempt,) I have gracefully acceded to his desire, and if you can put me up, will come at your earliest convenience.

Yours affectionately,
B.C.

P.S. I shall take the opportunity of getting clothes, (I am positively in rags,) so you will have to keep me some little time.

Edward came in shortly afterwards, looking much pleased with himself, and glanced slily at Bertha, thinking himself so clever that he could scarcely help laughing: had he not the habit of being most particular in his behaviour, he would undoubtedly have put his tongue in his cheek.

'With women, my dear sir, you must be firm. When you're putting them to a fence, close your legs and don't check 'em; but mind you keep 'em under control, or they'll lose their little heads. A man should always let a woman see that he's got her well in hand.'

Bertha was silent, able to eat nothing for luncheon; she sat opposite her husband, wondering how he could gorge so disgracefully when she was angry and unhappy. But in the afternoon her appetite returned and, going to the kitchen, she ate so many sandwiches that at dinner she could again touch nothing. She hoped Edward would notice that she refused all food, and be property alarmed and sorry. But he demolished enough for two, and never saw that his wife fasted.

At night Bertha went to bed and bolted herself in their room. Presently Edward came up and tried the door. Finding it locked, he knocked and cried to her to open it. She did not answer. He knocked again more loudly and shook the handle.

'I want to have my room to myself,' she cried out. 'I'm ill. Please don't try to come in.'

'What? Where am I to sleep?'

'Oh, you can sleep in one of the spare rooms.'

'Nonsense!' he said, and without further ado put his shoulder to the door. He was a strong man; one heave and the old hinges cracked. He entered laughing.

'If you wanted to keep me out, you ought to have barricaded yourself up with the furniture.'

Bertha was disinclined to treat the matter lightly. 'I'm not going to sleep with you,' she said.' If you come in here I shall go out.'

'Oh, no, you won't,' he said.

Bertha got up and put on a dressing-gown.

'I'll spend the night on the sofa then,' she said. 'I don't want to quarrel with you any more or to make a scene. I have written to Aunt Polly, and the day after tomorrow I shall go to London.'

'I was going to suggest that a change of air would do you good,' he replied. 'I think your nerves are a bit groggy.'

'It's very good of you to take an interest in my nerves,' she replied, with a scornful glance, settling herself on the sofa.

'Are you really going to sleep there?' he said, getting into bed.

'It looks like it.'

'You'll find it awfully cold.'

'I'd rather freeze than sleep with you.'

'You'll have the snuffles in the morning; but I daresay you'll think better of it in an hour. I'm going to turn the light out. Good night!'

Bertha did not answer, and in a few minutes she was angrily listening to his snores. Could he really be asleep? Did it mean nothing to him that she should refuse to share her bed, that she should arrange to go away? It was infamous that he slept so calmly.

'Edward,' she called.

There was no answer, but she could not bring herself to believe that he was sleeping. She could never even close her eyes. He must be pretending—to annoy her. She wanted to touch him, but feared that he would burst out laughing. She felt indeed horribly cold, and piled rugs and dresses over her. It required great fortitude not to sneak back to bed. She was extremely unhappy, and soon became very thirsty. Nothing is so horrid as the water in toilet-bottles, with the glass tasting of tooth-wash; she gulped some down, though it almost made her sick, and then walked about the room, turning over her manifold wrongs. Edward slept on insufferably. She made a noise to wake him, but he did not stir; she knocked down a table which made a clatter sufficient to disturb the dead, but her husband was insensible. Then she looked at the bed, wondering whether she dared lie down for an hour and trust to waking up before him. She was so cold that she determined to risk it, feeling certain that she would not sleep long; she walked to the bed.

'Coming to bed after all?' said Edward in a sleepy voice.

She stopped and her heart rose to her mouth.

'I was coming for my pillow,' she replied, indignantly, thanking her stars that he had not spoken a moment later.

She returned to the sofa, and eventually making herself very comfortable fell asleep. In this blissful condition she continued till the morning, and when she awoke Edward was drawing up the blinds.

'Slept well?' he asked.

'I haven't slept a wink.'

'Oh, what a crammer. I've been looking at you for the last hour.'

'I've had my eyes closed for about ten minutes, if that's what you mean.'

Bertha was quite justly annoyed that her husband should have caught her napping soundly; it robbed her proceeding of half its effect. Moreover, Edward was as fresh as a bird, while she felt old and haggard, and hardly dared look at herself in the glass.

In the middle of the morning came a telegram from Miss Ley, telling Bertha to come whenever she liked and hoping Edward would come too. Bertha left it in a conspicuous place, so that he could not fail to see it.

'So you're really going?' he said.

'I told you I was as able to keep my word as you.'

'Well, I think it'll do you no end of good. How long will you stay?'

'How do I know! Perhaps for ever.'

'That's a big word, though it has only two syllables.'

It cut Bertha to the heart that Edward should be so indifferent. He could not care for her at all. He seemed to think it natural that she should leave him. He pretended it was good for her health. Oh, what did she care about her health? As she made the needful preparations her courage failed her; she felt it impossible to leave him, and her tears came rapidly as she thought of the difference between their present state and the ardent love of a year ago. She would have welcomed the poorest excuse that forced her to stay and yet saved her self-respect. If Edward would only express grief at the parting it might not be too late. But her boxes were packed and her train was fixed; he told Miss Glover that his wife was going away for change of air, and regretted that his farm prevented him from accompanying her. The trap was brought to the door, and Edward jumped up, taking his seat. Now there was no hope, and go she must. She wished she had the courage to tell Edward that she could not leave him. She was afraid. They drove along in silence. Bertha waited for her husband to speak, herself daring to say nothing lest he should hear the tears in her voice. At last she made an effort.

'Are you sorry I'm going?'

'I think it's for your good, and I don't want to stand in the way of that.'

Bertha asked herself what love a man had for his wife who could bear her out of his sight, no matter what the necessity. She stifled a sigh.

They reached the station and he took her ticket. They waited in silence for the train, and Edward bought *Punch* and the *Sketch* from the newspaper boy. The horrible train steamed up, Edward helped her into a carriage, and the tears in her eyes now could not be concealed. She put out her lips.

'Perhaps for the last time,' she whispered.

CHAPTER XXII

72Eliot Mansions,
April 18 Chelsea, S.W.

DEAR Edward,

I think we were wise to part. We were too unsuited to one another, and our difficulties could only have increased. The knot of marriage between two persons of different temperament is so intricate that it can only be cut; you may try to unravel it, and think you are succeeding; but another turn shows you that the tangle is only worse than ever. Even time is powerless. Some things are impossible: you cannot heap water up like stones, you cannot measure one man by another man's rule. I am certain we were wise to separate. I see that if we had continued to live together our quarrels would have perpetually increased. It is horrible to look back upon those vulgar brawls. We wrangled like fish-wives. I cannot understand how my mouth could have uttered such things.

It is very bitter to look back and compare my anticipations with what has really happened. Did I expect too much from life? Ah, me, I only expected that my husband would love me. It is because I asked so little that I have received nothing; in this world you must ask much, you must spread your praises abroad, you must trample underfoot those that stand in your path, you must take up all the room you can, or you will be elbowed away. You must be irredeemably selfish, or you will be a thing of no account, a frippery that man plays with and flings aside.

Of course I expected the impossible. I was not satisfied with the conventional unity of marriage. I wanted to be really one with you. Oneself is the whole world and all other people are merely strangers. At first in my vehement desire I used to despair because I knew you so little; I was heart-broken at the impossibility of really understanding you, of getting right down into your heart of hearts. Never, to the best of my knowledge, have I seen your veritable self; you are really as much a stranger to me as if I had known you but an hour. I bared my soul to you, concealing nothing—there is in you a man I do not know and have never seen. We are so absolutely different, I don't know a single thing that we have in common; often when we have been talking and fallen into silence, our thoughts, starting from the same standpoint, have travelled in different directions, and on speaking again we found how widely they had diverged. I hoped to know you to the bottom of your soul; oh, I hoped that we should be united so as to have but one soul between us; and yet on the most commonplace occasion I can never know your thoughts. Perhaps it might have been different if we had had children; they might have formed between us a truer link, and perhaps in the delight of them I should have forgotten my impracticable dreams. But fate was against us, I come from a rotten stock; it is written in the book that the Leys should depart from the sight of man, and return to their mother earth to be incorporated with her; and who knows in the future what may be our lot? I like to think that in the course of ages I may be the wheat on a fertile plain or the smoke from a fire of brambles on the common. I wish I could be buried in the open fields, rather than in the grim coldness of a churchyard, so that I might anticipate the change and return more quickly to the life of Nature.

Believe me, separation was the only possible outcome. I loved you too passionately to be content with the cold regard which you gave me. Oh, of course I was exacting and tyrannical and unkind; I can confess all my faults now; my only excuse is that I was very unhappy. For all the pain I have caused you I beg you to forgive me. We may as well part friends, and I freely forgive you for all you have made me suffer. Now I can afford also to tell you how near I was to not carrying out my intention. Yesterday and this morning I scarcely held back my tears, the parting seemed too hard, I felt I could not leave you. If you had asked me not to go, if you had even showed the smallest sign of regretting my departure, I think I should have broken down. Yes, I can tell you now that I would have given anything to stay. Alas! I am so weak. In the train I cried bitterly. It is the first time we have been apart since our marriage, the first time that we have slept under different roofs. But now the worst is over. I have taken the step and I shall adhere to what I have done. I am sure I have acted for the best. I see no harm in our writing to one another occasionally if it pleases you to receive letters from me. I think I had better not see you—at all events for some time. Perhaps when we are both a good deal older we may without danger see one another now and then; but not yet. I should be afraid to see your face.

Aunt Polly has no suspicion. I can assure you it has been an effort to laugh and talk during the evening, and I was glad to get to my room. Now it is past midnight, and I am still writing to you. I felt I ought to let you know my thoughts, and I can tell them more easily by letter than by word of mouth. Does it not show how separated in heart we have become that I shall hesitate to say to you what I think? And I had hoped to have my heart always open to you; I fancied that I need never conceal a thing, nor hesitate to show you every emotion and every thought Good-bye.

Bertha.

72Eliot Mansions,
April 23 Chelsea, S.W.

My poor Edward,

You say you hope I shall soon get better and come back to Court Leys. You misunderstood my meaning so completely that I almost laughed. It is true. I was out of spirits and tired when I wrote, but that was not the reason of my letter. Cannot you conceive emotions not entirely due to one's physical condition? You cannot understand me, you never have; and yet I would not take up the vulgar and hackneyed position of a *femme incomprise.* There is nothing to understand about me. I am very simple and unmysterious; I only wanted love, and you could not give it me. No, our parting is final and irrevocable. What can you want me back for? You have Court Leys and your farms, everyone likes you in the neighbourhood, I was the only bar to your complete happiness. Court Leys I freely give you for my life; until you came it brought in nothing, and the income now arising from it is entirely due to your efforts; you earn it and I beg you to keep it. For me the small income I have from my mother is sufficient.

Aunt Polly still thinks I am on a visit, and constantly speaks of you; I throw dust in her eyes, but I cannot hope to keep her in ignorance for long. At present I am engaged in periodically seeing the doctor for an imaginary ill and getting one or two new things.

Shall we write to one another once a week? I know writing is a trouble to you; but I do not wish you to forget me altogether. If you like I will write to you every Sunday, and you may answer or not as you please.

Bertha.

P.S. Please do not think of any *rapprochement.* I am sure you will eventually see that we are both much happier apart.

72Eliot Mansions,
Chelsea, S.W.

May 15

My dear Eddie,

I was pleased to get your letter. I am a little touched at your wanting to see me. You suggest coming to town; perhaps it is fortunate that I shall be no longer here. If you had expressed such a wish before much might have gone differently. Aunt Polly, having let her flat to friends goes to Paris for the rest of the season; she starts tonight, and to Paris I have offered to accompany her, I am sick of London. I do not know whether she suspects anything, but I notice that she never mentions your name now; she looked a little sceptical the other day when I explained that I had long wished to go to Paris and that you were having the inside of Court Leys painted. Fortunately, however, she makes it a practice not to inquire into other people's business, and I can rest assured that she will never ask me a single question.

Forgive the shortness of this letter, but I am very busy packing.

Your affectionate wife,
Bertha,

41Rue des Ecoliers,
Paris.

May 16

My dearest Eddie,

I have been unkind to you. It is nice of you to want to see me, and my repugnance to it was, perhaps, unnatural. On consideration, I cannot think it will do any harm if we should see one another. Of course, I can never come back to Court Leys; there are some chains that, having broken, you can never weld together; and no fetters are so intolerable as those of love. But if you want to see me I will put no obstacle in your way, I will not deny that I also should like to see you. I am further away now, but if you care for me at all you will not hesitate to make the short journey.

We have here a very nice apartment, in the Latin Quarter, away from the rich people and the tourists. I do not know which is more vulgar, the average tripper or the part of Paris which he infests; I must say they become one another to a nicety. I loathe the shoddiness of the boulevards, with their gaudy cafés over-gilt and over-sumptuous, and their crowds of ill-dressed foreigners. But if you come I can show you a different Paris, a restful and old-fashioned Paris; theatres to which tourists do not go, gardens full of pretty children and nurse-maids with long ribbons to their caps. I can take you down innumerable grey streets with funny shops, in old churches where you see people praying; and it is all very quiet, calming to the nerves, and I can take you to the Louvre at hours when there are few visitors, and show you beautiful pictures and statues that have come from Italy and Greece, where the gods have their homes to this day. Come, Eddie.

Your ever loving wife,
Bertha.

41 Rue des Ecoliers,
Paris.

My dearest Eddie,

I am disappointed that you will not come. I should have thought, if you wanted to see me you could have found time to leave the farms for a few days. But perhaps it is really better that we should not meet. I cannot conceal from you that sometimes I long for you dreadfully. I forget all that has happened and desire with all my heart to be with you again.

What a fool I am. I know that we can never meet again, and you are never absent from my thoughts. I look forward to your letters almost madly, and your handwriting makes my heart beat as if I were a school-girl. Oh, you don't know how your letters disappoint me, they are so cold, you never say what I want you to say. It would be madness if we came together. I can only preserve my love to you by not seeing you. Does that sound horrible? And yet I would give anything to see you once more. I cannot help asking you to come here. It is not so very often I have asked you anything. Do come. I will meet you at the station and you wilt have no trouble or bother. Everything is perfectly simple, and Cook's interpreters are everywhere. I'm sure you would enjoy yourself so much.

If you love me, come.
Bertha.

Court Leys,
Blackstable, Kent.

May 30

My dearest Bertha,

Sorry I haven't answered yours of 25 inst before but I've been up to my eyes in work. You wouldn't think that there would be so much to do on a farm at this time of year unless you saw it with your own eyes. I can't possibly get away to Paris and besides I can't stomach the French. I don't want to see the capital and when I want a holiday London's good enough for me. You'd better come back here, people are asking after you and the place seems all topsy-turvy without you. Love to Aunt P.

In haste
Your affectionate husband
E. Craddock.

41 Rue des Ecoliers,
Paris.

June 1

My dearest, dearest Eddie,

You don't know bow disappointed I was to get your letter, and how I longed for it. Whatever you do, don't keep me waiting so long for an answer. I imagined all sorts of things—that you were ill or dying. I was on the point of wiring. I want you to promise me that if you are ever ill you will let me know. If you want me urgently I shall be pleased to come. But do not think that I can ever come back to Court Leys for good. Sometimes I feel ill and weak and I long for you, but I know I must not give way. I'm sure, for your good as well as for mine, I must never risk the unhappiness of our old life again. It was too degrading. With firm mind and the utmost resolution I swear that I will never, never return to Court Leys.

Your affectionate and loving wife,
Bertha.

Telegram.

Gare du Nord. 9 .50 a.m. June 2.
Craddock, Court Leys. Blackstable.
Arriving 7 .25 tonight. Bertha.

41 Rue des Ecoliers,
Paris.

My dear young Friend,

I am perturbed. Bertha, as you know, has for the last six weeks lived with me, for reasons the naturalness of which aroused my strongest suspicions. No one, I thought, would need so many absolutely conclusive motives to do so very simple a thing. I resisted the temptation to write to Edward (her husband—a nice man, but stupid!) to ask for an explanation, fearing that the reasons given me were the right ones (although I could not believe it), in which case I should have made myself ridiculous. Bertha in London pretended to go to a physician, but never was seen to take medicine, and I am certain no well-established specialist would venture to take two guineas from a *malade imaginaire* and not administer copious drugs. She accompanied me to Paris, ostensibly to get dresses, but has behaved as if their fit were of no more consequence than a change of ministry. She has taken great pains to conceal her emotions, and thereby made them the more conspicuous. I cannot tell you how often she has gone through the various stages from an almost hysterical elation to an equal despondency; she has mused as profoundly as it was fashionable for the young ladies of fifty years ago, (we were all young ladies then—not girls,) she has played *Tristan and Isolde* to the distraction of myself, she has snubbed an amorous French artist to the distraction of his wife; finally she has wept, and after weeping overpowdered her nose and eyes, which in a pretty woman is an infallible sign of extreme mental prostration.

This morning when I got up, I found at my door the following message: '*Don't think me an utter fool, but I couldn't stand another day away from Edward. Leaving by the* 10 *o'clock train. B.*' Now at 10.30 she had an appointment at Paquin's to try on the most ravishing dinner dress you could imagine.

I will not insult you by drawing inferences from all these facts. I know you would much sooner draw them yourself, and I have a sufficiently good opinion of you to be certain that they will coincide with mine.

Yours very sincerely,
Mary Ley.

CHAPTER XXIII

BERTHA'S relief was unmistakable when she landed on English soil; at last she was near Edward, and she had been extremely seasick. Though it was less than thirty miles from Dover to Blackstable, the communications were so bad that it was necessary to wait for hours at the port, or take the boat train to London and then come sixty miles down again. Bertha was exasperated at the delay, forgetting that she was now (thank Heaven!) in a free country, where the railways were not run for the convenience of the passengers, but the passengers necessary evils to earn dividends for an ill-managed company. Bertha's impatience was so great that she felt it impossible to wait at Dover, and made up her mind to go up to London and down again, thus saving herself ten minutes, rather than spend the afternoon in the dreary waiting-room or wandering about the town. The train seemed to crawl, and her restlessness became quite painful as she recognized the Kentish country, the fat meadows with trim hedges, the portly trees and the general air of prosperity.

Bertha had hoped, against her knowledge of him, that Edward would meet her at Dover, and it had been a disappointment not to see him; then she thought he might come up to London, though not explaining to herself how he could possibly have divined that she would be there; and her heart beat absurdly when she saw a back that might have been his. Still later, she comforted herself with the notion that he would certainly be at Faversley, which was the next station to Blackstable, and when they reached that place she put her head out of the window, looking along the platform—but he was not there.

'He might have come as far as this,' she thought.

Now, the train steaming on, she recognized the country more precisely, the desolate marsh and the sea. The line ran almost at the water's edge. The tide was out, leaving a broad expanse of shining mud, over which the sea-gulls flew, screeching. Then the houses were familiar, cottages beaten by wind and weather, 'The Jolly Sailor,' where in the old days many a smuggled keg of brandy had been hidden on its way to the cathedral city of Tercanbury. The coast-guard station was passed, low buildings painted pink; and finally they rattled across the bridge over the High Street, and the porters, with their Kentish drawl, called out, 'Blackstable, Blackstable.'

Bertha's emotions were always uncontrolled and so powerful as sometimes to unfit her for action. Now she had hardly strength to open the carriage door.

'At last!' she cried, with a gasp of relief.

She had never loved her husband so passionately as then; her love was a physical sensation that almost turned her faint. The arrival of the moment so anxiously awaited left her half afraid; she was of those who eagerly look for an opportunity and then can scarcely seize it. Bertha's heart was so full that she was afraid of bursting into tears when at last she should see Edward walking towards her; she had pictured the meeting so often, her husband advancing with his swinging stride, waving his stick, the dogs in front, rushing towards her, and barking furiously. The two porters waddled, with their seaman's walk, to the van to get out the luggage; people were stepping from the carriages. Next to her a pasty-faced clerk descended, in dingy black, with a baby in his arms; his pale-faced wife followed with another baby and innumerable parcels, then two or three children. A labourer sauntered down the platform, three or four sailors, and a couple of trim infantrymen. They all surged for the wicket at which stood the ticket collector. The porters got out the boxes and the train steamed off; an irascible city man was swearing volubly because his luggage had gone on to Margate. The station-master, in a decorated hat and a self-satisfied air, strolled up to see what was the matter. Bertha looked along the platform wildly. Edward was not there.

The station-master passed her and nodded patronisingly.

'Have you seen Mr Craddock?' she asked.

'No, I can't say I have. But I think there's a carriage below for you.'

Bertha began to tremble. A porter asked whether he should take her boxes; she nodded, unable to speak. She went down and found the brougham at the station door; the coachman touched his hat and gave her a note.

Dear Bertha,

Awfully sorry I can't come to meet you. I never expected you, so accepted an invitation of Lord Philip Dirk to a tennis tournament and a ball afterwards. He's going to sleep me, so I shan't be back till tomorrow. Don't get in a wax. See you in the morning.

E.C.

Bertha got into the carriage and huddled herself into one corner so that no one should see her. At first she hardly understood, she had spent the last hours on such a height of excitement that the disappointment deprived her of the power of thinking. She never took things reasonably and was now stunned. It was impossible. It seemed to be so callous that Edward should go playing tennis when she, looking forward so eagerly to seeing him, was coming home. And it was no ordinary homecoming, it was the first time she had ever left him, and then she had gone, hating him, as she thought for good. But her absence having revived her love, she had returned, yearning for reconciliation. And he was not there, he acted as though she had been to town for a day's shopping.

'Oh, God, what a fool I was to come!'

Suddenly she thought of going away, there and then. Would it not be easier? She felt she could not see him. But there were no trains. The London, Chatham and Dover Railway has perhaps saved many an elopement. But he must have known how bitterly disappointed she would be, and the notion flashed through her that he would leave the tournament and come home. Perhaps he was already at Court Leys, waiting; she took fresh courage and looked at the well-remembered scene. He might be at the gate. Oh, what joy it would be, what a relief! But they came to the gate and he was not there; they drove to the portico and he was not there. Bertha went into the house expecting to find him in the hall or in the drawing-room, not having heard the carriage; but he was nowhere to be found, and the servants corroborated his letter.

The house was empty, dull and inhospitable; the rooms had an uninhabited air, the furniture was primly rearranged, and Edward had caused antimacassars to be placed on the chairs; these Bertha, to the housemaid's surprise, took off one by one, and without a word threw into the empty fireplace. And still she thought it incredible that Edward should stay away. She sat down to dinner, expecting him every moment; she sat up very late, feeling sure that eventually he would come. But he did not.

'I wish to God I'd stayed away.'

Her thoughts went back to the struggle of the last few weeks. Pride, anger, reason, everything had been on one side and only love on the other; and love had conquered. The recollection of Edward had been seldom absent from her, and her dreams had been filled with his image. His letters had caused her an indescribable thrill, the sight of his handwriting had made her tremble; and she wanted to see him; she woke at night with his kisses on her lips. She begged him to come, and he would not, or could not. At last the yearning grew beyond control; and that very morning, not having received the letter she awaited, she had resolved to throw off all pretence of resentment and come. What did she care if Miss Ley laughed at her, or if Edward scored the victory in the struggle? She could not live without him. He still was her life and her love.

'Oh, God, I wish I hadn't come.'

She remembered how she had prayed that Edward might love her as she wished to be loved. The passionate rebellion after her child's death had ceased insensibly, and in her misery, in her loneliness, she had found a new faith. Belief with some comes and goes without reason; with them it is not a matter of conviction, but rather of sensibility; and Bertha found prayer easier in Catholic churches than in the cheerless meeting-houses she had been used to. She could not gabble prayers at stated hours with three hundred other people; the crowd caused her to shut away her emotions, and her heart could expand only in solitude. In Paris she had found quiet chapels, open at all hours, to which she could go for rest when the light without was over-dazzling; and in the evening, when the dimness, the fragrance of old incense and the silence were very restful. Then the only light came from the tapers, burning in gratitude or in hope, throwing a fitful, mysterious glimmer; and Bertha prayed earnestly for Edward and for herself.

But Edward would not let himself be loved. Her efforts all were useless. Her love was a jewel that he valued not at all, that he flung aside and cared not if he lost. But she was too unhappy, too broken in spirit to be angry. What was the use of anger? She knew that Edward would see nothing extraordinary in what he had done; he would return, confident, well-pleased with himself, having slept well, and entirely unaware that she had been grievously disappointed.

'I suppose the injustice is on my side. I am too exacting. I can't help it.' She only knew one way to love, and that, it appeared, was a foolish way. 'Oh, I wish,' she cried, 'I wish I could go away again now—for ever.'

She got up and ate a solitary breakfast, busying herself afterwards in the house. Edward had left word that he would be in to luncheon, and was it not his pride to keep his word? But all her impatience had gone, Bertha felt no particular anxiety now to see him. She was on the point of going out, the air was warm and balmy; but did not, in case Edward should return and be disappointed at her absence.

'What a fool I am to think of his feelings! If I'm not in he'll just go about his work and think nothing more about me till I appear.'

But, notwithstanding, she stayed in. He arrived at last, and she did not hurry to meet him; she was putting things a way in her bedroom, and continued, though she heard his voice below. The difference was curious between her intense and almost painful expectation of the previous day and her present indifference. She turned as he came in the room, but did not move towards him.

'So you've come back? Did you enjoy yourself?'

'Yes, rather.'

But I say, it's ripping to have you home. You weren't in a wax at my not being here?'

'Oh, no,' she said, smiling. 'I didn't mind at all.'

'That's all right. Of course I'd never been to Lord Philip's before, and I couldn't wire the last minute to say that my wife was coming home and I had to meet her.'

'Of course not, it would have made you appear too absurd.'

'But I was jolly sick, I can tell you. If you'd only let me know a week ago that you were coming, I should have refused the invitation.'

'My dear Edward, I'm so unpractical, I never know my own mind. I'm always doing things on the spur of the moment—to my own inconvenience and other people's. And I should never have expected you to deny yourself anything for my sake.'

Bertha had been looking at her husband since he came into the room, unable in astonishment to avert her eyes; she was perplexed, almost dismayed; she scarcely recognized him. In the three years of their common life Bertha had never noticed a change in him, and with her great faculty for idealization had carried in her mind always his image as he appeared when first she saw him, the slender, manly youth of eight-and-twenty. Miss Ley had discovered alterations, and spiteful feminine tongues had said that he was going off dreadfully; but his wife had seen nothing; and the separation had given further opportunity to her fantasy. In absence she had thought of him as the handsomest of men, delighting over his clear features, his fair hair, his inexhaustible youth and strength. The plain facts would have disappointed her even if Edward had retained the looks of his youth, but seeing now as well the other changes the shock was extreme. It was a different man she saw, almost a stranger. He did not wear well; though not thirty-one, he looked older. He had broadened and put on flesh; his features had lost their delicacy and the red of his cheeks was growing blotchy. He wore his clothes in a slovenly way and had fallen into a lumbering walk as if his boots were always heavy with clay; and there was in him besides the heartiness and intolerant joviality of the prosperous farmer. Edward's good looks had given her the keenest pleasure, and now, rushing, as was her habit, to the other extreme, she found him almost ugly. This was an exaggeration, for though he was no longer the slim youth of her first acquaintance, he was still in a heavy, massive way better looking than the majority of men.

Edward kissed her with marital calm, and the propinquity wafted to Bertha's nostrils the strong scents of the farmyard, which, no matter what his clothes, hung perpetually about him. She turned away, hardly concealing a little shiver of disgust; yet they were the same masculine odours as once had made her nearly faint with desire.

CHAPTER XXIV

BERTHA'S imagination seldom permitted her to see things in any but a false light; sometimes they were pranked out in the glamour of the ideal, and at others the process was reversed. It was astonishing that so short a break should have destroyed the habit of years; but the fact was plain that Edward had become a stranger, so that she felt it irksome to share the same room with him. She saw him now with jaundiced eyes, and told herself that at last she had discovered his true colours. Poor Edward was paying heavily because the furtive years had robbed him of his looks and given him in exchange a superabundance of fat, because responsibility, the east wind and good living had taken the edge off his features and turned his cheeks plethoric.

Bertha's love, indeed, had finally disappeared as suddenly as it had arisen, and she began to detest her husband. She had acquired a certain part of Miss Ley's analytic faculty, which now she employed upon Edward's character with destructive effect. Her absence had increased the danger to Edward's connubial happiness in another way, for the air of Paris had exhilarated her and sharpened her wits, she had bought many books, had been to the theatres, had read the French papers, whose sparkle offers at first a pleasing contrast to the sobriety of their British contemporaries; with the general result that her alertness to find fault was doubled and her impatience with the dull and the stupid, extreme.

And Bertha soon found that her husband's mind was not only commonplace, but common. His ignorance no longer seemed touching, but merely shameful; his prejudices no longer amusing, but contemptible. She was indignant at having humbled herself so abjectly before a man of such narrowness of mind and insignificance of character. She could not conceive how she had ever passionately loved him. He was bound by the stupidest routine; it irritated her beyond measure to see the regularity with which he went through the unvarying process of his toilet; nothing interfered with the order in which he washed his teeth and brushed his hair. She was indignant with his presumption and self-satisfaction and conscious rectitude. Edward's taste was contemptible in books, in pictures and in music; and his pretensions to judge upon such matters filled her with scorn. At first his deficiencies had not affected her, and later she had consoled herself with the obvious truism that a man may be ignorant of the arts and yet have every virtue under the sun. But now she was less charitable. Bertha wondered that because her husband could read and write as well as most board-scholars he should feel himself competent to judge books—even without reading them. Of course it was unreasonable to blame the poor man for a foible common to the vast majority of mankind. Everyone who can hold a pen is confident of his ability to criticize, and to criticize superciliously. It never occurs to the average citizen that, to speak modestly, almost as much art is needed to write a book as to adulterate a pound of tea; nor that the author has busied himself with style and contrast, characterization, light and shade, and many other things to which the practice of haberdashery, greengrocery, company promotion or pork-butchery is no sure key.

One day, Edward, coming in, caught sight of the yellow cover of a French book that Bertha was reading.

'What, reading again?' said he. 'You read too much, it's not good for people to be always reading.'

'Is that your opinion?'

'My idea is that a woman oughtn't to stuff her head with books. You'd be much better out in the open air or doing something useful.'

'Is that your opinion?'

'Well, I should like to know why you're always reading.'

'Sometimes to instruct myself; always to amuse myself.'

'Much instruction you'll get out of an indecent French novel.'

Bertha without answering handed him the book and showed the title; they were the letters of Madame de Sevigné.

'Well?' he said.

'You're no wiser, dear Edward?' she asked, with a smile; such a question in such a tone revenged her for much. 'I'm afraid you're very ignorant. You see I'm not reading a novel and it is not indecent. They are the letters of a mother to her daughter, models of epistolary style and feminine wisdom.'

Bertha purposely spoke in a somewhat formal and elaborate manner.

'Oh,' said Edward, looking mystified, feeling that he had been confounded but certain, none the less, that he was in the right. Bertha smiled provokingly. 'Of course, I've no objection to your reading if it amuses you.'

'It's very good of you to say so.'

'I don't pretend to have any book-learning. I'm a practical man and it's not required. In my business you find that the man who reads books comes a mucker.'

'You seem to think that ignorance is creditable.'

'It's better to have a good and pure heart, Bertha, and a clean mind than any amount of learning.'

'It's better to have a grain of wit than a collection of moral saws.'

'I don't know what you mean by that, but I'm quite content to be as I am, and I don't want to know a single foreign language. English is quite good enough for me.'

'So long as you're a good sportsman and wash yourself regularly you think you've performed the whole duty of man.'

'You can say what you like, but if there's one man I can't stick it's a measly book-worm.'

'I prefer him to the hybrid of a professional cricketer and a Turkish-bath man.'

'Does that mean me?'

'You can take it to yourself if you like,' said Bertha, smiling, 'or apply it to a whole class. Do you mind if I go on reading?'

Bertha took up her book; but Edward was the more argumentatively inclined since he saw he had not so far got the better of the contest.

'Well, what I must say is,' he rejoined, 'if you want to read, why can't you read English books? Surely there are enough. I think English people ought to stick to their own country. I don't pretend to have read any French books, but I've never heard anybody deny that at all events the great majority of them are indecent, and not the sort of thing a woman should read.'

'It's always incautious to judge from common report.' answered Bertha, without looking up.

'And now that the French are always behaving so badly to us, I should like to see every French book in the kingdom put into a huge bonfire. I'm sure it would be all the better for we English people. What we want now is purity and reconstitution of the national life. I'm in favour of English morals, English homes, English mothers and English habits.'

'What always astounds me, dear, is that though you invariably read the *Standard* you always talk like the *Daily Telegraph.*'

Bertha went on with her book and paid no further attention to Edward, who thereupon began to talk with his dogs. Like most frivolous persons, he found silence very onerous. Bertha thought it disconcerted him by rendering evident even to himself the vacuity of his mind. He talked with every animate thing, with the servants, with his pets, with the cat and the birds; he could not read even a newspaper without making a running commentary upon it. It was only a substantial meal that could induce in him even a passing taciturnity. Sometimes his unceasing chatter irritated Bertha so intensely that she was obliged to beg him, for Heaven's sake, to hold his tongue. Then he would look up with a good-natured laugh.

'Was I making a row? Sorry, I didn't know it.'

He remained quiet for ten minutes, and then began to hum a hackneyed melody, than which there is no more detestable habit.

Indeed the points of divergence between the couple were innumerable. Edward was a man who had the courage of his opinions; he disliked also whatever was not clear to his somewhat narrow intelligence, and was inclined to think it immoral. Bertha played the piano well and sang with a cultivated voice, but her performances were objectionable to her husband because whether she sang or whether she played there was never a rollicking tune that a fellow could get his teeth into. He had upbraided her for this singular taste, and could not help thinking that there was something wrong with a woman who shrugged her shoulders disdainfully at the music-hall ditties that everyone was singing. It must be confessed that Bertha exaggerated, for when a dull musical afternoon was given in the neighbourhood she took a malicious pleasure in playing a long recitative from a Wagner opera that no one could make head or tail of.

On such an occasion at the Glovers', the elder Miss Hancock turned to Edward and remarked upon his wife's admirable playing. Edward was a little annoyed, because everyone had vigorously applauded and to him the sounds had been meaningless.

'Well, I'm a plain man,' he said, 'and I don't mind confessing that I never can understand the stuff Bertha plays.'

'Oh, Mr Craddock, not even Wagner?' said Miss Hancock, who had been as bored as Edward, but, holding the contrary modest opinion that the only really admirable things are those you can't understand, would not for worlds have confessed it.

Bertha looked at him, remembering her dream that they should sit at the piano together in the evening and play for hour after hour; as a matter of fact he had always refused to budge from his chair, and gone to sleep regularly.

'My idea of music is like Dr Johnson's,' said Edward, looking round for approval.

'Is Saul also among the prophets?' murmured Bertha.

'When I hear a difficult piece I wish it was impossible.'

'You forget, dear,' said Bertha, 'that Dr Johnson was a very ill-mannered old man whom dear Fanny would not have allowed in her drawing-room for one minute.'

'You sing now, Edward,' said Miss Glover. 'We've not heard you for ever so long.'

'Oh, bless you,' he retorted, 'my singing's too old-fashioned. My songs have all got a tune in them and some feeling. They're only fit for the kitchen.'

'Oh, please give us "Ben Bolt,"' said Miss Hancock. 'We're all so fond of it.'

Edward's repertory was limited, and everyone knew his songs by heart.

'Anything to oblige,' he said; he was, as a matter of fact, very fond of singing, and applause was always grateful to his ears.

'Shall I accompany you, dear?' said Bertha.

> 'Oh! don't you remember sweet Alice, Ben Bolt,
> Sweet Alice with hai-air so brow-own?
> She wept with delight when you gave her a smile,
> And trembled with feaar at your frown.'

Once upon a time Bertha had found a subtle charm in these pleasing sentiments and in the honest melody that adorned them; but it was not strange that constant repetition had left her a little callous. Edward sang the ditty with a simple, homely style—which is the same as saying with no style at all—and he made use of much pathos. But Bertha's spirit was not forgiving; she owed him some return for the gratuitous attack on her playing; and the notion came to her to improve upon the accompaniment with little trills and flourishes that amused her immensely, but quite disconcerted her husband. Finally, just when his voice was growing flat with emotion over the grey-haired schoolmaster who had died, she wove in the strains of 'The Blue Bells of Scotland' and 'God Save the Queen,' so that Edward broke down. For once his even temper was disturbed.

'I say, I can't sing if you go playing the fool.'

'I'm very sorry,' smiled Bertha, 'I forgot what I was doing. Let's begin all over again.'

'No, I'm not going to sing any more. You spoil the whole thing.'

'Mrs Craddock has no heart,' said Miss Hancock.

'I don't think it's fair to laugh at an old song like this,' said Edward. 'After all, anyone can sneer. My idea of music is something that stirs one's heart. I'm not a sentimental chap, but "Ben Bolt" almost brings the tears to my eyes every time I sing it.'

Bertha difficultly abstained from retorting that sometimes she felt inclined to burst into tears over it herself—especially when he sang out of tune. Everyone looked at her as if she had behaved very badly; she smiled at Edward calmly, but she was not amused. On the way home she asked him if he knew why she had spoilt his song.

'I'm sure I don't know, unless you were in one of your beastly tempers. I suppose you're sorry now.'

'Not at all,' she answered.' I thought you were rude to me just before, and I wanted to punish you a little. Sometimes you're really too supercilious. And besides that, I object to being rowed in public. You will have the goodness in future to keep your strictures till we are alone.'

'I should have thought you could stand a bit of good-natured chaff by now,' he replied.

'Oh, I can, dear Edward. Only, perhaps you may have noticed that I am fairly quick at defending myself.'

'What d'you mean by that?'

'Merely that I can be horrid when I like, and you will be wise not to expose yourself to a public snub.'

Edward had never heard from his wife a threat so calmly administered, and it somewhat impressed him.

But as a general rule Bertha checked the sarcasms that constantly rose to her tongue. She treasured in her heart the wrath and hatred that her husband excited in her, feeling that it was a satisfaction at last to be free from love of him. Looking back, the fetters that had bound her were intolerably heavy. And it was a sweet revenge, although he knew nothing of it, to strip the idol of his ermine cloak and his crown and the gewgaws of his sovereignty. In his nakedness he was a pitiable figure. Edward was totally unconscious of all this. He was like a lunatic reigning in a madhouse over an imaginary kingdom. He did not see the curl of Bertha's lips upon some foolish remark of his, or the contempt with which she treated him. And since she was a great deal less exacting, he found himself far happier than before. The ironic philosopher might find some cause for moralizing in the fact that it was not till Bertha began to dislike Edward that he found marriage quite satisfactory. He told himself that his wife's stay abroad had done her no end of good and made her far more amenable to reason. Mr Craddock's principles, of course, were quite right; he had given her plenty of run and ignored her cackle, and now she had come home to roost. There is nothing like a knowledge of farming and an acquaintance with the habits of domestic animals to teach a man how to manage his wife.

CHAPTER XXV

If the gods, who scatter wit in sundry unexpected places, so that it is sometimes found beneath the bishop's mitre, and once in a thousand years beneath a king's crown, had given Edward two-pennyworth of that commodity he would undoubtedly have been a great as well as a good man. Fortune smiled upon him uninterruptedly; he enjoyed the envy of his neighbours, he farmed with profit, and having tamed the rebellious spirit of his wife he rejoiced in domestic happiness. And it must be noticed that he was rewarded only according to his deserts. He walked with upright spirit and contented mind along the path that it had pleased a merciful providence to set before him. He was lighted on the way by a strong sense of duty, by the principles that he had acquired at his mother's knee, and by a conviction of his own merit. Finally a deputation waited on him to propose that he should stand for the County Council election that was shortly to be held. He had been unofficially informed of the project, and received Mr Atthill Bacot with seven committee men in his frock-coat and a manner full of responsibility. He told them he could do nothing rashly, must consider the matter and would inform them of his decision. Edward had already made up his mind to accept, and having showed the deputation to the door went to Bertha.

'Things are looking up,' he said, having given her the details. The Blackstable district, for which Edward was invited to stand, being composed chiefly of fishermen, was intensely Radical. 'Old Bacot said I was the only moderate candidate who'd have a chance.'

Bertha was too much astonished to reply. She had so low an opinion of her husband that she could not understand why on carth they should make him such an offer. She turned over in her mind possible reasons.

'It's a ripping thing for me, isn't it?'

'But you're not thinking of accepting?'

'Not? Of course I am. What d'you think!'

This was not an inquiry, but an exclamation.

'You've never gone in for politics, you've never made a speech in your life.' She thought he would make an abject fool of himself, and for her sake, as well as his, decided to prevent him from standing. 'He's too stupid,' she thought.

'What! I've made speeches at cricket dinners; you set me on my legs and I'll say something.'

'But this is different; you know nothing about the County Council.'

'All you have to do is to look after steam-rollers and get glandered horses killed. I know all about it.'

There is nothing so difficult as to persuade men that they are ignorant. Bertha, exaggerating the seriousness of the affair, thought it charlatanry to undertake a post without knowledge and without capacity. Fortunately that is not the opinion of the majority, or the government of this enlightened country could not proceed.

'I should have thought you'd be glad to see me get a lift in the world,' said Edward.

'I don't want you to make a fool of yourself, Edward. You've told me often that you don't go in for book-learning; and it can't hurt your feelings when I say that you're not very well informed. I don't think it's honest to take a position you're not competent to fill.'

'Me—not competent?' cried Edward with surprise. 'That's a good one. Upon my word, I'm not given to boasting, but I must say I think myself competent to do most things. You just ask old Bacot what he thinks of me, and that'll open your eyes. The fact is, everyone appreciates me but you; but they say a man's never a hero to his valet.'

'Your proverb is most apt, dear Edward. But I have no intention of thwarting you in any of your plans. I only thought you didn't know what you were going in for and that I might save you some humiliation.'

'Humiliation, where? Oh, you think I shan't get elected. Well, look here, I bet you any money you like that I shall come out top of the poll.'

Next day Edward wrote to Mr Bacot expressing pleasure that he was able to fall in with the views of the Conservative Association; and Bertha, who knew that no argument could turn him from his purpose, determined to coach him, so that he should not make too arrant a fool of himself. Her fears were proportionate to her estimate of Edward's ability. She sent to London for pamphlets and blue-books on the rights and duties of the County Council, and begged Edward to read them. But in his self-confident manner he pooh-poohed her, and laughed when she read them herself in order to be able to teach him.

'I don't want to know all that rot,' he cried. 'All a man wants is gumption. Why, d'you suppose a man who goes in for Parliament knows anything about politics? Of course he doesn't.'

Bertha was indignant that her husband should be so satisfied in his own ignorance that he stoutly refused to learn. Happily men don't realize how stupid they are, or half the world would commit suicide. Knowledge is a will-of-the-wisp, fluttering ever out of the traveller's reach; and a weary journey must be endured before it is even seen. It is only when a man knows a good deal that he discovers how unfathomable is his ignorance. The man who knows nothing is satisfied that there is nothing to know, consequently that he knows everything; and you may more easily persuade him that the moon is made of green cheese than that he is not omniscient. The County Council elections in London were being held just then, and Bertha, hoping to give Edward useful hints, diligently read the oratory that they occasioned. But he refused to listen to her.

'I don't want to crib other men's stuff. I'm going to talk on my own.'

'Why don't you write out a speech and get it by heart?'

Bertha fancied that so she might influence him a little and spare herself and him the humiliation of utter ridicule.

'Old Bacot says when he makes a speech he always trusts to the spur of the moment. He says that Fox made his best speeches when he was blind drunk.'

'D'you know who Fox was?' asked Bertha.

'Some old buffer or other who made speeches.'

The day arrived when Edward was to make his first address in the Blackstable town hall; and for days placards had been pasted on every wall and displayed in every shop announcing the glad news. Mr Bacot came to Court Leys, rubbing his hands.

'We shall have a full house. It'll be a big success. The hall will hold four hundred people, and I think there won't be standing room. I daresay you'll have to address an overflow meeting at the Forester's Hall afterwards.'

'I'll address any number of meetings you like,' replied Edward.

Bertha grew more and more nervous. She anticipated a horrible collapse; they did not know—as she did—how limited was Edward's intelligence. She wanted to stay at home in order to avoid the ordeal, but Mr Bacot had reserved for her a prominent seat on the platform.

'Are you nervous, Eddie?' she said, feeling more kindly disposed to him from his approaching trial.

'Me—nervous? What have I got to be nervous about?'

The hall was indeed crammed with the most eager, smelly, enthusiastic crowd Bertha had ever seen. The gas-jets flared noisily, throwing ugly lights on the people, sailors, shopkeepers and farm hands. On the platform in a semi-circle like the immortal gods sat the notabilities of the neighbourhood; they were Conservative to the backbone. Bertha looked round with apprehension, but tried to calm herself with the thought that they were stupid people and she had no cause to tremble before them.

Presently the vicar took the chair, and in a few well-chosen words introduced Mr Craddock.

'Mr Craddock, like good wine, needs no bush. You all know him, and an introduction is superfluous. Still it is customary on such an occasion to say a few words on behalf of the candidate, and I have great pleasure, etc., etc. . . .'

Now Edward rose to his feet, and Bertha's blood ran cold. She dared not look at the audience. He advanced with his hands in his pockets; he had insisted on dressing himself up in a frock-coat and the most dismal pepper-and-salt trousers.

'Mr Chairman, Ladies and Gentlemen, unaccustomed to public speaking as I am. . . .'

Bertha looked up with a start. Could a man at the end of the nineteenth century seriously begin an oration with those words? But he was not joking; he went on gravely, and looking round, Bertha caught not the shadow of a smile. Edward was not in the least nervous; he quickly got into the swing of his speech: it was awful! He introduced every hackneyed phrase he knew, he mingled slang incongruously with pompous language, and his silly jokes, chestnuts of great antiquity, made Bertha sweat coldly. She wondered that he could go on with such self-possession; did he not see that be was making himself perfectly absurd? She dared not look up for fear of catching the sniggers of Mrs Branderton and the Hancocks: 'One sees what he was before he married Miss Ley. Of course, he's a quite uneducated man. I wonder his wife didn't prevent him from making such an exhibition of himself. The grammar of it, my dear; and the jokes and the stories!' Bertha clenched her hands, furious because the flush of shame would not leave her cheeks. The speech was even worse than she had expected. He used the longest words and, getting entangled in his own verbosity, was obliged to leave his sentence unfinished. He began a period with an elaborate flourish and waddled in confusion to the tamest commonplace; he was like a man who set out to explore the Andes and then, changing his mind, took a stroll in the Burlington Arcade. How long would it be, asked Bertha, before the audience broke into jeers and hisses? She blessed them for their patience. And what would happen afterwards? Would Mr Bacot ask Edward to withdraw his candidature? And supposing Edward refused, would it be necessary to tell him that he was really too great a fool? Bertha heard already the covert sneers of her neighbours.

'Oh, I wish he'd finish!' she muttered between her teeth. The agony, the humiliation of it, were unendurable.

But Edward was still talking and gave no sign of an approaching termination. Bertha thought miserably that he had always been long-winded; if he would only sit down quickly the failure might not be irreparable. He made a vile pun, and everyone cried, 'Oh! Oh!' Bertha shivered and set her teeth, she must bear it to the end now. Why wouldn't he sit down? Then Edward told an agricultural story, and the audience shouted with laughter. A ray of hope came to Bertha; perhaps his vulgarity might save him with the vulgar people who formed the great body of the audience. But what must the Brandertons and the Molsons and the Hancocks and all the rest of them be saying? They must utterly despise him.

But worse was to follow. Edward came to his peroration, and a few remarks on current politics (of which he knew nothing) brought him to his country, England, Home and Beauty. He turned the tap of patriotism full on; it gurgled out in a stream. He blew the penny trumpets of English purity, and the tin whistles of the British Empire, and he beat the big drum of the great Anglo-Saxon race. He thanked God he was an Englishman, and not as others are. Tommy Atkins and Jack Tar and Mr Rudyard Kipling danced a jig to the strains of the 'British Grenadiers' and Mr Joseph Chamberlain executed a *pas seul* to the tune of 'Yankee Doodle'. Metaphorically he waved the Union Jack.

The sentimentality and the bad taste and the vulgarity of what he said revolted Bertha; it was horrible to think how absolutely common must be the mind of a man who could foul his mouth with the expression of such sentiments.

He sat down. For one moment the audience were silent and then with one throat broke into thunderous applause. It was no perfunctory clapping of hands; they rose as one man and shouted and yelled with enthusiasm.

'Good old Teddy,' cried a voice. And then the air was filled with 'For he's a jolly good fellow.' Mrs Branderton stood on a chair and waved her handkerchief, Miss Glover clapped her hands as if she were no longer an automaton.

'Wasn't it perfectly splendid?' she whispered to Bertha.

Everyone on the platform was in a frenzy of delight. Mr Bacot warmly shook Edward's hand. Mrs Mayston Ryle fanned herself desperately. The scene might well have been described, in the language of journalists, as one of unparaleled enthusiasm. Bertha was dumbfounded.

Mr Bacot jumped to his feet.

'I must congratulate Mr Craddock on his excellent speech. I am sure it comes as a surprise to all of us that he should prove such a fluent speaker, with such a fund of humour and common-sense. And what is more valuable than these, his last words have proved to us that his heart—his heart, gentlemen—is in the right place, and that is saying a great deal. In fact I know nothing better to be said of a man than that his heart is in the right place. You know me, ladies and gentlemen, I have made many speeches to you since I had the honour of standing for the constituency in '85, but I must confess I couldn't make a better speech myself than the one you have just heard.'

'You could—you could!' cried Edward, modestly.

'No, Mr Craddock. No, I assert deliberately and I mean it, that I could not do better myself. From my shoulders I let fall the mantle, and give it—'

Here Mr Bacot was interrupted by the stentorian voice of the landlord of 'The Pig and Whistle' (a rabid conservative).

'Three cheers for good old Teddy!'

'That's right, my boys,' cried Mr Bacot, for once taking an interruption in good part,' three cheers for good old Teddy!'

The audience opened its mighty mouth and roared, and then burst again into 'For he's a jolly good fellow.' Arthur Branderton, when the tumult was subsiding, rose from his chair and called for more cheers. The object of all this enthusiasm sat calmly, with a well-satisfied look on his face, taking it all with his usual modest complacency. At last the meeting broke up, with cheers and 'God Save the Queen', and 'He's a jolly good fellow.' The committee and the personal friends of the Craddocks retired to the side room for light refreshment.

The ladies clustered round Edward, congratulating him. Arthur Branderton came to Bertha.

'Ripping speech, wasn't it?' he said. 'I had no idea he could jaw like that. By Jove, it simply stirred me right through.'

Before Bertha could answer, Mrs Mayston Ryle sailed in.

'Where's the man?' she cried in her loud voice. 'Where is he? Show him to me. My dear Mr Craddock, your speech was perfect. I say it.'

'And in such good taste,' said Miss Hancock, her eyes glowing. 'How proud you must be of your husband, Mrs Craddock!'

'There's no chance for the Radicals now,' said the vicar, rubbing his hands.

'Oh, Mr Craddock, let me come near you,' cried Mrs Branderton. 'I've been trying to get at you for twenty minutes. You've simply extinguished the horrid Radicals. I couldn't help crying, you were so pathetic.'

'One may say what one likes,' whispered Miss Glover to her brother,' but there's nothing in the world so beautiful as sentiment I felt my heart simply bursting.'

'Mr Craddock,' added Mrs Mayston Ryle, 'you've pleased me! Where's your wife, that I may tell her so?'

'It's the best speech we've ever had down here,' cried Mrs Branderton.

'That's the only true thing I've heard you say for twenty years, Mrs Branderton,' replied Mrs Mayston Ryle, looking very hard at Mr Atthill Bacot.

CHAPTER XXVI

WHEN Lord Rosebery makes a speech, even the journals of his own party report him in the first person and at full length; and this is said to be the politician's supreme ambition: when he has reached such distinction there is nothing left him but an honourable death and a public funeral in Westminster Abbey. Now, the *Blackstable Times* accorded this honour to Edward's first speech, it was printed with numberless I's peppered boldly over it, the grammar was corrected, and the stops inserted just as for the most important orators. Edward bought a dozen copies and read the speech right through in each, to see that his sentiments were correctly expressed and that there were no misprints. He gave it to Bertha and stood over her while she read it.

'Looks well, don't it?' he said.

'Splendid!'

'By the way, is Aunt Polly's address 72Eliot Mansions?'

'Yes. Why?'

Her jaw fell as she saw him roll up half a dozen copies of the *Blackstable Times* and address the wrapper.

'I'm sure she'd like to read my speech. And it might hurt her feelings if she heard about it and I'd not sent her the report.'

'Oh, I'm sure she'd like to see it very much. But if you send six copies you'll have none left—for other people.'

'Oh, I can easily get some more. The Editor chap told me I could have a thousand if I liked. I'm sending her six because I daresay she'd like to forward some to her friends.'

Almost by return of post came Miss Ley's reply.

My dear Edward,

I perused all six copies of your speech with the greatest interest; and I think you will agree with me that it is high proof of its merit that I was able to read it the sixth time with as unflagging attention as the first. The peroration, indeed, I am convinced that no acquaintance could stale. It is so true that 'every Englishman has a mother' (supposing, of course, that an untimely death has not robbed him of her). It is curious how one does not realize the truth of some things till they are set before one; when one's only surprise is at not having seen them before I hope it will not offend you if I suggest that Bertha's handiwork seems to me not invisible in some of the sentiments; (especially in that passage about the Union Jack); did you really write the whole speech yourself? Come, now, confess that Bertha helped you.

Yours very sincerely,
Mary Ley.

Edward read the letter and tossed it, laughing, to Bertha.

'What cheek her suggesting that you helped me! I like that.'

'I'll write at once and tell her that it was all your own.'

Bertha still could hardly believe genuine the admiration that her husband excited. Knowing his extreme incapacity, she was astounded that the rest of the world should think him an uncommonly clever fellow. To her his pretensions were merely ridiculous; she marvelled that he should venture to discuss with dogmatic glibness subjects of which he knew nothing; but she marvelled still more that people should be impressed thereby; he had an astonishing faculty for concealing his ignorance.

At last the polling-day arrived, and Bertha waited anxiously at Court Leys for the result. Edward eventually appeared, radiant.

'What did I tell you?' said he.

'I see you've got in.'

'Got in isn't the word for it! What did I tell you? My dear girl, I've simply knocked 'em all into a cocked hat. I got double the number of votes that the other chap did, and it's the biggest poll they've ever had. Aren't you proud that your hubby is a County Councillor? I tell you I shall be an M.P. before I die.'

'I congratulate you with all my heart,' said Bertha trying to be enthusiastic.

Edward in his excitement did not observe her coolness. He was walking up and down the room concocting schemes, asking himself how long it would be before Miles Campbell, the member, was confronted by the inevitable dilemma of the unopposed M.P., one horn of which is the kingdom of Heaven and the other the House of Lords.

Presently he stopped: 'I'm not a vain man,' he remarked, 'but I must say I don't think I've done badly.'

Edward for a while was somewhat overwhelmed by his own greatness, but the opinion came to his rescue that the rewards were only according to his deserts; and presently he entered energetically into the not very arduous duties of the County Councillor. Bertha continually expected to hear something to his disadvantage; but on the contrary everything seemed to proceed very satisfactorily, and Edward's aptitude for business, his keenness in making a bargain, his common-sense, were heralded abroad in a manner that should have been most gratifying to his wife. But as a matter of fact these constant praises exceedingly disquieted Bertha. She asked herself uneasily whether she was doing him an injustice. Was he really as clever, had he indeed the virtues that common report ascribed to him? Perhaps she was prejudiced, and perhaps—he was cleverer than she. The possibility of this made her wince; she had never doubted that her intellect was superior to Edward's; their respective knowledge was not comparable; she occupied herself with thoughts that Edward did not conceive. He never interested himself in abstract things, and his conversation was tedious as only the absence of speculation can make it. It was extraordinary that everyone but she should so highly esteem his intelligence. Bertha knew that his mind was paltry and his ignorance egregious. His pretentiousness made him a charlatan. One day he came to her, his head full of a new idea.

'I say, Bertha, I've been thinking it over, and it seems a pity that your name should be dropped entirely. And it sounds funny that people called Craddock should live at Court Leys.'

'D'you think so? I don't know how you can remedy it, unless you think of advertising for tenants with a more suitable name.'

'Well, I was thinking it wouldn't be a bad idea, and it would have a good effect on the county, if we took the name again.'

He looked at Bertha, who glared at him icily, but answered nothing.

'I've talked to old Bacot about it, and he thinks it would be just the thing, so I think we'd better do it.'

'I suppose you're going to consult me on the subject.'

'That's what I'm doing now.'

'Do you think of calling yourself Ley-Craddock or Craddock-Ley, or dropping the Craddock altogether?'

'Well, to tell you the truth, I hadn't gone so far as that yet.'

Bertha gave a little scornful laugh. 'I think the idea is utterly ridiculous.'

'I don't see that; I think it would be rather an improvement.'

'Really, Edward, if I was not ashamed to take your name, I don't think that you need be ashamed to keep it.'

'I say, I think you might be reasonable. You're always standing in my way.'

'I have no wish to do that. If you think my name will add to your importance, use it by all means. You may call yourself Tompkins for all I care.'

'What about you?'

'Oh, I—I shall continue to call myself Craddock.'

'I do think it's rough. You never do anything to help me.'

'I am sorry you're dissatisfied. But you forget that you have impressed one ideal on me for years; you have always given me to understand that your pattern of a female animal was the common or garden cow. I always regret that you didn't marry Fanny Glover. You would have suited one another admirably. And I think she would have worshipped you as you desire to be worshipped. I'm sure she would not have objected to your calling yourself Glover.'

'I shouldn't have wanted to take her name. That's no better than Craddock. The only thing in Ley is that it's an old county name and has belonged to your people.'

'That is why I don't choose that you should take it.'

CHAPTER XXVII

TIME passed slowly, slowly. Bertha wrapped her pride about her like a cloak, but sometimes it seemed too heavy to bear, and she nearly fainted. The restraint that she imposed upon herself was often intolerable; anger and hatred seethed within her, but she forced herself to preserve the smiling face that people had always seen. She suffered intensely from loneliness of spirit, for she had no one to whom she could tell her unhappiness; it is terrible to have no means of expressing oneself, to keep imprisoned always the anguish that gnaws at one's heart-strings; it is well enough for the writer; he can find solace in his words, he can tell his secret and yet not betray it; but the woman has only silence.

Bertha loathed Edward now with such an angry, physical repulsion that she could not bear his touch; and everyone she knew was his admiring friend. How could she tell Fanny Glover that Edward was a fool who bored her to death, when Fanny Glover thought him the best and most virtuous of mankind? She was annoyed that in the universal estimation Edward should have so entirely eclipsed her; once his only importance lay in the fact that he was her husband, but now the position was reversed. She found it very irksome thus to shine with reflected light, and at the same time despised herself for the petty jealousy.

At last she felt it impossible any longer to endure his company; he made her stupid and vulgar, she was ill and weak and she despaired. She made up her mind to go away again, this time for ever.

'If I stay, I shall kill myself.'

For two days Edward had been miserable; a favourite dog of his had died, and he was brought to the verge of tears. Bertha watched him contemptuously.

'You are more affected over the death of a wretched dog than you have ever been over a pain of mine.'

'Oh, don't rag me now, there's a good girl; I can't bear it.'

'Fool!' muttered Bertha under her breath.

He went about with hanging head and melancholy face, telling everyone the particulars of the beast's demise in a voice quivering with emotion.

'Poor fellow,' said Miss Glover, 'he has such a good heart.'

Bertha could hardly repress the bitter invective that rose to her lips. If people knew the coldness with which he had met her love, the indifference he had shown to her tears and to her despair. She despised herself when she remembered the utter self-abasement of the past.

'He made me drink the cup of humiliation to the very dregs.'

From the height of her disdain she summed him up for the thousandth time. It was inexplicable that she had been subject to a man so paltry in mind, so despicable in character. It made her blush with shame to think how servile had been her love.

Dr Ramsay, who was visiting Bertha for some trivial ill, happened to come in when she was engaged with such thoughts.

'Well,' he said, as soon as she had taken breath, 'and how is Edward today?'

'Good Heavens, how should I know?' she cried, beside herself, the words slipping out unawares after the long constraint.

'Hulloa, what's this? Have the turtle-doves had a tiff at last?'

'Oh, I'm sick of continually hearing Edward's praises. I'm sick of being treated as an appendage to him.'

'What's the matter with you, Bertha?' said the doctor, bursting into a shout of laughter. 'I always thought nothing pleased you more than to hear how much we all liked your husband.'

'Oh, my good doctor, you must be blind or an utter fool. I thought everyone knew by now that I loathe my husband.'

'What!' shouted Dr Ramsay; then, thinking Bertha was unwell: 'Come, come, I see you want a little medicine, my dear. You're out of sorts, and like all women you think the world is consequently coming to an end.'

Bertha sprang from the sofa. 'D'you think I should speak like this if I hadn't good cause? Don't you think I'd conceal my humiliation if I could? Oh, I've hidden it long enough; now I must speak. Oh, God, I can hardly help screaming with pain when I think of all I've suffered and bidden. I've never said a word to anyone but you, and now I can't help it. I tell you I loathe and abhor my husband and I utterly despise him. I can't live with him any more and I want to go away.'

Dr Ramsay opened his mouth and fell back in his chair; he looked at Bertha as if he expected her to have a fit.

'Well, I'm blowed. You're not serious?'

Bertha stamped her foot impatiently: 'Of course I'm serious. Do you think I'm a fool too? We've been miserable for years, and it can't go on. If you knew what I've had to suffer when everyone has congratulated me and said how pleased they were to see me so happy! Sometimes I've had to dig my nails in my hands to prevent myself from crying out the truth.'

Bertha walked up and down the room, letting herself go at last. The tears were streaming down her cheeks, but she took no notice of them. She was giving full vent to her passionate hatred.

'Oh, I've tried to love him. You know how I loved him once, how I adored him. I would have laid down my life for him with pleasure. I would have done anything he asked me; I used to search for the smallest indication of his wishes so that I might carry them out. I used to love to think that I was his abject slave. But he's destroyed every vestige of my love, and now I only despise him, I utterly despise him. Oh, I've tried to love him, but he's too great a fool.'

The last words Bertha said with such force that Dr Ramsay was startled.

'My dear Bertha!'

'Oh, I know you all think him wonderful. I've had his praises thrown at me for years. But you don't know what a man really is till you've lived with him, till you've seen him in every mood and in every circumstance. I know him through and through, and he's a fool. You can't conceive how stupid, how utterly brainless he is. He bores me to death.'

'Come now, you don't mean what you say. You're exaggerating as usual. You must expect to have little quarrels now and then; upon my word, I think it took me twenty years to get used to my wife.'

'Oh, for God's sake, don't be sententious,' Bertha interrupted fiercely. 'I've had enough moralizing in these five years. I might have loved Edward better if he hadn't been so moral. He's thrown his virtues in my face till I'm sick of them. He's made every goodness ugly to me till I sigh for vice just for a change. Oh, you can't imagine how frightfully dull is a really good man. Now I want to be free; I tell you I can't stand it any more.'

Bertha again walked up and down the room excitedly.

'Upon my word,' cried Dr Ramsay, 'I can't make head or tail of it.'

'I didn't expect you would. I knew you'd only preach at me.'

'What d'you want me to do? Shall I speak to him?'

'No! No! I've spoken to him endlessly. It's no good. D'you suppose your speaking to him will make him love me? He's incapable of it; all he can give me is esteem and affection. Good God, what do I want with esteem! It requires a certain intelligence to love, and he hasn't got it. I tell you he's a fool. Oh, when I think that I'm shackled to him for the rest of my life I feel I could kill myself.'

'Come now, he's not such a fool as all that. Everyone agrees that he's a very smart man of business. And I can't help saving that I've always thought you did uncommonly well when you insisted on marrying him.'

'It was all your fault,' cried Bertha. 'If you hadn't opposed me I might not have married so quickly. Oh, you don't know how I've regretted it. I wish I could see him dead at my feet.'

Dr Ramsay whistled. His mind worked somewhat slowly and he was becoming confused with the overthrow of his cherished opinions and the vehemence with which the unpleasant operation was conducted.

'I didn't know things were like this.'

'Of course you didn't!' said Bertha scornfully. 'Because I smiled and hid my sorrow you thought I was happy. When I look back on the misery I've gone through I wonder that I can ever have borne it.'

'I can't believe that this is very serious. You'll be of a different mind tomorrow and wonder that such things ever entered your head. You musn't mind an old fellow like me telling you you're very headstrong and impulsive. After all, Edward is a fine fellow, and I can't believe that he would willingly hurt your feelings.'

'Oh, for God's sake don't give me more of Edward's praises.'

'I wonder if you're a little jealous of the way he's got on?' asked the doctor, looking at her sharply.

Bertha flushed, for she had asked herself the same question; much scorn was needed to refute it.

'I? My dear doctor, you forget! Oh, don't you understand that it isn't a passing whim? It's dreadfully serious to me. I've borne the misery till I can bear it no longer. You must help me to get away. If you have any of your old affection for me, do what you can. I want to go away; but I don't want to have any more rows with Edward; I just want to leave him quietly. It's no good trying to make him understand that we're incompatible. He thinks that it's enough for my happiness just to be his wife. He's of iron and I am pitifully weak. I used to think myself so strong.'

'Am I to take it that you're absolutely serious? Do you want to take the extreme step of separating from your husband?'

'It's an extreme step that I've taken before. Last time I went with a flourish of trumpets, but now I want to go without any fuss at all. I still loved Edward then, but I have even ceased to hate him. Oh, I knew I was a fool to come back, but I couldn't help it. He asked me to return and I did.'

'Well, I don't know what I can do for you. I can't help thinking that if you wait a little things will get better.'

'I can't wait any longer. I've waited too long. I'm losing my whole life.'

'Why don't you go away for a few months, and then you can see? Miss Ley is going to Italy for the winter as usual, isn't she? Upon my word, I think it would do you good to go too.'

'I don't mind what I do as long as I can get away. I'm suffering too much.'

'Have you thought that Edward will miss you?' asked Dr Ramsay, gravely.

'No, he won't. Good Heavens, don't you think I know him by now? I know him through and through. And he's callous and selfish and stupid. And he's making me like himself. Oh, Dr Ramsay, please help me.'

'Does Miss Ley know?' asked the doctor, remembering what she had told him on her visit to Court Leys.

'No, I'm sure she doesn't. She thinks we adore one another. And I don't want her to know. I'm such a coward now. Years ago I never cared a straw for what anyone in the world thought of me; but my spirit is broken. Oh, get me away from here, Dr Ramsay, get me away.'

She burst into tears, weeping as she had been long unaccustomed to do; she was exhausted after the outburst of all that for years she had kept hid.

'I'm still so young, and I almost feel an old woman. Sometimes I should like to lie down and die, and have done with it all.'

A month later Bertha was in Rome. But at first she was hardly able to realize the change in her condition; for her life at Court Leys had impressed itself upon her with ghastly distinctness, so that she could not imagine its cessation. She was like a prisoner so long immured that freedom dazes him, and he looks for his chains and cannot understand that he is free.

They had taken an apartment in the Via Gregoriana, and Bertha, waking in the morning, did not know where she was. The relief was so great that she could not believe it true, and she lived in fear that her vision would be disturbed and she find herself again within the prison walls of Court Leys. It was a dream that she wandered in sunlit places, where the air was scented with violets and roses. The people were unreal, the models lounging on the steps of the Piazza di Spagna, the ragged urchins, quaintly costumed and importunate, the silver speech that caressed the air. How could she believe that life was true when it gave blue sky and sunshine, so that the heart thrilled with joy; when it gave rest and peace and the most delightful idleness. Real life was gloomy and strenuous; and its setting a Georgian mansion, surrounded by desolate, wind-swept fields. In real life everyone was deadly virtuous and deadly dull; the Ten Commandments hedged one round with the menace of hell-fire and eternal damnation. They are a dungeon more terrible because it has not walls, nor bars and bolts. But beyond those gloomy stones with the harsh 'thou shalt not' written upon them, is a land of fragrance and light, where the sunbeams send the blood running gaily through the veins, where the flowers give their perfume freely to the air, in token that riches must be spent and virtue must be squandered; where the amorets flutter here and there on the spring breezes, unknowing whither they go, uncaring. This land beyond the Ten Commandments is a land of olive-trees and pleasant shade, and the sea kisses the shore gently to show the youths how they must kiss the maidens; there lips are not vehicles for grotesque strenuosities, but Cupid's bows; and there dark eyes flash lambently, telling the traveller he need not fear, Love may be had for the asking. Blood is warm, and hands linger with grateful pressure in hands, and red lips ask for the kisses that are so sweet to give. There the flesh and the spirit walk side by side, and each is well satisfied with the other. Ah, give me the sunshine of this blissful country, and a garden of roses, and the murmur of a pleasant brook; give me a shady bank, and wine, and books, and the coral lips of Amaryllis, and I will live in complete felicity for at least ten days.

To Bertha the life in Rome seemed like a play. Miss Ley left her much freedom, and she wandered alone in strange places. She went often to the market and spent the morning wandering in and out of the booths, looking at a thousand things she did not want to buy; she fingered rich silks and antique bits of silver, smiling at the compliments of a friendly dealer. The people bustled round her, volubly talking, intensely alive, and yet, because she could not understand that what she saw was true, strangely unreal. She went to the galleries, to the Sistine Chapel or the Stanze of Raphael; and, lacking the hurry of the tourist and his sense of duty, she would spend a whole morning in front of one picture or in a corner of an old church, weaving with whatever she looked at the fantasies of her imagination.

And when she felt the need of her fellow-men she went to the Pincio and mingled with the throng that listened to the band. But the Franciscan monk in his brown cowl, standing apart, was a figure of a romantic play, and the soldiers in gay uniforms, the Bersaglieri with the bold cock's feathers in their hats, were the chorus of a comic opera. And there were black-robed priests, some old and fat, taking the sun and smoking cigarettes, at peace with themselves and the world; others young and restless, with the flesh unsubdued shining out of their dark eyes. And everyone seemed as happy as the children who romped and scampered with merry cries.

But gradually the shadows of the past fell away and Bertha was able more consciously to appreciate the beauty and the life that surrounded her. And knowing it fleeting, she set herself to enjoy it as best she could. Care and youth are difficultly yoked together, and merciful time wraps in oblivion the most gruesome misery. Bertha stretched out her arms to embrace the wonders of the living world, and she put away the dreadful thought that it must end so quickly. In the spring she spent long hours in the gardens that surround the city; the remains of ancient Rome mingled exotically with the half-tropical luxuriance, and excited in her new and subtle emotions. The flowers grew in the sarcophagi with a wild exuberance, wantoning, it seemed, in mockery of the tomb whence they sprang. Death is hideous, but life is always triumphant; the rose and the hyacinth arise from man's decay; and the dissolution of man is but the signal of other birth; and the world goes on, beautiful and ever new, revelling in its vigour.

Bertha went to the Villa Medici and sat where she could watch the light glowing on the mellow facade of the old palace and Syrinx peeping between the reeds; the students saw her and asked who was the beautiful woman who sat so long and so unconscious of the eyes that looked at her. She went to the Villa Doria-Pamphili, majestic and pompous, the fitting summer-house of princes in gorgeous habit, and bishops and cardinals. And the ruins of the Palatine, with its cypresses and well-kept walks, sent her thoughts back and back, and she pictured to herself the glories of bygone powers.

But the wildest garden of all, that of the Mattei, pleased her best. Here was a greater fertility and a greater abandonment; the distance and the difficulty of access kept strangers away, and Bertha could wander through it as if it were her own. She thought she had never enjoyed such exquisite moments as were given her by its solitude and its silence. Sometimes a troop of scarlet seminarists sauntered along the grass-grown avenues, vivid colour against the desolate verdure.

Then she went home, tired and happy; she sat at her open window and watched the setting sun. The sun set over St Peter's and the mighty cathedral was transfigured into a temple of fire and gold; the dome was radiant, formed no longer of solid stone, but of light and sunshine: it was the crown of a palace of Hyperion. Then with the night, St Peter's stood out in darkness, stood out in majestic profile against the splendour of heaven.

CHAPTER XXVIII

But after Easter Miss Ley proposed that they should travel slowly back to England. Bertha had dreaded the suggestion, not only because she regretted to leave Rome, but still more because it rendered necessary some explanation. The winter had passed comfortably enough with the excuse of indifferent health, but now another reason must be found to account for the continued absence from her husband's side, and Bertha's racked imagination gave her nothing. She was determined, however, under no circumstances to return to Court Leys; after the happy freedom of six months the confinement of body and soul would be doubly intolerable.

Edward had been satisfied with the pretext, and had let Bertha go without a word. As he said, he was not the man to stand in his wife's way when her health required her to leave him, and he could pig along all right by himself. Their letters had been fairly frequent, but on Bertha's side a constant effort. She was always telling herself that the only rational course was to make Edward a final statement of her intentions, then break off all communication; but the dread of fuss and bother, and of endless explanation, restrained her; and she compromised by writing as seldom as possible and adhering to the merest trivialities. She was surprised once or twice when she had delayed her answer, to receive from him a second letter, asking with some show of anxiety why she did not write.

Miss Ley had never mentioned Edward's name, and Bertha surmised that she knew much of the truth. But she kept her own counsel; blessed are they who mind their own business and hold their tongues! Miss Ley, indeed, was convinced that some catastrophe had occurred, but true to her habit of allowing people to work out their lives in their own way, without interference, took care to seem unobservant; which was really very noble, for she prided herself on nothing more than on her talent for observation.

'The most difficult thing for a wise woman to do,' she said, 'is to pretend to be a foolish one.'

She guessed Bertha's present difficulty; and it seemed easily surmountable.

'I wish you'd come back to London with me instead of going to Court Leys,' she said. 'You've never had a London season, have you? On the whole I think it's amusing; the opera is very good, and sometimes you see people who are quite well dressed.'

Bertha did not answer, and Miss Ley, seeing her wish to accept and at the same time her hesitation, suggested that she should come for a few weeks, well knowing that a woman's visit is apt to spin itself out for an indeterminate time.

'I'm sorry I shan't have room for Edward too,' said Miss Ley, smiling drily, 'but my flat is very small, you know.'

Irony is a gift of the gods, the most subtle of all the modes of speech. It is an armour and a weapon; it is a philosophy and a perpetual entertainment; it is food for the hungry of wit and drink to those thirsting for laughter. How much more elegant is it to slay your foe with the roses of irony than to massacre him with the axes of sarcasm or to belabour him with the bludgeons of invective. And the adept in irony enjoys its use when he alone is aware of his meaning, and he sniggers up his sleeve to see all and sundry, chained to their obtuseness, take him seriously. In a strenuous world it is the only safeguard of the flippant. To the man of letters it is a missile that he can fling in the reader's face to disprove the pestilent heresy that a man writes books for the subscriber to Mudie's Library, rather than for himself. Be not deceived gentle reader, no self-respecting writer cares a twopenny damn for you.

They had been settled a few days in the flat in Eliot Mansions, when Bertha, coming in to breakfast one morning, found Miss Ley in a great state of suppressed amusement. She was quivering all over like an uncoiled spring, and she pecked at her toast and her egg in a bird-like manner, which Bertha knew could only mean that someone, to the entertainment of her aunt, had made a fool of himself. Bertha began to laugh.

'Good Heavens,' she cried, 'what has happened?'

'My dear, a terrible catastrophe,' Miss Ley repressed a smile, but her eyes gleamed and danced as though she were a young woman. 'You don't know Gerald Vaudrey, do you? But you know who he is.'

'I believe he's a cousin of mine.'

Bertha's father, who made a practice of quarrelling with his relations, had found in General Vaudrey a brother-in-law as irascible as himself; so that the two families had never been on speaking terms.

'I've just had a letter from his mother to say that he's been philandering rather violently with her maid, and they're all in despair. The maid has been sent away in hysterics, his mother and his sisters are in tears, and the General's in a passion and says he won't have the boy in his house another day. And the little wretch is only nineteen. Disgraceful, isn't it?'

'Disgraceful,' said Bertha, smiling. 'I wonder what there is in a French n aid that small boys should invariably make love to her.'

'Oh, n y dear, if you only saw my sister's maid. She's forty if she's a day, and her complexion is like parchment very much the worse for wear. But the awful part of it is that your Aunt Betty beseeches me to look after the boy. He's going to Florida in a month, and meanwhile he's to stay in London. Now, what I want to know is how am I to keep a dissolute infant out of mischief? Is it the sort of thing that one would expect of me?'

Miss Ley waved her arms with comic desperation.

'Oh, but it'll be great fun. We'll reform him together. We'll lead him on to a path where French maids are not to be met at every turn and corner.'

'My dear, you don't know what he is. He's an utter young scamp. He was expelled from Rugby. He's been to half a dozen crammers, because they wanted him to go to Sandhurst, but he refused to work; and he's been ploughed in every exam, he's gone in for—even for the Militia. So now his father has given him five hundred pounds and told him to go to the devil.'

'How rude! But why should the poor boy go to Florida?'

'I suggested that. I know some people who've got an orange plantation there. And I daresay that the view of several miles of orange blossoms will suggest to him that promiscuous flirtation may have unpleasant results.'

'I think I shall like him,' said Bertha.

'I have no doubt you will; he's a perfect scamp and rather pretty.'

Next day, when Bertha was in the drawing-room, reading, Gerald Vaudrey was shown in. She got up smiling, to reassure him, and put out her hand in the friendliest manner; she thought he must be a little confused at meeting a stranger instead of Miss Ley, and unhappy in his disgrace.

'You don't know who I am?' she said.

'Oh, yes, I do,' he replied, with a very pleasant smile. 'The slavey told me Aunt Polly was out, but that you were here.'

'I'm glad you didn't go away.'

'I thought I shouldn't frighten you, you know.'

Bertha opened her eyes. He was certainly not at all shy, although he looked even younger than nineteen. He was quite a boy, very slight and not so tall as Bertha, with a small, girlish face. He had a tiny nose, but it was very straight, and his somewhat freckled complexion was admirable. His hair was dark and curly; he wore it long, evidently aware that it was very nice; and his handsome eyes had a charming expression. His sensual mouth was always smiling.

'What a pretty boy!' thought Bertha. 'I'm sure I shall like him.'

He began to talk as if he had known her all his life, and she was struck by the contrast between his innocent appearance and his shocking past. He looked about the room with boyish ease and stretched himself comfortably in a big armchair.

'Hulloa, that's new since I was here last,' he said, pointing to an Italian bronze.

'Have you been here often?'

'Rather! I used to come here whenever it got too hot for me at home. It's no good scrapping with your governor, because he's got the ooftish. It's a jolly unfair advantage that fathers have, but they always take it. So when the old chap flew into a passion, I used to say: "I won't argue with you. If you can't treat me like a gentleman, I shall go away for a week." And I used to come here. Aunt Polly always gave me five quid and said: "Don't tell me how you spend it, because I shouldn't approve, but come again when you want more." She is a ripper, ain't she?'

'I'm sorry she's not in.'

'I'm rather glad, because I can have a long talk with you till she comes. I've never seen you before, so I have such a lot to say.'

'Have you?' said Bertha laughing. 'That's rather unusual in young men.'

He looked so absurdly young that Bertha could not help treating him as a schoolboy; she was amused at his communicativeness. She wanted him to tell her all his escapades, but was afraid to ask.

'Are you very hungry?' She thought that boys always had appetites. 'Would you like some tea?'

'I'm starving.'

She poured him out a cup, and taking it and three jam sandwiches at once, he sat on a footstool at her feet. He made himself quite at home.

'You've never seen my Vaudrey cousins, have you?' he asked, with his mouth full. 'I can't stick 'em at any price, they're such frumps. I'll tell 'em all about you; it'll make them beastly sick.'

Bertha raised her eyebrows: 'And do you object to frumps?'

'I simply loathe them. At the last tutor's I was at the old chap's wife was the most awful old geyser you ever saw. So I wrote and told my mater that I was afraid my morals were being corrupted.'

'And did she take you away?'

'Well, by a curious coincidence, the old chap wrote the very same day and told the pater if he didn't remove me he'd give me the shoot. So I sent in my resignation and told him his cigars were poisonous and cleared out.'

'Don't you think you'd better sit on a chair?' said Bertha. 'You must be very uncomfortable on that footstool.'

'Oh, no, not at all. After a Turkey carpet and dining-room table, there's nothing so comfy as a footstool. A chair always makes me feel respectable, and dull.'

Bertha thought Gerald a nice name.

'How long are you staying in London?'

'Oh, only a month, worse luck. Then I've got to go to the States to make my fortune and reform.'

'I hope you will.'

'Which? One can't do both at once, you know. You make your money first and you reform afterwards if you've got time. But whatever happens, it'll be a damned sight better than sweating away at an everlasting crammer's. If there is one man I can't stick at any price it's the army crammer.'

'You have a large experience of them, I understand.'

'I wish you didn't know all my past history. Now I shan't have the sport of telling you.'

'I don't think it would be edifying.'

'Oh, yes, it would. It would show you how virtue is downtrodden (that's me) and how vice is triumphant. I'm awfully unlucky; people sort of conspire together to look at my actions from the wrong point of view. I've had jolly rough luck all through. First I was bunked from Rugby. Well, that wasn't my fault. I was quite willing to stay, and I'm blowed if I was worse than anybody else. The pater blackguarded me for six weeks and said I was bringing his grey hairs with sorrow to the grave. Well, you know, he's simply awfully bald, so at last I couldn't help saying that I didn't know where his grey hairs were going to; but it didn't much look as if he meant to accompany them. So after that he sent me to a crammer who played poker; well, he skinned me of every shilling I'd got, and then wrote and told the pater I was an immoral young dog and corrupting his house.'

'Isn't there something else we could talk about?'

'Oh, but you must have the sequel. The next place I went to, I found none of the other fellows knew poker; so of course I thought it a sort of merciful interposition of providence to help me to recoup myself. I told 'em not to lay up treasure in this world, and walloped 'em thirty quid in four days; then the old thingamyjig (I forget his name, but he was a parson) told me I was making his place into a gambling hell and he wouldn't have me another day in his house. So off I toddled, and I stayed at home for six months. That gave me the fair hump, I can tell you.'

The conversation was disturbed by the entrance of Miss Ley.

'You see we've made friends,' said Bertha.

'Gerald always does that with everybody. He's the most gregarious person. How are you, Lothario?'

'Flourishing, Belinda,' he replied, flinging his arms round Miss Ley's neck to her great delight and pretended indignation.

'You're irrepressible,' she said. 'I expected to find you in sackcloth and ashes, penitent and silent.'

'My dear Aunt Polly, ask me to do anything you like except to repent and to hold my tongue.'

'You know your mother has asked me to look after you.'

'I like being looked after. And is Bertha going to help?'

'I've been thinking it over,' added Miss Ley, 'and the only way I can see to keep you out of mischief is to make you spend your evenings with me. So you'd better go home now and dress. I know there's nothing you like better than changing your clothes.'

Meanwhile Bertha observed with astonishment that Gerald was devouring her with his eyes. It was impossible not to see his evident admiration.

'The boy must be mad,' she thought, but could not help feeling flattered.

'He's been telling me some dreadful stories,' she said to Miss Ley when he had gone. 'I hope they're not true.'

'Oh, I think you must take all Gerald says with a grain of salt. He exaggerates dreadfully, and all boys like to seem Byronic; so do most men, for the matter of that.'

'He looks so young, I can't believe that he's really very naughty.'

'Well, my dear, there's no doubt about his mother's maid. The evidence is of the most conclusive order. I know I should be dreadfully angry with him, but everyone is so virtuous nowadays that a change is quite refreshing. And he's so young, he may reform. Englishmen start galloping to the devil, but, as they grow older, they nearly always change horses and amble along gently to respectability, a wife and seventeen children.'

'I like the contrast of his green eyes and his dark hair.'

'My dear, it can't be denied that he's made to capture the feminine heart. I never try to resist him myself. He's never so convincing as when he tells you an outrageous fib.'

Bertha went to her room and looked at herself in the glass, then put on her most becoming dinner-dress.

'Good gracious,' said Miss Ley, 'you've not put that on for Gerald? You'll turn the boy's head; he's dreadfully susceptible.'

'It's the first one I came across,' replied Bertha innocently.

CHAPTER XXIX

'YOU'VE quite captured Gerald's heart,' said Miss Ley to Bertha a day or two later. 'He's confided in me that he thinks you perfectly stunning.'

'He's a very nice boy,' said Bertha, laughing.

The youth's outspoken admiration could not fail to increase her liking; and she was amused by the stare of his green eyes, which, with a woman's peculiar sense, she felt even when her back was turned. They followed her, they rested on her hair and on her beautiful hands; when she wore a low dress they burnt themselves on her neck and breast; she felt them travel along her arms and embrace her figure. They were the most caressing, smiling eyes, but with a certain mystery in their emerald depths. Bertha did not neglect to put herself in positions in which Gerald could see her to advantage; and when he looked at her hands she could not be expected to withdraw them as though she were ashamed. Few Englishmen see anything in a woman but her face, and it seldom occurs to them that her hand has the most delicate outlines, all grace and gentleness, with tapering fingers and rosy nails; they never look for the thousand things it has to say.

'Don't you know it's very rude to stare like that?' said Bertha, with a smile, turning round suddenly.

'I beg your pardon, I didn't know you were looking.'

'I wasn't, but I saw you all the same.'

She smiled at him most engagingly and she saw a sudden flame leap into his eyes. He was a pretty boy; of course a mere child.

A married woman is always gratified by the capture of a boy's fickle heart; it is an unsolicited testimonial to her charms, and has the advantage of being completely free from danger. She tells herself that there is no better training for a young man than to fall in love with a really nice woman a good deal older than himself. It teaches him how to behave and keeps him from getting into scrapes. How often have callow youths been known to ruin their lives by falling into the clutches of an adventuress with yellow hair and painted cheeks! Since she's old enough to be his mother, the really nice woman thinks there can be no harm in flirting with the poor boy, and it seems to please him; so she makes him fetch and carry, and dazzles him, and generally drives him quite distracted, till his youthful fickleness comes to the rescue and he falls passionately in love with a barmaid; when, of course, she calls him an ungrateful and low-minded wretch, regrets she was so mistaken in his character, and tells him never to come near her again. This, of course, only refers to the women whom men fall in love with; it is well known that the others have the strictest views on the subject and would sooner die than flirt.

Gerald had the charming gift of becoming intimate with people at the shortest notice, and a cousin is an agreeable relation (especially when she's pretty) with whom it is easy to get on. The relationship is not so close as to warrant chronic disagreeableness, and close enough to permit personalities, which are the most amusing part of conversation.

Within a week Gerald took to spending his whole day with Bertha, and she found the London season much more amusing than she had expected. She looked back with distaste to her only two visits to town; one had been her honeymoon, and the other the first separation from her husband; it was odd that in retrospect they both seemed equally dreary. Edward had almost disappeared from her thoughts, and she exulted like a captive free from chains. Her only worry was his often-expressed desire to see her. Why could he not leave her alone, as she left him? He was perpetually asking when she would return to Court Leys, and she had to invent excuses to prevent his coming to London. She loathed the idea of seeing him again.

But she put aside these thoughts when Gerald came. It is no wonder that the English are a populous race, when one observes how many are the resorts supplied by the munificence of governing bodies for the express purpose of philandering. On a hot day what spot can be more enchanting than the British Museum, cool, and silent, and roomy, with harmless statues that tell no tales and afford matter for conversation to break an awkward pause? The parks also are eminently suited for those whose fancy turns to thoughts of platonic love. Hyde Park is the fitting scene for an idyll in which Corydon wears patent-leather boots and a shiny top-hat, and Phyllis an exquisite frock. The well-kept lawns, the artificial water and the trim paths give a mock rurality that is infinitely amusing to persons who do not wish to take things too seriously. Here, in the summer mornings, Gerald and Bertha spent much time. It pleased her to listen to his chatter and to look into his green eyes; he was such a very nice boy, and seemed attached to her. Besides, he was only in London for a month, and she could afford to let him fall in love with her a little.

'Are you sorry you're going away so soon?' she asked.

'I shall be miserable at leaving you.'

'It's nice of you to say so,' she answered, smiling.

Bit by bit she extracted from him his discreditable history. Bertha was possessed by a cariosity to know details, which she elicited artfully, making him confess his iniquities so that she might pretend to be angry. It gave her a curious thrill, partly of admiration, to think that he was such a depraved young person, and she looked at him with a sort of amused wonder. He was very different from the virtuous Edward. A childlike innocence shone out of his handsome eyes, and yet he had already tasted the wine of many emotions. Bertha felt somewhat envious of the sex that gave opportunity, and the spirit that gave power, to seize life boldly and wring from it all it had to offer.

'I ought to refuse to speak to you any more,' she said; 'I ought to be ashamed of you.'

'But you're not. That's why you're such a ripper.'

How could she be angry with a boy who adored her? He might be utterly vicious, in fact he was; but his perversity fascinated her. Here was a man who would never hesitate to go to the devil for a woman, and Bertha was pleased at the compliment to her sex.

One evening Miss Ley was dining out, and Gerald asked Bertha to come to dinner with him, and then to the opera. She refused, thinking of the expense; but he was so eager, and she really so anxious to go, that at last she consented.

'Poor boy, he's going away so soon, I may as well be nice to him.'

Gerald arrived in high spirits. Evening clothes suited him admirably, but he looked even more boyish than usual.

'I'm really afraid to go out with you,' said Bertha. 'People will think you're my son. "Dear me, who'd have thought she was forty"!'

'What rot!' He looked at her beautiful gown. Like all nice women, Bertha was extremely careful to be always well dressed. 'By Jove, you are a stunner!'

'My dear child, I'm old enough to be your mother.'

They drove off, to a restaurant which Gerald, boy-like, had chosen because common report pronounced it the dearest in London. Bertha was amused by the bustle, the glitter of women in diamonds, the busy waiters gliding to and fro, the glare of the electric light; and her eyes rested with approval on the handsome lad in front of her. She could not keep in check the recklessness with which he insisted on ordering the most expensive things; and when they arrived at the opera she found he had a box.

'Oh, you wretch,' she cried. 'You must be utterly ruined.'

'Oh, I've got five hundred quid,' he replied, laughing. 'I must blue some of it.'

'But why on earth did you get a box?'

'I remembered that you hated any other part of the theatre.'

'But you promised to get cheap seats.'

'And I wanted to be alone with you.'

He was by nature a flatterer; and few women could withstand the cajolery of his eyes and his charming smile.

'He must be very fond of me,' thought Bertha, as they drove home, and she put her arm in his to express her thanks and her appreciation.

'It's very nice of you to have been so good to me. I always thought you were a nice creature.'

'I'd do more than that for you.'

He would have given the rest of his five hundred pounds for one kiss. She knew it and was pleased; but gave him no encouragement, and for once he was bashful. They separated at her doorstep with a discreet handshake.

'It's awfully kind of you to have come.'

He appeared immensely grateful to her. Her conscience pricked her now that he had spent so much money; but she liked him all the more. A woman would rather have a bunch of weeds that cost a fortune than a basket of roses that cost a shilling.

Gerald's month was nearly over, and Bertha was astonished that he occupied her thoughts so much. She did not know that she was so fond of him; it had never occurred to her that she would miss him.

'I wish he weren't going,' she said, and then quickly: 'But of course it's much better that he should.'

At that moment the boy appeared.

'This day week you'll be on the sea, Gerald,' she said. 'Then you'll be sorry for all your iniquities.'

'No,' he answered, sitting in the position he most affected, at Bertha's feet.

'No—which?'

'I shan't be sorry,' he replied, with a smile, 'and I'm not going away.'

'What d'you mean?'

'I've changed my plans. The man I'm going to said I could start at the end of this month or at the end of next. And I shall start at the end of next.'

'But why?' It was a foolish question, because she knew.

'I had nothing to stay for. Now I have, that's all.'

Bertha looked at him and caught his shining eyes, fixed intently upon her. She became grave.

'You're not angry?' he asked, changing his tone. 'I thought you wouldn't mind. I don't want to leave you.'

He looked at her earnestly, and tears were in his eyes. Bertha could not help being touched.

'I'm very glad that you should stay, dear. I didn't want you to go so soon. We've been such good friends.'

She passed her fingers through his curly hair and over his ears; but he started, and shivered.

'Don't do that,' he said, pushing her hand away.

'Why not?' she cried, laughing. 'Are you frightened of me?'

And caressingly she passed her hand over his ears again.

'Oh, you don't know what pain that gives me.'

He sprang up, and to her astonishment Bertha saw that he was pale and trembling.

'I feel I shall go mad when you touch me.'

Suddenly she saw the burning passion in his eyes: it was love that made him tremble. Bertha gave a little cry, and a curious sensation pressed her heart. Then without warning, the boy seized her hands and falling on his knees before her kissed them repeatedly. His hot breath made Bertha tremble too, and the kisses burnt themselves into her flesh. She snatched her hands away.

'I've wanted to do that so long,' he whispered.

She was too much moved to answer, but stood looking at him.

'You must be mad, Gerald.'

'Bertha!'

They stood very close together. He was about to put his arms around her, and for an instant she had an insane desire to let him do what he would, to let him kiss her lips as he had kissed her hands; she wanted to kiss his mouth and his curly hair and his cheek as soft as a girl's. But she recovered herself.

'Oh, it's absurd! Don't be silly, Gerald.'

He could not speak, he looked at her with his green eyes sparkling with desire.

'I love you,' he whispered.

'My dear boy, do you want me to succeed your mother's maid?'

'Oh!' He gave a groan and turned red.

'I'm glad you're staying on. You'll be able to see Edward, who's coming to town next week. You've never met my husband, have you?'

His lips twitched and he seemed to struggle to compose himself. Then he threw himself on a chair and buried his face in his hands. He seemed so little, so young—and he loved her. Bertha looked at him for a moment, and the tears came to her eyes. She put her hand on his shoulder.

'Gerald!' He did not look up. 'Gerald, I didn't mean to hurt your feelings. I'm sorry for what I said.'

She bent down and drew his hands away from his face.

'Are you cross with me?' he asked, almost tearfully.

'No,' she answered, caressingly. 'But you musn't be silly, dearest. You know I'm old enough to be your mother.'

He did not seem consoled, and she felt still that she had been horrid. She took his face between her hands and kissed his lips. And as if he were a little child she kissed away the teardrops that shone in his eyes.

CHAPTER XXX

BERTHA still felt on her hands Gerald's passionate kisses; they were like little patches of fire; and on her lips was still the touch of his boyish mouth. What magic current had passed from him to her that she should feel this sudden happiness? It was enchanting to think that Gerald loved her; she remembered how his eyes had sparkled, how his voice had grown hoarse so that he could hardly speak: ah, those were the signs of real love, of the love that is mighty and triumphant. Bertha put her hands to her heart with a rippling laugh of pure joy—for she was loved. The kisses tingled on her fingers so that she looked at them with surprise; she seemed almost to see a mark of burning. She was very grateful to him, she wanted to take his head in her hands and kiss his hair and his boyish eyes and again the soft lips. She told herself that she would be a mother to him.

The following day he had come to her almost shyly, afraid that she would be angry, and the bashfulness contrasting with his usual happy audacity had charmed her. It flattered her extremely to think that he was her humble slave, to see the pleasure he took in doing as she bade; but she could hardly believe it true that he loved her, and she wished to reassure herself. It gave her a queer thrill to see him turn white when she held his hand, to see him tremble when she leant on his arm. She stroked his hair, and was delighted with the anguish she saw in his eyes.

'Don't do that,' he cried. 'Please. You don't know how it hurts.'

'I was hardly touching you,' she replied, laughing.

She saw in his eyes glistening tears: they were tears of passion, and she could scarcely restrain a cry of triumph. At last she was loved as she wished; she gloried in her power: here at last was one who would not hesitate to lose his soul for her sake. She was grateful. But her heart grew cold when she thought that it was too late, that it was no good; he was only a boy, and she was married and nearly thirty.

But even then, why should she attempt to stop him? If it was the love she dreamt of, nothing could destroy it. And there was no harm; Gerald said nothing to which she might not listen, and he was so much younger than she; he was going away in less than a month and it would all be over. Why should she not enjoy the modest crumbs that the gods let fall from their table? It was little enough in all conscience! How foolish is he who will not bask in the sun of St Martin's summer because it heralds the winter as surely as the east wind!

They spent the whole day together, to Miss Ley's amusement, who for once did not use her sharp eyes to much effect.

'I'm so thankful to you, Bertha, for looking after the boy. His mother ought to be eternally grateful to you for keeping him out of mischief.'

'I'm very glad if I have,' said Bertha. 'He's such a nice boy and I'm so fond of him. I should be very sorry if he got into trouble. I'm rather anxious about him afterwards.'

'My dear, don't be; because he's certain to get into scrapes—it's his nature; but it's likewise his nature to get out of them. He'll swear eternal devotion to half a dozen fair damsels, and ride away rejoicing, while they are left to weep upon one another's bosoms. It's some men's nature to break women's hearts.'

'I think he's only a little wild; he means no harm.'

'Those sort of people never do; that's what makes their wrongdoing so much more fatal.'

'And he's so affectionate.'

'My dear, I shall really believe that you're in love with him.'

'I am,' said Bertha, 'madly!'

The plain truth is often the surest way to hoodwink people, more especially when it is told unconsciously. Women of fifty have an irritating habit of treating as contemporaries all persons of their own sex who are over twenty-five, and it never struck Miss Ley that Bertha might look upon Gerald as anything but a little boy.

But Edward could no longer be kept in the country. Bertha was astonished that he should wish to see her, and a little annoyed, for now of all times his presence would be importunate. She did not wish to have her dream disturbed, she knew it was nothing else; it was a mere spring day of happiness in the long winter of life.

She looked at Gerald now with a heavy heart, and she could not bear to think of the future. How empty would existence be without that joyous smile; above all, without that ardent passion! His love was wonderful; it surrounded her like a mystic fire and lifted her up so that she seemed to walk on air. But things always come too late or come by halves. Why should all her passion have been squandered and flung to the winds, so that now when a beautiful youth offered her his virgin heart she had nothing to give in exchange?

She was a little nervous at the meeting between him and Edward; she wondered what they would think of one another, and she watched—Gerald. Edward came in like a country wind, obstreperously healthy, jovial, large and rattier bald. Miss Ley trembled lest he should knock her china over as he went round the room. He kissed her on one cheek and Bertha on the other.

'Well, how are you all? And this is my young cousin, eh? How are you? Pleased to meet you.'

He wrung Gerald's hand, towering over him, beaming good-naturedly; then sat on a chair much too small for him, which creaked and grumbled at his weight. There are few sensations more amusing to a woman than to look at the husband she has once adored and to think how very unnecessary he is; but it is apt to make conversation a little difficult.

Miss Ley soon carried Gerald off, thinking that husband and wife should enjoy a little of that isolation to which marriage had indissolubly doomed them. Bertha had been awaiting, with great discomfort, the necessary ordeal. She had nothing to tell Edward, and she was much afraid that he would be sentimental.

'Where are you staying?' she asked.

'Oh, I'm putting up at the "Inns of Court", I always go there.'

'I thought you might care to go to the theatre tonight. I've got a box so that Aunt Polly and Gerald can come too.'

'I'm game for anything you like.'

'You always were the best-tempered man,' said Bertha, smiling gently.

'You don't seem to care very much for my society all the same.'

Bertha looked up quickly.' What makes you think that?'

'Well, you're a precious long time coming back to Court Leys,' he replied, laughing.

Bertha was relieved, for he was evidently not taking the matter seriously. She had not the courage to say that she meant never to return; the endless explanation, his wonder, the impossibility of making him understand, were more than she could bear.

'When are you coming back? We all miss you like anything.'

'Do you?' she said. 'I really don't know. We'll see after the season.'

'What? Aren't you coming for another couple of months?'

'I don't think Blackstable suits me very well. I'm always ill there.'

'Oh, nonsense. It's the finest air in England. Death-rate practically *nil.*'

'D'you think our life was very happy, Edward?'

She looked at him anxiously to see how he would take the tentative remark: but he was only astonished.

'Happy? Yes, rather. Of course we had our little tiffs. All people do. But they were chiefly at first; the road was a bit rough, and we hadn't got our tyres properly blown out. I'm sure I've got nothing to complain about.'

'That, of course, is the chief thing,' said Bertha.

'You look as well as anything now; I don't see why you shouldn't come back.'

'Well, we'll see later. We shall have plenty of time to talk it over.'

She was afraid to speak the words on the tip of her tongue; it would be easier by correspondence.

'I wish you'd give some fixed date, so that I could have things ready and tell people.'

'It depends upon Aunt Polly; I really can't say for certain; I'll write to you.'

They kept silence for a moment, and then an idea seized Bertha.

'What d'you say to going to the Natural History Museum? Don't you remember, we went there on our honeymoon?'

'Would *you* like to go?' asked Edward.

'I'm sure it would amuse you,' she replied.

Next day while Bertha was shopping with her husband, Gerald and Miss Ley sat alone.

'Are you very disconsolate without Bertha?' she asked.

'Utterly miserable!'

'That's very rude to me, dear boy.'

'I'm awfully sorry, but I can never be polite to more than one person at a time: and I've been using up all my good manners upon Mr Craddock.'

'I'm glad you like him,' replied Miss Ley, smiling.

'I don't!'

'He's a very worthy man.'

'If I hadn't seen Bertha for six months, I shouldn't take her off at once to see bugs.'

'Perhaps it was Bertha's suggestion.'

'She must find Mr Craddock precious dull if she prefers black-beetles and stuffed kangaroos.'

'You shouldn't draw such rapid conclusions, my friend.'

'D'you think she's fond of him?'

'My dear Gerald, what a question! Is it not her duty to love, honour and obey him?'

'If I were a woman I could never honour a man who was bald.'

'His locks are growing scanty; but he has a strong sense of duty.'

'It oozes out of him whenever he gets hot, like gum.'

'He is a County Councillor, and he makes speeches about the Union Jack, and he's virtuous.'

'I know that too. He simply reeks of the Ten Commandments; they stick out all over him, like almonds in a tipsy cake.'

'My dear Gerald, Edward is a model; he is the typical Englishman, as he flourishes in the country, upright and honest, healthy, dogmatic, moral and rather stupid. I esteem him enormously, and I ought to like him much better than you, who are a disgraceful scamp.'

'I wonder why you don't.'

'Because I'm a wicked old woman; and I've learnt by long experience that people generally keep their vices to themselves, but insist on throwing their virtues in your face. And if you don't happen to have any of your own, you get the worst of the encounter.'

'I think that's what's so comfortable in you, Aunt Polly, that you're not obstreperously good. You're charity itself.'

'My dear Gerald,' said Miss Ley, putting up an admonishing forefinger, 'women are by nature spiteful and intolerant; when you find one who exercises charity, it proves that she wants it very badly herself.'

Miss Ley was glad that Edward could not stay more than two days for she was always afraid of surprising him. Nothing is more tedious than to talk with persons who treat your most ordinary remarks as startling paradoxes; and Edward suffered likewise from that passion for argument which is the bad talker's substitute for conversation. People who cannot talk are always proud of their dialectic; they want to modify your most obvious statements, and if you do no more than observe that the day is fine insist on arguing it out. Miss Ley's opinion on the subject was that no woman under forty was worth talking to at all, and a man only if he was an attentive listener. Bertha, in her husband's presence, had suffered singular discomfort; it had been such a constraint that she found it an effort to talk with him, and had to rack her brain for subjects of conversation. Her heart was lightened when she returned from Victoria after seeing him off, and it gave her a thrill of pleasure to hear Gerald jump up when she came in. He ran towards her with glowing eyes.

'Oh, I'm so glad. I've hardly had a chance of speaking to you these last two days.'

'We have the whole afternoon before us.'

'Let's go for a walk, shall we?'

Bertha agreed, and like two school-fellows they sallied out, wandering by the river in the sunlight and the warmth: the banks of the Thames about Chelsea have a pleasing trimness, a levity that is infinitely grateful after the staidness of the rest of London. The embankments in spite of their novelty recall the days when the huge city was a great, straggling village, when the sedan-chair was a means of locomotion, and ladies wore patches and hoops; when epigram was the fashion and propriety was not.

Presently, as they watched the gleaming water, a penny-steamboat approaching the adjoining stage gave Bertha a sudden idea.

'Would you like to take me to Greenwich?' she cried. 'Aunt Polly's dining out; we can have dinner at the "Ship" and come back by train.'

'By Jove, it will be ripping.'

They bolted down the gangway and took their tickets; the boat started, and Bertha, panting, sank on a seat. She felt a little reckless, rather pleased with herself, and amused to see Gerald's unmeasured delight.

'I feel as if we were eloping,' she said with a laugh. 'I'm sure Aunt Polly will be dreadfully shocked.'

The boat went on, stopping every now and then to take people in. They came to the tottering wharves of Millbank, and then to the footstool turrets of St John's, the eight red blocks of St Thomas's Hospital and the Houses of Parliament. They passed Westminster Bridge and the massive strength of New Scotland Yard, the hotels and fiats and public buildings that line the Albert Embankment, the Temple Gardens: and opposite this grandeur, on the Surrey side, were the dingy warehouses and factories of

Lambeth. At London Bridge, Bertha found new interest in the varying scene; she stood in the bows with Gerald by her side, not speaking; they were happy in being near one another. The traffic became denser and their boat more crowded, with artisans, clerks, noisy girls, going eastwards to Rotherhithe and Deptford. Great merchantmen lay by the riverside or slowly made their way downstream under the Tower Bridge; and here the broad waters were crowded, with every imaginable craft, with lazy barges as picturesque, with their red sails, as the fishing-boats of Venice, with little tugs, puffing and blowing, with ocean tramps and with great liners. And as they passed in the penny-steamer, they had swift pictures of groups of naked boys, wallowing in the Thames mud, diving from the side of an anchored coal-barge.

A new atmosphere enveloped them now; grey warehouses that lined the river and the factories announced the commerce of a mighty nation, and the spirit of Charles Dickens gave to the passing scenes a Crash delight. How could they be prosaic when the great master had described them? An amiable stranger put names to the various places.

'Look, there's Wapping Old Stairs.'

And the words thrilled Bertha like poetry.

They passed innumerable wharves and docks, London Dock, John Cooper's Wharves and William Gibbs's Wharves (who are John Cooper and William Gibbs?), Limehouse Basin and West India Dock. Then with a great turn of the river they entered Limehouse Reach, and soon the noble lines of the Hospital, the immortal monument of Inigo Jones came in view, and they landed at Greenwich Pier.

CHAPTER XXXI

THEY stood for a while on a terrace by the side of the hospital. Immediately below them a crowd of boys were bathing, animated and noisy, chasing and ducking one another, running to and fro with many cries and splashing in the mud, a fine picture of youthful movement.

The river was stretched more widely before them. The sun played on the yellow wavelets so that they shone like gold. A tug grunted past with a long tail of barges, and a huge East Indiaman glided noiselessly. In the late afternoon there was over the scene an old-time air of ease and spaciousness. The stately flood carried the mind away, so that the onlooker followed it with his thoughts, and went down, as it broadened, crowded with traffic; and presently a sea-smell reached the nostrils, and the river, ever majestic, flowed into the sea; and the ships went East and West and South, bearing their merchandise to the uttermost parts of the earth, to Southern sunnier lands of palm trees and dark-skinned peoples, bearing the name and wealth of England. The Thames became an emblem of the power of the mighty Empire, and those who watched felt strong in its strength and proud of their name and the undiminished glory of their race.

But Gerald looked sadly.

'In a very little while it must take me away from you, Bertha.'

'But think of the freedom and the vastness. Sometimes in England one seems oppressed by the lack of room; one can hardly breathe.'

'It's the thought of leaving you.'

She put her hand on his arm, caressingly; and then, to take him away from his sadness, suggested that they should stroll about.

Greenwich is half London, half country town, and the unexpected union gives it a peculiar fascination. If the wharves and docks of London still preserve the spirit of Charles Dickens, here it is the happy breeziness of Captain Marryat that fills the imagination. Those tales of a freer life and of the sea-breezes come back amid the grey streets still peopled with the vivid characters of *Poor Jack*. In the park, by the side of the labourers asleep on the grass, navvies from the neighbouring docks, and the boys who play a primitive cricket, may be seen fantastic old persons who would have delighted the grotesque pen of the seaman-novelist.

Bertha and Gerald sat beneath the trees, looking at the people till it grew late; and then wandered back to the 'Ship' for dinner. It amused them immensely to sit in the old coffee-room and be waited on by a black waiter, who extolled absurdly the various dishes.

'We won't be economical today,' cried Bertha: 'I feel utterly reckless. It takes all the fun away if one counts the cost.'

'Well, for once let us be foolish and forget the morrow.'

And they drank champagne, which to women and boys is the acme of dissipation and magnificence. Presently Gerald's green eyes flashed more brightly, and Bertha turned red before their ardent gaze.

'I shall never forget today, Bertha,' said Gerald. 'As long as I live I shall look back upon it with regret.'

'Oh, don't dunk that it must come to an end; or we shall both be miserable.'

'You are the most beautiful woman I've ever seen.'

Bertha laughed, showing her exquisite teeth, and was glad that her own knowledge told her she looked her best.

'But come on the terrace again and smoke there. We'll watch the sunset.'

They sat alone, and the sun was already sinking. The heavy western clouds were rich and vivid red, and over the river the bricks and mortar stood out in ink-black masses. It was a sunset that singularly fitted the scene, combining in audacious colour with the river's strength. The murky wavelets danced like little flames of fire.

Bertha and the youth sat silently, very happy, but with the regret gnawing at their hearts that their hour of joy would have no morrow.

The night fell, and one by one the stars shone out. The river flowed noiselessly, restfully, and around them twinkled the lights of the riverside towns. They did not speak, but Bertha knew the boy thought of her, and she wanted to hear him say so.

'What are you thinking of, Gerald?'

'What should I be thinking of but you, and that I must leave you?'

Bertha could not help the pleasure that his words gave her: it was so delicious to be really loved; and she knew his love was real. She half turned her face, so that he saw her dark eyes, darker in the night.

'I wish I hadn't made a fool of myself before,' he whispered. 'I feel it was all horrible; you've made me so ashamed.'

'Oh, Gerald, you're not remembering what I said the other day. I didn't mean to hurt you. I've been so sorry ever since.'

'I wish you loved me. Oh, Bertha, don't stop me now. I've kept it in so long, and I can't any more. I don't want to go away without telling you.'

'Oh, my dear Gerald, don't,' said Bertha, her voice almost breaking. 'It's no good, and we shall both be dreadfully unhappy. My dear, you don't know how much older I am than you. Even if I weren't married, it would be impossible for us to love one another.'

'But I love you with all my heart. I wish I could tell you what I feel.'

He seized her hands and pressed them; she made no effort to resist.

'Don't you love me at all?' he asked.

Bertha did not answer, and he bent nearer to look into her eyes. Then, letting her hands go, he flung his arms about her and pressed her to his heart.

'Bertha, Bertha!'

He kissed her passionately.

'Oh, Bertha, say you love me. It would make me so happy.'

'My dearest,' she whispered, and taking his head in her hands, kissed him.

But the kiss that she had received had fired her blood, and she could not resist now from doing as she had wished. She kissed him on the lips and on the eyes, and she kissed his curly hair. But she tore herself away from him, and sprang to her feet.

'What fools we are! Let's go to the station, Gerald; it's growing late.'

'Oh, Bertha, don't go yet,' he pleaded.

'We must. I daren't stay.'

He tried to take her in his arms again, begging her passionately to remain.

'Please don't, Gerald,' she said. 'Don't ask me; you make me too unhappy. Don't you see how hopeless it is? What is the use of our loving one another? You're going away in a week and we shall never meet again. And even if you were staying, I'm married, and I'm twenty-six and you're only nineteen. My dearest, we should only make ourselves ridiculous.'

'But I can't go away. What do I care if you're older than I? And it's nothing if you're married; you don't care for your husband and he doesn't care two straws for you.'

'How do you know?'

'Oh, I saw it. I felt so sorry for you.'

'You dear boy!' murmured Bertha, almost crying. 'I've been dreadfully unhappy. It's true Edward never loved me, and he didn't treat me very well. Oh, I can't understand how I ever cared for him.'

'I'm glad.'

'I would never allow myself to fall in love again. I suffered too much. I wonder I didn't kill myself.'

'But I love you with all my heart, Bertha; don't you see I love you? Oh, this isn't like what I've felt before; it's something quite new and different. I can't live without you, Bertha. Oh, let me stay.'

'It's impossible. Come away, dearest; we've been here too long.'

'Kiss me again.'

Bertha, half smiling, half in tears, put her arm round his neck and kissed the soft, boyish lips.

'You are good to me,' he whispered.

Then they walked to the station, silently; and eventually reached Chelsea. At the fiat door Bertha held out her hand, and Gerald looked at her with a sadness that almost broke her heart; then he just touched her fingers and turned away.

But when Bertha was alone in her room she threw herself down on her bed and burst into tears. For she knew at last that she loved him. Gerald's kisses still burned on her lips and the touch of his hands was tremulous on her arms. Suddenly she knew that she had deceived herself; it was more than friendship that held her heart as in a vice, it was more than affection: it was eager, passionate love.

For a moment she was overjoyed, but quickly she remembered that she was married, that she was years older than he: to a boy of nineteen a woman of twenty-six must appear almost middle-aged. She seized a hand-mirror and looked at herself, she took it under the light so that the test might be more searching, and scrutinized her face for wrinkles and crow's-feet, the signs of departing youth.

'It's absurd,' she said. 'I'm making an utter fool of myself.'

Gerald was fickle; in a week he would be in love with some girl he met on the steamer. Well, what of it? He loved her now, with all his heart and with all his soul; he trembled with desire at her touch, and his passion was an agony that blanched his cheek. She could not mistake the eager longing of his eyes. Ah, that was the love she wanted, the love that kills and the love that engenders. She stood up, stretching out her arms in triumph, and in the empty room her lips formed the words:

'Come, my beloved, come, for I love you.'

But the morning brought an intolerable depression. Bertha saw then the futility of her love; her marriage, his departure, made it impossible; the disparity of age made it even grotesque. But she could not dull the aching of her heart, she could not stop her tears.

Gerald arrived about midday and found her alone. He approached almost timidly.

'You've been crying, Bertha.'

'I've been very unhappy,' she said. 'Oh, please, Gerald, forget our idiocy of yesterday. Don't say anything to me that I mustn't hear.'

'I can't help loving you.'

'Don't you see that it's all utter madness?'

'I can't leave you, Bertha. Let me stay.'

'It's impossible; you must go, now more than ever.'

They were interrupted by the appearance of Miss Ley. She began to talk; but to her surprise neither Bertha nor Gerald showed any vivacity.

'What is the matter with you both today?' she asked. 'You're usually attentive to my observations.'

'I'm tired,' said Bertha, 'and I have a headache.'

Miss Ley looked at Bertha more closely and fancied she had been crying; Gerald also seemed profoundly miserable. Surely—Then the truth dawned on her, and she could hardly conceal her astonishment.

'Good Heavens!' she thought, 'I must have been blind. How lucky he's going away in a week!'

Miss Ley now remembered a dozen occurrences that had escaped her notice. She was confounded.

'Upon my word,' she thought, 'I don't believe you can put a woman of seventy for five minutes in company of a boy of fourteen without their getting into mischief.'

The week to Gerald and to Bertha passed with terrible quickness. They scarcely had a moment alone, for Miss Ley, under the pretence of making much of her nephew, arranged little pleasure parties, so that all three might be continually together.

'We must spoil you a tittle before you go; and the harm it does you will be put right by the rocking of the boat.'

Bertha was in a torment. She knew that her love was impossible, but she knew also that it was beyond control. She tried to argue herself out of the infatuation, but without avail; Gerald was never absent from her thoughts, and she loved him with her whole soul. The temptation came to bid him stay. If he remained in England they might give rein to their passion and let it die of itself. But she dared not ask him. And his sorrow was more than she could bear; she looked into his eyes, and seemed there to see the grief of a breaking heart. It was horrible to think that he loved her and that she must continually distress him. And then a more terrible temptation beset her. There is one way in which a woman can bind a man to her for ever, there is one tie that is indissoluble; her very flesh cried out, and she trembled at the thought that she could give Gerald the inestimable gift of her body. Then he might go, but that would have passed between them which could not be undone; they might be separated by ten thousand miles, but there would always be the bond between them. Her flesh cried out to his flesh, and the desire was irresistible. How else could she prove to him her wonderful love? How else could she show her immeasurable gratitude? The temptation was very strong, incessantly recurring, and she was weak. It assailed her with all the violence of her fervid imagination. She drove it away with anger, she loathed it with all her heart; but she could not stifle the appalling hope that it would be too strong.

CHAPTER XXXII

AT last Gerald had but one day more. A long-standing engagement of Bertha and Miss Ley forced him to take leave of them in the afternoon, for he was to start from London at seven in the morning.

'I'm dreadfully sorry that you can't spend your last evening with us,' said Miss Ley. 'But the Trevor-Jones will never forgive us if we don't go to their dinner-party.'

'Of course it was my fault for not finding out before when I sailed.'

'What are you going to do with yourself this evening, you wretch?'

'I'm going to have one last unholy bust.'

'I'm afraid you're very glad that for one night we cant look after you.'

In a little while Miss Ley, looking at her watch, told Bertha that it was time to dress. Gerald got up, and kissing Miss Ley thanked her for her kindness.

'My dear boy, please don't sentimentalize. And you're not going for ever. You're sure to make a mess of things and come back; the Leys always do.'

Then Gerald turned to Bertha and held out his hand.

'You've been awfully good to me,' he said, smiling; but there was in his eyes a steadfast look that seemed intent on making her understand something. 'We've had a ripping time together.'

'I hope you won't forget me entirely. We've certainly kept you out of mischief.'

Miss Ley watched them, admiring their composure. She thought they took the parting very well.

'I daresay it was nothing but a little flirtation and not very serious. Bertha's so much older than he and so sensible that she's most unlikely to have made a fool of herself.'

But she had to fetch the gifts that she had prepared for Gerald.

'Wait just a moment, Gerald,' she said. 'I want to fetch something.

She left the room, and immediately the boy bent forward.

'Don't go out tonight, Bertha. I must see you again.'

Before Bertha could reply, Miss Ley called from the hall.

'Good-bye,' said Gerald aloud.

'Good-bye. I hope you'll have a nice journey.'

'Here's a little present for you, Gerald,' said Miss Ley, when he was outside. 'You're dreadfully extravagant; and as that's the only virtue you have I feel I ought to encourage it. And if you want money at any time, I can always scrape together a tenner, you know.'

She put into his hand two fifty-pound notes, and then, as if she were ashamed of herself, bundled him out of doors. She went to her room; and as she had somewhat seriously inconvenienced herself for the next six months, for an entirely unworthy object, she began to feel remarkably pleased.

In an hour Miss Ley returned to the drawing-room to wait for Bertha, who presently came in, dressed, but ghastly pale.

'Oh, Aunt Polly, I simply can't come tonight. I've got a racking headache, I can scarcely see. You must tell them that I am sorry, but I'm too ill.'

She sank on a chair and put her hands to her forehead. Miss Ley lifted her eyebrows; the affair was evidently more serious than she thought. However, the danger was over; it would ease Bertha to stay at home and cry it out. She thought it brave of her niece even to have dressed.

'You'll get no dinner,' she said. 'There's nothing in the place.'

'Oh, I want nothing to eat.'

Miss Ley expressed her concern, and promising to make excuses, went away. Bertha started up when she heard the door close, and went to the window. She looked round for Gerald, fearing he might be already there: he was incautious and eager; but if Miss Ley saw him, it would be fatal. The hansom drove away and Bertha breathed more freely. She could not help it, she too felt that she must see him; if they had to part it could not be under Miss Ley's cold eyes.

She waited at the window, but he did not come. Why did he delay? He was wasting the precious minutes; it was past eight. She walked up and down the room and looked again, but still he was not in sight. She fancied that while she watched he would not come, and forced herself to read, but how could she? Again she looked out of the window; and this time Gerald was there. He stood in the porch of the opposite house, looking up; and immediately he saw her crossed the street. She went to the door and opened it gently.

He slipped in, and on tip-toe they entered the drawing-room.

'Oh, it's so good of you,' he said. 'I couldn't leave you like that I knew you'd stay.'

'Why have you been so long? I thought you were never coming.'

'I dared not risk it before. I was afraid something might happen to stop Aunt Polly.'

'I said I had a headache. I dressed so that she might suspect nothing.'

The night was falling, and they sat together in the dimness. Gerald took her hands and kissed them.

'This week has been awful. I've never had the chance of saying a word to you. My heart has been breaking.'

'My dearest.'

'I wondered if you were sorry I was going.'

She looked at him and tried to smile; she could not trust herself to speak.

'Every day I thought you would tell me to stop, and you never did, and now it's too late. Oh, Bertha, if you loved me you wouldn't send me away.'

'I think I love you too much. Don't you see it's better that we should part?'

'I daren't think of tomorrow.'

'You are so young; in a little while you will fall in love with someone else.'

'I love you. Oh, I wish I could make you believe me. Bertha, Bertha, I can't leave you. I love you too much.'

'For God's sake don't talk like that. It's hard enough to bear already; don't make it harder.'

The night had fallen, and through the open window the summer breeze came in, and the softness of the air was like a kiss. They sat side by side in silence, the boy holding Bertha's hand; they could not speak, for words were powerless to express what was in their hearts. But presently a strange intoxication seized them and the mystery of passion wrapped them about invisibly. Bertha felt the trembling of Gerald's hand, and it passed to hers. She shuddered and tried to withdraw, but he would not let go. The silence became suddenly intolerable. Bertha tried to speak, but her throat was dry, and she could utter no word.

A weakness came to her limbs and her heart beat painfully. Her eyes met Gerald's, and they both looked aside, as if caught in some crime. Bertha began to breathe more quickly. Gerald's intense desire burned itself into her soul; she dared not move. She tried to implore God's help, but could not. The temptation, which all the week had terrified her, returned with double force, the temptation that she abhorred, but that she had a horrible longing not to resist.

And now she asked what it mattered. Her strength was dwindling; Gerald had but to say a word. And now she wished him to say the word; he loved her and she loved him. She gave way, she no longer wished to resist, flesh called to flesh, and there was no force on earth more powerful. Her whole frame was quivering with passion. She turned her face to Gerald, she leant towards him with parted lips.

'Bertha!' be whispered, and they were nearly in one another's arms.

But a fine sound pierced the silence; they started back and listened. They heard a key being put into the front door, and the door being opened.

'Take care,' whispered Bertha.

'It's Aunt Polly.'

Bertha pointed to the electric switch and, understanding, Gerald turned on the light. He looked round instinctively for some way to escape, but Bertha, with a woman's quick invention, sprang to the door and flung it open.

'Is that you, Aunt Polly?' she cried. 'How fortunate you came back! Gerald is here to bid us definitely good-bye.'

'He makes as many farewells as a *prima-donna,*' said Miss Ley.

She came in, breathless, with two spots of red on her cheeks.

'I thought you wouldn't mind if I came back here to wait till you returned,' said Gerald. 'And I found Bertha.'

'How funny that our thoughts should have been identical,' said Miss Ley. 'It occurred to me that you might come, and so I hurried home as quickly as I could.'

'You're quite out of breath,' said Bertha.

Miss Ley sank on a chair exhausted. As she was eating her fish and talking to a neighbour, it suddenly dawned upon her that Bertha's indisposition was assumed.

'Oh, what a fool I am! They've hoodwinked me as if I were a child. Good Heavens, what are they doing now?'

The dinner seemed interminable, but immediately afterwards she took leave of her astonished hostess and gave the cabman orders to drive furiously. She arrived, inveighing against the deceitfulness of the human race. She had never run up the stairs so quickly.

'How is your headache, Bertha?'

'Thanks, it's much better. Gerald has driven it away.'

This time Miss Ley's good-bye to the precocious youth was chilly; she was devoutly thankful that his boat sailed next morning.

'I'll show you out, Gerald,' said Bertha. 'Don't trouble, Aunt Polly, you must be dreadfully tired.'

They went into the hall, and Gerald put on his coat. He stretched out his hands to Bertha, without speaking; but she, with a glance at the drawing-room door, beckoned Gerald to follow her and slid out of the front door. There was no one on the stairs. She flung her arms around his neck and pressed her lips to his. She did not try to hide her passion now, she clasped him to her heart, their very souls flew to their lips and mingled. Their kiss was rapture, madness; it was an ecstasy beyond description, complete surrender; their senses were powerless to contain their pleasure. Bertha felt herself about to die. In the bliss, in the agony her spirit failed and she tottered; Gerald pressed her more closely to him.

But there was a sound of someone coming upstairs. She tore herself away.

'Good-bye for ever,' she whispered, and slipping in, closed the door between them.

She sank down half-fainting, but in fear struggled to her feet and dragged herself to her room. Her cheeks were glowing and her limbs trembled. Oh, now it was too late for prudence. What did she care for her marriage? What did she care that he was younger than she? She loved him, she loved him insanely; the present was there with its infinite joy, and if the future brought misery it was worth suffering. She could not let him go, he was hers; she stretched out her arms to take him in her embrace. She would surrender everything; she would bid him stay; she would follow him to the end of the earth. It was too late now for reason.

She walked up and down her room excitedly. She looked at the door; she had a mad desire to go to him now, to abandon everything for his sake. Her honour, her happiness, her station, were only precious because she could sacrifice them for him. He was her life and her love, he was her body and her soul. She listened at the door. Miss Ley would be watching, and she dared not go. Miss Ley knew or suspected.

'I'll wait,' said Bertha.

She tried to sleep, but could not. The thought of Gerald distracted her. She dozed, and his presence became more distinct. He seemed to be in the room, and she cried: 'At last, my dearest, at last!'

She woke and stretched out her hands to him; she could not realize that she had dreamt.

The day came, dim and grey at first, but lightening with the brilliant summer morning; the sun shone in the windows and the sunbeams danced in the room. Now the moments were very few, she must make up her mind quickly; and the sunbeams promised life and happiness and the glory of the unknown. Oh, what a fool she was to waste her life, to throw away her chance of happiness! How weak she was not to grasp the love thrown in her way! She thought of Gerald packing his things, getting off, the train speeding through the summer country. Her love was irresistible. She sprang up, and bathed, and dressed. She put her jewels and one or two things in a tiny handbag. It was past six; she slipped out of the room and made her way downstairs. The street was empty as in the night, but the sky was blue and the air fresh and sweet. She took a long breath and felt marvellously gay. She walked till she found a cab, and told the driver to go quickly to Euston. The cab crawled along, and she was in an agony of impatience. Supposing she arrived too late? She told the man to hurry.

The Liverpool train was full. Bertha walked up the crowded platform and quickly saw Gerald. He sprang towards her.

'Bertha, you've come. I felt certain you wouldn't let me go without seeing you.'

He took her hands and looked at her with eyes full of love.

'I'm so glad you've come so that I can say what I wanted. I meant to write to you. I shall always be grateful. I wanted to tell you how sorry I am that I've caused you unhappiness. I almost ruined your life. I was selfish and brutal; I forgot how much you had to lose. Of course I see now that it is all for the best that I'm going away. Will you forgive me?'

Bertha looked at him. She wanted to say that she adored him and would accompany him to the world's end, but the words stuck in her mouth. An inspector came along to look at the tickets.

'Is the lady going?' he asked.

'No,' said Gerald; and then when the man had passed on: 'You won't forget me, Bertha, will you? You won't think badly of me?'

Bertha's heart was breaking. He had only to ask her once more to go with him, and she would go. But he thought her refusal of the night before was final, and in his misery saw the obstacles that passion now hid from her.

'Gerald,' she murmured.

He had but to ask. She dared not speak. Did he want her? Was he repenting already? Was his love already on the wane? Oh, why did he not repeat that he adored her and say once more that he could not live without her? Bertha tried to make herself speak. She could not.

'Take your seats, please. Take your seats, please.'

A guard ran along the platform: 'Jump in, sir.'

'Right behind!'

'Good-bye,' said Gerald.

He kissed her quickly and jumped into the carriage.

'Right away!'

The guard blew his whistle and waved a flag, and the train puffed slowly out of the station.

CHAPTER XXXIII

MISS Ley was alarmed when she got up and found that Bertha had flown.

'Upon my word, I think that Providence is behaving scandalously. Am I not a harmless middle-aged woman who minds her own business? What have I done to deserve these shocks?'

She suspected that her niece had gone to the station; but the train started at seven, and it was ten. She started as it occurred to her that Bertha might have—eloped; and like a swarm of abominable little demons came thoughts of the scenes she must undergo if such were the case—the writing of the news to Edward, his consternation, the comfort that she must administer, and the fury of Gerald's father, the hysterics of his mother.

'She can't have done anything so stupid,' she cried in distraction. 'But if women can make fools of themselves, they always do.'

Miss Ley was extraordinarily relieved when at last she heard Bertha come in and go to her room.

Bertha for a long time had stood motionless on the platform, staring haggardly before her. She was stupefied. The excitement of the previous hours was followed by an utter blankness. Gerald was speeding to Liverpool, and she was still in London. She walked out of the station and turned towards Chelsea. The streets were endless and she was already tired, but she dragged herself along. She did not know the way, and wandered hopelessly, scarcely conscious. In Hyde Park she sat down to rest, feeling utterly exhausted; but the weariness of her body relieved the aching of her heart. She walked on after a while—it never occurred to her to take a cab—and eventually came to Eliot Mansions. The sun had grown hot and burned the crown of her head. Bertha crawled upstairs to her room, and throwing herself on the bed burst into tears of bitter anguish. She wept desperately.

'Oh, I daresay he was as worthless as the other,' she cried at last.

Miss Ley sent to inquire if she would eat, but Bertha had now really a bad headache, and could touch nothing. All day she spent in agony; she could not think; she was in despair. Sometimes she reproached herself for denying Gerald when he had asked her to let him stay; she had wilfully let go the happiness that was within her reach; and then, with a revulsion of feeling, she repeated that Gerald was worthless and thanked Heaven that she had escaped the danger. The dreary hours passed, and when the night came Bertha scarcely had strength to undress, and not till the morning did she get rest. But the early post brought a letter from Edward, repeating his wish that she should return to Court Leys. She read it listlessly.

'Perhaps it's the best thing to do,' she groaned.

She hated London now, and the flat; the rooms must be horribly bare without the joyous presence of Gerald. To return to Court Leys seemed the only course left to her, and there at least she would have quiet and solitude. She thought almost with longing of the desolate shore, the marshes and the dreary sea; she wanted rest and silence. But if she went she had better go at once; to stay in London was only to prolong her woe.

Bertha got up and dressed, and went into Miss Ley. Her face was deathly pale, and her eyes were heavy and red with weeping. She made no attempt to hide her distress.

'I'm going down to Court Leys today, Aunt Polly. I think it's the best thing I can do.'

'Edward will be pleased to see you.'

'I think he will.'

Miss Ley hesitated, looking at Bertha.

'You know, Bertha,' she said after a pause, 'in this world it is very difficult to know what to do. One struggles to know good from evil, but really they're often so very much alike. I always think those people fortunate who are content to stand, without question, by the Ten Commandments, knowing exactly how to conduct themselves and propped up by the hope of Paradise on the one hand and by the fear of a cloven-footed devil with pincers on the other. But we who answer *Why* to the crude *Thou shalt not* are like sailors on a wintry sea without a compass: reason and instinct say one thing, and convention says another; but the worst of it is that one's conscience has been reared on the Decalogue and fostered on hell-fire, and one's conscience has the last word. I daresay it's cowardly, but it's certainly discreet, to take it into consideration; it's like lobster salad: it's not immoral to eat it, but you will very likely have indigestion. One has to be very sure of oneself to go against the ordinary view of things; and if one isn't, perhaps it's better not to run any risks, but just to walk along the same secure old road as the common herd. It's not exhilarating, it's not brave, and it's rather dull; but it's eminently safe.'

Bertha sighed, but did not answer.

'You'd better tell Jane to pack your boxes,' said Miss Ley. 'Shall I wire to Edward?'

When Bertha had at last started, Miss Ley began to think.

'I wonder if I've done right,' she murmured, uncertain as ever. She was sitting on the piano-stool, and as she meditated, her finger passed idly over the keys. Presently her ears detected the beginning of a well-known melody, and almost unconsciously she began to play the air of Rigoletto. *La Donna è mobile,* the words ran, *Qual piuma al vento.* Miss Ley smiled: 'The fact is that few women can be happy with only one husband. I believe that the only solution of the marriage question is legalized polyandry.'

In the train at Victoria Bertha remembered with relief that the cattle-market was held at Tercanbury that day, and Edward would not come home till the evening; she would have the opportunity to settle herself at Court Leys without fuss or bother. Full of her painful thoughts, the journey passed quickly, and Bertha was surprised to find herself at Blackstable. She got out, wondering whether Edward would have sent the trap to meet her, but to her extreme surprise Edward himself was on the platform, and running up, helped her out of the carriage.

'Here you are at last!' he cried.

'I didn't expect you,' said Bertha. 'I thought you'd be at Tercanbury.'

'I got your wire just as I was starting, so of course I didn't go.'

'I'm sorry I prevented you.'

'Why? I'm jolly glad. You didn't think I was going to the cattle-market when my missus was coming home?'

She looked at him with astonishment; his honest, red face glowed with the satisfaction he felt at seeing her.

'By Jove, this is ripping!' he said. 'I'm tired of being a grass widower, I can tell you.'

They came to Corstal Hill, and he walked the horse.

'Just look behind you,' he said in an undertone. 'Notice anything?'

'What?'

'Look at Parker's hat.'

Parker was the footman. Bertha looked again and observed a cockade.

'What d'you think of that, eh?' Edward was almost exploding with laughter. 'I was elected Chairman of the Urban District Council yesterday; that means I'm *ex officio* J.P. So as soon as I beard you were coming I bolted off and got a cockade.'

When they reached Court Leys he helped Bertha out of the trap quite tenderly. She was taken aback to find the tea ready, flowers in the drawing-room, and everything possible done to make her comfortable.

'Are you tired?' asked Edward. 'Lie down on the sofa, and I'll give you your tea.'

He waited on her and pressed her to eat, and was, in fact, unceasing in his attentions.

'By Jove, I am glad to see you here again!'

His pleasure was obvious, and Bertha was touched.

'Are you too tired to come for a little walk in the garden? I want to show you what I've done for you, and just now the place is looking its best.'

He put a shawl round her shoulders, so that the evening air might not hurt her, and insisted on giving her his arm.

'Now, look here; I've planted rose trees outside the drawing-room window; I thought you'd like to see them when you sat in your favourite place, reading.'

He took her further to a place that offered a fine view of the sea.

'I've put a bench here between those two trees, so that you can sit down sometimes and look at the view.'

'It's very kind of you to be so thoughtful. Shall we sit there now?'

'Oh, I think you'd better not. There's a good deal of dew, and I don't want you to catch cold.'

For dinner Edward had ordered the dishes that he knew Bertha preferred, and he laughed joyously as she expressed her pleasure.

Afterwards when she lay down on the sofa he arranged the cushions for her. No one could have been kinder or more thoughtful.

'Ah, my dear,' she thought, 'if you'd been half as kind three years ago you might have kept my love.'

She wondered whether absence had increased his affection, or whether it was she who had changed. Was he not as unchanging as a rock? She knew that she was as unstable as water and variable as the summer winds. Had he always been kind and considerate; and had she, demanding a passion that it was not in him to feel, been blind to his deep tenderness? Expecting nothing from him now, she was astonished to find he had so much to offer. But she felt sorry if he loved her, for she could give him nothing in return but complete indifference; she was even surprised to find herself so utterly callous.

At bedtime she bade him good night, and kissed his cheek.

'I've had the spare bedroom arranged for me,' she said.

'Oh, I didn't know,' he replied; then, after glancing at her: 'I don't want to do anything that is disagreeable to you.'

There was no change in Blackstable; Bertha's friends still lived, for the death-rate of that fortunate place was their pride, and they could do nothing to increase it. Arthur Branderton had married a pretty, fluffy-haired girl, nicely bred and properly insignificant; but the only result of that was to give his mother a new topic of conversation. Bertha, resuming her old habits, had difficulty in realizing that she had ever been away. She set herself to forget Gerald, and was pleased to find the recollection of him not too importunate. A sentimentalist turned cynic has observed that a woman is only passionately devoted to her first lover, afterwards it is love itself of which she is enamoured; and certainly the wounds of second and subsequent attachments heal easily. Bertha was devoutly grateful to Miss Ley for her opportune return on Gerald's last night; she shuddered to think of what might have happened, and was thoroughly ashamed of the madness that had driven her to Euston intent upon the most dreadful courses. She could hardly forgive Gerald that, on his account, she had almost made herself ridiculous; she saw that he was a fickle boy, prepared to philander with every woman he met, and told herself scornfully that she had never really cared for him.

But in two weeks Bertha received a letter from America, forwarded by Miss Ley. She turned white as she recognized the handwriting; the old emotions came tumbling back, she thought of Gerald's green eyes, and of his boyish lips, and she felt sick with love. She looked at the address and at the post-mark, and then put the letter down.

'I told him not to write,' she murmured.

A feeling of anger seized her that the sight of a letter from Gerald should bring her such pain. She almost hated him now; and yet with all her heart she wished to kiss the paper and every word that was written upon it. But the violence of her emotion made her set her teeth, as it were, against giving way.

'I won't read it,' she said.

She wanted to prove to herself that she had strength, and this temptation at least she was determined to resist. Bertha lit a candle and took the letter in her hand to burn it, but then put it down again. That would settle the matter too quickly, and she wanted rather to prolong the trial so as to receive full assurance of her fortitude. With a strange pleasure at the pain she was preparing for herself, Bertha placed the letter on the chimney-piece of her room, prominently, so that whenever she went in or out she could not fail to see it. Wishing to punish herself her desire was to make the temptation as distressing as possible.

She watched the unopened envelope for a month, and sometimes the craving to open it was almost irresistible; sometimes she awoke in the middle of the night, thinking of Gerald, and told herself that she must know what he said. Ah, how well she could imagine it! He vowed he loved her, and he spoke of the kiss she had given him on that last day, and he said it was dreadfully hard to be without her. Bertha looked at the letter, clenching her hands so as not to seize it and tear it open; she had to hold herself forcibly back from covering it with kisses. But at last she conquered all desire; she was able to look at the handwriting indifferently; she scrutinized her heart and found no trace of emotion. The trial was complete.

'Now it can go,' she said.

Again she lit a candle, and held the letter to the flame till it was all consumed; and she gathered up the ashes, putting them in her hand, and blew them out of the window. She felt that by that act she had finished with the whole thing, and Gerald was definitely gone out of her life.

But rest did not come to Bertha's troubled soul. At first she found her life fairly tolerable; but she had now no emotions to distract her, and the routine of the day was unvarying. The weeks passed and the months; the winter came upon her, more dreary than she had ever known it. The country became insufferably dull.

The days were grey and cold, and the clouds so low that she could almost touch them. The broad fields, which had once offered such wonderful emotions, were now only tedious, and all the rural sights sank into her mind with a pitiless monotony; day after day, month after month, she saw the same things. She was bored to death.

Sometimes Bertha wandered to the sea-shore and looked across the desolate waste of water. She longed to travel as her eyes and her mind travelled, South, South to the azure skies, to the lands of beauty and sunshine beyond the greyness. Fortunately she did not know that she was looking almost directly North, and that if she really went on and on as she desired, she would reach no Southern lands of pleasure, but the North Pole.

She walked along the beach, among the countless shells; and not content with present disquietude, tortured herself with anticipation of the future. She could only imagine that it would bring an increase of this frightful ennui, and her head ached as she looked forward to the dull monotony of her life. She went home, entering the house with aversion as she thought of the tiresome evening.

Bertha was seized with restlessness. She would walk up and down her room in a fever of almost physical agony. She would sit at the piano, and cease playing after half a dozen bars; music seemed as futile as everything else. She seemed to have done everything so often. She tried to read, but could hardly bring herself to begin a new volume; the very sight of the printed pages was distasteful; the books of information told her things she did not want to know, the novels related deeds of persons about whom she could not raise the least interest. She read a few pages and threw the book down in disgust. Then she went out again—anything seemed preferable to what she was actually doing. She walked rapidly, but the motion, the country, the very atmosphere about her, were wearisome, and almost immediately she returned home.

Bertha was forced to take the same walks day after day, and the deserted roads, the trees, the hedges, the fields, impressed themselves on her mind with a dismal insistence. When she was driven to go out merely for exercise, she walked a certain number of miles, trying to get it over quickly. The winds of the early year blew that season more persistently than ever, and they impeded her steps, and chilled her to the bone.

Sometimes Bertha paid visits, and the restraint she had to put upon herself relieved her for the moment, but as soon as the door was closed behind her she felt more desperately bored than ever.

Yearning suddenly for society, she would send out invitations for some function, then, as it approached, felt it inexpressibly irksome to make preparations, and she loathed and abhorred her guests. For a long time she refused to see anyone, protesting her feeble health; and sometimes in the solitude she thought she would go mad. She turned to prayer as the only refuge of those who cannot act, but she only half believed, and therefore found no comfort. She accompanied Miss Glover on her district visiting, but she disliked the poor and hated their inane chatter.

Her head ached, and she put her hands to her temples, pressing them painfully; she felt she could take great wisps of her hair and tear it out. She threw herself on her bed and wept in the agony of boredom. Edward once found her thus and asked what was the matter.

'Oh, my head aches so that I feel I could kill myself.'

He sent for Ramsay, but Bertha knew that the doctor's remedies were useless. She imagined that there was no remedy for her ill—not even time—no remedy but death. She knew the terrible distress of waking in the morning with the thought that still another day must be gone through, she knew the relief of bedtime, with the thought that she would enjoy a few hours of unconsciousness. She was racked with the imagination of the future's frightful monotony: night would follow day, and day would follow night, the months passing one by one and the years slowly, slowly. They say that life is short: to those who look back perhaps it is; but to those who look forward it is long, horribly long, endless. Sometimes Bertha felt it impossible to endure. She prayed that she might fall asleep at night and never awake. How happy must be the lives of those people who can look forward to eternity! To Bertha the idea of living for ever and ever was merely ghastly; she desired nothing but the long rest, the rest of an endless sleep, the dissolution into nothing.

Once in her depression she wished to kill herself, but she was afraid. People say it requires no courage to commit suicide. Fools! They cannot realize the horror of the needful preparations, the anticipation of the pain, the terrible fear that one may regret when it is too late, when life is ebbing away. And there is the dread of the Unknown; above all, the awful fear of hell-fire. It is absurd and revolting, but so ingrained that no effort is sufficient entirely to destroy it; there is still, notwithstanding reason and argument, the fear that it may be true, the fear of a jealous God who will doom one to eternal punishment.

CHAPTER XXXIV

BUT if the human soul, or the heart, or the mind—call it what you will—is an instrument upon which countless melodies may be played, it is capable of responding to none for very long. Time dulls the most exquisite emotions and softens the most heartrending grief; the story is told of a philosopher who sought to console a woman in distress by the account of tribulations akin to hers, and upon losing his only son was sent by her a list of kings similarly bereaved. He read it, acknowledged its correctness, but wept none the less. Three months later the philosopher and the lady were surprised to find one another quite gay, and they erected a fine statue to Time, with the inscription: *A celui qui console.*

When Bertha vowed that life had lost all savour, that her ennui was unending, she exaggerated as usual; and almost grew angry on discovering that existence could be more supportable than she thought.

One gets used to all things. It is only very misanthropic persons who pretend that they cannot accustom themselves to the stupidity of their fellows; after a while one gets hardened to the most desperate bores, and monotony even ceases to be quite monotonous. Accommodating herself to circumstances, Bertha found life less tedious; it was a calm river, and presently she came to the conclusion that it ran more easily without the cascades and waterfalls, the eddies, whirlpools and rocks, that had disturbed its course. The man who can still humbug himself has before him a future not lacking in brightness.

The summer brought a certain variety, and Bertha found amusement in things that before had never interested her. She went to sheltered parts to see if favourite wild flowers had begun to blow: her love of liberty made her prefer the hedge-roses to the pompous blooms of the garden, the buttercups and daisies of the field to the prim geraniums, the calceolarias. Time fled, and she was surprised to find the year pass imperceptibly.

She began to read with greater zest, and in her favourite seat, on the sofa by the window, spent long hours of pleasure. She read as fancy prompted her, without a plan, because she wanted to, and not because she ought. She obtained pleasure by contrasting different writers, getting emotions out of the gravity of one and the frivolity of the next. She went from the latest novel to Orlando Furioso, from the Euphues of John Lyly (most entertaining and whimsical of books) to the tender melancholy of Verlaine. With a lifetime before her, the length of books was no hindrance, and she started boldly upon the eight volumes of the *Decline and Fall,* upon the many tomes of St Simon; and she never hesitated to put them aside after a hundred pages.

Bertha found reality tolerable when it was merely a background, a foil to the fantastic happenings of old books: she looked at the green trees, and the song of birds mingled agreeably with her thoughts, still occupied with the Dolorous Knight of La Mancha, with Manon Lescaut or the joyous band that wanders through the *Decameron.* With greater knowledge came greater curiosity, and she forsook the broad high-roads of literature for the mountain pathways of some obscure poet, for the bridle-track of the Spanish picaroon. She found unexpected satisfaction in the half-forgotten masterpieces of the past, in poets not quite divine whom fashion had left on one side, in the playwrights, novelists and essayist' whose remembrance lives only with the bookworm. It is a relief sometimes to look away from the bright sun of perfect achievement; and the writers who appealed to their age and not to posterity have by contrast a subtle charm. Undazzled by their splendour, one may discern more easily their individualities and the spirit of their time; they have pleasant qualities not always found among their betters, and there is even a certain pathos in their incomplete success.

In music also Bertha developed a taste for the half-known, the half-archaic. It suited the Georgian drawing-room, with its old pictures, with its Chippendale and chintz, to play the simple melodies of Couperin and Rameau; the rondos, the gavottes, the sonatinas in powder and patch that delighted the rococo lords and ladies of a past century.

Living away from the present, in an artificial paradise, Bertha was happy. She found indifference to the whole world a trusty armour: life was easy without love or hate, hope or despair, without ambition, desire of change or tumultuous passion. So bloom the flowers; unconscious, uncaring, the bud bursts from the endosing leaf, and opens to the sunshine, squanders its perfume to the breeze, and there is none to see its beauty; and then it dies.

Bertha found it possible to look back upon the past with something like amusement: it seemed now melodramatic to have loved the simple Edward with such violence; she was even able to smile at the contrast between her vivid expectations and the flat reality. Gerald was a pleasantly sentimental memory, she did not want to see him again, but she thought of him often, idealizing him until he became a mere figure in one of her favourite books. Her winter in Italy also formed the motive of some of her most delightful thoughts, and she determined never to spoil the impression by another visit. She had advanced a good deal in the science of life when she realized that pleasure came by surprise, that happiness was a spirit that descended unawares, and seldom when it was sought.

Edward had fallen into a life of such activity that his time was entirely taken up. He had added largely to the Ley estate, and, with the second-rate man's belief that you must do everything yourself to have it well done, he kept the farms under his immediate supervision. He was an important member of all the rural bodies: he was on the School Board, on the Board of Guardians, on the County

Council; he was Chairman of the Urban District Council, president of the local Cricket Club, and of the Football Club; patron of the Blackstable Regatta, on the committee of the Tercanbury Dog Show, and an enthusiastic supporter of the Mid-Kent Agricultural Exhibition. He was a pillar of the Blackstable Conservative Association, a magistrate, and a churchwarden. Finally, he was an ardent Freemason, and flew over Kent to attend the meetings of the half-dozen lodges of which he was a member. But the work did not disturb him.

'Lord bless you,' he said, 'I love work. You can't give me too much. If there's anything to be done, come to me and I'll do it, and say thank you for giving me the chance.'

Edward had always been even-tempered, but now his good nature was angelic. It became a by-word. His success was according to his deserts, and to have him concerned in any matter was an excellent insurance. He was always jovial and gay, contented with himself and with the world at large; he was a model squire, landlord, farmer, Conservative, man, Englishman. He did everything thoroughly, and his energy was such that he made a point of putting into every concern twice as much work as it really needed. He was busy from morning to night (as a rule quite unnecessarily), and he gloried in it.

'It shows I'm an excellent woman,' said Bertha to Miss Glover, 'to support his virtues with equanimity.'

'My dear, I think you ought to be very proud and happy. He's an example to the whole country. If he were my husband, I should be grateful to God.'

'I have much to be thankful for,' murmured Bertha.

Since he let her go her own way and she was only too pleased that he should go his, there was really no possibility of difference, and Edward, wise man, came to the conclusion that he had effectively tamed his wife. He thought, with good-humoured scorn, that he had been quite right when he likened women to chickens, animals which, to be happy, required no more than a good run, well fenced in, where they could scratch about to their heart's content.

'Feed 'em regularly, and let 'em cackle; and there you are!'

It is always satisfactory when experience proves the hypothesis that you formed in your youth.

One year, remembering by accident their wedding day, Edward gave his wife a bracelet; and feeling benevolent in consequence, and having dined well, he patted her hand and said:

'Time does fly, doesn't it?'

'I have heard people say so,' she replied, smiling.

'Well, who'd have thought we'd been married so many years; it doesn't seem above eighteen months to me. And we've got on very well, haven't we?'

'My dear Edward, you are such a model husband. It quite embarrasses me sometimes.'

'Ha, that's a good one! But I can say this for myself, I do try to do my duty. Of course at first we had our little tiffs, people have to get used to one another, and one can't expect to have all plain sailing just at once. But for years now—well, ever since you went to Italy, I think—we've been as happy as the day is long, haven't we?'

'Yes, dear.'

'When I look back at the little rumpuses we used to have, upon my word, I wonder what they were all about.'

'So do I.' And this Bertha said quite truthfully.

'I suppose it was just the weather.'

'I daresay.'

'Ah, well, all's well that ends well.'

'My dear Edward, you're a philosopher.'

'I don't know about that, but I think I'm a politician which reminds me that I've not read about the new men-of-war in today's paper. What I've been agitating about for years is more ships and more guns. I'm glad to see the Government have taken my advice at last.'

'It's very satisfactory, isn't it? It will encourage you to persevere. And of course it's well to know that the Cabinet read your speeches in the *Blackstable Times*.'

'I think it would be a good sight better for the country if those in power paid more attention to provincial opinions. It's men like me who really know the feeling of the nation. You might get me the paper, will you? It's in the dining-room.'

It seemed quite natural to Edward that Bertha should wait upon him: it was the duty of a wife. She handed him the *Standard,* and he began to read; he yawned once or twice.

'Lord, I am sleepy.'

Presently he could not keep his eyes open, the paper dropped from his hand and he sank back in his chair with his legs outstretched and his hands resting comfortably on his stomach; his head lolled to one side and his jaw dropped; he began to snore. Bertha read. After a while he woke with a start.

'Bless me, I do believe I've been asleep,' he cried. 'Well, I'm dead beat; I think I shall go to bed. I suppose you won't come up yet?'

'Not just yet.'

'Well, don't stay up too late, there's a good girl; it's not good for you; and put the lights out properly when you come.'

She turned her cheek to him, which he kissed, stifling a yawn; then roiled upstairs.

'There's one advantage in Edward,' murmured Bertha. 'No one could accuse him of being uxorious.'

Mariage à la Mode.

Bertha's solitary walk was to the sea. The shore between Blackstable and the mouth of the Thames was very wild. At distant intervals were the long, low buildings of the coastguard stations, and the prim gravel walk, the neat railings came as a surprise, but they made the surrounding desolation more forlorn. One could walk for miles without meeting a soul, and the country spread out from the sea low and flat and marshy. The beach was strewn with countless, shells, and they crumbled underfoot, and here and there were great banks of seaweed and bits of wood and rope, the jetsam of a thousand tides. In one spot, a few yards out at sea, high and dry at low water, were the remains of an old hulk, whose wooden ribs stood out weirdly like the skeleton of some huge sea-beast. And then all round was the grey sea, with never a ship nor even a fishing-smack in sight. In winter it was as if a spirit of loneliness, like a mystic shroud, had descended on the shore and the desert waters.

There in the melancholy, in the dreariness, Bertha found a bitter fascination. The sky was a lowering cloud, the wind tore along shouting and screaming and whistling; there was panic in the turbulent sea, murky and yellow; the waves leaped up, one at the other's heels, and beat down on the beach with an angry roar. It was desolate, desolate; the sea was so merciless that the very sight appalled one: it was a wrathful power, beating forwards, ever wrathfully beating forwards, roaring with pain when the chains that bound it wrenched it back; and after each desperate effort it shrank with a yell of pain. And the seagulls swayed above the waves in their disconsolate flight, rising and falling with the wind.

Bertha loved the calm of winter, when the sea-mist and the mist of heaven are one, when the sea is silent and heavy, and the solitary gull flies screeching over the grey waters, screeching mournfully. She loved the calm of summer, when the sky is cloudless and infinite. Then she spent long hours, lying at the water's edge, delighted with the solitude and the peace of her heart. The sea, placid as a lake, unmoved by the slightest ripple, was a looking-glass reflecting the glory of heaven, and it turned to fire when the sun sank in the west; it was a sea of molten copper, shining, so that the eyes were dazzled. A troop of seagulls slept on the water; there were hundreds of them, motionless, silent; one arose now and then, and flew for a moment with heavy whig, and sank down, and all was still.

Once the coolness was so tempting that Bertha could not resist it. Timidly, rapidly she slipped off her clothes, and looking round to see that there was really no one in sight, stepped in; the wavelets about her feet made her shiver a little, and then with a splash, stretching out her arms, she ran forward, and half fell, half dived into the water. Now it was delightful; she rejoiced in the freedom of her limbs; it was an unknown pleasure to swim unhampered by a bathing-dress. It gave her a wonderful sense of freedom, and the salt water lapping round her was so exhilarating that she felt a new strength. She wanted to sing aloud in the joy of her heart. Diving below the surface, she came up with a shake of the head and a little cry of delight; her hair was loosened, and with a motion it all came tumbling about her shoulders and trailed out in its ringlets over the water.

She swam out, a fearless swimmer; and it gave her a sense of power to have the deep waters all about her, the deep calm sea of summer. She turned on her back and floated, trying to look the sun in the face: the sea glimmered with the sunbeams and the sky was dazzling. Then, returning, Bertha floated again, quite near the shore; it amused her to lie on her back, rocked by the tiny waves, and to sink her ears so that she could hear the shingle rub together curiously with the ebb and Sow of the tide. She shook her long hair, and it stretched about her like an aureole.

She exulted in her youth—in her youth? Bertha felt no older than when she was eighteen, and yet she was thirty. The thought made her wince; she had never realized the passage of the years, she had never imagined that her youth was waning. Did people think her already old? The sickening fear came to her that she resembled Miss Hancock attempting by archness and by an assumption of frivolity to persuade her neighbours that she was juvenile. Bertha asked herself whether she was ridiculous when she rolled to the water like a young girl: you cannot play the mermaid with crow's-feet about your eyes and with wrinkles round your mouth. In a panic she dressed herself, and going home flew to a looking-glass. She scrutinized her features as she had never done before, searching anxiously for the signs she feared to see; she looked at her neck and at her eyes: her skin was as smooth as ever, her teeth as perfect. She gave a sigh of relief.

'I see no difference.'

Then, doubly to reassure herself, a fantastic idea seized Bertha to dress as though she were going to a great ball; she wished to see herself to all advantage. She chose the most splendid gown she had, and took out her jewels. The Leys had sold every vestige of their old magnificence, but their diamonds, with characteristic obstinacy, they had invariably refused to part with; and they lay aside, year after year unused, the stones in their old settings dulled with dust and neglect. The moisture still in Bertha's hair was an excuse to do it capriciously, and she placed in it the tiara that her grandmother had worn in the Regency. On her shoulders she wore two ornaments exquisitely set in gold-work, purloined by a great uncle from the saint of a Spanish church in the Peninsular War. She slipped a string of pearls round her neck, bracelets on her arms, and fastened a gleaming row of stars to her bosom. Knowing she had beautiful hands, Bertha disdained to wear rings, but now she covered her fingers with diamonds.

Finally she stood before the looking-glass, and gave a laugh of pleasure. She was not old yet.

But when she sailed into the drawing-room, Edward jumped up in surprise.

'Good Lord!' he cried. 'What on earth's up? Have we got people coming to dinner?'

'My dear, if we had I should not have dressed like this.'

'You're got up as if the Prince of Wales were coming. And I'm only in knickerbockers. It's not our wedding-day?'

'No.'

'Then I should like to know why you've got yourself up like that.'

'I thought it would please you,' she said, smiling.

'I wish you'd told me, I'd have dressed too. Are you sure no one's coming?'

'Quite sure.'

'Well, I think I ought to dress. It would look so queer if someone turned up.'

'If anyone does, I promise you I'll fly.'

They went in to dinner, Edward feeling very uncomfortable, and keeping his ear on the front-door bell. They ate their soup, and then was set on the table the remainder of a cold leg of mutton and some mashed poatoes. Bertha looked blank, and then, leaning back, burst into peal upon peal of laughter.

'Good Lord, what is the matter now?' asked Edward.

Nothing is more annoying than to have people violently hilarious over a joke that you cannot see. Bertha held her sides and tried to speak.

'I've just remembered that I told the servants they might go out tonight, there's a circus at Blackstable; and I said we'd just eat up the odds and ends.'

'I don't see any joke in that.'

And really there was none, but Bertha laughed again immoderately.

'I suppose there are some pickles,' said Edward.

Bertha repressed her gaiety and began to eat.

'That is my whole life,' she murmured under her breath, 'to eat cold mutton and mashed potatoes in a ball dress and all my diamonds.'

CHAPTER XXXV

BUT in the winter of that very year Edward, while hunting, had an accident. For years he had made a practice of riding unmanageable horses, and he never heard of a vicious brute without wishing to try it. He knew that he was a fine rider, and since he was never shy of parading his powers nor loth to taunt others with their inferior skill or courage, he preferred difficult animals. It gratified him to see people point to him and say: 'There's a good rider'; and his best joke with some person on a horse that pulled or refused was to cry: 'You don't seem friends with your gee; would you like to try mine?' And then, touching its sides with his spurs, he set it prancing. He was merciless with cautious hunters who looked for low parts of a hedge or tried to get through a gate instead of over it; and when anyone said a jump was dangerous, Edward with a laugh promptly went over it, shouting as he did so:

'I wouldn't try it if I were you. You might fall off.'

He had just bought a roan for a song, because it jumped un-uncertainly and had a trick of swinging a foreleg as it rose. He took it out on the earliest opportunity, and the first two hedges and a ditch the horse cleared easily; Edward thought that once again he had got for almost nothing a hunter that merely wanted riding properly to behave like a lamb. They rode on and came to a post and rail fence.

'Now, my beauty, this'll show what you're made of.'

He took his horse up in a canter and pressed his legs; the horse did not rise, but swerved round suddenly.

'No, you don't,' said Edward, taking him back.

He dug his spurs in, and the horse cantered up, but refused again. This time Edward got angry. Arthur Branderton came flying by, and having many old scores to pay, laughed loudly.

'Why don't you get down and walk over?' he shouted, as he passed Edward and took the jump.

'I'll either get over or weak my neck,' said Edward, setting his teeth.

But he did neither. He set the roan at the jump for the third time, hitting him over the head with his crop. The beast rose and then, displaying his habit of letting the fore-leg swing, came down with a crash. Edward fell heavily, and for a minute was stunned; when he recovered consciousness he found someone pouring brandy down his neck.

'Is the horse hurt?' he asked, not thinking of himself.

'No; he's all right How d'you feel?'

A young surgeon was in the field, and rode up.

'What's the matter? Anyone injured?'

'No,' said Edward, struggling to his feet, angry at the exhibition he thought he was making of himself. 'One would think none of you fellows had ever seen a man come down before. I've seen most of you come off often enough.'

He walked up to the horse and put his foot in the stirrup.

'You'd better go home, Craddock,' said the surgeon. 'I expect you're a bit shaken up.'

'Go home be damned. Blast!' As he tried to mount Edward felt a pain at the top of his chest 'I believe I've broken something.'

The surgeon went up to him and helped him off with his coat He twisted Edward's arm.

'Does that hurt?'

'A bit.'

'You've broken your collar-bone,' said the surgeon, after a moment's examination. 'You'll want a Sayer's strapping, my friend.'

'I thought I'd smashed something. How long will it take to mend?'

'Only three weeks. You needn't be alarmed.'

'I'm not alarmed, but I suppose I shall have to give up hunting for at least a month.'

Edward was driven to Dr Ramsay's, who bandaged him, and then went back to Court Leys. Bertha was surprised to see him in a dog-cart. He had by now recovered his good temper, and explained the occurrence laughing.

'It's nothing to make a fuss about. Only I'm bandaged up so that I feel like a mummy, and I don't know how I'm going to get a bath. That's what worries me.'

Next day Arthur Branderton came to see him.

'You've found your master at last, Craddock.'

'Me? Not much! I shall be all right in a month, and then out I go again.'

'I wouldn't ride him again if I were you. It's not worth it. With that trick of his of swinging his leg, you'll break your neck.'

'Bah,' said Edward scornfully. 'The horse hasn't been built that I can't ride.'

'You're a good weight now, and your bones aren't as supple as when you were twenty. The next fall you have will be a bad one.'

'Rot, man! One would think I was eighty. I've never funked a horse yet, and I'm not going to begin now.'

Branderton shrugged his shoulders and said nothing more at the time; but afterwards spoke to Bertha privately.

'You know, I think if I were you I'd persuade Edward to get rid of that horse. I don't think he ought to ride it again. It's not safe. However well he rides, it won't save him if the beast has got a bad trick.'

Bertha had in this particular great faith in her husband's skill. Whatever he could not do, he was certainly one of the finest riders in the country; but she spoke to him notwithstanding.

'Pooh, that's all rot!' he said.' I tell you what, on thc eleventh of next month we go over pretty well the same ground, and I'm going out, and I swear he's going over that post and rail in Coulter's Field.'

'You're very incautious.'

'No, I'm not. I know exactly what a horse can do. And I know that horse can jump it if he wants to, and by George, I'll make him. Why, if I funked it now I could never ride again. When a chap gets to be near forty and has a bad fall, the only thing is to go for it again at once, or he'll lose his nerve and never get it back. I've seen that over and over again.'

Miss Glover later on, when Edward's bandages were removed and he was fairly well, begged Bertha to use her influence with him.

'I've heard he's a most dangerous horse, Bertha. I think it would be madness for Edward to ride him.'

'I've begged him to sell it, but he merely laughs at me,' said Bertha. 'He's dreadfully obstinate, and I have very little power over him.'

'Aren't you frightened?'

Bertha laughed. 'No, I'm really not. You know, he always has ridden dangerous horses, and he's never come to any harm. When we were first married I used to go through agonies; every time he hunted I used to think he'd be brought home dead on a stretcher. But he never was, and I calmed down by degrees.'

'I wonder you could.'

'My dear, no one can keep on being frightfully agitated for ten years. People who live on volcanoes forget all about it; and you'd soon get used to sitting on barrels of gunpowder if you had no armchair.'

'Never!' said Miss Glover with conviction, seeing a vivid picture of herself in such a position.

Miss Glover was unaltered. Time passed over her head powerlessly; she still looked anything between five-and-twenty and forty, her hair was no more washed-out, her figure in its armour of black cloth was as young as ever, and not a new idea nor a thought had entered her mind. She was like Alice's queen who ran at the top of her speed and remained in the same place; but with Miss Glover the process was reversed: the world moved on, apparently faster and faster as the century drew near its end, but she remained fixed—an incarnation of the eighteen-eighties.

The day before the eleventh arrived. The hounds were to meet at 'The Share and Coulter', as when Edward had been thrown. He sent for Dr Ramsay to assure Bertha that he was quite fit; and after the examination brought him into the drawing-room.

'Dr Ramsay says my collar-bone is stronger than ever.'

'But I don't think he ought to ride the roan notwithstanding. Can't you persuade Edward not to, Bertha?'

Bertha looked from the doctor to Edward, smiling.

'I've done my best,' she said.

'Bertha knows better than to bother,' said Edward. 'She doesn't think much of me as a churchwarden, but where a horse is concerned she does trust me; don't you, dear?'

'I really do.'

'There,' said Edward, much pleased. 'That's what I call a good wife.'

Next day the horse was brought round and Bertha filled Edward's flask.

'You'll bury me nicely if I break my neck, won't you?' he said, laughing. 'You'll order a handsome tombstone.'

'My dear, you'll never do that. I feel certain you will die in your bed when you're a hundred and two, with a crowd of descendants weeping round you. You're just that sort of man.'

'I don't know where the descendants are coming in,' he laughed.

'I have a presentiment that I am doomed to make way for Fanny Glover. I'm sure there's a fatality about it. I've felt for years that you will eventually marry her; it's horrid of me to have kept you waiting so long, especially as she pines for you, poor thing.'

Edward laughed again. 'Well, good-bye!'

'Good-bye. Remember me to Mr Arthur.'

She stood at the window to see him mount, and as he flourished his crop at her waved her hand.

The winter day closed in, and Bertha, interested in the novel she was reading, was surprised to hear the clock strike. She wondered that Edward had not yet come in, and ringing for tea and the lamps, had the curtains drawn. He could not now be long.

'I wonder if he's had another fall,' she said with a smile. 'He really ought to give up hunting, he's getting too fat.'

She decided to wait no longer, but poured out her tea and arranged herself so that she could get at the scones and see comfortably to read. Then she heard a carriage drive up. Who could it be?

'What bores these' people are to call at this time!'

Bertha put down her book to receive the visitor, as the bell was rung. But no one was shown in; there was a confused sound of voices without. Could something have happened to Edward, after all? She sprang to her feet and walked half across the room. She heard an unknown voice in the hall.

'Where shall we take it?'

It. What was *it*—a corpse? Bertha felt a coldness travel through all her body; she put her hand on a chair, so that she might steady herself if she felt faint. The door was opened slowly by Arthur Branderton, and he closed it quietly behind him.

'I'm awfully sorry, but there's been an accident. Edward is rather hurt.'

She looked at him, growing pale; but found nothing to answer.

'You must nerve yourself, Bertha. I'm afraid he's very bad. You'd better sit down.'

He hesitated, and she turned to him with sudden anger.

'If he's dead, why don't you tell me?'

'I'm awfully sorry. We did all we could. He fell at the same post and rail fence as the other day. I think he must have lost his nerve.

I was dose by him. I saw him rash at it blindly, and then pull just as the horse was rising. They came down with a crash.'

'Is he dead?'

'Death must have been instantaneous.'

Bertha did not faint. She was a little horrified at the clearness with which she was able to understand Arthur Branderton. She seemed to feel nothing at all. The young man looked at her as if he expected that she would weep or swoon.

'Would you like me to send my wife to you?'

'No, thanks.'

Bertha understood quite well that her husband was dead, but the news seemed to make no impression upon her. She heard it as unmovedly as though it referred to a stranger. She found herself wondering what young Branderton thought of her unconcern.

'Won't you sit down?' he said, taking her arm and leading her to a chair. 'Shall I get you some brandy?'

'I'm all right, thanks. You need not trouble about me. Where is he?'

'I told them to take him upstairs. Shall I send Ramsay's assistant to you? He's here.'

'No,' she said in a low voice. 'I want nothing. Have they taken him up already?'

'Yes, but I don't think you ought to go to him. It'll upset you dreadfully.'

'I'll go to my room. Do you mind if I leave you? I should prefer to be alone.'

Branderton held the door open and Bertha walked out, her face very pale, but showing not the least trace of emotion. Branderton walked to Leanham Vicarage to send Miss Glover to Court Leys, and then home, where he told his wife that the wretched widow was absolutely stunned by the shock.

Bertha locked herself in her room. She heard the hum of voices in the house; Dr Ramsay came to the door, but she refused to open; then all was quite still.

She was aghast at the blankness of her heart; the calmness was inhuman and she wondered if she was going mad; she felt no emotion whatever. But she repeated to herself that Edward was killed; he was lying quite near at hand, dead, and she felt no grief. She remembered her anguish years before when she thought of his death, and now that it had taken place she did not faint, she did not weep, she was untroubled. Bertha had hidden herself to conceal her tears from strange eyes, and the tears did not come! After the sudden suspicion was confirmed she had experienced no emotion whatever; she was horrified that the tragic death affected her so little. She walked to the window and looked out, trying to gather her thoughts, trying to make herself care; but she was almost indifferent.

'I must be frightfully cruel,' she muttered.

Then the idea came of what her friends would say when they saw her calm and self-possessed. She tried to weep, but her eyes remained dry.

There was a knock at the door, and Miss Glover's voice.

'Bertha, Bertha, won't you let me in? It's me, Fanny.'

Bertha sprang to her feet, but did not answer. Miss Glover called again: her voice was broken with sobs. Why could Fanny Glover weep for Edward's death, who was a stranger, when she, Bertha, remained insensible?

'Bertha!'

'Yes.'

'Open the door for me. Oh, I'm so sorry for you. Please let me in.'

Bertha looked wildly at the door; she dared not let Miss Glover in.

'I can see no one now,' she cried hoarsely. 'Don't ask me.'

'I think I could comfort you.'

'I want to be alone.'

Miss Glover was silent for a minute, crying audibly.

'Shall I wait downstairs? You can ring if you want me. Perhaps you'll see me later.'

Bertha wanted to tell her to go away, but had not the courage.

'Do as you like,' she said.

A second voice was added to Miss Glover's, and Bertha heard a whispered conversation. There was another knock.

'Bertha, what do you wish done?'

'What can be done?'

'Oh, why don't you open the door? Don't you understand?' Miss Glover's voice shook. 'Shall we send for a woman to wash the body?'

Bertha paused, and the blood fled from her lips.

'Do whatever you like.'

There was silence again, an unearthly silence, more trying than hideous din. It was a silence that tightened the nerves and made them horribly sensitive: one dared not breathe for fear of breaking it.

And one thought came to Bertha, assailing her like a devil tormenting. She cried out in horror. This was more odious than anything. Intolerable. She threw herself on the bed and buried her face in the pillow to drive it away. For shame she put her hands to her ears in order not to hear the invisible fiends that whispered silently.

She was free.

'Has it come to this?' she murmured.

And then came back the recollection of the beginnings of her love. She recalled the passion that had thrown her blindly into Edward's arms, her bitter humiliation when she realized that he could not respond to her ardour; her love was a fire playing ineffectually over a rock of basalt. She recalled the hatred that followed the disillusion, and finally the indifference. It was the same indifference that chilled her heart now. Her life seemed all wasted when she compared her mad desire for happiness with the misery she had in fact endured. Bertha's many hopes stood out tike phantoms, and she looked at them despairingly. She had expected so much and got so little. She felt a terrible pain at her heart as she considered all she had gone through, her strength fell away, and, overcome by pity for herself, she sank to her knees and burst into tears.

'Oh, God,' she cried, 'what have I done that I should have been so unhappy?'

She sobbed aloud, not caring to restrain her grief.

Miss Glover, good soul, was waiting outside the room in case Bertha wanted her, crying silently. She knocked again when she heard the impetuous sobs within.

'Oh, Bertha, do let me in. You're tormenting yourself so much more because you won't see anybody.'

Bertha dragged herself to her feet and undid the door. Miss Glover entered, and throwing off all her reserve in her overwhelming sympathy clasped Bertha to her heart.

'Oh, my dear, my dear, it's utterly dreadful. I'm so sorry for you. I don't know what to say. I can only pray.'

Bertha sobbed unrestrainedly—not because Edward was dead.

'All you have now is God,' said Miss Glover.

At last Bertha tore herself away and dried her eyes.

'Don't try and be too brave, Bertha. It'll do you good to cry. He was such a good, kind man, and he loved you so.'

Bertha looked at her in silence.

'I must be horribly cruel,' she thought.

'Do you mind if I stay here tonight, dear?' said Miss Glover. 'I've sent word to Charles.'

'Oh, no, please don't. If you care for me, Fanny, let me be alone. I don't want to be unkind, but I can't bear to see anyone.'

Miss Glover was deeply pained, 'I don't want to be in the way. If you really wish me to go, I'll go.'

'I feel if I can't be alone I shall go mad,'

'Would you like to see Charles?'

'No, dear. Don't be angry. Don't think me unkind or ungrateful, but I want nothing but to be left entirely by myself.'

CHAPTER XXXVI

ALONE in her room once more, memories of the past crowded upon her. The last years passed from her mind, and Bertha saw vividly again the first days of her love, the visit to Edward at his farm, and the night at the gate of Court Leys when he asked her to marry him. She recalled the rapture with which she had flung herself into his arms. Forgetting the real Edward who had just died, she remembered the tall strong youth who had made her faint with love, and her passion returned, overwhelming. On the chimney-piece stood a photograph of Edward as he was then; it had been before her for years, but she had never noticed it. She took it and pressed it to her heart, and kissed it. A thousand things came back, and she saw him again standing before her as he was then, manly and strong so that she felt his love a protection against all the world.

But what was the use now?

'I should be mad if I began to love him again when it's too late.'

Bertha was appalled by the regret that she felt rising within her, a devil that wrung her heart in an iron grip. Oh, she could not risk the possibility of grief, she had suffered too much, and she must kill in herself the springs of pain. She dared not leave things that in future years might be the foundation of a new idolatry. Her only chance was to destroy everything that might recall him.

She took the photograph and, without daring to look again, withdrew it from its frame and quickly tore it in bits. She looked round the room.

'I musn't leave anything,' she muttered.

She saw on a table an album containing pictures of Edward at an ages, the child with long curls, the urchin in knickerbockers, the schoolboy, the lover of her heart. She had persuaded him to be photographed in London during their honeymoon, and he was there in half a dozen positions. Bertha thought her heart would break as she destroyed them one by one, and it needed all the strength she had to prevent her from covering them with passionate kisses. Her fingers ached with the tearing, but in a little while they were all in fragments in the fireplace. Then she added the letters Edward had written to her, and applied a match. She watched them curl and frizzle and burn; and presently they were ashes.

She sank on a chair, exhausted by the effort, but quickly roused herself. She drank some water nerving herself for a more terrible ordeal; she knew that on the next few hours depended her future peace.

By now the night was late, a stormy night with the wind howling through the leafless trees. Bertha started when it beat against the windows with a scream that was nearly human. A fear seized her of what she was about to do, but she was driven on by a greater fear. She took a candle, and opening the door listened. There was no one; the wind roared with its long, monotonous voice, and the branches of a tree beating against a window in the passage gave a ghastly tap-tap, as if unseen spirits were near.

The living in the presence of death feel that the air about them is full of something new and terrible. A greater sensitiveness perceives an inexplicable feeling of something present, or some horrible thing happening in visibly. Bertha walked to her husband's room, and for a while dared not enter. At last she opened the door; she lit the candles on the chimney-piece and on the dressing-table, then went to the bed. Edward was lying on his back, with a handkerchief bound round his jaw to hold it up, his hands crossed.

Bertha stood in front of the corpse and looked. The impression of the young man passed away, and she saw him as in truth he was, stout and red-faced; the vesicles of his cheeks stood out distinctly in a purple network; the sides of his face were bulgy as of late years they had become; and he had little side-whiskers. His skin was lined already and rough, the hair on the front of his head was scanty, and the scalp showed through, shining and white. The hands that had once delighted her by their strength, so that she compared them with the porphyry hands of an unfinished statue, now were repellent in their coarseness. For a long time their touch had a little disgusted her. This was the image Bertha wished to impress upon her mind. At last, turning away, she went out and returned to her own room.

Three days later was the funeral. All the morning wreaths and crosses of beautiful flowers had poured in, and now there was quite a large gathering in the drive in front of Ley House. The Blackstable Freemasons (Lodge No. 31,899), of which Edward at his death was Worshipful Master, had signified their intention of attending, and now lined the road, two and two, in white gloves and aprons. There were likewise representatives of the Tercanbury Lodge (4169), of the Provincial Grand Lodge, the Mark Masons and the Knights Templars. The Blackstable Unionist Association sent one hundred Conservatives who walked two and two after the Freemasons. There was some dispute as to precedence between Bro. G. W. Havelock, C.P.W.U., who led the Blackstable Lodge (31,899), and Mr Atthill Bacot, who marched at the head of the politicians; but it was settled in favour of the Lodge, as the older established body. Then came the members of the Local District Council, of which Edward had been chairman, and after them the carriages of the gentry. Mrs Mayston Ryle sent a landau and pair, but Mrs Branderton, the Molsons and the rest only broughams. It needed a prodigious amount of generalship to marshal these forces, and Arthur Branderton lost his temper because the Conservatives would start before they were wanted to.

'Ah,' said Bro. A. W. Rogers (the landlord of 'The Pig and Whistle '),' they want Craddock here now. He was the best organizer I've ever seen; he'd have got the procession into working order and the funeral over half an hour ago.'

The last carriage disappeared, and Bertha, alone at length, lay down by the window on the sofa. She was devoutly grateful to the old convention that prevented the widow's attendance at the funeral.

She looked with tired and listless eyes at the long avenue of elm trees, bare of leaf. The sky was grey and the clouds were heavy and low. Bertha was now a pale woman of more than thirty, still beautiful, with curly and abundant hair, but her dark eyes had under them still darker lines, and their fire was dimmed; between her brows was a little vertical line, and her tips had lost the joyousness of youth; the corner of her mouth turned down sadly. Her face was very thin. She seemed weary. Her apathetic eyes said that she had loved and found love wanting, that she had been a mother and that her child had died, and that now she desired nothing very much but to be left in peace.

Bertha was indeed tired out, in body and mind, tired of love and hate, tired of friendship and knowledge, tired of the passing years. Her thoughts wandered to the future, and she decided to leave Blackstable; she would let Court Leys, so that in no moment of weakness might she be tempted to return. And first she intended to travel; she wished more easily to forget the past, to live in places where she was unknown. Bertha's memory brought back Italy, the land of those who suffer in unfulfilled desire, the lotus-land; she would go there and she would go further, ever towards the sun. Now she bad no ties on earth, and at last, at last she was free.

The melancholy day closed in, and the great clouds hanging overhead darkened with the approach of night. Bertha remembered how ready in her girlhood she had been to give herself to the world. Feeling intense fellowship with all human beings, she wished to throw herself into their arms, thinking that they would stretch them out to receive her. Her life seemed to overflow into the lives of others, becoming one with theirs as the waters of rivers become one with the sea. But very soon the power she had felt of doing all this departed; she recognized a barrier between herself and human kind, and felt that they were strangers. Hardly understanding the impossibility of what she desired, she placed all her love, all her faculty of expansion, on one person, on Edward, making a final effort as it were to break the barrier of consciousness and unite her soul with his. She drew him towards her with all her might, Edward the man, seeking to know him in the depths of his heart, yearning to lose herself in him. But at last she saw that what she had striven for was unattainable. I myself stand on one side, and the rest of the world on the other. There is an abyss between that no power can cross, a strange barrier more insuperable than a mountain of fire. Husband and wife know nothing of one another. However ardently they love, however intimate their union, they are never one; they are scarcely more to one another than strangers.

And when she had discovered this, with many tears and after bitter heartache, Bertha retired into herself. But soon she found solace. In her silence she built a world of her own, and kept it from the eyes of every living soul, knowing that none could understand. And then all ties were irksome, all earthly attachments unnecessary.

Confusedly thinking these things, Bertha's thoughts reverted to Edward.

'If I had been keeping a diary of my emotions, I should dose it today with the words, "My husband has broken his neck".'

But she was pained at her own bitterness.

'Poor fellow,' she murmured. 'He was honest and kind and forbearing. He did all he could, and tried always to act like a gentleman. He was very useful in the world, and in his own way he was fond of me. His only fault was that I loved him—and ceased to do so.'

By her side lay the book she had been reading while waiting for Edward. Bertha had put it down open, face downwards, when she rose from the sofa to have tea; it had remained as she left it. She was tired of thinking and, taking it now, began reading quietly.

THE MAGICIAN

CHAPTER I

ARTHUR Burdon and Dr Porhoët walked in silence. They had lunched at a restaurant in the Boulevard Saint Michel, and were sauntering now in the gardens of the Luxembourg. Dr Porhoët walked with stooping shoulders, his hands behind him. He beheld the scene with the eyes of the many painters who have sought by means of the most charming garden in Paris to express their sense of beauty. The grass was scattered with the fallen leaves, but their wan decay little served to give a touch of nature to the artifice of all besides. The trees were neatly surrounded by bushes, and the bushes by trim beds of flowers. But the trees grew without abandonment, as though conscious of the decorative scheme they helped to form. It was autumn, and some were leafless already. Many of the flowers were withered. The formal garden reminded one of a light woman, no longer young, who sought, with faded finery, with powder and paint, to make a brave show of despair. It had those false, difficult smiles of uneasy gaiety, and the pitiful graces which attempt a fascination that the hurrying years have rendered vain.

Dr Porhoët drew more closely round his fragile body the heavy cloak which even in summer he could not persuade himself to discard. The best part of his life had been spent in Egypt, in the practice of medicine, and the frigid summers of Europe scarcely warmed his blood. His memory flashed for an instant upon those multi-coloured streets of Alexandria; and then, like a homing bird, it flew to the green woods and the storm-beaten coasts of his native Brittany. His brown eyes were veiled with sudden melancholy.

'Let us wait here for a moment,' he said.

They took two straw-bottomed chairs and sat near the octagonal water which completes with its fountain of Cupids the enchanting artificiality of the Luxembourg. The sun shone more kindly now, and the trees which framed the scene were golden and lovely. A balustrade of stone gracefully enclosed the space, and the flowers, freshly bedded, were very gay. In one corner they could see the squat, quaint towers of Saint Sulpice, and on the other side the uneven roofs of the Boulevard Saint Michel.

The palace was grey and solid. Nurses, some in the white caps of their native province, others with the satin streamers of the *nounou,* marched sedately two by two, wheeling perambulators and talking. Brightly dressed children trundled hoops or whipped a stubborn top. As he watched them, Dr Porhoët's lips broke into a smile, and it was so tender that his thin face, sallow from long exposure to subtropical suns, was transfigured. He no longer struck you merely as an insignificant little man with hollow cheeks and a thin grey beard; for the weariness of expression which was habitual to him vanished before the charming sympathy of his smile. His sunken eyes glittered with a kindly but ironic good-humour. Now passed a guard in the romantic cloak of a brigand in comic opera and a peaked cap like that of an *alguacil.* A group of telegraph boys in blue stood round a painter, who was making a sketch—notwithstanding half-frozen fingers. Here and there, in baggy corduroys, tight jackets, and wide-brimmed hats, strolled students who might have stepped from the page of Murger's immortal romance. But the students now are uneasy with the fear of ridicule, and more often they walk in bowler hats and the neat coats of the *boulevardier.*

Dr Porhoët spoke English fluently, with scarcely a trace of foreign accent, but with an elaboration which suggested that he had learned the language as much from study of the English classics as from conversation.

'And how is Miss Dauncey?' he asked, turning to his friend.

Arthur Burdon smiled.

'Oh, I expect she's all right. I've not seen her today, but I'm going to tea at the studio this afternoon, and we want you to dine with us at the Chien Noir.'

'I shall be much pleased. But do you not wish to be by yourselves?'

'She met me at the station yesterday, and we dined together. We talked steadily from half past six till midnight.'

'Or, rather, she talked and you listened with the delighted attention of a happy lover.'

Arthur Burdon had just arrived in Paris. He was a surgeon on the staff of St Luke's, and had come ostensibly to study the methods of the French operators; but his real object was certainly to see Margaret Dauncey. He was furnished with introductions from London surgeons of repute, and had already spent a morning at the Hotel Dieu, where the operator, warned that his visitor was a bold and skilful surgeon, whose reputation in England was already considerable, had sought to dazzle him by feats that savoured almost of legerdemain. Though the hint of charlatanry in the Frenchman's methods had not escaped Arthur Burdon's shrewd eyes, the audacious sureness of his hand had excited his enthusiasm. During luncheon he talked of nothing else, and Dr Porhoët, drawing upon his memory, recounted the more extraordinary operations that he had witnessed in Egypt.

He had known Arthur Burdon ever since he was born, and indeed had missed being present at his birth only because the Khedive Ismaïl had summoned him unexpectedly to Cairo. But the Levantine merchant who was Arthur's father had been his most intimate friend, and it was with singular pleasure that Dr Porhoët saw the young man, on his advice, enter his own profession and achieve a distinction which himself had never won.

Though too much interested in the characters of the persons whom chance threw in his path to have much ambition on his own behalf, it pleased him to see it in others. He observed with satisfaction the pride which Arthur took in his calling and the determination, backed by his confidence and talent, to become a master of his art. Dr Porhoët knew that a diversity of interests, though it adds charm to a man's personality, tends to weaken him. To excel one's fellows it is needful to be circumscribed. He did not regret, therefore, that Arthur in many ways was narrow. Letters and the arts meant little to him. Nor would he trouble himself with the graceful trivialities which make a man a good talker. In mixed company he was content to listen silently to others, and only something very definite to say could tempt him to join in the general conversation. He worked very hard, operating, dissecting, or lecturing at his hospital, and took pains to read every word, not only in English, but in French and German, which was published concerning his profession. Whenever he could snatch a free day he spent it on the golf-links of Sunningdale, for he was an eager and a fine player.

But at the operating-table Arthur was different. He was no longer the awkward man of social intercourse, who was sufficiently conscious of his limitations not to talk of what he did not understand, and sincere enough not to express admiration for what he did not like. Then, on the other hand, a singular exhilaration filled him; he was conscious of his power, and he rejoiced in it. No unforeseen accident, was able to confuse him. He seemed to have a positive instinct for operating, and his hand and his brain worked in a manner that appeared almost automatic. He never hesitated, and he had no fear of failure. His success had been no less than his courage, and it was plain that soon his reputation with the public would equal that which he had already won with the profession.

Dr Porhoët had been making listless patterns with his stick upon the gravel, and now, with that charming smile of his, turned to Arthur.

'I never cease to be astonished at the unexpectedness of human nature,' he remarked. 'It is really very surprising that a man like you should fall so deeply in love with a girl like Margaret Dauncey.'

Arthur made no reply, and Dr Porhoët, fearing that his words might offend, hastened to explain.

'You know as well as I do that I think her a very charming young person. She has beauty and grace and sympathy. But your characters are more different than chalk and cheese. Notwithstanding your birth in the East and your boyhood spent amid the very scenes of the *Thousand and One Nights*, you are the most matter-of-fact creature I have ever come across.'

'I see no harm in your saying insular,' smiled Arthur. 'I confess that I have no imagination and no sense of humour. I am a plain, practical man, but I can see to the end of my nose with extreme clearness. Fortunately it is rather a long one.'

'One of my cherished ideas is that it is impossible to love without imagination.'

Again Arthur Burdon made no reply, but a curious look came into his eyes as he gazed in front of him. It was the look which might fill the passionate eyes of a mystic when he saw in ecstasy the Divine Lady of his constant prayers.

'But Miss Dauncey has none of that narrowness of outlook which, if you forgive my saying so, is perhaps the secret of your strength. She has a delightful enthusiasm for every form of art. Beauty really means as much to her as bread and butter to the more soberly-minded. And she takes a passionate interest in the variety of life.'

'It is right that Margaret should care for beauty, since there is beauty in every inch of her,' answered Arthur.

He was too reticent to proceed to any analysis of his feelings; but he knew that he had cared for her first on account of the physical perfection which contrasted so astonishingly with the countless deformities in the study of which his life was spent. But one phrase escaped him almost against his will.

'The first time I saw her I felt as though a new world had opened to my ken.'

The divine music of Keats's lines rang through Arthur's remark, and to the Frenchman's mind gave his passion a romantic note that foreboded future tragedy. He sought to dispel the cloud which his fancy had cast upon the most satisfactory of love affairs.

'You are very lucky, my friend. Miss Margaret admires you as much as you adore her. She is never tired of listening to my prosy stories of your childhood in Alexandria, and I'm quite sure that she will make you the most admirable of wives.'

'You can't be more sure than I am,' laughed Arthur.

He looked upon himself as a happy man. He loved Margaret with all his heart, and he was confident in her great affection for him. It was impossible that anything should arise to disturb the pleasant life which they had planned together. His love cast a glamour upon his work, and his work, by contrast, made love the more entrancing.

'We're going to fix the date of our marriage now,' he said. 'I'm buying furniture already.'

'I think only English people could have behaved so oddly as you, in postponing your marriage without reason for two mortal years.'

'You see, Margaret was ten when I first saw her, and only seventeen when I asked her to marry me. She thought she had reason to be grateful to me and would have married me there and then. But I knew she hankered after these two years in Paris, and I didn't feel it was fair to bind her to me till she had seen at least something of the world. And she seemed hardly ready for marriage, she was growing still.'

'Did I not say that you were a matter-of-fact young man?' smiled Dr Porhoët.

'And it's not as if there had been any doubt about our knowing our minds. We both cared, and we had a long time before us. We could afford to wait.'

At that moment a man strolled past them, a big stout fellow, showily dressed in a check suit; and he gravely took off his hat to Dr Porhoët. The doctor smiled and returned the salute.

'Who is your fat friend?' asked Arthur.

'That is a compatriot of yours. His name is Oliver Haddo.'

'Art-student?' inquired Arthur, with the scornful tone he used when referring to those whose walk in life was not so practical as his own.

'Not exactly. I met him a little while ago by chance. When I was getting together the material for my little book on the old alchemists I read a great deal at the library of the Arsenal, which, you may have heard, is singularly rich in all works dealing with the occult sciences.'

Burden's face assumed an expression of amused disdain. He could not understand why Dr Porhoët occupied his leisure with studies so profitless. He had read his book, recently published, on the more famous of the alchemists; and, though forced to admire the profound knowledge upon which it was based, he could not forgive the waste of time which his friend might have expended more usefully on topics of pressing moment.

'Not many people study in that library,' pursued the doctor, 'and I soon knew by sight those who were frequently there. I saw this gentleman every day. He was immersed in strange old books when I arrived early in the morning, and he was reading them still when I left, exhausted. Sometimes it happened that he had the volumes I asked for, and I discovered that he was studying the same subjects as myself. His appearance was extraordinary, but scarcely sympathetic; so, though I fancied that he gave me opportunities to address him, I did not avail myself of them. One day, however, curiously enough, I was looking up some point upon which it seemed impossible to find authorities. The librarian could not help me, and I had given up the search, when this person brought me the very book I needed. I surmised that the librarian had told him of my difficulty. I was very grateful to the stranger. We left together that afternoon, and our kindred studies gave us a common topic of conversation. I found that his reading was extraordinarily wide, and he was able to give me information about works which I had never even heard of. He had the advantage over me that he could apparently read Hebrew as well as Arabic, and he had studied the Kabbalah in the original.'

'And much good it did him, I have no doubt,' said Arthur. 'And what is he by profession?'

Dr Porhoët gave a deprecating smile.

'My dear fellow, I hardly like to tell you, I tremble in every limb at the thought of your unmitigated scorn.'

'Well?'

'You know, Paris is full of queer people. It is the chosen home of every kind of eccentricity. It sounds incredible in this year of grace, but my friend Oliver Haddo claims to be a magician. I think he is quite serious.'

'Silly ass!' answered Arthur with emphasis.

CHAPTER II

MARGARET Dauncey shared a flat near the Boulevard du Montparnasse with Susie Boyd; and it was to meet her that Arthur had arranged to come to tea that afternoon. The young women waited for him in the studio. The kettle was boiling on the stove; cups and *petits fours* stood in readiness on a model stand. Susie looked forward to the meeting with interest. She had heard a good deal of the young man, and knew that the connexion between him and Margaret was not lacking in romance. For years Susie had led the monotonous life of a mistress in a school for young ladies, and had resigned herself to its dreariness for the rest of her life, when a legacy from a distant relation gave her sufficient income to live modestly upon her means. When Margaret, who had been her pupil, came, soon after this, to announce her intention of spending a couple of years in Paris to study art, Susie willingly agreed to accompany her. Since then she had worked industriously at Colarossi's Academy, by no means under the delusion that she had talent, but merely to amuse herself. She refused to surrender the pleasing notion that her environment was slightly wicked. After the toil of many years it relieved her to be earnest in nothing; and she found infinite satisfaction in watching the lives of those around her.

She had a great affection for Margaret, and though her own stock of enthusiasms was run low, she could enjoy thoroughly Margaret's young enchantment in all that was exquisite. She was a plain woman; but there was no envy in her, and she took the keenest pleasure in Margaret's comeliness. It was almost with maternal pride that she watched each year add a new grace to that exceeding beauty. But her common sense was sound, and she took care by good-natured banter to temper the praises which extravagant admirers at the drawing-class lavished upon the handsome girl both for her looks and for her talent. She was proud to think that she would hand over to Arthur Burdon a woman whose character she had helped to form, and whose loveliness she had cultivated with a delicate care.

Susie knew, partly from fragments of letters which Margaret read to her, partly from her conversation, how passionately he adored his bride; and it pleased her to see that Margaret loved him in return with a grateful devotion. The story of this visit to Paris touched her imagination. Margaret was the daughter of a country barrister, with whom Arthur had been in the habit of staying; and when he died, many years after his wife, Arthur found himself the girl's guardian and executor. He sent her to school; saw that she had everything she could possibly want; and when, at seventeen, she told him of her wish to go to Paris and learn drawing, he at once consented. But though he never sought to assume authority over her, he suggested that she should not live alone, and it was on this account that she went to Susie. The preparations for the journey were scarcely made when Margaret discovered by chance that her father had died penniless and she had lived ever since at Arthur's entire expense. When she went to see him with tears in her eyes, and told him what she knew, Arthur was so embarrassed that it was quite absurd.

'But why did you do it?' she asked him. 'Why didn't you tell me?'

'I didn't think it fair to put you under any obligation to me, and I wanted you to feel quite free.'

She cried. She couldn't help it.

'Don't be so silly.' he laughed. 'You owe me nothing at all. I've done very little for you, and what I have done has given me a great deal of pleasure.'

'I don't know how I can ever repay you.'

'Oh, don't say that,' he cried. 'It makes it so much harder for me to say what I want to.'

She looked at him quickly and reddened. Her deep blue eyes were veiled with tears.

'Don't you know that I'd do anything in the world for you?' she cried.

'I don't want you to be grateful to me, because I was hoping—I might ask you to marry me some day.'

Margaret laughed charmingly as she held out her hands.

'You must know that I've been wanting you to do that ever since I was ten.'

She was quite willing to give up her idea of Paris and be married without delay, but Arthur pressed her not to change her plans. At first Margaret vowed it was impossible to go, for she knew now that she had no money, and she could not let her lover pay.

'But what does it matter?' he said. 'It'll give me such pleasure to go on with the small allowance I've been making you. After all, I'm pretty well-to-do. My father left me a moderate income, and I'm making a good deal already by operating.'

'Yes, but it's different now. I didn't know before. I thought I was spending my own money.'

'If I died tomorrow, every penny I have would be yours. We shall be married in two years, and we've known one another much too long to change our minds. I think that our lives are quite irrevocably united.'

Margaret wished very much to spend this time in Paris, and Arthur had made up his mind that in fairness to her they could not marry till she was nineteen. She consulted Susie Boyd, whose common sense prevented her from paying much heed to romantic notions of false delicacy.

'My dear, you'd take his money without scruple if you'd signed your names in a church vestry, and as there's not the least doubt that you'll marry, I don't see why you shouldn't now. Besides, you've got nothing whatever to live on, and you're equally unfitted to be a governess or a typewriter. So it's Hobson's choice, and you'd better put your exquisite sentiments in your pocket.'

Miss Boyd, by one accident after another, had never seen Arthur, but she had heard so much that she looked upon him already as an old friend. She admired him for his talent and strength of character as much as for his loving tenderness to Margaret. She had seen portraits of him, but Margaret said he did not photograph well. She had asked if he was good-looking.

'No, I don't think he is,' answered Margaret, 'but he's very paintable.'

'That is an answer which has the advantage of sounding well and meaning nothing,' smiled Susie.

She believed privately that Margaret's passion for the arts was a not unamiable pose which would disappear when she was happily married. To have half a dozen children was in her mind much more important than to paint pictures. Margaret's gift was by no means despicable, but Susie was not convinced that callous masters would have been so enthusiastic if Margaret had been as plain and old as herself.

Miss Boyd was thirty. Her busy life had not caused the years to pass easily, and she looked older. But she was one of those plain women whose plainness does not matter. A gallant Frenchman had to her face called her a *belle laide,* and, far from denying the justness of his observation, she had been almost flattered. Her mouth was large, and she had little round bright eyes. Her skin was colourless and much disfigured by freckles. Her nose was long and thin. But her face was so kindly, her vivacity so attractive, that no one after ten minutes thought of her ugliness. You noticed then that her hair, though sprinkled with white, was pretty, and that her figure was exceedingly neat. She had good hands, very white and admirably formed, which she waved continually in the fervour of her gesticulation. Now that her means were adequate she took great pains with her dress, and her clothes, though they cost much more than she could afford, were always beautiful. Her taste was so great, her tact so sure, that she was able to make the most of herself. She was determined that if people called her ugly they should be forced in the same breath to confess that she was perfectly gowned. Susie's talent for dress was remarkable, and it was due to her influence that Margaret was arrayed always in the latest mode. The girl's taste inclined to be artistic, and her sense of colour was apt to run away with her discretion. Except for the display of Susie's firmness, she would scarcely have resisted her desire to wear nondescript garments of violent hue. But the older woman expressed herself with decision.

'My dear, you won't draw any the worse for wearing a well-made corset, and to surround your body with bands of grey flannel will certainly not increase your talent.'

'But the fashion is so hideous,' smiled Margaret.

'Fiddlesticks! The fashion is always beautiful. Last year it was beautiful to wear a hat like a pork-pie tipped over your nose; and next year, for all I know, it will be beautiful to wear a bonnet like a sitz-bath at the back of your head. Art has nothing to do with a smart frock, and whether a high-heeled pointed shoe commends itself or not to the painters in the quarter, it's the only thing in which a woman's foot looks really nice.'

Susie Boyd vowed that she would not live with Margaret at all unless she let her see to the buying of her things.

'And when you're married, for heaven's sake ask me to stay with you four times a year, so that I can see after your clothes. You'll never keep your husband's affection if you trust to your own judgment.'

Miss Boyd's reward had come the night before, when Margaret, coming home from dinner with Arthur, had repeated an observation of his.

'How beautifully you're dressed!' he had said. 'I was rather afraid you'd be wearing art-serges.'

'Of course you didn't tell him that I insisted on buying every stitch you'd got on,' cried Susie.

'Yes, I did,' answered Margaret simply. 'I told him I had no taste at all, but that you were responsible for everything.'

'That was the least you could do,' answered Miss Boyd.

But her heart went out to Margaret, for the trivial incident showed once more how frank the girl was. She knew quite well that few of her friends, though many took advantage of her matchless taste, would have made such an admission to the lover who congratulated them on the success of their costume.

There was a knock at the door, and Arthur came in.

'This is the fairy prince,' said Margaret, bringing him to her friend.

'I'm glad to see you in order to thank you for all you've done for Margaret,' he smiled, taking the proffered hand.

Susie remarked that he looked upon her with friendliness, but with a certain vacancy, as though too much engrossed in his beloved really to notice anyone else; and she wondered how to make conversation with a man who was so manifestly absorbed. While Margaret busied herself with the preparations for tea, his eyes followed her movements with a doglike, touching devotion. They travelled from her smiling mouth to her deft hands. It seemed that he had never seen anything so ravishing as the way in which she bent over the kettle. Margaret felt that he was looking at her, and turned round. Their eyes met, and they stood for an appreciable time gazing at one another silently.

'Don't be a pair of perfect idiots,' cried Susie gaily. 'I'm dying for my tea.'

The lovers laughed and reddened. It struck Arthur that he should say something polite.

'I hope you'll show me your sketches afterwards, Miss Boyd. Margaret says they're awfully good.'

'You really needn't think it in the least necessary to show any interest in me,' she replied bluntly.

'She draws the most delightful caricatures,' said Margaret. 'I'll bring you a horror of yourself, which she'll do the moment you leave us.'

'Don't be so spiteful, Margaret.'

Miss Boyd could not help thinking all the same that Arthur Burdon would caricature very well. Margaret was right when she said that he was not handsome, but his clean-shaven face was full of interest to so passionate an observer of her kind. The lovers were silent, and Susie had the conversation to herself. She chattered without pause and had the satisfaction presently of capturing their attention. Arthur seemed to become aware of her presence, and laughed heartily at her burlesque account of their fellow-students at Colarossi's. Meanwhile Susie examined him. He was very tall and very thin. His frame had a Yorkshireman's solidity, and his bones were massive. He missed being ungainly only through the serenity of his self-reliance. He had high cheek-bones and a long, lean face. His nose and mouth were large, and his skin was sallow. But there were two characteristics which fascinated her, an imposing strength of purpose and a singular capacity for suffering. This was a man who knew his mind and was determined to achieve his desire; it refreshed her vastly after the extreme weakness of the young painters with whom of late she had mostly consorted. But those quick dark eyes were able to express an anguish that was hardly tolerable, and the mobile mouth had a nervous intensity which suggested that he might easily suffer the very agonies of woe.

Tea was ready, and Arthur stood up to receive his cup.

'Sit down,' said Margaret. 'I'll bring you everything you want, and I know exactly how much sugar to put in. It pleases me to wait on you.'

With the grace that marked all her movements she walked across the studio, the filled cup in one hand and the plate of cakes in the other. To Susie it seemed that he was overwhelmed with gratitude by Margaret's condescension. His eyes were soft with indescribable tenderness as he took the sweetmeats she gave him. Margaret smiled with happy pride. For all her good-nature, Susie could not prevent the pang that wrung her heart; for she too was capable of love. There was in her a wealth of passionate affection that none had sought to find. None had ever whispered in her ears the charming nonsense that she read in books. She recognised that she had no beauty to help her, but once she had at least the charm of vivacious youth. That was gone now, and the freedom to go into the world had come too late; yet her instinct told her that she was made to be a decent man's wife and the mother of children. She stopped in the middle of her bright chatter, fearing to trust her voice, but Margaret and Arthur were too much occupied to notice that she had ceased to speak. They sat side by side and enjoyed the happiness of one another's company.

'What a fool I am!' thought Susie.

She had learnt long ago that common sense, intelligence, good-nature, and strength of character were unimportant in comparison with a pretty face. She shrugged her shoulders.

'I don't know if you young things realise that it's growing late. If you want us to dine at the Chien Noir, you must leave us now, so that we can make ourselves tidy.'

'Very well,' said Arthur, getting up. 'I'll go back to my hotel and have a wash. We'll meet at half-past seven.'

When Margaret had closed the door on him, she turned to her friend.

'Well, what do you think?' she asked, smiling.

'You can't expect me to form a definite opinion of a man whom I've seen for so short a time.'

'Nonsense!' said Margaret.

Susie hesitated for a moment.

'I think he has an extraordinarily good face,' she said at last gravely. 'I've never seen a man whose honesty of purpose was so transparent.'

Susie Boyd was so lazy that she could never be induced to occupy herself with household matters and, while Margaret put the tea things away, she began to draw the caricature which every new face suggested to her. She made a little sketch of Arthur, abnormally lanky, with a colossal nose, with the wings and the bow and arrow of the God of Love, but it was not half done before she thought it silly. She tore it up with impatience. When Margaret came back, she turned round and looked at her steadily.

'Well?' said the girl, smiling under the scrutiny.

She stood in the middle of the lofty studio. Half-finished canvases leaned with their faces against the wall; pieces of stuff were hung here and there, and photographs of well-known pictures. She had fallen unconsciously into a wonderful pose, and her beauty gave her, notwithstanding her youth, a rare dignity. Susie smiled mockingly.

'You look like a Greek goddess in a Paris frock,' she said.

'What have you to say to me?' asked Margaret, divining from the searching look that something was in her friend's mind.

Susie stood up and went to her.

'You know, before I'd seen him I hoped with all my heart that he'd make you happy. Notwithstanding all you'd told me of him, I was afraid. I knew he was much older than you. He was the first man you'd ever known. I could scarcely bear to entrust you to him in case you were miserable.'

'I don't think you need have any fear.'

'But now I hope with all my heart that you'll make *him* happy. It's not you I'm frightened for now, but him.'

Margaret did not answer; she could not understand what Susie meant.

'I've never seen anyone with such a capacity for wretchedness as that man has. I don't think you can conceive how desperately he might suffer. Be very careful, Margaret, and be very good to him, for you have the power to make him more unhappy than any human being should be.'

'Oh, but I want him to be happy,' cried Margaret vehemently. 'You know that I owe everything to him. I'd do all I could to make him happy, even if I had to sacrifice myself. But I can't sacrifice myself, because I love him so much that all I do is pure delight.'

Her eyes filled with tears and her voice broke. Susie, with a little laugh that was half hysterical, kissed her.

'My dear, for heaven's sake don't cry! You know I can't bear people who weep, and if he sees your eyes red, he'll never forgive me.'

CHAPTER III

THE Chien Noir, where Susie Boyd and Margaret generally dined, was the most charming restaurant in the quarter. Downstairs was a public room, where all and sundry devoured their food, for the little place had a reputation for good cooking combined with cheapness; and the *patron,* a retired horse-dealer who had taken to victualling in order to build up a business for his son, was a cheery soul whose loud-voiced friendliness attracted custom. But on the first floor was a narrow room, with three tables arranged in a horse-shoe, which was reserved for a small party of English or American painters and a few Frenchmen with their wives. At least, they were so nearly wives, and their manner had such a matrimonial respectability, that Susie, when first she and Margaret were introduced into this society, judged it would be vulgar to turn up her nose. She held that it was prudish to insist upon the conventions of Notting Hill in the Boulevard de Montparnasse. The young women who had thrown in their lives with these painters were modest in demeanour and quiet in dress. They were model housewives, who had preserved their self-respect notwithstanding a difficult position, and did not look upon their relation with less seriousness because they had not muttered a few words before *Monsieur le Maire.*

The room was full when Arthur Burdon entered, but Margaret had kept him an empty seat between herself and Miss Boyd. Everyone was speaking at once, in French, at the top of his voice, and a furious argument was proceeding on the merit of the later

Impressionists. Arthur sat down, and was hurriedly introduced to a lanky youth, who sat on the other side of Margaret. He was very tall, very thin, very fair. He wore a very high collar and very long hair, and held himself like an exhausted lily.

'He always reminds me of an Aubrey Beardsley that's been dreadfully smudged,' said Susie in an undertone. 'He's a nice, kind creature, but his name is Jagson. He has virtue and industry. I haven't seen any of his work, but he has absolutely no talent.'

'How do you know, if you've not seen his pictures?' asked Arthur.

'Oh, it's one of our conventions here that nobody has talent,' laughed Susie. 'We suffer one another personally, but we have no illusions about the value of our neighbour's work.'

'Tell me who everyone is.'

'Well, look at that little bald man in the corner. That is Warren.'

Arthur looked at the man she pointed out. He was a small person, with a pate as shining as a billiard-ball, and a pointed beard. He had protruding, brilliant eyes.

'Hasn't he had too much to drink?' asked Arthur frigidly.

'Much,' answered Susie promptly, 'but he's always in that condition, and the further he gets from sobriety the more charming he is. He's the only man in this room of whom you'll never hear a word of evil. The strange thing is that he's very nearly a great painter. He has the most fascinating sense of colour in the world, and the more intoxicated he is, the more delicate and beautiful is his painting. Sometimes, after more than the usual number of *apéritifs,* he will sit down in a café to do a sketch, with his hand so shaky that he can hardly hold a brush; he has to wait for a favourable moment, and then he makes a jab at the panel. And the immoral thing is that each of these little jabs is lovely. He's the most delightful interpreter of Paris I know, and when you've seen his sketches—he's done hundreds, of unimaginable grace and feeling and distinction—you can never see Paris in the same way again.'

The little maid who looked busily after the varied wants of the customers stood in front of them to receive Arthur's order. She was a hard-visaged creature of mature age, but she looked neat in her black dress and white cap; and she had a motherly way of attending to these people, with a capacious smile of her large mouth which was full of charm.

'I don't mind what I eat,' said Arthur. 'Let Margaret order my dinner for me.'

'It would have been just as good if I had ordered it,' laughed Susie.

They began a lively discussion with Marie as to the merits of the various dishes, and it was only interrupted by Warren's hilarious expostulations.

'Marie, I precipitate myself at your feet, and beg you to bring me a *poule au riz.*'

'Oh, but give me one moment, *monsieur*,' said the maid.

'Do not pay any attention to that gentleman. His morals are detestable, and he only seeks to lead you from the narrow path of virtue.'

Arthur protested that on the contrary the passion of hunger occupied at that moment his heart to the exclusion of all others.

'Marie, you no longer love me,' cried Warren. There was a time when you did not look so coldly upon me when I ordered a bottle of white wine.'

The rest of the party took up his complaint, and all besought her not to show too hard a heart to the bald and rubicund painter.

'Mais si, je vous aime, Monsieur Warren,' she cried, laughing, *'Je vous aime tous, tous.'*

She ran downstairs, amid the shouts of men and women, to give her orders.

'The other day the Chien Noir was the scene of a tragedy,' said Susie. 'Marie broke off relations with her lover, who is a waiter at Lavenue's, and would have no reconciliation. He waited till he had a free evening, and then came to the room downstairs and ordered dinner. Of course, she was obliged to wait on him, and as she brought him each dish he expostulated with her, and they mingled their tears.'

'She wept in floods,' interrupted a youth with neatly brushed hair and fat nose. 'She wept all over our food, and we ate it salt with tears. We besought her not to yield; except for our encouragement she would have gone back to him; and he beats her.'

Marie appeared again, with no signs now that so short a while ago romance had played a game with her, and brought the dishes that had been ordered. Susie seized once more upon Arthur Burdon's attention.

'Now please look at the man who is sitting next to Mr Warren.'

Arthur saw a tall, dark fellow with strongly-marked features, untidy hair, and a ragged black moustache.

'That is Mr O'Brien, who is an example of the fact that strength of will and an earnest purpose cannot make a painter. He's a failure, and he knows it, and the bitterness has warped his soul. If you listen to him, you'll hear every painter of eminence come under his lash. He can forgive nobody who's successful, and he never acknowledges merit in anyone till he's safely dead and buried.'

'He must be a cheerful companion,' answered Arthur. 'And who is the stout old lady by his side, with the flaunting hat?'

'That is the mother of Madame Rouge, the little palefaced woman sitting next to her. She is the mistress of Rouge, who does all the illustrations for *La Semaine.* At first it rather tickled me that the old lady should call him *mon gendre,* my son-in-law, and take the irregular union of her daughter with such a noble unconcern for propriety; but now it seems quite natural.'

The mother of Madame Rouge had the remains of beauty, and she sat bolt upright, picking the leg of a chicken with a dignified gesture. Arthur looked away quickly, for, catching his eye she gave him an amorous glance. Rouge had more the appearance of a prosperous tradesman than of an artist; but he carried on with O'Brien, whose French was perfect, an argument on the merits of Cézanne. To one he was a great master and to the other an impudent charlatan. Each hotly repeated his opinion, as though the mere fact of saying the same thing several times made it more convincing.

'Next to me is Madame Meyer,' proceeded Susie. 'She was a governess in Poland, but she was much too pretty to remain one, and now she lives with the landscape painter who is by her side.'

Arthur's eyes followed her words and rested on a clean-shaven man with a large quantity of grey, curling hair. He had a handsome face of a deliberately aesthetic type and was very elegantly dressed. His manner and his conversation had the flamboyance of the romantic thirties. He talked in flowing periods with an air of finality, and what he said was no less just than obvious. The gay little lady who shared his fortunes listened to his wisdom with an admiration that plainly flattered him.

Miss Boyd had described everyone to Arthur except young Raggles, who painted still life with a certain amount of skill, and Clayson, the American sculptor. Raggles stood for rank and fashion at the Chien Noir. He was very smartly dressed in a horsey way, and he walked with bowlegs, as though he spent most of his time in the saddle. He alone used scented pomade upon his neat smooth hair. His chief distinction was a great-coat he wore, with a scarlet lining; and Warren, whose memory for names was defective, could only recall him by that peculiarity. But it was understood that he knew duchesses in fashionable streets, and occasionally dined with them in solemn splendour.

Clayson had a vinous nose and a tedious habit of saying brilliant things. With his twinkling eyes, red cheeks, and fair, pointed beard, he looked exactly like a Franz Hals; but he was dressed like the caricature of a Frenchman in a comic paper. He spoke English with a Parisian accent.

Miss Boyd was beginning to tear him gaily limb from limb, when the door was flung open, and a large person entered. He threw off his cloak with a dramatic gesture.

'Marie, disembarrass me of this coat of frieze. Hang my sombrero upon a convenient peg.'

He spoke execrable French, but there was a grandiloquence about his vocabulary which set everyone laughing.

'Here is somebody I don't know,' said Susie.

'But I do, at least, by sight,' answered Burdon. He leaned over to Dr Porhoët who was sitting opposite, quietly eating his dinner and enjoying the nonsense which everyone talked. 'Is not that your magician?'

'Oliver Haddo,' said Dr Porhoët, with a little nod of amusement.

The new arrival stood at the end of the room with all eyes upon him. He threw himself into an attitude of command and remained for a moment perfectly still.

'You look as if you were posing, Haddo,' said Warren huskily.

'He couldn't help doing that if he tried,' laughed Clayson.

Oliver Haddo slowly turned his glance to the painter.

'I grieve to see, O most excellent Warren, that the ripe juice of the *aperitif* has glazed your sparkling eye.'

'Do you mean to say I'm drunk, sir?'

'In one gross, but expressive, word, drunk.'

The painter grotesquely flung himself back in his chair as though he had been struck a blow, and Haddo looked steadily at Clayson.

'How often have I explained to you, O Clayson, that your deplorable lack of education precludes you from the brilliancy to which you aspire?'

For an instant Oliver Haddo resumed his effective pose; and Susie, smiling, looked at him. He was a man of great size, two or three inches more than six feet high; but the most noticeable thing about him was a vast obesity. His paunch was of imposing dimensions. His face was large and fleshy. He had thrown himself into the arrogant attitude of Velasquez's portrait of Del Borro in the Museum of Berlin; and his countenance bore of set purpose the same contemptuous smile. He advanced and shook hands with Dr Porhoët.

'Hail, brother wizard! I greet in you, if not a master, at least a student not unworthy my esteem.'

Susie was convulsed with laughter at his pompousness, and he turned to her with the utmost gravity.

'Madam, your laughter is more soft in mine ears than the singing of Bulbul in a Persian garden.'

Dr Porhoët interposed with introductions. The magician bowed solemnly as he was in turn made known to Susie Boyd, and Margaret, and Arthur Burdon. He held out his hand to the grim Irish painter.

'Well, my O'Brien, have you been mixing as usual the waters of bitterness with the thin claret of Bordeaux?'

'Why don't you sit down and eat your dinner?' returned the other, gruffly.

'Ah, my dear fellow, I wish I could drive the fact into this head of yours that rudeness is not synonymous with wit. I shall not have lived in vain if I teach you in time to realize that the rapier of irony is more effective an instrument than the bludgeon of insolence.'

O'Brien reddened with anger, but could not at once find a retort, and Haddo passed on to that faded, harmless youth who sat next to Margaret.

'Do my eyes deceive me, or is this the Jagson whose name in its inanity is so appropriate to the bearer? I am eager to know if you still devote upon the ungrateful arts talents which were more profitably employed upon haberdashery.'

The unlucky creature, thus brutally attacked, blushed feebly without answering, and Haddo went on to the Frenchman, Meyer as more worthy of his mocking.

'I'm afraid my entrance interrupted you in a discourse. Was it the celebrated harangue on the greatness of Michelangelo, or was it the searching analysis of the art of Wagner?'

'We were just going,' said Meyer, getting up with a frown.

'I am desolated to lose the pearls of wisdom that habitually fall from your cultivated lips,' returned Haddo, as he politely withdrew Madame Meyer's chair.

He sat down with a smile.

'I saw the place was crowded, and with Napoleonic instinct decided that I could only make room by insulting somebody. It is cause for congratulation that my gibes, which Raggles, a foolish youth, mistakes for wit, have caused the disappearance of a person who lives in open sin; thereby vacating two seats, and allowing me to eat a humble meal with ample room for my elbows.'

Marie brought him the bill of fare, and he looked at it gravely.

'I will have a vanilla ice, O well-beloved, and a wing of a tender chicken, a fried sole, and some excellent pea-soup.'

'Bien, un potage, une sole, one chicken, and an ice.'

'But why should you serve them in that order rather than in the order I gave you?'

Marie and the two Frenchwomen who were still in the room broke into exclamations at this extravagance, but Oliver Haddo waved his fat hand.

'I shall start with the ice, O Marie, to cool the passion with which your eyes inflame me, and then without hesitation I will devour the wing of a chicken in order to sustain myself against your smile. I shall then proceed to a fresh sole, and with the pea-soup I will finish a not unsustaining meal.'

Having succeeded in capturing the attention of everyone in the room, Oliver Haddo proceeded to eat these dishes in the order he had named. Margaret and Burdon watched him with scornful eyes, but Susie, who was not revolted by the vanity which sought to attract notice, looked at him curiously. He was clearly not old, though his corpulence added to his apparent age. His features were good, his ears small, and his nose delicately shaped. He had big teeth, but they were white and even. His mouth was large, with heavy moist lips. He had the neck of a bullock. His dark, curling hair had retreated from the forehead and temples in such a way as to give his clean-shaven face a disconcerting nudity. The baldness of his crown was vaguely like a tonsure. He had the look of a very wicked, sensual priest. Margaret, stealing a glance at him as he ate, on a sudden violently shuddered; he affected her with an uncontrollable dislike. He lifted his eyes slowly, and she looked away, blushing as though she had been taken in some indiscretion. These eyes were the most curious thing about him. They were not large, but an exceedingly pale blue, and they looked at you in a way that was singularly embarrassing. At first Susie could not discover in what precisely their peculiarity lay, but in a moment she found out: the eyes of most persons converge when they look at you, but Oliver Haddo's, naturally or by a habit he had acquired for effect, remained parallel. It gave the impression that he looked straight through you and saw the wall beyond. It was uncanny. But another strange thing about him was the impossibility of telling whether he was serious. There was a mockery in that queer glance, a sardonic smile upon the mouth, which made you hesitate how to take his outrageous utterances. It was irritating to be uncertain whether, while you were laughing at him, he was not really enjoying an elaborate joke at your expense.

His presence cast an unusual chill upon the party. The French members got up and left. Warren reeled out with O'Brien, whose uncouth sarcasms were no match for Haddo's bitter gibes. Raggles put on his coat with the scarlet lining and went out with the tall Jagson, who smarted still under Haddo's insolence. The American sculptor paid his bill silently. When he was at the door, Haddo stopped him.

'You have modelled lions at the Jardin des Plantes, my dear Clayson. Have you ever hunted them on their native plains?'

'No, I haven't.'

Clayson did not know why Haddo asked the question, but he bristled with incipient wrath.

'Then you have not seen the jackal, gnawing at a dead antelope, scamper away in terror when the King of Beasts stalked down to make his meal.'

Clayson slammed the door behind him. Haddo was left with Margaret, and Arthur Burdon, Dr Porhoët, and Susie. He smiled quietly.

'By the way, are *you* a lion-hunter?' asked Susie flippantly.

He turned on her his straight uncanny glance.

'I have no equal with big game. I have shot more lions than any man alive. I think Jules Gérard, whom the French of the nineteenth century called *Le Tueur de Lions,* may have been fit to compare with me, but I can call to mind no other.'

This statement, made with the greatest calm, caused a moment of silence. Margaret stared at him with amazement.

'You suffer from no false modesty,' said Arthur Burdon.

'False modesty is a sign of ill-breeding, from which my birth amply protects me.'

Dr Porhoët looked up with a smile of irony.

'I wish Mr Haddo would take this opportunity to disclose to us the mystery of his birth and family. I have a suspicion that, like the immortal Cagliostro, he was born of unknown but noble parents, and educated secretly in Eastern palaces.'

'In my origin I am more to be compared with Denis Zachaire or with Raymond Lully. My ancestor, George Haddo, came to Scotland in the suite of Anne of Denmark, and when James I, her consort, ascended the English throne, he was granted the estates in Staffordshire which I still possess. My family has formed alliances with the most noble blood of England, and the Merestons, the Parnabys, the Hollingtons, have been proud to give their daughters to my house.'

'Those are facts which can be verified in works of reference,' said Arthur dryly.

'They can,' said Oliver.

'And the Eastern palaces in which your youth was spent, and the black slaves who waited on you, and the bearded sheikhs who imparted to you secret knowledge?' cried Dr Porhoët.

'I was educated at Eton, and I left Oxford in 1896.'

'Would you mind telling me at what college you were?' said Arthur.

'I was at the House.'

'Then you must have been there with Frank Hurrell.'

'Now assistant physician at St Luke's Hospital. He was one of my most intimate friends.'

'I'll write and ask him about you.'

'I'm dying to know what you did with all the lions you slaughtered,' said Susie Boyd.

The man's effrontery did not exasperate her as it obviously exasperated Margaret and Arthur. He amused her, and she was anxious to make him talk.

'They decorate the floors of Skene, which is the name of my place in Staffordshire.' He paused for a moment to light a cigar. 'I am the only man alive who has killed three lions with three successive shots.'

'I should have thought you could have demolished them by the effects of your oratory,' said Arthur.

Oliver leaned back and placed his two large hands on the table.

'Burkhardt, a German with whom I was shooting, was down with fever and could not stir from his bed. I was awakened one night by the uneasiness of my oxen, and I heard the roaring of lions close at hand. I took my carbine and came out of my tent. There was only the meagre light of the moon. I walked alone, for I knew natives could be of no use to me. Presently I came upon the carcass of an antelope, half-consumed, and I made up my mind to wait for the return of the lions. I hid myself among the boulders twenty paces from the prey. All about me was the immensity of Africa and the silence. I waited, motionless, hour after hour, till the dawn was nearly at hand. At last three lions appeared over a rock. I had noticed, the day before, spoor of a lion and two females.'

'May I ask how you could distinguish the sex?' asked Arthur, incredulously.

'The prints of a lion's fore feet are disproportionately larger than those of the hind feet. The fore feet and hind feet of the lioness are nearly the same size.'

'Pray go on,' said Susie.

'They came into full view, and in the dim light, as they stood chest on, they appeared as huge as the strange beasts of the Arabian tales. I aimed at the lioness which stood nearest to me and fired. Without a sound, like a bullock felled at one blow, she dropped. The lion gave vent to a sonorous roar. Hastily I slipped another cartridge in my rifle. Then I became conscious that he had seen me. He lowered his head, and his crest was erect. His lifted tail was twitching, his lips were drawn back from the red gums, and I saw his great white fangs. Living fire flashed from his eyes, and he growled incessantly. Then he advanced a few steps, his head held low; and his eyes were fixed on mine with a look of rage. Suddenly he jerked up his tail, and when a lion does this he charges. I got a quick sight on his chest and fired. He reared up on his hind legs, roaring loudly and clawing at the air, and fell back dead. One lioness remained, and through the smoke I saw her spring to her feet and rush towards me. Escape was impossible, for behind me were high boulders that I could not climb. She came on with hoarse, coughing grunts, and with desperate courage I fired my remaining barrel. I missed her clean. I took one step backwards in the hope of getting a cartridge into my rifle, and fell, scarcely two lengths in front of the furious beast. She missed me. I owed my safety to that fall. And then suddenly I found that she had collapsed. I had hit her after all. My bullet went clean through her heart, but the spring had carried her forwards. When I scrambled to my feet I found that she was dying. I walked back to my camp and ate a capital breakfast.'

Oliver Haddo's story was received with astonished silence. No one could assert that it was untrue, but he told it with a grandiloquence that carried no conviction. Arthur would have wagered a considerable sum that there was no word of truth in it. He had never met a person of this kind before, and could not understand what pleasure there might be in the elaborate invention of improbable adventures.

'You are evidently very brave,' he said.

'To follow a wounded lion into thick cover is probably the most dangerous proceeding in the world,' said Haddo calmly. 'It calls for the utmost coolness and for iron nerve.'

The answer had an odd effect on Arthur. He gave Haddo a rapid glance, and was seized suddenly with uncontrollable laughter. He leaned back in his chair and roared. His hilarity affected the others, and they broke into peal upon peal of laughter. Oliver watched them gravely. He seemed neither disconcerted nor surprised. When Arthur recovered himself, he found Haddo's singular eyes fixed on him.

'Your laughter reminds me of the crackling of thorns under a pot,' he said.

Haddo looked round at the others. Though his gaze preserved its fixity, his lips broke into a queer, sardonic smile.

'It must be plain even to the feeblest intelligence that a man can only command the elementary spirits if he is without fear. A capricious mind can never rule the sylphs, nor a fickle disposition the undines.'

Arthur stared at him with amazement. He did not know what on earth the man was talking about. Haddo paid no heed.

'But if the adept is active, pliant, and strong, the whole world will be at his command. He will pass through the storm and no rain shall fall upon his head. The wind will not displace a single fold of his garment. He will go through fire and not be burned.'

Dr Porhoët ventured upon an explanation of these cryptic utterances.

'These ladies are unacquainted with the mysterious beings of whom you speak, *cher ami*. They should know that during the Middle Ages imagination peopled the four elements with intelligences, normally unseen, some of which were friendly to man and others hostile. They were thought to be powerful and conscious of their power, though at the same time they were profoundly aware that they possessed no soul. Their life depended upon the continuance of some natural object, and hence for them there could be no immortality. They must return eventually to the abyss of unending night, and the darkness of death afflicted them always. But it was thought that in the same manner as man by his union with God had won a spark of divinity, so might the sylphs, gnomes, undines, and salamanders by an alliance with man partake of his immortality. And many of their women, whose beauty was more than human, gained a human soul by loving one of the race of men. But the reverse occurred also, and often a love-sick youth lost his immortality because he left the haunts of his kind to dwell with the fair, soulless denizens of the running streams or of the forest airs.'

'I didn't know that you spoke figuratively,' said Arthur to Oliver Haddo.

The other shrugged his shoulders.

'What else is the world than a figure? Life itself is but a symbol. You must be a wise man if you can tell us what is reality.'

'When you begin to talk of magic and mysticism I confess that I am out of my depth.'

'Yet magic is no more than the art of employing consciously invisible means to produce visible effects. Will, love, and imagination are magic powers that everyone possesses; and whoever knows how to develop them to their fullest extent is a magician. Magic has but one dogma, namely, that the seen is the measure of the unseen.'

'Will you tell us what the powers are that the adept possesses?'

'They are enumerated in a Hebrew manuscript of the sixteenth century, which is in my possession. The privileges of him who holds in his right hand the Keys of Solomon and in his left the Branch of the Blossoming Almond are twenty-one. He beholds God face to face without dying, and converses intimately with the Seven Genii who command the celestial army. He is superior to every affliction and to every fear. He reigns with all heaven and is served by all hell. He holds the secret of the resurrection of the dead, and the key of immortality.'

'If you possess even these you have evidently the most varied attainments,' said Arthur ironically.

'Everyone can make game of the unknown,' retorted Haddo, with a shrug of his massive shoulders.

Arthur did not answer. He looked at Haddo curiously. He asked himself whether he believed seriously these preposterous things, or whether he was amusing himself in an elephantine way at their expense. His manner was earnest, but there was an odd expression about the mouth, a hard twinkle of the eyes, which seemed to belie it. Susie was vastly entertained. It diverted her enormously to hear occult matters discussed with apparent gravity in this prosaic tavern. Dr Porhoët broke the silence.

'Arago, after whom has been named a neighbouring boulevard, declared that doubt was a proof of modesty, which has rarely interfered with the progress of science. But one cannot say the same of incredulity, and he that uses the word impossible outside of pure mathematics is lacking in prudence. It should be remembered that Lactantius proclaimed belief in the existence of antipodes inane, and Saint Augustine of Hippo added that in any case there could be no question of inhabited lands.'

'That sounds as if you were not quite sceptical, dear doctor,' said Miss Boyd.

'In my youth I believed nothing, for science had taught me to distrust even the evidence of my five senses,' he replied, with a shrug of the shoulders. 'But I have seen many things in the East which are inexplicable by the known processes of science. Mr Haddo has given you one definition of magic, and I will give you another. It may be described merely as the intelligent utilization of forces which are unknown, contemned, or misunderstood of the vulgar. The young man who settles in the East sneers at the ideas of magic which surround him, but I know not what there is in the atmosphere that saps his unbelief. When he has sojourned for some years among Orientals, he comes insensibly to share the opinion of many sensible men that perhaps there is something in it after all.'

Arthur Burdon made a gesture of impatience.

'I cannot imagine that, however much I lived in Eastern countries, I could believe anything that had the whole weight of science against it. If there were a word of truth in anything Haddo says, we should be unable to form any reasonable theory of the universe.'

'For a scientific man you argue with singular fatuity,' said Haddo icily, and his manner had an offensiveness which was intensely irritating. 'You should be aware that science, dealing only with the general, leaves out of consideration the individual cases that contradict the enormous majority. Occasionally the heart is on the right side of the body, but you would not on that account ever put your stethoscope in any other than the usual spot. It is possible that under certain conditions the law of gravity does not apply, yet you will conduct your life under the conviction that it does so invariably. Now, there are some of us who choose to deal only with these exceptions to the common run. The dull man who plays at Monte Carlo puts his money on the colours, and generally black or red turns up; but now and then zero appears, and he loses. But we, who have backed zero all the time, win many times our stake. Here and there you will find men whose imagination raises them above the humdrum of mankind. They are willing to lose their all if only they have chance of a great prize. Is it nothing not only to know the future, as did the prophets of old, but by making it to force the very gates of the unknown?'

Suddenly the bantering gravity with which he spoke fell away from him. A singular light came into his eyes, and his voice was hoarse. Now at last they saw that he was serious.

'What should you know of that lust for great secrets which consumes me to the bottom of my soul!'

'Anyhow, I'm perfectly delighted to meet a magician,' cried Susie gaily.

'Ah, call me not that,' he said, with a flourish of his fat hands, regaining immediately his portentous flippancy. 'I would be known rather as the Brother of the Shadow.'

'I should have thought you could be only a very distant relation of anything so unsubstantial,' said Arthur, with a laugh.

Oliver's face turned red with furious anger. His strange blue eyes grew cold with hatred, and he thrust out his scarlet lips till he had the ruthless expression of a Nero. The gibe at his obesity had caught him on the raw. Susie feared that he would make so insulting a reply that a quarrel must ensure.

'Well, really, if we want to go to the fair we must start,' she said quickly. 'And Marie is dying to be rid of us.'

They got up, and clattered down the stairs into the street.

CHAPTER IV

THEY came down to the busy, narrow street which led into the Boulevard du Montparnasse. Electric trams passed through it with harsh ringing of bells, and people surged along the pavements.

The fair to which they were going was held at the Lion de Belfort, not more than a mile away, and Arthur hailed a cab. Susie told the driver where they wanted to be set down. She noticed that Haddo, who was waiting for them to start, put his hand on the horse's neck. On a sudden, for no apparent reason, it began to tremble. The trembling passed through the body and down its limbs till it shook from head to foot as though it had the staggers. The coachman jumped off his box and held the wretched creature's head. Margaret and Susie got out. It was a horribly painful sight. The horse seemed not to suffer from actual pain, but from an extraordinary fear. Though she knew not why, an idea came to Susie.

'Take your hand away, Mr Haddo,' she said sharply.

He smiled, and did as she bade him. At the same moment the trembling began to decrease, and in a moment the poor old cab-horse was in its usual state. It seemed a little frightened still, but otherwise recovered.

'I wonder what the deuce was the matter with it,' said Arthur.

Oliver Haddo looked at him with the blue eyes that seemed to see right through people, and then, lifting his hat, walked away. Susie turned suddenly to Dr Porhoët.

'Do you think he could have made the horse do that? It came immediately he put his hand on its neck, and it stopped as soon as he took it away.'

'Nonsense!' said Arthur.

'It occurred to me that he was playing some trick,' said Dr Porhoët gravely. 'An odd thing happened once when he came to see me. I have two Persian cats, which are the most properly conducted of all their tribe. They spend their days in front of my fire, meditating on the problems of metaphysics. But as soon as he came in they started up, and their fur stood right on end. Then they began to run madly round and round the room, as though the victims of uncontrollable terror. I opened the door, and they bolted out. I have never been able to understand exactly what took place.'

Margaret shuddered.

'I've never met a man who filled me with such loathing,' she said. 'I don't know what there is about him that frightens me. Even now I feel his eyes fixed strangely upon me. I hope I shall never see him again.'

Arthur gave a little laugh and pressed her hand. She would not let his go, and he felt that she was trembling. Personally, he had no doubt about the matter. He would have no trifling with credibility. Either Haddo believed things that none but a lunatic could, or else he was a charlatan who sought to attract attention by his extravagances. In any case he was contemptible. It was certain, at all events, that neither he nor anyone else could work miracles.

'I'll tell you what I'll do,' said Arthur. 'If he really knows Frank Hurrell I'll find out all about him. I'll drop a note to Hurrell tonight and ask him to tell me anything he can.'

'I wish you would,' answered Susie, 'because he interests the enormously. There's no place like Paris for meeting queer folk. Sooner or later you run across persons who believe in everything. There's no form of religion, there's no eccentricity or enormity, that hasn't its votaries. Just think what a privilege it is to come upon a man in the twentieth century who honestly believes in the occult.'

'Since I have been occupied with these matters, I have come across strange people,' said Dr Porhoët quietly, 'but I agree with Miss Boyd that Oliver Haddo is the most extraordinary. For one thing, it is impossible to know how much he really believes what he says. Is he an impostor or a madman? Does he deceive himself, or is he laughing up his sleeve at the folly of those who take him seriously? I cannot tell. All I know is that he has travelled widely and is acquainted with many tongues. He has a minute knowledge of alchemical literature, and there is no book I have heard of, dealing with the black arts, which he does not seem to know.' Dr Porhoët shook his head slowly. 'I should not care to dogmatize about this man. I know I shall outrage the feelings of my friend Arthur, but I am bound to confess it would not surprise me to learn that he possessed powers by which he was able to do things seemingly miraculous.'

Arthur was prevented from answering by their arrival at the Lion de Belfort.

The fair was in full swing. The noise was deafening. Steam bands thundered out the popular tunes of the moment, and to their din merry-go-rounds were turning. At the door of booths men vociferously importuned the passers-by to enter. From the shooting saloons came a continual spatter of toy rifles. Linking up these sounds, were the voices of the serried crowd that surged along the central avenue, and the shuffle of their myriad feet. The night was lurid with acetylene torches, which flamed with a dull unceasing roar. It was a curious sight, half gay, half sordid. The throng seemed bent with a kind of savagery upon amusement, as though, resentful of the weary round of daily labour, it sought by a desperate effort to be merry.

The English party with Dr Porhoët, mildly ironic, had scarcely entered before they were joined by Oliver Haddo. He was indifferent to the plain fact that they did not want his company. He attracted attention, for his appearance and his manner were remarkable, and Susie noticed that he was pleased to see people point him out to one another. He wore a Spanish cloak, the *capa,* and he flung the red and green velvet of its lining gaudily over his shoulder. He had a large soft hat. His height was great, though less noticeable on account of his obesity, and he towered over the puny multitude.

They looked idly at the various shows, resisting the melodramas, the circuses, the exhibitions of eccentricity, which loudly clamoured for their custom. Presently they came to a man who was cutting silhouettes in black paper, and Haddo insisted on posing for him. A little crowd collected and did not spare their jokes at his singular appearance. He threw himself into his favourite attitude of proud command. Margaret wished to take the opportunity of leaving him, but Miss Boyd insisted on staying.

'He's the most ridiculous creature I've ever seen in my life,' she whispered. 'I wouldn't let him out of my sight for worlds.'

When the silhouette was done, he presented it with a low bow to Margaret.

'I implore your acceptance of the only portrait now in existence of Oliver Haddo,' he said.

'Thank you,' she answered frigidly.

She was unwilling to take it, but had not the presence of mind to put him off by a jest, and would not be frankly rude. As though certain she set much store on it, he placed it carefully in an envelope. They walked on and suddenly came to a canvas booth on which was an Eastern name. Roughly painted on sail-cloth was a picture of an Arab charming snakes, and above were certain words in Arabic. At the entrance, a native sat cross-legged, listlessly beating a drum. When he saw them stop, he addressed them in bad French.

'Does not this remind you of the turbid Nile, Dr Porhoët?' said Haddo. 'Let us go in and see what the fellow has to show.'

Dr Porhoët stepped forward and addressed the charmer, who brightened on hearing the language of his own country.

'He is an Egyptian from Assiut,' said the doctor.

'I will buy tickets for you all,' said Haddo.

He held up the flap that gave access to the booth, and Susie went in. Margaret and Arthur Burdon, somewhat against their will, were obliged to follow. The native closed the opening behind them. They found themselves in a dirty little tent, ill-lit by two smoking lamps; a dozen stools were placed in a circle on the bare ground. In one corner sat a fellah woman, motionless, in ample robes of dingy black. Her face was hidden by a long veil, which was held in place by a queer ornament of brass in the middle of the forehead, between the eyes. These alone were visible, large and sombre, and the lashes were darkened with kohl: her fingers were brightly stained with henna. She moved slightly as the visitors entered, and the man gave her his drum. She began to rub it with her hands, curiously, and made a droning sound, which was odd and mysterious. There was a peculiar odour in the place, so that Dr Porhoët was for a moment transported to the evil-smelling streets of Cairo. It was an acrid mixture of incense, of attar of roses, with every imaginable putrescence. It choked the two women, and Susie asked for a cigarette. The native grinned when he heard the English tongue. He showed a row of sparkling and beautiful teeth.

'My name Mohammed,' he said. 'Me show serpents to Sirdar Lord Kitchener. Wait and see. Serpents very poisonous.'

He was dressed in a long blue gabardine, more suited to the sunny banks of the Nile than to a fair in Paris, and its colour could hardly be seen for dirt. On his head was the national tarboosh.

A rug lay at one side of the tent, and from under it he took a goatskin sack. He placed it on the ground in the middle of the circle formed by the seats and crouched down on his haunches. Margaret shuddered, for the uneven surface of the sack moved strangely. He opened the mouth of it. The woman in the corner listlessly droned away on the drum, and occasionally uttered a barbaric cry. With a leer and a flash of his bright teeth, the Arab thrust his hand into the sack and rummaged as a man would rummage in a sack of corn. He drew out a long, writhing snake. He placed it on the ground and for a moment waited, then he passed his hand over it: it became immediately as rigid as a bar of iron. Except that the eyes, the cruel eyes, were open still, there might have been no life in it.

'Look,' said Haddo. 'That is the miracle which Moses did before Pharaoh.'

Then the Arab took a reed instrument, not unlike the pipe which Pan in the hills of Greece played to the dryads, and he piped a weird, monotonous tune. The stiffness broke away from the snake suddenly, and it lifted its head and raised its long body till it stood almost on the tip of its tail, and it swayed slowly to and fro.

Oliver Haddo seemed extraordinarily fascinated. He leaned forward with eager face, and his unnatural eyes were fixed on the charmer with an indescribable expression. Margaret drew back in terror.

'You need not be frightened,' said Arthur. 'These people only work with animals whose fangs have been extracted.'

Oliver Haddo looked at him before answering. He seemed to consider each time what sort of man this was to whom he spoke.

'A man is only a snake-charmer because, without recourse to medicine, he is proof against the fangs of the most venomous serpents.'

'Do you think so?' said Arthur.

'I saw the most noted charmer of Madras die two hours after he had been bitten by a cobra,' said Haddo. 'I had heard many tales of his prowess, and one evening asked a friend to take me to him. He was out when we arrived, but we waited, and presently, accompanied by some friends, he came. We told him what we wanted. He had been at a marriage-feast and was drunk. But he sent for his snakes, and forthwith showed us marvels which this man has never heard of. At last he took a great cobra from his sack and began to handle it. Suddenly it darted at his chin and bit him. It made two marks like pin-points. The juggler started back.

'"I am a dead man," he said.

'Those about him would have killed the cobra, but he prevented them.

'"Let the creature live," he said. "It may be of service to others of my trade. To me it can be of no other use. Nothing can save me."

'His friends and the jugglers, his fellows, gathered round him and placed him in a chair. In two hours he was dead. In his drunkenness he had forgotten a portion of the spell which protected him, and so he died.'

'You have a marvellous collection of tall stories,' said Arthur. 'I'm afraid I should want better proof that these particular snakes are poisonous.'

Oliver turned to the charmer and spoke to him in Arabic. Then he answered Arthur.

'The man has a horned viper, *cerastes* is the name under which you gentlemen of science know it, and it is the most deadly of all Egyptian snakes. It is commonly known as Cleopatra's Asp, for that is the serpent which was brought in a basket of figs to the paramour of Caesar in order that she might not endure the triumph of Augustus.'

'What are you going to do?' asked Susie.

He smiled but did not answer. He stepped forward to the centre of the tent and fell on his knees. He uttered Arabic words, which Dr. Porhoët translated to the others.

'O viper, I adjure you, by the great God who is all-powerful, to come forth. You are but a snake, and God is greater than all snakes. Obey my call and come.'

A tremor went through the goatskin bag, and in a moment a head was protruded. A lithe body wriggled out. It was a snake of light grey colour, and over each eye was a horn. It lay slightly curled.

'Do you recognize it?' said Oliver in a low voice to the doctor.

'I do.'

The charmer sat motionless, and the woman in the dim background ceased her weird rubbing of the drum. Haddo seized the snake and opened its mouth. Immediately it fastened on his hand, and the reptile teeth went deep into his flesh. Arthur watched him for signs of pain, but he did not wince. The writhing snake dangled from his hand. He repeated a sentence in Arabic, and, with the peculiar suddenness of a drop of water falling from a roof, the snake fell to the ground. The blood flowed freely. Haddo spat upon the bleeding place three times, muttering words they could not hear, and three times he rubbed the wound with his fingers. The bleeding stopped. He stretched out his hand for Arthur to look at.

'That surely is what a surgeon would call healing by first intention,' he said.

Burdon was astonished, but he was irritated, too, and would not allow that there was anything strange in the cessation of the flowing blood.

'You haven't yet shown that the snake was poisonous.'

'I have not finished yet,' smiled Haddo.

He spoke again to the Egyptian, who gave an order to his wife. Without a word she rose to her feet and from a box took a white rabbit. She lifted it up by the ears, and it struggled with its four quaint legs. Haddo put it in front of the horned viper. Before anyone could have moved, the snake darted forward, and like a flash of lightning struck the rabbit. The wretched little beast gave a slight scream, a shudder went through it, and it fell dead.

Margaret sprang up with a cry.

'Oh, how cruel! How hatefully cruel!'

'Are you convinced now?' asked Haddo coolly.

The two women hurried to the doorway. They were frightened and disgusted. Oliver Haddo was left alone with the snake-charmer.

CHAPTER V

DR Porhoët had asked Arthur to bring Margaret and Miss Boyd to see him on Sunday at his apartment in the Île Saint Louis; and the lovers arranged to spend an hour on their way at the Louvre. Susie, invited to accompany them, preferred independence and her own reflections.

To avoid the crowd which throngs the picture galleries on holidays, they went to that part of the museum where ancient sculpture is kept. It was comparatively empty, and the long halls had the singular restfulness of places where works of art are gathered together. Margaret was filled with a genuine emotion; and though she could not analyse it, as Susie, who loved to dissect her state of mind, would have done, it strangely exhilarated her. Her heart was uplifted from the sordidness of earth, and she had a sensation of freedom which was as delightful as it was indescribable. Arthur had never troubled himself with art till Margaret's enthusiasm taught him that there was a side of life he did not realize. Though beauty meant little to his practical nature, he sought, in his great love for Margaret, to appreciate the works which excited her to such charming ecstasy. He walked by her side with docility and listened, not without deference, to her outbursts. He admired the correctness of Greek anatomy, and there was one statue of an athlete which attracted his prolonged attention, because the muscles were indicated with the precision of a plate in a surgical textbook. When Margaret talked of the Greeks' divine repose and of their blitheness, he thought it very clever because she said it; but in a man it would have aroused his impatience.

Yet there was one piece, the charming statue known as *La Diane de Gabies,* which moved him differently, and to this presently he insisted on going. With a laugh Margaret remonstrated, but secretly she was not displeased. She was aware that his passion for this figure was due, not to its intrinsic beauty, but to a likeness he had discovered in it to herself.

It stood in that fair wide gallery where is the mocking faun, with his inhuman savour of fellowship with the earth which is divine, and the sightless Homer. The goddess had not the arrogance of the huntress who loved Endymion, nor the majesty of the cold mistress of the skies. She was in the likeness of a young girl, and with collected gesture fastened her cloak. There was nothing divine in her save a sweet strange spirit of virginity. A lover in ancient Greece, who offered sacrifice before this fair image, might forget easily that it was a goddess to whom he knelt, and see only an earthly maid fresh with youth and chastity and loveliness. In Arthur's eyes Margaret had all the exquisite grace of the statue, and the same unconscious composure; and in her also breathed the spring odours of ineffable purity. Her features were chiselled with the clear and divine perfection of this Greek girl's; her ears were as delicate and as finely wrought. The colour of her skin was so tender that it reminded you vaguely of all beautiful soft things, the radiance of sunset and the darkness of the night, the heart of roses and the depth of running water. The goddess's hand was raised to her right shoulder, and Margaret's hand was as small, as dainty, and as white.

'Don't be so foolish,' said she, as Arthur looked silently at the statue.

He turned his eyes slowly, and they rested upon her. She saw that they were veiled with tears.

'What on earth's the matter?'

'I wish you weren't so beautiful,' he answered, awkwardly, as though he could scarcely bring himself to say such foolish things. 'I'm so afraid that something will happen to prevent us from being happy. It seems too much to expect that I should enjoy such extraordinarily good luck.'

She had the imagination to see that it meant much for the practical man so to express himself. Love of her drew him out of his character, and, though he could not resist, he resented the effect it had on him. She found nothing to reply, but she took his hand.

'Everything has gone pretty well with me so far,' he said, speaking almost to himself. 'Whenever I've really wanted anything, I've managed to get it. I don't see why things should go against me now.'

He was trying to reassure himself against an instinctive suspicion of the malice of circumstances. But he shook himself and straightened his back.

'It's stupid to be so morbid as that,' he muttered.

Margaret laughed. They walked out of the gallery and turned to the quay. By crossing the bridge and following the river, they must come eventually to Dr. Porhoët's house.

Meanwhile Susie wandered down the Boulevard Saint Michel, alert with the Sunday crowd, to that part of Paris which was dearest to her heart. L'Île Saint Louis to her mind offered a synthesis of the French spirit, and it pleased her far more than the garish boulevards in which the English as a rule seek for the country's fascination. Its position on an island in the Seine gave it a compact charm. The narrow streets, with their array of dainty comestibles, had the look of streets in a provincial town. They had a quaintness which appealed to the fancy, and they were very restful. The names of the streets recalled the monarchy that passed away in bloodshed, and in *poudre de riz*. The very plane trees had a greater sobriety than elsewhere, as though conscious they stood in a Paris where progress was not. In front was the turbid Seine, and below, the twin towers of Notre Dame. Susie could have kissed the hard paving stones of the quay. Her good-natured, plain face lit up as she realized the delight of the scene upon which her eyes rested; and it was with a little pang, her mind aglow with characters and events from history and from fiction, that she turned away to enter Dr Porhoët's house.

She was pleased that the approach did not clash with her fantasies. She mounted a broad staircase, dark but roomy, and, at the command of the *concierge,* rang a tinkling bell at one of the doorways that faced her. Dr Porhoët opened in person.

'Arthur and Mademoiselle are already here,' he said, as he led her in.

They went through a prim French dining-room, with much woodwork and heavy scarlet hangings, to the library. This was a large room, but the bookcases that lined the walls, and a large writing-table heaped up with books, much diminished its size. There were books everywhere. They were stacked on the floor and piled on every chair. There was hardly space to move. Susie gave a cry of delight.

'Now you mustn't talk to me. I want to look at all your books.'

'You could not please me more,' said Dr Porhoët, 'but I am afraid they will disappoint you. They are of many sorts, but I fear there are few that will interest an English young lady.'

He looked about his writing-table till he found a packet of cigarettes. He gravely offered one to each of his guests. Susie was enchanted with the strange musty smell of the old books, and she took a first glance at them in general. For the most part they were in paper bindings, some of them neat enough, but more with broken backs and dingy edges; they were set along the shelves in serried rows, untidily, without method or plan. There were many older ones also in bindings of calf and pigskin, treasure from half the bookshops in Europe; and there were huge folios like Prussian grenadiers; and tiny Elzevirs, which had been read by patrician ladies in Venice. Just as Arthur was a different man in the operating theatre, Dr Porhoët was changed among his books. Though he preserved the amiable serenity which made him always so attractive, he had there a diverting brusqueness of demeanour which contrasted quaintly with his usual calm.

'I was telling these young people, when you came in, of an ancient Korân which I was given in Alexandria by a learned man whom I operated upon for cataract.' He showed her a beautifully-written Arabic work, with wonderful capitals and headlines in gold.

'You know that it is almost impossible for an infidel to acquire the holy book, and this is a particularly rare copy, for it was written by Kaït Bey, the greatest of the Mameluke Sultans.'

He handled the delicate pages as a lover of flowers would handle rose-leaves.

'And have you much literature on the occult sciences?' asked Susie.

Dr Porhoët smiled.

'I venture to think that no private library contains so complete a collection, but I dare not show it to you in the presence of our friend Arthur. He is too polite to accuse me of foolishness, but his sarcastic smile would betray him.'

Susie went to the shelves to which he vaguely waved, and looked with a peculiar excitement at the mysterious array. She ran her eyes along the names. It seemed to her that she was entering upon an unknown region of romance. She felt like an adventurous princess who rode on her palfrey into a forest of great bare trees and mystic silences, where wan, unearthly shapes pressed upon her way.

'I thought once of writing a life of that fantastic and grandiloquent creature, Philippus Aureolus Theophrastus Paracelsus Bombast von Hohenheim,' said Dr Porhoët, 'and I have collected many of his books.'

He took down a slim volume in duodecimo, printed in the seventeenth century, with queer plates, on which were all manner of cabbalistic signs. The pages had a peculiar, musty odour. They were stained with iron-mould.

'Here is one of the most interesting works concerning the black art. It is the *Grimoire of Honorius,* and is the principal textbook of all those who deal in the darkest ways of the science.'

Then he pointed out the *Hexameron* of Torquemada and the *Tableau de l'Inconstance des Démons,* by Delancre; he drew his finger down the leather back of Delrio's *Disquisitiones Magicæ* and set upright the *Pseudomonarchia Daemonorum* of Wierus; his eyes rested for an instant on Hauber's *Acta et Scripta Magica,* and he blew the dust carefully off the most famous, the most infamous, of them all, Sprenger's *Malleus Malefikorum.*

'Here is one of my greatest treasures. It is the *Clavicula Salomonis*; and I have much reason to believe that it is the identical copy which belonged to the greatest adventurer of the eighteenth century, Jacques Casanova. You will see that the owner's name had been cut out, but enough remains to indicate the bottom of the letters; and these correspond exactly with the signature of Casanova which I have found at the Bibliothéque Nationale. He relates in his memoirs that a copy of this book was seized among his effects when he was arrested in Venice for traffic in the black arts; and it was there, on one of my journeys from Alexandria, that I picked it up.'

He replaced the precious work, and his eye fell on a stout volume bound in vellum.

'I had almost forgotten the most wonderful, the most mysterious, of all the books that treat of occult science. You have heard of the Kabbalah, but I doubt if it is more than a name to you.'

'I know nothing about it at all,' laughed Susie, 'except that it's all very romantic and extraordinary and ridiculous.'

'This, then, is its history. Moses, who was learned in all the wisdom of Egypt, was first initiated into the Kabbalah in the land of his birth; but became most proficient in it during his wanderings in the wilderness. Here he not only devoted the leisure hours of forty years to this mysterious science, but received lessons in it from an obliging angel. By aid of it he was able to solve the difficulties which arose during his management of the Israelites, notwithstanding the pilgrimages, wars, and miseries of that most unruly nation. He covertly laid down the principles of the doctrine in the first four books of the Pentateuch, but withheld them from Deuteronomy. Moses also initiated the Seventy Elders into these secrets, and they in turn transmitted them from hand to hand. Of all who formed the unbroken line of tradition, David and Solomon were the most deeply learned in the Kabbalah. No one, however, dared to write it down till Schimeon ben Jochai, who lived in the time of the destruction of Jerusalem; and after his death the

Rabbi Eleazar, his son, and the Rabbi Abba, his secretary, collected his manuscripts and from them composed the celebrated treatise called *Zohar.*'

'And how much do you believe of this marvellous story?' asked Arthur Burdon.

'Not a word,' answered Dr Porhoët, with a smile. 'Criticism has shown that *Zohar* is of modern origin. With singular effrontery, it cites an author who is known to have lived during the eleventh century, mentions the Crusades, and records events which occurred in the year of Our Lord 1264. It was some time before 1291that copies of *Zohar* began to be circulated by a Spanish Jew named Moses de Leon, who claimed to possess an autograph manuscript by the reputed author Schimeon ben Jochai. But when Moses de Leon was gathered to the bosom of his father Abraham, a wealthy Hebrew, Joseph de Avila, promised the scribe's widow, who had been left destitute, that his son should marry her daughter, to whom he would pay a handsome dowry, if she would give him the original manuscript from which these copies were made. But the widow (one can imagine with what gnashing of teeth) was obliged to confess that she had no such manuscript, for Moses de Leon had composed *Zohar* out of his own head, and written it with his own right hand.'

Arthur got up to stretch his legs. He gave a laugh.

'I never know how much you really believe of all these things you tell us. You speak with such gravity that we are all taken in, and then it turns out that you've been laughing at us.'

'My dear friend, I never know myself how much I believe,' returned Dr Porhoët.

'I wonder if it is for the same reason that Mr Haddo puzzles us so much,' said Susie.

'Ah, there you have a case that is really interesting,' replied the doctor. 'I assure you that, though I know him fairly intimately, I have never been able to make up my mind whether he is an elaborate practical joker, or whether he is really convinced he has the wonderful powers to which he lays claim.'

'We certainly saw things last night that were not quite normal,' said Susie. 'Why had that serpent no effect on him though it was able to kill the rabbit instantaneously? And how are you going to explain the violent trembling of that horse, Mr. Burdon?'

'I can't explain it,' answered Arthur, irritably, 'but I'm not inclined to attribute to the supernatural everything that I can't immediately understand.'

'I don't know what there is about him that excites in me a sort of horror,' said Margaret. 'I've never taken such a sudden dislike to anyone.'

She was too reticent to say all she felt, but she had been strangely affected last night by the recollection of Haddo's words and of his acts. She had awakened more than once from a nightmare in which he assumed fantastic and ghastly shapes. His mocking voice rang in her ears, and she seemed still to see that vast bulk and the savage, sensual face. It was like a spirit of evil in her path, and she was curiously alarmed. Only her reliance on Arthur's common sense prevented her from giving way to ridiculous terrors.

'I've written to Frank Hurrell and asked him to tell me all he knows about him,' said Arthur. 'I should get an answer very soon.'

'I wish we'd never come across him,' cried Margaret vehemently. 'I feel that he will bring us misfortune.'

'You're all of you absurdly prejudiced,' answered Susie gaily. 'He interests me enormously, and I mean to ask him to tea at the studio.'

'I'm sure I shall be delighted to come.'

Margaret cried out, for she recognized Oliver Haddo's deep bantering tones; and she turned round quickly. They were all so taken aback that for a moment no one spoke. They were gathered round the window and had not heard him come in. They wondered guiltily how long he had been there and how much he had heard.

'How on earth did you get here?' cried Susie lightly, recovering herself first.

'No well-bred sorcerer is so dead to the finer feelings as to enter a room by the door,' he answered, with his puzzling smile. 'You were standing round the window, and I thought it would startle you if I chose that mode of ingress, so I descended with incredible skill down the chimney.'

'I see a little soot on your left elbow,' returned Susie. 'I hope you weren't at all burned.'

'Not at all, thanks,' he answered, gravely brushing his coat.

'In whatever way you came, you are very welcome,' said Dr Porhoët, genially holding out his hand.

But Arthur impatiently turned to his host.

'I wish I knew what made you engage upon these studies,' he said. 'I should have thought your medical profession protected you from any tenderness towards superstition.'

Dr Porhoët shrugged his shoulders.

'I have always been interested in the oddities of mankind. At one time I read a good deal of philosophy and a good deal of science, and I learned in that way that nothing was certain. Some people, by the pursuit of science, are impressed with the dignity of man, but I was only made conscious of his insignificance. The greatest questions of all have been threshed out since he acquired the beginnings of civilization and he is as far from a solution as ever. Man can know nothing, for his senses are his only means of knowledge, and they can give no certainty. There is only one subject upon which the individual can speak with authority, and that is his own mind, but even here he is surrounded with darkness. I believe that we shall always be ignorant of the matters which it most behoves us to know, and therefore I cannot occupy myself with them. I prefer to set them all aside, and, since knowledge is unattainable, to occupy myself only with folly.'

'It is a point of view I do not sympathize with,' said Arthur.

'Yet I cannot be sure that it is all folly,' pursued the Frenchman reflectively. He looked at Arthur with a certain ironic gravity. 'Do you believe that I should lie to you when I promised to speak the truth?'

'Certainly not.'

'I should like to tell you of an experience that I once had in Alexandria. So far as I can see, it can be explained by none of the principles known to science. I ask you only to believe that I am not consciously deceiving you.'

He spoke with a seriousness which gave authority to his words. It was plain, even to Arthur, that he narrated the event exactly as it occurred.

'I had heard frequently of a certain shiekh who was able by means of a magic mirror to show the inquirer persons who were absent or dead, and a native friend of mine had often begged me to see him. I had never thought it worth while, but at last a time came when I was greatly troubled in my mind. My poor mother was an old woman, a widow, and I had received no news of her for many weeks. Though I wrote repeatedly, no answer reached me. I was very anxious and very unhappy. I thought no harm could come if I sent for the sorcerer, and perhaps after all he had the power which was attributed to him. My friend, who was interpreter to the French Consulate, brought him to me one evening. He was a fine man, tall and stout, of a fair complexion, but with a dark brown beard. He was shabbily dressed, and, being a descendant of the Prophet, wore a green turban. In his conversation he was affable and unaffected. I asked him what persons could see in the magic mirror, and he said they were a boy not arrived at puberty, a virgin, a black female slave, and a pregnant woman. In order to make sure that there was no collusion, I despatched my servant to an intimate friend and asked him to send me his son. While we waited, I prepared by the magician's direction frankincense and coriander-seed, and a chafing-dish with live charcoal. Meanwhile, he wrote forms of invocation on six strips of paper. When the boy arrived, the sorcerer threw incense and one of the paper strips into the chafing-dish, then took the boy's right hand and drew a square and certain mystical marks on the palm. In the centre of the square he poured a little ink. This formed the magic mirror. He desired the boy to look steadily into it without raising his head.

The fumes of the incense filled the room with smoke. The sorcerer muttered Arabic words, indistinctly, and this he continued to do all the time except when he asked the boy a question.

'"Do you see anything in the ink?" he said.

'"No," the boy answered.

'But a minute later, he began to tremble and seemed very much frightened.

'"I see a man sweeping the ground," he said.

'"When he has done sweeping, tell me," said the sheikh.

'"He has done," said the boy.

'The sorcerer turned to me and asked who it was that I wished the boy should see.

'"I desire to see the widow Jeanne-Marie Porhoët."

'The magician put the second and third of the small strips of paper into the chafing-dish, and fresh frankincense was added. The fumes were painful to my eyes. The boy began to speak.

'"I see an old woman lying on a bed. She has a black dress, and of her head is a little white cap. She has a wrinkled face and her eyes are closed. There is a band tied round her chin. The bed is in a sort of hole, in the wall, and there are shutters to it."

'The boy was describing a Breton bed, and the white cap was the *coiffe* that my mother wore. And if she lay there in her black dress, with a band about her chin, I knew that it could mean but one thing.

'"What else does he see?" I asked the sorcerer.

'He repeated my question, and presently the boy spoke again.

'"I see four men come in with a long box. And there are women crying. They all wear little white caps and black dresses. And I see a man in a white surplice, with a large cross in his hands, and a little boy in a long red gown. And the men take off their hats. And now everyone is kneeling down."

'"I will hear no more," I said. "It is enough."

'I knew that my mother was dead.

'In a little while, I received a letter from the priest of the village in which she lived. They had buried her on the very day upon which the boy had seen this sight in the mirror of ink.'

Dr Porhoët passed his hand across his eyes, and for a little while there was silence.

'What have you to say to that?' asked Oliver Haddo, at last.

'Nothing,' answered Arthur.

Haddo looked at him for a minute with those queer eyes of his which seemed to stare at the wall behind.

'Have you ever heard of Eliphas Levi?' he inquired. 'He is the most celebrated occultist of recent years. He is thought to have known more of the mysteries than any adept since the divine Paracelsus.'

'I met him once,' interrupted Dr Porhoët. 'You never saw a man who looked less like a magician. His face beamed with good-nature, and he wore a long grey beard, which covered nearly the whole of his breast. He was of a short and very corpulent figure.'

'The practice of black arts evidently disposes to obesity,' said Arthur, icily.

Susie noticed that this time Oliver Haddo made no sign that the taunt moved him. His unwinking, straight eyes remained upon Arthur without expression.

'Levi's real name was Alphonse-Louis Constant, but he adopted that under which he is generally known for reasons that are plain to the romantic mind. His father was a boot-maker. He was destined for the priesthood, but fell in love with a damsel fair and married her. The union was unhappy. A fate befell him which has been the lot of greater men than he, and his wife presently abandoned the marital roof with her lover. To console himself he began to make serious researches in the occult, and in due course published a vast number of mystical works dealing with magic in all its branches.'

'I'm sure Mr Haddo was going to tell us something very interesting about him,' said Susie.

'I wished merely to give you his account of how he raised the spirit of Apollonius of Tyana in London.'

Susie settled herself more comfortably in her chair and lit a cigarette.

'He went there in the spring of 1856 to escape from internal disquietude and to devote himself without distraction to his studies. He had letters of introduction to various persons of distinction who concerned themselves with the supernatural, but, finding them trivial and indifferent, he immersed himself in the study of the supreme Kabbalah. One day, on returning to his hotel, he found a note in his room. It contained half a card, transversely divided, on which he at once recognized the character of Solomon's Seal, and a tiny slip of paper on which was written in pencil: *The other half of this card will be given you at three o'clock tomorrow in front of Westminster Abbey.* Next day, going to the appointed spot, with his portion of the card in his hand, he found a baronial equipage waiting for him. A footman approached, and, making a sign to him, opened the carriage door. Within was a lady in black satin, whose face was concealed by a thick veil. She motioned him to a seat beside her, and at the same time displayed the other part of the card he had received. The door was shut, and the carriage rolled away. When the lady raised her veil, Eliphas Levi saw that she was of mature age; and beneath her grey eyebrows were bright black eyes of preternatural fixity.'

Susie Boyd clapped her hands with delight.

'I think it's delicious, and I'm sure every word of it is true,' she cried. 'I'm enchanted with the mysterious meeting at Westminster Abbey in the Mid-Victorian era. Can't you see the elderly lady in a huge crinoline and a black poke bonnet, and the wizard in a ridiculous hat, a bottle-green frock-coat, and a flowing tie of black silk?'

'Eliphas remarks that the lady spoke French with a marked English accent,' pursued Haddo imperturbably. 'She addressed him as follows: "Sir, I am aware that the law of secrecy is rigorous among adepts; and I know that you have been asked for phenomena, but have declined to gratify a frivolous curiosity. It is possible that you do not possess the necessary materials. I can show you a complete magical cabinet, but I must require of you first the most inviolable silence. If you do not guarantee this on your honour, I will give the order for you to be driven home."'

Oliver Haddo told his story not ineffectively, but with a comic gravity that prevented one from knowing exactly how to take it.

'Having given the required promise Eliphas Levi was shown a collection of vestments and of magical instruments. The lady lent him certain books of which he was in need; and at last, as a result of many conversations, determined him to attempt at her house the experience of a complete evocation. He prepared himself for twenty-one days, scrupulously observing the rules laid down by the Ritual. At length everything was ready. It was proposed to call forth the phantom of the divine Apollonius, and to question it upon two matters, one of which concerned Eliphas Levi and the other, the lady of the crinoline. She had at first counted on assisting at the evocation with a trustworthy person, but at the last moment her friend drew back; and as the triad or unity is rigorously prescribed in magical rites, Eliphas was left alone. The cabinet prepared for the experiment was situated in a turret. Four concave mirrors were hung within it, and there was an altar of white marble, surrounded by a chain of magnetic iron. On it was engraved the sign of the Pentagram, and this symbol was drawn on the new, white sheepskin which was stretched beneath. A copper brazier stood on the altar, with charcoal of alder and of laurel wood, and in front a second brazier was placed upon a tripod. Eliphas Levi was clothed in a white robe, longer and more ample than the surplice of a priest, and he wore upon his head a chaplet of vervain leaves entwined about a golden chain. In one hand he held a new sword and in the other the Ritual.'

Susie's passion for caricature at once asserted itself, and she laughed as she saw in fancy the portly little Frenchman, with his round, red face, thus wonderfully attired.

'He set alight the two fires with the prepared materials, and began, at first in a low voice, but rising by degrees, the invocations of the Ritual. The flames invested every object with a wavering light. Presently they went out. He set more twigs and pefumes on the brazier, and when the flame started up once more, he saw distinctly before the altar a human figure larger than life, which dissolved and disappeared. He began the invocations again and placed himself in a circle, which he had already traced between the altar and the tripod. Then the depth of the mirror which was in front of him grew brighter by degrees, and a pale form arose, and it seemed gradually to approach. He closed his eyes, and called three times upon Apollonius. When he opened them, a man stood before him, wholly enveloped in a winding sheet, which seemed more grey than black. His form was lean, melancholy, and beardless. Eliphas felt an intense cold, and when he sought to ask his questions found it impossible to speak. Thereupon, he placed his hand on the Pentagram, and directed the point of his sword toward the figure, adjuring it mentally by that sign not to terrify, but to obey him. The form suddenly grew indistinct and soon it strangely vanished. He commanded it to return, and then felt, as it were, an air pass by him; and, something having touched the hand which held the sword, his arm was immediately benumbed as far as the shoulder. He supposed that the weapon displeased the spirit, and set it down within the circle. The human figure at once reappeared, but Eliphas experienced such a sudden exhaustion in all his limbs that he was obliged to sit down. He fell into a deep coma, and dreamed strange dreams. But of these, when he recovered, only a vague memory remained to him. His arm continued for several days to be numb and painful. The figure had not spoken, but it seemed to Eliphas Levi that the questions were answered in his own mind. For to each an inner voice replied with one grim word: dead.'

'Your friend seems to have had as little fear of spooks as you have of lions,' said Burdon. 'To my thinking it is plain that all these preparations, and the perfumes, the mirrors, the pentagrams, must have the greatest effect on the imagination. My only surprise is that your magician saw no more.'

'Eliphas Levi talked to me himself of this evocation,' said Dr Porhoët. 'He told me that its influence on him was very great. He was no longer the same man, for it seemed to him that something from the world beyond had passed into his soul.'

'I am astonished that you should never have tried such an interesting experiment yourself,' said Arthur to Oliver Haddo.

'I have,' answered the other calmly. 'My father lost his power of speech shortly before he died, and it was plain that he sought with all his might to tell me something. A year after his death, I called up his phantom from the grave so that I might learn what I took to be a dying wish. The circumstances of the apparition are so similar to those I have just told you that it would only bore you if I repeated them. The only difference was that my father actually spoke.'

'What did he say?' asked Susie.

'He said solemnly: *"Buy Ashantis, they are bound to go up."* I did as he told me; but my father was always unlucky in speculation, and they went down steadily. I sold out at considerable loss, and concluded that in the world beyond they are as ignorant of the tendency of the Stock Exchange as we are in this vale of sorrow.'

Susie could not help laughing. But Arthur shrugged his shoulders impatiently. It disturbed his practical mind never to be certain if Haddo was serious, or if, as now, he was plainly making game of them.

CHAPTER VI

Two days later, Arthur received Frank Hurrell's answer to his letter. It was characteristic of Frank that he should take such pains to reply at length to the inquiry, and it was clear that he had lost none of his old interest in odd personalities. He analysed Oliver Haddo's character with the patience of a scientific man studying a new species in which he is passionately concerned.

My dear Burdon:

It is singular that you should write just now to ask what I know of Oliver Haddo, since by chance I met the other night at dinner at Queen Anne's Gate a man who had much to tell me of him. I am curious to know why he excites your interest, for I am sure his peculiarities make him repugnant to a person of your robust common sense. I can with difficulty imagine two men less capable of getting on together. Though I have not seen Haddo now for years, I can tell you, in one way and another, a good deal about him. He erred when he described me as his intimate friend. It is true that at one time I saw much of him, but I never ceased cordially to dislike him. He came up to Oxford from Eton with a reputation for athletics and eccentricity. But you know that there is nothing that arouses the ill-will of boys more than the latter, and he achieved an unpopularity which was remarkable. It turned out that he played football admirably, and except for his rather scornful indolence he might easily have got his blue. He sneered at the popular enthusiasm for games, and was used to say that cricket was all very well for boys but not fit for the pastime of men. (He was then eighteen!) He talked grandiloquently of big-game shooting and of mountain climbing as sports which demanded courage and self-reliance. He seemed, indeed, to like football, but he played it with a brutal savagery which the other persons concerned naturally resented. It became current opinion in other pursuits that he did not play the game. He did nothing that was manifestly unfair, but was capable of taking advantages which most people would have thought mean; and he made defeat more hard to bear because he exulted over the vanquished with the coarse banter that youths find so difficult to endure.

What you would hardly believe is that, when he first came up, he was a person of great physical attractions. He is now grown fat, but in those days was extremely handsome. He reminded one of those colossal statues of Apollo in which the god is represented with a feminine roundness and delicacy. He was very tall and had a magnificent figure. It was so well-formed for his age that one might have foretold his precious corpulence. He held himself with a dashing erectness. Many called it an insolent swagger. His features were regular and fine. He had a great quantity of curling hair, which was worn long, with a sort of poetic grace: I am told that now he is very bald; and I can imagine that this must be a great blow to him, for he was always exceedingly vain. I remember a peculiarity of his eyes, which could scarcely have been natural, but how it was acquired I do not know. The eyes of most people converge upon the object at which they look, but his remained parallel. It gave them a singular expression, as though he were scrutinising the inmost thought of the person with whom he talked. He was notorious also for the extravagance of his costume, but, unlike the aesthetes of that day, who clothed themselves with artistic carelessness, he had a taste for outrageous colours. Sometimes, by a queer freak, he dressed himself at unseasonable moments with excessive formality. He is the only undergraduate I have ever seen walk down the High in a tall hat and a closely-buttoned frock-coat.

I have told you he was very unpopular, but it was not an unpopularity of the sort which ignores a man and leaves him chiefly to his own society. Haddo knew everybody and was to be found in the most unlikely places. Though people disliked him, they showed a curious pleasure in his company, and he was probably entertained more than any man in Oxford. I never saw him but he was surrounded by a little crowd, who abused him behind his back, but could not resist his fascination.

I often tried to analyse this, for I felt it as much as anyone, and though I honestly could not bear him, I could never resist going to see him whenever opportunity arose. I suppose he offered the charm of the unexpected to that mass of undergraduates who, for all their matter-of-fact breeziness, are curiously alive to the romantic. It was impossible to tell what he would do or say next, and you were kept perpetually on the alert. He was certainly not witty, but he had a coarse humour which excited the rather gross sense of the ludicrous possessed by the young. He had a gift for caricature which was really diverting, and an imperturbable assurance. He had also an ingenious talent for profanity, and his inventiveness in this particular was a power among youths whose imaginations stopped at the commoner sorts of bad language. I have heard him preach a sermon of the most blasphemous sort in the very accents of the late Dean of Christ Church, which outraged and at the same time irresistibly amused everyone who heard it. He had a more varied knowledge than the greater part of undergraduates, and, having at the same time a retentive memory and considerable quickness, he was able to assume an attitude of omniscience which was as impressive as it was irritating. I have never heard him confess that he had not read a book. Often, when I tried to catch him, he confounded me by quoting the identical words of a passage in some work which I could have sworn he had never set eyes on. I daresay it was due only to some juggling, like the conjuror's sleight of hand that apparently lets you choose a card, but in fact forces one on you; and he brought the conversation round cleverly to a point when it was obvious I should mention a definite book. He talked very well, with an entertaining flow of rather pompous language which made the amusing things he said particularly funny. His passion for euphuism contrasted strikingly with the simple speech of those with whom he consorted. It certainly added authority to what he said. He was proud of his family and never hesitated to tell the curious of his distinguished descent. Unless he has much altered, you will already have heard of his relationship with various noble houses. He is, in fact, nearly connected with persons of importance, and his ancestry is no less distingushed than he asserts. His father is dead, and he owns a place in Staffordshire which is almost historic. I have seen photographs of it, and it is certainly very fine. His forebears have been noted in the history of England since the days of the courtier who accompanied Anne of Denmark to Scotland, and, if he is proud of his stock, it is not without cause. So he passed his time at Oxford, cordially disliked, at the same time respected and mistrusted; he had the reputation of a liar and a rogue, but it could not be denied that he had considerable influence over others. He amused, angered, irritated, and interested everyone with whom he came in contact. There was always something mysterious about him, and he loved to wrap himself in a romantic impenetrability. Though he knew so many people, no one knew him, and to the end he remained a stranger in our midst. A legend grew up around him, which he fostered sedulously, and it was reported that he had secret vices which could only be whispered with bated breath. He was said to intoxicate himself with Oriental drugs, and to haunt the vilest opium-dens in the East of London. He kept the greatest surprise for the last, since, though he was never seen to work, he managed, to the universal surprise, to get a first. He went down, and to the best of my belief was never seen in Oxford again.

I have heard vaguely that he was travelling over the world, and, when I met in town now and then some of the fellows who had known him at the 'Varsity, weird rumours reached me. One told me that he was tramping across America, earning his living as he went; another asserted that he had been seen in a monastry in India; a third assured me that he had married a ballet-girl in Milan; and someone else was positive that he had taken to drink. One opinion, however, was common to all my informants, and this was that he did something out of the common. It was clear that he was not the man to settle down to the tame life of a country gentleman which his position and fortune indicated. At last I met him one day in Piccadilly, and we dined together at the Savoy. I hardly recognized him, for he was become enormously stout, and his hair had already grown thin. Though he could not have been more than twenty-five, he looked considerably older. I tried to find out what he had been up to, but, with the air of mystery he affects, he would go into no details. He gave me to understand that he had sojourned in lands where the white man had never been before, and had learnt esoteric secrets which overthrew the foundations of modern science. It seemed to me that he had coarsened in mind as well as in appearance. I do not know if it was due to my own development since the old days at Oxford, and to my greater knowledge of the world, but he did not seem to me so brilliant as I remembered. His facile banter was rather stupid. In fact he bored me. The pose which had seemed amusing in a lad fresh from Eton now was intolerable, and I was glad to leave him. It was characteristic that, after asking me to dinner, he left me in a lordly way to pay the bill.

Then I heard nothing of him till the other day, when our friend Miss Ley asked me to meet at dinner the German explorer Burkhardt. I dare say you remember that Burkhardt brought out a book a little while ago on his adventures in Central Asia. I knew that Oliver Haddo was his companion in that journey and had meant to read it on this account, but, having been excessively busy, had omitted to do so. I took the opportunity to ask the German about our common acquaintance, and we had a long talk. Burkhardt had met him by chance at Mombasa in East Africa, where he was arranging an expedition after big game, and they agreed to go together. He told me that Haddo was a marvellous shot and a hunter of exceptional ability. Burkhardt had been rather suspicious of a man who boasted so much of his attainments, but was obliged soon to confess that he boasted of nothing unjustly. Haddo has had an extraordinary experience, the truth of which Burkhardt can vouch for. He went out alone one night on the trail of three lions and killed them all before morning with one shot each. I know nothing of these things, but from the way in which Burkhardt spoke, I judge it must be a unique occurrence. But, characteristically enough, no one was more conscious than Haddo of the singularity of his feat, and he made life almost insufferable for his fellow-traveller in consequence. Burkhardt assures me that Haddo is really remarkable in pursuit of big game. He has a sort of instinct which leads him to the most unlikely places, and a wonderful feeling for country, whereby he can cut across, and head off animals whose spoor he has noticed. His courage is very great. To follow a wounded lion into thick cover is the most dangerous proceeding in the world, and demands the utmost coolness.

The animal invariably sees the sportsman before he sees it, and in most cases charges. But Haddo never hesitated on these occasions, and Burkhardt could only express entire admiration for his pluck. It appears that he is not what is called a good sportsman. He kills wantonly, when there can be no possible excuse, for the mere pleasure of it; and to Burkhardt's indignation frequently shot beasts whose skins and horns they did not even trouble to take. When antelope were so far off that it was impossible to kill them, and the approach of night made it useless to follow, he would often shoot, and leave a wretched wounded beast to die by inches. His selfishness was extreme, and he never shared any information with his friend that might rob him of an uninterrupted pursuit of game. But notwithstanding all this, Burkhardt had so high an opinion of Haddo's general capacity and of his resourcefulness that, when he was arranging his journey in Asia, he asked him to come also. Haddo consented, and it appears that Burkhardt's book gives further proof, if it is needed, of the man's extraordinary qualities. The German confessed that on more than one occasion he owed his life to Haddo's rare power of seizing opportunities. But they quarrelled at last through Haddo's over-bearing treatment of the natives. Burkhardt had vaguely suspected him of cruelty, but at length it was clear that he used them in a manner which could not be defended. Finally he had a desperate quarrel with one of the camp servants, as a result of which the man was shot dead. Haddo swore that he fired in self-defence, but his action caused a general desertion, and the travellers found themselves in a very dangerous predicament. Burkhardt thought that Haddo was clearly to blame and refused to have anything more to do with him. They separated. Burkhardt returned to England; and Haddo, pursued by the friends of the murdered man, had great difficulty in escaping with his life. Nothing has been heard of him since till I got your letter.

Altogether, an extraordinary man. I confess that I can make nothing of him. I shall never be surprised to hear anything in connexion with him. I recommend you to avoid him like the plague. He can be no one's friend. As an an acquaintance he is treacherous and insincere; as an enemy, I can well imagine that he would be as merciless as he is unscrupulous.

An immensely long letter!

Goodbye, my son. I hope that your studies in French methods of surgery will have added to your wisdom. Your industry edifies me, and I am sure that you will eventually be a baronet and the President of the Royal College of Surgcons; and you shall relieve royal persons of their vermiform appendix.

Yours ever,
FRANK HURRELL

Arthur, having read this letter twice, put it in an envelope and left it without comment for Miss Boyd. Her answer came within a couple of hours: 'I've asked him to tea on Wednesday, and I can't put him off. You must come and help us; but please be as polite to him as if, like most of us, he had only taken mental liberties with the Ten Commandments.'

CHAPTER VII

ON the morning of the day upon which they had asked him to tea, Oliver Haddo left at Margaret's door vast masses of chrysanthemums. There were so many that the austere studio was changed in aspect. It gained an ephemeral brightness that Margaret, notwithstanding pieces of silk hung here and there on the walls, had never been able to give it. When Arthur arrived, he was dismayed that the thought had not occurred to him.

'I'm so sorry,' he said. 'You must think me very inconsiderate.'

Margaret smiled and held his hand.

'I think I like you because you don't trouble about the common little attentions of lovers.'

'Margaret's a wise girl,' smiled Susie. 'She knows that when a man sends flowers it is a sign that he has admired more women than one.'

'I don't suppose that these were sent particularly to me.'

Arthur Burdon sat down and observed with pleasure the cheerful fire. The drawn curtains and the lamps gave the place a nice cosiness, and there was the peculiar air of romance which is always in a studio. There is a sense of freedom about it that disposes the mind to diverting speculations. In such an atmosphere it is possible to be serious without pompousness and flippant without inanity.

In the few days of their acquaintance Arthur and Susie had arrived at terms of pleasant familiarity. Susie, from her superior standpoint of an unmarried woman no longer young, used him with the good-natured banter which she affected. To her, he was a foolish young thing in love, and she marvelled that even the cleverest man in that condition could behave like a perfect idiot. But Margaret knew that, if her friend chaffed him, it was because she completely approved of him. As their intimacy increased, Susie learnt to appreciate his solid character. She admired his capacity in dealing with matters that were in his province, and the simplicity with which he left alone those of which he was ignorant. There was no pose in him. She was touched also by an ingenuous candour which gave a persuasive charm to his abruptness. And, though she set a plain woman's value on good looks, his appearance, rough hewn like a statue in porphyry, pleased her singularly. It was an index of his character. The look of him gave you the whole man, strong yet gentle, honest and simple, neither very imaginative nor very brilliant, but immensely reliable and trustworthy to the bottom of his soul. He was seated now with Margaret's terrier on his knees, stroking its ears, and Susie, looking at him, wondered with a little pang why no man like that had even cared for her. It was evident that he would make a perfect companion, and his love, once won, was of the sort that did not alter.

Dr Porhoët came in and sat down with the modest quietness which was one of his charms. He was not a great talker and loved most to listen in silence to the chatter of young people. The dog jumped down from Arthur's knee, went up to the doctor, and rubbed itself in friendly fashion against his legs. They began to talk in the soft light and had forgotten almost that another guest was expected. Margaret hoped fervently that he would not come. She had never looked more lovely than on this afternoon, and she busied herself with the preparations for tea with a housewifely grace that added a peculiar delicacy to her comeliness. The dignity which encompassed the perfection of her beauty was delightfully softened, so that you were reminded of those sweet domestic saints who lighten here and there the passionate records of the Golden Book.

'*C'est tellement intime ici,*' smiled Dr Porhoët, breaking into French in the impossibility of expressing in English the exact feeling which that scene gave him.

It might have been a picture by some master of *genre.* It seemed hardly by chance that the colours arranged themselves in such agreeable tones, or that the lines of the wall and the seated persons achieved such a graceful decoration. The atmosphere was extraordinarily peaceful.

There was a knock at the door, and Arthur got up to open. The terrier followed at his heels. Oliver Haddo entered. Susie watched to see what the dog would do and was by this time not surprised to see a change come over it. With its tail between its legs, the friendly little beast slunk along the wall to the furthermost corner. It turned a suspicious, frightened eye upon Haddo and then hid its head. The visitor, intent upon his greetings, had not noticed even that there was an animal in the room. He accepted with a simple courtesy they hardly expected from him the young woman's thanks for his flowers. His behaviour surprised them. He put aside his poses. He seemed genuinely to admire the cosy little studio. He asked Margaret to show him her sketches and looked at them with unassumed interest. His observations were pointed and showed a certain knowledge of what he spoke about. He described himself as an amateur, that object of a painter's derision: the man 'who knows what he likes'; but his criticism, though generous, showed that he was no fool. The two women were impressed. Putting the sketches aside, he began to talk, of the many places he had seen. It was evident that he sought to please. Susie began to understand how it was that, notwithstanding his affectations, he had acquired so great an influence over the undergraduates of Oxford. There was romance and laughter in his conversation; and though, as Frank Hurrell had said, lacking in wit, he made up for it with a diverting pleasantry that might very well have passed for humour. But Susie, though amused, felt that this was not the purpose for which she had asked him to come. Dr Porhoët had lent her his entertaining work on the old alchemists, and this gave her a chance to bring their conversation to matters on which Haddo was expert. She had read the book with delight and, her mind all aflame with those strange histories wherein fact and fancy were so wonderfully mingled, she was eager to know more. The long toil in which so many had engaged, always to lose their fortunes, often to suffer persecution and torture, interested her no less than the accounts, almost authenticated, of those who had succeeded in their extraordinary quest.

She turned to Dr Porhoët.

'You are a bold man to assert that now and then the old alchemists actually did make gold,' she said.

'I have not gone quite so far as that,' he smiled. 'I assert merely that, if evidence as conclusive were offered of any other historical event, it would be credited beyond doubt. We can disbelieve these circumstantial details only by coming to the conclusion beforehand that it is impossible they should be true.'

'I wish you would write that life of Paracelsus which you suggest in your preface.'

Dr Porhoët, smiling shook his head.

'I don't think I shall ever do that now,' he said. 'Yet he is the most interesting of all the alchemists, for he offers the fascinating problem of an immensely complex character. It is impossible to know to what extent he was a charlatan and to what a man of serious science.'

Susie glanced at Oliver Haddo, who sat in silence, his heavy face in shadow, his eyes fixed steadily on the speaker. The immobility of that vast bulk was peculiar.

'His name is not so ridiculous as later associations have made it seem,' proceeded the doctor, 'for he belonged to the celebrated family of Bombast, and they were called Hohenheim after their ancient residence, which was a castle near Stuttgart in Würtemberg. The most interesting part of his life is that which the absence of documents makes it impossible accurately to describe. He travelled in Germany, Italy, France, the Netherlands, in Denmark, Sweden, and Russia. He went even to India. He was taken prisoner by the Tartars, and brought to the Great Khan, whose son he afterwards accompanied to Constantinople. The mind must be dull indeed that is not thrilled by the thought of this wandering genius traversing the lands of the earth at the most eventful date of the world's history. It was at Constantinople that, according to a certain *aureum vellus* printed at Rorschach in the sixteenth century, he received the philosopher's stone from Solomon Trismosinus. This person possessed also the *Universal Panacea,* and it is asserted that he was seen still alive by a French traveller at the end of the seventeenth century. Paracelsus then passed through the countries that border the Danube, and so reached Italy, where he served as a surgeon in the imperial army. I see no reason why he should not have been present at the battle of Pavia. He collected information from physicians, surgeons and alchemists; from executioners, barbers, shepherds, Jews, gipsies, midwives, and fortune-tellers; from high and low, from learned and vulgar. In the sketch I have given of his career in that volume you hold, I have copied out a few words of his upon the acquirement of knowledge which affect me with a singular emotion.'

Dr Porhoët took his book from Miss Boyd and opened it thoughtfully. He read out the fine passage from the preface of the *Paragranum*:

> 'I went in search of my art, often incurring danger of life. I have not been ashamed to learn that which seemed useful to me even from vagabonds, hangmen, and barbers. We know that a lover will go far to meet the woman he adores; how much more will the lover of Wisdom be tempted to go in search of his divine mistress.'

He turned the page to find a few more lines further on:

> 'We should look for knowledge where we may expect to find it, and why should a man be despised who goes in search of it? Those who remain at home may grow richer and live more comfortably than those who wander; but I desire neither to live comfortably nor to grow rich.'

'By Jove, those are fine words,' said Arthur, rising to his feet.

Their brave simplicity moved him as no rhetoric could have done, and they made him more eager still to devote his own life to the difficult acquisition of knowledge. Dr Porhoët gave him his ironic smile.

'Yet the man who could write that was in many ways a mere buffoon, who praised his wares with the vulgar glibness of a quack. He was vain and ostentatious, intemperate and boastful. Listen:

> 'After me, O Avicenna, Galen, Rhases and Montagnana! After me, not I after you, ye men of Paris, Montpellier, Meissen, and Cologne; all you that come from the countries along the Danube and the Rhine, and you that come from the islands of the sea. It is not for me to follow you, because mine is the lordship. The time will come when none of you shall remain in his dark corner who will not be an object of contempt to the world, because I shall be the King, and the Monarchy will be mine.'

Dr Porhoët closed the book.

'Did you ever hear such gibberish in your life? Yet he did a bold thing. He wrote in German instead of in Latin, and so, by weakening the old belief in authority, brought about the beginning of free thought in science. He continued to travel from place to place, followed by a crowd of disciples, some times attracted to a wealthy city by hope of gain, sometimes journeying to a petty court at the invitation of a prince. His folly and the malice of his rivals prevented him from remaining anywhere for long. He wrought many wonderful cures. The physicians of Nuremberg denounced him as a quack, a charlatan, and an impostor. To refute them he asked the city council to put under his care patients that had been pronounced incurable. They sent him several cases of elephantiasis, and he cured them: testimonials to that effect may still be found in the archives of Nuremberg. He died as the result of a tavern brawl and was buried at Salzburg. Tradition says that, his astral body having already during physical existence become selfconscious, he is now a living adept, residing with others of his sort in a certain place in Asia. From there he still influences the minds of his followers and at times even appears to them in visible and tangible substance.'

'But look here,' said Arthur, 'didn't Paracelsus, like most of these old fellows, in the course of his researches make any practical discoveries?'

'I prefer those which were not practical,' confessed the doctor, with a smile. 'Consider for example the *Tinctura Physicorum,* which neither Pope nor Emperor could buy with all his wealth. It was one of the greatest alchemical mysteries, and, though mentioned under the name of *The Red Lion* in many occult works, was actually known to few before Paracelsus, except Hermes Trismegistus and Albertus Magnus. Its preparation was extremely difficult, for the presence was needed of two perfectly harmonious persons whose skill was equal. It was said to be a red ethereal fluid. The least wonderful of its many properties was its power to transmute all inferior metals into gold. There is an old church in the south of Bavaria where the tincture is said to be still buried in the ground. In the year 1698 some of it penetrated through the soil, and the phenomenon was witnessed by many people, who believed it to be a miracle. The church which was thereupon erected is still a well-known place for pilgrimage. Paracelsus concludes his directions for its manufacture with the words: *But if this be incomprehensible to you, remember that only he who desires with his whole heart will find, and to him only who knocks vehemently shall the door be opened.'*

'I shall never try to make it,' smiled Arthur.

'Then there was the *Electrum Magicum,* of which the wise made mirrors wherein they were able to see not only the events of the past and of the present, but the doings of men in daytime and at night. They might see anything that had been written or spoken, and the person who said it, and the causes that made him say it. But I like best the *Primum Ens Melissæ.* An elaborate prescription is given for its manufacture. It was a remedy to prolong life, and not only Paracelsus, but his predecessors Galen, Arnold of Villanova, and Raymond Lulli, had laboured studiously to discover it.'

'Will it make me eighteen again?' cried Susie.

'It is guaranteed to do so,' answered Dr Porhoët gravely. 'Lesebren, a physician to Louis XIV, gives an account of certain experiments witnessed by himself. It appears that one of his friends prepared the remedy, and his curiosity would not let him rest until he had seen with his own eyes the effect of it.'

'That is the true scientific attitude,' laughed Arthur.

'He took every morning at sunrise a glass of white wine tinctured with this preparation; and after using it for fourteen days his nails began to fall out, without, however, causing him any pain. His courage failed him at this point, and he gave the same dose to an old female servant. She regained at least one of the characteristics of youth, much to her astonishment, for she did not know that she had been taking a medicine, and, becoming frightened, refused to continue. The experimenter then took some grain, soaked it in the tincture, and gave it to an aged hen. On the sixth day the bird began to lose its feathers, and kept on losing them till it was naked as a newborn babe; but before two weeks had passed other feathers grew, and these were more beautifully coloured than any that fortunate hen had possessed in her youth. Her comb stood up, and she began again to lay eggs.'

Arthur laughed heartily.

'I confess I like that story much better than the others. The *Primum Ens Melissæ* at least offers a less puerile benefit than most magical secrets.'

'Do you call the search for gold puerile?' asked Haddo, who had been sitting for a long time in complete silence.

'I venture to call it sordid.'

'You are very superior.'

'Because I think the aims of mystical persons invariably gross or trivial? To my plain mind, it is inane to raise the dead in order to hear from their phantom lips nothing but commonplaces. And I really cannot see that the alchemist who spent his life in the attempted manufacture of gold was a more respectable object than the outside jobber of modern civilization.'

'But if he sought for gold it was for the power it gave him, and it was power he aimed at when he brooded night and day over dim secrets. Power was the subject of all his dreams, but not a paltry, limited dominion over this or that; power over the whole world, power over all created things, power over the very elements, power over God Himself. His lust was so vast that he could not rest till the stars in their courses were obedient to his will.'

For once Haddo lost his enigmatic manner. It was plain now that his words intoxicated him, and his face assumed a new, a strange, expression. A peculiar arrogance flashed in his shining eyes.

'And what else is it that men seek in life but power? If they want money, it is but for the power that attends it, and it is power again that they strive for in all the knowledge they acquire. Fools and sots aim at happiness, but men aim only at power. The magus, the sorcerer, the alchemist, are seized with fascination of the unknown; and they desire a greatness that is inaccessible to mankind. They think by the science they study so patiently, but endurance and strength, by force of will and by imagination, for these are the great weapons of the magician, they may achieve at last a power with which they can face the God of Heaven Himself.'

Oliver Haddo lifted his huge bulk from the low chair in which he had been sitting. He began to walk up and down the studio. It was curious to see this heavy man, whose seriousness was always problematical, caught up by a curious excitement.

'You've been talking of Paracelsus,' he said. 'There is one of his experiments which the doctor has withheld from you. You will find it neither mean nor mercenary, but it is very terrible. I do not know whether the account of it is true, but it would be of extraordinary interest to test it for oneself.'

He looked round at the four persons who watched him intently. There was a singular agitation in his manner, as though the thing of which he spoke was very near his heart.

'The old alchemists believed in the possibility of spontaneous generation. By the combination of psychical powers and of strange essences, they claim to have created forms in which life became manifest. Of these, the most marvellous were those strange beings, male and female, which were called *homunculi.* The old philosophers doubted the possibility of this operation, but Paracelsus asserts positively that it can be done. I picked up once for a song on a barrow at London Bridge a little book in German. It was dirty and thumbed, many of the pages were torn, and the binding scarcely held the leaves together. It was called *Die Sphinx* and was edited by a certain Dr Emil Besetzny. It contained the most extraordinary account I have ever read of certain spirits generated by Johann-Ferdinand, Count von Küffstein, in the Tyrol, in 1775. The sources from which this account is taken consist of masonic manuscripts, but more especially of a diary kept by a certain James Kammerer, who acted in the capacity of butler and famulus to the Count. The evidence is ten times stronger than any upon which men believe the articles of their religion. If it related to less wonderful subjects, you would not hesitate to believe implicitly every word you read. There were ten *homunculi*—James Kammerer calls them prophesying spirits—kept in strong bottles, such as are used to preserve fruit, and these were filled with water. They were made in five weeks, by the Count von Küffstein and an Italian mystic and rosicrucian, the Abbé Geloni. The bottles were closed with a magic seal. The spirits were about a span long, and the Count was anxious that they should grow. They were therefore buried under two cartloads of manure, and the pile daily sprinkled with a certain liquor prepared with great trouble by the adepts. The pile after such sprinklings began to ferment and steam, as if heated by a subterranean fire. When the bottles were removed, it was found that the spirits had grown to about a span and a half each; the male *homunculi* were come into possession of heavy beards, and the nails of the fingers had grown. In two of the bottles there was nothing to be seen save clear water, but when the Abbé knocked thrice at the seal upon the mouth, uttering at the same time certain Hebrew words, the water turned a mysterious colour, and the spirits showed their faces, very small at first, but growing in size till they attained that of a human countenance. And this countenance was horrible and fiendish.'

Haddo spoke in a low voice that was hardly steady, and it was plain that he was much moved. It appeared as if his story affected him so that he could scarcely preserve his composure. He went on.

'These beings were fed every three days by the Count with a rose-coloured substance which was kept in a silver box. Once a week the bottles were emptied and filled again with pure rain-water. The change had to be made rapidly, because while the *homunculi* were exposed to the air they closed their eyes and seemed to grow weak and unconscious, as though they were about to die. But with the spirits that were invisible, at certain intervals blood was poured into the water; and it disappeared at once, inexplicably, without colouring or troubling it. By some accident one of the bottles fell one day and was broken. The *homunculus* within died after a few painful respirations in spite of all efforts to save him, and the body was buried in the garden. An attempt to generate another, made by the Count without the assistance of the Abbé, who had left, failed; it produced only a small thing like a leech, which had little vitality and soon died.'

Haddo ceased speaking, and Arthur looked at him with amazement. 'But taking for granted that the thing is possible, what on earth is the use of manufacturing these strange beasts?' he exclaimed.

'Use!' cried Haddo passionately. 'What do you think would be man's sensations when he had solved the great mystery of existence, when he saw living before him the substance which was dead? These *homunculi* were seen by historical persons, by Count Max Lemberg, by Count Franz-Josef von Thun, and by many others. I have no doubt that they were actually generated. But with our modern appliances, with our greater skill, what might it not be possible to do now if we had the courage? There are chemists toiling away in their laboratories to create the primitive protoplasm from matter which is dead, the organic from the inorganic.

I have studied their experiments. I know all that they know. Why shouldn't one work on a larger scale, joining to the knowledge of the old adepts the scientific discovery of the moderns? I don't know what would be the result. It might be very strange and very wonderful. Sometimes my mind is verily haunted by the desire to see a lifeless substance move under my spells, by the desire to be as God.'

He gave a low weird laugh, half cruel, half voluptuous. It made Margaret shudder with sudden fright. He had thrown himself down in the chair, and he sat in complete shadow. By a singular effect his eyes appeared blood-red, and they stared into space, strangely parallel, with an intensity that was terrifying. Arthur started a little and gave him a searching glance. The laugh and that uncanny glance, the unaccountable emotion, were extraordinarily significant. The whole thing was explained if Oliver Haddo was mad.

There was an uncomfortable silence. Haddo's words were out of tune with the rest of the conversation. Dr Porhoët had spoken of magical things with a sceptical irony that gave a certain humour to the subject, and Susie was resolutely flippant. But Haddo's vehemence put these incredulous people out of countenance. Dr Porhoët got up to go. He shook hands with Susie and with Margaret. Arthur opened the door for him. The kindly scholar looked round for Margaret's terrier . . .

'I must bid my farewells to your little dog.'

He had been so quiet that they had forgotten his presence.

'Come here, Copper,' said Margaret.

The dog slowly slunk up to them, and with a terrified expression crouched at Margaret's feet.

'What on earth's the matter with you?' she asked.

'He's frightened of me,' said Haddo, with that harsh laugh of his, which gave such an unpleasant impression.

'Nonsense!'

Dr Porhoët bent down, stroked the dog's back, and shook its paw. Margaret lifted it up and set it on a table.

'Now, be good,' she said, with lifted finger.

Dr Porhoët with a smile went out, and Arthur shut the door behind him. Suddenly, as though evil had entered into it, the terrier sprang at Oliver Haddo and fixed its teeth in his hand. Haddo uttered a cry, and, shaking it off, gave it a savage kick. The dog rolled over with a loud bark that was almost a scream of pain, and lay still for a moment as if it were desperately hurt. Margaret cried out with horror and indignation. A fierce rage on a sudden seized Arthur so that he scarcely knew what he was about. The wretched brute's suffering, Margaret's terror, his own instinctive hatred of the man, were joined together in frenzied passion.

'You brute,' he muttered.

He hit Haddo in the face with his clenched fist. The man collapsed bulkily to the floor, and Arthur, furiously seizing his collar, began to kick him with all his might. He shook him as a dog would shake a rat and men violently flung him down. For some reason Haddo made no resistance. He remained where he fell in utter helplessness. Arthur turned to Margaret. She was holding the poor hurt dog in her hands, crying over it, and trying to comfort it in its pain. Very gently he examined it to see if Haddo's brutal kick had broken a bone. They sat down beside the fire. Susie, to steady her nerves, lit a cigarette. She was horribly, acutely conscious of that man who lay in a mass on the floor behind them. She wondered what he would do. She wondered why he did not go. And she was ashamed of his humiliation. Then her heart stood still; for she realized that he was raising himself to his feet, slowly, with the difficulty of a very fat person. He leaned against the wall and stared at them. He remained there quite motionless. His stillness got on her nerves, and she could have screamed as she felt him look at them, look with those unnatural eyes, whose expression now she dared not even imagine.

At last she could no longer resist the temptation to turn round just enough to see him. Haddo's eyes were fixed upon Margaret so intently that he did not see he was himself observed. His face, distorted by passion, was horrible to look upon. That vast mass of flesh had a malignancy that was inhuman, and it was terrible to see the satanic hatred which hideously deformed it. But it changed. The redness gave way to a ghastly pallor. The revengeful scowl disappeared; and a torpid smile spread over the features, a smile that was even more terrifying than the frown of malice. What did it mean? Susie could have cried out, but her tongue cleaved to her throat. The smile passed away, and the face became once more impassive. It seemed that Margaret and Arthur realized at last the power of those inhuman eyes, and they became quite still. The dog ceased its sobbing. The silence was so great that each one heard the beating of his heart. It was intolerable.

Then Oliver Haddo moved. He came forward slowly.

'I want to ask you to forgive me for what I did,' he said.

'The pain of the dog's bite was so keen that I lost my temper. I deeply regret that I kicked it. Mr Burdon was very right to thrash me. I feel that I deserved no less.'

He spoke in a low voice, but with great distinctness. Susie was astounded. An abject apology was the last thing she expected.

He paused for Margaret's answer. But she could not bear to look at him. When she spoke, her words were scarcely audible. She did not know why his request to be forgiven made him seem more detestable.

'I think, if you don't mind, you had better go away.'

Haddo bowed slightly. He looked at Burdon.

'I wish to tell you that I bear no malice for what you did. I recognize the justice of your anger.'

Arthur did not answer at all. Haddo hesitated a moment, while his eyes rested on them quietly. To Susie it seemed that they flickered with the shadow of a smile. She watched him with bewildered astonishment.

He reached for his hat, bowed again, and went.

CHAPTER VIII

SUSIE could not persuade herself that Haddo's regret was sincere. The humility of it aroused her suspicion. She could not get out of her mind the ugly slyness of that smile which succeeded on his face the first passionate look of deadly hatred. Her fancy suggested various dark means whereby Oliver Haddo might take vengeance on his enemy, and she was at pains to warn Arthur. But he only laughed.

'The man's a funk,' he said. 'Do you think if he'd had anything in him at all he would have let me kick him without trying to defend himself?'

Haddo's cowardice increased the disgust with which Arthur regarded him. He was amused by Susie's trepidation.

'What on earth do you suppose he can do? He can't drop a brickbat on my head. If he shoots me he'll get his head cut off, and he won't be such an ass as to risk that!'

Margaret was glad that the incident had relieved them of Oliver's society. She met him in the street a couple of days later, and since he took off his hat in the French fashion without waiting for her to acknowledge him, she was able to make her cut more pointed.

She began to discuss with Arthur the date of their marriage. It seemed to her that she had got out of Paris all it could give her, and she wished to begin a new life. Her love for Arthur appeared on a sudden more urgent, and she was filled with delight at the thought of the happiness she would give him.

A day or two later Susie received a telegram. It ran as follows:

> Please meet me at the Gare du Nord, 2:40.
>
> NANCY CLERK

It was an old friend, who was apparently arriving in Paris that afternoon. A photograph of her, with a bold signature, stood on the chimney-piece, and Susie gave it an inquisitive glance. She had not seen Nancy for so long that it surprised her to receive this urgent message.

'What a bore it is!' she said. 'I suppose I must go.'

They meant to have tea on the other side of the river, but the journey to the station was so long that it would not be worth Susie's while to come back in the interval; and they arranged therefore to meet at the house to which they were invited. Susie started a little before two.

Margaret had a class that afternoon and set out two or three minutes later. As she walked through the courtyard she started nervously, for Oliver Haddo passed slowly by. He did not seem to see her. Suddenly he stopped, put his hand to his heart, and fell heavily to the ground. The *concierge,* the only person at hand, ran forward with a cry. She knelt down and, looking round with terror, caught sight of Margaret.

'Oh, mademoiselle, venez vile!' she cried.

Margaret was obliged to go. Her heart beat horribly. She looked down at Oliver, and he seemed to be dead. She forgot that she loathed him. Instinctively she knelt down by his side and loosened his collar. He opened his eyes. An expression of terrible anguish came into his face.

'For the love of God, take me in for one moment,' he sobbed. 'I shall die in the street.'

Her heart was moved towards him. He could not go into the poky den, evil-smelling and airless, of the *concierge.* But with her help Margaret raised him to his feet, and together they brought him to the studio. He sank painfully into a chair.

'Shall I fetch you some water?' asked Margaret.

'Can you get a pastille out of my pocket?'

He swallowed a white tabloid, which she took out of a case attached to his watch-chain.

'I'm very sorry to cause you this trouble,' he gasped. 'I suffer from a disease of the heart, and sometimes I am very near death.'

'I'm glad that I was able to help you,' she said.

He seemed able to breathe more easily. She left him to himself for a while, so that he might regain his strength. She took up a book and began to read. Presently, without moving from his chair, he spoke.

'You must hate me for intruding on you.'

His voice was stronger, and her pity waned as he seemed to recover. She answered with freezing indifference.

'I couldn't do any less for you than I did. I would have brought a dog into my room if it seemed hurt.'

'I see that you wish me to go.'

He got up and moved towards the door, but he staggered and with a groan tumbled to his knees. Margaret sprang forward to help him. She reproached herself bitterly for those scornful words. The man had barely escaped death, and she was merciless.

'Oh, please stay as long as you like,' she cried. 'I'm sorry, I didn't mean to hurt you.'

He dragged himself with difficulty back to the chair, and she, conscience-stricken, stood over him helplessly. She poured out a glass of water, but he motioned it away as though he would not be beholden to her even for that.

'Is there nothing I can do for you at all?' she exclaimed, painfully.

'Nothing, except allow me to sit in this chair,' he gasped.

'I hope you'll remain as long as you choose.'

He did not reply. She sat down again and pretended to read. In a little while he began to speak. His voice reached her as if from a long way off.

'Will you never forgive me for what I did the other day?'

She answered without looking at him, her back still turned.

'Can it matter to you if I forgive or not?'

'You have not pity. I told you then how sorry I was that a sudden uncontrollable pain drove me to do a thing which immediately I bitterly regretted. Don't you think it must have been hard for me, under the actual circumstances, to confess my fault?'

'I wish you not to speak of it. I don't want to think of that horrible scene.'

'If you knew how lonely I was and how unhappy, you would have a little mercy.'

His voice was strangely moved. She could not doubt now that he was sincere.

'You think me a charlatan because I aim at things that are unknown to you. You won't try to understand. You won't give me any credit for striving with all my soul to a very great end.'

She made no reply, and for a time there was silence. His voice was different now and curiously seductive.

'You look upon me with disgust and scorn. You almost persuaded yourself to let me die in the street rather than stretch out to me a helping hand. And if you hadn't been merciful then, almost against your will, I should have died.'

'It can make no difference to you how I regard you,' she whispered.

She did not know why his soft, low tones mysteriously wrung her heartstrings. Her pulse began to beat more quickly.

'It makes all the difference in the world. It is horrible to think of your contempt. I feel your goodness and your purity. I can hardly bear my own unworthiness. You turn your eyes away from me as though I were unclean.'

She turned her chair a little and looked at him. She was astonished at the change in his appearance. His hideous obesity seemed no longer repellent, for his eyes wore a new expression; they were incredibly tender now, and they were moist with tears. His mouth was tortured by a passionate distress. Margaret had never seen so much unhappiness on a man's face, and an overwhelming remorse seized her.

'I don't want to be unkind to you,' she said.

'I will go. That is how I can best repay you for what you have done.'

The words were so bitter, so humiliated, that the colour rose to her cheeks.

'I ask you to stay. But let us talk of other things.'

For a moment he kept silence. He seemed no longer to see Margaret, and she watched him thoughtfully. His eyes rested on a print of *La Gioconda* which hung on the wall. Suddenly he began to speak. He recited the honeyed words with which Walter Pater expressed his admiration for that consummate picture.

> 'Hers is the head upon which all the ends of the world are come, and the eyelids are a little weary. It is a beauty wrought out from within upon the flesh, the deposit, little cell by cell, of strange thoughts and fantastic reveries and exquisite passions. Set it for a moment beside one of those white Greek goddesses or beautiful women of antiquity, and how would they be troubled by this beauty, into which the soul with all its maladies has passed. All the thoughts and experience of the world have etched and moulded there, in that which they have of power to refine and make expressive the outward form, the animalism of Greece, the lust of Rome, the mysticism of the Middle Ages, with its spiritual ambition and imaginative loves, the return of the Pagan world, the sins of the Borgias.'

His voice, poignant and musical, blended with the suave music of the words so that Margaret felt she had never before known their divine significance. She was intoxicated with their beauty. She wished him to continue, but had not the strength to speak. As if he guessed her thought, he went on, and now his voice had a richness in it as of an organ heard afar off. It was like an overwhelming fragrance and she could hardly bear it.

> 'She is older than the rocks among which she sits; like the vampire, she has been dead many times, and learned the secrets of the grave; and has been a diver in deep seas,

> and keeps their fallen day about her; and trafficked for strange evils with Eastern merchants; and, as Leda, was the mother of Helen of Troy, and, as Saint Anne, the mother of Mary; and all this has been to her but as the sound of lyres and flutes, and lives only in the delicacy with which it has moulded the changing lineaments, and tinged the eyelids and the hands.'

Oliver Haddo began then to speak of Leonardo da Vinci, mingling with his own fantasies the perfect words of that essay which, so wonderful was his memory, he seemed to know by heart. He found exotic fancies in the likeness between Saint John the Baptist, with his soft flesh and waving hair, and Bacchus, with his ambiguous smile. Seen through his eyes, the seashore in the Saint Anne had the airless lethargy of some damasked chapel in a Spanish nunnery, and over the landscapes brooded a wan spirit of evil that was very troubling. He loved the mysterious pictures in which the painter had sought to express something beyond the limits of painting, something of unsatisfied desire and of longing for unhuman passions. Oliver Haddo found this quality in unlikely places, and his words gave a new meaning to paintings that Margaret had passed thoughtlessly by. There was the portrait of a statuary by Bronzino in the Long Gallery of the Louvre. The features were rather large, the face rather broad. The expression was sombre, almost surly in the repose of the painted canvas, and the eyes were brown, almond-shaped like those of an Oriental; the red lips were exquisitely modelled, and the sensuality was curiously disturbing; the dark, chestnut hair, cut short, curled over the head with an infinite grace. The skin was like ivory softened with a delicate carmine. There was in that beautiful countenance more than beauty, for what most fascinated the observer was a supreme and disdainful indifference to the passion of others. It was a vicious face, except that beauty could never be quite vicious; it was a cruel face, except that indolence could never be quite cruel. It was a face that haunted you, and yet your admiration was alloyed with an unreasoning terror. The hands were nervous and adroit, with long fashioning fingers; and you felt that at their touch the clay almost moulded itself into gracious forms. With Haddo's subtle words, the character of that man rose before her, cruel yet indifferent, indolent and passionate, cold yet sensual; unnatural secrets dwelt in his mind, and mysterious crimes, and a lust for the knowledge that was arcane. Oliver Haddo was attracted by all that was unusual, deformed, and monstrous, by the pictures that represented the hideousness of man or that reminded you of his mortality. He summoned before Margaret the whole array of Ribera's ghoulish dwarfs, with their cunning smile, the insane light of their eyes, and their malice: he dwelt with a horrible fascination upon their malformations, the humped backs, the club feet, the hydrocephalic heads. He described the picture by Valdes Leal, in a certain place at Seville, which represents a priest at the altar; and the altar is sumptuous with gilt and florid carving. He wears a magnificent cope and a surplice of exquisite lace, but he wears them as though their weight was more than he could bear; and in the meagre trembling hands, and in the white, ashen face, in the dark hollowness of the eyes, there is a bodily corruption that is terrifying. He seems to hold together with difficulty the bonds of the flesh, but with no eager yearning of the soul to burst its prison, only with despair; it is as if the Lord Almighty had forsaken him and the high heavens were empty of their solace. All the beauty of life appears forgotten, and there is nothing in the world but decay. A ghastly putrefaction has attacked already the living man; the worms of the grave, the piteous horror of mortality, and the darkness before him offer naught but fear. Beyond, dark night is seen and a turbulent sea, the dark night of the soul of which the mystics write, and the troublous sea of life whereon there is no refuge for the weary and the sick at heart.

Then, as if in pursuance of a definite plan, he analysed with a searching, vehement intensity the curious talent of the modern Frenchman, Gustave Moreau. Margaret had lately visited the

Luxembourg, and his pictures were fresh in her memory. She had found in them little save a decorative arrangement marred by faulty drawing; but Oliver Haddo gave them at once a new, esoteric import. Those effects as of a Florentine jewel, the clustered colours, emerald and ruby, the deep blue of sapphires, the atmosphere of scented chambers, the mystic persons who seem ever about secret, religious rites, combined in his cunning phrases to create, as it were, a pattern on her soul of morbid and mysterious intricacy. Those pictures were filled with a strange sense of sin, and the mind that contemplated them was burdened with the decadence of Rome and with the passionate vice of the Renaissance; and it was tortured, too, by all the introspection of this later day.

Margaret listened, rather breathlessly, with the excitement of an explorer before whom is spread the plain of an undiscovered continent. The painters she knew spoke of their art technically, and this imaginative appreciation was new to her. She was horribly fascinated by the personality that imbued these elaborate sentences. Haddo's eyes were fixed upon hers, and she responded to his words like a delicate instrument made for recording the beatings of the heart. She felt an extraordinary languor. At last he stopped. Margaret neither moved nor spoke. She might have been under a spell. It seemed to her that she had no power in her limbs.

'I want to do something for you in return for what you have done for me,' he said.

He stood up and went to the piano.

'Sit in this chair,' he said.

She did not dream of disobeying. He began to play. Margaret was hardly surprised that he played marvellously. Yet it was almost incredible that those fat, large hands should have such a tenderness of touch. His fingers caressed the notes with a peculiar suavity, and he drew out of the piano effects which she had scarcely thought possible. He seemed to put into the notes a troubling, ambiguous passion, and the instrument had the tremulous emotion of a human being. It was strange and terrifying. She was vaguely familiar with the music to which she listened; but there was in it, under his fingers, an exotic savour that made it harmonious with all that he had said that afternoon. His memory was indeed astonishing. He had an infinite tact to know the feeling that occupied Margaret's heart, and what he chose seemed to be exactly that which at the moment she imperatively needed. Then he began to play things she did not know. It was music the like of which she had never heard, barbaric, with a plaintive weirdness that brought to her fancy the moonlit nights of desert places, with palm trees mute in the windless air, and tawny distances. She seemed to know tortuous narrow streets, white houses of silence with strange moon-shadows, and the glow of yellow light within, and the tinkling of uncouth instruments, and the acrid scents of Eastern perfumes. It was like a procession passing through her mind of persons who were not human, yet existed mysteriously, with a life of vampires. Mona Lisa and Saint John the Baptist, Bacchus and the mother of Mary, went with enigmatic motions. But the daughter of Herodias raised her hands as though, engaged for ever in a mystic rite, to invoke outlandish gods. Her face was very pale, and her dark eyes were sleepless; the jewels of her girdle gleamed with sombre fires; and her dress was of colours that have long been lost. The smile, in which was all the sorrow of the world and all its wickedness, beheld the wan head of the Saint, and with a voice that was cold with the coldness of death she murmured the words of the poet:

> 'I am amorous of thy body, Iokanaan! Thy body is white like the lilies of a field that the mower hath never mowed. Thy body is white like the snows that lie on the mountains of Judæa, and come down into the valleys. The roses in the garden of the Queen of Arabia are not so white as thy body. Neither the roses in the garden of the Queen of Arabia, the garden of spices of the Queen of Arabia, nor the feet of the dawn when they light on the leaves, nor the breast of the moon when she lies on the breast of the sea . . . There is nothing in the world so white as thy body. Suffer me to touch thy body.'

Oliver Haddo ceased to play. Neither of them stirred. At last Margaret sought by an effort to regain her self-control.

'I shall begin to think that you really are a magician,' she said, lightly.

'I could show you strange things if you cared to see them,' he answered, again raising his eyes to hers.

'I don't think you will ever get me to believe in occult philosophy,' she laughed.

'Yet it reigned in Persia with the magi, it endowed India with wonderful traditions, it civilised Greece to the sounds of Orpheus's lyre.'

He stood before Margaret, towering over her in his huge bulk; and there was a singular fascination in his gaze. It seemed that he spoke only to conceal from her that he was putting forth now all the power that was in him.

'It concealed the first principles of science in the calculations of Pythagoras. It established empires by its oracles, and at its voice tyrants grew pale upon their thrones. It governed the minds of some by curiosity, and others it ruled by fear.'

His voice grew very low, and it was so seductive that Margaret's brain reeled. The sound of it was overpowering like too sweet a fragrance.

'I tell you that for this art nothing is impossible. It commands the elements, and knows the language of the stars, and directs the planets in their courses. The moon at its bidding falls blood-red from the sky. The dead rise up and form into ominous words the night wind that moans through their skulls. Heaven and Hell are in its province; and all forms, lovely and hideous; and love and hate. With Circe's wand it can change men into beasts of the field, and to them it can give a monstrous humanity. Life and death are in the right hand and in the left of him who knows its secrets. It confers wealth by the transmutation of metals and immortality by its quintessence.'

Margaret could not hear what he said. A gradual lethargy seized her under his baleful glance, and she had not even the strength to wish to free herself. She seemed bound to him already by hidden chains.

'If you have powers, show them,' she whispered, hardly conscious that she spoke.

Suddenly he released the enormous tension with which he held her. Like a man who has exerted all his strength to some end, the victory won, he loosened his muscles, with a faint sigh of exhaustion. Margaret did not speak, but she knew that something horrible was about to happen. Her heart beat like a prisoned bird, with helpless flutterings, but it seemed too late now to draw back. Her words by a mystic influence had settled something beyond possibility of recall.

On the stove was a small bowl of polished brass in which water was kept in order to give a certain moisture to the air. Oliver Haddo put his hand in his pocket and drew out a little silver box. He tapped it, with a smile, as a man taps a snuff-box, and it opened. He took an infinitesimal quantity of a blue powder that it contained and threw it on the water in the brass bowl. Immediately a bright flame sprang up, and Margaret gave a cry of alarm. Oliver looked at her quickly and motioned her to remain still. She saw that the water was on fire. It was burning as brilliantly, as hotly, as if it were common gas; and it burned with the same dry, hoarse roar. Suddenly it was extinguished. She leaned forward and saw that the bowl was empty.

The water had been consumed, as though it were straw, and not a drop remained. She passed her hand absently across her forehead.

'But water cannot burn,' she muttered to herself.

It seemed that Haddo knew what she thought, for he smiled strangely.

'Do you know that nothing more destructive can be invented than this blue powder, and I have enough to burn up all the water in Paris? Who dreamt that water might burn like chaff?'

He paused, seeming to forget her presence. He looked thoughtfully at the little silver box.

'But it can be made only in trivial quantities, at enormous expense and with exceeding labour; it is so volatile that you cannot keep it for three days. I have sometimes thought that with a little ingenuity I might make it more stable, I might so modify it that, like radium, it lost no strength as it burned; and then I should possess the greatest secret that has ever been in the mind of man. For there would be no end of it. It would continue to burn while there was a drop of water on the earth, and the whole world would be consumed. But it would be a frightful thing to have in one's hands; for once it were cast upon the waters, the doom of all that existed would be sealed beyond repeal.'

He took a long breath, and his eyes glittered with a devilish ardour. His voice was hoarse with overwhelming emotion.

'Sometimes I am haunted by the wild desire to have seen the great and final scene when the irrevocable flames poured down the river, hurrying along the streams of the earth, searching out the moisture in all growing things, tearing it even from the eternal rocks; when the flames poured down like the rushing of the wind, and all that lived fled from before them till they came to the sea; and the sea itself was consumed in vehement fire.'

Margaret shuddered, but she did not think the man was mad. She had ceased to judge him. He took one more particle of that atrocious powder and put it in the bowl. Again he thrust his hand in his pocket and brought out a handful of some crumbling substance that might have been dried leaves, leaves of different sorts, broken and powdery. There was a trace of moisture in them still, for a low flame sprang up immediately at the bottom of the dish, and a thick vapour filled the room. It had a singular and pungent odour that Margaret did not know. It was difficult to breathe, and she coughed. She wanted to beg Oliver to stop, but could not. He took the bowl in his hands and brought it to her.

'Look,' he commanded.

She bent forward, and at the bottom saw a blue fire, of a peculiar solidity, as though it consisted of molten metal. It was not still, but writhed strangely, like serpents of fire tortured by their own unearthly ardour.

'Breathe very deeply.'

She did as he told her. A sudden trembling came over her, and darkness fell across her eyes. She tried to cry out, but could utter no sound. Her brain reeled. It seemed to her that Haddo bade her cover her face. She gasped for breath, and it was as if the earth spun under her feet. She appeared to travel at an immeasurable speed. She made a slight movement, and Haddo told her not to look round. An immense terror seized her. She did not know whither she was borne, and still they went quickly, quickly; and the hurricane itself would have lagged behind them. At last their motion ceased, and Oliver was holding her arm.

'Don't be afraid,' he said. 'Open your eyes and stand up.'

The night had fallen; but it was not the comfortable night that soothes the troubled minds of mortal men; it was a night that agitated the soul mysteriously so that each nerve in the body tingled. There was a lurid darkness which displayed and yet distorted the objects that surrounded them. No moon shone in the sky, but small stars appeared to dance on the heather, vague night-fires like spirits of the damned. They stood in a vast and troubled waste, with huge stony boulders and leafless trees, rugged and gnarled like tortured souls in pain. It was as if there had been a devastating storm, and the country reposed after the flood of rain and the tempestuous wind and the lightning. All things about them appeared dumbly to suffer, like a man racked by torments who has not the strength even to realize that his agony has ceased. Margaret heard the flight of monstrous birds, and they seemed to whisper strange things on their passage. Oliver took her hand. He led her steadily to a cross-road, and she did not know if they walked amid rocks or tombs.

She heard the sound of a trumpet, and from all parts, strangely appearing where before was nothing, a turbulent assembly surged about her. That vast empty space was suddenly filled by shadowy forms, and they swept along like the waves of the sea, crowding upon one another's heels. And it seemed that all the mighty dead appeared before her; and she saw grim tyrants, and painted courtesans, and Roman emperors in their purple, and sultans of the East. All those fierce evil women of olden time passed by her side, and now it was Mona Lisa and now the subtle daughter of Herodias. And Jezebel looked out upon her from beneath her painted brows, and Cleopatra turned away a wan, lewd face; and she saw the insatiable mouth and the wanton eyes of Messalina, and Fustine was haggard with the eternal fires of lust. She saw cardinals in their scarlet, and warriors in their steel, gay gentlemen in periwigs, and ladies in powder and patch. And on a sudden, like leaves by the wind, all these were driven before the silent throngs of the oppressed; and they were innumerable as the sands of the sea. Their thin faces were earthy with want and cavernous from disease, and their eyes were dull with despair. They passed in their tattered motley, some in the fantastic rags of the beggars of Albrecht Dürer and some in the grey cerecloths of Le Nain; many wore the blouses and the caps of the rabble in France, and many the dingy, smoke-grimed weeds of English poor. And they surged onward like a riotous crowd in narrow streets flying in terror before the mounted troops. It seemed as though all the world were gathered there in strange confusion.

Then all again was void; and Margaret's gaze was riveted upon a great, ruined tree that stood in that waste place, alone, in ghastly desolation; and though a dead thing, it seemed to suffer a more than human pain. The lightning had torn it asunder, but the wind of centuries had sought in vain to drag up its roots. The tortured branches, bare of any twig, were like a Titan's arms, convulsed with intolerable anguish. And in a moment she grew sick with fear, for a change came into the tree, and the tremulousness of life was in it; the rough bark was changed into brutish flesh and the twisted branches into human arms. It became a monstrous, goat-legged thing, more vast than the creatures of nightmare. She saw the horns and the long beard, the great hairy legs with their hoofs, and the man's rapacious hands. The face was horrible with lust and cruelty, and yet it was divine. It was Pan, playing on his pipes, and the lecherous eyes caressed her with a hideous tenderness.

But even while she looked, as the mist of early day, rising, discloses a fair country, the animal part of that ghoulish creature seemed to fall away, and she saw a lovely youth, titanic but sublime, leaning against a massive rock. He was more beautiful than the Adam of Michelangelo who wakes into life at the call of the Almighty; and, like him freshly created, he had the adorable languor of one who feels still in his limbs the soft rain on the loose brown earth. Naked and full of majesty he lay, the outcast son of the morning; and she dared not look upon his face, for she knew it was impossible to bear the undying pain that darkened it with ruthless shadows. Impelled by a great curiosity, she sought to come nearer, but the vast figure seemed strangely to dissolve into a cloud; and immediately she felt herself again surrounded by a hurrying throng. Then came all legendary monsters and foul beasts of a madman's fancy; in the darkness she saw enormous toads, with paws pressed to their flanks, and huge limping scarabs, shelled creatures the like of which she had never seen, and noisome brutes with horny scales and round crabs' eyes, uncouth primeval things, and winged serpents, and creeping animals begotten of the slime. She heard shrill cries and peals of laughter and the terrifying rattle of men at the point of death. Haggard women, dishevelled and lewd, carried wine; and when they spilt it there were stains like the stains of blood. And it seemed to Margaret that a fire burned in her veins, and her soul fled from her body; but a new soul came in its place, and suddenly she knew all that was obscene. She took part in some festival of hideous lust, and the wickedness of the world was patent to her eyes. She saw things so vile that she screamed in terror, and she heard Oliver laugh in derision by her side. It was a scene of indescribable horror, and she put her hands to her eyes so that she might not see.

She felt Oliver Haddo take her hands. She would not let him drag them away. Then she heard him speak.

'You need not be afraid.'

His voice was quite natural once more, and she realized with a start that she was sitting quietly in the studio. She looked around her with frightened eyes. Everything was exactly as it had been.

The early night of autumn was fallen, and the only light in the room came from the fire. There was still that vague, acrid scent of the substance which Haddo had burned.

'Shall I light the candles?' he said.

He struck a match and lit those which were on the piano. They threw a strange light. Then Margaret suddenly remembered all that she had seen, and she remembered that Haddo had stood by her side. Shame seized her, intolerable shame, so that the colour, rising to her cheeks, seemed actually to burn them. She hid her face in her hands and burst into tears.

'Go away,' she said. 'For God's sake, go.'

He looked at her for a moment; and the smile came to his lips which Susie had seen after his tussle with Arthur, when last he was in the studio.

'When you want me you will find me in the Rue de Vaugiraud, number 209,' he said. 'Knock at the second door on the left, on the third floor.'

She did not answer. She could only think of her appalling shame.

'I'll write it down for you in case you forget.'

He scribbled the address on a sheet of paper that he found on the table. Margaret took no notice, but sobbed as though her heart would break. Suddenly, looking up with a start, she saw that he was gone. She had not heard him open the door or close it. She sank down on her knees and prayed desperately, as though some terrible danger threatened her.

But when she heard Susie's key in the door, Margaret sprang to her feet. She stood with her back to the fireplace, her hands behind her, in the attitude of a prisoner protesting his innocence. Susie was too much annoyed to observe this agitation.

'Why on earth didn't you come to tea?' she asked. 'I couldn't make out what had become of you.'

'I had a dreadful headache,' answered Margaret, trying to control herself.

Susie flung herself down wearily in a chair. Margaret forced herself to speak.

'Had Nancy anything particular to say to you?' she asked.

'She never turned up,' answered Susie irritably. 'I can't understand it. I waited till the train came in, but there was no sign of her. Then I thought she might have hit upon that time by chance and was not coming from England, so I walked about the station for half an hour.'

She went to the chimneypiece, on which had been left the telegram that summoned her to the Gare du Nord, and read it again. She gave a little cry of surprise.

'How stupid of me! I never noticed the postmark. It was sent from the Rue Littré.'

'This was less than ten minutes' walk from the studio. Susie looked at the message with perplexity.

'I wonder if someone has been playing a silly practical joke on me.' She shrugged her shoulders. 'But it's too foolish. If I were a suspicious woman,' she smiled, 'I should think you had sent it yourself to get me out of the way.'

The idea flashed through Margaret that Oliver Haddo was the author of it. He might easily have seen Nancy's name on the photograph during his first visit to the studio. She had no time to think before she answered lightly.

'If I wanted to get rid of you, I should have no hesitation in saying so,'

'I suppose no one has been here?' asked Susie.

'No one.'

The lie slipped from Margaret's lips before she had made up her mind to tell it. Her heart gave a great beat against her chest. She felt herself redden.

Susie got up to light a cigarette. She wished to rest her nerves. The box was on the table and, as she helped herself, her eyes felt carelessly on the address that Haddo had left. She picked it up and read it aloud.

'Who on earth lives there?' she asked.

'I don't know at all,' answered Margaret.

She braced herself for further questions, but Susie, without interest, put down the sheet of paper and struck a match.

Margaret was ashamed. Her nature was singularly truthful, and it troubled her extraordinarily that she had lied to her greatest friend. Something stronger than herself seemed to impel her. She would have given much to confess her two falsehoods, but had not the courage. She could not bear that Susie's implicit trust in her straightforwardness should be destroyed; and the admission that Oliver Haddo had been there would entail a further acknowledgment of the nameless horrors she had witnessed. Susie would think her mad.

There was a knock at the door; and Margaret, her nerves shattered by all that she had endured, could hardly restrain a cry of terror. She feared that Haddo had returned. But it was Arthur Burdon. She greeted him with a passionate relief that was unusual, for she was by nature a woman of great self-possession. She felt excessively weak, physically exhausted as though she had gone a long journey, and her mind was highly wrought. Margaret remembered that her state had been the same on her first arrival in Paris, when, in her eagerness to get a preliminary glimpse of its marvels, she had hurried till her bones ached from one celebrated monument to another. They began to speak of trivial things. Margaret tried to join calmly in the conversation, but her voice sounded unnatural, and she fancied that more than once Arthur gave her a curious look. At length she could control herself no longer and burst into a sudden flood of tears. In a moment, uncomprehending but affectionate, he caught her in his arms. He asked tenderly what was the matter. He sought to comfort her. She wept ungovernably, clinging to him for protection.

'Oh, it's nothing,' she gasped. 'I don't know what is the matter with me. I'm only nervous and frightened.'

Arthur had an idea that women were often afflicted with what he described by the old-fashioned name of vapours, and was not disposed to pay much attention to this vehement distress. He soothed her as he would have done a child.

'Oh, take care of me, Arthur. I'm so afraid that some dreadful thing will happen to me. I want all your strength. Promise that you'll never forsake me.'

He laughed, as he kissed away her tears, and she tried to smile.

'Why can't we be married at once?' she asked. 'I don't want to wait any longer. I shan't feel safe till I'm actually your wife.'

He reasoned with her very gently. After all, they were to be married in a few weeks. They could not easily hasten matters, for their house was not yet ready, and she needed time to get her clothes. The date had been fixed by her. She listened sullenly to his words. Their wisdom was plain, and she did not see how she could possibly insist. Even if she told him all that had passed he would not believe her; he would think she was suffering from some trick of her morbid fancy.

'If anything happens to me,' she answered, with the dark, anguished eyes of a hunted beast, 'you will be to blame.'

'I promise you that nothing will happen.'

CHAPTER IX

MARGARET'S night was disturbed, and next day she was unable to go about her work with her usual tranquillity. She tried to reason herself into a natural explanation of the events that had happened. The telegram that Susie had received pointed to a definite scheme on Haddo's part, and suggested that his sudden illness was but a device to get into the studio. Once there, he had used her natural sympathy as a means whereby to exercise his hypnotic power, and all she had seen was merely the creation of his own libidinous fancy. But though she sought to persuade herself that, in playing a vile trick on her, he had taken a shameful advantage of her pity, she could not look upon him with anger. Her contempt for him, her utter loathing, were alloyed with a feeling that aroused in her horror and dismay. She could not get the man out of her thoughts. All that he had said, all that she had seen, seemed, as though it possessed a power of material growth, unaccountably to absorb her. It was as if a rank weed were planted in her heart and slid long poisonous tentacles down every artery, so that each part of her body was enmeshed. Work could not distract her, conversation, exercise, art, left her listless; and between her and all the actions of life stood the flamboyant, bulky form of Oliver Haddo. She was terrified of him now as never before, but curiously had no longer the physical repulsion which hitherto had mastered all other feelings. Although she repeated to herself that she wanted never to see him again, Margaret could scarcely resist an overwhelming desire to go to him. Her will had been taken from her, and she was an automaton. She struggled, like a bird in the fowler's net with useless beating of the wings; but at the bottom of her heart she was dimly conscious that she did not want to resist. If he had given her that address, it was because he knew she would use it. She did not know why she wanted to go to him; she had nothing to say to him; she knew only that it was necessary to go. But a few days before she had seen the *Phèdre* of Racine, and she felt on a sudden all the torments that wrung the heart of that unhappy queen; she, too, struggled aimlessly to escape from the poison that the immortal gods poured in her veins. She asked herself frantically whether a spell had been cast over her, for now she was willing to believe that Haddo's power was all-embracing. Margaret knew that if she yielded to the horrible temptation nothing could save her from destruction. She would have cried for help to Arthur or to Susie, but something, she knew not what, prevented her. At length, driven almost to distraction, she thought that Dr Porhoët might do something for her. He, at least, would understand her misery. There seemed not a moment to lose, and she hastened to his house. They told her he was out. Her heart sank, for it seemed that her last hope was gone. She was like a person drowning, who clings to a rock; and the waves dash against him, and beat upon his bleeding hands with a malice all too human, as if to tear them from their refuge.

Instead of going to the sketch-class, which was held at six in the evening, she hurried to the address that Oliver Haddo had given her. She went along the crowded street stealthily, as though afraid that someone would see her, and her heart was in a turmoil. She desired with all her might not to go, and sought vehemently to prevent herself, and yet withal she went. She ran up the stairs and knocked at the door. She remembered his directions distinctly. In a moment Oliver Haddo stood before her. He did not seem astonished that she was there. As she stood on the landing, it occurred to her suddenly that she had no reason to offer for her visit, but his words saved her from any need for explanation.

'I've been waiting for you,' he said.

Haddo led her into a sitting-room. He had an apartment in a *maison meublée,* and heavy hangings, the solid furniture of that sort of house in Paris, was unexpected in connexion with him. The surroundings were so commonplace that they seemed to emphasise his singularity. There was a peculiar lack of comfort, which suggested that he was indifferent to material things. The room was large, but so cumbered that it gave a cramped impression. Haddo dwelt there as if he were apart from any habitation that might be his. He moved cautiously among the heavy furniture, and his great obesity was somehow more remarkable. There was the acrid perfume which Margaret remembered a few days before in her vision of an Eastern city.

Asking her to sit down, he began to talk as if they were old acquaintances between whom nothing of moment had occurred. At last she took her courage in both hands.

'Why did you make me come here?' she asked suddenly.

'You give me credit now for very marvellous powers,' he smiled.

'You knew I should come.'

'I knew.'

'What have I done to you that you should make me so unhappy? I want you to leave me alone.'

'I shall not prevent you from going out if you choose to go. No harm has come to you. The door is open.'

Her heart beat quickly, painfully almost, and she remained silent. She knew that she did not want to go. There was something that drew her strangely to him, and she was ceasing to resist. A strange feeling began to take hold of her, creeping stealthily through her limbs; and she was terrified, but unaccountably elated.

He began to talk with that low voice of his that thrilled her with a curious magic. He spoke not of pictures now, nor of books, but of life. He told her of strange Eastern places where no infidel had been, and her sensitive fancy was aflame with the honeyed fervour of his phrase. He spoke of the dawn upon sleeping desolate cities, and the moonlit nights of the desert, of the sunsets with their splendour, and of the crowded streets at noon. The beauty of the East rose before her. He told her of many-coloured webs and of silken carpets, the glittering steel of armour damascened, and of barbaric, priceless gems. The splendour of the East blinded her eyes. He spoke of frankincense and myrrh and aloes, of heavy perfumes of the scent-merchants, and drowsy odours of the Syrian gardens. The fragrance of the East filled her nostrils. And all these things were transformed by the power of his words till life itself seemed offered to her, a life of infinite vivacity, a life of freedom, a life of supernatural knowledge. It seemed to her that a comparison was drawn for her attention between the narrow round which awaited her as Arthur's wife and this fair, full existence. She shuddered to think of the dull house in Harley Street and the insignificance of its humdrum duties. But it was possible for her also to enjoy the wonder of the world. Her soul yearned for a beauty that the commonalty of men did not know. And what devil suggested, a warp as it were in the woof of Oliver's speech, that her exquisite loveliness gave her the right to devote herself to the great art of living? She felt a sudden desire for perilous adventures. As though fire passed through her, she sprang to her feet and stood with panting bosom, her flashing eyes bright with the multicoloured pictures that his magic presented.

Oliver Haddo stood too, and they faced one another. Then, on a sudden, she knew what the passion was that consumed her. With a quick movement, his eyes more than ever strangely staring, he took her in his arms, and he kissed her lips. She surrendered herself to him voluptuously. Her whole body burned with the ecstasy of his embrace.

'I think I love you,' she said, hoarsely.

She looked at him. She did not feel ashamed.

'Now you must go,' he said.

He opened the door, and, without another word, she went. She walked through the streets as if nothing at all had happened. She felt neither remorse nor revulsion.

Then Margaret felt every day that uncontrollable desire to go to him; and, though she tried to persuade herself not to yield, she knew that her effort was only a pretence: she did not want anything to prevent her. When it seemed that some accident would do so, she could scarcely control her irritation. There was always that violent hunger of the soul which called her to him, and the only happy hours she had were those spent in his company. Day after day she felt that complete ecstasy when he took her in his huge arms, and kissed her with his heavy, sensual lips. But the ecstasy was extraordinarily mingled with loathing, and her physical attraction was allied with physical abhorrence.

Yet when he looked at her with those pale blue eyes, and threw into his voice those troubling accents, she forgot everything. He spoke of unhallowed things. Sometimes, as it were, he lifted a corner of the veil, and she caught a glimpse of terrible secrets. She understood how men had bartered their souls for infinite knowledge. She seemed to stand upon a pinnacle of the temple, and spiritual kingdoms of darkness, principalities of the unknown, were spread before her eyes to lure her to destruction. But of Haddo himself she learned nothing. She did not know if he loved her. She did not know if he had ever loved. He appeared to stand apart from human kind. Margaret discovered by chance that his mother lived, but he would not speak of her.

'Some day you shall see her,' he said.

'When?'

'Very soon.'

Meanwhile her life proceeded with all outward regularity. She found it easy to deceive her friends, because it occurred to neither that her frequent absence was not due to the plausible reasons she gave. The lies which at first seemed intolerable now tripped glibly off her tongue. But though they were so natural, she was seized often with a panic of fear lest they should be discovered; and sometimes, suffering agonies of remorse, she would lie in bed at night and think with utter shame of the way she was using Arthur. But things had gone too far now, and she must let them take their course. She scarcely knew why her feelings towards him had so completely changed. Oliver Haddo had scarcely mentioned his name and yet had poisoned her mind. The comparison between the two was to Arthur's disadvantage. She thought him a little dull now, and his commonplace way of looking at life contrasted with Haddo's fascinating boldness. She reproached Arthur in her heart because he had never understood what was in her. He narrowed her mind. And gradually she began to hate him because her debt of gratitude was so great. It seemed unfair that he should have done so much for her. He forced her to marry him by his beneficence. Yet Margaret continued to discuss with him the arrangement of their house in Harley Street. It had been her wish to furnish the drawing-room in the style of Louis XV; and together they made long excursions to buy chairs or old pieces of silk with which to cover them. Everything should be perfect in its kind. The date of their marriage was fixed, and all the details were settled. Arthur was ridiculously happy. Margaret made no sign. She did not think of the future, and she spoke of it only to ward off suspicion. She was inwardly convinced now that the marriage would never take place, but what was to prevent it she did not know. She watched Susie and Arthur cunningly. But though she watched in order to conceal her own secret, it was another's that she discovered. Suddenly Margaret became aware that Susie was deeply in love with Arthur Burdon. The discovery was so astounding that at first it seemed absurd.

'You've never done that caricature of Arthur for me that you promised,' she said, suddenly.

'I've tried, but he doesn't lend himself to it,' laughed Susie.

'With that long nose and the gaunt figure I should have thought you could make something screamingly funny.'

'How oddly you talk of him! Somehow I can only see his beautiful, kind eyes and his tender mouth. I would as soon do a caricature of him as write a parody on a poem I loved.'

Margaret took the portfolio in which Susie kept her sketches. She caught the look of alarm that crossed her friend's face, but Susie had not the courage to prevent her from looking. She turned the drawings carelessly and presently came to a sheet upon which, in a more or less finished state, were half a dozen heads of Arthur. Pretending not to see it, she went on to the end. When she closed the portfolio Susie gave a sigh of relief.

'I wish you worked harder,' said Margaret, as she put the sketches down. 'I wonder you don't do a head of Arthur as you can't do a caricature.'

'My dear, you mustn't expect everyone to take such an overpowering interest in that young man as you do.'

The answer added a last certainty to Margaret's suspicion. She told herself bitterly that Susie was no less a liar than she. Next day, when the other was out, Margaret looked through the portfolio once more, but the sketches of Arthur had disappeared. She was seized on a sudden with anger because Susie dared to love the man who loved her.

The web in which Oliver Haddo enmeshed her was woven with skilful intricacy. He took each part of her character separately and fortified with consummate art his influence over her. There was something satanic in his deliberation, yet in actual time it was almost incredible that he could have changed the old abhorrence with which she regarded him into that hungry passion. Margaret could not now realize her life apart from his. At length he thought the time was ripe for the final step.

'It may interest you to know that I'm leaving Paris on Thursday,' he said casually, one afternoon.

She started to her feet and stared at him with bewildered eyes.

'But what is to become of me?'

'You will marry the excellent Mr Burdon.'

'You know I cannot live without you. How can you be so cruel?'

'Then the only alternative is that you should accompany me.'

Her blood ran cold, and her heart seemed pressed in an iron vice.

'What do you mean?'

'There is no need to be agitated. I am making you an eminently desirable offer of marriage.'

She sank helplessly into her chair. Because she had refused to think of the future, it had never struck her that the time must come when it would be necessary to leave Haddo or to throw in her lot with his definitely. She was seized with revulsion. Margaret realized that, though an odious attraction bound her to the man, she loathed and feared him. The scales fell from her eyes. She remembered on a sudden Arthur's great love and all that he had done for her sake. She hated herself. Like a bird at its last gasp beating frantically against the bars of a cage, Margaret made a desperate effort to regain her freedom. She sprang up.

'Let me go from here. I wish I'd never seen you. I don't know what you've done with me.'

'Go by all means if you choose,' he answered.

He opened the door, so that she might see he used no compulsion, and stood lazily at the threshold, with a hateful smile on his face. There was something terrible in his excessive bulk. Rolls of fat descended from his chin and concealed his neck. His cheeks were huge, and the lack of beard added to the hideous nakedness of his face. Margaret stopped as she passed him, horribly repelled yet horribly fascinated. She had an immense desire that he should take her again in his arms and press her lips with that red voluptuous mouth. It was as though fiends of hell were taking revenge upon her loveliness by inspiring in her a passion for this monstrous creature. She trembled with the intensity of her desire. His eyes were hard and cruel.

'Go,' he said.

She bent her head and fled from before him. To get home she passed through the gardens of the Luxembourg, but her legs failed her, and in exhaustion she sank upon a bench. The day was sultry. She tried to collect herself. Margaret knew well the part in which she sat, for in the enthusiastic days that seemed so long gone by she was accustomed to come there for the sake of a certain tree upon which her eyes now rested. It had all the slim delicacy of a Japanese print. The leaves were slender and fragile, half gold with autumn, half green, but so tenuous that the dark branches made a pattern of subtle beauty against the sky. The hand of a draughtsman could not have fashioned it with a more excellent skill. But now Margaret could take no pleasure in its grace. She felt a heartrending pang to think that thenceforward the consummate things of art would have no meaning for her. She had seen Arthur the evening before, and remembered with an agony of shame the lies to which she had been forced in order to explain why she could not see him till late that day. He had proposed that they should go to Versailles, and was bitterly disappointed when she told him they could not, as usual on Sundays, spend the whole day together. He accepted her excuse that she had to visit a sick friend. It would not have been so intolerable if he had suspected her of deceit, and his reproaches would have hardened her heart. It was his entire confidence which was so difficult to bear.

'Oh, if I could only make a clean breast of it all,' she cried.

The bell of Saint Sulpice was ringing for vespers. Margaret walked slowly to the church, and sat down in the seats reserved in the transept for the needy. She hoped that the music she must hear there would rest her soul, and perhaps she might be able to pray. Of late she had not dared. There was a pleasant darkness in the place, and its large simplicity was soothing. In her exhaustion, she watched listlessly the people go to and fro. Behind her was a priest in the confessional. A little peasant girl, in a Breton *coiffe,* perhaps a maid-servant lately come from her native village to the great capital, passed in and knelt down. Margaret could hear her muttered words, and at intervals the deep voice of the priest. In three minutes she tripped neatly away. She looked so fresh in her plain black dress, so healthy and innocent, that Margaret could not restrain a sob of envy. The child had so little to confess, a few puny errors which must excite a smile on the lips of the gentle priest, and her candid spirit was like snow. Margaret would have given anything to kneel down and whisper in those passionless ears all that she suffered, but the priest's faith and hers were not the same. They spoke a different tongue, not of the lips only but of the soul, and he would not listen to the words of an heretic.

A long procession of seminarists came in from the college which is under the shadow of that great church, two by two, in black cassocks and short white surplices. Many were tonsured already. Some were quite young. Margaret watched their faces, wondering if they were tormented by such agony as she. But they had a living faith to sustain them, and if some, as was plain, were narrow and obtuse, they had at least a fixed rule which prevented them from swerving into treacherous byways. One of two had a wan ascetic look, such as the saints may have had when the terror of life was known to them only in the imaginings of the cloister. The canons of the church followed in their more gorgeous vestments, and finally the officiating clergy.

The music was beautiful. There was about it a staid, sad dignity; and it seemed to Margaret fit thus to adore God. But it did not move her. She could not understand the words that the priests chanted; their gestures, their movements to and fro, were strange to her. For her that stately service had no meaning. And with a great cry in her heart she said that God had forsaken her. She was alone in an alien land. Evil was all about her, and in those ceremonies she could find no comfort. What could she expect when the God of her fathers left her to her fate? So that she might not weep in front of all those people, Margaret with down-turned face walked to the door. She felt utterly lost. As she walked along the interminable street that led to her own house, she was shaken with sobs.

'God has forsaken me,' she repeated. 'God has foresaken me.'

Next day, her eyes red with weeping, she dragged herself to Haddo's door. When he opened it, she went in without a word. She sat down, and he watched her in silence.

'I am willing to marry you whenever you choose,' she said at last.

'I have made all the necessary arrangements.'

'You have spoken to me of your mother. Will you take me to her at once.'

The shadow of a smile crossed his lips.

'If you wish it.'

Haddo told her that they could be married before the Consul early enough on the Thursday morning to catch a train for England. She left everything in his hands.

'I'm desperately unhappy,' she said dully.

Oliver laid his hands upon her shoulders and looked into her eyes.

'Go home, and you will forget your tears. I command you to be happy.'

Then it seemed that the bitter struggle between the good and the evil in her was done, and the evil had conquered. She felt on a sudden curiously elated. It seemed no longer to matter that she deceived her faithful friends. She gave a bitter laugh, as she thought how easy it was to hoodwink them.

Wednesday happened to be Arthur's birthday, and he asked her to dine with him alone.

'We'll do ourselves proud, and hang the expense,' he said.

They had arranged to eat at a fashionable restaurant on the other side of the river, and soon after seven he fetched her. Margaret was dressed with exceeding care. She stood in the middle of the room, waiting for Arthur's arrival, and surveyed herself in the glass. Susie thought she had never been more beautiful.

'I think you've grown more pleasing to look upon than you ever were,' she said. 'I don't know what it is that has come over you of late, but there's a depth in your eyes that is quite new. It gives you an odd mysteriousness which is very attractive.'

Knowing Susie's love for Arthur, she wondered whether her friend was not heartbroken as she compared her own plainness with the radiant beauty that was before her. Arthur came in, and Margaret did not move. He stopped at the door to look at her. Their eyes met. His heart beat quickly, and yet he was seized with awe. His good fortune was too great to bear, when he thought that this priceless treasure was his. He could have knelt down and worshipped as though a goddess of old Greece stood before him. And to him also her eyes had changed. They had acquired a burning passion which disturbed and yet enchanted him. It seemed that the lovely girl was changed already into a lovely woman. An enigmatic smile came to her lips.

'Are you pleased?' she asked.

Arthur came forward and Margaret put her hands on his shoulders.

'You have scent on,' he said.

He was surprised, for she had never used it before. It was a faint, almost acrid perfume that he did not know. It reminded him vaguely of those odours which he remembered in his childhood in the East. It was remote and strange. It gave Margaret a new and troubling charm. There had ever been something cold in her statuesque beauty, but this touch somehow curiously emphasized her sex, Arthur's lips twitched, and his gaunt face grew pale with passion. His emotion was so great that it was nearly pain. He was puzzled, for her eyes expressed things that he had never seen in them before.

'Why don't you kiss me?' she said.

She did not see Susie, but knew that a quick look of anguish crossed her face. Margaret drew Arthur towards her. His hands began to tremble. He had never ventured to express the passion that consumed him, and when he kissed her it was with a restraint that was almost brotherly. Now their lips met. Forgetting that anyone else was in the room, he flung his arms around Margaret. She had never kissed him in that way before, and the rapture was intolerable. Her lips were like living fire. He could not take his own away. He forgot everything. All his strength, all his self-control, deserted him. It crossed his mind that at this moment he would willingly die. But the delight of it was so great that he could scarcely withhold a cry of agony. At length Susie's voice reminded him of the world.

'You'd far better go out to dinner instead of behaving like a pair of complete idiots.'

She tried to make her tone as flippant as the words, but her voice was cut by a pang of agony. With a little laugh, Margaret withdrew from Arthur's embrace and lightly looked at her friend. Susie's brave smile died away as she caught this glance, for there was in it a malicious hatred that startled her. It was so unexpected that she was terrified. What had she done? She was afraid, dreadfully afraid, that Margaret had guessed her secret. Arthur stood as if his senses had left him, quivering still with the extremity of passion.

'Susie says we must go,' smiled Margaret.

He could not speak. He could not regain the conventional manner of polite society. Very pale, like a man suddenly awaked from deep sleep, he went out at Margaret's side. They walked along the passage. Though the door was closed behind them and they were out of earshot, Margaret seemed not withstanding to hear Susie's passionate sobbing. It gave her a horrible delight.

The tavern to which they went was on the Boulevard des Italiens, and at this date the most frequented in Paris. It was crowded, but Arthur had reserved a table in the middle of the room. Her radiant loveliness made people stare at Margaret as she passed, and her consciousness of the admiration she excited increased her beauty. She was satisfied that amid that throng of the best-dressed women in the world she had cause to envy no one. The gaiety was charming. Shaded lights gave an opulent cosiness to the scene, and there were flowers everywhere. Innumerable mirrors reflected women of the world, admirably gowned, actresses of renown, and fashionable courtesans. The noise was very great. A Hungarian band played in a distant corner, but the music was drowned by the loud talking of excited men and the boisterous laughter of women. It was plain that people had come to spend their money with a lavish hand. The vivacious crowd was given over with all its heart to the pleasure of the fleeting moment. Everyone had put aside grave thoughts and sorrow.

Margaret had never been in better spirits. The champagne went quickly to her head, and she talked all manner of charming nonsense. Arthur was enchanted. He was very proud, very pleased, and very happy. They talked of all the things they would do when they were married. They talked of the places they must go to, of their home and of the beautiful things with which they would fill it. Margaret's animation was extraordinary. Arthur was amused at her delight with the brightness of the place, with the good things they ate, and with the wine. Her laughter was like a rippling brook. Everything tended to take him out of his usual reserve. Life was very pleasing, at that moment, and he felt singularly joyful.

'Let us drink to the happiness of our life,' he said.

They touched glasses. He could not take his eyes away from her.

'You're simply wonderful tonight,' he said. 'I'm almost afraid of my good fortune.'

'What is there to be afraid of?' she cried.

'I should like to lose something I valued in order to propitiate the fates. I am too happy now. Everything goes too well with me.'

She gave a soft, low laugh and stretched out her hand on the table. No sculptor could have modelled its exquisite delicacy. She wore only one ring, a large emerald which Arthur had given her on their engagement. He could not resist taking her hand.

'Would you like to go on anywhere?' he said, when they had finished dinner and were drinking their coffee.

'No, let us stay here. I must go to bed early, as I have a tiring day before me tomorrow.'

'What are you going to do?' he asked.

'Nothing of any importance,' she laughed.

Presently the diners began to go in little groups, and Margaret suggested that they should saunter towards the Madeleine. The night was fine, but rather cold, and the broad avenue was crowded. Margaret watched the people. It was no less amusing than a play. In a little while, they took a cab and drove through the streets, silent already, that led to the quarter of the Montparnasse. They sat in silence, and Margaret nestled close to Arthur. He put his arm around her waist. In the shut cab that faint, oriental odour rose again to his nostrils, and his head reeled as it had before dinner.

'You've made me very happy, Margaret,' he whispered. 'I feel that, however long I live, I shall never have a happier day than this.'

'Do you love me very much?' she asked, lightly.

He did not answer, but took her face in his hands and kissed her passionately. They arrived at Margaret's house, and she tripped up to the door. She held out her hand to him, smiling.

'Goodnight.'

'It's dreadful to think that I must spend a dozen hours without seeing you. When may I come?'

'Not in the morning, because I shall be too busy. Come at twelve.'

She remembered that her train started exactly at that hour. The door was opened, and with a little wave of the hand she disappeared.

CHAPTER X

SUSIE stared without comprehension at the note that announced Margaret's marriage. It was a *petit bleu* sent off from the Gare du Nord, and ran as follows:

> When you receive this I shall be on my way to London. I was married to Oliver Haddo this morning. I love him as I never loved Arthur. I have acted in this manner because I thought I had gone too far with Arthur to make an explanation possible. Please tell him.
>
> MARGARET

Susie was filled with dismay. She did not know what to do nor what to think. There was a knock at the door, and she knew it must be Arthur, for he was expected at midday. She decided quickly that it was impossible to break the news to him then and there. It was needful first to find out all manner of things, and besides, it was incredible. Making up her mind, she opened the door.

'Oh, I'm so sorry Margaret isn't here,' she said. 'A friend of hers is ill and sent for her suddenly.'

'What a bore!' answered Arthur. 'Mrs Bloomfield as usual, I suppose?'

'Oh, you know she's been ill?'

'Margaret has spent nearly every afternoon with her for some days.'

Susie did not answer. This was the first she had heard of Mrs Bloomfield's illness, and it was news that Margaret was in the habit of visiting her. But her chief object at this moment was to get rid of Arthur.

'Won't you come back at five o'clock?' she said.

'But, look here, why shouldn't we lunch together, you and I?'

'I'm very sorry, but I'm expecting somebody in.'

'Oh, all right. Then I'll come back at five.'

He nodded and went out. Susie read the brief note once more, and asked herself if it could possibly be true. The callousness of it was appalling. She went to Margaret's room and saw that everything was in its place. It did not look as if the owner had gone on a journey. But then she noticed that a number of letters had been destroyed. She opened a drawer and found that Margaret's trinkets were gone. An idea struck her. Margaret had bought lately a number of clothes, and these she had insisted should be sent to her dressmaker, saying that it was needless to cumber their little apartment with them. They could stay there till she returned to England a few weeks later for her marriage, and it would be simpler to despatch them all from one place. Susie went out. At the door it occurred to her to ask the *concierge* if she knew where Margaret had gone that morning.

'Parfaitement, Mademoiselle,' answered the old woman. 'I heard her tell the coachman to go to the British Consulate.'

The last doubt was leaving Susie. She went to the dressmaker and there discovered that by Margaret's order the boxes containing her things had gone on the previous day to the luggage office of the Gare du Nord.

'I hope you didn't let them go till your bill was paid,' said Susie lightly, as though in jest.

The dressmaker laughed.

'Mademoiselle paid for everything two or three days ago.'

With indignation, Suise realised that Margaret had not only taken away the trousseau bought for her marriage with Arthur; but, since she was herself penniless, had paid for it with the money which he had generously given her. Susie drove then to Mrs Bloomfield, who at once reproached her for not coming to see her.

'I'm sorry, but I've been exceedingly busy, and I knew that Margaret was looking after you.'

'I've not seen Margaret for three weeks,' said the invalid.

'Haven't you? I thought she dropped in quite often.'

Susie spoke as though the matter were of no importance. She asked herself now where Margaret could have spent those afternoons. By a great effort she forced herself to speak of casual things with the garrulous old lady long enough to make her visit seem natural. On leaving her, she went to the Consulate, and her last doubt was dissipated. Then nothing remained but to go home and wait for Arthur. Her first impulse had been to see Dr Porhoët and ask for his advice; but, even if he offered to come back with her to the studio, his presence would be useless. She must see Arthur by himself. Her heart was wrung as she thought of the man's agony when he knew the truth. She had confessed to herself long before that she loved him passionately, and it seemed intolerable that she of all persons must bear him this great blow.

She sat in the studio, counting the minutes, and thought with a bitter smile that his eagerness to see Margaret would make him punctual. She had eaten nothing since the *petit déjeuner* of the morning, and she was faint with hunger. But she had not the heart to make herself tea. At last he came. He entered joyfully and looked around.

'Is Margaret not here yet?' he asked, with surprise.

'Won't you sit down?'

He did not notice that her voice was strange, nor that she kept her eyes averted.

'How lazy you are,' he cried. 'You haven't got the tea.'

'Mr Burdon, I have something to say to you. It will cause you very great pain.'

He observed now the hoarseness of her tone. He sprang to his feet, and a thousand fancies flashed across his brain. Something horrible had happened to Margaret. She was ill. His terror was so great that he could not speak. He put out his hands as does a blind man. Susie had to make an effort to go on. But she could not. Her voice was choked, and she began to cry. Arthur trembled as though he were seized with ague. She gave him the letter.

'What does it mean?'

He looked at her vacantly. Then she told him all that she had done that day and the places to which she had been.

'When you thought she was spending every afternoon with Mrs Bloomfield, she was with that man. She made all the arrangements with the utmost care. It was quite premeditated.'

Arthur sat down and leaned his head on his hand. He turned his back to her, so that she should not see his face. They remained in perfect silence. And it was so terrible that Susie began to cry quietly. She knew that the man she loved was suffering an agony greater than the agony of death, and she could not help him. Rage flared up in her heart, and hatred for Margaret.

'Oh, it's infamous!' she cried suddenly. 'She's lied to you, she's 'been odiously deceitful. She must be vile and heartless. She must be rotten to the very soul.'

He turned round sharply, and his voice was hard.

'I forbid you to say anything against her.'

Susie gave a little gasp. He had never spoken to her before in anger. She flashed out bitterly.

'Can you love her still, when she's shown herself capable of such vile treachery? For nearly a month this man must have been making love to her, and she's listened to all we said of him. She's pretended to hate the sight of him, I've seen her cut him in the street. She's gone on with all the preparations for your marriage. She must have lived in a world of lies, and you never suspected anything because you had an unalterable belief in her love and truthfulness. She owes everything to you. For four years she's lived on your charity. She was only able to be here because you gave her money to carry out a foolish whim, and the very clothes on her back were paid for by you.'

'I can't help it if she didn't love me,' he cried desperately.

'You know just as well as I do that she pretended to love you. Oh, she's behaved shamefully. There can be no excuse for her.'

He looked at Susie with haggard, miserable eyes.

'How can you be so cruel? For God's sake don't make it harder.'

There was an indescribable agony in his voice. And as if his own words of pain overcame the last barrier of his self-control, he broke down. He hid his face in his hands and sobbed. Susie was horribly conscience-stricken.

'Oh, I'm so sorry,' she said. 'I didn't mean to say such hateful things. I didn't mean to be unkind. I ought to have remembered how passionately you love her.'

It was very painful to see the effort he made to regain his self-command. Susie suffered as much as he did. Her impulse was to throw herself on her knees, and kiss his hands, and comfort him; but she knew that he was interested in her only because she was Margaret's friend. At last he got up and, taking his pipe from his pocket, filled it silently. She was terrified at the look on his face. The first time she had ever seen him, Susie wondered at the possibility of self-torture which was in that rough-hewn countenance; but she had never dreamed that it could express such unutterable suffering. Its lines were suddenly changed, and it was terrible to look upon.

'I can't believe it's true,' he muttered. 'I can't believe it.'

There was a knock at the door, and Arthur gave a startled cry.

'Perhaps she's come back.'

He opened it hurriedly, his face suddenly lit up by expectation; but it was Dr Porhoët.

'How do you do?' said the Frenchman. 'What is happening?'

He looked round and caught the dismay that was on the faces of Arthur and Susie.

'Where is Miss Margaret? I thought you must be giving a party.'

There was something in his manner that made Susie ask why.

'I received a telegram from Mr Haddo this morning.'

He took it from his pocket and handed it to Susie. She read it and passed it to Arthur. It said:

Come to the studio at five. High jinks.

OLIVER HADDO

'Margaret was married to Mr Haddo this morning,' said Arthur, quietly. 'I understand they have gone to England.'

Susie quickly told the doctor the few facts they knew. He was as surprised, as distressed, as they.

'But what is the explanation of it all?' he asked.

Arthur shrugged his shoulders wearily.

'She cared for Haddo more than she cared for me, I suppose. It is natural enough that she should go away in this fashion rather than offer explanations. I suppose she wanted to save herself a scene she thought might be rather painful.'

'When did you see her last?'

'We spent yesterday evening together.'

'And did she not show in any way that she contemplated such a step?'

Arthur shook his head.

'You had no quarrel?'

'We've never quarrelled. She was in the best of spirits. I've never seen her more gay. She talked the whole time of our house in London, and of the places we must visit when we were married.'

Another contraction of pain passed over his face as he remembered that she had been more affectionate than she had ever been before. The fire of her kisses still burnt upon his lips. He had spent a night of almost sleepless ecstasy because he had been certain for the first time that the passion which consumed him burnt in her heart too. Words were dragged out of him against his will.

'Oh, I'm sure she loved me.'

Meanwhile Susie's eyes were fixed on Haddo's cruel telegram. She seemed to hear his mocking laughter.

'Margaret loathed Oliver Haddo with a hatred that was almost unnatural. It was a physical repulsion like that which people sometimes have for certain animals. What can have happened to change it into so great a love that it has made her capable of such villainous acts?'

'We mustn't be unfair to him,' said Arthur. 'He put our backs up, and we were probably unjust. He has done some very remarkable things in his day, and he's no fool. It's possible that some people wouldn't mind the eccentricities which irritated us. He's certainly of very good family and he's rich. In many ways it's an excellent match for Margaret.'

He was trying with all his might to find excuses for her. It would not make her treachery so intolerable if he could persuade himself that Haddo had qualities which might explain her infatuation. But as his enemy stood before his fancy, monstrously obese, vulgar, and overbearing, a shudder passed through him. The thought of Margaret in that man's arms tortured him as though his flesh were torn with iron hooks.

'Perhaps it's not true. Perhaps she'll return,' he cried.

'Would you take her back if she came to you?' asked Susie.

'Do you think anything she can do has the power to make me love her less? There must be reasons of which we know nothing that caused her to do all she has done. I daresay it was inevitable from the beginning.'

Dr Porhoët got up and walked across the room.

'If a woman had done me such an injury that I wanted to take some horrible vengeance, I think I could devise nothing more subtly cruel than to let her be married to Oliver Haddo.'

'Ah, poor thing, poor thing!' said Arthur. 'If I could only suppose she would be happy! The future terrifies me.'

'I wonder if she knew that Haddo had sent that telegram,' said Susie.

'What can it matter?'

She turned to Arthur gravely.

'Do you remember that day, in this studio, when he kicked Margaret's dog, and you thrashed him? Well, afterwards, when he thought no one saw him, I happened to catch sight of his face. I never saw in my life such malignant hatred. It was the face of a fiend of wickedness. And when he tried to excuse himself, there was a cruel gleam in his eyes which terrified me. I warned you; I told you that he had made up his mind to revenge himself, but you laughed at me. And then he seemed to go out of our lives and I thought no more about it. I wonder why he sent Dr Porhoët here today. He must have known that the doctor would hear of his humiliation, and he may have wished that he should be present at his triumph. I think that very moment he made up his mind to be even with you, and he devised this odious scheme.'

'How could he know that it was possible to carry out such a horrible thing?' said Arthur.

'I wonder if Miss Boyd is right,' murmured the doctor. 'After all, if you come to think of it, he must have thought that he couldn't hurt you more. The whole thing is fiendish. He took away from you all your happiness. He must have known that you wanted nothing in the world more than to make Margaret your wife, and he has not only prevented that, but he has married her himself. And he can only have done it by poisoning her mind, by warping her very character. Her soul must be horribly besmirched; he must have entirely changed her personality.'

'Ah, I feel that,' cried Arthur. 'If Margaret has broken her word to me, if she's gone to him so callously, it's because it's not the Margaret I know. Some devil must have taken possession of her body.'

'You use a figure of speech. I wonder if it can possibly be a reality.'

Arthur and Dr Porhoët looked at Susie with astonishment.

'I can't believe that Margaret could have done such a thing,' she went on. 'The more I think of it, the more incredible it seems. I've known Margaret for years, and she was incapable of deceit. She was very kind-hearted. She was honest and truthful. In the first moment of horror, I was only indignant, but I don't want to think too badly of her. There is only one way to excuse her, and that is by supposing she acted under some strange compulsion.'

Arthur clenched his hands.

'I'm not sure if that doesn't make it more awful than before. If he's married her, not because he cares, but in order to hurt me, what life will she lead with him? We know how heartless he is, how vindictive, how horribly cruel.'

'Dr Porhoët knows more about these things than we do,' said Susie. 'Is it possible that Haddo can have cast some spell upon her that would make her unable to resist his will? Is it possible that he can have got such an influence over her that her whole character was changed?'

'How can I tell?' cried the doctor helplessly. 'I have heard that such things may happen. I have read of them, but I have no proof. In these matters all is obscurity. The adepts in magic make strange claims. Arthur is a man of science, and he knows what the limits of hypnotism are.'

'We know that Haddo had powers that other men have not,' answered Susie. 'Perhaps there was enough truth in his extravagant pretensions to enable him to do something that we can hardly imagine.'

Arthur passed his hands wearily over his face.

'I'm so broken, so confused, that I cannot think sanely. At this moment everything seems possible. My faith in all the truths that have supported me is tottering.'

For a while they remained silent Arthur's eyes rested on the chair in which Margaret had so often sat. An unfinished canvas still stood upon the easel. It was Dr Porhoët who spoke at last.

'But even if there were some truth in Miss Boyd's suppositions, I don't see how it can help you. You cannot do anything. You have no remedy, legal or otherwise. Margaret is apparently a free agent, and she has married this man. It is plain that many people will think she has done much better in marrying a country gentleman than in marrying a young surgeon. Her letter is perfectly lucid. There is no trace of compulsion. To all intents and purposes she has married him of her own free-will, and there is nothing to show that she desires to be released from him or from the passion which we may suppose enslaves her.'

What he said was obviously true, and no reply was possible.

'The only thing is to grin and bear it,' said Arthur, rising.

'Where are you going?' said Susie.

'I think I want to get away from Paris. Here everything will remind me of what I have lost. I must get back to my work.'

He had regained command over himself, and except for the hopeless woe of his face, which he could not prevent from being visible, he was as calm as ever. He held out his hand to Susie.

'I can only hope that you'll forget,' she said.

'I don't wish to forget,' he answered, shaking his head. 'It's possible that you will hear from Margaret. She'll want the things that she has left here, and I daresay will write to you. I should like you to tell her that I bear her no ill-will for anything she has done, and I will never venture to reproach her. I don't know if I shall be able to do anything for her, but I wish her to know that in any case and always I will do everything that she wants.'

'If she writes to me, I will see that she is told,' answered Susie gravely.

'And now goodbye.'

'You can't go to London till tomorrow. Shan't I see you in the morning?'

'I think if you don't mind, I won't come here again. The sight of all this rather disturbs me.'

Again a contraction of pain passed across his eyes, and Susie saw that he was using a superhuman effort to preserve the appearance of composure. She hesitated a moment.

'Shall I never see you again?' she said. 'I should be sorry to lose sight of you entirely.'

'I should be sorry, too,' he answered. 'I have learned how good and kind you are, and I shall never forget that you are Margaret's friend. When you come to London, I hope that you will let me know.'

He went out. Dr Porhoët, his hands behind his back, began to walk up and down the room. At last he turned to Susie.

'There is one thing that puzzles me,' he said. 'Why did he marry her?'

'You heard what Arthur said,' answered Susie bitterly. 'Whatever happened, he would have taken her back. The other man knew that he could only bind her to him securely by going through the ceremonies of marriage.'

Dr Porhoët shrugged his shoulders, and presently he left her. When Susie was alone she began to weep broken-heartedly, not for herself, but because Arthur suffered an agony that was hardly endurable.

CHAPTER XI

ARTHUR went back to London next day.

Susie felt it impossible any longer to stay in the deserted studio, and accepted a friend's invitation to spend the winter in Italy. The good Dr Porhoët remained in Paris with his books and his occult studies.

Susie travelled slowly through Tuscany and Umbria. Margaret had not written to her, and Susie, on leaving Paris, had sent her friend's belongings to an address from which she knew they would eventually be forwarded. She could not bring herself to write. In answer to a note announcing her change of plans, Arthur wrote briefly that he had much work to do and was delivering a new course of lectures at St. Luke's; he had lately been appointed visiting surgeon to another hospital, and his private practice was increasing. He did not mention Margaret. His letter was abrupt, formal, and constrained. Susie, reading it for the tenth time, could make little of it. She saw that he wrote only from civility, without interest; and there was nothing to indicate his state of mind. Susie and her companion had made up their minds to pass some weeks in Rome; and here, to her astonishment, Susie had news of Haddo and his wife. It appeared that they had spent some time there, and the little English circle was talking still of their eccentricities. They travelled in some state, with a courier and a suite of servants; they had taken a carriage and were in the habit of driving every afternoon on the Pincio. Haddo had excited attention by the extravagance of his costume, and Margaret by her beauty; she was to be seen in her box at the opera every night, and her diamonds were the envy of all beholders. Though people had laughed a good deal at Haddo's pretentiousness, and been exasperated by his arrogance, they could not fail to be impressed by his obvious wealth. But finally the pair had disappeared suddenly without saying a word to anybody. A good many bills remained unpaid, but these, Susie learnt, had been settled later. It was reported that they were now in Monte Carlo.

'Did they seem happy?' Susie asked the gossiping friend who gave her this scanty information.

'I think so. After all, Mrs Haddo has almost everything that a woman can want, riches, beauty, nice clothes, jewels. She would be very unreasonable not to be happy.'

Susie had meant to pass the later spring on the Riviera, but when she heard that the Haddos were there, she hesitated. She did not want to run the risk of seeing them, and yet she had a keen desire to find out exactly how things were going. Curiosity and distaste struggled in her mind, but curiosity won; and she persuaded her friend to go to Monte Carlo instead of to Beaulieu. At first Susie did not see the Haddos; but rumour was already much occupied with them, and she had only to keep her ears open. In that strange place, where all that is extravagant and evil, all that is morbid, insane, and fantastic, is gathered together, the Haddos were in fit company. They were notorious for their assiduity at the tables and for their luck, for the dinners and suppers they gave at places frequented by the very opulent, and for their eccentric appearance. It was a complex picture that Susie put together from the scraps of information she collected. After two or three days she saw them at the tables, but they were so absorbed in their game that she felt quite safe from discovery. Margaret was playing, but Haddo stood behind her and directed her movements. Their faces were extraordinarily intent. Susie fixed her attention on Margaret, for in what she had heard of her she had been quite unable to recognize the girl who had been her friend. And what struck her most now was that there was in Margaret's expression a singular likeness to Haddo's. Notwithstanding her exquisite beauty, she had a curiously vicious look, which suggested that somehow she saw literally with Oliver's eyes. They had won great sums that evening, and many persons watched them. It appeared that they played always in this fashion, Margaret putting on the stakes and Haddo telling her what to do and when to stop. Susie heard two Frenchmen talking of them. She listened with all her ears. She flushed as she heard one of them make an observation about Margaret which was more than coarse. The other laughed.

'It is incredible,' he said.

'I assure you it's true. They have been married six months, and she is still only his wife in name. The superstitious through all the ages have believed in the power of virginity, and the Church has made use of the idea for its own ends. The man uses her simply as a mascot.'

The men laughed, and their conversation proceeded so grossly that Susie's cheeks burned. But what she had heard made her look at Margaret more closely still. She was radiant. Susie could not deny that something had come to her that gave a new, enigmatic savour to her beauty. She was dressed more gorgeously than Susie's fastidious taste would have permitted; and her diamonds, splendid in themselves, were too magnificent for the occasion. At last, sweeping up the money, Haddo touched her on the shoulder, and she rose. Behind her was standing a painted woman of notorious disreputability. Susie was astonished to see Margaret smile and nod as she passed her.

Susie learnt that the Haddos had a suite of rooms at the most expensive of the hotels. They lived in a whirl of gaiety. They knew few English except those whose reputations were damaged, but seemed to prefer the society of those foreigners whose wealth and eccentricities made them the cynosure of that little world. Afterwards, she often saw them, in company of Russian Grand-Dukes and their mistresses, of South American women with prodigious diamonds, of noble gamblers and great ladies of doubtful fame, of strange men overdressed and scented. Rumour was increasingly busy with them. Margaret moved among all those queer people with a cold mysteriousness that excited the curiosity of the sated idlers. The suggestion which Susie overheard was repeated more circumstantially. But to this was joined presently the report of orgies that were enacted in the darkened sitting-room of the hotel, when all that was noble and vicious in Monte Carlo was present. Oliver's eccentric imagination invented whimsical festivities. He had a passion for disguise, and he gave a fancy-dress party of which fabulous stories were told. He sought to revive the mystical ceremonies of old religions, and it was reported that horrible rites had been performed in the garden of the villa, under the shining moon, in imitation of those he had seen in Eastern places. It was said that Haddo had magical powers of extraordinary character, and the tired imagination of those pleasure-seekers was tickled by his talk of black art. Some even asserted that the blasphemous ceremonies of the Black Mass had been celebrated in the house of a Polish Prince, People babbled of satanism and of necromancy. Haddo was thought to be immersed in occult studies for the performance of a magical operation; and some said that he was occupied with the *Magnum Opus,* the greatest and most fantastic of alchemical experiments. Gradually these stories were narrowed down to the monstrous assertion that he was attempting to create living beings. He had explained at length to somebody that magical receipts existed for the manufacture of *homunculi.*

Haddo was known generally by the name he was pleased to give himself, The Brother of the Shadow; but most people used it in derision, for it contrasted absurdly with his astonishing bulk. They were amused or outraged by his vanity, but they could not help talking about him, and Susie knew well enough by now that nothing pleased him more. His exploits as a lion-hunter were well known, and it was reported that human blood was on his hands. It was soon discovered that he had a queer power over animals, so that in his presence they were seized with unaccountable terror. He succeeded in surrounding himself with an atmosphere of the fabulous, and nothing that was told of him was too extravagant for belief. But unpleasant stories were circulated also, and someone related that he had been turned out of a club in Vienna for cheating at cards. He played many games, but here, as at Oxford, it was found that he was an unscrupulous opponent. And those old rumours followed him that he took strange drugs. He was supposed to have odious vices, and people whispered to one another of scandals that had been with difficulty suppressed. No one quite understood on what terms he was with his wife, and it was vaguely asserted that he was at times brutally cruel to her. Susie's heart sank when she heard this; but on the few occasions upon which she caught sight of Margaret, she seemed in, the highest spirits. One story inexpressibly shocked her. After lunching at some restaurant, Haddo gave a bad louis among the money with which he paid the bill, and there was a disgraceful altercation with the waiter. He refused to change the coin till a policeman was brought in. His guests were furious, and several took the first opportunity to cut him dead. One of those present narrated the scene to Susie, and she was told that Margaret laughed unconcernedly with her neighbour while the sordid quarrel was proceeding. The man's blood was as good as his fortune was substantial, but it seemed to please him to behave like an adventurer. The incident was soon common property, and gradually the Haddos found themselves cold-shouldered. The persons with whom they mostly consorted had reputations too delicate to stand the glare of publicity which shone upon all who were connected with him, and the suggestion of police had thrown a shudder down many a spine. What had happened in Rome happened here again: they suddenly disappeared.

Susie had not been in London for some time, and as the spring advanced she remembered that her friends would be glad to see her. It would be charming to spend a few weeks there with an adequate income; for its pleasures had hitherto been closed to her, and she looked forward to her visit as if it were to a foreign city. But though she would not confess it to herself, her desire to see Arthur was the strongest of her motives. Time and absence had deadened a little the intensity of her feelings, and she could afford to acknowledge that she regarded him with very great affection. She knew that he would never care for her, but she was content to be his friend. She could think of him without pain.

Susie stayed in Paris for three weeks to buy some of the clothes which she asserted were now her only pleasure in life, and then went to London.

She wrote to Arthur, and he invited her at once to lunch with him at a restaurant. She was vexed, for she felt they could have spoken more freely in his own house; but as soon as she saw him, she realized that he had chosen their meeting-place deliberately. The crowd of people that surrounded them, the gaiety, the playing of the band, prevented any intimacy of conversation. They were forced to talk of commonplaces. Susie was positively terrified at the change that had taken place in him. He looked ten years older; he had lost flesh, and his hair was sprinkled with white. His face was extraordinarily drawn, and his eyes were weary from lack of sleep. But what most struck her was the change in his expression. The look of pain which she had seen on his face that last evening in the studio was now become settled, so that it altered the lines of his countenance. It was harrowing to look at him. He was more silent than ever, and when he spoke it was in a strange low voice that seemed to come from a long way off. To be with him made Susie curiously uneasy, for there was a strenuousness in him which deprived his manner of all repose. One of the things that had pleased her in him formerly was the tranquillity which gave one the impression that here was a man who could be relied on in difficulties. At first she could not understand exactly what had happened, but in a moment saw that he was making an unceasing effort at self-control. He was never free from suffering and he was constantly on the alert to prevent anyone from seeing it. The strain gave him a peculiar restlessness.

But he was gentler than he had ever been before. He seemed genuinely glad to see her and asked about her travels with interest. Susie led him to talk of himself, and he spoke willingly enough of his daily round. He was earning a good deal of money, and his professional reputation was making steady progress. He worked hard. Besides his duties at the two hospitals with which he was now connected, his teaching, and his private practice, he had read of late one or two papers before scientific bodies, and was editing a large work on surgery.

'How on earth can you find time to do so much?' asked Susie.

'I can do with less sleep than I used,' he answered. 'It almost doubles my working-day.'

He stopped abruptly and looked down. His remark had given accidentally some hint at the inner life which he was striving to conceal. Susie knew that her suspicion was well-founded. She thought of the long hours he lay awake, trying in vain to drive from his mind the agony that tortured him, and the short intervals of troubled sleep. She knew that he delayed as long as possible the fatal moment of going to bed, and welcomed the first light of day, which gave him an excuse for getting up. And because he knew that he had divulged the truth he was embarrassed. They sat in awkward silence. To Susie, the tragic figure in front of her was singularly impressive amid that lighthearted throng: all about them happy persons were enjoying the good things of life, talking, laughing, and making merry. She wondered what refinement of self-torture had driven him to choose that place to come to. He must hate it.

When they finished luncheon, Susie took her courage in both hands.

'Won't you come back to my rooms for half an hour? We can't talk here.'

He made an instinctive motion of withdrawal, as though he sought to escape. He did not answer immediately, and she insisted.

'You have nothing to do for an hour, and there are many things I want to speak to you about.'

'The only way to be strong is never to surrender to one's weakness,' he said, almost in a whisper, as though ashamed to talk so intimately.

'Then you won't come?'

'No.'

It was not necessary to specify the matter which it was proposed to discuss. Arthur knew perfectly that Susie wished to talk of Margaret, and he was too straightforward to pretend otherwise. Susie paused for one moment.

'I was never able to give Margaret your message. She did not write to me.'

A certain wildness came into his eyes, as if the effort he made was almost too much for him.

'I saw her in Monte Carlo,' said Susie. 'I thought you might like to hear about her.'

'I don't see that it can do any good,' he answered.

Susie made a little hopeless gesture. She was beaten.

'Shall we go?' she said.

'You are not angry with me?' he asked. 'I know you mean to be kind. I'm very grateful to you.'

'I shall never be angry with you,' she smiled.

Arthur paid the bill, and they threaded their way among the tables. At the door she held out her hand.

'I think you do wrong in shutting yourself away from all human comradeship,' she said, with that good-humoured smile of hers. 'You must know that you will only grow absurdly morbid.'

'I go out a great deal,' he answered patiently, as though he reasoned with a child. 'I make a point of offering myself distractions from my work. I go to the opera two or three times a week.'

'I thought you didn't care for music.'

'I don't think I did,' he answered. 'But I find it rests me.'

He spoke with a weariness that was appalling. Susie had never beheld so plainly the torment of a soul in pain.

'Won't you let me come to the opera with you one night?' she asked. 'Or does it bore you to see me?'

'I should like it above all things,' he smiled, quite brightly. 'You're like a wonderful tonic. They're giving *Tristan* on Thursday. Shall we go together?'

'I should enjoy it enormously.'

She shook hands with him and jumped into a cab.

'Oh, poor thing!' she murmured. 'Poor thing! What can I do for him?'

She clenched her hands when she thought of Margaret. It was monstrous that she should have caused such havoc in that good, strong man.

'Oh, I hope she'll suffer for it,' she whispered vindictively. 'I hope she'll suffer all the agony that he has suffered.'

Susie dressed herself for Covent Garden as only she could do. Her gown pleased her exceedingly, not only because it was admirably made, but because it had cost far more than she could afford. To dress well was her only extravagance. It was of taffeta silk, in that exquisite green which the learned in such matters call *Eau de Nil;* and its beauty was enhanced by the old lace which had formed not the least treasured part of her inheritance. In her hair she wore an ornament of Spanish paste, of exquisite workmanship, and round her neck a chain which had once adorned that of a madonna in an Andalusian church. Her individuality made even her plainness attractive. She smiled at herself in the glass ruefully, because Arthur would never notice that she was perfectly dressed.

When she tripped down the stairs and across the pavement to the cab with which he fetched her, Susie held up her skirt with a grace she flattered herself was quite Parisian. As they drove along, she flirted a little with her Spanish fan and stole a glance at herself in the glass. Her gloves were so long and so new and so expensive that she was really indifferent to Arthur's inattention.

Her joyous temperament expanded like a spring flower when she found herself in the Opera House. She put up her glasses and examined the women as they came into the boxes of the Grand Tier. Arthur pointed out a number of persons whose names were familiar to her, but she felt the effort he was making to be amiable. The weariness of his mouth that evening was more noticeable because of the careless throng. But when the music began he seemed to forget that any eye was upon him; he relaxed the constant tension in which he held himself; and Susie, watching him surreptitiously, saw the emotions chase one another across his face. It was now very mobile. The passionate sounds ate into his soul, mingling with his own love and his own sorrow, till he was taken out of himself; and sometimes he panted strangely. Through the interval he remained absorbed in his emotion. He sat as quietly as before and did not speak a word. Susie understood why Arthur, notwithstanding his old indifference, now showed such eager appreciation of music; it eased the pain he suffered by transferring it to an ideal world, and his own grievous sorrow made the music so real that it gave him an enjoyment of extraordinary vehemence. When it was all over and Isolde had given her last wail of sorrow, Arthur was so exhausted that he could hardly stir.

But they went out with the crowd, and while they were waiting in the vestibule for space to move in, a common friend came up to them. This was Arbuthnot, an eye-specialist, whom Susie had met on the Riviera and who, she presently discovered, was a colleague of Arthur's at St Luke's. He was a prosperous bachelor with grey hair and a red, contented face, well-to-do, for his practice was large, and lavish with his money. He had taken Susie out to luncheon once or twice in Monte Carlo; for he liked women, pretty or plain, and she attracted him by her good-humour. He rushed up to them now and wrung their hands. He spoke in a jovial voice.

'The very people I wanted to see! Why haven't you been to see me, you wicked woman? I'm sure your eyes are in a deplorable condition.'

'Do you think I would let a bold, bad man like you stare into them with an ophthalmoscope?' laughed Susie.

'Now look here, I want you both to do me a great favour. I'm giving a supper party at the Savoy, and two of my people have suddenly failed me. The table is ordered for eight, and you must come and take their places.'

'I'm afraid I must get home,' said Arthur. 'I have a deuce of a lot of work to do.'

'Nonsense,' answered Arbuthnot 'You work much too hard, and a little relaxation will do you good.' He turned to Susie: 'I know you like curiosities in human nature; I'm having a man and his wife who will positively thrill you, they're so queer, and a lovely actress, and an awfully jolly American girl.'

'I should love to come,' said Susie, with an appealing look at Arthur, 'if only to show you how much more amusing I am than lovely actresses.'

Arthur, forcing himself to smile, accepted the invitation. The specialist patted him cheerily on the back, and they agreed to meet at the Savoy.

'It's awfully good of you to come,' said Susie, as they drove along. 'Do you know, I've never been there in my life, and I'm palpitating with excitement.'

'What a selfish brute I was to refuse!' he answered.

When Susie came out of the dressing-room, she found Arthur waiting for her. She was in the best of spirits.

'Now you must say you like my frock. I've seen six women turn green with envy at the sight of it. They think I must be French, and they're sure I'm not respectable.'

'That is evidently a great compliment,' he smiled.

At that moment Arbuthnot came up to them in his eager way and seized their arms.

'Come along. We're waiting for you. I'll just introduce you all round, and then we'll go in to supper.'

They walked down the steps into the *foyer,* and he led them to a group of people. They found themselves face to face with Oliver Haddo and Margaret.

'Mr Arthur Burdon—Mrs Haddo. Mr Burdon is a colleague of mine at St Luke's; and he will cut out your appendix in a shorter time than any man alive.'

Arbuthnot rattled on. He did not notice that Arthur had grown ghastly pale and that Margaret was blank with consternation. Haddo, his heavy face wreathed with smiles, stepped forward heartily. He seemed thoroughly to enjoy the situation.

'Mr Burdon is an old friend of ours,' he said. 'In fact, it was he who introduced me to my wife. And Miss Boyd and I have discussed Art and the Immortality of the Soul with the gravity due to such topics.'

He held out his hand, and Susie took it. She had a horror of scenes, and, though this encounter was as unexpected as it was disagreeable, she felt it needful to behave naturally. She shook hands with Margaret.

'How disappointing!' cried their host. 'I was hoping to give Miss Boyd something quite new in the way of magicians, and behold! she knows all about him.'

'If she did, I'm quite sure she wouldn't speak to me,' said Oliver, with a bantering smile.

They went into the supper-room.

'Now, how shall we sit?' said Arbuthnot, glancing round the table.

Oliver looked at Arthur, and his eyes twinkled.

'You must really let my wife and Mr Burdon be together. They haven't seen one another for so long that I'm sure they have no end of things to talk about.' He chuckled to himself. 'And pray give me Miss Boyd, so that she can abuse me to her heart's content.'

This arrangement thoroughly suited the gay specialist, for he was able to put the beautiful actress on one side of him and the charming American on the other. He rubbed his hands.

'I feel that we're going to have a delightful supper.'

Oliver laughed-boisterously. He took, as was his habit, the whole conversation upon himself, and Susie was obliged to confess that he was at his best. There was a grotesque drollery about him that was very diverting, and it was almost impossible to resist him. He ate and drank with tremendous appetite. Susie thanked her stars at that moment that she was a woman who knew by long practice how to conceal her feelings, for Arthur, overcome with dismay at the meeting, sat in stony silence. But she talked gaily. She chaffed Oliver as though he were an old friend, and laughed vivaciously. She noticed meanwhile that Haddo, more extravagantly dressed than usual, had managed to get an odd fantasy into his evening clothes: he wore knee-breeches, which in itself was enough to excite attention; but his frilled shirt, his velvet collar, and oddly-cut satin waistcoat gave him the appearance of a comic Frenchman. Now that she was able to examine him more closely, she saw that in the last six months he was grown much balder; and the shiny whiteness of his naked crown contrasted oddly with the redness of his face. He was stouter, too, and the fat hung in heavy folds under his chin; his paunch was preposterous. The vivacity of his movements made his huge corpulence subtly alarming. He was growing indeed strangely terrible in appearance. His eyes had still that fixed, parallel look, but there was in them now at times a ferocious gleam. Margaret was as beautiful as ever, but Susie noticed that his influence was apparent in her dress; for there could be no doubt that it had crossed the line of individuality and had degenerated into the eccentric. Her gown was much too gorgeous. It told against the classical character of her beauty. Susie shuddered a little, for it reminded her of a courtesan's.

Margaret talked and laughed as much as her husband, but Susie could not tell whether this animation was affected or due to an utter callousness. Her voice seemed natural enough, yet it was inconceivable that she should be so lighthearted. Perhaps she was trying to show that she was happy. The supper proceeded, and the lights, the surrounding gaiety, the champagne, made everyone more lively. Their host was in uproarious spirits. He told a story or two at which everyone laughed. Oliver Haddo had an amusing anecdote handy. It was a little risky, but it was so funnily narrated that everyone roared but Arthur, who remained in perfect silence. Margaret had been drinking glass after glass of wine, and no sooner had her husband finished than she capped his story with another. But whereas his was wittily immoral, hers was simply gross. At first the other women could not understand to what she was tending, but when they saw, they looked down awkwardly at their plates. Arbuthnot, Haddo, and the other man who was there laughed very heartily; but Arthur flushed to the roots of his hair. He felt horribly uncomfortable. He was ashamed. He dared not look at Margaret. It was inconceivable that from her exquisite mouth such indecency should issue. Margaret, apparently quite unconscious of the effect she had produced, went on talking and laughing.

Soon the lights were put out, and Arthur's agony was ended. He wanted to rush away, to hide his face, to forget the sight of her and her gaiety, above all to forget that story. It was horrible, horrible.

She shook hands with him quite lightly.

'You must come and see us one day. We've got rooms at the Carlton.'

He bowed and did not answer. Susie had gone to the dressing-room to get her cloak. She stood at the door when Margaret came out.

'Can we drop you anywhere?' said Margaret. 'You must come and see us when you have nothing better to do.'

Susie threw back her head. Arthur was standing just in front of them looking down at the ground in complete abstraction.

'Do you see him?' she said, in a low voice quivering with indignation. That is what you have made him.'

He looked up at that moment and turned upon them his sunken, tormented eyes. They saw his wan, pallid face with its took of hopeless woe.

'Do you know that he's killing himself on your account? He can't sleep at night. He's suffered the tortures of the damned. Oh, I hope you'll suffer as he's suffered!'

'I wonder that you blame me,' said Margaret. 'You ought to be rather grateful.'

'Why?'

'You're not going to deny that you've loved him passionately from the first day you saw him? Do you think I didn't see that you cared for him in Paris? You care for him now more than ever.'

Susie felt suddenly sick at heart. She had never dreamt that her secret was discovered. Margaret gave a bitter little laugh and walked past her.

CHAPTER XII

ARTHUR Burdon spent two or three days in a state of utter uncertainty, but at last the idea he had in mind grew so compelling as to overcome all objections. He went to the Carlton and asked for Margaret. He had learnt from the porter that Haddo was gone out and so counted on finding her alone. A simple device enabled him to avoid sending up his name. When he was shown into her private room Margaret was sitting down. She neither read nor worked.

'You told me I might call upon you,' said Arthur.

She stood up without answering, and turned deathly pale.

'May I sit down?' he asked.

She bowed her head. For a moment they looked at one another in silence. Arthur suddenly forgot all he had prepared to say. His intrusion seemed intolerable.

'Why have you come?' she said hoarsely.

They both felt that it was useless to attempt the conventionality of society. It was impossible to deal with the polite commonplaces that ease an awkward situation.

'I thought that I might be able to help you,' he answered gravely.

'I want no help. I'm perfectly happy. I have nothing to say to you.'

She spoke hurriedly, with a certain nervousness, and her eyes were fixed anxiously on the door as though she feared that someone would come in.

'I feel that we have much to say to one another,' he insisted. 'If it is inconvenient for us to talk here, will you not come and see me?'

'He'd know,' she cried suddenly, as if the words were dragged out of her. 'D'you think anything can be hidden from him?'

Arthur glanced at her. He was horrified by the terror that was in her eyes. In the full light of day a change was plain in her expression. Her face was strangely drawn, and pinched, and there was in it a constant look as of a person cowed. Arthur turned away.

'I want you to know that I do not blame you in the least for anything you did. No action of yours can ever lessen my affection for you.'

'Oh, why did you come here? Why do you torture me by saying such things?'

She burst on a sudden into a flood of tears, and walked excitedly up and down the room.

'Oh, if you wanted me to be punished for the pain I've caused you, you can triumph now. Susie said she hoped I'd suffer all the agony that I've made you suffer. If she only knew!'

Margaret gave a hysterical laugh. She flung herself on her knees by Arthur's side and seized his hands.

'Did you think I didn't see? My heart bled when I looked at your poor wan face and your tortured eyes. Oh, you've changed. I could never have believed that a man could change so much in so few months, and it's I who've caused it all. Oh, Arthur, Arthur, you must forgive me. And you must pity me.'

'But there's nothing to forgive, darling,' he cried.

She looked at him steadily. Her eyes now were shining with a hard brightness.

'You say that, but you don't really think it. And yet if you only knew, all that I have endured is on your account.'

She made a great effort to be calm.

'What do you mean?' said Arthur.

'He never loved me, he would never have thought of me if he hadn't wanted to wound you in what you treasured most. He hated you, and he's made me what I am so that you might suffer. It isn't I who did all this, but a devil within me; it isn't I who lied to you and left you and caused you all this unhappiness.'

She rose to her feet and sighed deeply.

'Once, I thought he was dying, and I helped him. I took him into the studio and gave him water. And he gained some dreadful power over me so that I've been like wax in his hands. All my will has disappeared, and I have to do his bidding. And if I try to resist . . .'

Her face twitched with pain and fear.

'I've found out everything since. I know that on that day when he seemed to be at the point of death, he was merely playing a trick on me, and he got Susie out of the way by sending a telegram from a girl whose name he had seen on a photograph. I've heard him roar with laughter at his cleverness.'

She stopped suddenly, and a look of frightful agony crossed her face.

'And at this very minute, for all I know, it may be by his influence that I say this to you, so that he may cause you still greater suffering by allowing me to tell you that he never cared for me. You know now that my life is hell, and his vengeance is complete.'

'Vengeance for what?'

'Don't you remember that you hit him once, and kicked him unmercifully? I know him well now. He could have killed you, but he hated you too much. It pleased him a thousand times more to devise this torture for you and me.'

Margaret's agitation was terrible to behold. This was the first time that she had ever spoken to a soul of all these things, and now the long restraint had burst as burst the waters of a dam. Arthur sought to calm her.

'You're ill and overwrought. You must try to compose yourself. After all, Haddo is a human being like the rest of us.'

'Yes, you always laughed at his claims. You wouldn't listen to the things he said. But I *know.* Oh, I can't explain it; I daresay common sense and probability are all against it, but I've seen things with my own eyes that pass all comprehension. I tell you, he has powers of the most awful kind. That first day when I was alone with him, he seemed to take me to some kind of sabbath.

I don't know what it was, but I saw horrors, vile horrors, that rankled for ever after like poison in my mind; and when we went up to his house in Staffordshire, I recognized the scene; I recognized the arid rocks, and the trees, and the He of the land. I knew I'd been there before on that fatal afternoon. Oh, you must believe me! Sometimes I think I shall go mad with the terror of it all.'

Arthur did not speak. Her words caused a ghastly suspicion to flash through his mind, and he could hardly contain himself. He thought that some dreadful shock had turned her brain. She buried her face in her hands.

'Look here,' he said, 'you must come away at once. You can't continue to live with him. You must never go back to Skene.'

'I can't leave him. We're bound together inseparably.'

'But it's monstrous. There can be nothing to keep you to him. Come back to Susie. Shell be very kind to you; she'll help you to forget all you've endured.'

'It's no use. You can do nothing for me.'

'Why not?'

'Because, notwithstanding, I love him with all my soul.'

'Margaret!'

'I hate him. He fills me with repulsion. And yet I do not know what there is in my blood that draws me to him against my will. My flesh cries out for him.'

Arthur looked away in embarrassment. He could not help a slight, instinctive movement of withdrawal.

'Do I disgust you?' she said.

He flushed slightly, but scarcely knew how to answer. He made a vague gesture of denial.

'If you only knew,' she said.

There was something so extraordinary in her tone that he gave her a quick glance of surprise. He saw that her cheeks were flaming. Her bosom was panting as though she were again on the point of breaking into a passion of tears.

'For God's sake, don't look at me!' she cried.

She turned away and hid her face. The words she uttered were in a shamed, unnatural voice.

'If you'd been at Monte Carlo, you'd have heard them say, God knows how they knew it, that it was only through me he had his luck at the tables. He's contented himself with filling my soul with vice. I have no purity in me. I'm sullied through and through. He has made me into a sink of iniquity, and I loathe myself. I cannot look at myself without a shudder of disgust.'

A cold sweat came over Arthur, and he grew more pale than ever. He realized now he was in the presence of a mystery that he could not unravel She went on feverishly.

'The other night, at supper, I told a story, and I saw you wince with shame. It wasn't I that told it. The impulse came from him, and I knew it was vile, and yet I told it with gusto. I enjoyed the telling of it; I enjoyed the pain I gave you, and the dismay of those women. There seem to be two persons in me, and my real self, the old one that you knew and loved, is growing weaker day by day, and soon she will be dead entirely. And there will remain only the wanton soul in the virgin body.'

Arthur tried to gather his wits together. He felt it an occasion on which it was essential to hold on to the normal view of things.

'But for God's sake leave him. What you've told me gives you every ground for divorce. It's all monstrous. The man must be so mad that he ought to be put in a lunatic asylum.'

'You can do nothing for me,' she said.

'But if he doesn't love you, what does he want you for?'

'I don't know, but I'm beginning to suspect.'

She looked at Arthur steadily. She was now quite calm.

'I think he wishes to use me for a magical operation. I don't know if he's mad or not. But I think he means to try some horrible experiment, and I am needful for its success. That is my safeguard.'

'Your safeguard?'

'He won't kill me because he needs me for that. Perhaps in the process I shall regain my freedom.'

Arthur was shocked at the callousness with which she spoke. He went up to her and put his hands on her shoulders.

'Look here, you must pull yourself together, Margaret. This isn't sane. If you don't take care, your mind will give way altogether. You must come with me now. When you're out of his hands, you'll soon regain your calmness of mind. You need never see him again. If you're afraid, you shall be hidden from him, and lawyers shall arrange everything between you.'

'I daren't.'

'But I promise you that you can come to no harm. Be reasonable. We're in London now, surrounded by people on every side. How do you think he can touch you while we drive through the crowded streets? I'll take you straight to Susie. In a week you'll laugh at the idle fears you had.'

'How do you know that he is not in the room at this moment, listening to all you say?'

The question was so sudden, so unexpected, that Arthur was startled. He looked round quickly.

'You must be mad. You see that the room is empty.'

'I tell you that you don't know what powers he has. Have you ever heard those old legends with which nurses used to frighten our childhood, of men who could turn themselves into wolves, and who scoured the country at night?' She looked at him with staring eyes. 'Sometimes, when he's come in at Skene in the morning, with bloodshot eyes, exhausted with fatigue and strangely discomposed, I've imagined that he too . . .' She stopped and threw back her head, 'You're right, Arthur, I think I shall go mad.'

He watched her helplessly. He did not know what to do. Margaret went on, her voice quivering with anguish.

'When we were married, I reminded him that he'd promised to take me to his mother. He would never speak of her, but I felt I must see her. And one day, suddenly, he told me to get ready for a journey, and we went a long way, to a place I did not know, and we drove into the country. We seemed to go miles and miles, and we reached at last a large house, surrounded by a high wall, and the windows were heavily barred. We were shown into a great empty room. It was dismal and cold like the waiting-room at a station. A man came in to us, a tall man, in a frock-coat and gold spectacles. He was introduced to me as Dr Taylor, and then, suddenly, I understood.'

Margaret spoke in hurried gasps, and her eyes were staring wide, as though she saw still the scene which at the time had seemed the crowning horror of her experience.

'I knew it was an asylum, and Oliver hadn't told me a word. He took us up a broad flight of stairs, through a large dormitory—oh, if you only knew what I saw there! I was so horribly frightened, I'd never been in such a place before—to a cell. And the walls and the floor were padded.'

Margaret passed her hand across her forehead to chase away the recollection of that awful sight.

'Oh, I see it still. I can never get it out of my mind.'

She remembered with a morbid vividness the vast misshapen mass which she had seen heaped strangely in one corner. There was a slight movement in it as they entered, and she perceived that it was a human being. It was a woman, dressed in shapeless brown flannel; a woman of great stature and of a revolting, excessive corpulence. She turned upon them a huge, impassive face; and its unwrinkled smoothness gave it an appearance of aborted childishness. The hair was dishevelled, grey, and scanty. But what most terrified Margaret was that she saw in this creature an appalling likeness to Oliver.

'He told me it was his mother, and she'd been there for five-and-twenty years.'

Arthur could hardly bear the terror that was in Margaret's eyes. He did not know what to say to her. In a little while she began to speak again, in a low voice and rapidly, as though to herself, and she wrung her hands.

'Oh, you don't know what I've endured! He used to spend long periods away from me, and I remained alone at Skene from morning till night, alone with my abject fear. Sometimes, it seemed that he was seized with a devouring lust for the gutter, and he would go to Liverpool or Manchester and throw himself among the very dregs of the people. He used to pass long days, drinking in filthy pot-houses. While the bout lasted, nothing was too depraved for him. He loved the company of all that was criminal and low. He used to smoke opium in foetid dens—oh, you have no conception of his passion to degrade himself—and at last he would come back, dirty, with torn clothes, begrimed, sodden still with his long debauch; and his mouth was hot with the kisses of the vile women of the docks. Oh, he's so cruel when the fit takes him that I think he has a fiendish pleasure in the sight of suffering!'

It was more than Arthur could stand. His mind was made up to try a bold course. He saw on the table a whisky bottle and glasses. He poured some neat spirit into a tumbler and gave it to Margaret.

'Drink this,' he said.

'What is it?'

'Never mind! Drink it at once.'

Obediently she put it to her lips. He stood over her as she emptied the glass. A sudden glow filled her.

'Now come with me.'

He took her arm and led her down the stairs. He passed through the hall quickly. There was a cab just drawn up at the door, and he told her to get in. One or two persons stared at seeing a woman come out of that hotel in a teagown and without a hat. He directed the driver to the house in which Susie lived and looked round at Margaret. She had fainted immediately she got into the cab.

When they arrived, he carried Margaret upstairs and laid her on a sofa. He told Susie what had happened and what he wanted of her. The dear woman forgot everything except that Margaret was very ill, and promised willingly to do all he wished.

For a week Margaret could not be moved. Arthur hired a little cottage in Hampshire, opposite the Isle of Wight, hoping that amid the most charming, restful scenery in England she would quickly regain her strength; and as soon as it was possible Susie took her down. But she was much altered. Her gaiety had disappeared and with it her determination. Although her illness had been neither long nor serious, she seemed as exhausted, physically and mentally, as if she had been for months at the point of death. She took no interest in her surroundings; and was indifferent to the shady lanes through which they drove and to the gracious trees and the meadows. Her old passion for beauty was gone, and she cared neither for the flowers which filled their little garden nor for the birds that sang continually. But at last it seemed necessary to discuss the future. Margaret acquiesced in all that was suggested to her, and agreed willingly that the needful steps should be taken to procure her release from Oliver Haddo. He made apparently no effort to trace her, and nothing had been heard of him. He did not know where Margaret was, but he might have guessed that Arthur was responsible for her flight, and Arthur was easily to be found. It made Susie vaguely uneasy that there was no sign of his existence. She wished that Arthur were not kept by his work in London.

At last a suit for divorce was instituted.

Two days after this, when Arthur was in his consulting-room, Haddo's card was brought to him. Arthur's jaw set more firmly.

'Show the gentleman in,' he ordered.

When Haddo entered, Arthur, standing with his back to the fireplace, motioned him to sit down.

'What can I do for you?' he asked coldly.

'I have not come to avail myself of your surgical skill, my dear Burden,' smiled Haddo, as he fell ponderously into an armchair.

'So I imagined.'

'You perspicacity amazes me. I surmise that it is to you I owe this amusing citation which was served on me yesterday.'

'I allowed you to come in so that I might tell you I will have no communication with you except through my solicitors.'

'My dear fellow, why do you treat me with such discourtesy? It is true that you have deprived me of the wife of my bosom, but you might at least so far respect my marital rights as to use me civilly.'

'My patience is not as good as it was,' answered Arthur, 'I venture to remind you that once before I lost my temper with you, and the result you must have found unpleasant.'

'I should have thought you regretted that incident by now, O Burdon,' answered Haddo, entirely unabashed.

'My time is very short,' said Arthur.

'Then I will get to my business without delay. I thought it might interest you to know that I propose to bring a counterpetition against my wife, and I shall make you co-respondent.'

'You infamous blackguard!' cried Arthur furiously. 'You know as well as I do that your wife is above suspicion.'

'I know that she left my hotel in your company, and has been living since under your protection.'

Arthur grew livid with rage. He could hardly restrain himself from knocking the man down. He gave a short laugh.

'You can do what you like. I'm really not frightened.'

'The innocent are so very incautious. I assure you that I can make a good enough story to ruin your career and force you to resign your appointments at the various hospitals you honour with your attention.'

'You forget that the case will not be tried in open court,' said Arthur.

Haddo looked at him steadily. He did not answer for a moment.

'You're quite right,' he said at last, with a little smile. 'I had forgotten that.'

'Then I need not detain you longer.'

Oliver Haddo got up. He passed his hand reflectively over his huge face. Arthur watched him with scornful eyes. He touched a bell, and the servant at once appeared.

'Show this gentleman out.'

Not in the least disconcerted, Haddo strolled calmly to the door.

Arthur gave a sigh of relief, for he concluded that Haddo would not show fight. His solicitor indeed had already assured him that Oliver would not venture to defend the case.

Margaret seemed gradually to take more interest in the proceedings, and she was full of eagerness to be set free. She did not shrink from the unpleasant ordeal of a trial. She could talk of Haddo with composure. Her friends were able to persuade themselves that in a little while she would be her old self again, for she was growing stronger and more cheerful; her charming laughter rang through the little house as it had been used to do in the Paris studio. The case was to come on at the end of July, before the long vacation, and Susie had agreed to take Margaret abroad as soon as it was done.

But presently a change came over her. As the day of the trial drew nearer, Margaret became excited and disturbed; her gaiety deserted her, and she fell into long, moody silences. To some extent this was comprehensible, for she would have to disclose to callous ears the most intimate details of her married life; but at last her nervousness grew so marked that Susie could no longer ascribe it to natural causes. She thought it necessary to write to Arthur about it.

My Dear Arthur:

I don't know what to make of Margaret, and I wish you would come down and see her. The good-humour which I have noticed in her of late has given way to a curious irritability. She is so restless that she cannot keep still for a moment Even when she is sitting down her body moves in a manner that is almost convulsive. I am beginning to think that the strain from which she suffered is bringing on some nervous disease, and I am really alarmed. She walks about the house in a peculiarly aimless manner, up and down the stairs, in and out of the garden. She has grown suddenly much more silent, and the look has come back to her eyes which they had when first we brought her down here. When I beg her to tell me what is troubling her, she says: 'I'm afraid that something is going to happen.' She will not or cannot explain what she means. The last few weeks have set my own nerves on edge, so that I do not know how much of what I observe is real, and how much is due to my fancy; but I wish you would come and put a little courage into me. The oddness of it all is making me uneasy, and I am seized with preposterous terrors. I don't know what there is in Haddo that inspires me with this unaccountable dread. He is always present to my thoughts. I seem to see his dreadful eyes and his cold, sensual smile. I wake up at night, my heart beating furiously, with the consciousness that something quite awful has happened.

Oh, I wish the trial were over, and that we were happy in Germany.

Yours ever
SUSAN BOYD

Susie took a certain pride in her common sense, and it was humiliating to find that her nerves could be so distraught. She was worried and unhappy. It had not been easy to take Margaret back to her bosom as if nothing had happened. Susie was human; and, though she did ten times more than could be expected of her, she could not resist a feeling of irritation that Arthur sacrificed her so calmly. He had no room for other thoughts, and it seemed quite natural to him that she should devote herself entirely to Margaret's welfare.

Susie walked some way along the road to post this letter and then went to her room. It was a wonderful night, starry and calm, and the silence was like balm to her troubles. She sat at the window for a long time, and at last, feeling more tranquil, went to bed. She slept more soundly than she had done for many days. When she awoke the sun was streaming into her room, and she gave a deep sigh of delight. She could see trees from her bed, and blue sky. All her troubles seemed easy to bear when the world was so beautiful, and she was ready to laugh at the fears that had so affected her.

She got up, put on a dressing-gown, and went to Margaret's room. It was empty. The bed had not been slept in. On the pillow was a note.

> It's no good; I can't help myself. I've gone back to him. Don't trouble about me any more. It's quite hopeless and useless.
>
> M

Susie gave a little gasp. Her first thought was for Arthur, and she uttered a wail of sorrow because he must be cast again into the agony of desolation. Once more she had to break the dreadful news. She dressed hurriedly and ate some breakfast. There was no train till nearly eleven, and she had to bear her impatience as best she could. At last it was time to start, and she put on her gloves. At that moment the door was opened, and Arthur came in.

She gave a cry of terror and turned pale.

'I was just coming to London to see you,' she faltered. 'How did you find out?'

'Haddo sent me a box of chocolates early this morning with a card on which was written: *I think the odd trick is mine.*'

This cruel vindictiveness, joined with a schoolboy love of taunting the vanquished foe, was very characteristic. Susie gave Arthur Burdon the note which she had found in Margaret's room. He read it and then thought for a long time.

'I'm afraid she's right,' he said at length. 'It seems quite hopeless. The man has some power over her which we can't counteract.'

Susie wondered whether his strong scepticism was failing at last. She could not withstand her own feeling that there was something preternatural about the hold that Oliver had over Margaret. She had no shadow of a doubt that he was able to affect his wife even at a distance, and was convinced now that the restlessness of the last few days was due to this mysterious power. He had been at work in some strange way, and Margaret had been aware of it. At length she could not resist and had gone to him instinctively: her will was as little concerned as when a chip of steel flies to a magnet.

'I cannot find it in my heart now to blame her for anything she has done,' said Susie. 'I think she is the victim of a most lamentable fate. I can't help it. I must believe that he was able to cast a spell on her; and to that is due all that has happened. I have only pity for her great misfortunes.'

'Has it occurred to you what will happen when she is back in Haddo's hands?' cried Arthur. 'You know as well as I do how revengeful he is and how hatefully cruel. My heart bleeds when I think of the tortures, sheer physical tortures, which she may suffer.'

He walked up and down in desperation.

'And yet there's nothing whatever that one can do. One can't go to the police and say that a man has cast a magic spell on his wife.'

'Then you believe it too?' said Susie.

'I don't know what I believe now,' he cried. 'After all, we can't do anything if she chooses to go back to her husband. She's apparently her own mistress.' He wrung his hands. 'And I'm imprisoned in London! I can't leave it for a day. I ought not to be here now, and I must get back in a couple of hours. I can do nothing, and yet I'm convinced that Margaret is utterly wretched.'

Susie paused for a minute or two. She wondered how he would accept the suggestion that was in her mind.

'Do you know, it seems to me that common methods are useless. The only chance is to fight him with his own weapons. Would you mind if I went over to Paris to consult Dr Porhoët? You know that he is learned in every branch of the occult, and perhaps he might help us.'

But Arthur pulled himself together.

'It's absurd. We mustn't give way to superstition. Haddo is merely a scoundrel and a charlatan. He's worked on our nerves as he's worked on poor Margaret's. It's impossible to suppose that he has any powers greater than the common run of mankind.'

'Even after all you've seen with your own eyes?'

'If my eyes show me what all my training assures me is impossible, I can only conclude that my eyes deceive me.'

'Well, I shall run over to Paris.'

CHAPTER XIII

SOME weeks later Dr Porhoët was sitting among his books in the quiet, low room that overlooked the Seine. He had given himself over to a pleasing melancholy. The heat beat down upon the noisy streets of Paris, and the din of the great city penetrated even to his fastness in the Île Saint Louis. He remembered the cloud-laden sky of the country where he was born, and the south-west wind that blew with a salt freshness. The long streets of Brest, present to his fancy always in a drizzle of rain, with the lights of cafés reflected on the wet pavements, had a familiar charm. Even in foul weather the sailor-men who trudged along them gave one a curious sense of comfort. There was delight in the smell of the sea and in the freedom of the great Atlantic. And then he thought of the green lanes and of the waste places with their scented heather, the fair broad roads that led from one old sweet town to another, of the *Pardons* and their gentle, sad crowds. Dr Porhoët gave a sigh.

'It is good to be born in the land of Brittany,' he smiled.

But his *bonne* showed Susie in, and he rose with a smile to greet her. She had been in Paris for some time, and they had seen much of one another. He basked in the gentle sympathy with which she interested herself in all the abstruse, quaint matters on which he spent his time; and, divining her love for Arthur, he admired the courage with which she effaced herself. They had got into the habit of eating many of their meals together in a quiet house opposite the Cluny called La Reine Blanche, and here they had talked of so many things that their acquaintance was grown into a charming friendship.

'I'm ashamed to come here so often,' said Susie, as she entered. 'Matilde is beginning to look at me with a suspicious eye.'

'It is very good of you to entertain a tiresome old man,' he smiled, as he held her hand. 'But I should have been disappointed if you had forgotten your promise to come this afternoon, for I have much to tell you.'

'Tell me at once,' she said, sitting down.

'I have discovered an MS. at the library of the Arsenal this morning that no one knew anything about.'

He said this with an air of triumph, as though the achievement were of national importance. Susie had a tenderness for his innocent mania; and, though she knew the work in question was occult and incomprehensible, congratulated him heartily.

'It is the original version of a book by Paracelsus. I have not read it yet, for the writing is most difficult to decipher, but one point caught my eye on turning over the pages. That is the gruesome fact that Paracelsus fed the *homunculi* he manufactured on human blood. One wonders how he came by it.'

Susie gave a little start, which Dr Porhoët noticed.

'What is the matter with you?'

'Nothing,' she said quickly.

He looked at her for a moment, then proceeded with the subject that strangely fascinated him.

'You must let me take you one day to the library of the Arsenal. There is no richer collection in the world of books dealing with the occult sciences. And of course you know that it was at the Arsenal that the tribunal sat, under the suggestive name of *chambre ardente*, to deal with cases of sorcery and magic?'

'I didn't,' smiled Susie.

'I always think that these manuscripts and queer old books, which are the pride of our library, served in many an old trial. There are volumes there of innocent appearance that have hanged wretched men and sent others to the stake. You would not believe how many persons of fortune, rank, and intelligence, during the great reign of Louis XIV, immersed themselves in these satanic undertakings.'

Susie did not answer. She could not now deal with these matters in an indifferent spirit. Everything she heard might have some bearing on the circumstances which she had discussed with Dr Porhoët times out of number. She had never been able to pin him down to an affirmation of faith. Certain strange things had manifestly happened, but what the explanation of them was, no man could say. He offered analogies from his well-stored memory. He gave her books to read till she was saturated with occult science. At one moment, she was inclined to throw them all aside impatiently, and, at another, was ready to believe that everything was possible.

Dr Porhoët stood up and stretched out a meditative finger. He spoke in that agreeably academic manner which, at the beginning of their acquaintance, had always entertained Susie, because it contrasted so absurdly with his fantastic utterances.

'It was a strange dream that these wizards cherished. They sought to make themselves beloved of those they cared for and to revenge themselves on those they hated; but, above all, they sought to become greater than the common run of men and to wield the power of the gods. They hesitated at nothing to gain their ends. But Nature with difficulty allows her secrets to be wrested from her. In vain they lit their furnaces, and in vain they studied their crabbed books, called up the dead, and conjured ghastly spirits. Their reward was disappointment and wretchedness, poverty, the scorn of men, torture, imprisonment, and shameful death. And yet, perhaps after all, there may be some particle of truth hidden away in these dark places.'

'You never go further than the cautious perhaps,' said Susie. 'You never give me any definite opinion.'

'In these matters it is discreet to have no definite opinion,' he smiled, with a shrug of the shoulders. 'If a wise man studies the science of the occult, his duty is not to laugh at everything, but to seek patiently, slowly, perseveringly, the truth that may be concealed in the night of these illusions.'

The words were hardly spoken when Matilde, the ancient *bonne,* opened the door to let a visitor come in. It was Arthur Burdon. Susie gave a cry of surprise, for she had received a brief note from him two days before, and he had said nothing of crossing the Channel.

'I'm glad to find you both here,' said Arthur, as he shook hands with them.

'Has anything happened?' cried Susie.

His manner was curiously distressing, and there was a nervousness about his movements that was very unexpected in so restrained a person.

'I've seen Margaret again,' he said.

'Well?'

He seemed unable to go on, and yet both knew that he had something important to tell them. He looked at them vacantly, as though all he had to say was suddenly gone out of his mind.

'I've come straight here,' he said, in a dull, bewildered fashion. 'I went to your hotel, Susie, in the hope of finding you; but when they told me you were out, I felt certain you would be here.'

'You seem worn out, *cher ami,*' said Dr Porhoët, looking at him. 'Will you let Matilde make you a cup of coffee?'

'I should like something,' he answered, with a look of utter weariness.

'Sit still for a minute or two, and you shall tell us what you want to when you are a little rested.'

Dr Porhoët had not seen Arthur since that afternoon in the previous year when, in answer to Haddo's telegram, he had gone to the studio in the Rue Campagne Première. He watched him anxiously while Arthur drank his coffee. The change in him was extraordinary; there was a cadaverous exhaustion about his face, and his eyes were sunken in their sockets. But what alarmed the good doctor most was that Arthur's personality seemed thoroughly thrown out of gear. All that he had endured during these nine months had robbed him of the strength of purpose, the matter-of-fact sureness, which had distinguished him. He was now unbalanced and neurotic.

Arthur did not speak. With his eyes fixed moodily on the ground, he wondered how much he could bring himself to tell them. It revolted him to disclose his inmost thoughts, yet he was come to the end of his tether and needed the doctor's advice. He found himself obliged to deal with circumstances that might have existed in a world of nightmare, and he was driven at last to take advantage of his friend's peculiar knowledge.

Returning to London after Margaret's flight, Arthur Burdon had thrown himself again into the work which for so long had been his only solace. It had lost its savour; but he would not take this into account, and he slaved away mechanically, by perpetual toil seeking to deaden his anguish. But as the time passed he was seized on a sudden with a curious feeling of foreboding, which he could in no way resist; it grew in strength till it had all the power of an obsession, and he could not reason himself out of it. He was sure that a great danger threatened Margaret. He could not tell what it was, nor why the fear of it was so persistent, but the idea was there always, night and day; it haunted him like a shadow and pursued him like remorse. His anxiety increased continually, and the vagueness of his terror made it more tormenting. He felt quite certain that Margaret was in imminent peril, but he did not know how to help her. Arthur supposed that Haddo had taken her back to Skene; but, even if he went there, he had no chance of seeing her. What made it more difficult still, was that his chief at St Luke's was away, and he was obliged to be in London in case he should be suddenly called upon to do some operation. But he could think of nothing else. He felt it urgently needful to see Margaret. Night after night he dreamed that she was at the point of death, and heavy fetters prevented him from stretching out a hand to help her. At last he could stand it no more. He told a brother surgeon that private business forced him to leave London, and put the work into his hands. With no plan in his head, merely urged by an obscure impulse, he set out for the village of Venning, which was about three miles from Skene.

It was a tiny place, with one public-house serving as a hotel to the rare travellers who found it needful to stop there, and Arthur felt that some explanation of his presence was necessary. Having seen at the station an advertisement of a large farm to let, he told the inquisitive landlady that he had come to see it. He arrived late at night. Nothing could be done then, so he occupied the time by trying to find out something about the Haddos.

Oliver was the local magnate, and his wealth would have made him an easy topic of conversation even without his eccentricity. The landlady roundly called him insane, and as an instance of his queerness told Arthur, to his great dismay, that Haddo would have no servants to sleep in the house: after dinner everyone was sent away to the various cottages in the park, and he remained alone with his wife. It was an awful thought that Margaret might be in the hands of a raving madman, with not a soul to protect her. But if he learnt no more than this of solid fact, Arthur heard much that was significant. To his amazement the old fear of the wizard had grown up again in that lonely place, and the garrulous woman gravely told him of Haddo's evil influence on the crops and cattle of farmers who had aroused his anger. He had had an altercation with his bailiff, and the man had died within a year. A small free-holder in the neighbourhood had refused to sell the land which would have rounded off the estate of Skene, and a disease had attacked every animal on his farm so that he was ruined. Arthur was impressed because, though she reported these rumours with mock scepticism as the stories of ignorant yokels and old women, the innkeeper had evidently a terrified belief in their truth. No one could deny that Haddo had got possession of the land he wanted; for, when it was put up to auction, no one would bid against him, and he bought it for a song.

As soon as he could do so naturally, Arthur asked after Margaret. The woman shrugged her shoulders. No one knew anything about her. She never came out of the park gates, but sometimes you could see her wandering about inside by herself. She saw no one. Haddo had long since quarrelled with the surrounding gentry; and though one old lady, the mother of a neighbouring landowner, had called when Margaret first came, she had not been admitted, and the visit was never returned.

'She'll come to no good, poor lady,' said the hostess of the inn. 'And they do say she's a perfect picture to look at.'

Arthur went to his room. He longed for the day to come. There was no certain means of seeing Margaret. It was useless to go to the park gates, since even the tradesmen were obliged to leave their goods at the lodge; but it appeared that she walked alone, morning and afternoon, and it might be possible to see her then. He decided to climb into the park and wait till he came upon her in some spot where they were not likely to be observed.

Next day the great heat of the last week was gone, and the melancholy sky was dark with lowering clouds. Arthur inquired for the road which led to Skene, and set out to walk the three miles which separated him from it. The country was grey and barren. There was a broad waste of heath, with gigantic boulders strewn as though in pre-historic times Titans had waged there a mighty battle. Here and there were trees, but they seemed hardly to withstand the fierce winds of winter; they were old and bowed before the storm. One of them attracted his attention. It had been struck by lightning and was riven asunder, leafless; but the maimed branches were curiously set on the trunk so that they gave it the appearance of a human being writhing in the torture of infernal agony. The wind whistled strangely. Arthur's heart sank as he walked on. He had never seen a country so desolate.

He came to the park gates at last and stood for some time in front of them. At the end of a long avenue, among the trees, he could see part of a splendid house. He walked along the wooden palisade that surrounded the park. Suddenly he came to a spot where a board had been broken down. He looked up and down the road. No one was in sight. He climbed up the low, steep bank, wrenched down a piece more of the fence, and slipped in.

He found himself in a dense wood. There was no sign of a path, and he advanced cautiously. The bracken was so thick and high that it easily concealed him. Dead owners had plainly spent much care upon the place, for here alone in the neighbourhood were trees in abundance; but of late it had been utterly neglected. It had run so wild that there were no traces now of its early formal arrangement; and it was so hard to make one's way, the vegetation was so thick, that it might almost have been some remnant of primeval forest. But at last he came to a grassy path and walked along it slowly. He stopped on a sudden, for he heard a sound. But it was only a pheasant that flew heavily through the low trees. He wondered what he should do if he came face to face with Oliver. The innkeeper had assured him that the squire seldom came out, but spent his days locked in the great attics at the top of the house. Smoke came from the chimneys of them, even in the hottest days of summer, and weird tales were told of the devilries there committed.

Arthur went on, hoping in the end to catch sight of Margaret, but he saw no one. In that grey, chilly day the woods, notwithstanding their greenery, were desolate and sad. A sombre mystery seemed to hang over them. At last he came to a stone bench at a cross-way among the trees, and, since it was the only resting-place he had seen, it struck him that Margaret might come there to sit down. He hid himself in the bracken. He had forgotten his watch and did not know how the time passed; he seemed to be there for hours.

But at length his heart gave a great beat against his ribs, for all at once, so silently that he had not heard her approach, Margaret came into view. She sat on the stone bench. For a moment he dared not move in case the sound frightened her. He could not tell how to make his presence known. But it was necessary to do something to attract her attention, and he could only hope that she would not cry out.

'Margaret,' he called softly.

She did not move, and he repeated her name more loudly. But still she made no sign that she had heard. He came forward and stood in front of her.

'Margaret.'

She looked at him quietly. He might have been someone she had never set eyes on, and yet from her composure she might have expected him to be standing there.

'Margaret, don't you know me?'

'What do you want?' she answered placidly.

He was so taken aback that he did not know what to say. She kept gazing at him steadfastly. On a sudden her calmness vanished, and she sprang to her feet.

'Is it you really?' she cried, terribly agitated. 'I thought it was only a shape that mimicked you.'

'Margaret, what do you mean? What has come over you?'

She stretched out her hand and touched him.

'I'm flesh and blood all right,' he said, trying to smile.

She shut her eyes for a moment, as though in an effort to collect herself.

'I've had hallucinations lately,' she muttered. 'I thought it was some trick played upon me.'

Suddenly she shook herself.

'But what are you doing here? You must go. How did you come? Oh, why won't you leave me alone?'

'I've been haunted by a feeling that something horrible was going to happen to you. I was obliged to come.'

'For God's sake, go. You can do me no good. If he finds out you've been here—'

She stopped, and her eyes were dilated with terror. Arthur seized her hands.

'Margaret, I can't go—I can't leave you like this. For Heaven's sake, tell me what is the matter. I'm so dreadfully frightened.'

He was aghast at the difference wrought in her during the two months since he had seen her last. Her colour was gone, and her face had the greyness of the dead. There were strange lines on her forehead, and her eyes had an unnatural glitter. Her youth had suddenly left her. She looked as if she were struck down by mortal illness.

'What is that matter with you?' he asked.

'Nothing.' She looked about her anxiously. 'Oh, why don't you go? How can you be so cruel?'

'I must do something for you,' he insisted.

She shook her head.

'It's too late. Nothing can help me now.' She paused; and when she spoke again it was with a voice so ghastly that it might have come from the lips of a corpse. 'I've found out at last what he's going to do with me He wants me for his great experiment, and the time is growing shorter.'

'What do you mean by saying he wants you?'

'He wants—my life.'

Arthur gave a cry of dismay, but she put up her hand.

'It's no use resisting. It can't do any good—I think I shall be glad when the moment comes. 'I shall at least cease to suffer.'

'But you must be mad.'

'I don't know. I know that he is.'

'But if your life is in danger, come away for God's sake. After all, you're free. He can't stop you.'

'I should have to go back to him, as I did last time,' she answered, shaking her head. 'I thought I was free then, but gradually I knew that he was calling me. I tried to resist, but I couldn't. I simply had to go to him.'

'But it's awful to think that you are alone with a man who's practically raving mad.'

'I'm safe for today,' she said quietly. 'It can only be done in the very hot weather. If there's no more this year, I shall live till next summer.'

'Oh, Margaret, for God's sake don't talk like that. I love you—I want to have you with me always. Won't you come away with me and let me take care of you? I promise you that no harm shall come to you.'

'You don't love me any more; you're only sorry for me now.'

'It's not true.'

'Oh yes it is. I saw it when we were in the country. Oh, I don't blame you. I'm a different woman from the one you loved. I'm not the Margaret you knew.'

'I can never care for anyone but you.'

She put her hand on his arm.

'If you loved me, I implore you to go. You don't know what you expose me to. And when I'm dead you must marry Susie. She loves you with all her heart, and she deserves your love.'

'Margaret, don't go. Come with me.'

'And take care. He will never forgive you for what you did. If he can, he will kill you.'

She started violently, as though she heard a sound. Her face was convulsed with sudden fear.

'For God's sake go. go!'

She turned from him quickly, and, before he could prevent her, had vanished. With heavy heart he plunged again into the bracken.

When Arthur had given his friends some account of this meeting, he stopped and looked at Dr Porhoët. The doctor went thoughtfully to his bookcase.

'What is it you want me to tell you?' he asked.

'I think the man is mad,' said Arthur. 'I found out at what asylum his mother was, and by good luck was able to see the superintendent on my way through London. He told me that he had grave doubts about Haddo's sanity, but it was impossible at present to take any steps. I came straight here because I wanted your advice. Granting that the man is out of his mind, is it possible that he may be trying some experiment that entails a sacrifice of human life?'

'Nothing is more probable,' said Dr Porhoët gravely.

Susie shuddered. She remembered the rumour that had reached her ears in Monte Carlo.

'They said there that he was attempting to make living creatures by a magical operation.' She glanced at the doctor, but spoke to Arthur. 'Just before you came in, our friend was talking of that book of Paracelsus in which he speaks of feeding the monsters he has made on human blood.'

Arthur gave a horrified cry.

'The most significant thing to my mind is that fact about Margaret which we are certain of,' said Dr Porhoët. 'All works that deal with the Black Arts are unanimous upon the supreme efficacy of the virginal condition.'

'But what is to be done?' asked Arthur is desperation. 'We can't leave her in the hands of a raving madman.' He turned on a sudden deathly white. 'For all we know she may be dead now.'

'Have you ever heard of Gilles de Rais?' said Dr Porhoët, continuing his reflections. That is the classic instance of human sacrifice. I know the country in which he lived; and the peasants to this day dare not pass at night in the neighbourhood of the ruined castle which was the scene of his horrible crimes.'

'It's awful to know that this dreadful danger hangs over her, and to be able to do nothing.'

'We can only wait,' said Dr Porhoët.

'And if we wait too long, we may be faced by a terrible catastrophe.'

'Fortunately we live in a civilized age. Haddo has a great care of his neck. I hope we are frightened unduly.'

It seemed to Susie that the chief thing was to distract Arthur, and she turned over in her mind some means of directing his attention to other matters.

'I was thinking of going down to Chartres for two days with Mrs Bloomfield,' she said. 'Won't you come with me? It is the most lovely cathedral in the world, and I think you will find it restful to wander about it for a little while. You can do no good, here or in London. Perhaps when you are calm, you will be able to think of something practical.'

Dr Porhoët saw what her plan was, and joined his entreaties to hers that Arthur should spend a day or two in a place that had no associations for him. Arthur was too exhausted to argue, and from sheer weariness consented. Next day Susie took him to Chartres. Mrs Bloomfield was no trouble to them, and Susie induced him to linger for a week in that pleasant, quiet town. They passed many hours in the stately cathedral, and they wandered about the surrounding country. Arthur was obliged to confess that the change had done him good, and a certain apathy succeeded the agitation from which he had suffered so long. Finally Susie persuaded him to spend three or four weeks in Brittany with Dr Porhoët, who was proposing to revisit the scenes of his childhood. They returned to Paris. When Arthur left her at the station, promising to meet her again in an hour at the restaurant where they were going to dine with Dr Porhoët, he thanked her for all she had done.

'I was in an absurdly hysterical condition,' he said, holding her hand. 'You've been quite angelic. I knew that nothing could be done, and yet I was tormented with the desire to do something. Now I've got myself in hand once more. I think my common sense was deserting me, and I was on the point of believing in the farrago of nonsense which they call magic. After all, it's absurd to think that Haddo is going to do any harm to Margaret. As soon as I get back to London, I'll see my lawyers, and I daresay something can be done. If he's really mad, we'll have to put him under restraint, and Margaret will be free. I shall never forget your kindness.'

Susie smiled and shrugged her shoulders.

She was convinced that he would forget everything if Margaret came back to him. But she chid herself for the bitterness of the thought. She loved him, and she was glad to be able to do anything for him.

She returned to the hotel, changed her frock, and walked slowly to the Chien Noir. It always exhilarated her to come back to Paris; and she looked with happy, affectionate eyes at the plane trees, the yellow trams that rumbled along incessantly, and the lounging people. When she arrived, Dr Porhoët was waiting, and his delight at seeing her again was flattering and pleasant. They talked of Arthur. They wondered why he was late.

In a moment he came in. They saw at once that something quite extraordinary had taken place.

'Thank God, I've found you at last!' he cried.

His face was moving strangely. They had never seen him so discomposed.

'I've been round to your hotel, but I just missed you. Oh, why did you insist on my going away?'

'What on earth's the matter?' cried Susie.

'Something awful has happened to Margaret.'

Susie started to her feet with a sudden cry of dismay.

'How do you know?' she asked quickly.

He looked at them for a moment and flushed. He kept his eyes upon them, as though actually to force his listeners into believing what he was about to say.

'I feel it,' he answered hoarsely.

'What do you mean?'

'It came upon me quite suddenly, I can't explain why or how. I only know that something has happened.'

He began again to walk up and down, prey to an agitation that was frightful to behold. Susie and Dr Porhoët stared at him helplessly. They tried to think of something to say that would calm him.

'Surely if anything had occurred, we should have been informed.'

He turned to Susie angrily.

'How do you suppose we could know anything? She was quite helpless. She was imprisoned like a rat in a trap.'

'But, my dear friend, you mustn't give way in this fashion,' said the doctor. 'What would you say of a patient who came to you with such a story?'

Arthur answered the question with a shrug of the shoulders.

'I should say he was absurdly hysterical.'

'Well?'

'I can't help it, the feeling's there. If you try all night you'll never be able to argue me out of it. I feel it in every bone of my body. I couldn't be more certain if I saw Margaret lying dead in front of me.'

Susie saw that it was indeed useless to reason with him. The only course was to accept his conviction and make the best of it.

'What do you want us to do?' she asked.

'I want you both to come to England with me at once. If we start now we can catch the evening train.'

Susie did not answer, but she got up. She touched the doctor on the arm.

'Please come,' she whispered.

He nodded and untucked the napkin he had already arranged over his waistcoat.

'I've got a cab at the door,' said Arthur.

'And what about clothes for Miss Susie?' said the doctor.

'Oh, we can't wait for that,' cried Arthur. 'For God's sake, come quickly.'

Susie knew that there was plenty of time to fetch a few necessary things before the train started, but Arthur's impatience was too great to be withstood.

'It doesn't matter,' she said. 'I can get all I want in England.'

He hurried them to the door and told the cabman to drive to the station as quickly as ever he could.

'For Heaven's sake, calm down a little,' said Susie. 'You'll be no good to anyone in that state.'

'I feel certain we're too late.'

'Nonsense! I'm convinced that you'll find Margaret safe and sound.'

He did not answer. He gave a sigh of relief as they drove into the courtyard of the station.

CHAPTER XIV

SUSIE never forgot the horror of that journey to England. They arrived in London early in the morning and, without stopping, drove to Euston. For three or four days there had been unusual heat, and even at that hour the streets were sultry and airless. The train north was crowded, and it seemed impossible to get a breath of air. Her head ached, but she was obliged to keep a cheerful demeanour in the effort to allay Arthur's increasing anxiety. Dr Porhoët sat in front of her. After the sleepless night his eyes were heavy and his face deeply lined. He was exhausted. At length, after much tiresome changing, they reached Venning. She had expected a greater coolness in that northern country; but there was a hot blight over the place, and, as they walked to the inn from the little station, they could hardly drag their limbs along.

Arthur had telegraphed from London that they must have rooms ready, and the landlady expected them. She recognized Arthur. He passionately desired to ask her whether anything had happened since he went away, but forced himself to be silent for a while. He greeted her with cheerfulness.

'Well, Mrs Smithers, what has been going on since I left you?' he cried.

'Of course you wouldn't have heard, sir,' she answered gravely.

He began to tremble, but with an almost superhuman effort controlled his voice.

'Has the squire hanged himself?' he asked lightly.

'No sir—but the poor lady's dead.'

He did not answer. He seemed turned to stone. He stared with ghastly eyes.

'Poor thing!' said Susie, forcing herself to speak. 'Was it—very sudden?'

The woman turned to Susie, glad to have someone with whom to discuss the event. She took no notice of Arthur's agony.

'Yes, mum; no one expected it. She died quite sudden like. She was only buried this morning.'

'What did she die of?' asked Susie, her eyes on Arthur.

She feared that he would faint. She wanted enormously to get him away, but did not know how to manage it.

'They say it was heart disease,' answered the landlady. 'Poor thing! It's a happy release for her.'

'Won't you get us some tea, Mrs Smithers? We're very tired, and we should like something immediately.'

'Yes, miss. I'll get it at once.'

The good woman bustled away. Susie quickly locked the door. She seized Arthur's arm.

'Arthur, Arthur.'

She expected him to break down. She looked with agony at Dr Porhoët, who stood helplessly by.

'You couldn't have done anything if you'd been here. You heard what the woman said. If Margaret died of heart disease, your suspicions were quite without ground.'

He shook her away, almost violently.

'For God's sake, speak to us,' cried Susie.

His silence terrified her more than would have done any outburst of grief. Dr Porhoët went up to him gently.

'Don't try to be brave, my friend. You will not suffer as much if you allow yourself a little weakness.'

'For Heaven's sake leave me alone!' said Arthur, hoarsely.

They drew back and watched him silently. Susie heard their hostess come along to the sitting-room with tea, and she unlocked the door. The landlady brought in the things. She was on the point of leaving them when Arthur stopped her.

'How do you know that Mrs Haddo died of heart disease?' he asked suddenly.

His voice was hard and stern. He spoke with a peculiar abruptness that made the poor woman look at him in amazement.

'Dr Richardson told me so.'

'Had he been attending her?'

'Yes, sir. Mr Haddo had called him in several times to see his lady.'

'Where does Dr Richardson live?'

'Why, sir, he lives at the white house near the station.'

She could not make out why Arthur asked these questions.

'Did Mr Haddo go to the funeral?'

'Oh yes, sir. I've never seen anyone so upset'

'That'll do. You can go.'

Susie poured out the tea and handed a cup to Arthur. To her surprise, he drank the tea and ate some bread and butter. She could not understand him. The expression of strain, and the restlessness which had been so painful, were both gone from his face, and it was set now to a look of grim determination. At last he spoke to them.

'I'm going to see this doctor. Margaret's heart was as sound as mine.'

'What are you going to do?'

'Do?'

He turned on her with a peculiar fierceness.

'I'm going to put a rope round that man's neck, and if the law won't help me, by God, I'll kill him myself.'

'Mais, mon ami, vous êtes fou,' cried Dr Porhoët, springing up.

Arthur put out his hand angrily, as though to keep him back. The frown on his face grew darker.

'You *must* leave me alone. Good Heavens, the time has gone by for tears and lamentation. After all I've gone through for months, I can't weep because Margaret is dead. My heart is dried up. But I know that she didn't die naturally, and I'll never rest so long as that fellow lives.'

He stretched out his hands and with clenched jaws prayed that one day he might hold the man's neck between them, and see his face turn livid and purple as he died.

'I am going to this fool of a doctor, and then I shall go to Skene.'

'You must let us come with you,' said Susie.

'You need not be frightened,' he answered. 'I shall not take any steps of my own till I find the law is powerless.'

'I want to come with you all the same.'

'As you like.'

Susie went out and ordered a trap to ge got ready. But since Arthur would not wait, she arranged that it should be sent for them to the doctor's door. They went there at once, on foot.

Dr Richardson was a little man of five-and-fifty, with a fair beard that was now nearly white, and prominent blue eyes. He spoke with a broad Staffordshire accent. There was in him something of the farmer, something of the well-to-do tradesman, and at the first glance his intelligence did not impress one.

Arthur was shewn with his two friends into the consulting-room, and after a short interval the doctor came in. He was dressed in flannels and had an old-fashioned racket in his hand.

'I'm sorry to have kept you waiting, but Mrs Richardson has got a few lady-friends to tea, and I was just in the middle of a set.'

His effusiveness jarred upon Arthur, whose manner by contrast became more than usually abrupt.

'I have just learnt of the death of Mrs Haddo. I was her guardian and her oldest friend. I came to you in the hope that you would be able to tell me something about it.'

Dr Richardson gave him at once the suspicious glance of a stupid man.

'I don't know why you come to me instead of to her husband. He will be able to tell you all that you wish to know.'

'I came to you as a fellow-practitioner,' answered Arthur. 'I am at St Luke's Hospital.' He pointed to his card, which Dr Richardson still held. 'And my friend is Dr Porhoët, whose name will be familiar to you with respect to his studies in Malta Fever.'

'I think I read an article of yours in the *B. M. I.*,' said the country doctor.

His manner assumed a singular hostility. He had no sympathy with London specialists, whose attitude towards the general practitioner he resented. He was pleased to sneer at their pretensions to omniscience, and quite willing to pit himself against them.

'What can I do for you, Mr Burdon?'

'I should be very much obliged if you would tell me as exactly as possible how Mrs Haddo died.'

'It was a very simple case of endocarditis.'

'May I ask how long before death you were called in?'

The doctor hesitated. He reddened a little.

'I'm not inclined to be cross-examined,' he burst out, suddenly making up his mind to be angry. 'As a surgeon I daresay your knowledge of cardiac diseases is neither extensive nor peculiar. But this was a very simple case, and everything was done that was possible. I don't think there's anything I can tell you.'

Arthur took no notice of the outburst.

'How many times did you see her?'

'Really, sir, I don't understand your attitude. I can't see that you have any right to question me.'

'Did you have a post-mortem?'

'Certainly not. In the first place there was no need, as the cause of death was perfectly clear, and secondly you must know as well as I do that the relatives are very averse to anything of the sort. You gentlemen in Harley Street don't understand the conditions of private practice. We haven't the time to do post-mortems to gratify a needless curiosity.'

Arthur was silent for a moment. The little man was evidently convinced that there was nothing odd about Margaret's death, but his foolishness was as great as his obstinacy. It was clear that several motives would induce him to put every obstacle in Arthur's way, and chief of these was the harm it would do him if it were discovered that he had given a certificate of death carelessly. He would naturally do anything to avoid social scandal. Still Arthur was obliged to speak.

'I think I'd better tell you frankly that I'm not satisfied, Dr Richardson. I can't persuade myself that this lady's death was due to natural causes.'

'Stuff and nonsense!' cried the other angrily. 'I've been in practice for hard upon thirty-five years, and I'm willing to stake my professional reputation on it.'

'I have reason to think you are mistaken.'

'And to what do you ascribe death, pray?' asked the doctor.

'I don't know yet.'

'Upon my soul, I think you must be out of your senses. Really, sir, your behaviour is childish. You tell me that you are a surgeon of some eminence . . .'

'I surely told you nothing of the sort.'

'Anyhow, you read papers before learned bodies and have them printed. And you come with as silly a story as a Staffordshire peasant who thinks someone has been trying to poison him because he's got a stomach-ache. You may be a very admirable surgeon, but I venture to think I am more capable than you of judging in a case which I attended and you know nothing about.'

'I mean to take the steps necessary to get an order for exhumation, Dr Richardson, and I cannot help thinking it will be worth your while to assist me in every possible way.'

'I shall do nothing of the kind. I think you very impertinent, sir. There is no need for exhumation, and I shall do everything in my power to prevent it. And I tell you as chairman of the board of magistrates, my opinion will have as great value as any specialist's in Harley Street.'

He flounced to the door and held it open. Susie and Dr Porhoët walked out; and Arthur, looking down thoughtfully, followed on their heels. Dr Richardson slammed the street-door angrily.

Dr Porhoët slipped his arm in Arthur's.

'You must be reasonable, my friend,' he said. 'From his own point of view this doctor has all the rights on his side. You have nothing to justify your demands. It is monstrous to expect that for a vague suspicion you will be able to get an order for exhumation.'

Arthur did not answer. The trap was waiting for them.

'Why do you want to see Haddo?' insisted the doctor. 'You will do no more good than you have with Dr Richardson.'

'I have made up my mimd to see him,' answered Arthur shortly. 'But there is no need that either of you should accompany me.'

'If you go, we will come with you,' said Susie.

Without a word Arthur jumped into the dog-cart, and Susie took a seat by his side. Dr Porhoët, with a shrug of the shoulders, mounted behind. Arthur whipped up the pony, and at a smart trot they traversed the three miles across the barren heath that lay between Venning and Skene.

When they reached the park gates, the lodgekeeper, as luck would have it, was standing just inside, and she held one of them open for her little boy to come in. He was playing in the road and showed no inclination to do so. Arthur jumped down.

'I want to see Mr Haddo,' he said.

'Mr Haddo's not in,' she answered roughly.

She tried to close the gate, but Arthur quickly put his foot inside.

'Nonsense! I have to see him on a matter of great importance.'

'Mr Haddo's orders are that no one is to be admitted.'

'I can't help that, I'm proposing to come in, all the same.'

Susie and Dr Porhoët came forward. They promised the small boy a shilling to hold their horse.

'Now then, get out of here,' cried the woman. 'You're not coming in, whatever you say.'

She tried to push the gate to, but Arthur's foot prevented her. Paying no heed to her angry expostulations, he forced his way in. He walked quickly up the drive. The lodge-keeper accompanied him, with shrill abuse. The gate was left unguarded, and the others were able to follow without difficulty.

'You can go to the door, but you won't see Mr Haddo,' the woman cried angrily. 'You'll get me sacked for letting you come.'

Susie saw the house. It was a fine old building in the Elizabethan style, but much in need of repair; and it had the desolate look of a place that has been uninhabited. The garden that surrounded it had been allowed to run wild, and the avenue up which they walked was green with rank weeds. Here and there a fallen tree, which none had troubled to remove, marked the owner's negligence. Arthur went to the door and rang a bell. They heard it clang through the house as though not a soul lived there. A man came to the door, and as soon as he opened it, Arthur, expecting to be refused admission, pushed in. The fellow was as angry as the virago, his wife, who explained noisily how the three strangers had got into the park.

'You can't see the squire, so you'd better be off. He's up in the attics, and no one's allowed to go to him.'

The man tried to push Arthur away.

'Be off with you, or I'll send for the police.'

'Don't be a fool,' said Arthur. 'I mean to find Mr Haddo.'

The housekeeper and his wife broke out with abuse, to which Arthur listened in silence. Susie and Dr Porhoët stood by anxiously. They did not know what to do. Suddenly a voice at their elbows made them start, and the two servants were immediately silent.

'What can I do for you?'

Oliver Haddo was standing motionless behind them. It startled Susie that he should have come upon them so suddenly, without a sound. Dr Porhoët, who had not seen him for some time, was astounded at the change which had taken place in him. The corpulence which had been his before was become now a positive disease. He was enormous. His chin was a mass of heavy folds distended with fat, and his cheeks were puffed up so that his eyes were preternaturally small. He peered at you from between the swollen lids. All his features had sunk into that hideous obesity. His ears were horribly bloated, and the lobes were large and swelled. He had apparently a difficulty in breathing, for his large mouth, with its scarlet, shining lips, was constantly open. He had grown much balder and now there was only a crescent of long hair stretching across the back of his head from ear to ear. There was something terrible about that great shining scalp. His paunch was huge; he was a very tall man and held himself erect, so that it protruded like a vast barrel. His hands were infinitely repulsive; they were red and soft and moist. He was sweating freely, and beads of perspiration stood on his forehead and on his shaven lip.

For a moment they all looked at one another in silence. Then Haddo turned to his servants.

'Go,' he said.

As though frightened out of their wits, they made for the door and with a bustling hurry flung themselves out. A torpid smile crossed his face as he watched them go. Then he moved a step nearer his visitors. His manner had still the insolent urbanity which was customary to him.

'And now, my friends, will you tell me how I can be of service to you?'

'I have come about Margaret's death,' said Arthur.

Haddo, as was his habit, did not immediately answer. He looked slowly from Arthur to Dr Porhoët, and from Dr Porhoët to Susie. His eyes rested on her hat, and she felt uncomfortably that he was inventing some gibe about it.

'I should have thought this hardly the moment to intrude upon my sorrow,' he said at last. 'If you have condolences to offer, I venture to suggest that you might conveniently send them by means of the penny post.'

Arthur frowned.

'Why did you not let me know that she was ill?' he asked.

'Strange as it may seem to you, my worthy friend, it never occurred to me that my wife's health could be any business of yours.'

A faint smile flickered once more on Haddo's lips, but his eyes had still the peculiar hardness which was so uncanny. Arthur looked at him steadily.

'I have every reason to believe that you killed her,' he said.

Haddo's face did not for an instant change its expression.

'And have you communicated your suspicions to the police?'

'I propose to.'

'And, if I am not indiscreet, may I inquire upon what you base them?'

'I saw Margaret three weeks ago, and she told me that she went in terror of her life.'

'Poor Margaret! She had always the romantic temperament. I think it was that which first brought us together.'

'You damned scoundrel!' cried Arthur.

'My dear fellow, pray moderate your language. This is surely not an occasion when you should give way to your lamentable taste for abuse. You outrage all Miss Boyd's susceptibilities.' He turned to her with an airy wave of his fat hand. 'You must forgive me if I do not offer you the hospitality of Skene, but the loss I have so lately sustained does not permit me to indulge in the levity of entertaining.'

He gave her an ironical, low bow; then looked once more at Arthur.

'If I can be of no further use to you, perhaps you would leave me to my own reflections. The lodgekeeper will give you the exact address of the village constable.'

Arthur did not answer. He stared into vacancy, as if he were turning over things in his mind. Then he turned sharply on his heel and walked towards the gate. Susie and Dr Porhoët, taken completely aback, did not know what to do; and Haddo's little eyes twinkled as he watched their discomfiture.

'I always thought that your friend had deplorable manners,' he murmured.

Susie, feeling very ridiculous, flushed, and Dr Porhoët awkwardly took off his hat. As they walked away, they felt Haddo's mocking gaze fixed upon them, and they were heartily thankful to reach the gate. They found Arthur waiting for them.

'I beg your pardon,' he said, 'I forgot that I was not alone.'

The three of them drove slowly back to the inn.

'What are you going to do now?' asked Susie.

For a long time Arthur made no reply, and Susie thought he could not have heard her. At last he broke the silence.

'I see that I can do nothing by ordinary methods. I realize that it is useless to make a public outcry. There is only my own conviction that Margaret came to a violent end, and I cannot expect anyone to pay heed to that.'

'After all, it's just possible that she really died of heart disease.'

Arthur gave Susie a long look. He seemed to consider her words deliberately.

'Perhaps there are means to decide that conclusively,' he replied at length, thoughtfully, as though he were talking to himself.

'What are they?'

Arthur did not answer. When they came to the door of the inn, he stopped.

'Will you go in? I wish to take a walk by myself,' he said.

Susie looked at him anxiously.

'You're not going to do anything rash?'

'I will do nothing till I have made quite sure that Margaret was foully murdered.'

He turned on his heel and walked quickly away. It was late now, and they found a frugal meal waiting for them in the little sitting-room. It seemed no use to delay it till Arthur came back, and silently, sorrowfully, they ate. Afterwards, the doctor smoked cigarettes, while Susie sat at the open window and looked at the stars. She thought of Margaret, of her beauty and her charming frankness, of her fall and of her miserable end; and she began to cry quietly. She knew enough of the facts now to be aware that the wretched girl was not to blame for anything that had happened. A cruel fate had fallen upon her, and she had been as powerless as in the old tales Phaedra, the daughter of Minos, or Myrrha of the beautiful hair. The hours passed, and still Arthur did not return. Susie thought now only of him, and she was frightfully anxious.

But at last he came in. The night was far advanced. He put down his hat and sat down. For a long while he looked silently at Dr. Porhoët.

'What is it, my friend?' asked the good doctor at length.

'Do you remember that you told us once of an experiment you made in Alexandria?' he said, after some hesitation.

He spoke in a curious voice.

'You told us that you took a boy, and when he looked in a magic mirror, he saw things which he could not possibly have known.'

'I remember very well,' said the doctor.

'I was much inclined to laugh at you at the time. I was convinced that the boy was a knave who deceived you.'

'Yes?'

'Of late I've thought of that story often. Some hidden recess of my memory has been opened, and I seem to remember strange things. Was I the boy who looked in the ink?'

'Yes,' said the doctor quietly.

Arthur did not say anything. A profound silence fell upon them, while Susie and the doctor watched him intently. They wondered what was in his mind.

'There is a side of my character which I did not know till lately,' Arthur said at last. 'When first it dawned upon me, I fought against it. I said to myself that deep down in all of us, a relic from the long past, is the remains of the superstition that blinded our fathers; and it is needful for the man of science to fight against it with all his might. And yet it was stronger than I. Perhaps my birth, my early years, in those Eastern lands where everyone believes in the supernatural, affected me although I did not know it. I began to remember vague, mysterious things, which I never knew had been part of my knowledge. And at last one day it seemed that a new window was opened on to my soul, and I saw with extraordinary clearness the incident which you had described. I knew suddenly it was part of my own experience. I saw you take me by the hand and pour the ink on my palm and bid me look at it. I felt again the strange glow that thrilled me, and with an indescribable bitterness I saw things in the mirror which were not there before. I saw people whom I had never seen. I saw them perform certain actions. And some force I knew not, obliged me to speak. And at length everything grew dim, and I was as exhausted as if I had not eaten all day.'

He went over to the open window and looked out. Neither of the others spoke. The look on Arthur's face, curiously outlined by the light of the lamp, was very stern. He seemed to undergo some mental struggle of extraordinary violence. He breath came quickly. At last he turned and faced them. He spoke hoarsely, quickly.

'I *must* see Margaret again.'

'Arthur, you're mad!' cried Susie.

He went up to Dr Porhoët and, putting his hands on his shoulders, looked fixedly into his eyes.

'You have studied this science. You know all that can be known of it. I want you to show her to me.'

The doctor gave an exclamation of alarm.

'My dear fellow, how can I? I have read many books, but I have never practised anything. I have only studied these matters for my amusement.'

'Do you believe it can be done?'

'I don't understand what you want.'

'I want you to bring her to me so that I may speak with her, so that I may find out the truth.'

'Do you think I am God that I can raise men from the dead?'

Arthur's hands pressed him down in the chair from which he sought to rise. His fingers were clenched on the old man's shoulders so that he could hardly bear the pain.

'You told us how once Eliphas Levi raised a spirit. Do you believe that was true?'

'I don't know. I have always kept an open mind. There was much to be said on both sides.'

'Well, now you *must* believe. You must do what he did.'

'You must be mad, Arthur.'

'I want you to come to that spot where I saw her last. If her spirit can be brought back anywhere, it must be in that place where she sat and wept. You know all the ceremonies and all the words that are necessary.'

But Susie came forward and laid her hand on his arm. He looked at her with a frown.

'Arthur, you know in your heart that nothing can come of it. You're only increasing your unhappiness. And even if you could bring her from the grave for a moment, why can you not let her troubled soul rest in peace?'

'If she died a natural death we shall have no power over her, but if her death was violent perhaps her spirit is earth-bound still. I tell you I must be certain. I want to see her once more, and afterwards I shall know what to do.'

'I cannot, I cannot,' said the doctor.

'Give me the books and I will do it alone.'

'You know that I have nothing here.'

'Then you must help me,' said Arthur. 'After all, why should you mind? We perform a certain operation, and if nothing happens we are no worse off then before. On the other hand, if we succeed. . . . Oh, for God's sake, help me! If you have any care for my happiness do this one thing for me.'

He stepped back and looked at the doctor. The Frenchman's eyes were fixed upon the ground.

'It's madness,' he muttered.

He was intensely moved by Arthur's appeal. At last he shrugged his shoulders.

'After all, if it is but a foolish mummery it can do no harm.'

'You will help me?' cried Arthur.

'If it can give you any peace or any satisfaction, I am willing to do what I can. But I warn you to be prepared for a great disappointment.'

CHAPTER XV

ARTHUR wished to set about the invocation then and there, but Dr Porhoët said it was impossible. They were all exhausted after the long journey, and it was necessary to get certain things together without which nothing could be done. In his heart he thought that a night's rest would bring Arthur to a more reasonable mind. When the light of day shone upon the earth he would be ashamed of the desire which ran counter to all his prepossessions. But Arthur remembered that on the next day it would be exactly a week since Margaret's death, and it seemed to him that then their spells might have a greater efficacy.

When they came down in the morning and greeted one another, it was plain that none of them had slept.

'Are you still of the same purpose as last night?' asked Dr Porhoët gravely.

'I am.'

The doctor hesitated nervously.

'It will be necessary, if you wish to follow out the rules of the old necromancers, to fast through the whole day.'

'I am ready to do anything.'

'It will be no hardship to me,' said Susie, with a little hysterical laugh. 'I feel I couldn't eat a thing if I tried.'

'I think the whole affair is sheer folly,' said Dr Porhoët.

'You promised me you would try.'

The day, the long summer day, passed slowly. There was a hard brilliancy in the sky that reminded the Frenchman of those Egyptian heavens when the earth seemed crushed beneath a bowl of molten fire. Arthur was too restless to remain indoors and left the others to their own devices. He walked without aim, as fast as he could go; he felt no weariness. The burning sun beat down upon him, but he did not know it. The hours passed with lagging feet. Susie lay on her bed and tried to read. Her nerves were so taut that, when there was a sound in the courtyard of a pail falling on the cobbles, she cried out in terror. The sun rose, and presently her window was flooded with quivering rays of gold. It was midday. The day passed, and it was afternoon. The evening came, but it brought no freshness. Meanwhile Dr Porhoët sat in the little parlour, with his head between his hands, trying by a great mental effort to bring back to his memory all that he had read. His heart began to beat more quickly. Then the night fell, and one by one the stars shone out. There was no wind. The air was heavy. Susie came downstairs and began to talk with Dr Porhoët. But they spoke in a low tone, as if they were afraid that someone would overhear. They were faint now with want of food. The hours went one by one, and the striking of a clock filled them each time with a mysterious apprehension. The lights in the village were put out little by little, and everybody slept. Susie had lighted the lamp, and they watched beside it. A cold shiver passed through her.

'I feel as though someone were lying dead in the room,' she said. 'Why does not Arthur come?'

They spoke inconsequently, and neither heeded what the other said. The window was wide open, but the air was difficult to breathe. And now the silence was so unusual that Susie grew strangely nervous. She tried to think of the noisy streets in Paris, the constant roar of traffic, and the shuffling of the crowds toward evening as the work people returned to their homes. She stood up.

'There's no air tonight. Look at the trees. Not a leaf is moving.'

'Why does not Arthur come?' repeated the doctor.

'There's no moon tonight. It will be very dark at Skene.'

'He's walked all day. He should be here by now.'

Susie felt an extraordinary oppression, and she panted for breath. At last they heard a step on the road outside, and Arthur stood at the window.

'Are you ready to come?' he said.

"We've been waiting for you.'

They joined him, bringing the few things that Dr Porhoët had said were necessary, and they walked along the solitary road that led to Skene. On each side the heather stretched into the dark night, and there was a blackness about it that was ominous. There was no sound save that of their own steps. Dimly, under the stars, they saw the desolation with which they were surrounded. The way seemed very long. They were utterly exhausted, and they could hardly drag one foot after the other.

'You must let me rest for a minute,' said Susie.

They did not answer, but stopped, and she sat on a boulder by the wayside. They stood motionless in front of her, waiting patiently till she was ready. After a little while she forced herself to get up.

'Now I can go,' she said.

Still they did not speak, but walked on. They moved like figures in a dream, with a stealthy directness, as though they acted under the influence of another's will. Suddenly the road stopped, and they found themselves at the gates of Skene.

'Follow me very closely,' said Arthur.

He turned on one side, and they followed a paling. Susie could feel that they walked along a narrow path. She could see hardly two steps in front of her. At last he stood still.

'I came here earlier in the night and made the opening easier to get through.'

He turned back a broken piece of railing and slipped in. Susie followed, and Dr Porhoët entered after her.

'I can see nothing,' said Susie.

'Give my your hand, and I will lead you.'

They walked with difficulty through the tangled bracken, among closely planted trees. They stumbled, and once Dr Porhoët fell. It seemed that they went a long way. Susie's heart beat fast with anxiety. All her weariness was forgotten.

Then Arthur stopped them, and he pointed in front of him. Through an opening in the trees, they saw the house. All the windows were dark except those just under the roof, and from them came bright lights.

'Those are the attics which he uses as a laboratory. You see, he is working now. There is no one else in the house.'

Susie was curiously fascinated by the flaming lights. There was an awful mystery in those unknown labours which absorbed Oliver Haddo night after night till the sun rose. What horrible things were done there, hidden from the eyes of men? By himself in that vast house the madman performed ghastly experiments; and who could tell what dark secrets he trafficked in?

'There is no danger that he will come out,' said Arthur. 'He remains there till the break of day.'

He took her hand again and led her on. Back they went among the trees, and presently they were on a pathway. They walked along with greater safety.

'Are you all right, Porhoët?' asked Arthur.

'Yes.'

But the trees grew thicker and the night more sombre. Now the stars were shut out, and they could hardly see in front of them.

'Here we are,' said Arthur.

They stopped, and found that there was in front of them a green space formed by four cross-ways. In the middle a stone bench gleamed vaguely against the darkness.

'This is where Margaret sat when last I saw her.'

'I can see to do nothing here,' said the doctor.

They had brought two flat bowls of brass to serve as censers, and these Arthur gave to Dr Porhoët. He stood by Susie's side while the doctor busied himself with his preparations. They saw him move to and fro. They saw him bend to the ground. Presently there was a crackling of wood, and from the brazen bowls red flames shot up. They did not know what he burnt, but there were heavy clouds of smoke, and a strong, aromatic odour filled the air. Now and again the doctor was sharply silhouetted against the light. His slight, bowed figure was singularly mysterious. When Susie caught sight of his face, she saw that it was touched with a strong emotion. The work he was at affected him so that his doubts, his fears, had vanished. He looked like some old alchemist busied with unnatural things. Susie's heart began to beat painfully. She was growing deperately frightened and stretched out her hand so that she might touch Arthur. Silently he put his arm through hers. And now the doctor was tracing strange signs upon the ground. The flames died down and only a glow remained, but he seemed to have no difficulty in seeing what he was about. Susie could not discern what figures he drew. Then he put more twigs upon the braziers, and the flames sprang up once more, cutting the darkness sharply as with a sword.

'Now come,' he said.

But, inexplicably, a sudden terror seized Susie. She felt that the hairs of her head stood up, and a cold sweat broke out on her body. Her limbs had grown on an instant inconceivably heavy so that she could not move. A panic such as she had never known came upon her, and, except that her legs would not carry her, she would have fled blindly. She began to tremble. She tried to speak, but her tongue clave to her throat.

'I can't, I'm afraid,' she muttered hoarsely.

'You must. Without you we can do nothing,' said Arthur.

She could not reason with herself. She had forgotten everything except that she was frightened to death. Her heart was beating so quickly that she almost fainted. And now Arthur held her, so firmly that she winced.

'Let me go,' she whispered. 'I won't help you. I'm afraid.'

'You must,' he said. 'You must.'

'No.'

'I tell you, you must come.'

'Why?'

Her deadly fear expressed itself in a passion of sudden anger.

'Because you love me, and it's the only way to give me peace.'

She uttered a low wail of pain, and her terror gave way to shame. She blushed to the roots of her hair because he too knew her secret. And then she was seized again with anger because he had the cruelty to taunt her with it. She had recovered her courage now, and she stepped forward. Dr. Porhoët told her where to stand. Arthur took his place in front of her.

'You must not move till I give you leave. If you go outside the figure I have drawn, I cannot protect you.'

For a moment Dr Porhoët stood in perfect silence. Then he began to recite strange words in Latin. Susie heard him but vaguely. She did not know the sense, and his voice was so low that she could not have distinguished the words. But his intonation had lost that gentle irony which was habitual to him, and he spoke with a trembling gravity that was extraordinarily impressive. Arthur stood immobile as a rock. The flames died away, and they saw one another only by the glow of the ashes, dimly, like persons in a vision of death. There was silence. Then the necromancer spoke again, and now his voice was louder. He seemed to utter weird invocations, but they were in a tongue that the others knew not. And while he spoke the light from the burning cinders on a sudden went out.

It did not die, but was sharply extinguished, as though by invisible hands. And now the darkness was more sombre than that of the blackest night. The trees that surrounded them were hidden from their eyes, and the whiteness of the stone bench was seen no longer. They stood but a little way one from the other, but each might have stood alone. Susie strained her eyes, but she could see nothing. She looked up quickly; the stars were gone out, and she could see no further over her head than round about. The darkness was terrifying. And from it, Dr Porhoët's voice had a ghastly effect. It seemed to come, wonderfully changed, from the void of bottomless chaos. Susie clenched her hands so that she might not faint.

All at once she started, for the old man's voice was cut by a sudden gust of wind. A moment before, the utter silence had been almost intolerable, and now a storm seemed to have fallen upon them. The trees all around them rocked in the wind; they heard the branches creak; and they heard the hissing of the leaves. They were in the midst of a hurricane. And they felt the earth sway as it resisted the straining roots of great trees, which seemed to be dragged up by the force of the furious gale. Whistling and roaring, the wind stormed all about them, and the doctor, raising his voice, tried in vain to command it. But the strangest thing of all was that, where they stood, there was no sign of the raging blast. The air immediately about them was as still as it had been before, and not a hair on Susie's head was moved. And it was terrible to hear the tumult, and yet to be in a calm that was almost unnatural.

On a sudden, Dr Porhoët raised his voice, and with a sternness they had never heard in it before, cried out in that unknown language. Then he called upon Margaret. He called her name three times. In the uproar Susie could scarcely hear. Terror had seized her again, but in her confusion she remembered his command, and she dared not move.

'Margaret, Margaret, Margaret.'

Without a pause between, as quickly as a stone falls to the ground, the din which was all about them ceased. There was no gradual diminution. But at one moment there was a roaring hurricane and at the next a silence so complete that it might have been the silence of death.

And then, seeming to come out of nothingness, extraordinarily, they heard with a curious distinctness the sound of a woman weeping. Susie's heart stood still. They heard the sound of a woman weeping, and they recognized the voice of Margaret. A groan of anguish burst from Arthur's lips, and he was on the point of starting forward. But quickly Dr Porhoët put out his hand to prevent him. The sound was heartrending, the sobbing of a woman who had lost all hope, the sobbing of a woman terrified. If Susie had been able to stir, she would have put her hands to her ears to shut out the ghastly agony of it.

And in a moment, notwithstanding the heavy darkness of the starless night, Arthur saw her. She was seated on the stone bench as when last he had spoken with her. In her anguish she sought not to hide her face. She looked at the ground, and the tears fell down her cheeks. Her bosom heaved with the pain of her weeping.

Then Arthur knew that all his suspicions were justified.

CHAPTER XVI

ARTHUR would not leave the little village of Venning. Neither Susie nor the doctor could get him to make any decision. None of them spoke of the night which they had spent in the woods of Skene; but it coloured all their thoughts, and they were not free for a single moment from the ghastly memory of it. They seemed still to hear the sound of that passionate weeping. Arthur was moody. When he was with them, he spoke little; he opposed a stubborn resistance to their efforts at diverting his mind. He spent long hours by himself, in the country, and they had no idea what he did. Susie was terribly anxious. He had lost his balance so completely that she was prepared for any rashness. She divined that his hatred of Haddo was no longer within the bounds of reason. The desire for vengeance filled him entirely, so that he was capable of any violence.

Several days went by.

At last, in concert with Dr Porhoët, she determined to make one more attempt. It was late at night, and they sat with open windows in the sitting-room of the inn. There was a singular oppressiveness in the air which suggested that a thunderstorm was at hand. Susie prayed for it; for she ascribed to the peculiar heat of the last few days much of Arthur's sullen irritability.

'Arthur, you *must* tell us what you are going to do,' she said. 'It is useless to stay here. We are all so ill and nervous that we cannot consider anything rationally. We want you to come away with us tomorrow.'

'You can go if you choose,' he said. 'I shall remain till that man is dead.'

'It is madness to talk like that. You can do nothing. You are only making yourself worse by staying here.'

'I have quite made up my mind.'

'The law can offer you no help, and what else can you do?'

She asked the question, meaning if possible to get from him some hint of his intentions; but the grimness of his answer, though it only confirmed her vague suspicions, startled her.

'If I can do nothing else, I shall shoot him like a dog.'

She could think of nothing to say, and for a while they remained in silence. Then he got up.

'I think I should prefer it if you went,' he said. 'You can only hamper me.'

'I shall stay here as long as you do.'

'Why?'

'Because if you do anything, I shall be compromised. I may be arrested. I think the fear of that may restrain you.'

He looked at her steadily. She met his eyes with a calmness which showed that she meant exactly what she said, and he turned uneasily away. A silence even greater than before fell upon them. They did not move. It was so still in the room that it might have been empty. The breathlessness of the air increased, so that it was horribly oppressive. Suddenly there was a loud rattle of thunder, and a flash of lightning tore across the heavy clouds. Susie thanked Heaven for the storm which would give presently a welcome freshness. She felt excessively ill at ease, and it was a relief to ascribe her sensation to a state of the atmoshere. Again the thunder rolled. It was so loud that it seemed to be immediately above their heads. And the wind rose suddenly and swept with a long moan through the trees that surrounded the house. It was a sound so human that it might have come from the souls of dead men suffering hopeless torments of regret.

The lamp went out, so suddenly that Susie was vaguely frightened. It gave one flicker, and they were in total darkness. It seemed as though someone had leaned over the chimney and blown it out. The night was very black, and they could not see the window which opened on to the country. The darkness was so peculiar that for a moment no one stirred.

Then Susie heard Dr Porhoët slip his hand across the table to find matches, but it seemed that they were not there. Again a loud peal of thunder startled them, but the rain would not fall. They panted for fresh air. On a sudden Susie's heart gave a bound, and she sprang up.

'There's someone in the room.'

The words were no sooner out of her mouth than she heard Arthur fling himself upon the intruder. She knew at once, with the certainty of an intuition, that it was Haddo. But how had he come in? What did he want? She tried to cry out, but no sound came from her throat. Dr Porhoët seemed bound to his chair. He did not move. He made no sound. She knew that an awful struggle was proceeding. It was a struggle to the death between two men who hated one another, but the most terrible part of it was that nothing was heard. They were perfectly noiseless. She tried to do something, but she could not stir. And Arthur's heart exulted, for his enemy was in his grasp, under his hands, and he would not let him go while life was in him. He clenched his teeth and tightened his straining muscles. Susie heard his laboured breathing, but she only heard the breathing of one man. She wondered in abject terror what that could mean. They struggled silently, hand to hand, and Arthur knew that his strength was greater. He had made up his mind what to do and directed all his energy to a definite end. His enemy was extraordinarily powerful, but Arthur appeared to create some strength from the sheer force of his will. It seemed for hours that they struggled. He could not bear him down.

Suddenly, he knew that the other was frightened and sought to escape from him. Arthur tightened his grasp; for nothing in the world now would he ever loosen his hold. He took a deep, quick breath, and then put out all his strength in a tremendous effort. They swayed from side to side. Arthur felt as if his muscles were being torn from the bones, he could not continue for more than a moment longer; but the agony that flashed across his mind at the thought of failure braced him to a sudden angry jerk. All at once Haddo collapsed, and they fell heavily to the ground. Arthur was breathing more quickly now. He thought that if he could keep on for one instant longer, he would be safe. He threw all his weight on the form that rolled beneath him, and bore down furiously on the man's arm. He twisted it sharply, with all his might, and felt it give way. He gave a low cry of triumph; the arm was broken. And now his enemy was seized with panic; he struggled madly, he wanted only to get away from those long hands that were killing him. They seemed to be of iron. Arthur seized the huge bullock throat and dug his fingers into it, and they sunk into the heavy rolls of fat; and he flung the whole weight of his body into them. He exulted, for he knew that his enemy was in his power at last; he was strangling him, strangling the life out of him. He wanted light so that he might see the horror of that vast face, and the deadly fear, and the staring eyes. And still he pressed with those iron hands. And now the movements were strangely convulsive. His victim writhed in the agony of death. His struggles were desperate, but the avenging hands held him as in a vice. And then the movements grew spasmodic, and then they grew weaker. Still the hands pressed upon the gigantic throat, and Arthur forgot everything. He was mad with rage and fury and hate and sorrow. He thought of Margaret's anguish and of her fiendish torture, and he wished the man had ten lives so that he might take them one by one. And at last all was still, and that vast mass of flesh was motionless, and he knew that his enemy was dead. He loosened his grasp and slipped one hand over the heart. It would never beat again. The man was stone dead. Arthur got up and straightened himself. The darkness was intense still, and he could see nothing. Susie heard him, and at length she was able to speak.

'Arthur what have you done?'

'I've killed him,' he said hoarsely.

'O God, what shall we do?'

Arthur began to laugh aloud, hysterically, and in the darkness his hilarity was terrifying.

'For God's sake let us have some light.'

'I've found the matches,' said Dr Porhoët.

He seemed to awake suddenly from his long stupor. He struck one, and it would not light. He struck another, and Susie took off the globe and the chimney as he kindled the wick. Then he held up the lamp, and they saw Arthur looking at them. His face was ghastly. The sweat ran off his forehead in great beads, and his eyes were bloodshot. He trembled in every limb. Then Dr Porhoët advanced with the lamp and held it forward. They looked down on the floor for the man who lay there dead. Susie gave a sudden cry of horror.

There was no one there.

Arthur stepped back in terrified surprise. There was no one in the room, living or dead, but the three friends. The ground sank under Susie's feet, she felt horribly ill, and she fainted. When she awoke, seeming difficultly to emerge from an eternal night, Arthur was holding down her head.

'Bend down,' he said. 'Bend down.'

All that had happened came back to her, and she burst into tears. Her self-control deserted her, and, clinging to him for protection, she sobbed as though her heart would break. She was shaking from head to foot. The strangeness of this last horror had overcome her, and she could have shrieked with fright.

'It's all right,' he said. 'You need not be afraid.'

'Oh, what does it mean?'

'You must pluck up courage. We're going now to Skene.'

She sprang to her feet, as though to get away from him; her heart beat wildly.

'No, I can't; I'm frightened.'

'We must see what it means. We have no time to lose, or the morning will be upon us before we get back.'

Then she sought to prevent him.

'Oh, for God's sake, don't go, Arthur. Something awful may await you there. Don't risk your life.'

'There is no danger. I tell you the man is dead.'

'If anything happened to you . . .'

She stopped, trying to restrain her sobs; she dared not go on. But he seemed to know what was in her mind.

'I will take no risks, because of you. I know that whether I live or die is not a—matter of indifference to you.'

She looked up and saw that his eyes were fixed upon her gravely. She reddened. A curious feeling came into her heart.

'I will go with you wherever you choose,' she said humbly.

'Come, then.'

They stepped out into the night. And now, without rain, the storm had passed away, and the stars were shining. They walked quickly. Arthur went in front of them. Dr Porhoët and Susie followed him, side by side, and they had to hasten their steps in order not to be left behind. It seemed to them that the horror of the night was passed, and there was a fragrancy in the air which was wonderfully refreshing. The sky was beautiful. And at last they came to Skene. Arthur led them again to the opening in the palisade, and he took Susie's hand. Presently they stood in the place from which a few days before they had seen the house. As then, it stood in massive blackness against the night and, as then, the attic windows shone out with brilliant lights. Susie started, for she had expected that the whole place would be in darkness.

'There is no danger, I promise you,' said Arthur gently. 'We are going to find out the meaning of all this mystery.'

He began to walk towards the house.

'Have you a weapon of some sort?' asked the doctor.

Arthur handed him a revolver.

'Take this. It will reassure you, but you will have no need of it. I bought it the other day when—I had other plans.'

Susie gave a little shudder. They reached the drive and walked to the great portico which adorned the façade of the house. Arthur tried the handle, but it would not open.

'Will you wait here?' he said. 'I can get through one of the windows, and I will let you in.'

He left them. They stood quietly there, with anxious hearts; they could not guess what they would see. They were afraid that something would happen to Arthur, and Susie regretted that she had not insisted on going with him. Suddenly she remembered that awful moment when the light of the lamp had been thrown where all expected to see a body, and there was nothing.

'What do you think it meant?' she cried suddenly, 'What is the explanation?'

'Perhaps we shall see now,' answered the doctor.

Arthur still lingered, and she could not imagine what had become of him. All sorts of horrible fancies passed through her mind, and she dreaded she knew not what. At last they heard a footstep inside the house, and the door was opened.

'I was convinced that nobody slept here, but I was obliged to make sure. I had some difficulty in getting in.'

Susie hesitated to enter. She did not know what horrors awaited her, and the darkness was terrifying.

'I cannot see,' she said.

'I've brought a torch,' said Arthur.

He pressed a button, and a narrow ray of bright light was cast upon the floor. Dr Porhoët and Susie went in. Arthur carefully closed the door, and flashed the light of his torch all round them. They stood in a large hall, the floor of which was scattered with the skins of lions that Haddo on his celebrated expedition had killed in Africa. There were perhaps a dozen, and their number gave a wild, barbaric note. A great oak staircase led to the upper floors.

'We must go through all the rooms,' said Arthur.

He did not expect to find Haddo till they came to the lighted attics, but it seemed needful nevertheless to pass right through the house on their way. A flash of his torch had shown him that the walls of the hall were decorated with all manner of armour, ancient swords of Eastern handiwork, barbaric weapons from central Africa, savage implements of medieval warfare; and an idea came to him. He took down a huge battle-axe and swung it in his hand.

'Now come.'

Silently, holding their breath as though they feared to wake the dead, they went into the first room. They saw it difficultly with their scant light, since the thin shaft of brilliancy, emphasising acutely the surrounding darkness, revealed it only piece by piece. It was a large room, evidently unused, for the furniture was covered with holland, and there was a mustiness about it which suggested that the windows were seldom opened. As in many old houses, the rooms led not from a passage but into one another, and they walked through many till they came back into the hall. They had all a desolate, uninhabited air. Their sombreness was increased by the oak with which they were panelled. There was panelling in the hall too, and on the stairs that led broadly to the top of the house. As they ascended, Arthur stopped for one moment and passed his hand over the polished wood.

'It would burn like tinder,' he said.

They went through the rooms on the first floor, and they were as empty and as cheerless. Presently they came to that which had been Margaret's. In a bowl were dead flowers. Her brushes were still on the toilet table. But it was a gloomy chamber, with its dark oak, and, so comfortless that Susie shuddered. Arthur stood for a time and looked at it, but he said nothing. They found themselves again on the stairs and they went to the second storey. But here they seemed to be at the top of the house.

'How does one get up to the attics?' said Arthur, looking about him with surprise.

He paused for a while to think. Then he nodded his head.

'There must be some steps leading out of one of the rooms.'

They went on. And now the ceilings were much lower, with heavy beams, and there was no furniture at all. The emptiness seemed to make everything more terrifying. They felt that they were on the threshold of a great mystery, and Susie's heart began to beat fast. Arthur conducted his examination with the greatest method; he walked round each room carefully, looking for a door that might lead to a staircase; but there was no sign of one.

'What will you do if you can't find the way up?' asked Susie.

'I shall find the way up,' he answered.

They came to the staircase once more and had discovered nothing. They looked at one another helplessly.

'It's quite clear there is a way,' said Arthur, with impatience. 'There must be something in the nature of a hidden door somewhere or other.'

He leaned against the balustrade and meditated. The light of his lantern threw a narrow ray upon the opposite wall.

'I feel certain it must be in one of the rooms at the end of the house. That seems the most natural place to put a means of ascent to the attics.'

They went back, and again he examined the panelling of a small room that had outside walls on three sides of it. It was the only room that did not lead into another.

'It must be here,' he said.

Presently he gave a little laugh, for he saw that a small door was concealed by the woodwork. He pressed it where he thought there might be a spring, and it flew open. Their torch showed them a narrow wooden staircase. They walked up and found themselves in front of a door. Arthur tried it, but it was locked. He smiled grimly.

'Will you get back a little,' he said.

He lifted his axe and swung it down upon the latch. The handle was shattered, but the lock did not yield. He shook his head. As he paused for a moment, an there was a complete silence, Susie distinctly heard a slight noise. She put her hand on Arthur's arm to call his attention to it, and with strained ears they listened. There was something alive on the other side of the door. They heard its curious sound: it was not that of a human voice, it was not the crying of an animal, it was extraordinary.

It was the sort of gibber, hoarse and rapid, and it filled them with an icy terror because it was so weird and so unnatural.

'Come away, Arthur,' said Susie. 'Come away.'

'There's some living thing in there,' he answered.

He did not know why the sound horrified him. The sweat broke out on his forehead.

'Something awful will happen to us,' whispered Susie, shaking with uncontrollable fear.

'The only thing is to break the door down.'

The horrid gibbering was drowned by the noise he made. Quickly, without pausing, he began to hack at the oak door with all his might. In rapid succession his heavy blows rained down, and the sound echoed through the empty house. There was a crash, and the door swung back. They had been so long in almost total darkness that they were blinded for an instant by the dazzling light. And then instinctively they started back, for, as the door opened, a wave of heat came out upon them so that they could hardly breathe. The place was like an oven.

They entered. It was lit by enormous lamps, the light of which was increased by reflectors, and warmed by a great furnace. They could not understand why so intense a heat was necessary. The narrow windows were closed. Dr Porhoët caught sight of a thermometer and was astounded at the temperature it indicated. The room was used evidently as a laboratory. On broad tables were test-tubes, basins and baths of white porcelain, measuring-glasses, and utensils of all sorts; but the surprising thing was the great scale upon which everything was. Neither Arthur nor Dr Porhoët had ever seen such gigantic measures nor such large test-tubes. There were rows of bottles, like those in the dispensary of a hospital, each containing great quanties of a different chemical. The three friends stood in silence. The emptiness of the room contrasted so oddly with its appearance of being in immediate use that it was uncanny. Susie felt that he who worked there was in the midst of his labours, and might return at any moment; he could have only gone for an instant into another chamber in order to see the progress of some experiment. It was quite silent. Whatever had made those vague, unearthly noises was hushed by their approach.

The door was closed between this room and the next. Arthur opened it, and they found themselves in a long, low attic, ceiled with great rafters, as brilliantly lit and as hot as the first. Here too were broad tables laden with retorts, instruments for heating, huge test-tubes, and all manner of vessels. The furnace that warmed it gave a steady heat. Arthur's gaze travelled slowly from table to table, and he wondered what Haddo's experiments had really been. The air was heavy with an extraordinary odour: it was not musty, like that of the closed rooms through which they had passed, but singularly pungent, disagreeable and sickly. He asked himself what it could spring from. Then his eyes fell upon a huge receptacle that stood on the table nearest to the furnace. It was covered with a white cloth. He took it off. The vessel was about four feet high, round, and shaped somewhat like a washing tub, but it was made of glass more than an inch thick. In it a spherical mass, a little larger than a football, of a peculiar, livid colour. The surface was smooth, but rather coarsely grained, and over it ran a dense system of blood-vessels. It reminded the two medical men of those huge tumours which are preserved in spirit in hospital museums. Susie looked at it with an incomprehensible disgust. Suddenly she gave a cry.

'Good God, it's moving!'

Arthur put his hand on her arm quickly to quieten her and bent down with irresistible curiosity. They saw that it was a mass of flesh unlike that of any human being; and it pulsated regularly. The movement was quite distinct, up and down, like the delicate heaving of a woman's breast when she is asleep. Arthur touched the thing with one finger and it shrank slightly.

'Its quite warm,' he said.

He turned it over, and it remained in the position in which he had placed it, as if there were neither top nor bottom to it. But they could see now, irregularly placed on one side, a few short hairs. They were just like human hairs.

'Is it alive?' whispered Susie, struck with horror and amazement.

'Yes!'

Arthur seemed fascinated. He could not take his eyes off the loathsome thing. He watched it slowly heave with even motion.

'What can it mean?' he asked.

He looked at Dr Porhoët with pale startled face. A thought was coming to him, but a thought so unnatural, extravagant, and terrible that he pushed it from him with a movement of both hands, as though it were a material thing. Then all three turned around abruptly with a start, for they heard again the wild gibbering which had first shocked their ears. In the wonder of this revolting object they had forgotten all the rest. The sound seemed extraordinarily near, and Susie drew back instinctively, for it appeared to come from her very side.

'There's nothing here,' said Arthur. 'It must be in the next room.'

'Oh, Arthur, let us go,' cried Susie. 'I'm afraid to see what may be in store for us. It is nothing to us, and what we see may poison our sleep for ever.'

She looked appealingly at Dr Porhoët. He was white and anxious. The heat of that place had made the sweat break out on his forehead.

'I have seen enough. I want to see no more,' he said.

'Then you may go, both of you,' answered Arthur. 'I do not wish to force you to see anything. But I shall go on. Whatever it is, I wish to find out.'

'But Haddo? Supposing he is there, waiting? Perhaps you are only walking into a trap that he has set for you.'

'I am convinced that Haddo is dead.'

Again that unintelligible jargon, unhuman and shrill, fell upon their ears, and Arthur stepped forward. Susie did not hesitate. She was prepared to follow him anywhere. He opened the door, and there was a sudden quiet. Whatever made those sounds was there. It was a larger room than any on the others and much higher, for it ran along the whole front of the house. The powerful lamps showed every corner of it at once, but, above, the beams of the open ceiling were dark with shadow. And here the nauseous odour, which had struck them before, was so overpowering that for a while they could not go in. It was indescribably foul. Even

Arthur thought it would make him sick, and he looked at the windows to see if it was possible to open them; but it seemed they were hermetically closed. The extreme warmth made the air more overpowering. There were four furnaces here, and they were all alight. In order to give out more heat and to burn slowly, the fronts of them were open, and one could see that they were filled with glowing coke.

The room was furnished no differently from the others, but to the various instruments for chemical operations on a large scale were added all manner of electrical appliances. Several books were lying about, and one had been left open face downwards on the edge of a table. But what immediately attracted their atention was a row of those large glass vessels like that which they had seen in the adjoining room. Each was covered with a white cloth. They hesitated a moment, for they knew that here they were face to face with the great enigma. At last Arthur pulled away the cloth from one. None of them spoke. They stared with astonished eyes. For here, too, was a strange mass of flesh, almost as large as a new-born child, but there was in it the beginnings of something ghastly human. It was shaped vaguely like an infant, but the legs were joined together so that it looked like a mummy rolled up in its coverings. There were neither feet nor knees. The trunk was formless, but there was a curious thickening on each side; it was as if a modeller had meant to make a figure with the arms loosely bent, but had left the work unfinished so that they were still one with the body. There was something that resembled a human head, covered with long golden hair, but it was horrible; it was an uncouth mass, without eyes or nose or mouth. The colour was a kind of sickly pink, and it was almost transparent. There was a very slight movement in it, rhythmical and slow. It was living too.

Then quickly Arthur removed the covering from all the other jars but one; and in a flash of the eyes they saw abominations so awful that Susie had to clench her fists in order not to scream.

There was one monstrous thing in which the limbs approached nearly to the human. It was extraordinarily heaped up, with fat tiny arms, little bloated legs, and an absurd squat body, so that it looked like a Chinese mandarin in porcelain. In another the trunk was almost like that of a human child, except that it was patched strangely with red and grey. But the terror of it was that at the neck it branched hideously, and there were two distinct heads, monstrously large, but duly provided with all their features. The features were a caricature of humanity so shameful that one could hardly bear to look. And as the light fell on it, the eyes of each head opened slowly. They had no pigment in them, but were pink, like the eyes of white rabbits; and they stared for a moment with an odd, unseeing glance. Then they were shut again, and what was curiously terrifying was that the movements were not quite simultaneous; the eyelids of one head fell slowly just before those of the other. And in another place was a ghastly monster in which it seemed that two bodies had been dreadfully entangled with one another. It was a creature of nightmare, with four arms and four legs, and this one actually moved. With a peculiar motion it crawled along the bottom of the great receptacle in which it was kept, towards the three persons who looked at it. It seemed to wonder what they did. Susie started back with fright, as it raised itself on its four legs and tried to reach up to them.

Susie turned away and hid her face. She could not look at those ghastly counterfeits of humanity. She was terrified and ashamed.

'Do you understand what this means?' said Dr Porhoët to Arthur, in an awed voice. 'It means that he has discovered the secret of life.'

'Was it for these vile monstrosities that Margaret was sacrificed in all her loveliness?'

The two men looked at one another with sad, wondering eyes.

'Don't you remember that he talked of the manufacture of human beings? It's these misshapen things that he's succeeding in producing,' said the doctor.

'There is one more that we haven't seen,' said Arthur.

He pointed to the covering which still hid the largest of the vases. He had a feeling that it contained the most fearful of all these monsters; and it was not without an effort that he drew the cloth away. But no sooner had he done this than something sprang up, so that instinctively he started back, and it began to gibber in piercing tones. These were the unearthly sounds that they had heard. It was not a voice, it was a kind of raucous crying, hoarse yet shrill, uneven like the barking of a dog, and appalling. The sounds came forth in rapid succession, angrily, as though the being that uttered them sought to express itself in furious words. It was mad with passion and beat against the glass walls of its prison with clenched fists. For the hands were human hands, and the body, though much larger, was of the shape of a new-born child. The creature must have stood about four feet high. The head was horribly misshapen. The skull was enormous, smooth and distended like that of a hydrocephalic, and the forehead protruded over the face hideously. The features were almost unformed, preternaturally small under the great, overhanging brow; and they had an expression of fiendish malignity.

The tiny, misshapen countenance writhed with convulsive fury, and from the mouth poured out a foaming spume. It raised its voice higher and higher, shrieking senseless gibberish in its rage. Then it began to hurl its whole body madly against the glass walls and to beat its head. It appeared to have a sudden incomprehensible hatred for the three strangers. It was trying to fly at them. The toothless gums moved spasmodically, and it threw its face into horrible grimaces. That nameless, loathsome abortion was the nearest that Oliver Haddo had come to the human form.

'Come away,' said Arthur. 'We must not look at this.'

He quickly flung the covering over the jar.

'Yes, for God's sake let us go,' said Susie.

'We haven't done yet,' answered Arthur. 'We haven't found the author of all this.'

He looked at the room in which they were, but there was no door except that by which they had entered. Then he uttered a startled cry, and stepping forward fell on his knee.

On the other side of the long tables heaped up with instruments, hidden so that at first they had not seen him, Oliver Haddo lay on the floor, dead. His blue eyes were staring wide, and they seemed larger than they had ever been. They kept still the expression of terror which they had worn in the moment of his agony, and his heavy face was distorted with deadly fear. It was purple and dark, and the eyes were injected with blood.

'He died of suffocation,' whispered Dr Porhoët.

Arthur pointed to the neck. There could be seen on it distinctly the marks of the avenging fingers that had strangled the life out of him. It was impossible to hesitate.

'I told you that I had killed him,' said Arthur.

Then he remembered something more. He took hold of the right arm. He was convinced that it had been broken during that desperate struggle in the darkness. He felt it carefully and listened. He heard plainly the two parts of the bone rub against one another. The dead man's arm was broken just in the place where he had broken it. Arthur stood up. He took one last look at his enemy. That vast mass of flesh lay heaped up on the floor in horrible disorder.

'Now that you have seen, will you come away?' said Susie, interrupting him.

The words seemed to bring him suddenly to himself.

'Yes, we must go quickly.'

They turned away and with hurried steps walked through those bright attics till they came to the stairs.

'Now go down and wait for me at the door,' said Arthur. 'I will follow you immediately.'

'What are you going to do?' asked Susie.

'Never mind. Do as I tell you. I have not finished here yet.'

They went down the great oak staircase and waited in the hall. They wondered what. Arthur was about. Presently he came running down.

'Be quick!' he cried. 'We have no time to lose.'

'What have you done, Arthur?'

'There's no time to tell you now.'

He hurried them out and slammed the door behind him. He took Susie's hand.

'Now we must run. Come.'

She did not know what his haste signified, but her heart beat furiously. He dragged her along. Dr Porhoët hurried on behind them. Arthur plunged into the wood. He would not leave them time to breathe.

'You must be quick,' he said.

At last they came to the opening in the fence, and he helped them to get through. Then he carefully replaced the wooden paling and, taking Susie's arm began to walk rapidly towards their inn.

'I'm frightfully tired,' she said. 'I simply can't go so fast.'

'You must. Presently you can rest as long as you like.'

They walked very quickly for a while. Now and then Arthur looked back. The night was still quite dark, and the stars shone out in their myriads. At last he slackened their pace.

'Now you can go more slowly,' he said.

Susie saw the smiling glance that he gave her. His eyes were full of tenderness. He put his arm affectionately round her shoulders to support her.

'I'm afraid you're quite exhausted, poor thing,' he said. 'I'm sorry to have had to hustle you so much.'

'It doesn't matter at all.'

She leaned against him comfortably. With that protecting arm about her, she felt capable of any fatigue. Dr Porhoët stopped.

'You must really let me roll myself a cigarette,' he said.

'You may do whatever you like,' answered Arthur.

There was a different ring in his voice now, and it was soft with a good-humour that they had not heard in it for many months. He appeared singularly relieved. Susie was ready to forget the terrible past and give herself over to the happiness that seemed at last in store for her. They began to saunter slowly on. And now they could take pleasure in the exquisite night. The air was very suave, odorous with the heather that was all about them, and there was an enchanting peace in that scene which wonderfully soothed their weariness. It was dark still, but they knew the dawn was at hand, and Susie rejoiced in the approaching day. In the east the azure of the night began to thin away into pale amethyst, and the trees seemed gradually to stand out from the darkness in a ghostly beauty. Suddenly birds began to sing all around them in a splendid chorus. From their feet a lark sprang up with a rustle of wings and, mounting proudly upon the air, chanted blithe canticles to greet the morning. They stood upon a little hill.

'Let us wait here and see the sun rise,' said Susie.

'As you will.'

They stood all three of them, and Susie took in deep, joyful breaths of the sweet air of dawn. The whole land, spread at her feet, was clothed in the purple dimness that heralds day, and she exulted in its beauty. But she noticed that Arthur, unlike herself and Dr Porhoët, did not look toward the east. His eyes were fixed steadily upon the place from which they had come. What did he look for in the darkness of the west? She turned round, and a cry broke from her lips, for the shadows there were lurid with a deep red glow.

'It looks like a fire,' she said.

'It is. Skene is burning like tinder.'

And as he spoke it seemed that the roof fell in, for suddenly vast flames sprang up, rising high into the still night air; and they saw that the house they had just left was blazing furiously. It was a magnificent sight from the distant hill on which they stood to watch the fire as it soared and sank, as it shot scarlet tongues along like strange Titanic monsters, as it raged from room to room. Skene was burning. It was beyond the reach of human help. In a little while there would be no trace of all those crimes and all those horrors. Now it was one mass of flame. It looked like some primeval furnace, where the gods might work unheard-of miracles.

'Arthur, what have you done?' asked Susie, in a tone that was hardly audible.

He did not answer directly. He put his arm about her shoulder again, so that she was obliged to rurn round.

'Look, the sun is rising.'

In the east, a long ray of light climbed up the sky, and the sun, yellow and round, appeared upon the face of the earth.

SUGGESTED READING

CALDER, ROBERT. *Willie: The Life of W. Somerset Maugham.* London: Heinemann, 1989.

CONNOR, BRYAN. *Somerset Maugham and the Maugham Dynasty.* London: Sinclair-Stevenson, 1997.

CURTIS, ANTHONY, AND JOHN WHITEHEAD, EDS. *W. Somerset Maugham: The Critical Heritage.* London: Routledge, 1987.

HOLDEN, PHILIP. *Orienting Masculinity, Orienting Nation: W. Somerset Maugham's Exotic Fiction.* Westport, Conn.: Greenwood, 1996.

MAUGHAM, W. SOMERSET. *Cakes and Ale: Or, the Skeleton in the Cupboard.* London: Heinemann, 1930.

---. *The Complete Short Stories of W. Somerset Maugham: 3 Volumes.* London: Heinemann, 1951.

---. *The Moon and Sixpence.* London: Heinemann, 1919.

---. *Of Human Bondage.* New York: Barnes & Noble Books, 2005.

---. *The Painted Veil.* London: Heinemann, 1925.

---. *Points of View.* London: Heinemann, 1960

---. *The Summing Up.* London: Heinemann, 1948.

---. *Ten Novels and Their Authors.* London: Heinemann, 1954.

---. *A Writer's Notebook.* London: Heinemann, 1949.

---. *The Razor's Edge*. London: Heinemann, 1944.

MEYERS, JEFFREY. *Somerset Maugham: A Life.* New York: Knopf, 2004.

MORGAN, TED. *Maugham.* New York: Simon and Schuster, 1980.

ROGAL, SAMUEL J. *A William Somerset Maugham Encyclopedia.* Westport, Conn.: Greenwood, 1997.